This space reserved for excerpts from critics' raving, glowing reviews
of REVOLUTION (should any such reviews ever be written).

OTHER TITLES BY DAVID DORROUGH:

REVOLUTION

A NOVEL

DAVID DORROUGH

For Karen

REVOLUTION

Chapter 1

On an unusually warm April morning in Los Angeles, Bill Smede stepped onto the sidewalk in front of his home and immediately began to whine. Unfortunately for his wife Yvonne, she was only a few steps ahead and had to listen to it.

"God, it's fucking hot out here! I can't believe it's already this hot and it's not even 9 A.M. What's it going to feel like this afternoon?"

Yvonne didn't reply, although she was tempted to, knowing Bill's question was purely rhetorical and that any response to it would irritate him. Instead she continued to focus on her new PaceTek Ultra, a device clearly intended to encourage either exercising a lot or losing one's mind in utter bewilderment and frustration. Since strapping it onto her wrist an hour ago, Yvonne had been doing mainly the latter.

At the end of the block, she finally managed to bring her step count up on the tiny screen. She frowned—a paltry 375 steps so far today. Bill came up alongside, fiddling with his own device, a PaceTek Nano.

"How are your steps?" he asked.

"Lousy."

"Yeah, mine too. Want to make this one a double?"

"Sounds good."

One loop around the neighborhood was somewhere between 2,000 and 2,500 steps, depending on whose device was asked and on which day. Major streets, like Santa Monica Boulevard, were to be avoided because of the sounds and smells of the hundreds of cars slowly passing along them during any given minute, and anyway crossing them was too much of a hassle. So Bill and Yvonne had designed the loop to provide the maximum possible length without ever reaching any of these major streets. It went south on their street, Wexler Avenue, then east on Oklahoma Avenue, north on Underwood Avenue, west on Utah

Avenue, and finally south on Wexler again, back to their building.

The section of L.A. where Bill and Yvonne lived, a sprawling patch of territory far bigger than most cities, was known affectionately by its residents as the Westside (or The WestSide by its most affectionate ones) and included many famous places like the Playboy Mansion. Judging by the cost of housing, L.A. ranked among the very most desirable American cities in which to live. And, by that same measure, the Westside was apparently the most desirable part of L.A.

Bill harbored serious doubts about both. Despite the fact that he could never hope to buy even the smallest, most dilapidated house in his neighborhood (he and Yvonne had scrimped and saved for their rather non-luxurious 2-bedroom condo), it seemed a bit of a dump. The sidewalks were always dirty, with their slabs cracked and pushed up by tree roots; parked cars, in widely varying condition, perpetually lined both sides of every street; many houses and apartment buildings had fallen into major disrepair; dubious characters roamed around at all hours of the day and night...

It was a list that could go on and on. And indeed, in Bill's mind, it did. As he grudgingly completed each loop to ensure the logging of precious steps, he was constantly refining and expanding his collection of gripes.

For her part, Yvonne acknowledged the shortcomings of the neighborhood but didn't let them get under her skin. She also acknowledged quite gracefully that her husband could be a hypersensitive, overreacting grump. She enjoyed his company anyway. He had a good sense of humor, including about himself, and their walking loops were primarily filled with lighthearted banter and shared chuckles (often at the expense of their dearly loved but easily ridiculed friends and family).

On Oklahoma, as they walked past a tiny old dwelling next door to a gigantic new one, Bill and Yvonne spotted Mrs. Harris about three houses down, in her trademark green sweatpants and slightly-different-shade-of-green sweatshirt, coming toward them. As usual, she had her cocker spaniel mix, Max, with her. Also as usual, Max was not on a leash.

Mrs. Harris noticed Bill and Yvonne, too. She'd seen them walking their loops many times before and had made mental notes, later transferred into written ones, of all their distinguishing characteristics. Two middle-aged, moderately overweight, caucasian individuals, both with light-colored hair.   Occasionally one of them would be out alone but usually they were together. Both had a slightly scruffy, unkempt appearance, but not of the sort that suggested homelessness or destitution, just lack of concern. The man always wore a hat and sunglasses to conceal his identity. The woman, oddly, seldom wore either. Like many other neighborhood residents on whom Mrs. Harris kept detailed notes, she found these two very suspicious. She wasn't sure, yet, what they were up to... but definitely something not good.

Bill and Yvonne did not know that Mrs. Harris found them suspicious, nor even that her name was Mrs. Harris. They didn't know her dog's name was Max. All they knew about her was that she never made any effort to move out of their way, never smiled at them, and never seemed to care when her pet rubbed its snout all over their ankles.

As the two pairs drew close to each other, Bill muttered "I'll go behind you," and he and Yvonne swiftly moved into single-file formation, hugged the righthand edge of the sidewalk and quickened their pace. They both cast a brief nod and smile at the scowling face of Mrs. Harris as it whizzed past them on the left and some part of Max brushed lightly against their legs. Then it was over.

For Bill and Yvonne, there was nothing very special about Mrs. Harris. During a typical loop they encountered two dozen people, half of whom had dogs (though usually leashed (though it made almost no difference)) and 90% of whom were oblivious to the concept of a sidewalk being a shared space. 99% never smiled or spoke, even though 75% of these crossed paths with Bill and Yvonne regularly.

Making their way along Underwood, Bill and Yvonne's conversation turned to the subject of their teenage daughter.

"Alice seemed funny last night," said Yvonne.

Bill thought back to the previous evening, but all he could remember was how annoyed he'd felt with the loud music coming through the floor from the condo below them, and also with accidentally bashing his elbow against the frame of the bathroom door as he walked through it.

"What do you mean?" he asked.

"Well, she was really quiet at dinner and then she went straight to her room after, and we didn't see her the rest of the night."

Bill pondered this. "Hmm... Yeah, you're right. Kinda weird."

It did not occur to either of them that Alice had always been quiet during dinner and hardly ever made any after-dinner appearances.

"I wonder if she's upset about something," Yvonne mused.

Bill got pensive for a moment, then suddenly grimaced. "I hope she didn't take some kind of drug," he said.

"God. Yeah, me too."

They both chewed on this in silence for a couple of minutes. Then Yvonne's mind drifted to things that were going on at work, and she related some of these to Bill. After that they discussed a movie they'd recently watched together, concluding that it was a "threshold flick"— the least interesting a movie could possibly be while still interesting enough to watch all the way to the end.

Rounding the corner from Utah onto Wexler, Bill and Yvonne came upon the building where their friends Gary and Scott lived. It was a soaring tower (meaning, in most residential neighborhoods (including this one), it had five stories), finished in stucco painted two contrasting shades of gray, with glass-walled balconies. Though over twenty years old at this point, it still looked pretty trendy. Bill and Yvonne's two-story building just down the street was more than twice as old, with an all-wood exterior desperately in need of painting, and didn't look the least bit trendy. But they weren't much concerned with aesthetics, compared to practicality (and price).

Gary was in the driveway, holding a piece of cloth and rubbing it furiously against the roof of his cherry red 1985 Toyota Supra. Technically the color of the car was "Super Deep Red," but nobody except Gary knew this (even though he'd told many people many times).

"Morning, Gary," Bill called out as he and Yvonne approached.

Gary Williams had a certain positive vibe about him. Somehow he exuded energy and physical fitness. In part this could be objectively observed, simply by looking at his lean, toned limbs and the speed and precision with which they moved. But there was more to it than that. His voice, his facial expressions, the way he held himself—his whole style of existing—all worked in concert to create the vibe. Being handsome didn't hurt, either. Most people who met Gary agreed he looked like a young Clifton Davis. Or anyway they would've, if they'd known who Clifton Davis was.

Gary's vibe was always there, and this morning was no exception. He looked up at Bill and Yvonne, a big grin breaking out across his face, even as his right arm continued buffing the Supra's new coat of wax.

"Oh, hey guys!" he exclaimed. "Good morning!"

"Polishing up your baby, huh?" asked Yvonne in the most enthusiastic tone she could manage. (She'd never understood how anyone could get excited about a car.)

"Oh yeah, you know it! Getting her all shiny and perfect. They're doing one of those 'Cars and Donuts' events in Mar Vista this morning, so I thought I'd take her down there and show her off a little."

Having just reminded himself he needed to be somewhere, Gary abruptly glanced down at his phone, lying next to him on the concrete.

"Uh-oh, I'm running late," he said with a little chuckle, then hurriedly began gathering up his car beautification paraphernalia.

"Well it looks fantastic," said Bill. "Enjoy your Cars and Donuts."

"Thanks! You guys have a great morning!"

"Bye, Gary."

Bill and Yvonne continued along Wexler. Nearing their building, they both hesitated and glanced at each other. Perhaps one loop was enough for now? No, no—they'd decided on two and their plan was sound. A quick unspoken exchange and it was agreed. They passed by their home and carried on down the street toward Oklahoma.

Two days later, Scott Portcullis walked into his kitchen at 6:04 A.M., which was the same time he entered his kitchen every morning. Many things about Scott were exactly the same every morning—the slicked back, plastered down hair (which was actually a dull light brown color but appeared shiny dark brown with all the product in it); the meticulously shaved face, smooth as a baby's bottom; the "uniform": black leather lace-ups, dark khakis (black, gray or navy blue, never brown or tan), black leather belt, and white or off-white open-collar shirt.

After popping four slices of bread into the toaster and retrieving butter and eggs from the fridge, Scott stationed himself in front of the range and began his fry work. He stood three stories directly above the front bumper of the Supra, which was currently blocked in by his car, a Chevrolet Cruze. Scott and Gary, like so many residents of L.A., enjoyed a lifestyle feature known as "tandem" parking.

Scott was a tall, slender man who walked with a slightly awkward gait and his wide, bright blue eyes constantly darting, which made him seem more nervous than he actually was. In fact Scott was very comfortable in his own skin and had a fairly low level of resting anxiety. But he was always alert, and always wary—of everything and everyone.

At 6:11 Scott emerged from the kitchen carrying two plates and set them down on the table where a suit-clad Gary had just taken a seat and was fiddling with his phone.

"Mmm, smells great, babe," said Gary, smiling and looking up from the phone as his food arrived in front of him. "Wow, a hot breakfast. Lucky me!"

Ordinarily Gary was not even awake by this time, but today he was meeting up early with his colleague Frank Barnes for a trip to Bakersfield to conduct what was known as an Annual Retail Service Evaluation—a yearly audit that all CuppaJoe franchisees were required to undergo.

"So," said Scott, taking a seat, "the double-team road trip. Worried about it? You normally work alone."

"Nah, it'll be fine," said Gary. "Should be fun, actually. This Frank guy seems like quite a character."

"He's new, right?"

"Well, he's been with the company for like a year I think, but I never met him until last week. He just got promoted to Associate. Just started at the regional office, reporting to Jim."

Scott raised an eyebrow. "So why doesn't he shadow Jim on one of these things? Why you?"

"I don't know. I think Jim was stuck in the office for a couple of weeks. Or maybe it was a scheduling thing. Anyway I don't mind. Should be fun."

"Cool," Scott said, managing a weak smile.

Gary went back to his phone but continued talking. "Frank's supposed to meet me here, but it was kind of weird. He didn't want to come here in a car for some reason."

"Oh?"

"Yeah. He explained why, but it was complicated. It didn't really make sense. So anyway he said he's going to *run* here."

Scott's eyes got even wider. "Run?"

"Yep." Gary chuckled and shook his head. "I know, I know. Weird, right? I'm calling him now to see where he is."

After a couple of rings the call was picked up and Gary's ear was blasted by what sounded like gale-force winds. Then came Frank's voice, with its quick pacing and flat tone, cutting through the background noise.

"Gare-ree. How's it going, partner?"

"Hi, Frank! Good morning!" Gary replied. "Hey, listen, I just wanted to check on your situation. You on your way here?"

"Negative, my friend. There's been a lot of unfortunate trouble this morning on my street. With the trash collection."

"The trash?"

"Yep, yep. Typical stuff, standard stuff. So yeah, I've been trying to deal with that. Nightmare, Gary, I'm telling you. Nightmare."

Wearing a puzzled face but still smiling, Gary glanced across the table at Scott, who was now tapping on his own phone and seemed oblivious.

"Okay," Gary said to Frank, "so when do you think you can make it here? We were planning to get on the road at 6:30."

"Impossible to say, man. Depends on a wide variety of factors."

"Hmm... Well, what if I head out right now and come down there and pick you up?"

"Uh..." Frank went silent for several seconds, then resumed. "I'd be delighted. Yep, that would be just splendid, Gare old buddy."

"Okay, great, I should be there in about twenty, twenty-five minutes. Send me your address, okay?"

By 6:28, Gary was guiding the Supra up the on-ramp of the 405. Freeways were so highly regarded in L.A. that their names were always preceded with "the." Nobody ever took 10 to go downtown; they took The 10.

At the same moment, Scott was guiding the Cruze out of their building's garage, slightly miffed that he was fully three minutes late departing for work (thanks to his unplanned visit to the garage a few minutes earlier to move his car out of his hurried husband's way).

Scott's destination in El Segundo, the offices of Lathrop Halliday where he'd worked as an engineer for many years, was not very far from Gary's destination in Inglewood.

After exiting the 405 and making a few turns, Gary slowed down as his phone announced that Frank's place was coming up on the right. Then, out of the corner of his eye, he saw somebody running the opposite direction on the other side of the street. It was Frank, decked out in shorts and a windbreaker, with a large fluorescent lime green sash bouncing around on his shoulder. Gary made a quick U-turn and pulled up beside him.

"Frank!" Gary called out with a smile as he lowered his passenger-side window. Frank didn't seem to notice and continued to run, staring straight ahead with a look of intense concentration on his face. Seconds passed. The car slowly rolled along, keeping pace with Frank.

Gary was about to call out again when Frank abruptly stopped running and turned toward the car.

"Aha. Gary, my man. There you are," he said, approaching the car and pulling open the passenger door. "About time. We gotta make tracks, my friend." He climbed in and shut the door.

"Frank, good morning! Good to see you," said Gary. "So, you want to grab your stuff from your house quickly?"

Frank scrunched up his face. "Huh? What stuff?" he asked.

"Like your computer. And, uh… don't you want to change your clothes?"

"No need," Frank replied with a dismissive wave of his hand. "Fancy clothes are just a crutch. You know, to help people project their identity. I don't need that."

He tapped his temple with his index finger. "My mind, Gare. My mind *is* my clothes." A short pause, then he added with a tiny grin, "And my computer, too."

Another short pause as Frank glanced over at Gary, looking him up and down. "But no offense, man. Your suit is very spiffy." His grin was gone but he made a quick thumbs-up gesture.

Gary was slightly taken aback by all this, but found Frank's style oddly charming.

"Well alright, then!" he exclaimed, putting the car in gear and pulling away from the curb. "Self-confidence. I like it!"

Most Angelenos agreed that, if given the choice between getting a root canal and driving their car from one side of the city to the other, they'd have a tough time choosing. But Gary was different. The stop-and-go of heavy traffic didn't bother him, nor did the noises and fumes. The unpredictable and rough road conditions, the maniac drivers, the spaced-out drivers, the tight squeezes, the confusing signs, the perpetually shifting array of walkers and runners and cyclists and electric scooter riders—Gary didn't mind any of these things. He was always perfectly comfortable and content sitting in the car (any car—it did not need to be his prized Supra). He loved driving.

This trait served Gary well in his line of work, although on this particular journey he didn't desperately need it. Early in the morning, traveling up the 405 to the northernmost part of L.A. tended to be relatively quick and painless, and indeed so it was for Gary and Frank today. From there they joined the 5 (the main artery up and down the west coast) for about 60 miles before forking off onto the 99, which took them into Bakersfield.

At 8:57, Gary pulled into a parking space at the Ming Avenue CuppaJoe and cut the engine. He smiled and sighed contentedly— they'd arrived on time for their appointment despite the earlier delay.

Frank, who'd been asleep since two minutes after getting in the car, suddenly sprang back to life.

"Let's do this," he said. "I sure hope you brought your 'A' game, buddy." Then he opened his door and jumped out.

Paige Lena Turner, though not at all an arrogant or proud woman, had always deeply valued her entrepreneurial prowess, and had been honing it nearly her entire life. Before even reaching a double-digit age, she'd become the only child in history (as far as she knew) to operate a consistently profitable neighborhood lemonade stand—with paid employees—three summers in a row. During high school she'd set up a primitive version of an app-based ride-hailing service, which connected local youngsters who needed to get places but didn't have a license with other local youngsters who had access to a vehicle but were short on money. In college, Paige had devoted far less time to her coursework than to running her "vice brokerage," which efficiently connected folks with any tobacco, alcohol and marijuana products they desired and were legally entitled to consume. Eventually she'd dropped out to pursue this venture full time. But after a couple of years, with dwindling margins and the perpetual annoyance of red tape, she'd decided to give up on it.

After that, Paige had set about building her current business empire, becoming the first CuppaJoe franchisee outside of metro Los Angeles. A big believer in slow but steady growth, she'd started with a single store and opened a new one every three years, like clockwork, over the past decade and a half.

Frugality had always been paramount. She had no desire to flaunt her wealth, nor to fill her life with vast amounts of luxury or even convenience. All her worldly possessions could have—and, in fact, did—fit inside of a large automobile. Specifically, Paige's Cadillac Escalade (she'd reluctantly gone for the prestigious brand, acknowledging that keeping up appearances was a necessary evil in the world of business). The mattress in the back was perfectly comfortable (and easy to conceal from clients riding up front). Her compact propane grill was quick to set up and take down (although many of her meals were purchased from CuppaJoe—a great way to re-invest). She had a fabulous laundromat where she'd been taking her clothes for years. She showered at the gym. And why would anyone require a personal toilet when there were so many public ones available for free?

On this sunny Monday morning, Paige stood inside her original store on Ming Avenue, awaiting the arrival of the "boys from corporate" (as they were nearly always boys) for their routine annual audit.

"Right on time—good," she muttered to herself as she spotted two of them through the window, emerging from a surprisingly old, funny-looking red sports coupe and making their way across the parking lot toward the entrance.

Over the next several hours, Gary led the three of them through all the standard procedures, tapping away on his tablet throughout. He asked Paige a lot of questions, and she asked him a few. They went around Bakersfield, visiting all of Paige's locations, inspecting equipment and chatting with employees at each one. Gary talked Paige through the planned sales promotions over the next year, a few upcoming corporate policy changes, and a software update that was in the works. The whole affair went swimmingly, Gary felt, and he was impressed with Paige—a consummate professional, and in full compliance.

Frank's frequent interjections perturbed Gary at first, but he gradually grew more comfortable as he began to conclude that Frank was offering some valid insights and developing quite a good rapport with Paige (neither of which was true). By the time they were finished, Gary was delighted with Frank's performance.

"Well that went great," Gary enthused as the two men got in the car.

"Yep, it went okay," Frank replied. "She'll definitely think twice before pulling any shit, you know?"

Gary did not know, but he ignored it and continued his enthusing. "You were great, Frank! A really strong showing your first time out."

Frank glanced over at Gary, staying silent for a moment before responding, "Yep."

Frank stayed awake on the drive back to L.A. and Gary found him an engaging conversation partner. As expected, Frank had a unique perspective on every subject. In addition to the designer coffee industry, they discussed music, sports, their favorite movies, and Gary's recently-acquired passion for classic Toyota models. Eventually Gary asked Frank about his running.

"So, you do a lot of running? I used to be a runner myself, actually."

Frank cocked an eyebrow. "Used to be? What happened, Gary? You know, running is the single healthiest thing you can do for your body. It heals and strengthens everything, my friend. Bones, muscles, nerves. Your heart, your brain, your gut. I'm telling you, it's like magic medicine."

"Really?" Gary replied with a laugh. "Wow. That's pretty cool."

"Very cool, Gare. Very cool."

"Yeah well, I was really into it for a while, maybe like five or ten years ago. I mean *super* into it. Ran marathons and everything." Gary paused, thinking back to those days. "Can't really remember why I stopped. Guess I got burnt out or something..."

"Well it's time for you to get back into it, my friend. I mean training, running races, the whole nine yards."

Gary chuckled. "Maybe so, maybe so."

"Definitely so," said Frank. "There's a very special event that I'm training for, and it's right up your alley, buddy. It's a marathon, but not just any marathon, no sir. It's *the* marathon. The marathon to end all marathons. Happening next summer, in North Virginia."

"North Virginia? You mean northern Virginia, like Washington D.C. area?"

"Yep, exactly. But listen up, Gary. This is the mother of all marathons. You can't just go sign up for it willy-nilly. You gotta qualify. By running other marathons."

"Right, yeah I remember that sort of thing from back in the day. Like you had to get a decent time on New York in order to even qualify to run Boston."

Frank shook his head. "No, not like that. This is the real deal, my friend. You have to run ten other marathons to qualify for the mother. And you have to run 'em, you know, fast. Lightning fast."

Gary chuckled again, smiling broadly, and shook his head slowly. "Wow," he said. Gary liked Frank's passion, and enjoyed his intense, fast-paced, overly serious speaking style.

"I got all the literature in my desk at work," Frank continued. "I'll hook you up tomorrow morning."

"Great! Thanks, Frank."

"You and me, Gary. We're in this together. It's called the Pot of Gold Classic. We're gonna tear up the road, my friend."

Gary was feeling the energy. "Okay, Frank," he said with another big smile. "Sounds great!"

He thought about it for a second, then added, "Pot of Gold, huh? Is it like an Irish thing?"

"Beats me, Gare. Beats the hell outta me."

As Yvonne Smede laid her hairbrush down on the counter of her tiny bathroom and stepped into her tiny bedroom, she heard her husband's voice coming through the paper-thin wall from the living room.

"Goddammit, fucking piece of shit," he said.

Yvonne rolled her eyes. Bill was probably having issues booting up his computer.

It was almost time to head off to work, and Yvonne was decked out in her standard office outfit of dark slacks, not-too-dressy-but-not-too-casual blouse, and sensible shoes. Thinking of how she wished both the slacks and the blouse could be a couple of sizes smaller, Yvonne checked her step count. Off to a good start, she thought. She'd already been up for two hours, cooked and eaten a healthy breakfast, and walked the neighborhood loop with Bill twice. Their mornings typically featured this kind of responsible, wellness-oriented behavior. The evenings were the danger time.

Officially, this condominium unit was classified as a "two bedroom plus den." The rather narrow, rather short hallway that connected the master suite to the second bedroom included three other doorways. On one side of the hall was a bathroom and an entrance to the front half of the condo (which was basically just one giant room). On the other side of the hall, behind a sliding shoji-style door, was a little alcove that could just barely be used as a bedroom, and indeed, just barely was used as one, by Alice Smede.

Yvonne came out of the master and strolled past the "den" on her way to the other end of the hall. The shoji door was open and the den currently unoccupied. Inside it, Alice's bed, dresser and belongings were impeccably tidy, as usual.

Now standing before the other bedroom's closed door, Yvonne knocked on it.

"Patrick?"

Silence from behind the door. She knocked again, louder and longer.

"Patrick, you up?"

Still nothing. She tried the doorknob. Locked. She banged on the door a third time.

"Patrick! Don't forget you have that eight o'clock interview this morn—"

The door abruptly swung open and Yvonne's son stood before her, sporting crazy hair, a groggy face and clothes he'd obviously slept in.

"Nah, it got moved to tomorrow morning," he said, rubbing his eyes.

Yvonne frowned. Since Patrick had begun "freelancing" (at what, exactly, was unclear to his parents) several months ago, the amount of time he spent working had been rather minimal, as had his income.

"So, what are you up to today, then?" Yvonne asked.

Patrick shrugged. "Not sure," he said. Then, after a lengthy yawn, "Might meet up with Len later, try to hash out some ideas and stuff."

Len was Patrick's best friend and a stiff competitor in the field of accomplishing nothing. Yvonne knew the "ideas" the two young men were planning to discuss were most likely related to launching a small business of some kind. She wasn't thrilled about this, but concentrated hard on literally turning her frown upside-down, with some success.

"Okay," was the best she could manage to say.

Patrick smiled down at his mother. He was a full head taller than her, with a gigantic, unwieldy mop of dark brown hair and eyes that were equally dark, slightly beady, and accentuated by a pair of long, bushy, very expressive eyebrows. He looked nothing like any other family member. Yvonne had struggled to think, on many occasions, whom she might've slept with around the time Patrick was conceived. But Bill was the only one. Patrick was definitely their child. The mysteries of DNA, she mused.

"Have a good day, Mom," said Patrick before giving Yvonne a quick kiss on the forehead and then disappearing again behind his bedroom door. Yvonne sighed, turned and headed for the living room.

She got there just in time to see her daughter opening the front door of the apartment to leave for school, and would've tried to say a quick goodbye, but knew there was no point—Alice's back was turned and she was wearing her bluetooth earbuds. A moment later the door was shut and she was gone.

Alice rode a bus each morning, but not a school bus, a city bus. L.A.U.S.D. only provided bus service to students who traveled a great distance; those who actually lived in the correct, designated residential area for their school were left to their own devices. Yvonne and Bill had made a hard choice: ultimately the anxiety of allowing their 16-year-old child to use urban public transport had been deemed lesser than the anxiety of driving that child through the urban jungle themselves (which involved, after all, trying to get from one side of the 405 to the other during rush hour).

Yvonne retrieved her laptop bag from the corner of the sofa and hoisted it onto her shoulder.

"Well I'm heading out too," she said to Bill, who was sitting at their dining table (which doubled as his desk), glaring at his own laptop with a frown and a furrowed brow, clicking furiously on his mouse.

"What the fuck?!" he blurted out.

"Oh, sorry," said Yvonne, smirking. "Didn't realize my leaving for work was such a big issue for you."

Bill snapped out of his cyber-rage spell and turned to her. "Sorry," he said with a sigh and a faint smile. "Hope you have a good one. See you tonight."

Yvonne departed and Bill turned back to his screen and his never-ending struggle with the confounding forces of digital technology. Not spyware or ransomware or phishing—he could cope with those. They were simply malicious. What really made his head spin and whipped him into fits of profanity was all the idiotic stuff: frozen screens, momentarily dropped Internet, unexplained lags, two-factor authentications where the second "factor" just decides to give it a miss, mandatory password-protected screen locking every two minutes.

Currently his computer was rebooting itself without his permission and with very little notice. Apparently this was unavoidable because, as the computer had explained to him, his I.T. department urgently needed to install some updates on this machine.

As he sat, impotent, watching this process unfold, his angry astonishment somehow drained away and was replaced with the amused kind. He smiled and shook his head. "Fucking computers," he muttered.

Bill, who worked for CompDynCorp (a small, unknown R&D company with big, well-known clients) creating statistical modeling software, thought his job was pretty much the best possible job he could ever ask for. He hated it.

The working arrangement—entirely from home, with the corporate headquarters that he was almost never required to visit located thousands of miles away in New York—suited Bill, for three reasons. He didn't have to endure an L.A. commute, he didn't have to interact with a bunch of irritating people in an office, and, best of all, he could spend a large portion of each workday ignoring his work and getting on with more important things.

Down on the street, Yvonne was walking north on Wexler and spotted Gary in his driveway, his body contorted into a shape she suspected her own body could only achieve by getting run over by a car. But Gary was just stretching. He was wearing a tightly-clinging, fluorescent sky-blue t-shirt, shiny jet-black shorts, and a pair of brand-new, brightly-colored running shoes.

"Morning, Gary," Yvonne called out. "Going for a run?"

Gary looked up, smiled, and un-contorted himself.

"Oh, hey guys!" he then exclaimed. "Good morning! Yes indeed, going for a run! My training begins today. Very excited about it!"

"Cool," replied Yvonne, not slowing her brisk stride at all. "Sorry, can't talk right now, but you can tell me all about it Friday at dinner."

"I will certainly do that. You have a great day!"

"You too," she replied, then added over her shoulder as she moved away up the sidewalk, "Hey, I don't think you're supposed to stretch before you run. Just after."

Gary was already midway through another stretch, but abruptly stopped when he heard this. Really? he thought with a puzzled frown, then resolved to do some serious research into this running stuff after work tonight, or maybe just ask Frank about it.

Yvonne continued up Wexler, past Utah, until she arrived outside the building where Morris Batz lived. Yvonne and Morris had discovered, after working together for nearly three years in the I.T. department at Beth Universal Mount Zion Medical Center, that they lived down the street from each other. Ever since then they'd been carpooling to the office. Morris, who drove them every day, liked the arrangement because it got him a discount on his parking. Yvonne liked it because it meant she never had to drive to work.

After standing next to the building's driveway scarcely more than 30 seconds, Yvonne heard the whirring of the subterranean garage gate rolling back, and a moment later Morris's Jeep Grand Cherokee came roaring up the ramp and stopped beside her. Yvonne had never had to wait more than three minutes for Morris, and he had never had to wait for her at all. They were a well-oiled carpooling machine. She hopped into the car, a quick greeting was exchanged, and off they went.

The journey was not pleasant for Yvonne. Morris kept all his car windows open at all times, regardless of the weather, and never ran the air conditioning or the heat. His passenger seat contained two inexplicable bumps, one protruding from the middle of the seat cushion and another from the middle of the seat back. His radio was always on, playing either jazz (which Yvonne hated) quite loudly or news (which she liked) too quietly to hear what was said.

But Morris was no chatterbox, for which Yvonne was grateful. The two of them knew remarkably little about one another, considering all the years they'd been riding in the same car, working in the same office, and living on the same street. Yvonne didn't care, and as far as she could tell, neither did Morris. Some people just weren't meant to be friends with each other.

After five miles and 37 minutes on the chaos-filled streets of Los Angeles, the Jeep arrived at their Wilshire Boulevard office tower and began its spiral descent to level B-5 of the parking garage. This building was not part of the main hospital campus—being non-clinical personnel, most of Yvonne's job duties could be carried out sitting at a computer a mile away (or any distance, really), but occasionally she did need to go over to the hospital to meet with people. This was done either by walking or taking the shuttle, and was generally a pain, but could be a welcome relief on those days when the office environment got especially stifling.

Morris, a member of the Security Team, got off the elevator at the 5th floor. Yvonne continued up to the 17th floor, home of the Lab Team, whose job it was to ensure that all the digital data related to the ordering of lab tests, and the results of those tests, found its way into the correct instruments and the correct computer systems and the correct people's faces, quickly and accurately.

The 17th was open-plan, with 360 degrees of floor-to-ceiling windows, offering quite a spectacular view of the city. From here a person was able to see many, many streets simultaneously, confirming that traffic jams existed even when they weren't stuck in one. They were also provided a good look at the smog.

Yvonne strode from the elevator to her desk, located in what once had been a little aisle containing six cubicles. But all of the thin, fabric-covered half-walls had long ago been removed (following cubicles' falling out of fashion), so now it was just a row of three desks pushed up against each other right behind another row of three desks pushed up against each other.

Yvonne's colleague and friend, Amy Lee, who occupied the desk next to Yvonne's, had also just arrived and was getting settled in.

"Good morning!" Amy said in her typical high-energy style.

"Good morning," replied Yvonne in her own typical (lower energy) style. "How are you?"

"Good, I'm doing good," said Amy. "Mmmf, last night was kinda crazy around our place. Jake was supposed to pick up the kids, you know, because I had that late meeting. So anyways—Oh! Before I forget. Happy hour tonight."

Yvonne raised an eyebrow. "Again?"

"Yes! What do you mean, again?" Amy gave Yvonne a playful shove. "You're funny. Yes, *again*. We haven't had one since last… when was it? I don't know, whatevs. But we have to do it tonight because I just found out they have three-dollar margaritas on Wednesdays at Taco Loco!" Amy had been smiling the entire time, but broke into a bigger grin as "Lo-co" slowly rolled off her tongue.

Yvonne couldn't help smiling back. She liked Amy very much, and she did enjoy "happy hour" (a charitable term for what usually ended up including dinner and lasting for about five hours), but it seemed to happen so frequently, and tended to be quite hard on both the wallet and the waistline.

"Is Laura on board?" Yvonne asked. Laura was their partner in crime and also their manager.

"Yes. She will be." Amy grinned again and somehow conveyed a wink of the eye, although she might not have literally winked.

Yvonne hesitated. "Well, let me talk to Bill…"

"You're going!" said Amy, giving her another little shove.

Yvonne knew it was true. She was going.

Gary and Scott were busily engaged in one of their favorite shared activities: preparing for dinner guests. Gary enjoyed it because of the artistry involved, and the anticipation of socializing. Scott liked the meticulous planning and flawless execution of that plan.

For both men, it also didn't hurt that they saw eye-to-eye on nearly every aspect of hosting, and worked very smoothly together on it. Gary created the menu, oversaw the layout of the table (including associated decorations) and managed the evening's musical selections. He also made the dessert. Scott acted as head chef, orchestrating the timing of all kitchen tasks and performing most of the measuring, chopping and stirring. This harmony between them relieved stress and gave rise to a feeling of camaraderie and even a bit of romance.

The prep for this particular dinner was especially nice because of who was coming over. Friends were always easier to handle than family, and the Smedes were among the easiest of all friends. Their quiet, low-key style was appreciated by Scott, who would've preferred never to interact with any other type of person (his husband notwithstanding). It also appealed to Gary, a refreshing change from nearly everyone he encountered in the sales world. But the Smedes could also be a lot of fun once they were drawn out. Added bonuses: they never seemed to have any expectations and never overstayed their welcome.

Gary felt fortunate to know the Smedes, and indeed, also felt they were very fortunate to know him. These folks were not an easy pair to get to know; a few years back, Gary had waged a tough campaign to befriend them, which lasted several weeks and was sometimes touch-and-go. He'd noticed them repeatedly out on the neighborhood sidewalks and somehow sensed, just by looking at them, that they were good and interesting people. His extremely brief "chance" meetings with them reinforced this sense. Ever so gradually, over the course of many such brief meetings, Gary had gained their trust and built a little framework of a rapport with them. They'd finally agreed to come over for tea the third time he'd invited them, then they'd canceled, then accepted his fourth invitation and that time actually did show up. And they'd had a great cup of tea together. And the rest, as Gary liked to say, was history. The beginning of a beautiful friendship.

One other great thing about the Smedes, thought Gary as the doorbell rang, was that they always showed up exactly on time. Scott buzzed them in and a moment later the four friends were standing together, exchanging the usual pleasantries. Gary gratefully took the bottle of wine Bill was holding and set it on a nearby bookshelf, then transferred it to the wine rack a few minutes later. Yvonne made a mental note that they really should stop bringing wine, as she could see all the bottles they'd ever brought sitting in that rack each time they came over.

These dinners, which happened roughly every six weeks, were the only substantial interaction the two couples had with each other. So their conversations mostly consisted of catching up on what'd been going on in their lives since the last one. Tonight, as always, Gary drove it, because everyone else at the table was an introvert.

Work was typically a big topic. Gary loved explaining the excitement of the franchise coffee business, and also loved hearing all the details of other people's jobs. Scott found his own work fascinating but didn't much care to discuss it, and had very little interest in anyone else's. Yvonne fell somewhere in the middle; she enjoyed both sharing and listening, but not with the same appetite as Gary. Bill found his own job extremely boring and others' jobs even more so. But he did enjoy a good workplace anecdote (if it was accessible to somebody outside that particular industry), and always waited patiently—and usually in vain—for one to arise.

This evening Gary was delighted to find that all three of his companions were more talkative than usual. Scott spoke with mild excitement (which was a lot for him) about his newly-conceived quest to achieve "MasterBlaster" status this year in Cooperstown Universe (a stunningly complex online baseball trivia and statistics game with a surprisingly large following (meaning more than zero)).

Yvonne described a recent looping experience in which she and Bill were followed by another couple who yacked loudly, incessantly and oh so inanely; despite changing their route and pace repeatedly, they'd not been able to shake this annoying pair for the entirety of their walk.

Bill related his recent confrontation with the L.A. Parking Violations Bureau, who'd ticketed him for "blocking" a driveway when the back bumper of his car extended a mere two inches past where the curb began to curve downwards. He'd mailed them a lengthy letter accompanied by photos, but had ultimately lost the fight and paid the fine.

But the "main event" tonight was Gary's newfound (or, technically, newly rediscovered) passion for long-distance running.

"So Yvonne tells me you're training for some event, like a 5K?" Bill enquired.

"Yes indeed!" Gary exclaimed. "Not a 5K, a marathon. Multiple marathons, actually. Which hopefully will lead to a grand climax of running this super-prestigious, really special marathon next year. Hardly anyone qualifies for it. It's called... What's it called again, babe?"

"The Golden Road Championship Classic," said Scott.

"So anyway," Gary continued, "qualifying for this race is pretty tough. I've gotta run like three or four other marathons before I can run that one. Really specific ones, in a certain order. And I have to get really good times on them. Or else I'm out!" He made a slicing gesture across his throat and chuckled.

"All the marathons are color-coded," Scott explained, "according to when they take place, and maybe geography too. They're all over the world and happening all throughout the year. But I think the way it works is you just have to complete one from each color group." He paused. "The rules are actually pretty confusing."

"They sure are," Gary agreed. "But I am jazzed! I'm ready!" He laughed again. "Bring it on," he added with a big grin and a little fist-pump.

"Sounds great," said Bill.

"So you must be training pretty hard, huh?" asked Yvonne. "When's your first race?"

"Good question," said Scott, pulling out his phone. "We were trying to figure that out. I think we ended up with one in northern California in late June..." He began tapping away, looking for his notes.

"Yeah, the training's going to be intense," Gary said. "I was looking into some local running groups I could join, but Frank suggested I should train at altitude with a personal coach. That's how the elite runners do it."

"So," Bill ventured, "the idea is you get used to breathing the thin air and then when you run the actual race, at a lower elevation...?"

"Exactly! It's like an energy boost. The same time and distance feels easier. Like walking on the moon!"

"Wow, cool," said Bill, but privately suspected it was a huge waste of time.

"A personal trainer sounds expensive," said Yvonne.

"It is," Scott muttered.

"Well, yeah, kind of," Gary conceded. "But hey, I'm in it to win it! Plus Frank wants to split the cost. And he's got some good connections in the running world."

"Oh, yeah?"

"Yeah, totally. He knows a guy whose cousin is friends with Bob Larsen. Hoping he can hook us up. Wouldn't that just be so great?" Gary flashed another big grin.

"Who's Bob Larsen?" Yvonne asked.

"Big-name running coach. Former UCLA cross-country coach. He trained Meb!"

"Meb?"

"Oh, you don't know Meb? He's a really famous runner."

"There are no really famous runners," said Bill.

"Hah-hah. Fine. He's pretty famous. Olympic silver medalist. And he won the New York *and* Boston marathons. A truly great runner."

"Apparently so," said Yvonne.

Gary continued, "Partly because of great coaching! So anyway, if we can get Bob Larsen that'll be super exciting."

Everyone was silent for a moment. Then Scott said, "Don't worry, guys—Gary didn't know who those people were either, until five minutes ago when he started this running fad."

Gary wasn't offended but did immediately voice his disagreement. "Oh, it's no fad," he said, smiling. "This is real. Running isn't just a hobby. It's a lifestyle!"

There was another moment of silence. Then Yvonne asked, "So where are you going to do this altitude training? Big Bear?"

"Nope. Colorado, baby! The Rocky Mountains. Nothing but the best!"

"Wow," said Bill, "are you going to drive your Supra all the way out there?"

It was common knowledge among everyone who knew Gary that he was afraid of flying and always drove everywhere he went, no matter how far.

Gary pondered Bill's question for a few seconds. Lately he hadn't been feeling the same level of passion for his car. He also wondered what sort of price such a fine specimen might fetch—money that could help fund his marathon efforts.

"Yeah, maybe," he finally said. "I don't know. It might be time for me to look into getting something more practical."

A barely audible "Hmm" escaped from Scott's throat.

Chapter 2

Amy Lee tended to make an impression whenever she entered a room.

"What's up, bitches!" she exclaimed as she entered this one—the reception and bar area of Souper Trouper—on a Tuesday evening in late April.

Amy was not a conventionally attractive woman. She was at least 40 pounds overweight, with slightly crooked teeth, an oddly shaped nose and eyes a bit too far apart. But she was abundantly self-confident, which had a huge impact on how people saw her. Everything about Amy's style—how she walked, how she talked, how she dressed, the way she'd spontaneously break into song (with a fantastic voice)—was all about expression and freedom and fun. Everyone could tell she felt sexy, and she brought them all along with her on that.

The bitches she was addressing, seated around a small, circular, high table not far from the entrance, were Laura Johnson, Yvonne Smede and Desdemona "Mona" Knox.

"We put our name in," Laura informed Amy. "They said it'd be about ten minutes."

"But that was about fifteen minutes ago," added Yvonne.

"Okay, whatevs," Amy replied. "We've got our drinks, so we're all good, right?" She quickly eyed up Laura's gin and tonic, Yvonne's glass of white wine, and Mona's Diet Coke.

"Except for me!" she added with a grin. "Better fix that. B.R.B. ladies!" And she scurried off to the bar.

The four women were all members of the Lab Team, with Laura overseeing the other three. Laura was an adventurer, curious about almost everything, but rather quiet and unassuming. She had a fundamentally innocent approach to the world, implicitly trusting of every person, place and situation. Yet she was largely indifferent about matters moral, and about her fellow humans generally. She enjoyed light socializing, but tended not to feel much love, or even much like, for others.

So she'd surprised herself several years ago by becoming good friends with a couple of people, and especially these particular ones— the brash, bombastic Amy and the cynical, shy-but-sharp-tongued Yvonne. Laura's promotion to management a few years later had changed her official duties, but had affected her professional interactions with the other two very little, and their personal relationships not at all.

Mona smiled weakly at Yvonne and Laura as she sipped on her soda through a straw. They both smiled back at her. All three women's minds were racing, trying to think of something to say, but they were all failing.

After a minute, Amy rescued them by returning. "Okay, let's get this party started," she said, pulling up a stool and setting her Negroni down on the table. "So, any hubbies joining us? Laura, where's Mike?"

"He was working until noon, so he's been sleeping. But he said he might try to come later."

"Bill should be here soon," offered Yvonne. "He texted me like an hour ago saying he was heading out."

Amy's gaze turned to Mona. "How 'bout you, Mona-My-Sharona? What's your husband's name again? Is it Don?"

"Oh, Don definitely won't be joining us," Mona replied, a bit startled. "We separated a few months ago."

"Oh, that's right!" Amy said, chuckling and smacking herself on the forehead. "Oops."

Laura asked Mona, "How have you been doing?"

"Good," said Mona, and the others silently kept their attention on her for several seconds, expecting her to say more. But she didn't.

Mona did not usually join these after-work gatherings, but this time she'd decided to give it a try after some energetic prodding from Amy. Mona didn't particularly enjoy being out in public, or drinking, or even conversation. But she nursed a small hope that she might be able to penetrate the "triumvirate" (her private pet name for them), or at least gain some insight into their inner workings, or at the very least, endear herself to them a little. Mona had always suspected that the other members of the team believed her to be quite boring and a bit stupid. And she was right (and so were they).

"Laura, party of five!" called out a cheerful voice suddenly, and the Lab Team women turned to see the beaming face of Oleanna Arrandami, who was standing at the host station holding a stack of menus. They all stood and headed that way.

"One of our party hasn't arrived yet," Laura informed Oleanna.

"Not a problem," she replied with a smile. "I'll seat the four of you now, and when your fifth arrives I will bring them right to you!"

Oleanna then led the others swiftly through the labyrinthine main dining room, making three left turns and two right turns (not in that order), stopping at a relatively small round table with five place settings.

"Here you are, ladies," she said, gesturing at the table with genuine pleasure.

Amy said "Why thank you, ma'am!" and the other three said nothing as they all took their seats.

"I'm your server this evening," said Oleanna, handing out the menus. "My name is Oleanna and I aim to please. I'll check on you frequently, unless you ask me not to, in which case I won't. But in between checks, if there is anything you need or want, anything whatsoever, you flag me down. And if you don't see me, flag down another staff member and tell them to find me A.S.A.P."

Correctly sensing that her guests had no requests to make of her at the moment, Oleanna then took her leave of them.

And Oleanna's guests sensed correctly that she meant every word she said and that all of her enthusiasm was completely sincere. Her heart soared when she provided diners with excellent service and saw what pleasure they took from the experience. It had always been Oleanna's dream to one day wait tables in a top-tier L.A. restaurant. At eighteen she'd moved here from Oklahoma to pursue that dream, and every day she pursued it relentlessly. Of course, she wasn't there yet, and struggled to make ends meet working as a server in less prestigious places like Souper Trouper. So she supported herself by taking temporary jobs acting in movies and television shows.

"So," said Amy as they were all settling in and glancing over the menu, "anyone got any big plans for the weekend?"

"The weekend is still four days off," Mona pointed out.

"Ugh, my dad is coming for a visit," sighed Yvonne. "I invite him over for dinner and then he just invites himself to come for the entire weekend. So frustrating. He only lives twenty minutes away!"

"He's probably lonely."

"Hmm, maybe. Hard to imagine Dad feeling lonely. He hates people."

Amy laughed. "I'm sure that's not true," she said.

Laura was staring into her phone. Mona was staring at a spot on the table in front of her where a phone might have been but wasn't.

"Oh!" said Amy, suddenly remembering a good story. "Speaking of parents, I got a call from my mom the other day."

Laura and Mona looked up.

"So, she calls me up all excited and she says, she says"—Amy put on a dopey-sounding voice—" 'Aim-ee, I must tear you about sum-fing very wun-der-fur'…"

Yvonne laughed very quietly, muffling it.

"That's terrible!" said Mona.

"What?" asked Amy with a slightly defiant smirk.

"Well, pretty racist," Laura chided, "with stereotyping plus mocking. Also you shouldn't make fun of your own mother."

Amy fired back: "It's *because* she's my own mother that it's okay! And anyways, that's what she sounds like. You've met her, right? That's what she sounds like, bless her heart. I'm just tellin' it like it is.

"Besides," she added with a small giggle, "I'm allowed to be racist on Asians because I'm Asian."

Taking this remark more seriously than it was intended, Laura said, "No, actually that doesn't follow." She felt no moral outrage but was a sucker for light philosophical debate. It was like a sport.

She continued, "Being a member of a marginalized group doesn't exempt you from treating that group with respect. If anything, you have a greater responsibility than the population at large."

"Okay, professor," said Amy with a grin. "But back to my story! So my mom says she has this supposed great news and then she starts rambling on and on about how she got in touch with some other Chinese chick through some kind of, like genealogy website or something, and they've been doing research, digging into the history of my mom's home village where she grew up…

"And I'm thinking like, 'What could the good news be? Did she find out she's inheriting a bunch of money or something?' But no, that's not it. She finally gets to the point, and it's: she thinks she's found my biological father."

"You're adopted?" asked Mona.

"Yeah, totally. You didn't know that? Yep, I was adopted when I was a baby." Amy glanced at Yvonne and Laura. "You guys knew that, right?"

Laura nodded yes. Yvonne just smiled. Neither of them could remember if they knew or not.

"It's no biggie," Amy continued. "My parents are my parents. Always were. I don't care if I didn't get my DNA from them, you know? They're my parents. And I've never had any interest in finding my biological ones. Not that I have a grudge against them or anything, I just... you know, never had any interest. But apparently my mom did. So she found out, through this online research nerd pal of hers, about this dude from her village that she thinks is my bio father.

"Well, actually, let me back up. She actually already knew who this guy was. So, way, way back, when she lived over there, everybody in the village knew who this guy was. He was from a wealthy family that ran a big rice business, farming and processing it, for generations. They were like, the wealthiest and most well-known and well-respected family in the village, by far. And this guy was like the biggest star from that family, even. Mom said he was all charismatic and generous and just like, involved in everything. He was a businessman, but he was also a community organizer and a local politician and a philanthropist and a lecturer and... you name it. He was like a rock star there."

"Can I get anybody anything?" asked Oleanna, who had reappeared beside the table, Amy felt, almost by magic.

Then Amy noticed that Bill was here now, too, having stealthily slid into the formerly empty chair between Yvonne and Mona.

"Oh, hey, Bill!" she said. "Didn't see ya there. Welcome to our little shindig!"

"Thanks," Bill replied with a face he hoped looked like a smile but in fact looked more like a grimace.

Everybody was drinkless at this point except Mona, who still had three quarters of her Diet Coke. The other women asked Oleanna for refills and Bill asked her for an old fashioned. Then food was discussed briefly, but nobody had made any decisions yet apart from Amy, who ordered three appetizers for the table: fried breaded mozzarella, fried breaded mushrooms and fried breaded rye toast. After ensuring there were no further requests, Oleanna vanished again.

"How was your walk?" Yvonne asked Bill.

"Terrible," he replied, "but better than driving. And I got tons of steps!"

Yvonne and Bill both hated driving in L.A., and generally walked to any destination less than five miles away unless there was a lot of stuff to carry. (Once a week they grudgingly drove the two miles (about 20 minutes) each way to the local Hank's for their big grocery shopping session.)

"What was terrible about it?" asked Laura.

"Well the worst thing was, I almost got run over by one of those electric scooters."

"Oh, I hate those," said Amy.

"Yeah, the fucker just whizzes past me like I'm not there. A kid, of course. Comes within millimeters…"

Mona winced at the word "fucker."

"Scared the shit out of me," Bill continued. Another wince from Mona.

"Were you wearing your earphones?" asked Yvonne in a playful "Tsk, tsk" tone.

"Well, yeah," Bill replied with a small smile and eyeroll. "Of course. I need my music. I can't walk without my music."

"Those scooters shouldn't exist," said Laura. "Or they should have their own dedicated lane or something. They're dangerous on the street and they're dangerous on the sidewalk."

"I wholeheartedly agree," said Bill. "All the electric scooters should be thrown into the mouth of an active volcano. With the riders still attached to them."

Bill went on to explain other issues he'd encountered on his journey, including being deprived of his precious music for the last half-mile (post-scooter-incident) because his battery had died. Not his phone battery—unlike most self-respecting members of the 21st century, Bill continued to listen to music on a small, screenless, well-over-a-decade-old iPod (the first—and, to date, last—Apple product he'd understood how to operate). Nobody knew the reason for this, but it was suspected to be related to his technophobia and short temper.

After a few minutes, Oleanna returned with everyone's drinks, giving Amy an opportunity to interrupt Bill's enumeration of all his gripes from his walk.

"So anyways, Bill, I was telling the gals here about this thing with my mom."

"Oh, yeah, I think I caught the tail end of it. Some guy who was kind of a celebrity back in the day, in her village in China?"

"Yes, exactly. His name was, uh, Chang, I think…"

Amy picked up her phone and, after a few seconds, found the link her mother had sent.

"Yep, Arnold Chang. Well that's his American name, anyways. That's him."

The phone was passed around the table and everyone glanced at the picture, which was part of a short news article and showed an elderly man in a suit, standing behind a lectern, apparently speaking, with one arm gesturing behind him, perhaps to an unseen whiteboard or projection screen.

"Check out his wrist," said Amy. In the photo, the man's wrist protruded a bit from the shirt sleeve of his outstretched arm. "There's a little blob there. Hard to make out. I mean it could be anything—it could be a freakin' shadow, or, whatever…"

She held up her own wrist for her companions to see. "But my mom thinks it's this."

It was a reddish-purple birthmark, about two inches long, with a shape somewhat resembling a seahorse.

Everybody was briefly dumbstruck. Then Yvonne said, "That's it? She thinks you two have the same birthmark and therefore he's your father?"

"Are birthmarks even hereditary?" asked Bill, prompting Laura to pick up her phone and begin investigating.

"Doesn't matter," said Amy. "In my mother's mind, they are. Oh, but it's not just the birthmark, to answer your question, Yvonne. She also has it, 'on good authority,' "—Amy made air quotes with her fingers—"that Mr. Chang there immigrated to the U.S. after their village was destroyed in a fire."

"The whole village burned down?"

"Yep. It was literally wiped off the map. Huge, out-of-control fire. Like forty-some years ago, when my mom was a teenager. Everyone who didn't die had to move somewhere else. Actually I think that fire was one of the reasons my mom immigrated, too."

"Nope, they're not hereditary," Laura announced.

"What?" asked Amy.

"Birthmarks. They're not hereditary."

"Yeah, good luck convincing my mom. She knows what she knows. So yeah, according to this woman she connected with online, this guy Chang, my supposed father, came to the U.S., to the state of Michigan—which is where I was adopted from—and he had a daughter, around the same time I was born, and he gave up the daughter for adoption."

"Hmm," said Yvonne, "her case still seems pretty weak."

"I know, right?"

Oleanna reappeared, performed a sleek delivery of the appetizers, checked nobody needed another drink, then disappeared again.

"Mmm, these look delicious," said Amy.

"Yes!" Laura agreed. They both enthusiastically piled up their little appetizer plates and began to dig in. Mona piled up and began munching, too, but without the enthusiasm.

Bill and Yvonne glanced at each other. Once again, they found themselves facing the "happy hour dilemma": give in to the forces of evil and have an evening of pleasure followed by a day of regret, or perform a Herculean act of self-restraint and suffer through an evening of hunger, sobriety and envy.

In theory there was a third way, a middle path of moderation. This was the sensible, smart course. But in practice it was never going to happen. When one drink is gone, it must be replaced with another. And as the drinks flow, the desire to wolf down food increases, while the desire to behave sensibly decreases. Diabolical.

However, there was also a fourth way: just leave. This was the option Bill and Yvonne had privately discussed earlier in the day, and on which they now silently agreed with facial expressions. Sometimes the fourth way was blocked by the formidable social jujitsu of some members of "The Evils" (a squad comprising Amy (the captain), Laura (the lieutenant), their husbands (the foot soldiers), and the Smedes (unconsenting draftees)). But with sufficient tenacity, it could be done.

Amy had just swallowed a bite of app and was poised to launch back into her story.

"Well," said Yvonne, standing up, "we're going to head out."

"Aw, we only just got here," said Laura, as Amy simultaneously said, "What?! No you're not."

Bill jumped up too. "Yeah, 'fraid so. I am super tired, and I still need to help Alice with her homework." These were both lies.

"And we've got dinner waiting in the slow cooker," Yvonne added. This was true.

As Amy and Laura stammered (having been caught off guard),

on the brink of their next maneuver, Bill and Yvonne began walking briskly away from the table.

"I'll Venmo you for this, just let me know how much," Yvonne called over her shoulder. Then they were gone.

"Those two," said a bemused Laura, shaking her head.

Amy shrugged. "Life goes on, baby. We got eats, we got drinks. The night is young!"

Mona made a loud slurping noise with her straw as she reached the bottom of her Diet Coke.

Out on the street a few minutes later, Yvonne and Bill were grinning at each other as they climbed into the back of an Uber.

"That was a close one," said Bill.

"Yeah," Yvonne replied. "Want to have a celebratory drink when we get home?"

"Definitely."

It was Friday morning and Bill was standing inside Mail and Ship, which (as hinted at by its name) rented out mailboxes, provided shipping services, and sold supplies used in the sending and receiving of stuff. The small shop was owned and operated entirely by one person, named Lev Rockman (though no customer had ever known his name), a humorless man with a permanently expressionless face who didn't hesitate to charge people very high prices for everything and lie to them about how much the post office would charge. But Mail and Ship was only a 15-minute walk from home for Bill.

Having just completed his distasteful transaction with Lev, which was to send a faulty computer smart card reader back to CompDyn-Corp, Bill inserted his earphones, stepped out onto Santa Monica Boulevard and turned left. He quickly arrived at the corner of Roper

Boulevard and, despite needing to cross both streets, stood there for nearly a minute with neither walk signal on, underneath a billboard promoting a "non-invasive" surgical procedure to render a person's underarm sweat glands non-functional. Meanwhile one of the cars sitting at the light had its stereo at maximum volume and all its windows down, so Bill was unable to hear the music he'd chosen for himself and was treated to somebody else's instead. The offender sat calmly behind the wheel, in plain sight, utterly shameless. This situation was not at all unusual, but Bill scowled and muttered "Goddammit" anyway.

Eventually the lights got through their entire cycle, the obnoxious driver was gone, and Bill made it across both streets, then continued a short distance on the south side of Santa Monica, past a couple of palm trees, before turning down Landon Avenue into the neighborhood adjacent to his own. Whenever Bill needed to walk north or south through this part of the street grid, he chose Landon because of its unique scenery: for three blocks, the front of every single property, houses and apartment buildings alike, was themed for a specific year in history—the year matching its address.

Bill strolled along slowly, turning his head left and right, taking it all in. The folks living at 1744 had created a desert scene, with a collection of colorfully decorated tents and a flag containing a white crescent moon on a solid green background. The entire apartment block at 1789 looked like a medieval fortress and its front yard was littered with replicas of muskets and cannons, pieces of torn clothing, and three signs with single-word exclamations like "Fraternité!" printed on them.

Bill crossed Utah Avenue and continued his whirlwind history lesson. In front of 1804 was a huge model of a train engine, with a long stretch of track extending out from under it. 1818 looked like it was ready for Halloween, with a yard done up like a spooky mad-scientist-style laboratory and featuring a huge, hulking statue of a humanoid creature with two electrodes protruding from its neck. The front wall of 1859 had a map of the world painted onto it with a red line indicating routes traveled, like in an Indiana Jones movie; on the grass sat a sequence of cardboard silhouettes, their shapes progressing from a monkey-like creature on the far left to a person on the far right.

Crossing Wyoming Avenue brought Bill's idyll into the 20th century. The humble house at 1908 Landon looked like it might have been built in 1908 (though it had actually been built in 1927), and parked in its driveway was a mint condition Ford Model T. The extra-wide driveway at 1955 contained three cars parked side by side: an early Porsche with the word "Continental" stamped on it, a first-generation Ford Thunderbird, and a DeLorean. These were flanked by a giant pair of mouse ears on one side and a giant pair of golden arches on the other.

At the end of this block, Bill turned onto Arkansas Avenue rather than continuing down Landon. On that next block, the majority of properties were not participating in the program, some for unknown reasons and others because their year had not yet arrived, making the choice of theme a tricky one indeed. Besides, there was a light at the intersection of Arkansas and Boswick Boulevard, allowing Bill to easily cross Boswick into his neighborhood.

He never got tired of Landon Avenue, especially as many of the buildings made frequent changes, ranging from minor adjustments to major enhancements and occasionally a complete re-do with a new focus. He lamented the fact that many years were not represented (each block had only ten lots on each side), and found the absence of 1776, 1865, 1918 and 1945 particularly regrettable.

As Bill began crossing Whitmore Avenue, he noticed, lounging on the sidewalk on the opposite side, Rufus Fletcher, a homeless man who could often be found lounging on the sidewalk. Bill didn't know Rufus's last name and, at this point in his life, neither did Rufus. But the two men did know each other's first names, and always exchanged a greeting when they met under these circumstances (which were the only times they met).

"Good morning, Bill," Rufus called out as Bill approached.

Bill pulled his earphones out. "Morning, Rufus. How are the squirrels?"

Bill had learned long ago not to bother asking "How are you?" of Rufus, because he always insisted that how he was didn't matter, all that mattered was how the squirrels were. Rufus loved the squirrels, which seemed to populate these neighborhoods in even greater numbers than humans or dogs. He loathed the crows, which were also undoubtedly among the four most common species in the area.

"Pretty well today," Rufus replied. "Roderick knocked a piece of bread right out of the beak of one of those bastards, and then scurried off with it. A beautiful sight to behold!"

"I'll bet."

Rufus firmly believed that the squirrels and the crows were locked in eternal battle over resources, tree occupation rights, and probably ideology too. Good versus evil. The noble squirrels all had names (e.g. Roderick), a few of which they'd been kind enough to share with Rufus. The foul crows didn't mess around with individual names, regarding themselves as undistinguished components of one massive, dark whole; they were simply Crow.

Bill felt neutral about the squirrels, but he agreed with Rufus that the crows sucked. Their perpetual squawking featured prominently on his list of neighborhood annoyances.

"Talk to you later," said Rufus.

"Okay, later," Bill replied, re-inserting his earphones and carrying on along Arkansas. He smiled. He was quite fond of Rufus, who, in all their encounters, had never asked for anything and had never said the same thing twice. "A thinking man's bum," Bill called him (to a very select few people).

The rest of Bill's walk along Arkansas was mercifully uneventful, apart from someone using their car horn to brutally punish another driver (and everyone in the vicinity—collateral damage) for an unknown slight, right next to Bill as he made his way across Boswick. Having arrived back in his own neighborhood, Bill turned left onto Wexler and was soon climbing the stairs to the door of his condo.

Checking his step count as he entered, Bill was startled to look up and see a man standing in the middle of the living room. The man was white, fairly slender for the most part but with a sizeable gut, appeared to be approximately 75 years of age, and sported a clean-shaven face with shaggy gray hair around the sides and none on top. The man was Bill's father-in-law.

"Hello, Billy," he said.

There was only one person on earth who'd ever called Bill by this name (and that was one too many). Even his own parents had never called him Billy when he was growing up. For the first eighteen years of his life he'd been known only as William. Then, in his first year of college, his friend Matt had branded him Bill and somehow it had stuck.

"Oh, hey, Al. Wasn't expecting you."

"I prefer Mr. Forrester."

"Yeah, you probably prefer a lot of things," Bill said silently in his own mind. Out loud he just said, "Right."

Al, who was known (somewhat) affectionately to the Smede family as Gramps, said "Yvonne didn't tell you I was coming?"

"Yeah, but she said for the weekend. I assumed you'd be arriving tonight, or maybe tomorrow morning."

"Never assume, never the tomb. Thomas J. Watson said that."

"Did he?"

"Where's that granddaughter of mine? Is she home?"

"No, she's at school right now. Strangest thing, she always seems to be there on weekdays during school hours."

"What about Patrick? Is he home?"

"Yeah, of course he's home," said Bill, taking out his phone. "It's before noon."

"What are you doing?" asked Gramps.

"Just letting Yvonne know you're here."

Gramps reached out for the phone. "I want to talk to her," he said.

"I'm just texting her."

"Text, schmext. That's all you kids ever do these days. What a bunch of crap. Just call her!"

"But, she's working."

"It won't take long. People get phone calls at work all the time, don't they?"

"Okay, okay," said Bill, who pretty much never argued with anyone about anything. He dialed Yvonne.

She picked up almost immediately with a quiet, flat "Hey, what's up?" (This was her "I'm at work" voice.)

"Hey," said Bill. "You'll never guess who's here. Oh no, wait, hang on—you'll guess easily."

"He's early even by his standards," Yvonne said.

"He wants to say hello," said Bill, handing the phone to Gramps.

"Hi darling. I'm here at your apartment... Yes, pretty good. Billy's been rude to me but that's expected... Okay, great. I'll be here when you get here. Love you. Bye."

He gave the phone back to Bill without hanging up. Bill put it to his ear but Yvonne was gone.

"Well I really need to get some work done," said Bill, heading for the table where his open laptop sat.

"Yes, you'd better get on with that. I'm going to go see Patrick."

"Good idea. You guys spend some quality time together."

Gramps headed for the back of the condo. Bill sat down and unlocked his screen, upon which he was horrified to discover that his boss had been messaging him and that an unexpected conference call had been scheduled, starting in five minutes.

"Fuck," he said.

A loud, high-pitched noise abruptly pierced Yvonne's consciousness and brought her wandering mind back to her immediate surroundings. She was sitting on a sofa next to Amy. Across from them, Amy's husband Jake sat on a dining chair he'd pulled up. Jake's mouth was moving, and Yvonne remembered that she'd been attempting to pay attention to the seemingly endless stream of drivel it was emitting. She resumed this attempt.

"...So I said, 'How could he possibly be on track to get all those reports done on time?' I mean, damn! I mean, just, every time I turn around, he's on a smoke break or a bathroom break. Oh, speaking of bathrooms, don't use our half-bath. It's out of order. You can use the one in the back if you need to."

Yvonne intended to say "Okay, thanks" but missed her five-millisecond window of opportunity by inhaling first.

"Yeah, hah, it was funny," Jake continued. "The toilet in there just kept having trouble! And it was, on and on, this thing and that thing. The flusher and, just on and on. So we finally decided, okay, we're just gonna go for it and get that darn thing out of there and get rid of it. And get a new toilet."

"Two new toilets," Amy interjected. "They had a special on toilets at Home Depot. Buy one get one half off. And the other one wasn't in great shape either so we figured, what the hell."

It crossed Yvonne's mind that Amy and Jake were a somewhat odd couple, with both members being so aggressively talkative every waking moment. How did they manage to satisfactorily carve up the air time? Yvonne had also always felt that Amy was probably brighter than Jake, and more successful in her career. And more attractive. But they'd been together ever since college, and seemed quite happy with each other.

"What the hell, what the hell," echoed Jake. "So we brought the new toilets home and then we started working on the installation."

"You started working on it," Amy corrected him. "I said we should hire somebody to do it. And I was right."

"No you weren't," said Jake. "Everything was going fine removing that toilet in there"—he gestured toward the half-bath—"but then, something was just wrong with that toilet. I mean, it just wasn't right! A couple of those gasket thingies were warped, and one was missing. I tried every trick in the book…"

Amy had begun to chuckle and shake her head.

"But now, uh, it's stuck," Jake continued. "It won't come off and it won't go back on right. And we had to shut off the water flow to it because it's just leaking all over the place. I mean leaking bad!" He chuckled too.

The same loud, high-pitched noise that had jarred Yvonne out of her reverie a few minutes ago happened again, and this time she realized that it was created by two young children racing through the room screaming at each other. They were Brandon, age four, and his sister Jennifer, age seven. Yvonne suppressed the urge to scrunch up her face in disgust.

"Jake, can you round up those little rascals, honey?" asked Amy.

"Yes, ma'am," he replied, rising from his seat and making a move in the direction his son and daughter had just darted. "Hey you two," he called out as he gave chase, "it's bath time!"

Jake Lee had an energy about him, a physical energy that seemed to constantly fill him up and animate him and radiate out. Despite being more than a hundred pounds overweight, he moved rather quickly and was limber enough to avoid tripping over the numerous objects that littered the floor of his home as he made his way to his brats' bedroom, where he cornered them.

Everywhere within Yvonne's field of view—the lounge in which she sat, the adjoining kitchen and dining area, the little corridor that led back to the bedrooms—was loaded with clutter, wall-to-wall and floor-to-ceiling. A decent portion of this comprised clothes, books and food, but primarily it was various toys and amusements.

There were the kids' toys, of course, but there were also a fair number of items designed for the cats to play with and climb on. Yvonne wasn't sure how many cats lived here. At least two, because she could see one lounging on a window sill while glimpsing another one out of the corner of her eye which cruised along the edge of the room and then disappeared.

Finally there was a third type of toy: Jake's. Many of the shelves and some of the smaller tables were piled up with never-opened packages of vintage action figures. Star Wars, Star Trek, G.I. Joe—he loved them all. He also loved comic books, and owned dozens of cardboard boxes filled with them, hundreds of comics per box, that were stacked up in nearly every corner of his tiny house. And he was always on the hunt for more—shortly after Yvonne had arrived this evening, he'd regaled her with the story of his burning desire to obtain a copy of an extremely rare issue of Field Marshal Wield-Partial.

The series, which had begun in the late 1970s, followed the adventures of a military-style superhero who inherited powers from both of his mysterious, long-deceased parents, policeman Fletcher Wield and nurse Dorothy-Ann Partial. The first issue was very rare. But another issue, published in limited quantities in the mid-1980s, was the most rare of all. It was called "Number Zero" and contained juicy details of the main character's childhood and his parents' backstories. This was the issue Jake longed to lay his hands on.

Yvonne turned her attention to Amy, who'd picked up the telling of the toilet story: "So we arranged for somebody to come out and install the new toilets for us. But when the guy got here, the new toilets were nowhere to be found."

Yvonne raised her eyebrows as Amy paused for dramatic effect.

"They were in Jake's freakin' car! He never took them out. And then he took his car in for service, and it's still there, in the shop, and they're closed on Sundays, and then they were closed today too for some weird-ass reason."

Yvonne was laughing now.

"So that's where we are with that," Amy said in conclusion.

After a moment Yvonne said, "Oh, hey, what's the latest with that thing with your mom?"

"Oh yeah! So wild," Amy said, chuckling. "So I don't know if I told you all of Mom's crazy theory. She not only thinks this Chang guy is my father, she thinks *she's* related to him, too!"

"Really?"

"Yeah, he came from some really famous family from that village. They'd been wealthy and influential for generations. For like, hundreds of years. Everyone knew who they were. And, in my mom's family, there was always this idea—like, folklore, I guess—that their family was related to this other family, the rich and famous one."

"Okay," said Yvonne.

"And, get this. There was supposed to be proof of the connection in some ancient ancestry book. Some super old, handwritten book where the village elders or council or whatever had always kept records of all the families there. And they were still doing it, like, when my mom was a kid. Adding more entries to this old-ass book, keeping it up to date."

"So, the villagers couldn't look at the book?"

"Nope. It was kept under lock and key. 'Need to know only' type thing. And it was destroyed in the fire, when the village burned down."

"Hmm," said Yvonne.

"But, there might have been copies made at some unknown time in the past. And rumor has it—according to my mom, according to her crazy pen-pal friend—rumor has it that mysterious Mr. Chang took one of those copies when he fled."

"Hmm," said Yvonne again.

Jake returned, carrying the bottle of wine they'd opened when the women arrived.

"Kids are in the bath," he announced. "Refills, ladies?"

"Oh yes, please," said Amy, holding out her glass.

Yvonne hesitated but relented. She felt the standard trap springing.

Morris had left work early today for a dental appointment, and the initial plan had been that Bill, who'd taken the day off work to (very grudgingly) attend an afternoon performance of The Ultra-Realistic Natural Theatre (which included no stage or seating and seamlessly incorporated the audience members into every scene) with his mother and sister, would swing by Yvonne's office on his way home and pick her up. But he'd called two hours ago to inform her he'd been detained by an unanticipated encore, so she'd decided to just Uber home. But then Amy had hatched the plan of bringing Yvonne back to the Lee residence after work (and then Bill could pick her up from there later). So now here she was.

"Anyways," said Amy as Jake was pouring, "I haven't found any contact info for this guy. Not that I tried very hard—hah! That's

Mom's job. Anyways, all I know is he's like a history professor or something, and he's giving some lecture in Michigan in July. So guess what? I'm going to that freakin' lecture!"

"Seriously?" asked Yvonne.

"Dead serious. My mom insists I gotta talk to this guy, and that's the only way I can." She paused for a moment, then said, "Hey, I'm going to Michigan!"

"To Michigan!" Jake cried abruptly, grinning and raising his glass.

"To Michigan!" repeated Amy.

Yvonne, slightly bewildered, opted out of the impromptu chant but joined in the toast, raising her glass and clinking it against the other two.

Chapter 3

"I'm living the dream," Irene Hoffman said quietly and sincerely, in between taking a gulp from the coffee mug she held in her right hand and a drag from the cigarette in her left. She stood alone on the back patio of her house, gazing at the brick wall fifteen feet in front of her that separated her property from the one behind, but somehow gazing far beyond it too. She thought about her beautiful house, sitting here in one of the most desirable spots on the planet; about the two fine automobiles parked in its garage; about her four young children, each being molded for greatness, whose muffled shouts and laughter from inside the house were the only sound currently penetrating Irene's backyard sanctuary; about her passion for—and skill at—innovation and entrepreneurship. She had always felt that she was the master of her own fate, that the sky was the limit—and had always taken great satisfaction from this feeling.

Irene lived in Orange County, California. Relative to neighboring Los Angeles County, Orange was slightly south on the map, a fair bit to the right politically, several decades newer, and light years ahead on the Boring Sameness scale. The county consisted of a giant grid of streets forming 1,600 half-mile-square blocks surrounded by six-feet-tall sand-colored brick walls. At the corners of these blocks were gas stations, supermarkets and strip malls. Inside each block were 600 single-family homes with standardized floorplans, difficult to distinguish from each other and from the ones inside the other 1,599 blocks. The residents of the county had been enormously pleased by the advent of GPS, prior to which they'd found it quite a struggle to navigate themselves home each day.

It was at Orange County High School, so long ago, longer than she cared to remember, that young, awkward, nerdy Irene Morales had befriended young, awkward, nerdy William Smede. She and William had been close, almost inseparable, those final two years of childhood. After high school, he'd run off to UCLA, changed his name to Bill, and never returned.

"William," she muttered, then a quick puff on her cigarette, then, "Silly boy." Why would someone want to move away from the best place on earth? Shame. She'd never been interested in him romantically or sexually, but he was a good friend. Her favorite friend. Would've been cool, she thought, if they'd ended up in identical Orange County houses next door to each other, raising their kids side by side.

But they still got together a few times a year for a couple of hours, went for a bite to eat and got caught up with each other. One such meet-up had been arranged for this morning, which was why he was on Irene's mind. And she was excited to tell him all about her latest business venture.

"Fuckin' A," she said, for no reason except to formally end her little sunrise session of solitude. She dropped her cigarette butt into an old coffee can lying next to her on the concrete, opened the sliding glass door and stepped through.

It was a circus inside. All the noises that had been muffled were now coming through loud and clear, accompanied by visuals. 14-year-old Keith Hoffman, Junior (whom Irene called Junior but everyone else (including Keith Senior) called Keith) and 12-year-old Luke were sprawled on the living room carpet, their eyes glued to the massive T.V. screen in front of them, fingers punching feverishly on Xbox controllers, lobbing playful obscenities at each other. Their game characters were engaged in a hand-to-hand fight to the death. Irene was impressed with the graphics, and also with the soundtrack, which included an instrumental arrangement of the 1970s rock classic "Peace of Mind."

"Cut out the foul language," she barked. "And turn down the volume!" To herself she muttered, "This music is wasted on you knuckleheads, anyway…"

Irene's youngest, 8-year-old Connor, was standing in the kitchen, facing off against his father in a battle of wills, and winning.

"You've had enough toast," said Keith, pulling up the toaster lever that Connor had just pushed down. "And you've made a total mess in here."

"*You've* had enough toast," Connor shot back, laughing and pushing the lever down again. "Now go to your room!"

Keith looked relieved as he spotted Irene approaching. "Mommy's not going to be happy about this mess, or that you're still in your pajamas," he said to Connor.

Irene rolled her eyes as she quickly passed through the kitchen area, then asked over her shoulder, "Where's Alex?"

"Um, I don't know," Keith replied. "Hey, honey, can you help me out here? Connor is really out of control this morning."

Irene ignored her husband and continued into the hallway, singing quietly and mindlessly to herself: "Now everybody's got advice they just keep on giving, doesn't mean too much to me…"

She stopped in the doorway of her 10-year-old daughter's bedroom. Alexandra Isabella Corina Hoffman was sitting at her combo desk/dressing table, browsing an issue of Newport Lifestyle magazine.

"Ah, there you are, princess," said Irene. "What're you up to?"

"Not much," Alex replied, looking up and smiling gently.

"Listen, I'm going out for breakfast with an old friend. Could you hold down the fort while I'm gone? Help Daddy tame those wild beasts, okay?"

"Sure, Mommy."

Meanwhile, Bill was making his way southward on the 405 in the Cadillac ATS he shared with Yvonne, used for their weekly grocery run and very occasional trips elsewhere, like this one. They'd acquired the car during a moment of weakness, briefly succumbing to the L.A. ethos and agreeing that they would enjoy (and deserved) something with a bit of luxury, a bit of cachet. They'd chosen Cadillac on the notion that it might marginally stand out in a sea of Mercedes and BMW. Immediately after they'd made the purchase, G.M. had duly discontinued the ATS and announced production of its sexier successor, the CT4.

"*Fuck!*" Bill yelled, realizing he was about to get routed onto the 710 North. In his hurried attempt to remedy this situation, he moved the Cadillac into a lane that somebody else, driving an orange Ford Mustang, believed they owned, temporarily stopping them from doing exactly as they wanted, exactly when they wanted.

The other driver responded to this grievous slight relatively mildly, first with a long, hard blast on the horn, then by swerving left, flipping Bill off while passing him, and swerving right again, causing him to slam on the brakes.

"Douche," muttered Bill, somewhat dispassionately. L.A. freeway justice didn't really concern him. But punctuality did, and, glancing at the clock, he realized that he was almost definitely going to be late. Even at this early hour and on a weekend, the 405 traffic was a force to be reckoned with, and one he'd underestimated.

Bill felt a little, but not very, resentful that his hangouts with Irene happened entirely according to her parameters. He'd set out while it was still dark this morning because she always insisted on breakfast, and an early one at that. And he always went to her, never the other way around. She chose the restaurant every time, too. It wasn't a big deal, though. Bill was easygoing (about some things), and he knew that Irene had younger kids, a busier schedule, and an anxious, needy husband who would've preferred she didn't have any friends at all, much less male ones.

Driving across the county line, Bill could instantly see, hear and feel the change in the road surface. It was newer, cleaner, smoother, quieter. The traffic began to thin out, too, almost as if by magic. Off to the right he saw a gigantic shopping mall, and to the left, a gigantic mini-golf and waterslide park. The sky seemed slightly more blue, and all the rooftops shimmered majestically in the early May sunshine.

A few minutes later, he pulled up in front of Irene's house and spotted her standing on the front walk, examining a nearby bush with a look of skepticism, a lit cigarette protruding from her lips. Filthy habit, thought Bill, but a tiny corner of the back of his mind found it sexy, too. He watched her another moment as she absentmindedly lowered the cigarette from her mouth and flicked away the ash from its tip. She'd aged well. Hints of crow's feet now flanked her round, dark brown eyes, but otherwise she had the same clear, smooth, deep tan skin. She'd always kept her look simple, no-nonsense. Her long hair was pulled back into her trademark ponytail. She wore little or no makeup, a slightly baggy white cotton button-up shirt, untucked, with the sleeves rolled up, and gray three-quarter-length casual pants. On her feet she always had either sneakers or a pair of basic, unobtrusive one-inch heels. Today it was sneakers.

Bill cut the engine, got out of the car and began walking up the driveway.

"You're late, dumbass," Irene said, not taking her eyes off the shrubbery.

"Nice to see you, too," said Bill, coming up beside her on the front path.

"You see any lemons on this goddamn thing?" asked Irene.

"Hmm, no," said Bill, giving his eyes a quick, token aim at the small tree next to them. He doubted anyone in the world cared less than he did about horticulture or gardening.

"They said it'd be blowing up with lemons. Fucking lemons up the wazoo."

Irene abruptly turned toward the house. "Anyway, whatever," she said, discarding her cigarette butt in an old coffee can sitting on the concrete next to her front door. "So, you hungry?"

"Yeah."

"Okay, I'll drive."

Irene went inside. After a few seconds, the garage door opened and a huge family-style vehicle backed out onto the driveway. Bill climbed in and off they went.

Half an hour later, sitting across from Bill with two recently-arrived plates of food (his avocado toast and her eggs benedict) sitting between them, having caught him up on work stuff and family stuff, Irene launched with relish into the most exciting subject.

"Okay, listen," she said, "I've come up with a new business idea and it's the best one I've ever had. So, so cool. I've been thinking it through and doing some strategizing and..." She paused and grinned, a sparkle in her eye. "I really think it's gonna work. I think it's gonna be big."

Irene had never had a shred of doubt that she would found a phenomenally successful business. After each of her dozen failed attempts to do so, she'd remained supremely confident that the next one would be *the* one.

Bill's level of doubt about this lay at the far opposite end of the spectrum. But he tried very, very hard, as Irene looked across the table at him, to convey receptivity, or at least blankness.

She continued, "Everyone knows V.R., right? Virtual reality. Well there's also this thing called A.R.—augmented reality. Heard of it?"

"Yeah."

"So with A.R., you're still experiencing the actual, real world around you, but it's got extra stuff thrown in by a computer, to make it more informative or more interesting or whatever. It's being *augmented*." Irene pronounced the final word slowly and accompanied it with a small, meaningless hand gesture.

"Right," said Bill, a tad impatient for her to get to the point.

"Except usually, the augmentation is with words and images. My idea is, augmentation with sound. With music, to be more precise."

"Uh, haven't they done that already?"

"Well, yes, but only as part of something bigger and more complex. What I'm talking about isn't a game, or a tool, or even entertainment, really. It's more basic than that. It's just... the soundtrack to your life."

"The soundtrack to your life?"

"Yeah. It's just music, to accompany you in whatever you're doing or seeing or experiencing. The right music for each moment. You know how in a movie, there's always music playing to match whatever's going on? Well that's what this is. You're the star of your own movie, all the time, complete with music!"

Bill was still puzzled. "But isn't that just, listening to your iPod while you do stuff? I hate to break it to you, but people have been doing that for a long time."

Irene smiled and shook her head. "No, no," she said.

Bill continued, chuckling, "'Fraid Apple thought of your business idea before you did, Irene. And Sony thought of it before them, way back in the 80s."

"Shut up," said Irene, not angrily, still smiling. "You stupid piece of shit. Shut up and listen, okay? Hear me out. This is different because the music matches your environment. It enhances the mood, the feeling of whatever situation you're in. Just like in a movie. That's where the technology comes into it."

"Okay, I think I get what you're talking about," said Bill.

"Yeah—it happens to me all the time, I hear the music in my head that'd be perfect for whatever moment I'm in. Like last weekend when I was gearing up for go-karts, my mental stereo was playing the Top Gun Anthem. And a few days ago, walking through the park in the afternoon, it was so beautiful and peaceful, and, I hate to admit it, but, Theme from 'A Summer Place' was running through my brain..."

Bill smiled. He was starting to come around to this wacky idea.

"Remember that time we were wandering around Balboa and saw all those bikers and party people hanging out on that bar patio? The Boys are Back in Town!"

"Exactly! You've got it, William my friend."

"Sounds pretty complicated, though," Bill said, "I mean, even just from the technical perspective of creating the software, never mind all the other things you'll have to figure out…"

"Don't you worry your pretty little head about it," said Irene with a smug smile as she pulled out a cigarette and a lighter. "I'm all over this."

"You can't smoke in here," Bill reminded her, astounded.

"Right," she said, grimacing and rolling her eyes.

"It's only been a law here for like, three decades, Irene. You probably live in the first place on earth that banned smoking."

"Well, it's perfect here except for that," she said, standing up. "Join me in the alley?"

Bill shrugged and also stood up. "Sure."

As the two friends made their way single-file through the dining room toward the side door, passing in front of the tall, wide windows that looked out over the ocean, Bill began thinking about everything he needed to do when he got home.

In the early afternoon four days later, two women and two men stood around a circular conference table, looking down at a large sheet of paper that had been unrolled across the table's surface. On the paper were detailed technical diagrams of a thick band of soft plastic, attached to which were several straps, hooks and buckles, along with two interlocking, sliding, harder plastic pieces. The paper also contained less technical images depicting this contraption with a smartphone embedded in it, a pair of wireless earphones, and a human head adorned with all of the above.

"Nice," said Irene, then, looking across the table at Stan Wojcik, "Very nice indeed. You've still got it, old pal."

They'd met their first year at U.C. Irvine, at which point Stan was already a computer whiz kid, arriving there age sixteen with a full scholarship. These days, although officially employed at a software company called SteelTrap, he was effectively a free-lance expert (he called it "dabbling") in nearly all things technological. Irene, who hadn't actually spoken to Stan in the preceding five years, had been thrilled when he'd agreed to serve as Chief Software Architect (meaning the entire software department) for her new product, and further thrilled when he'd, unsolicited, produced ("cobbled together," in his words) the hardware design now spread out before them.

"Um, thanks," muttered an embarrassed Stan with a small smile, casting his eyes at the ground and pulling part of his massive cornrow mane (which was never tied back) out of his face with his hand and flipping it back over his shoulder.

Irene turned to her left. "It's nice, isn't it?" she said to Donald Piper, her office assistant of many years.

"Yes," he replied reflexively, then nodded his head a couple of times in an unconscious effort to alter the reality that he had no considered opinion on the matter and that nobody would've cared if he did.

Donald had been with Irene, providing perfect mindless support for her one-woman accounting firm, since the days when she worked out of her home. She considered him a godsend—fastidiously taking care of all the menial tasks she hated, never butting into the real work, never complaining and, oddly, never quitting. As an added bonus, he was so short, skinny, ugly and boring that Keith had never felt threatened by him.

Turning to her right, Irene said, "Judy, what've you got for me?"

"Working on the patent applications," said Judy. "All the stuff Stan's provided will make it pretty easy. I should be able to get those filed within nineteen days."

Judy Goldstein was one of Orange County's non-premier personal injury attorneys. Irene had hired her seven years ago after suffering whiplash in a traffic accident, and the two had become fast friends while working on the case together. Ultimately the parents of the reckless youngster who'd rear-ended Irene had shelled out $50,000 to cover the cost of her therapeutic treatments from an elite neuro-skeleto-muscular neck specialist. Since then, Judy had become Irene's go-to person for all legal matters, and in fact, her go-to person for any matters requiring research that she didn't feel like doing. Irene had once commented, during the early days, that if they lost the case she'd want nothing more to do with Judy, ever, but she'd said this entirely in jest. Probably.

"Money!" snapped Irene. "I mean, patents are nice and all, Judy, but what I really need is cash. What've you got for me with the money?"

"Ah, yes—the funding," said Judy. "Well, honestly, I've reached out to a lot of V.C. firms and they have not been showing much enthusiasm."

Thus far, the people helping Irene on this project had been paid only with promises. Meanwhile, her family income had dwindled as she shifted her focus to the new business and spent less and less time on her accounting work. So the personal credit card debt had been mounting. Irene had loved Judy's suggestion of going after venture capital money, and had immediately volunteered Judy to spearhead the effort.

"They've been telling me, basically," Judy continued, "that it's too big a departure from existing products, while at the same time not offering enough that's truly new."

Irene frowned.

"Uh, they're wrong, of course," Judy stammered. "And actually, I do seem to have my foot in the door at one place. It's called LeVay Say. Clever name, actually." She smiled in amusement. "It's French. 'Vay' is the letter V in French, and 'say' is the letter C. So it's 'The V.C.'" She drew the letters in the air with her finger as she spoke.

Irene found it less amusing. "What'd they say?" she asked.

"Well, they don't like mounting the phone in—"

"Goddammit," said Irene as the sound of bells came through from the front of the office suite. "I told you to lock the door, Donald."

"You did?" Donald replied with confusion and a bit of panic.

"Hello?" called out a man's voice from the reception area.

"Go get rid of him," Irene commanded. "And lock the damn door."

Donald scurried out of the room.

"Judy, continue," said Irene.

"Well, they don't like mounting the phone in the headpiece. They think it's too awkward, people won't like messing around with it, plus people want to have their phone at their fingertips at all times."

"Hmm," said Irene, absorbing this.

Judy went on, "So they want you to use a separate, external camera. If you'll agree to this change then they'll consider giving you some limited funding to complete your prototype."

Irene smiled slightly.

"But they want to meet you in person," Judy added.

Irene put her hand on her chin and spent several seconds processing all the new information while slowly nodding her head, moving her eyes left and right along the floor and muttering "Okay... okay." Then she looked up at the group and clasped her hands together.

"Sounds good to me!" she said. "Stan, this makes your software a little more complicated, no?"

Stan smiled. "Not really," he said quietly. "A camera's a camera. External versus built-in, doesn't make much difference."

"Great. That's what I like to hear," said Irene. "And you can get these designs updated pronto, right?"

"Sure thing," Stan replied.

"Cool. Good stuff. Stacy, you still there?"

"Yes," said the voice of Stacy Parabola, coming out of Judy's phone, which was lying on the conference table. Stacy was a friend of Judy's who worked for a small plastics manufacturing company.

"This change isn't a problem for you, is it?" asked Irene.

"Nope," said Stacy's voice. "As long as you send all the details, it can be built however you want. Just remember, *I* might work pro bono but my materials and machinery don't. You're going to get invoiced for any actual production."

Donald re-entered the room, carrying a stack of manila folders under his arm, each one crammed to capacity with papers.

"What the fuck?" said Irene.

"Sorry, way it goes," came the voice from the phone.

"Oh, no, not you, Stacy. I was talking to my secretary here. Yeah, I understand you gotta get paid for making stuff. Not a problem."

"Uh, the guy gave me these," said Donald.

"What guy?" snapped Irene.

"The guy you told me to get rid of. The customer."

"Oh, right, well... Take care of it. File it, or whatever. I don't need to tell you how to do your job."

Donald departed again.

"Okay, well I think we're done here, everyone," said Irene. "You've all got your marching orders. Any questions?"

Judy, Stan, and Judy's phone were all silent.

"Okay, class dismissed," said Irene. "Good work, everyone. Christ, I need a cigarette."

Irene strode swiftly out of the conference room, down the corridor and across the reception area. When she reached the door leading out to the sidewalk and pushed against it, the door didn't move. Irene's body and face smacked into the glass with a loud thud.

"Aargh!" she screamed. "Who locked the fucking door?"

The following week, Bill and Yvonne strolled side by side down Wexler Avenue at 4:30 on Thursday afternoon, nearing the completion of their fifth loop together that day. As usual, they were not holding hands. Neither Bill nor Yvonne went in for public displays of affection, or even private ones very much, a quality each of them admired and appreciated in the other. It wasn't that they didn't feel a deep fondness and strong sense of romance for each other; they simply believed that in a healthy, secure relationship, these feelings needn't be expressed very often (and, in fact, could be radically cheapened by over-expression).

Yvonne had just finished an anecdote about a recent comedy of errors at the office, primarily driven by her well-intentioned but bumbling teammate, Fred Nguyen, who, if only he'd been lazier, would've caused far fewer issues.

There was a short lull in the conversation. Then Yvonne spoke again. "So, let's have a little wager," she said.

Bill smiled. This was one of their standard games.

"Will Patrick stick around and have a drink with us?"

The topic was different each time they played. It could be anything, provided it had a predictable outcome. Bill always started by answering honestly.

"No," he said, "he'll politely decline and then go out for the whole evening."

"Ooh, sorry," said Yvonne, "I'm taking that one, so you'll have to take something else."

Bill chuckled. He liked how the repeated sharing of a joke could evolve into something so rich, a connection between two people, bringing a warm sense of joy each time; this special kind of joke never got old, and actually became more funny than it had been originally.

"Go on," said Yvonne, her straight face starting to crack. "It can be anything else. Anything at all."

"Okay," said Bill, "I'll go with, uh... he *does* have a drink with us, and he has dinner with us, and he washes all the dishes."

"Alright then," said Yvonne. "Who will be right? Hmm. It's anyone's guess."

Passing by a palm tree as they neared their building, they spotted Wilfred "Wally" Wallace kneeling on the sidewalk in front of his condo, hunched over with his face an inch from the ground, staring intensely at it. Wally was an obsessed government conspiracy theorist who lived in Number Two, and that was all Yvonne and Bill knew about him, because his theories were the only thing he ever talked about. Sometimes he kept it mercifully brief and cryptic, other times long-winded and very detailed.

Their most recent encounter had fallen into the latter category, as Wally had explained how, although he didn't personally agree with the aims of a particular obscure conservative Christian municipal activism group—a coalition of doctors calling themselves Physicians Against Physicists (or P.A.P. for short)—he was nevertheless appalled by the top-secret and highly unethical efforts of the mayor's office to undermine and silence them. Remembering that painful experience, Bill and Yvonne glanced at each other now and silently agreed it'd be best if Wally could be completely avoided this time.

The building consisted of six nearly identical units. The Smedes lived in Number Four, which was on the upper level at the north end of the building, and they were approaching from the north. Number Two was in the middle, on the ground level. Thus, Yvonne and Bill would be turning off the sidewalk before they reached the point where Wally was kneeling. So there was a chance. Without speaking, they tiptoed the last few steps to the concrete footpath, turned and crept along it, inching ever nearer the staircase that led up to safety.

"Stealth movements," yelled Wally. "Nice! Just like I taught you. The word 'never' is only truly accurate in one case: you can never be too careful."

Bill stopped at the foot of the stairs and turned toward Wally. "Hah, you know it," he forced himself to say.

Bill hated awkwardness so much that he would put himself through virtually any amount of torture to ensure interactions with other people went smoothly. Yvonne, though quite sensitive to such things, was no match for Bill. She proceeded up the stairs, ignoring Wally completely.

"I bet you're wondering what I'm doing," Wally said.

"Yes," Bill replied.

In a quiet voice, from the top of the stairs, Yvonne said, with a speaking-to-a-baby-or-pet style, "Oh yes you *are*, Bill, you're wondering oh so much..."

Bill stifled a laugh.

"Well," Wally continued, "to tell you the truth, the less you know about this, the better off you are. Suffice it to say, the nodes they—" He stopped himself. "Um, suffice it to say, I haven't discovered any evidence of anything to get too worried about. Yet."

Yvonne had already gone inside, leaving the door open for Bill's quick, easy access. He began to sprint up the stairs, saying, "Okay, Wally, sounds good. See you later."

"Remember," called Wally as Bill disappeared into his condo, "if you see a red scarf and a blue scarf tied to a sycamore tree on a street corner, that means the feds are going ahead with Operation P."

"Got it!" shouted Bill as he shut the door.

Working remotely from home, as Yvonne did every Thursday, provided no guarantee of avoiding an after-work happy hour. This fact had been demonstrated two hours ago, when Amy and Laura had informed Yvonne in a group chat that the festivities would begin at 5:30 and that she would be hosting.

Bill and Yvonne went about preparing their home for guests— tidying up the living room, checking the liquor inventory, wiping down tabletops, setting out glassware. Throughout this process they continually reassured each other that it would just be an hour or two of slow sipping and pleasant conversation. Just a couple of drinks, three at the most. No unhealthy snacks. No drunkenness. Then everyone would leave because they all had stuff to do, after which it'd be a simple dinner of leftovers zapped in the microwave (spicy mushroom loaf and kale cakes from Sunday night) and then off to bed nice and early. By the time Laura and her husband, Mike, arrived at 5:25, Yvonne and

Bill had almost convinced themselves of all this.

Laura and Mike brought a jumbo bag of potato chips, a tub of creamy onion dip and a can of cashews, all of which were promptly laid out on the coffee table. They also brought four different types of bourbon that Mike wanted Bill to sample, a bottle of Laura's favorite pinot grigio and a bottle of Laura's favorite pinot noir. By 6:15, the men were lining up their third pour of whiskey, the women were both approaching the bottom of their second glass of wine, and everybody was vigorously tucking into the food.

At that moment, Patrick emerged from the back of the condo, smiled and nodded at the group, and began awkwardly shuffling in the general direction of the front door.

"Hey, Patrick," said Bill. "Want to join us for a drink?"

"Um, no, thank you." More smiling, nodding and shuffling. "I, um, there are some things I need to do. So I, um, need to get going."

"Okay, have fun."

"Thank you. Nice seeing all of you!" Then he was gone.

Amy arrived, alone, at 6:40. The original plan had been for her to come with Jake, Jennifer and Brandon, and for the kids to eat their Happy Meals and watch cartoons on a laptop at the dining table while the grown-ups did their grown-uppy stuff at the opposite end of the room. But the plan had changed when Amy'd arrived home from work to find both children tired, grumpy and rowdy. At this point she'd volunteered Jake to stay behind with them while she bravely bore the full weight of the evening's socializing on her own shoulders.

Food and drink were free-flowing. Everybody was having a good time, and gradually having an even better time. The highlight of this portion of the evening, in Mike's mind at least, was when he shared with the others that he hadn't paid for his breakfast once in the past six weeks, after perfecting a sneaky strategy whereby he obtained it gratis from a Holiday Inn Express located near his apartment.

At 7:30, Laura suggested ordering delivery from Bo Thai, a place Amy and Jake sometimes liked to order from. Amy and Mike thought this was a great idea. Yvonne and Bill thought it was an okay idea. Amy used her phone to place the order.

Alice came through the front door at 8:05, wearing her backpack and earbuds. She sensed the presence of the five revelers but headed directly into the back of the condo without looking at them or speaking. Nobody noticed her.

The Thai food arrived at 8:30, just as people were starting to feel a bit panicked because all the chips, dip and nuts had run out ten minutes earlier. Everyone eagerly got on with the business of gorging, and all agreed that it was incredibly delicious.

At 9:30, Bill realized that the two bottles of wine Laura had brought were empty, and so was the bottle Amy had brought. He also noticed that all three women's glasses were dangerously low. Springing into action, he retrieved two bottles from the rack, swiftly opened both of them, and placed them on the coffee table, ready for use. Then he rewarded himself with another bourbon on the rocks. He also rewarded Mike (for moral support) in the same fashion.

By 10:30, the group had again begun feeling desperate cravings for salt and fat which they mistook for hunger. Mike suggested they order pizza, and everyone else thought this was a great idea. It occurred to Yvonne that there were some DiGiorno pizzas in the freezer, but she quickly dismissed this idea because it entailed far more physical effort than delivery. Amy used her phone to place the order.

When Patrick returned at midnight, he was startled to see that his parents and their guests were still gathered around the coffee table, talking and laughing. He was also somewhat startled by the tower of food containers stacked up next to them.

"Um, hello again," he stammered as he crossed the living room toward the back of the condo. "It's getting pretty late... I'm, um, going to bed. Nice seeing all of you!"

"Pretty late indeed," said Yvonne, looking at the clock on her phone. The first pangs of regret hit her.

Bill had completely lost track of the time. Now that he knew it, thoughts of how tomorrow morning was going to feel were doing an astounding job of sobering him up.

"Evil," he muttered very quietly.

"One last round and then we'll call it a night!" Amy exclaimed with a big grin.

Fifteen hours later and 300 miles away, Irene Hoffman and Judy Goldstein sat next to each other on a sofa composed of a single large, seamless, sofa-shaped piece of white plastic with red velvet cushions. The massive room contained several other similar pieces of furniture, but no other people. The walls were white and bare, the floor covered in white tile, and the ceiling consisted of one continuous bank of fluorescent light fixtures. Around the perimeter of the room were two wide openings leading to corridors, and eight identical closed doors, all solid red with no windows, signs or labels. On the far wall directly across from the sofa, a huge window offered a magnificent second-floor view of the entire Saratoga, California cityscape.

Irene and Judy had come through at least one of the two corridors today, and had been behind a few of the red doors, but at this point they had no idea which ones. They'd spent the last five hours here, at the offices of LeVay Say, meeting with various attorneys and people whose title was Vice President. None of them were the Vice President *of* anything specific, just Vice President. Irene thought that, for a company with only 35 people in total, they certainly had a lot of vice presidents.

Now there was only one meeting remaining, and both women were impatiently awaiting it. Irene fidgeted with her nicotine patch as she halfheartedly surveyed the white plastic table in front of them. Stacked on top of it were two dozen magazines, all of them devoted to business or technology, and an iPad on which folks who were fed up with print could read electronic versions of the same magazines. The iPad was attached to the base of the table with a cable.

"Untrusting fuckers," muttered Irene to herself.

Judy looked over at her. "Nervous?" she asked.

"Nope. Why would I be?"

"I'm nervous," Judy said.

"Nope," Irene continued, "not nervous. Bored, yes. Annoyed, yes. Getting more annoyed with each passing minute. I mean, let's get on with it. Let's do this shit." Then, finally absorbing what Judy had said, "Wait, *you're* nervous? What are *you* nervous about?"

"I don't know... It's kind of a big thing..."

"Look, you've got nothing to worry about, Judy. You know your shit. You're not some hack lawyer, right?"

Judy thought about this.

"Anyway, it doesn't matter what you or I say or do, 'cause our product kicks ass. *He's* the one who should be nervous, 'cause he's the one in danger of missing out on an amazing opportunity!"

"True," said Judy.

Irene hated the patch but felt immensely grateful to Judy for thinking of it and supplying it. Her cigarettes had been confiscated downstairs at the security checkpoint. Use of tobacco products, including vape, anywhere on the premises was strictly prohibited. A dense network of cameras, smoke detectors and highly advanced chemical sensors blanketed the entire facility, including the outdoor walkways and parking areas. There were, however, special designated locations for smoking weed and micro-dosing LSD.

The iPad suddenly began to vibrate. Then its screen lit up and a female voice coming out of it said, "Mr. LeVay will see you now." Irene wasn't sure if it was a synthesized voice, a recording of a real woman, or a live feed. In any case, it was creepy.

As she and Judy stood up, one of the red doors opened and a man stepped out, smiling.

"Hello, my friends," he said. "I'm Derek LeVay. Please come into my office."

At first glance, the only thing remarkable about LeVay's appearance was his little Hitler-style mustache. Apart from that, he was a very ordinary-looking middle-aged white man. Average height, average build, medium-length brown hair, brown eyes, a face nobody would notice in a crowd. He wore loafers, dark gray slacks and a light blue shirt with the collar open. No jacket.

At second glance, which Irene and Judy got as they approached LeVay and he turned around to walk back into his office, he did have one other noteworthy feature: a long, bushy mullet hanging down over his neck and the top of his back. The women gave each other a quick look of bemusement as they strode through the open red door.

The rather small office contained no works of art, no fish tanks, no plants, nor anything else remotely decorative except for a large, old, threadbare oriental rug covering the majority of the floor. Derek LeVay deliberately kept things simple and humble. He was just a regular, down-to-earth guy who'd pulled himself up by his bootstraps, in his opinion. Through decades of hard work, focus, self-belief, and perhaps a little luck, he'd managed to inherit his father's entire $300 million fortune.

Once LeVay had closed the door, and Irene and Judy had declined his offer of herbal tea or scotch, the three of them settled into chairs around his desk.

"Now," he said with a smile, "this is just a formality—sort of. All the details of our arrangement have been hammered out already, and everybody's already signed everything. But it's very important for you and me to sit down like this, Irene, and look into each other's face, and shake each other's hand."

He reached across the desk. Irene took his hand in hers and shook it.

"We need to feel okay about each other," he continued, "as human beings. You're not really making a deal with my company, Irene. You're making a deal with me. I am your partner now. We're in this together. Just the two of us. You and me. That's the only way to go. That's what every successful business is, at its core. Personal."

"Yes, absolutely," Irene replied with a solemn face.

Judy found LeVay's speech fascinating and hoped he would say more. Irene hoped he wouldn't. Judy got her wish.

"I alone made the decision to invest in your fantastic idea. Just me. Because that's what I do. The other people who work here, they do a lot of analysis, but what they don't do is… judgment. I must make the judgments myself. I gather up all the information, provided by my own people and by the entrepreneur." He made gathering motions with his arms on the surface of the desk. "I gather it all up and then I use it to make my judgment, of whether or not the idea is worthy. And I judged your idea… worthy!"

"Thanks," said Irene.

"Awesome," said Judy.

"But," LeVay went on with a smile of self-admiration, "it's not just a simple 'yea' or 'nay.' Sometimes—in fact, always—it's a 'yea, but.' See, I'm not just judging the basic merit of an idea, I'm also judging how the entire process is going to unfold, *and* I'm also judging how to structure protections against potential flaws in that very judgment."

Irene couldn't stop herself from frowning slightly. She hated having to ask for money, because, no matter what the situation, you're always beholden in some way to the provider of that money. And being beholden to somebody inevitably means taking shit from them. Like keeping your mouth shut while they deliver a lengthy and lame monologue.

LeVay had hit his stride and didn't notice the frown. "Which is why," he went on, "we are taking baby steps, as I'm sure you already know. You see, I'm sort of like an insurance underwriter. They're the ones who work behind the scenes on crafting the exact details of the policy, you know?"

"Right," said Irene.

"Yes," said Judy.

"Just like them, I have to figure out, very carefully... what's the situation, what might happen. Or else I'll lose my shirt." He grinned as if something amusing had been said. "The only difference is, I do it in reverse order. The money part, I mean. You see, I pay out to you right at the beginning, then later you pay me. Or so we both hope! Yep, I'm a reverse underwriter. And a damn good one, too, I might add. You should be more optimistic than ever, Irene. Because I chose you."

Irene smiled, mainly because LeVay was now taking the longest break from speaking since they'd met him. Perhaps he was finished.

"So," he finally said, "what questions do you have for me?"

"Are you French?" asked Judy.

"Judy, what the f—" Irene halted, then started again. "What on earth, Judy?"

LeVay had become distracted by a sheet of paper lying on his desk. "Hmm," he said, reading it.

Then he looked up at the women and asked, "Have either of you heard of a company called Peloton?"

"Of course," said Irene.

"No," said Judy.

"It says here they're a..."—he looked back down at the paper—"a 'technology fitness media design software retail product apparel experience logistics' company... Now that just sounds terrific to me. I wonder if they'd be interested in a little outside investment..."

"I think you're too late," said Irene.

LeVay looked down again and noticed that the memo regarding Peloton was dated over four years ago. He emitted another "Hmm."

Then he looked up and said, "Sorry, my friends—I believe you asked me a question?"

"Oh," said Judy, "I was, uh, just curious about the name. Of your company."

"Ah, yes—it's rather... imperious, isn't it? *I* have the say. *I* call the shots. True, though."

"Was it your idea?" Judy asked.

"Actually, no. My ex-wife came up with it."

"Oh, you're still friendly with your ex-wife?"

"No. She was my current wife at the time."

"So, what do we do next?" Irene asked impatiently.

"Next," said LeVay, "you take the money I'm supplying today. Use it however you need to in order to get your prototype built. Then, when I come to see you on the date we agreed—sometime in July, right?—you demo the heck out of it. Dazzle me."

"Yeah, but then what? I'll need a lot more money to actually roll this thing out. We've got advertising, manufacturing, distribution. We'll need an ongoing software effort for maintenance and support…"

"Of course. Be sure to draw up plans for all those things, to show me next time. Detailed plans. Very important to think through all the details."

"Yeah, I did already, and I brought those plans with me today…"

"Irene," said LeVay, raising one finger as a hushing gesture. "Remember, baby steps."

"But—"

"Irene." Again he raised one admonishing finger.

"Okay," said Irene, rising to go. "Fine. Thank you."

Judy stood up too, smiling at LeVay, then giving Irene a disapproving look.

Irene stopped suddenly. "Uh, you never actually gave me the money."

LeVay smiled. "Stop by the cashier's window on your way out. They'll have a check for you. They can also validate your parking."

Chapter 4

Bill Smede grunted and grimaced, shifting awkwardly in his seat. It was 2:00 on a gorgeous Sunday afternoon in late May, and he found himself in his least favorite location for such a time—outdoors. He reached up and pulled the brim of his baseball cap even more snugly against the top of his sunglasses. Sweat trickled down his back, slid under his jeans and began working its way into the waistband of his underwear. The cushionless wrought-iron patio chair pressed uncomfortably against his butt and shoulder blades.

The sounds of voices continuously entered Bill's ears on the left and the right, but at this point they were just meaningless noise passing through; the effort of processing them had become too tedious for his poor brain nearly an hour ago. Anyway it didn't matter, he told himself, because their chatter was meant for each other's benefit, not his.

The voice on the left belonged to Bill's twin sister, Debbie Smede. They'd always had a good relationship, but never an extremely close one. Too different, even at a very young age—the carefree, outspoken, optimistic people-lover and the quiet, brooding, reclusive cynic. Bill doubted a wider personality gap had ever existed in the history of humanity between two people who were born on the same day, to the same parents, and then lived under the same roof for the next 18 years. The mysteries of DNA, he mused.

The voice on the right came from their mother, Catherine Smede, who, after divorcing their father, rather acrimoniously, almost thirty years ago, had always kept his name. Nobody, including Catherine herself, really knew why. The top three candidates in her children's minds were, in increasing order of likelihood: wanting to have the same name as them, unconsciously still carrying a torch for Richard, and laziness.

For most of her life she'd been known as Cathy, but in recent times she'd switched to being called "Mamsy." The name had been coined by Patrick when he was two years old, but had gradually spread (like a virus, said Bill), not just to new grandchildren as they arrived but to the whole world—first all of her family, then all her friends, and ultimately everybody with whom she came in contact, because she took to introducing herself as Mamsy. Even Debbie, these days, mainly called her own mother Mamsy. Bill stubbornly stuck with the name Mom, which he'd used since before he could remember.

As it happened, she was currently talking about her own name.

"My girl says I should pronounce it 'Mam-*zay*' and spell it with two *E*s and one of those, oh, what are they called? Apostrophes?"

"Oh, that's silly," Debbie replied with a giggle. "Just keep it the way it is."

Bill had just tuned back in. Why would she ever spell that name? he thought. Then he said, "Your 'girl'? Who's your girl?"

"You know, the girl who does my hair. Oh, Debbie, you should come with me sometime. She's very good. And they have this cucumber water that is, mmm, so refreshing."

"Do they do nails there, too?" Debbie asked.

Bill tuned out again.

The three of them were sitting on the back patio of Debbie's house in Cerritos (an L.A. suburb worryingly close to, but not actually behind, the Orange Curtain), watching her daughters, Raylene and Anika, play in the yard. Bill couldn't identify the game they were playing. It involved no equipment but plenty of running, screaming, laughing, and gently slapping one another. Tag? In any case, it irritated him.

"Aren't they kind of old for this game?" he said to nobody in particular, and nobody responded. Bill didn't actually know their ages. (Raylene was eleven years old and Anika was nine.)

Bill's phone rang. He grabbed it eagerly, jumped up, and headed for the sliding glass door that led into the house.

"Sorry," he said, "gotta take this. It's Yvonne."

"Tell her I said 'Hi'!" both women called out, in unison, as he disappeared inside.

"Hey," said Bill, answering the call from Debbie's kitchen area.

"Hey," said Yvonne, "thought maybe you could use a little break."

"Yes, indeed," Bill said while smiling at Grace Hogg, Debbie's wife, as she glided past him carrying a fresh pitcher of iced tea for the patio dwellers.

"Much appreciated," he continued. "So, how are you?"

"Mmm, not great, to be honest. Juice postponed, so I had to rearrange my schedule. And I cut myself on a kitchen knife making lunch."

"Aw, sorry."

"Well I don't blame you *entirely*."

Bill chuckled.

Yvonne continued, "So what's been happening at the Fem Den?"

"Not much." He glanced around, confirming that everyone else was currently on the opposite side of the closed slider. "You know, the usual. Very dull. I think at some point Debbie's going to make the girls show all of us this little dance routine they've been working on. So that should be a blast."

"Yes. Shame I won't be there for it."

"Yeah... Oh, I guess you could've been—you said Juice postponed? Hey, you still could! Why don't you get your ass down here and rescue me?"

Yvonne laughed. "Nope! She just pushed it back by a few hours. I'm on my way there now."

"Crap."

Bill had nearly avoided today's get-together with extended family, informing them that Yvonne would be taking the car for a girls' day with her friend Juice, so he'd be stranded at home. But his mother had offered, cheerfully and without hesitation, to come pick him up and take him to Cerritos. This detour added 55 miles to her journey (or 110 total, assuming she took him home afterward), a ludicrous amount that Bill himself would've only ever considered doing in three situations: a *very* special occasion (e.g. wedding, funeral); a matter of life and death; Yvonne asked him to.

But Mamsy loved getting together with her kids. She also loved driving, constantly spending countless hours crisscrossing the whole metro area, and happy as a clam doing so. She reminded Bill of Gary Williams in that respect.

"But I'll be thinking of you," said Yvonne, "and wishing I was there."

"Yeah!"

"Yep, thinking of you sitting around, not getting any steps. I got in another two loops today after you left."

"Now you're just being cruel."

The slider opened and Grace poked her head in. "Bill," she said, "Mamsy wants you."

"Uh, okay, thanks," Bill replied, then, to Yvonne, "I'm being summoned."

"Well, you'd better get going then!"

"Okay, talk to you later."

"Bye."

As the call ended, Yvonne saw that Tampa Avenue, her exit from the 101, was coming up. She steered the ATS onto the off-ramp and, five minutes later, rolled up in front of the home of Juice Hughes-Newton. Yvonne and Juice had met when they were both students at Washington State University. Yvonne smiled, thinking back on those times and about the random chance events that shape everyone's lives.

Like almost any two people who ever met, she and Juice could so easily not have. Yvonne, an outstanding high school student, had been admitted to the more prestigious University of Washington, located barely ten miles away from the home she'd grown up in. But she'd chosen instead to move 280 miles away, to the desolate eastern side of the state, precisely because it was so far away. Juice was a year older and not even from Washington, but had ended up at WSU, as a transfer student, after something (to this day Yvonne didn't really understand what) had gone horribly wrong for her at Cal Poly San Luis Obispo.

They'd met on the first day of the term, in a psychology class that Yvonne had been enrolled in by mistake and transferred out of that same week. But they'd learned that they resided just one floor apart in the same dorm. The following day they'd bumped into each other on the stairs, Juice had invited Yvonne to a small party in a third girl's room, Yvonne had reluctantly accepted, and the two had quickly become close friends—so close, in fact, that after graduation, Yvonne had essentially followed Juice to Southern California.

That was a *long* time ago, Yvonne thought as she stepped out of the car and noticed, without surprise, that it was ten degrees hotter here than back home on Wexler Avenue. Juice lived in Tarzana, a district in the San Fernando Valley (or just the Valley, for short). Although situated immediately north of the city of L.A. (and technically part of it), the Valley offered a distinct, hazy atmosphere, in the literal sense but also figuratively—a jumbled-up hybrid of urban and suburban. Some swollen-headed, bland academic types had coined the term "supersuburban" for such an environment, but no normal person ever used it.

Yvonne started up the red brick path toward Juice's front door. The ranch-style house, not intended as anything special by its original builder back in the 1950s, had been heavily renovated several times, including a couple of extensions and the addition of an in-ground swimming pool. It was also extremely well maintained, inside and out, by a large coterie of specialists, including hired help but also including Juice's ex-husband, Paul Newton, and their children, Henry and Lateesha. Queen Juice ran a tight ship. Yvonne couldn't recall ever seeing a crooked blade of grass, a speck of dust on a piece of furniture, a tiny crack in a wood, glass, or tile surface, or any other imperfection here at this mini-palace. For privacy, a perfectly manicured hedge, twelve feet tall and four feet thick, surrounded the property on three sides; in the front, due to city ordinance, a three-feet-high wall had to suffice.

Yvonne reached the heavy, dark wood door, opened it (Juice never locked the house and expected all visitors to let themselves in), went through into the foyer and continued toward the family room and kitchen area, from which the sound of a T.V. was emanating. She glanced at various family photos as she passed them. Every wall in the house, as well as most tables and shelves, contained at least one, typically four or five. Even though Paul had moved out eight years ago, when Lateesha was a toddler, he still appeared in many of the displayed photos. This was not because Juice still loved him.

Yvonne found her old friend exactly as expected: cross-legged on the sofa, cradling a bag of potato chips, wearing a purple tracksuit, dividing her attention equally between the little phone screen in her hand, with its perpetual notifications, and the big one in front of her, currently offering an entertainment news program doing a segment about a recent episode of a celebrity talk show in which they'd discussed highlights from a celebrity reality show.

"Hi, Juice."

"Hey, girl," Juice replied without looking at Yvonne. "Make yourself comfortable. Grab a drink from the kitchen. You know where they are, right?"

"I'm fine, thanks," said Yvonne, taking a seat next to Juice. "So, what's on our agenda? Shopping? Late lunch somewhere?"

"Umm," Juice replied vaguely, distracted by the larger of her two screens.

"What was that place you said you wanted to try?" Yvonne asked. "The new Indian, in Canoga Park?"

Juice looked over at her. "Huh? Oh yeah, on Sherman Way, down the street from Paul's apartment. I think it's called Bombay Bombast. Looks pretty nice."

"Well… are you hungry?"

"Um, yeah," said Juice, now looking down at her phone. "But, I don't know…" She popped a chip into her mouth and crunched away on it for a few seconds, then swallowed and looked up at Yvonne again.

"I'm just not really feeling it right now. Maybe we should order in. What do you think?"

Yvonne shrugged. "Yeah, sure, I guess."

"Oh!" Juice suddenly exclaimed. "I haven't told you about this shit with Nancy!"

"Nancy?"

"Nancy Parsons. This total bitch I knew in high school. I've told you about her before. Nasty Nancy, remember? We were BFFs, for a while, until the little cunt turned against me."

"Oh yeah, I think I remember," lied Yvonne. Many people in Juice's life had (apparently) turned against her over the years.

"Well, check this out," said Juice, scanning the surrounding area. "Oh, grab that laptop, would you?" She gestured toward a side table located nearer to herself than to Yvonne.

After retrieving the computer, handing it to Juice and settling back into her spot on the sofa, Yvonne looked at the screen, which showed a blown-up image, obviously clipped from a website. The image contained a photo of a white woman with wavy, shoulder-length dirty blonde hair, dark eyes and eyebrows, and a thin nose, wearing a lot of makeup and a very wide, fake-looking smile. Under the photo was a line of text reading "Shayla Jennings," and, under that, another line of text reading "1 Mutual Friend."

"After all these years," said Juice, "yesterday, out of the blue, she pops up again!"

"She got in touch with you?"

"Hell, no! That shitty-ass skank would never get in touch with me. She wouldn't dare! No—Facebook got in touch with me, *about* her.

Suggested her as a *friend*. Hah! Can you believe it?"

"Funny," said Yvonne with a small laugh. "So—Shayla? Thought you said her name was Nancy…"

"Right. Nancy is her real name. And her last name is Parsons, not Jennings. Or was, back then at least. And her middle name wasn't Shayla, either. It was Jane. I remember. But name changes are exactly the kind of shady, underhanded thing she would do."

"Well, are you sure this is her? I mean, it's been a long time."

"Oh, it's definitely her. Not a doubt in my mind. I'd recognize Nasty Nancy anywhere."

"I guess it doesn't matter anyway," said Yvonne. "It's not as if you'd try to friend her."

"Oh, yes I would! I did! That bitch and I, we have some unfinished business. Being reminded of her existence has brought back all the memories of how she treated me."

"You two were so young when all that stuff happened. I'm sure she's a different person now."

"Doubt it," said Juice. "You don't know this girl. She's a bitch to the core. It's in her DNA. But even if she did change, I don't care—I want justice."

Yvonne smiled. "What are you going to do? Kick her ass?"

"Damn right I am! Not physically. But it's gonna feel the same when I let her know what a worthless piece of shit she is. And when I rub it in her face how great my life is now."

"You certainly do have some incredible friends now," Yvonne remarked with a smirk.

Juice ignored her and continued: "She's gonna be so jealous when she finds out I'm a doctor."

"Maybe she's a doctor, too."

Juice laughed. "Puh-lease! Not a chance. Nancy's dumb as a rock and lazy as fuck. She's probably got ten kids with four different fathers and she's on food stamps."

Both women were silent for a moment while Juice fantasized about Nancy's fate. Then she said, "I also want my necklace back."

"She borrowed a necklace from you?"

"Borrowed? No—she stole it in cold blood. I had this necklace that my Aunt Rhoda gave me for my 13th birthday. A silver chain with a diamond pendant. Nancy found it in a drawer in my bedroom one day when we were hanging out, I think it was the summer before senior year. She asked if she could borrow it but I said no, it was too special. But she just took it anyway. Sneakily. I didn't realize it was missing until like a week later."

"So that was the end of your friendship?" asked Yvonne.

"No, no. But I think it was the beginning of the end. I'd say the friendship died a slow death throughout most of senior year, as we gradually liked each other less and less... and trusted each other less and less!" Juice laughed about this and then paused for a few seconds, thinking.

"Actually," she continued, "I think she was the one who stopped liking and I was the one who stopped trusting. But I still thought she was cool as hell, hated the idea of losing her as a friend. God, what an idiot I was!" Juice laughed again and Yvonne joined in.

"So anyway, I confronted her about the necklace and she denied taking it. But I just let it go. Then later I confronted her again—while she was wearing the damn thing!—and she *still* denied it. Just said it wasn't the same necklace. Unbelievable."

"She does sound like a bitch," Yvonne conceded.

"Yep. But I just let her walk all over me. Until finally, the last straw was when she kissed my boyfriend at a party. I was so angry and so... just devastated. I remember crying and screaming at her. I made a huge scene in front of everybody, oh my goodness..." They shared another laugh.

Reflecting further on the incident, Juice added, "But actually, you know... I think it was the last straw for *her*. Not for me. 'Cause I remember her telling me, right then and there, that our friendship was over. And it was a real slap in the face."

"Wow," said Yvonne.

"And that was that. We never spoke again."

"Until now."

"Yep, until now." Juice paused, then grinned and said, "Revenge!"

"I don't know, Juice," said Yvonne. "High school? I mean, isn't that stuff all water under the bridge now?"

Juice, still grinning, said, "A dish best served cold!"

"She probably doesn't have the necklace anymore," added Yvonne.

"I think she does."

"Did she accept your friend request?"

"No, not so far. She never will if she's smart. But that's okay. I can track her down. Justice *will* be mine, oh yes."

"I guess you could start with that one mutual friend you two have."

"Yes! Great idea. There you go, my girl—now you're getting into the spirit of things!"

Juice chuckled delightedly. Yvonne smiled at her with a mixture of affection, amusement, and astonishment.

Tapping the laptop mousepad to open a new browser window, Juice said, "Alright, then—let's figure out what we want to stuff our faces with."

Sitting in her office chair three days later, Yvonne glanced over at her cell phone and saw that she had a missed call. While continuing to listen to the equal parts confused and confusing sequence of words currently flowing out of Mona's mouth, and maintaining the "I'm focused and fascinated" facial expression, she slowly reached for the phone and checked it. The missed call was from Juice. Must be an emergency, Yvonne thought sarcastically.

Mona's inane chatter had been solicited, as part of the "Titanium Ten," an informal daily status meeting. Each morning at 10:00, Laura came out of her private office and stood among the six desks of her underlings. All the Lab Team members present would then turn their seats around 180 degrees to face each other, listen to Laura's updates, and give quick updates of their own in turn. This process, although intended to last ten minutes, typically dragged on for at least half an hour. Wednesdays were particularly rough because nobody worked remotely on Wednesdays. Today, however, Amy had temporarily left the office to attend a special show-and-tell event at her son's pre-school.

The updates always began with Rob Harkin, who sat across from Yvonne, then proceeded clockwise around the desks. Everyone on the team liked the cheerful, mild-mannered, 63-year-old Rob, but only the foolish ones relied on him to get anything done, much less to get it done right. In discussions of drawers containing knives, nobody ever linked the word "sharpest" with Rob's name. Yet it was a tricky task judging exactly how much of his weak job performance owed itself to a weak intellect, because Rob also enjoyed world-class ranking in apathy and laziness. Despite sitting next to a major aisle from which anybody who worked on the 17th floor and happened to be passing by could clearly see his huge computer screen, he normally had it completely filled with an active game of solitaire.

Today, like most days, Rob had given a mercifully brief status report consisting of describing a randomly selected "ongoing issue" from his list of four or five such alleged issues. The list never changed, and every item on it was either already resolved, wasn't actually a problem, or wasn't even true. Somehow Yvonne was the only member of the team who knew this.

"That's all I have," said Mona, concluding her bewildering delivery. Mona, who sat next to Rob, generally delivered updates nearly as predictable as his, equally useful, and far more long-winded, always ending with "That's all I have."

"Um, okay," said Laura, after pausing to check nobody else had any response. "Let's take that offline, okay?"

Mona smiled and nodded. Yvonne knew the probability of an "offline" follow-up discussion about Mona's tangled mess of nonsensical concerns was zero. Laura unconsciously believed it to be 50/50. Mona believed it was 100% but would very shortly forget all about it.

Fred, sitting at the desk between Mona's and the window, began his update. Although substantially brighter than Rob and Mona, Fred often got in over his head at work, largely due to his taking on too many things and struggling with the English language (he'd immigrated from Vietnam as a teenager). Curiously for a person with such poor speaking skills, he loved to talk and routinely gave the lengthiest report of all during the Titanium Ten.

As Fred was describing in great detail the eighth task, out of eleven, currently on his plate, Yvonne received a text from Juice. It read, "Call me! Progress on nasty Nancy!"

Slowly, still trying to listen to Fred, Yvonne responded with "I'm at work."

Another text arrived almost immediately: "So am I! Call me ASAP!"

When Fred reached the end of his list, Mona and Laura requested a few clarifications, which he attempted to provide. Rob, who hadn't been listening and anyway wouldn't have understood much or cared at all, asked no questions. Neither did Yvonne, who'd already known everything about all eleven of Fred's items before he began. She had learned from his update, however, that Fred himself misunderstood several of them, and made a mental note to closely monitor his group emails about these.

There were also no questions from Jack Sutton, who occupied the other window desk, across from Fred. And the entire team would've been stunned if there had been any—Jack never asked questions. He seldom spoke at all unless forced to, wrote very few emails, refrained from making eye contact with others, and generally gave the impression of disliking his job, as well as all human beings.

It was Jack's turn now and, as usual, he said "I have nothing new to report." Laura didn't bat an eyelid at this; she'd made peace with Jack's way and its immutability. Long gone were the days of lecturing and coaxing him. Long gone, even, were the days following those, when she'd sighed and rolled her eyes. These were the days of no concern, no reaction.

Jack wasn't stupid, or ignorant, or lazy. Yet his contribution to the team was quite small indeed. As small as it possibly could be without risking getting fired. He relentlessly, methodically ensured this, with his every action and every decision. Like oppositely charged magnetic poles, Jack's devotion to not working matched Fred's to working.

Jack organized his entire life around the principle of "value efficiency." He'd once explained this to Yvonne, in a rare unguarded moment in the break room. People are tricked into wasting so much of their life, Jack believed, because it feels infinite. But in reality, every second is precious. Every second must be used for something valuable. Which is why enlightened folks don't spend any time doing stuff they hate, or stuff that bores them, or pointless stuff like exchanging pleasantries and making idle chitchat. When Yvonne had asked him how it was valuable for him to spend time telling her all of this, he'd stared at her, bug-eyed and speechless, for five seconds and then scurried away.

Today Yvonne's update followed Jack's (since Amy, whose desk was in between theirs, was absent). Yvonne hesitated to bring up the same subject yet again, but decided to go for it.

"The main thing I want to mention," she said, "which some of you might recall I've mentioned before, is that we should actively lobby the nurses to dock their glucometers. And that means we *don't* re-send messages when they complain about the patient not being recognized."

Nurses, when preparing to conduct a blood sugar test using a portable device called a glucometer, began by letting the device know whose blood they were about to draw, by scanning the patient's wristband barcode. Occasionally, the glucometer would complain that it didn't recognize the patient, upon which the nurse called the I.T. Help Desk, which in turn assigned the issue (or "ticket") to whomever from the Lab Team was currently on call (a responsibility that rotated weekly among five of them (the exempted being Laura, as the manager, and Amy, as a special person who demanded it)).

The glucometer lacked any wireless communication ability, meaning that if the patient had been registered recently enough, i.e. since the nurse removed the glucometer from its docking station and began carrying it around with them, it would have no way of knowing about that registration. So the solution to the nurses' "problem" was simply to dock their glucometers momentarily in order to update them, and the solution to the Lab Team's problem of being assigned these tickets was to ensure the nurses understood this.

But, most team members (all except Jack (who simply ignored every case until it was automatically re-assigned to someone else) and Yvonne) instead handled these incidents by logging into the patient registration system and forcing it to re-send the patient's information over to the lab system, then informing the nurse of what they'd done. This approach did nothing to solve the problem while simultaneously perpetuating the myth that solving it required Lab Team intervention.

"Yes," said Laura, "a very good idea. Thanks, Yvonne. I will write that up in an email to the whole team. I'll also post a Protocol Note about it in SCUM." (Support Case Utility Management, a computer system for tracking work.)

"Great, thanks," said Yvonne. "That's it for me."

"Does anyone have anything else?" Laura asked.

Nobody did.

"Okay, thanks, everyone. Great meeting!"

Yvonne watched Laura stroll back across the main aisle and into her office, which featured a very non-sound-proof wall and door, both made of clear glass. Yvonne wondered why they even existed. To prevent other employees from stealing the boss's red pen? She suspected it was purely symbolic. Not that Laura personally subscribed to such thinking. Always down-to-earth and approachable, she'd not changed how she treated anybody when she'd been promoted.

Yvonne felt skeptical, though, of Laura's managerial prowess. Looking through the glass wall at the cluttered, chaotic desk, strewn with dozens of individual sheets of paper varying in size from legal down to Post-It, Yvonne sighed. Hopelessly disorganized, she thought. Belongs in the trenches with the rest of us. She rated the chances of the promised team email and Protocol Note actually happening at slim to none.

Turning back to her computer screen, Yvonne saw an alert pop up in the corner indicating the arrival of an email from Juice (subject: "Nasty Nancy!"). She clicked over to Outlook to find she also had several unread work-related emails, but couldn't resist reading Juice's right away.

It began: "Fine girl, ignore all my texts and calls! Just want you to know I've been super-sleuthing it in my Quest for Vengeance! :-) The mutual friend was a bust, some bitch named Carol Clucker or some shit, I don't know who the fuck she is (I have thousands of friends (of course!) BUT, check this out. I dug deeper! That's right, I did me some deep Google digging and found every person out there named Shayla Jennings!"

Juice went on to say that the mysterious Facebook photo she'd shown Yvonne on Sunday was not to be found anywhere else on the Internet, but the vast majority of people named Shayla Jennings did have photos available and could be ruled out that way. There were four exceptions:

1. Shayla S. Jennings – no phone, no email, age unknown, looks to be active on a Chicago area dating app called Shy-Town

2. shayla.jennings@netknot.org – no phone, age unknown, location unknown

3. Shayla Jennings – no phone, no email, age unknown, works as office manager at some place called CoxBox in San Diego

4. Shayla Jean Jennings – no phone, no email, correct age, lives at 223 Redbud Drive, Hendersonville, TN

She sure is on a mission, thought Yvonne, shaking her head and smiling.

I think #4 is Nancy! She's the right age, and Nancy's family was originally from Nashville... (a bunch of honky-tonk rednecks, haha) And Hendersonville is a suburb of Nashville!

I realized trying to friend her, as me, was a big mistake. She'll never knowingly talk to me. Lesson learned! From now on, I gotta disguise my identity when I reach out to these girls.

Juice's email then detailed how she planned to pursue each of the four candidates. For her prime suspect out in Tennessee, she'd pretend to be organizing a high school reunion and try to draw out an admission of having attended their high school and/or being known as Nancy back then. Ideally this would be done over the phone, but if continued efforts to discover a phone number failed, it could always be done through old-fashioned snail mail.

Juice also hoped to obtain a phone number for CoxBox, which she'd then use to contact Shayla #3, multiple times, if necessary, using multiple fake identities, and try to extract sufficient info to rule her out (or, perhaps, in).

Juice had already sent an email to Shayla #2 (using a new account she'd created under a false name), employing the same high school reunion ruse also intended for Shayla #4. So far, no response.

For Shayla #1, Juice planned to sign up with the same dating app and take a look at the woman's profile there (which surely would include a photo).

Yvonne marveled at the length of the email, and Juice's overall dedication to her cause, dubious though its worth might be. Figuring Juice would be on her case fervently until she replied, she quickly banged out "Sounds great! Nice job!" and hit Send. Then she turned her attention back to work matters.

A series of emails with the subject "RE: [1092746] patinet not found" had accumulated in Yvonne's inbox prior to the Titanium Ten, when she'd been focused on resolving an interface issue (which, like most interface issues, should've been fixed by—and was caused in the first place by—the Interface Team). The first email came from Deepa Ramakrishnan, who earlier had opened a ticket because her glucometer claimed not to recognize the patient on whom she needed to perform a blood sugar test. After hearing nothing back for a couple of hours, she'd replied to the initial Help Desk email (a useless auto-generated message simply acknowledging her issue) and copied the entire Lab Team, asking for the status.

The next email, from Fred, had arrived one minute after Deepa's. It stated that re-sending a patient registration message to the lab system was the prescribed solution for this situation, and that he'd just done this.

Mona had replied next, five minutes later, saying that she was unsure how to help Deepa and asking her teammates for advice. She'd used Reply-All, so Deepa was included.

Another email from Fred had come in, one minute after Mona's, beginning with "Good Morning Mona," then reiterating verbatim everything from his previous email, and then providing pasted-in step-by-step instructions for re-sending the message.

Five minutes after that, Deepa had sent another email indicating that the patient was still not recognized.

The next email from Fred had come in one minute after Deepa's and informed her that he'd performed another re-send.

Mona had chimed in again, ten minutes after Fred, to let everyone know she'd figured out the re-send procedure and had successfully completed it. Her email ended with a smiley emoticon.

After that, the thread had gone quiet for nearly half an hour, at which point there'd been one more from Deepa, saying she'd taken a break and, when she got back and tried scanning the patient's wristband again, the glucometer had recognized the patient and she'd been able to complete her blood test. She expressed immense gratitude to the Lab Team for all their help.

"She docked it," muttered Yvonne under her breath, through gritted teeth, as another email, with the same subject, came in.

The new arrival, from Rob, was a reply to Deepa's very first email. It said, "Message needs to be re-sent from registration."

After a minute of holding her head in her hands, and another minute of editing (pasting in Rob's contribution, removing patient details, and adding "See what I have to put up with?" at the top), Yvonne forwarded the entire thread to Bill.

He replied a few minutes later with "Ugh, tell me about it. I was forced to go on a conference call this morning about some stuff I needed input on. I tried to get out of it but I just couldn't."

"Hello?" said the voice of Paul Newton, coming out of Juice's speakers. "Are you still there?"

Juice was distracted, curious about a bumper sticker on the car in front of her and attempting to read it.

"Yeah," she said.

"Well?" asked Paul.

Juice was now following dangerously closely and squinting hard at the little blue sticker with white lettering. She couldn't read any of the words yet, but suspected the picture next to them of being either a gun or a Christian cross.

"Well what?" she snapped after a long pause.

"I asked if you could pick up the kids an hour earlier on Sunday. The church called and they want me to cover for Greg while he's recovering from back surgery."

"Dammit!" shouted Juice, because the car in front of her was exiting the freeway and now she'd never know what the sticker said. Although Juice had no particular political leanings herself, she enjoyed the spectacle of others expressing theirs, especially in passionate ways about controversial subjects. But in this instance, had Juice succeeded in glimpsing the other driver's bumper-mounted message, she would've found it disappointingly boring. The rapidly departing sticker in fact simply contained the words "Moss Ivy Preparatory School" with an image of intertwined vines and leaves.

"Okay, you don't have to get all uppity about it," said Paul. "I was just asking."

"Asking what?"

"If you could pick up the kids early on Sunday!"

"Nope, can't. In fact I might be late getting them. I've got a thing." As Juice suspected while saying this, but couldn't really remember for sure, she had no plans for Sunday.

Paul sighed. "Hmm, okay, well I guess I can—"

"I'm going to have to let you go, Paul," said Juice, wary of any sort of childcare negotiations and also bored.

"Oh, um, okay, I guess I'll—"

"Bye!" said Juice, and pressed the red hang-up button on her dashboard touchscreen.

After ten more minutes of driving, which passed uneventfully, she pulled into the parking lot of CoxBox Corp, found a spot (easily), turned off the engine and hopped out into the Friday afternoon San Diego sunshine. One of the perks of Juice's job (as a family practice physician on staff at South Valley General Hospital), which she'd seized on the moment she became eligible after five years of service, was the optional four-day work week. It meant less money, but having a long weekend every single weekend made the financial sacrifice totally worthwhile (especially as a portion of every dollar she made went to Paul). Most Fridays she spent sitting around the house, with the occasional bit of eating out or shopping. But today, she was on a mission.

Despite feeling very confident that Shayla #4 (in Tennessee) was actually her longtime nemesis Nancy Parsons, Juice knew that until she confirmed this, it'd be prudent to track down the other three Shaylas and definitively cross them off the list. After several awkward, frustrating phone calls with CoxBox, during which she'd gotten Shayla on the phone a couple of times but had never managed to learn much about her, Juice had decided to quit messing around and just make the 3-hours-each-way journey for an in-person visit.

"With my luck, this'll be Shayla's day off," she muttered to herself as she strode toward the red brick building.

Juice was a naturally beautiful, full-figured black woman. She had large eyes, high cheekbones, very subtly distinctive curvature of nose and lips, and perhaps the most perfectly symmetrical face humankind had ever possessed. Her beauty arsenal also included a keen fashion sense, superb makeup skills, and a crack team of hair and nail specialists who provided their services at least once a week. Though she was always carrying between 30 and 50 pounds of excess weight, she dressed herself masterfully (when in public) to accentuate breasts, thighs and buttocks while totally concealing belly and upper arms. Nobody was more keenly aware of Juice's gorgeousness than Juice herself, who derived constant delight and smugness from it.

Her phone pinged as she reached the glass double doors and flung one of them open. Stepping inside, she looked at her email to find that Shayla #2 had finally replied:

> *Dear Ms. Wilson,*
>
> *Thank you so much for your very kind and friendly e-letter! Reading it made me wish that I had attended Hawthorne High School, but alas, I did not. It must have been a lovely experience for you and your classmates. I had a wonderful vacation once, in nearby Torrance Beach. So beautiful.*
>
> *Of course, the mountains have their appeal, too. After living all my life back east, I moved to Hemet, California, last year with my husband, Juan. We have found it truly delightful here.*
>
> *Best wishes for your upcoming reunion!*
> *Sincerely yours,*
> *Shayla T. Jennings*

"Mmm-hmm," said Juice to herself. Cross that one off the list. No way in hell Nancy would ever write anything like that. How old was this girl, anyway, like 90?

Immediately inside the front door of CoxBox was a 20-feet-long corridor. Juice traversed it and came out into a modest reception area containing two desks and, behind these, two doorways through which she could see office workers milling around and doing office work. The reception area also contained a third doorway, on the near side of the desks, whose door was shut and bore a sign reading "Unisex Restroom." Hanging on one wall was a large portrait of a non-descript middle-aged white man wearing a suit.

Atop both desks sat nameplates, one reading "Tina Hecht" and the other "Shayla Jennings." Tina's desk was currently unoccupied. A young woman who looked nothing like Nancy sat at Shayla's desk, staring into her lap. She seemed unaware of Juice's presence.

"Excuse me," said Juice, stepping up to the desk, from where she could see that the woman was playing a game on a phone. "Shayla?"

The woman looked up. "Oh, hi!" she exclaimed with a big smile. "No, I'm Tina. Can I help you with something?"

"Why aren't you sitting at your own desk?" asked Juice, slightly annoyed.

Still smiling, Tina replied, "What did you say your name was?"

"My name's Janet Jones. I need to speak with Shayla. She's expecting me."

"Um, okay, let me see if I can find her," Tina said, then jumped up and disappeared through one of the doors into the office workers' area.

Juice's phone emitted a notification sound, informing her that something new had just happened on the Shy-Town dating app. Signing up for it Wednesday afternoon, Juice had imagined that eliminating Shayla #1 from contention would be quick and easy, but had then discovered that Shy-Town was a specialty app for extremely timid, anxious, self-conscious people.

She'd also experienced a setback after initially creating a male profile, then discovering that Shayla #1 preferred women. But ultimately, under the pseudonym Natasha Nelson, Juice had struck up a flirtatious conversation with Shayla, who quickly admitted to using a pseudonym herself and whose real name was Nancy. Pure coincidence, Juice suspected, but definitely worth following through on, and she'd been pressing Shayla/Nancy relentlessly for a picture. Now it had arrived at last.

A grainy photo, with terrible lighting and washed-out colors, but clearly not Nancy Parsons. Wrong age, wrong race, wrong size, wrong shape. Wrong everything. Another check in a box. Juice couldn't stop a small smirk from forming on her mouth as she marveled at her own devious, methodical genius.

Tina returned, taking a seat at her own desk this time.

"Shayla's on her way out," she said.

"Thanks," said Juice, then turned her attention to the giant portrait, noticing a small plaque underneath it containing two lines of text: "Our Founder" and, under that, "Raymond J. Norshein."

"Oh," she said, turning back toward Tina, "I assumed your founder was somebody named, uh, Mr. Cox... or Ms. Cox, or whatever."

"Oh, uh-huh," laughed Tina. "No, the reason we're called CoxBox is we make boxes for coxes."

"What are you talking about? Where's Shayla?"

"In competitive rowing," Tina explained, "the person who sits at the end of the boat and directs the activity of the rowers is called the coxswain, or just cox for short. We make different types of special storage boxes for those people to keep their stuff in."

"Great," said Juice in a tone that hinted at her boredom and impatience.

"Yep," Tina continued, smiling enthusiastically, "Ray there has always adored the sport. And he's a big fan of the cox! So, one day, he had this idea of how he could help out and, presto, our company was born!" She judiciously refrained from mentioning the pending lawsuit against them from Nielsen Kellerman, a much older company that had trademarked the name "CoxBox."

A woman walked into the room from one of the office workers' area doors and said to Juice, "Hi there. May I help you with something?"

"Shayla Jennings?" Juice enquired.

"Yes," Shayla replied.

Without another word, Juice turned on her heel and strode quickly out of the room, down the corridor and out the main door into the parking lot. CoxBox Shayla was obviously not Hawthorne Nancy, and Juice didn't want to waste another second of her time here.

She'd nearly reached her car when her phone rang. Seeing it was a Tennessee number, she got very excited and answered immediately. "Hello?" she said.

A deep, masculine voice with a thick southern drawl came over the line. "Hello. This is Shayla Jennings. I'm trying to reach Sharon Smith."

"Oh my god," said Juice.

"Ma'am, is everything alright?"

"You're Shayla Jennings?"

"Yes, ma'am."

"You are a woman, right?"

A long pause. Then, "Uh, yes, ma'am."

Juice sighed. "You never went to high school in Southern California, did you?"

"No, ma'am. As a matter of fact, that's the reason I'm calling you today. I got this mess—"

Juice hung up, sighed again, reflected for a moment, then went back into her phone and quickly blocked calls from that number. Then, continuing to assess the current state of her quest for vengeance, she slowly slumped against the side of her car, a frown forming on her face.

"What the fuck am I gonna do now..."

Chapter 5

Standing amidst the early June, mid-afternoon weekend chaos of the Venice Beach boardwalk, with the sun cooking the back of his neck, watching a tall, shaggy-haired, rail-thin man with pasty white skin purchase a hot dog, Bill Smede felt a rare pang of fondness and love (momentarily interrupting the default irritation and anxiety). The customer was Matt Spratt, Bill's closest friend for over 25 years, and the snack he'd just obtained was officially considered a sausage by the discerning folks producing them at Joni Macaroni the Sausage Queen.

Chewing delightedly, Matt made his way out of the throng of people clustered around the vendors' little shack-bungalows and rejoined Bill in the throng of people swarming every which way on the massive concrete footpath that ran alongside the vendors.

Matt swallowed, grinned widely and said, "You should get one of these, too."

"Can't," Bill replied. "You used the last of my cash."

"Oh. Well, you can share mine," Matt offered, extending his arm so that his newly-acquired prize nearly touched Bill's nose. "Go on, have a bite, dude. It's awesome!"

"Uh, no thanks," said Bill, waving it away with his hand. "I'm not hungry."

"Suit yourself," said Matt, bringing the hot dog back over next to his own face. "But it's not really about hunger." He took another bite, then added, through closed lips, "Mmm."

The two men began walking south along the footpath, continuing a circuit they'd started from Matt's home two hours ago which had included lunch at The Sidewalk Cafe, a Venice Beach institution (where, as usual, Bill had happily offered to pay and Matt had happily accepted).

To their left was a seemingly never-ending row of ramshackle eateries and souvenir shops, punctuated by the occasional palm tree, cross-street, or small, decrepit apartment building (typically occupied by around five dozen people, all between the ages of 21 and 24).

To their right sat the mobile vendors, operating from tents, blankets and chairs they set up and took down each day, hawking their primarily artsy and homemade wares such as jewelry, paintings, knittings and bongs. Behind these lay a vast stretch of sand with a paved bicycle path winding through it. Beyond that, the waves of the Pacific crashed rhythmically against the shore. This place could be really beautiful, thought Bill, surveying his surroundings. If it weren't for all the people.

"So what do they call that one?" he asked, gesturing at the rapidly disappearing treat clutched in Matt's hand.

"This one is known as Joni's Spicy Special Curving Pork Cutlass," Matt replied with a grin. "It's my favorite."

"Aha," said Bill. "So I guess all the names begin with 'Joni's'? But wouldn't that go without saying?"

Matt made a "Mmph" sound as he chewed another chunk of cutlass, then swallowed and said, "No, actually some of them are other people's. Like they've got this long, thin one called Marco's Italian Hot Beef Needle." They both laughed.

Matt continued, "And some other ones, too. I guess these are folks who helped out Joni with her recipes." He paused. "Or naming them, at least."

"If Joni's even a real person," added Bill.

"Hah! Right," said Matt.

As the two friends made their way slowly down the crowded boardwalk, anybody watching (which nobody was) would've been struck by the contrast between them. The six-inch height difference. Matt's utterly carefree stride versus Bill's tense, rigid movements. Matt clad in just baggy tank top, baggy shorts and flip-flops, versus the comparatively decked-out Bill with his running shoes (so his feet wouldn't hurt), jeans (to prevent his legs from getting burned), polo shirt (because every shirt he owned was a polo), sunglasses, hat, and PaceTek Nano which he compulsively glanced at seven times per minute.

And indeed, Matt and Bill were very different people, or at least had been when they'd first met, as freshmen at UCLA, where Matt had arrived on a surfing scholarship and Bill had begun with an undeclared major because he hadn't made up his mind yet between math and computer science.

Since that time, they'd become considerably more alike, having shared so many experiences and influenced each other's personalities. Bill had learned from Matt how to lighten up and relax a bit (a fact some people who'd met Bill later on found hard to believe), and to better appreciate playfulness and whimsy. In turn, Bill had sharpened up Matt's sense of humor and generally broadened Matt's awareness of the world and its ideas.

But fundamentally, they were still an innocent, happy wanderer and a fretful, sensitive philosopher—which, oddly enough, was part of why they enjoyed spending time together.

Glancing at a collection of pottery laid out on a carpet as they passed it, Matt commented, "You know, I've been thinking I might try my hand at selling my clay pots here."

"Your clay pots?" Bill asked, puzzled.

"Yeah, seems like it wouldn't be too bad, sitting out here, you know, of an afternoon... chilling out, watching all the people go by. Maybe make a couple bucks."

"Maybe," said Bill, thinking he'd be hard-pressed to come up with a more miserable activity that didn't involve weapons or surgical tools. "But, I didn't know you were a potter."

"Oh, well I'm not, yet. But seems like it'd be fun. It's not that hard, actually. I saw a thing on YouTube. They teach you how to do it in like five minutes. Painting designs on them and everything."

Bill looked at him.

"What?" said Matt with a little laugh. "I might do it. Seriously."

After another half mile on the boardwalk, during which Matt obtained the phone number of a young woman after she accidentally stepped on his foot, they turned left onto 25th Avenue and headed toward the small network of canals, inspired by the older Venice, that had been a neighborhood trademark for well over a century.

It was quite a beautiful scene—largely inaccessible to automobiles, lined with flowering plants and a mix of quaint houses and quirky ones. Still, both Bill and Matt suspected that the look and feel of this place differed vastly from that of its Italian namesake. They crossed over a footbridge on their way into the canals area, then another one on their way out, and, after several more minutes and a few more twists and turns, arrived at the house on Clark Avenue where Matt lived.

The somewhat ugly, single-story house, surrounded by overgrown shrubs, clad in aluminum siding on all four sides and painted a dull, faded bluish-gray (except for a few random spots that were a dull, faded yellow), had been built in the 1940s and, since then, had received the bare minimum amount of renovation and maintenance to remain habitable under L.A. County codes. One exception: in the 1970s it had been split into a duplex, with a new entrance added to one half and a new kitchen and shower to the other.

Matt's uncle, who owned the property, allowed Matt to occupy the left side essentially rent-free. The right side housed real (albeit usually terrible) tenants, who rotated through at an average rate of twice per year.

Bill and Matt crossed the weed-riddled front yard, climbed the two steps onto the porch, and entered the house. Like Juice, Matt never locked his door. But unlike her, if a visitor knocked, he would happily come open it for them.

Matt went through to the kitchen as Bill took a seat on one of the battered, stained old couches (first moving some magazines, a floppy elastic band intended for arm exercises, a dinner plate, and a small teddy bear, to make space for his butt), across from the always-on television which was currently showing an episode of "The Simpsons" from 1997. The dirty, cluttered, totally disorganized state of Matt's living room never surprised Bill, though it did occasionally surprise Matt himself.

It resembled the stereotypical college kid's dwelling. Every square inch of flat surface that didn't contain an object was covered in a thick layer of dust, but this didn't add up to very many square inches because every surface was also littered with coffee cups, soda cans, beer bottles, papers, coins, kitchenware, miscellaneous boardwalk-style trinkets, playing cards, makeshift ashtrays and proper ashtrays. None of the furniture matched, most of it was older than Bill's son Patrick, and some of it sat in seemingly arbitrary locations, at seemingly arbitrary angles. The two-decades-old carpet, which at the time of its installation had been the cheapest Matt's uncle could find, had been vacuumed exactly five times, most recently three years ago, by Bill.

"Hey Bill, you want a beer?" Matt called out from the kitchen.

"No, thanks," Bill replied. "I'm good. Hey, you mind if I turn off the T.V.?"

No response.

Matt's "work station"—a folding chair and a flimsy child's desk holding a monitor, keyboard and mouse, with a PC on the floor underneath—occupied a corner fairly near where Bill was sitting. The aging computer wouldn't have been able to handle live streams or newer games very well, but it sufficed for Matt's needs: browsing obscure websites, playing older non-Internet games, and watching the occasional YouTube video. The Wi-Fi came from the other half of the duplex or, in a pinch, the house next door. Ever the friendly, charming neighbor, Matt had never failed to persuade anyone to share their password with him.

Bill noticed some pictures on sheets of paper, taped to the wall behind the desk, and leaned forward to examine them more closely. They were all photos of the same woman, and the computer screen showed an image of her as well. Bill didn't recognize the woman, but wondered if perhaps he should. She looked like an old-timey glamorous Hollywood celebrity, and the photos themselves seemed extremely old.

The bathroom door opened abruptly and a stark naked woman stepped into the tiny hallway connecting the living room to the bedroom. She was nearly as thin as Matt, but with much darker and somewhat wrinklier skin. Her breasts were unusually large for her body size and shape, but hung very naturally. Her hair, currently wet and frizzy and shoulder-length, appeared light brown, the same color as her eyes. She had a small tattoo on her right thigh and a larger one, of a pistol, on her abdomen. Although Bill found the view very pleasant, his enjoyment was severely compromised by his feelings of shock, confusion and embarrassment. He wondered if she could be, but doubted she was, the woman from the photos.

Seeing Bill, the woman smiled and said, "Oh, hi," then paused, chuckled and added, "Sorry, I didn't know anyone was here."

"Neither did I," was all Bill could think to say in response.

At that moment, Matt re-entered, carrying two bottles of beer by their necks with his right hand while balancing a plate containing a sandwich on his forearm, and holding a lit joint in his left hand.

"Well hey there, little lady," he exclaimed. "When did you get here?"

"A while ago," the woman replied, grinning, clearly pleased to see Matt. "I got bored, so I took a shower."

"Cool," said Matt after taking a puff on his joint, then, "Oh, Bill, have you met my girlfriend, Sherrie?"

"Uh, no, I don't believe I have," stammered Bill, awkwardly rising from his seat as he realized Sherrie was walking toward him. He could now see that her smaller tattoo was a peace symbol.

The two shook hands as Matt, now standing next to them, casually transferred his food and drink to a small, low table nearby.

"Nice to meet you, Bill," Sherrie said, then let out a small giggle.

"You too."

She turned toward Matt, grabbed him by the head with both hands and pulled him in for a long, deep, passionate kiss. When their faces finally separated, Matt's carried a tiny hint of embarrassment (Sherrie's did not). He took another drag from his joint, then offered it to her.

"No thanks, babe," she said. "But I'll take one of those beers."

"Sure thing," said Matt, snatching up one of the beers and handing it to her. "Now you should probably get some clothes on. Poor Bill here, he's the respectable sort."

"Aw, don't be so hard on him," Sherrie said, smiling at Bill. "He doesn't look all that respectable."

"No," said Bill.

Sherrie turned and sauntered off toward the bedroom, receiving a playful slap on the butt from Matt as she departed. Bill sat down again, feeling at last that it was safe to do so.

Matt picked up the remaining beer and held it out to Bill.

"Here, you take this one, man," he said. "I'll grab myself another one from the fridge."

"No, thanks. I'm good."

Extending the joint toward Bill, Matt said, "Don't suppose you're interested in this, either..."

Bill chuckled. "No. But thank you."

"Okay, whatever—ya square," teased Matt.

He extinguished the joint after taking one last puff, then took a swig of beer, then plopped himself down on the couch next to Bill and began eyeing up his sandwich.

"So, who's the woman in the photos there?" asked Bill, pointing.

"Ah, glad you asked!" Matt replied, eyes twinkling. He was no longer interested in the sandwich. "That woman..."—a short dramatic pause—"...is probably the sexiest movie star of all time."

"Oh yeah?"

"Yes. Her name is Marion Davies."

Bill thought for a few seconds. "Hmm, the name sounds very familiar," he said. "Was she in anything I would've seen?"

Matt had swiftly moved to the computer and was clicking away furiously. "Not if you're a time snob," he said, "which I bet you are."

More images of Davies were popping up all over the screen, along with articles about her and lists of her films.

Matt continued, "Sadly, Marion retired from acting over 80 years ago." He sighed.

"Oh," said Bill, standing up and moving toward the computer himself.

"I could almost hate her," Matt went on, "for robbing the world of her awesomeness so soon. But, who could hate *her*?"

Bill looked over Matt's shoulder at another picture of Davies, a painting this time, in a window Matt was now maximizing to fill the entire screen as he sighed again.

"She's lovely," said Bill. "So, you're obsessed with her, huh?"

"Indeed I am," said Matt. "How could I not be? I'm only human."

Matt clicked around a few more times and a slide-show of Marion Davies images began. Some were portraits, others were stills from her movies.

"I've been learning everything I can about her," he said. "About her movies, about her life, about who she was. You know, who she really was, as a person."

Bill started to feel a bit bored and a bit worried.

"Like, for example, she was so concerned for the well-being of the horses at Hearst Castle that she wrote to the guy in charge there—you know, after it was turned over to the state—asking him to do all these nice things for them, like enlarge their paddock and stuff..."

"Uh, okay..."

"Oh, and her movies are just the best! Luckily, most of her stuff is available on DVD. Even the silent stuff. If you know where to look. Which I do!"

Matt jumped out of the chair, giggling, and went to the other side of the room, where his ancient T.V. (still showing The Simpsons) and a DVD player were perched on a particleboard stand of the flat-pack, self-assembly variety. He knelt down and began perusing the DVD titles stored on the lower level of the stand.

"I've already managed to collect quite a few of them," he said excitedly over his shoulder.

Bill's mind was racing now, trying to think of a suitable excuse to leave. But he couldn't come up with anything.

"Hey!" said Matt, clapping his hands together and turning to look at Bill. "I've got a great idea! You and me and Sherrie are going to have ourselves a little Marion Davies film festival."

And so they did.

———————

That same afternoon, Yvonne Smede was also meeting up with a friend, Francisco, who lived just a few miles away in Century City but whom she managed to see only three or four times a year. They both led busy lives (or so they both told themselves, anyway) and, it seemed to Yvonne, there was always something more important going on.

Strolling eastward along Santa Monica Boulevard, passing under a billboard on which some organization (whose name wasn't clearly specified) encouraged its potential future customers to "Learn screenwriting from the best," Yvonne thought: When they live nearby you always think, "Well I can see them anytime." She knew more blame lay with her than with Francisco, particularly this time around—he'd been pestering her for several weeks about getting together.

She'd finally made the arrangement after learning that Bill was heading off today for yet another rendezvous with one of his VIPs. Though a little ashamed of it, Yvonne couldn't entirely suppress her twinges of jealousy and resentment over Bill's constant dalliances with the likes of Matt, Irene, his sister, his mother, etc. Granted, he usually invited Yvonne to come along on these outings. But she didn't really like any of those people.

Glancing at her PaceTek Ultra as she waited to cross Beverly Glen Boulevard, Yvonne saw that she'd already racked up over 8,000 steps today. "Nice," she said to herself, then made a mental note not to let Francisco give her a lift home, which she suspected he would try to insist on. Allowing it would constitute an unacceptably massive sacrifice of steps.

It then occurred to Yvonne that she and Francisco might well find themselves in a state of mismatched formality of attire today. She looked down at her outfit of t-shirt, shorts, and tennis shoes. Francisco was the sort who tended to get rather dressed up for any activity whatsoever, and generally Bill and Yvonne tried to make a token effort in this direction whenever they met up with him. Oh well, she thought. If he wants to dress inappropriately, that's on him.

The signal finally changed and, after making way for a wheelchair-bound man and his caregiver, and nearly getting sandwiched between a maniac kid on a scooter and a maniac adult on a bicycle, Yvonne cautiously stepped off the curb and began crossing. As with many L.A. intersections, the distance to the opposite side was substantial, and the countdown timer offered only barely enough seconds for a typical pedestrian to make it. So Yvonne and her fellow street adventurers moved briskly and with great focus.

As she reached the safety of the curb with exactly zero seconds remaining, Yvonne heard an unfamiliar pinging sound from her phone. Checking it, she discovered a notification from the recently-installed Version 7 of the eJackal app, informing her that she'd received an e-postcard from Laura, who was currently vacationing with Mike in their favorite spot, the Saint Geert Islands (or SGI, as they called it for short).

The cluster of islands, located in the South Atlantic and originally colonized by the Dutch in the 18th century, had been the subject of international territorial disputes almost continuously ever since. More than two dozen countries (some of which no longer existed) from four continents had laid claim to part or all of the small archipelago at some point in time.

In recent decades, it had operated semi-autonomously under a provisional government jointly established and monitored by The Netherlands, Namibia, Uruguay, and the United States. Roughly every two years, meetings were held by diplomats from these nations, usually in a Swiss resort town, to try to hash out a roadmap for the future. Each time, no progress was made and all sides departed very satisfied with the outcome. But through the political turmoil, the islands had always maintained a safe, peaceful environment and a thriving tourism industry.

Laura and Mike were hugely enamored of SGI, to a degree none of their acquaintances understood. (Bill had once remarked on the subject: "Tons of places have sun, sand, surf, booze and food. Why do you need to go all the way out there?") For them, these islands offered a unique, indescribable vibe. In fact, each individual island offered a slightly different one, and they'd made it a goal to eventually visit all ten. But only one island per trip, otherwise they'd be unable to fully savor it. For this trip, their eighth, they'd selected the island called Nieuw Leeuwarden.

Yvonne began scrolling through the postcard photos as she continued walking, now making her way up a gentle incline toward Century Park West. Every picture featured Laura and Mike, his right arm entwined with her left, both smiling widely for the camera and looking genuinely very happy. The only variables were which beautiful seascape served as their backdrop and which fruity cocktail each of them clutched in their other hand. Yvonne smiled.

Mike and Laura were indeed having a fantastic vacation together, as their photos suggested. The pair made a rather unlikely couple on paper—both borderline misanthropes, one gregarious and a bit goofy, the other (Laura) rather subdued and serious-minded, both of whom had always struggled with dating and relationships, and who'd come from very different backgrounds.

Laura Jean Johnson had grown up in Brooklyn, the only child of white middle-class parents who raised her lovingly but not too lovingly. After a dull, nerdy, rather isolated but fairly happy childhood, she'd gone to college at SUNY Stony Brook, then started a career in I.T. which had taken her to many locales around the country. Her eventual arrival in Southern California, however, had not been for a job but for a man. She'd followed her boyfriend, Ivan, whom she'd only been dating for four months, when he got a job transfer from Akron, Ohio to Gardena. They'd broken up six months after moving, but Laura had stayed put, fond of the mild weather and her recently-acquired job.

Michael James Howell came from a working-class black family in suburban Atlanta, the middle child of seven. All of Mike's siblings had always fit in perfectly with the household ethos established by their disciplinarian parents: hard work, integrity, devotion to God, and most of all, seriousness. Jokes, tomfoolery and horseplay were strictly forbidden. Laughter, on those very rare occasions when it occurred, was met with reprimands or at least disapproving scowls. Smiling, if well justified (e.g. news of a birth or wedding), was tolerated. Apart from quick, dull meals, every family member's every waking moment was occupied with either work, school, church, chores, or childcare.

But Mike, a natural prankster and layabout, had always felt like a square peg in a round hole and had spent his entire childhood pushing back and getting into perpetual trouble with every authority figure. He'd left home at eighteen, ostensibly to attend college but really to escape. The next two decades he'd spent somewhat adrift—nine different occupations in as many states, and twice as many domestic partners. He'd finally begun to feel like he was settling down after qualifying as a paramedic in San Bernardino, California, joining a model airplane club and getting a pet cat. Meeting Laura had been the final piece of his puzzle.

This had happened at a volunteer L.A. beach cleanup effort that neither one was actually interested in helping with. Laura had been pushed into participating by her do-gooder friend, Bunny, and Mike had shown up in the hopes of getting his hands on some precious metal and/or re-sellable scrap metal. Despite the apparently long odds of them even bumping into each other, much less having great chemistry when they did, both happened. Their chemistry, in fact, was astronomical. Nobody who knew them had ever known any other couple so frictionless, so completely, continuously content.

After flipping through all seventeen of the vacation pics Laura'd sent, Yvonne put away her phone and turned her attention to navigating the final few blocks to Francisco's building. Despite owning multiple houses in far-flung parts of the L.A. metro area, he spent most of his time at a rented apartment in a Century City high-rise ("closer to all the action," he reasoned). Every building in Century City (which was not actually a city in its own right, just a district of the city of L.A.) was a high-rise, most of them standing very high indeed. The two tallest buildings outside of downtown, and ten of the tallest forty in all of Los Angeles, could be found here, packed into a patch of land measuring only a half mile square. So it felt kind of like a downtown, minus most of the character—like an artificial downtown that, rather than evolving over numerous decades, had been willed into existence overnight.

Sixty-seven minutes after leaving her condo, with 10,265 steps on the clock, quite sweaty, Yvonne stood in front of Francisco's door, number 2408. She knocked. There was a doorbell button mounted on the wall, but she didn't feel entirely comfortable using it—somehow a doorbell seemed excessive, potentially disruptive, when standing in a windowless passageway surrounded on all sides by people's stacked-up box-homes. No, doorbells were for single-family homes with lots of open space around them.

Yvonne's eyes wandered over the opulent yet tasteful, immaculate, narrow corridor, bending its way toward the similarly spiffy elevator she'd rode up here in (and off to parts unknown in the other direction). Everything about this building felt elegant, dignified, organized, sleek. The man at the security desk, James, had recognized Yvonne instantly (even though she hadn't been here for nearly a year and had no clue who he was) and ushered her through, warmly and eloquently welcoming her back and assuring her that her host waited eagerly upstairs. It was all very impressive and rather appealing, but also foreign and a bit intimidating, and perhaps even—Yvonne wasn't quite sure—absurd, somehow?

It crossed her mind that this was actually, probably, the 23rd floor she was standing on. The mere fact they named it the 24th did not make it so. Those poor saps who live on the so-called 14th, she mused. Too lazy, or dumb, to realize they're doomed to bad luck. Hmm, or is it the entire building that's unlucky, simply because it possesses a thirteenth floor? Ah, but it doesn't—just look at the buttons in the elevator. Hah, take that, cosmos! You're outsmarted.

Just as Yvonne began to reconsider her position on ringing the bell, believing it'd been two minutes since knocking when in fact it'd been fifteen seconds, the door opened. There stood Francisco Danilo Rosario, his twinkling brown eyes and broad smile both projecting great warmth. He was naturally handsome, with a subtle, distinguishing hook in his nose, and his appearance was always enhanced by flawless arrangement of his jet-black hair and perfectly-fitting clothing (at the moment, a three-piece navy blue Armani suit). Yet, there was always something slightly awkward about his posture, his facial expressions, the way he held himself, the way he moved.

"Yvonne!" he exclaimed. "It is a great pleasure to see you."

Before she could finish saying "You too," he'd lurched forward with outstretched arms, almost making contact with her but then hesitating, one millimeter of air separating them.

Yvonne grudgingly extended her own arms, moved that final millimeter and brought the hug to completion. Francisco tucked his chin over her shoulder and clapped both hands against her back. Then, as they pulled away again, he gave her a kiss on the cheek which, although very quick, was somehow also very wet.

"Please, come in," Francisco said with a small laugh. "I am so happy that you are here." Then he turned and started walking back through the foyer. Yvonne wiped her cheek with her hand, stepped inside, closed the door, and followed Francisco through to the main section of the apartment.

The vastness and luxuriousness of this place always struck Yvonne anew each time she visited. The kitchen—decked out in sprawling swaths of mahogany and granite, with two double-wide sinks, three ovens, eight gas burners of various sizes, and a fridge and freezer you might be able to park motorcycles in—had about the same square footage as the front half of her condo. But it was dwarfed by the adjacent lounge, which featured an informal dining alcove (the real dining room was a separate space, around the corner), two distinct sitting areas (the larger of which included a sofa that could comfortably accommodate sixteen butts), a handful of isolated armchairs with little side tables, a massive wet bar, a massive fireplace, and big wide-open spaces between all these things. On the far side of the room, a gigantic window—stretching from floor to twelve-foot ceiling and 25 feet across—provided a spectacular view of the skyscraper next to this one.

"Please, have a little something," said Francisco, gesturing toward a kitchen island on which a large set of hors d'oeuvres had been beautifully laid out—several types of crackers and crispy breads (all snooty-looking), pâté, cheddar, brie, gouda, lox, grapes, berries, sliced melon, and three varieties of olive.

Feeling it would be impolite to decline, especially as the impressive spread appeared completely untouched, Yvonne picked up one of the little plates stacked next to the food and began putting a few items on it.

"Wow," she said with a smile. "Are you expecting others?"

"It will just be you and me," Francisco replied. Then, realizing the reason for Yvonne's question, he added, "When I arranged for the food, I thought Bill might be joining us."

"Ah, right," said Yvonne, with a slightly nervous chuckle. "Yeah, shame he couldn't. You know, because of that thing with Matt. He, uh, wanted to come up and say a quick hello, but, you know how tough it is to park around here." (For the sake of her step count, she'd lied to Francisco when they were planning this, saying that Bill was dropping her off after shopping.)

"I have a spare parking space," said Francisco, who'd taken a seat on one of the sofas. "You and Bill are always welcome to avail yourselves of it."

"Thanks."

"You do have the code for the garage, do you not? I feel certain I provided it to you."

"Uh, yeah, I think I do," Yvonne replied as she sat down on a loveseat that formed a right angle with the sofa, holding her plate of haute bites.

"I will provide it again, just in case," said Francisco, taking out his phone.

As he was sending the text, Yvonne took a bite of cheese-and-cracker and chewed thoughtfully on it.

"Mmm," she grunted after a few seconds, then swallowed and said, "Delicious. Aren't you having any?"

"No," said Francisco, "I am not hungry. I am, however, very pleased that you are enjoying it."

Then he leaned forward and asked, in a way that made it clear he really wanted to know, "So, Yvonne, how are you?"

"I'm good."

"Well," Francisco replied.

A moment of silence followed, during which Yvonne raised both eyebrows and gave him an expectant/puzzled/bemused (and ever so slightly annoyed) face.

"You are well," he finally said, then followed it with a small, ashamed laugh.

"I'm well and good, Francisco," she replied with an assertive tone and a small, tight smirk. She intended her words and face to let him know that he should tread lightly but that he needn't panic—yet.

Francisco got the message. "Wonderful," he said.

They both knew this whole thing was off to a rocky start, but they also both knew it would most likely smooth out and ultimately evolve into a nice afternoon together.

"How are Patrick and Alice doing?"

Yvonne's smile softened and she said, "They're both doing great, thank you." She liked how Francisco (who'd never been a father) always asked about her children and, despite having had virtually no interaction with them, always remembered their names and other basic facts about them.

"Alice is a sophomore in high school now, correct?"

"Yes, just finishing up her sophomore year. Good memory."

"How time flies. And Patrick? Attending college, not attending college... Dabbling in various endeavors... Finding himself...?"

"Yes, all of the above," said Yvonne, and they both laughed.

Then she asked, "How's Felicia? You're still seeing her, I assume?"

"Felaecia—" Francisco reflexively said, then stopped abruptly. His girlfriend of many years, Felaecia Berg-Weinberg, pronounced the second syllable of her unusual first name with a long 'A' sound. Nobody ever got this right, which irritated Francisco immensely (but didn't bother Felaecia in the least).

He continued, "Yes, we are still seeing each other, and she is well. Thank you for asking."

Then he paused again and fidgeted in his seat a bit. After a few seconds, he said, "I need to ask your advice about something, Yvonne. I was planning to wait until a little later, after we had become more comfortable and settled into our shared time today, but I suppose, as we are speaking of Felaecia, I might as well go ahead with it now."

Oh god, thought Yvonne. "Okay," she said.

Francisco drew in a deep breath, then exhaled slowly, collecting his thoughts. Having done a rather poor job of this, he then asked, "Would you rather suck on a woman's nipples, or nibble on her buttocks?"

"Excuse me?"

"What I mean is... What is your favorite part of the female anatomy?"

"The brain."

"No, your favorite external part. No, scratch that. What I mean is... What qualities in a woman would make you want to go to bed with her?"

"Francisco, are you hoping to have a threesome with Felicia and another woman?"

He sighed. "Yes, correct."

"But she doesn't want to."

"Yes, correct, essentially. She is open to the idea, but I would like for her to truly *embrace* it."

"Well I don't think I can help you with that. Every woman is unique. You need to discuss it further with Felicia."

Francisco sighed again. "Unfortunately, I believe that approach has fully run its course."

"Well, hmm… Maybe you could… I don't know… seek another male perspective?"

Francisco sighed a third time. "Yes," he said, "I suppose you are right. Thank you, Yvonne. Thank you."

Yvonne shrugged and forced a smile as she looked across at Francisco's pensive expression. But, to her great relief, the awkward silence was brief, Francisco changed the subject, the conversation grew easier and more natural, and the exchange they'd just had remained the low point of her afternoon.

In fact, it was followed by a very pleasant couple of hours together, which included browsing the shops of the nearby outdoor mall and enjoying a glass of wine on the veranda of one of its many upscale eateries, as the sounds and smells of the never-ending traffic jam floated up from Santa Monica Boulevard.

A little past 5:00, as they sat gazing at the mountains rising out of the concrete jungle a few miles to the north, Yvonne received a text from Bill, complaining that he was being forced to watch hundred-year-old silent movies. She sent a reply of sarcastic sympathy.

Then, a minute later, she sent him another text saying, "Hey btw, Francisco wants to talk to you about something serious."

"What is it?" came Bill's reply, accompanied by a frowning emoji.

"I have no idea."

Three days later at 12 noon, Bill was sitting in front of his computer at his "desk," fuming at what a rotten morning he'd had. Tuesday was already his least favorite day of the work week, because of the standing 7:30 A.M. (or, for all his New York colleagues, a far more convenient 10:30) conference call, on which the five people who loved the sound of their own voice took turns speaking (as the other four of them planned what they would say next) while the remaining eight participants silently wondered how large an unemployment check they might be eligible for. But today, that call had been followed by a mandatory training session on emergency preparedness in the workplace, which had been followed by an awkward one-on-one status meeting with his boss.

Meanwhile, the sounds of hammers and drills and electric saws had been coming through the front wall of the condo, it seemed, louder, longer, more frequently, and starting earlier, than usual. These sounds were produced by a construction crew putting up a new McMansion across the street, a project that had begun over a year ago and, despite feverish work taking place six days a week ever since, showed no signs of nearing completion. Bill suspected the effort had been commissioned by a shadowy organization called Team Kill Bill whose mission was to make his home and neighborhood environment as horrible as possible. Though the existence of such an outfit made no sense and had no supporting evidence whatsoever, Bill felt almost certain of it.

Glancing at his wrist and his calendar, he discovered two more things that didn't help his mood: a very low step count and another meeting, at 1:30 (to talk about a very simple issue that had already been thoroughly covered in an email thread), arranged by an abrasive blowhard named Ted Bonar ("Just the sort of asshole who'd schedule something at 4:30 in the afternoon," Bill said to himself). It was time for a loop, he decided.

Angry, frustrated, and with a sense of urgency, Bill hurriedly gathered up his phone, hat, sunglasses, iPod, and earphones, but not his key. He realized his mistake almost, but not quite, immediately, just as he rounded the bend halfway down the stairs, 2.8 seconds after his front door closed behind him.

"Fuck!" he shouted, which drew the attention of a dog passing by on the sidewalk (but not its owner, who was too mesmerized by a phone screen).

He dashed back up and tried the door, then, upon confirming it was indeed locked, began pacing around in front of it, swearing some more and mentally running through his options. Locksmith? Only as a last resort. Too much time, too much money. Even jogging all the way over to College High School, pulling Alice out of class and taking her key would probably be preferable.

What about neighbors? No, none of them had a key. Long ago Yvonne had given one to kindly old Mrs. Wax in Number One, but she'd died three years back and her son had turned the unit into a rental, after which the 10-member, recently-immigrated-from-Belarus Lifshitz family—with whom the Smedes had no contact (and also did not know their name, number, or country of origin), owing to both families being antisocial, as well as a language barrier—had moved in.

Then it hit him—Patrick! The lazy so-and-so, whom Bill hadn't yet seen today, must still be in his bedroom. He quickly dialed him, but after ten rings it went to voicemail. "Fuck," he said. Then he tried again, with the same result. "Fuck," he said.

What else? Yvonne would be too busy at the office to make a trip back here, and anyway she didn't have a car. The thought of breaking in through a window crossed Bill's mind, but he doubted he had the strength or skill to pull it off, plus afterward he'd probably have to repair damage he'd caused.

He returned to the Patrick idea. His son was probably asleep, Bill figured, with his phone on vibrate. So the new plan was to throw rocks and sticks at Patrick's window until it got his attention. Unfortunately, this would require climbing over a seven-foot fence. Bill didn't relish the task, but felt he was up to it.

After fourteen failed attempts to get on top of the fence, which included scraped up hands, ripped jeans and copious swearing, Bill succeeded. The downward journey on the other side should have been the easy part, especially while grabbing onto tree branches for extra support, but a branch snapped off and Bill ended up lying face-down in a patch of mud with his earphone wire snapped in two.

Watching all of this unfold from her third story balcony in the building next door was alarming for Faye Mussley, who didn't recognize Bill despite having seen him hundreds of times before. She decided calling the police would be the prudent thing to do.

Bill spent twenty minutes underneath Patrick's window (and directly in front of another window belonging to Number Three), searching for things to throw, throwing them, missing most of the time, and inventing new swears. He even threw his phone once, in desperation, and landed a solid hit, the satisfying sound of technology smacking against a pane of glass floating down to his eager ears. And the phone survived this abuse completely intact. But Patrick never appeared.

Finally giving up on the window idea, and with no other ideas left, Bill slowly trudged through the gate, back out to the front of the property, dirty, sweaty, and despairing. He reached the sidewalk just as a police cruiser pulled up. Two officers leapt out, guns drawn, on high alert, and confronted Bill very aggressively at first, but quickly mellowed (and holstered their weapons) upon realizing that he was a white, middle-aged man.

During the five minutes Bill then spent on the sidewalk, chatting with the cops and explaining the situation to them, he felt as if the whole world descended on him. Faye made a brief appearance, to give him a good look-over (she still didn't recognize him) and receive reassurances. Mrs. Harris passed by (with Max) and eyed him up disapprovingly. Wally popped out of Number Two just long enough to inform the police that he had no comment and to whisper "This is how it starts!" in Bill's ear.

A car heading north on Wexler slowed down and the driver began ogling the scene. Then the car came to a complete stop and Bill realized that he knew the face of the man behind the wheel. It was Morris Batz. Suddenly Bill remembered that Yvonne was coming home early today because of some kind of maintenance work happening at her office. He heard the passenger door shut, Morris gave a faint smile and pulled away, and there she was, standing in the road, her sparkling bright blue eyes looking straight at Bill, one eyebrow cocked, lips curled into a smirk.

"Sorry about my husband, officers," she said as she began walking toward them. "I know I'm not supposed to leave him unsupervised."

"Forgot my key," Bill said to her with a grin and a shoulder shrug.

"Mmm-hmm," said Yvonne (in the mocking, judgmental way where the "hmm" part is stressed and higher pitched) as she stepped onto the curb and joined the three others.

After another five minutes of conversation, the police, who'd grown ever friendlier the whole time they'd been here, ultimately behaving almost as if they didn't want to leave, finally did. Just as they were pulling away, Bill spotted a scooter zooming toward him from the opposite direction, a couple of blocks away but closing fast.

"I hate it when they ride on the fucking sidewalk," he said, sort of to Yvonne. Then he turned and yelled to the cops, "Hey! Wait!"

He waved his arms at them and pointed emphatically down the sidewalk toward the approaching offender. They ignored him and drove off.

Bill glanced at Yvonne and, seeing that another smirk had appeared on her face, said, "It's illegal and dangerous."

But she was watching the scooter, which was very close now and rapidly decelerating. Bill turned around just as it came to a halt right next to him, and grimaced at the rider's identity.

"Hi," said Patrick, dismounting and removing his earbuds. "What happened? Was there a break-in?"

"Attempted," said Yvonne.

Bill was very agitated and didn't know where to begin. "I thought you were in your room," he stammered.

"Nope," said Patrick, then added, "I was out."

"Why didn't you answer your phone?" his father demanded.

"Oh, it died."

"Again? Patrick, would you *please* get your act together with keeping your phone charged? It's important."

"Well, I think something's wrong with the phone," said Patrick. "It charges, like, super slow. I think I need a new one."

"You're not getting a new one," said Yvonne.

"Hang on a sec," said Bill suddenly. "How did you rent the scooter if your phone was dead?"

Patrick looked up again. His expression had been pretty much blank this entire time, but now he wore a sly grin. "Oh, there are ways, Dad," he said.

"So, were you out looking for a job today?" asked Yvonne.

"Don't need to," Patrick replied, his face returning to blank mode. "Len and I have something lined up already. It's going to be awesome."

Bill and Yvonne looked at each other, then back at their son.

"Well, I gotta go," said Patrick. "I told them I was gonna be online." Then, without waiting for a response, he bolted away, flew up the stairs and disappeared into the condo.

Bill sighed. "Before all this insanity," he said to Yvonne, "I was about to do a loop. Feel like doing one with me?"

"Sure," she said, "just let me stick my laptop inside."

By the time they'd reached Underwood Avenue, Bill had noticed eleven separate instances of artifacts from canine bowel movements, four of which were on the sidewalk stones, two of which he'd narrowly avoided stepping in, and all of which he'd complained bitterly about.

"God, I can't believe how much fucking dog shit there is all over the place," he said as they walked past a tree with yet another fresh pile in the grass next to it, swarming with flies.

"Really, you still can't believe it?" was Yvonne's response.

To their credit, the majority of dog owners did bag up their pet's excrement the majority of the time. But this led to another form of neighborhood blight, as many liked to rid themselves of the filled bag A.S.A.P., depositing it almost anywhere.

Bill encountered these on his walks even more frequently than the unbagged stuff—on top of low walls, on top of dumpsters that were padlocked, on top of household garbage bins that weren't ("How hard is it to just lift the fucking lid?" he would mutter), tossed into overflowing recycle bins that had the words "NO DOG POOP" spray-painted down the side. Sometimes a bag was hanging on the rim of, or lying on the ground next to, a receptacle, as if a careless fling of the arm while speeding past was all the bagger could be bothered to do. Sometimes Bill saw what a dog had left behind sitting in the exact spot where the dog had left it, but inside a bag.

Shortly after the Smedes had crossed Arkansas Avenue, a scooter went past them in the street, then slowed down, turned into a driveway and came to a stop a few yards directly in front of them. It was Matt Spratt. Smoke curled up from a joint pinched between two of his fingers and one of the scooter handlebars.

"Hey you two crazy kids," he called out, grinning.

"Hi Matt," said Yvonne as she and Bill reached the spot where he'd stopped. "How are you?"

"Doing great!" replied Matt, then took a drag on his joint.

"Did you ride all the way over here from Venice?" asked Bill.

"Yep," said Matt, stepping off the scooter. "I found out something really cool about Marion. As if she wasn't already, like, stratosphere cool!"

"Marion?" Yvonne queried.

"Yeah," Matt continued. "Get this. She literally buried a treasure chest in the sand. Right there on the beach in Santa Monica."

"Marion Davies," said Bill to Yvonne. "An old silent movie star."

"Ah, right," she said, making the link with Bill's gripes from Saturday.

"Have you ever seen any of her stuff, Vonnie?" Matt asked. "She did some talkies, too. Not many, but some. Before she… retired." He sighed, dropped his eyes and shook his head sadly.

Even after all these years, Matt's nickname for Yvonne rankled her each time she heard it. But nothing could be done: he was not a man who changed his ways, and one of his ways was to reduce everyone's name to a single syllable (and for the women, append the "ie" sound).

"Uh, no," she said, "I don't think so."

"Well, you should. Seriously. You'd love her movies. I mean, you might not dig her sex appeal like me and Bill do, but, her beauty and her charm, and, her acting ability… and she is so funny…" He seemed to drift away into a private reverie.

"So what's this about a treasure chest?" asked Bill.

Instantly Matt was back with them. "Right!" he exclaimed. "Can you believe it? Buried treasure. Like one of those old pirate stories. And there's a map and everything. And nobody knows about it!"

"If nobody knows about it, how do *you* know about it?"

Matt grinned. "Solid detective work," he said, and winked. "So I found this article online that said some guy who knew her did a T.V. interview with CBS, like, forever ago… like 50 years ago or something. And in the interview this guy was talking about how there was a buried treasure on the beach, and there was a map for finding it, and Marion was the one who buried it."

Bill and Yvonne looked at each other, then back at their friend.

"Anyway," Matt continued after a puff on his joint, "I think it's all true. And I'm gonna get a copy of that interview. It's nowhere to be found on YouTube, but, my girlfriend Lonnie—remember her? Anyway, her cousin works at CBS. So I figure she can hook me up."

"Cool," said Yvonne.

"So, you came all the way over here just to tell us that?" asked Bill.

"Yeah," said Matt. "Well, I thought maybe we could have dinner together too."

"We were planning on cooking a roast chicken dinner at home tonight," said Yvonne.

"Cool, that sounds great!" said Matt.

"Hey, Matt," Bill said, "you don't have a smartphone. So how did you rent that scooter?"

"Oh, there are ways," Matt replied with a sly grin. "If you—"

"Goddammit!" Bill suddenly shouted. "My 1:30 meeting. I

completely forgot about it. What time is it?"

Matt shrugged. Yvonne looked at her phone.

"1:28," she said. "Better run along, then."

"Shit, fuck, dammit," said Bill as he sprang into motion and sprinted off down the sidewalk toward home.

"Heh, Bill is a trip," Matt said, chuckling. Then he took another drag on his joint.

Chapter 6

It was a scorching hot June day: 85 degrees in El Segundo, despite its location right next to the ocean. Unfortunately for the employees of Lathrop Halliday, the corporate philosophy took a dim view of both teleworking and routine air conditioner maintenance, so the cooling had failed that morning and now, mid-afternoon, hundreds sitting inside the building were suffering and drenched in sweat.

The emergency system, used strictly to cool the server room, was completely independent from the main system and was still functioning without any issue. Cody Tang and Lance Korprill, the only people whose desks sat inside the server room, had been receiving a lot of visitors today who'd arrived with unclear purposes and stayed with them for stretches of 20–30 minutes, saying very little at all and nearly nothing related to work.

One such person, Wendy Adams, who'd recently taken her leave of Cody and Lance, after which she'd visited the soda machine and the restroom, now strolled past a bank of elevators and entered a long aisle lined on both sides with 6-foot cubicle walls (another feature of the somewhat behind-the-times corporate culture). Stopping next to the second one on the right, she pulled off the plastic nameplate reading "Scott Portcullis" (backed with a velcro strip for adhering to the fabric-covered wall), turned it upside-down, and stuck it back on.

"Cut it out, Wendy," said Scott from inside the cubicle. This was a prank she played on him five to ten times per week, but usually while he was away from his desk.

She chuckled, stepped inside Scott's mini-pseudo-office, plopped her butt down on the edge of the desk, and opened her can of Diet Coke. After taking a sip, she said, "So what's the latest, darling?"

Scott, staring absentmindedly at his computer screen, sighed and said "Not much," then turned to look at Wendy. "How about you?"

"Just trying to beat the heat," she said. "Had to go check up on Lance and Cody for a while. Keep 'em honest, you know."

He smiled and nodded. "Having a corner cube by the windows doesn't seem like such a great idea anymore, does it? I always told you, better to be tucked away inconspicuously near the nice, insulated center of the building."

"Uh-huh," said Wendy, rolling her eyes. "Hey, did you see the Dodgers last night?"

"No."

"They won."

"Yeah, I know. Five to three. They did well. Cincinnati is tough to beat, especially with Castillo pitching."

Scott had been Wendy's favorite co-worker, by far, ever since she'd started at Lathrop five years ago. Endlessly patient, calm, and kind, he'd taken her under his wing and shown her the ropes, only revealing his cynical side after many months working together, once she'd become secure in both the job and their friendship. Almost everybody here (with a couple of very frustrating exceptions) was smart, but it seemed only Scott would actually listen to what someone else had to say. And he loved baseball—wow. Wendy had often wished—and occasionally even suspected—that he was straight.

"How's it going with C.U.?" she asked. "Are you a Blaster yet?"

"Nah, still a Slugger. Getting close, though."

"Cool."

Scott's cell phone lit up and started vibrating against the surface of his desk. He glanced at it, hesitated for a split second, then reached for it. "Sorry, I'd better take this."

"No problem. Later!" said Wendy and departed.

Scott answered the call, speaking in his usual quiet, calm, matter-of-fact tone. "Hi, Gary."

Gary's voice carried considerably more emotion (though not a huge amount). "Hey, babe," he said with a sigh.

"I'm not very comfortable with phone conversations at work," Scott reminded his husband.

"Yeah, I know. I know. I just... I felt bad about last night and, well, I guess about everything lately. I, um... I hate when things are like this between us. I really need you in my corner."

They'd gone to bed angry last night, after a huge argument,

and hadn't spoken since. Scott resented all the time Gary had devoted to his marathon training recently; these feelings included some jealousy (related to Gary's running mentor Frank Barnes), though Scott couldn't quite admit so, even to himself. He was particularly peeved at the fact that his entire annual bonus, which had originally been earmarked for funding most of a Hawaiian vacation planned for next winter, had instead been blown on a "romantic getaway" (Gary's term) in Estes Park, Colorado.

"I mean, I'm so jazzed," Gary continued. "Just... so, *so* jazzed about this weekend. But, it's just not the same if you aren't jazzed too. You're my partner in... jazzitude." He chuckled nervously.

"I understand," said Scott. "I don't like fighting, either."

There was a long silence. Then Gary spoke again. "And... I'm sorry. About Colorado. You were right all along, babe. T-Dub was a huge waste of time and money."

The corners of Scott's serious mouth curled up slightly. "It wasn't your fault," he said. "Frank's just a complete idiot."

Gary and Scott had jointly coined the nickname T.W., short for Third Wheel, one Saturday evening after an especially disruptive afternoon with Gary's high-altitude trainer, Bobbi Larson. Scott had a collection of other nicknames for her that he kept to himself. The mood dampening for which she was noted might've been forgivable if she'd actually done her job well; but her training program was totally unorthodox, utterly disorganized, immensely confusing, and on several occasions had left Gary incapacitated for a couple of days with exhaustion or injury. To top it off, she'd delivered all this in the most miserable, grumpy fashion imaginable, and had charged an obscene fee for the privilege.

"Aw, you're too hard on poor Frank," said Gary. "Anyone could've made that mistake. And he's still gonna pay for his half." (Gary couldn't see Scott putting his hand over his eyes and slowly shaking his head.)

"Well," Scott said, "anyway, don't worry about it. I shouldn't have let everything get under my skin like I did."

"Aw, babe... You wouldn't be you if you didn't. And I love you just the way you are!"

Scott had reached his threshold. "Thanks for calling, Gary. Really. I'll see you tonight."

"Okay, see you then."

Gary hung up and smiled, feeling heartwarmed and relieved. He knew, despite Scott's awkward and terse side of the conversation, that all was forgiven.

He turned his attention back to a very dull set of reports he'd been working on all day with virtually no progress, but found himself still unable to focus on them even though he'd cleared the air with Scott. He was just too excited about presiding over the grand opening of a new CuppaJoe store on Friday and then running his first marathon Sunday.

The office door suddenly flew open and Martha Reyes strolled in. Gary's promotion to Senior Associate two years ago had entitled him to move from the open-plan semi-cubicle farm where most employees toiled into a personal office with real walls and a door. He'd gleefully accepted this new perk, though he cared more about the achievement it symbolized than any practical enhancements of privacy or solitude it offered.

In theory it should've provided him a window, too, as all the offices were located around the perimeter of the seventh floor, on the outside wall of the building. However, this particular office was slightly L-shaped, with a portion of what would've been Gary's window belonging to the coat closet of the (far more luxurious) office next door, and the other portion lined up perfectly with a massive vertical support pillar attached to the side of the building, which would've obscured any view through a window. So this office did not have one.

"Hi, Martha!" Gary said with a big smile, though he was not happy to see her.

Martha's role had evolved over the many, many years she'd worked here, but through it all she'd maintained a consistently high standard of laziness, rudeness and incompetence. Long ago she'd been somebody's personal secretary. Then, as more and more of the tasks of that job could be facilitated—or outright taken over—by new technologies (the adoption of which at CuppaJoe was largely driven by Martha's presence there), she'd become the administrative assistant to a team of people, then multiple teams, then the entire company.

Eventually all of her duties had been phased out and she'd ended up with the title "Manager," with what or whom she allegedly managed not known to anybody except (possibly) her. But she still had ample opportunity to practice at least one of her three trademark qualities in the office each day.

"Hello," she said with a scowl, then strode to the edge of Gary's desk, picked up a coffee-themed snow globe that was sitting there and began handling it idly.

"Um, can I help you with something?" Gary asked.

"Doubt it," said Martha.

Gary chuckled, then waited a few seconds for her to say more, but she didn't. Instead she became intensely interested in the snow globe and began tipping it upside-down then right-side up repeatedly in rapid succession.

"Well," Gary finally said, "it sure is nice to see you. Um, to what do I owe the pleasure?"

Martha abruptly stopped playing with the globe and looked at Gary with an expression of sneering contempt. "Tony's been looking for you. And Frank."

"Tony's looking for both of us?"

"No," said Martha. She rolled her eyes and slapped the globe back down onto Gary's desk. "*Listen* to what I'm saying—if you can. Tony's looking for you. Frank's looking for you. They're both looking for you."

Gary made one last attempt at civility and lightheartedness. "Aha, gotcha. Well, here I am!" He let out a little laugh.

Martha turned and walked out of the room, leaving the door open.

Ten minutes later, Gary was sitting on the floor in the office of Jim Jamb, another Senior Associate who'd joined the company around the same time as Gary and had advanced at around the same pace. The two had always gotten along very well.

Jim was lying on the floor on his side, head resting in his hand, an open laptop a few inches away—his standard position on hot days. Hyper-conscious of the need to do his part to protect the environment, Jim kept his personal office thermostat set to 83, then tried to stay as comfortable as he could by keeping very low to the ground (where he thought the coolest air would be located).

"Tony and Frank are both supposed to be in, according to their calendars," said Gary, "but seems neither of them are. Knocked on Tony's door, no answer, so I looked in. Lights were off and his computer was missing."

"Yeah, he was invited to the board meeting on Eight," said Jim. "Probably'll be up there the rest of the day."

Tony Nicotini was Regional Director, the highest-ranking person on the seventh floor and the only one ever allowed to visit the eighth, where CuppaJoe had just conference rooms, waiting rooms, and the office of the CEO, Hortense Prieger, to whom Tony reported directly.

"I stopped by Frank's office, too," said Gary. (Frank had recently been promoted to Senior Associate.) "He had that 'Be Right Back' sign of his stuck up—you know, with the little clock?"

"Uh-huh."

"But the clock was set to 7:30, which doesn't really make sense."

"Yeah, not sure what's going on. He was a no-show for a meeting earlier, too."

"Hmm. Well, anyway, Martha said they were both looking for me. You know anything about that?"

Jim laughed. "Martha," he repeated. "No, I don't. But, uh…" He hesitated briefly and glanced down at the floor. "I do know that Tony's been a little disappointed with your numbers lately. And he's kind of annoyed that you're taking tomorrow off."

"Oh, really? Wow. Ouch." Gary paused, mulling it over. "So, how do you know? Did he tell you?"

"No, Frank did."

"Frank? Well how did *he* know?"

Jim tried to make a shrugging gesture while still propping himself up with one arm. "Not sure," he said. "But Frank does seem to have a way of knowing stuff."

"He sure does," agreed Gary, smiling. Then he said, smile fading, "But anyway, Jim, about tomorrow. I've got no choice. I've gotta be there first thing Friday morning and it's like an 8-hour drive."

"Gary, for Pete's sake. Why don't you just fly?"

"I can't fly. You know that."

"Mmm, I know you *won't*. 'Can't' is a strong word. Maybe… maybe you should think about working on your phobia, hmm?"

"Yeah, maybe," Gary sighed.

"Also," said Jim, using his elbows to propel himself along like a secret agent crawling through a ventilation duct, "you should try and join the conference call tomorrow from the road…"

He arrived next to his desk, opened the bottom drawer and took out a manila folder. "About the new packaging proposal?"

"Oh, right," said Gary. "Yeah, I should be able to join."

"Here's some stuff to bring you up to speed," Jim said, and slid the folder across the office floor over to Gary.

"Thanks, Jim."

It felt like the world's most crowded, brightly-lit sauna to Gary as he emerged from the main doors of the U.S. Bank Tower onto Fifth Street shortly after 5 P.M. The Tower had been the tallest building in Los Angeles for nearly 30 years, until it was finally overtaken in 2016 by the Wilshire Grand Center. But, as many CuppaJoe employees proudly knew, their address was still number one in terms of actual roof height; the usurping of the title had been achieved through the underhanded tactic of bolting a purely decorative sail-shaped structure onto what otherwise would've been the top of the W.G.C.

For most of its long history, the CuppaJoe company had traditionally kept its headquarters (technically "regional office," though they had only one region) in L.A.'s tallest building, whatever that was at the time. In 1963, the founder, Chester Knorr Giugnere (who went by C. Knorr), had rented them a small space inside the City Hall building, which had grown steadily larger until the city had kicked them out in 1972. At this point, the founder's son, C. Knorr Junior, had managed to move their offices into a collection of disconnected storage rooms sprinkled throughout the newly-built twin skyscrapers on the 500 block of Flower Street. This arrangement had lasted three years, after which he'd moved them again, into the bottom two floors of the Aon Center on Wilshire. There they'd remained until 1991, when C. Knorr III had relocated the company to the U.S. Bank Tower.

Gary, decked out in his running clothes with all his work stuff crammed into a tiny, snug-fitting backpack, had intended to run the 12 miles back to his condo. As he paced around on the sidewalk in the sweltering heat, debating whether to go through with the plan, his phone rang.

"Frank!" Gary exclaimed happily as he answered the call. "How are you? *Where* are you?"

"Top of the evening to you, Gare old buddy," Frank said. "Ready for Reno, my friend?"

"I sure am! It's—"

"Listen, Gary, I need you to do something for me. It's big. I wouldn't ask if we weren't so tight, you know?"

"Yeah, of course, Frank. What is it?"

"I need you to grab my comb. From my office."

"Your comb?"

"That's right, buddy. Very important. I would do it myself but I'm dealing with some things right now and I can't get there."

"Um, okay. Is it in your desk?"

"Affirmative, Gary. Desk drawer. A little black plastic mustache comb. I'm counting on you, pal."

"Yeah, sure thing, Frank. So I'll—"

"Bring it to Reno. I will see you there, my friend. Bright and early Sunday morning. And then we're gonna do this thing."

"Hah! Yes we are indeed! Um, Frank… you were gonna register us both, right? For the race?"

"Already done, Gare, already done. I sent you all the details. Check your email."

"Oh. I did check it, several times. I didn't see anything…"

"Check it again. Carefully, buddy, carefully. Sounds like you might be getting scammed."

"Well, I, um—"

"Gotta go, Gary. Things are starting to get hairy here. See you Sunday. And do not forget the comb."

"Okay, Frank! See you then!" Gary said, but the call had already dropped.

Forty-eight hours later, as Gary was wrapping up very successful CuppaJoe grand opening festivities in Truckee, California, Rufus Fletcher watched three pedestrians slowly ambling toward the spot on the Utah Avenue sidewalk where he was lounging in the (rather limited) shade of a palm tree. A squirrel named Bartholomew stood on the grass six inches from Rufus's left hand, which held an acorn, trying to formulate a strategy for safely obtaining it.

The people approaching were Bill and Yvonne Smede and Albert Forrester. To Bill's delight, immediately upon arriving home from work Yvonne had proposed they do a neighborhood loop together. But then, to their horror, Gramps, who was visiting for the weekend, had volunteered to accompany them.

Doing the loop with any third person was challenging (because the sidewalk was not wide enough for three to walk abreast), and all the more so with this particular one. They'd set out with Gramps in the back and the other two in the front. But as he seldom remained silent for more than five seconds, especially if somebody else was speaking, and addressed everything he said only to his daughter, the configuration had shifted mid-loop and now Bill was bringing up the rear.

"I knew there were a lot of homeless people around here," Gramps commented loudly upon noticing Rufus, interrupting Yvonne's attempt to respond to his previous remark (about parking regulations). "But I thought they stuck to the big, major streets."

Bill's face flushed, but Rufus, completely unfazed, smiled as they arrived next to him and gave a little hello wave with his right hand (still clutching the acorn in his left).

"Good evening, Bill!" he said cheerfully. "I thought that was you, hiding back there behind your fan club."

"Hi, Rufus," said Bill, feeling slightly, but not much, more relaxed. "Uh, I think you've met my wife, Yvonne, before. And this is her father, Al."

"Pleasure," said Rufus, nodding at each of them in turn.

"Hi," said Yvonne.

Gramps scowled and pointed at Bartholomew. "You should get the hell away from that disgusting creature before it bites you and gives you a disease," he said.

Bill went red-faced again.

Rufus momentarily stopped smiling, looked in Bartholomew's direction, and flicked the acorn onto the grass. Then he looked back at the humans and his smile returned.

"Roderick's not disgusting," he said. (Rufus couldn't tell the different squirrels apart as well as he thought he could.) "He's a beautiful, noble soul. And a good friend!"

Bartholomew inched forward, grabbed the acorn, and scurried away.

"Hmmf," said Gramps. "Don't let the cute bushy tail fool you. Squirrels are vermin. When I was managing an HVAC warehouse up in Seattle, they used to always try to get in there. Had to use traps, poison, the whole nine yards to keep those little demons at bay."

Rufus was aghast. "Sir, I must tell you that I regard such behavior as barbaric," he said.

"Well, you can regard it however you want. But facts are facts. They share 95% of their DNA with rats. You wouldn't hesitate to kill a rat, would you?"

"As a matter of fact, I would," Rufus replied.

Gramps shrugged. Yvonne grabbed his arm and gave it a little tug. "Come on, Dad," she said. "We should be heading back now."

"Okay, darling," he replied. Then, as the two of them began walking away, he turned back toward Rufus and said, "You be careful out here."

Bill lingered for several seconds. "Sorry about that," he stammered. "Al can be a bit, uh…"

"Aw, don't worry about it," Rufus said with a smile. "Good seeing you, Bill."

"Yeah, you too. Bye."

A moment later, approaching Dimvale Avenue just as his wife and father-in-law were about to start crossing it, Bill's attention was captured by an object standing at the corner, roughly the same size and shape as a mailbox, with a similar little door near the top, but painted yellow and bearing the logo of Concerned Angelenos Community Action, a local volunteer group. He'd seen it, and others like it, a few times recently but hadn't taken a close look at one.

"Hey, check this out," he called to Yvonne as he left the sidewalk and headed for the strange box. "Have you noticed these things have been popping up lately?"

Yvonne stopped and turned toward Bill. Gramps continued walking.

"If only there were a vast network of computers," said Yvonne, "containing virtually all information known to humankind…"

Bill smiled. This was a standard ribbing for him to receive.

"And if only," she continued, "there were software specially designed for searching all that information for the specific info you wanted…"

"Yeah, yeah," he replied, circling the mystery box and examining it.

"And if only there were a device that you carried around with you all the time, and it gave you easy access to all of that."

"Looks like maybe it's a special place for people to dump dog shit," Bill speculated. "If so, I wish they'd start fucking using it."

Yvonne took out her phone and snapped a picture, then said, "We'll find out. Now come on, let's finish this loop."

"Okay."

Bill abandoned his investigation and they both hustled off to catch up with Gramps.

When they did, he was in the midst of purchasing a plastic cup full of pineapple chunks from a mobile fruit vendor stationed at the corner of Utah and Tappan Avenue. For many years Bill had been observing these folks with puzzlement as they'd set up shop for many hours at a time in relatively low-foot-traffic residential locations. This was the first time he'd ever seen one of them make a sale.

"Keep the change," said Gramps, handing five dollars to the miserable-looking fellow manning the vending cart.

Glancing at the placard bolted onto the cart's front, Bill noticed that the price of a fruit cup was exactly $5.

An hour later back at the condo, the three loopers and the two youngest members of the clan were taking their seats around the dining table, about to share a tri-generational family meal of fish and chips. Although Gramps had grown up in a non-denominational (and very non-devout) Protestant household and then led an almost entirely non-religious adult life, at some point in his thirties, inspired by a neighbor family, he'd latched onto the idea of eating fish on Friday nights, and had never let go of it. So when he joined the Smedes for a Friday dinner, it was understood by all what type of dinner it must be. (He also always insisted on having spaghetti on Saturdays, because it was "the kids' favorite" (it wasn't).)

"Mmm, delicious," said Gramps after taking his first bite. "You've done it again, darling."

"Actually," said Yvonne, "Bill—"

Cutting her off and ignoring her, Gramps said "So, how's my favorite granddaughter been doing?"

For a moment it was not clear to anyone at the table whether Alice, eyes cast downward and earbuds in (she'd promised her parents no music would be piped to them during meals, it was simply convenient to keep them in), had heard the question. This behavior was completely in-character, so it didn't lead any of her tablemates to suspect the mild resentment she felt over always being relegated to the sofa when Gramps spent the night (and over never having been given the bedroom her parents had agreed would pass to her when her brother finished high school). Curiously, though, neither had being told flat-out by Alice how she felt multiple times in the past.

Finally she looked up at Gramps very briefly, and another moment later, after swallowing her food, quietly and emotionlessly uttered "Fine."

Gramps chuckled delightedly. "That's great," he said. "Just great."

No matter how many grandchildren Al Forrester had ended up with, Alice most likely would always have been his true favorite. But in fact he'd only ever had the two sitting here with him now (so he was quite safe in openly identifying her as the favorite female one). Yvonne's only sibling, her older sister Becky, had died without having children (and without ever moving out of her parents' house) at the age of 33, after a short battle with phylomyrilatrophaegiosis, an extremely rare and little understood—though believed correlated with a (mentally and physically) sedentary lifestyle—degenerative disease with some symptoms similar to both dementia and severe depression. In a bizarre and cruel twist of fate, this had happened just five years after their mother, Janice, had succumbed to the very same illness (despite it not being the least bit contagious or hereditary).

"How about you, Patrick?" asked Gramps. "How's the main man?"

Patrick grinned. He enjoyed his grandfather's daffy attempts to meet the young generation on their own turf.

"I'm doing pretty good, Gramps," he said. "Aunt Debbie got me a subscription to BizNTeen for my birthday. It's pretty sick. Me and Len are—"

"It's an online platform for creating business—" Yvonne interjected, trying to explain, but was almost immediately interrupted herself.

"Ah, yes, your Aunt Debbie," said Gramps. "Billy's identical twin." He looked at Bill and chuckled smugly at his witty turn.

Indeed, through the years, many of Bill's friends who'd met his sister had noted that she looked like a female version of him. Bill didn't think it was true. Yvonne knew it was, but had never admitted so.

"They can't be identical twins, Gramps," said Patrick. "That's scientifically impossible."

"Are you sure?" Gramps replied. "They both have no balls and they both dig chicks."

He laughed heartily, and his grandson joined him. Bill and Yvonne couldn't help laughing too, though they mostly stifled theirs. Alice's only reaction was a quick glance around the table at the other four; her face remained expressionless.

Gramps continued riffing. "Poor Cathy is a great gal, too. Didn't deserve Pansy-Pants over here and a carpet muncher."

"Dad," Yvonne said, frowning.

Patrick stopped laughing but continued smiling. "Um, Gramps, I think you've got some unfair bias against the LGBTQQIP2SAA community," he said gently.

Alice continued to eat and to ignore the others. Bill had now followed her lead.

"Hmmf," muttered Gramps. "Community."

For a couple of minutes, everyone ate in silence and Bill felt the atmosphere gradually becoming more relaxed. Eventually he decided to speak.

"Hey, Yvonne, I think Sunday is Gary's first marathon."

"Yes, that's right!" she said. "In Reno. He's already gone, went up there early for some work thing."

"We should call him tomorrow. Or text him at least. Wish him well."

"Yeah."

Gramps had been listening intently. "Gary," he said. "Is he one of those faggots who live up the street?"

The next morning, Gary awoke in the quaint, serene B&B he'd selected for himself on the western shore of Lake Tahoe feeling very happy. His mood soon took a big nosedive, however, when he logged onto G.T.R. (Get The Runs, the running site that in recent times had become his go-to online spot for info and gab) to discover posts that seemed to imply the Reno marathon was in fact taking place today, not tomorrow. It got even worse when a rigorous checking of email turned up nothing from Frank, who was also not answering Gary's calls.

"Scott!" Gary cried down the phone line in a panic. "What am I gonna do? Is there any way I can still run this race?"

"Hey, it's okay. Calm down," said Scott, who was himself very calm indeed (partly because he got a small kick out of playing the wise, cool-headed savior), sitting down at his computer to investigate. "We'll figure this out. Don't worry."

Over the next ten minutes, they (mainly Scott) did figure it out—at least what the current situation was—and Gary's standard optimism returned. They'd somehow been mistaken about the exact date of the Reno marathon, which was indeed happening today as suggested on G.T.R. Since Gary didn't even know if he was registered for it, and it had already started, this was no longer an option for him.

However, there was another marathon in the same Golden Road Championship color category (yellow) slated for the very next day in Missoula, Montana.

"I want to do it!" exclaimed Gary. "I've been so psyched up to run a marathon this weekend, I just gotta run one!"

"Well..." said Scott, tapping away on his keyboard.

"Can we still sign me up?" Gary asked eagerly.

"Hmm. Unfortunately it looks like online registration has already closed..."

"Dangit!"

"But..." Scott said. Long pauses, filled with flurries of tapping and clicking, punctuated his speech. "Possibly, you... might be allowed to register... at the starting line. Yes. Yes, looks like it's possible. But they can't guarantee it, you just have to show up and cross your fingers."

"Hah-hah, yes!" Gary shouted excitedly.

"But Gary, your other issue is: how do you get there?"

"I'll drive there, babe."

"I'm looking at flights..."

"No! No flights. I'll just drive. It'll be fine."

"Gary, it's a 14-hour drive. The race starts tomorrow morning at 7 A.M."

"That's okay," said Gary as the non-stop sound of tapping and clicking continued to come over the line. "Not a problem. I can get on the road right now. There's plenty of time!"

Scott's fingers stopped and he said, "We can get you a ticket for $350. Leaves Reno at 2:30 this afternoon, lands in Missoula around five o'clock, local time."

Gary wouldn't budge. "No, no, no. I appreciate it, babe. But it's totally fine. I'll head out now. I'll be fine. I promise. Love you!"

Scott sighed. "Okay. Love you too."

"Bye, babe."

"Hey, Gary?"

"Yeah?"

"Uh... nothing. Drive safe. Bye."

They hung up. Scott had nearly revealed his now-ruined plan to show up by surprise to cheer Gary on (including a flight to Reno purchased several weeks back), but had thought better of it.

After seven hours on the road, Gary was starting to feel quite bored and frustrated. The Supra (which he'd still not gotten around to selling) didn't have satellite radio; it didn't even have a CD player. Typically when driving all over Southern California, Gary listened to good old-fashioned terrestrial radio, and this had been mostly available during his journey on Thursday, too. But today he was making his way through the most middle part of the middle of nowhere, and all the stations had disappeared nearly 200 miles back.

For a while he'd tried talking to himself, then singing to himself. After that he'd listened to both sides of both of his cassettes (Kool and the Gang's 1996 comeback album "State of Affairs" and the third tape (out of eight) of the audio edition of Dean Koontz's 1993 thriller/horror novel "Dragon Tears"), twice each. Finally he'd resorted to silently scanning the horizon for anything remotely interesting that might pop into view.

Just as Gary finished marveling at a tumbleweed gently rolling along in the dirt parallel to the roadway, a distant vehicle appeared in his rearview mirror, gaining on him rapidly. He'd seen very few other cars on US-95 and began gleefully anticipating all the things he could observe about this one—make, model, color, home state, the people riding inside—when it overtook him.

This happened three minutes later, at which point Gary discovered that his latest highway companions were two white adults, probably in their twenties, traveling in a dark blue Toyota Corolla with California plates. "Hey, California!" he said to himself, grinning.

Gary'd noticed them put on their left turn signal as they came up behind him, and once they'd gone past and slid back into his lane and started to zoom away, he saw that it was still there, blinking away.

"Whoops," he said, shaking his head and smiling. "Better give 'em a helping hand!" He put on his own left turn signal.

Gary had developed this little "Good Samaritan" trick long ago. The idea was for the other driver to notice whatever strange, out-of-place feature appeared on your car, and it would cue them to then notice the same thing about their own.

Reggie Volkenstadt, the driver of the Corolla, did notice Gary's blinker (though it took him a couple of minutes, by which time the Supra had receded quite far into the distance behind him).

"Hey, check out that dumbshit back there behind us," he sneered. "Got his signal on like a fuckin' retard."

His girlfriend, Lilah Wanks, wriggled her body around in the passenger seat to face out the back, just in time to catch a glimpse of Gary's car before it became a tiny, undiscernible speck on the horizon.

"Oh yeah," she chuckled. "Stupid piece of shit."

She turned around again and began fiddling with the stereo, then glanced idly at Reggie's side of the dashboard.

"Hey!" she shouted abruptly. "Who's the retard now?"

"What?"

Lilah burst out laughing and pointed at the little flashing light next to the speedometer. "You've got *your* fucking signal on!"

Reggie's face turned bright red as he switched off the signal. "Shut up!" he screamed.

"Stupid dipshit," said Lilah. "Watching other people, fuckin' making fun of them, don't even notice you're doing the same fucking thing." All the while her paroxysmal laughing continued.

"I said shut *up*!" yelled Reggie. "Stop fucking laughing at me, you stupid bitch!"

After another minute, during which relations between the two young philosophers continued to deteriorate, the Corolla careened off the left side of the highway and, by a stroke of phenomenally bad luck, collided with the only obstacle in the vicinity, a "Welcome to Oregon" sign, then rolled onto its side, slid twenty feet, tipped onto its roof, and finally came to a stop, sitting upside-down in the dirt.

By the time Gary came past the empty wreck three hours later (its occupants long since ferried away by ambulance), sitting in the cab of a tow truck, he'd forgotten he knew the Corolla and wasn't paying attention anyway. All his energy was focused on pestering the driver, Alan Kammell, with incessant questions.

"Is it normal not to have any cell service out here?" Gary asked.

"Yes," Alan replied.

"But there'll be service in town, right?"

"Yeah. Well there should be. I guess it might depend on who your carrier is."

"How far away are we now?"

"From phone service? I dunno, maybe half an hour."

"No, I mean, how far 'til... um, your place. Your shop, or whatever..."

"Keep your hat on, pal—we've only been driving for five minutes. So we're five minutes closer than when you asked me before."

"Right, sorry," said Gary, making a mental note to try to calm down.

"Should be about an hour," Alan added. "You wanna listen to some music?"

"Oh, yes, please!"

From the curb outside the tiny office of Alan's eponymous tow service in downtown Boise, Idaho, Gary began working with Scott on a new plan of action. The Supra's engine had very suddenly died at 55 miles per hour, could not be revived roadside, and was definitely going to be out of action and not even diagnosed until Monday morning (when the mechanic returned to work) at the soonest. None of this surprised Scott, who couldn't resist gently reminding Gary that the car had been way overdue for service, and was much too old to be constantly driving all over hell and gone anyway, and that he'd reminded Gary of these things several times previously.

For $700, they discovered, a ticket could be bought for a flight that would depart Boise at 11 P.M. and get Gary into Missoula around midnight. Scott favored this approach but Gary hated it.

They investigated rental cars, but curiously, none were available. Querying this online, the best explanation Scott could find was that people apparently had flocked there from all around to attend the home opener of the Boise Hawks (a minor league baseball team).

Gary considered simply giving up on the race, but when they found there were no hotel rooms available either, he finally agreed to fly and they booked it (along with a hotel room in Missoula (where there were plenty) for him to crash in for a few hours).

The next morning at 6:25, a very-much-the-worse-for-wear Gary trudged into the administration tent near the starting line of the Missoula Marathon and approached the folding table behind which volunteer Wilma Deering-Rogers sat.

"Good morning," said Gary, without the special energy he nearly always exuded. "I would really like to run this marathon, but I'm not registered yet. Can I register with you right now?"

Wilma smiled. "No, I'm sorry," she said. "Registration is closed. We had a very strict final deadline of 5:30 this morning."

Gary's face fell and he went silent for a moment, but then found a small reserve of hope and will.

"Please, ma'am," he said quietly and slowly. "I have made my way here from California, racing against the clock, overcoming many obstacles. I have just experienced one of the most stressful, sleepless, and terrifying nights of my entire life."

Gary's flight had been delayed by five hours while they awaited the arrival of the aircraft (which had been detained by U.S. Customs in Edmonton), during which time he'd tried, extremely unsuccessfully, to sleep on seats near the gate. Once airborne, they'd encountered severe turbulence almost immediately, and it hadn't let up until a few minutes before touching down in Missoula. Gary's fingernails had left permanent marks on both his armrests.

"The taxi that picked me up at the airport," he continued, his tone calm and gentle, "had to drop me off three miles from here, because all the roads were already barricaded for the race. I walked here from there.

"So, I'm begging you. I dearly, *dearly* want to run this marathon. Is there any way, at all, you could see your way clear to... to letting me?" He managed a weak smile.

Wilma regarded him in silence for 30 seconds with a scowl frozen on her face. Then she shrugged and said, "Okay."

Standing in the farthest back and most crowded of the seven starting pens 20 minutes later, Gary glanced up from a session of mental self-coaching and gasped with shock. Could he be hallucinating? Just a few feet away, separated from him by an elderly man and a teenage girl who were both wearing knee-high socks but didn't seem to know each other, stood Frank Barnes.

"Frank!" Gary exclaimed, beaming.

Frank looked over at him with a face that conveyed no surprise at all, and responded in his usual quick, clipped, serious style.

"Gary," he said. "Good to see you, my man."

Gary squeezed through the crowd and came up right next to Frank.

"Good to see you too, buddy!" he said, grinning and clapping his friend on the shoulder. "But, uh... what are you doing here?"

"No time to be glib, Gare," said Frank. "We need to focus now. One hundred and ten percent. It's almost go-time."

"Um... Yes, absolutely. You know it!"

"Let's do this thing, partner."

"Let's do it. We are in it to win it!"

"Four hours, Gary. That's what it means to win it today, my friend. We gotta do it in four hours or less."

"Oh, really? You mean to qualify, for the Golden Road thing?"

"That's affirmative. Have you got what it takes, Gare?"

Gary chuckled. "Why yes, I believe I do. And I'm very pleased to have you by my side!"

At 7:30, the rope across the pen came down and the two men, along with hundreds of other runners, filed out onto the race course and began their marathon. Gary felt on top of the world, like lightning was coursing through his veins.

By 7:40, he had no idea where Frank was.

Chapter 7

Sometimes Bill and Yvonne Smede resigned themselves to the inevitability of devoting an entire, very long, evening to the aggressive ravaging of their bodies with booze and decadent foods. Each had privately speculated, on occasion, that such resignation might in fact be the smartest approach every time, as it freed them to attend fully to savoring the experience, and to relax while doing so, with usually the exact same end result.

However, as often happened with these gatherings, they both still felt a wee bit resentful toward the organizer of this one (Amy, of course) for, it seemed, manipulating them with a combination of concealment and coercion. She'd sprung tonight on them rather last-minute, after they'd joined her, just a few days earlier, in some very similar over-the-top revelry (in celebration of the Fourth of July), and she'd framed this evening's event as some kind of very special, very obligatory, self-thrown going-away party—one last hurrah for a close-knit group of friends before one of them left town for 72 whole hours.

"Clever party bitch," muttered Yvonne as she stood in her living room, looking at her phone screen, setting up pizza delivery for the kids (who were perfectly capable of arranging their own pizza but preferred having it done for them).

"Yep, she is sneaky A.F.," agreed Bill, who was standing next to her, face in his own phone, working on ordering an Uber.

As if deliberately twisting the knife, Amy had scheduled the shindig for a Thursday, the one day each week that Yvonne worked from home, at a venue near the office. Initially, Yvonne had intended to leave her desk early so she and Bill could walk there (about two hours) and still arrive only fashionably late. But, the hospital lab interface fates had intervened, keeping her working long past her normal quitting time, and their plan had shifted to using Uber and sacrificing the 10,000+ extra steps that would've partially offset the huge number of calories on the night's agenda. They were able, though, to retain the part about arriving fashionably late.

Still, it'll be fun, thought Bill, surprising himself. He smiled and said, "Still, it'll be fun."

Yvonne smiled too. "Yeah," she said.

Jake Lee enjoyed the sound of human voices, his own and everyone else's. If he was in a conversation—almost totally regardless of with whom or about what—he was happy. Right now the whom was Mike Howell (seated next to Jake) and the what was whiskey.

"I like it smoky, myself," Jake said. "Mmm, just that, that hint of smokiness. Not too much, not too much. But just, you know... that, that hint of smoke." He held up one hand, fingers arranged into a meaningless configuration. "Do you like a smoky whiskey?"

Mike spoke more slowly than Jake, with considerably less intensity and enthusiasm, but felt perfectly content with their chat. "Well, yeah. Sure," he replied. "I like different flavors. But I find the character—"

"Oh!" cried Jake, spotting their server nearby and waving to him. "Hey, Todd! Can we, uh..." He turned back to Mike. "What was that one you recommended to me?"

Mike's eyebrows went up, but in the most casual way. "Recommended?"

The server, whose name wasn't Todd, came over to them.

"Yeah," said Jake. "You, the other, a few days ago... or, last month... We were at that one place, and you said, like... You said I should try it. But they didn't have it there. It was a single malt."

"Oh, Scotch? The Glenspoodgerie, probably," said Mike.

"That's it! Yes!" Jake grinned and looked up at the server. "Do you have Glen-joops... uh, what my friend just said. Do you have it here?"

"Yes, sir," the server replied with a (fake) warm smile. "We have 12, 15 and 18."

"Oh, just one shot," Jake chuckled. "Just a single. For now, at least. Gotta pace myself!"

"It's the age, not the size," said Mike. "18 years is the best. You won't be disappointed with that."

"Great! 18 it is. You want one too?"

"Yeah, sure. What the hell."

"Two, please," Jake beamed.

"Coming right up, gentlemen," said the server. "Ladies, anything for you?"

Mike's wife, Laura, was sitting next to him. They'd arrived first (the only ones to arrive on time) and secured the table. On the other side of Laura sat Amy Lee, the instigator. She and Jake had come in together and, initially, sat together. But after a few minutes, Jake, fed up with listening to the women talk about their work, had moved himself over to the opposite side and begun talking about his work to Mike.

"I'll take another Negroni," said Amy, then did a little top-half-of-the-body-only dance and added, "Cel-uh-bray-tion!"

The server looked at Laura expectantly.

"Um," she said, "yeah, I'll have another too." She paused for a second, then clarified, "Another, also."

"The same? The pinot?"

"Yes, please."

"Okay, great. Those will be right up."

"Ooh, wait!" said Amy. "We should order for Yvonne, too. And Bill. Then they don't have to wait around once they get here. And we can have a toast, all six of us!"

"Okay," said Laura, "so, another pinot for Yvonne..."

"Okay," said the server.

"Bill likes Negronis," said Amy. "Bring another one of these for him."

"He likes whiskey," said Jake. "I think we should get him one of those Glen whatchamacallits that me and Mike are having!"

The server stood silently, his quizzical gaze slowly moving around from one member of the group to another.

Finally Amy said, "Aw, screw it. Bring both. This is a party!" She grinned widely at her companions and lifted her glass toward them.

The server smiled, nodded, and departed.

Yvonne and Bill arrived at Bolognese Ways five minutes later and took their seats at the table just as the drinks were delivered, and Amy got her wish of participating in—and also being the object of—a six-way toast.

Bolognese Ways, long before becoming a pricey restaurant in the Miracle Mile district, had been a pretentious food and lifestyle website. Before that it had been a cooking magazine. And way, way back, it had started its life as basically a community newsletter with some recipes. The founder, Enrico Palazzo, had immigrated from Italy in 1975 as an enterprising young man with no interests or skills. Today he presided over a small empire and enjoyed nationwide celebrity chef status.

"So, when do you ship out?" Bill asked Amy after everyone had clinked and gulped.

"Tomorrow night!" she answered excitedly. Then, in a sing-songy voice, "Takin' the midnight train to Georgia." Then, switching back to normal speech, "Except it's a plane, and it's Michigan. Hah!"

"Late flight, huh?"

"Yep. Well, late arrival, anyways. That is one long-ass flight! Plus a three-hour time change."

"Really? Shit," said Bill. "I thought Michigan was like in the middle of the country. Near the Great Lakes."

"I know, right? So did I. Until I started planning this trip." She took a quick sip of Negroni, then put the glass down and held up her right palm.

"Actually," she said, pointing with her left hand all around the perimeter of her right, "all of this is Great Lakes, surrounding almost the whole freakin' state. So that part is true. But it is *much* farther east than I thought. Or hoped!"

"Wow, interesting," said Bill, though he was losing interest rapidly and made a quick mental calculation that he'd prefer just to assume Michigan must be shaped roughly like a human hand than try to confirm this through further discussion.

Laura and Yvonne, who'd already been briefed on all things Michigan back at the office, smiled politely.

Mike slowly nodded, recalling a brief time in the mid-1990s when he'd lived in southeast Michigan.

Jake nodded too, enthusiastically and with a big grin, but hadn't really been listening for the past minute; he'd been thinking about how cool trains were since hearing his wife utter the word "train."

"Hey honey," he said, "remember that time when we took that cross-country train trip? Aw, that was just..."

"Oh, when we took the train to San Diego a couple years ago? Yeah, that was fun."

"Just so beautiful," Jake continued. "And just... watching it through the window. Most people have never actually been on a train, and they just..."

"Oh!" Amy suddenly exclaimed, and then somehow seemed to make eye contact with both of the other women simultaneously, even though they were sitting on opposites sides of her. "I didn't tell you what went down on that call with the Security Team!"

None of the men listened as Amy proceeded to fill her colleagues in. Jake observed that Mike had begun tapping on his phone, while Bill was simply staring at the untouched Negroni in front of him, wondering whose it was.

"So, Bill," said Jake, "have you ever ridden on a train?"

"Hmm, good question," said Bill, trying to recall if he'd ever actually set foot on a big, real, long-distance type train. (He assumed light rail, like the L.A. Metro, didn't count, but then, thinking harder, he wasn't even sure if he'd ever been on that kind, either.)

"Have you ever worked with model trains?" Jake asked.

"Uh, no."

"Well, if you ever decide to, let me know. I can guide you through it. Most people just don't realize how... just, how complex... I mean, you've got... all these decisions you have to make. Me and my dad, we used to—"

"Oh, crap! Jake!" Amy suddenly said, interrupting her own story and his. "We forgot about Jennifer and Brandon."

"I'm on it!" Jake cried, leaping up from his chair, which then fell over.

Turning to see what he'd done and breaking into a laugh, he unknowingly smacked Mike in the face with his butt. Bill cracked up. Jake, his eyes meeting Bill's, gave a quick flash of conspiratorial glee.

"Oops!" he said as he righted the chair. "That's just... just, me..." Then he darted off across the dining room and exited the restaurant.

"Oh my god, I am so silly!" said Amy. "The day care will keep them until seven, and I thought we'd easily be done here before then. I should've known better. Oh, dear..." She chuckled and took a sip of her drink.

Nobody else could think of anything to say, so Amy continued. "So, now we need to decide what we're gonna do about food, guys."

"Eat some!" said Mike with a chuckle. "Eat a lot!"

"Yes, Mike!" Amy replied. "I like the way you think!"

Over the next few minutes, the group concocted a plan. Amy took the lead on this, with Mike providing some input, Laura offering encouragement to both of them, and the Smedes supplying their (silent) assent. Everyone wanted to sample the (presumed delicious) cuisine of Bolognese Ways, but didn't want Jake to miss out. So, they determined, they'd order on his behalf, get all six dinners to go, and then head back (to Amy's) home to eat. But first, some appetizers and another round of drinks (which would give Jake a chance to get the kids home, feed them, and get them ready for bed).

Two hours later, having re-assembled at the Lee residence, a mile from the restaurant, the six were sitting around the dining table, their take-out boxes in front of them, ready to dig in. Bill and Yvonne, who'd made the journey on foot, had suggested Amy join them, but she'd opted instead to ride in the back of Mike's ambulance. (Mike, an employee of the City of Bell Gardens, had a unique arrangement whereby he owned and maintained a single ambulance which he leased to a company called Southern California Ambulance Masters (who were contracted with the Bell Gardens E.M.S. Department), and always worked alongside the same partner (his friend Chazz), who was the sole employee of Mike's own company, Howell Enterprises.)

"Mmm, delicious!" said Jake with his mouth full of his first bite. Then, after swallowing, he added, "Just so good, so authentic."

Everybody had ordered the same thing—tagliatelle al ragù, the specialty of the house—on Jake's strong recommendation (which he'd based on a blog he'd read). As each of the other five took a taste, they all stated their agreement that it was indeed very good, and none of them were lying.

"So it occurred to me," said Amy, "only just like, I guess it was just last week—there's another way for me to look into whether I'm related to this Chang guy. Besides just chasing him. I can chase myself!"

"Right!" said Jake with a laugh.

The other four looked at Amy quizzically.

"Investigate my own adoption," she continued. "Try and find out who I was adopted from. I mean, I don't know what the rules are about that kind of thing. You know, about, giving out that information to the, um, the kid. But I figure, it's worth a try, right?"

Some nods and grunts of agreement from around the table.

"So, it turns out the actual adoption agency my parents worked with is out of business, long ago. Like 20 years ago or something. But, from what I can tell looking online, when they closed down, all their records would've been handed over to the State of Michigan, to the Department of Health and Human Services."

A meek voice suddenly came from the other side of the room. Although it was soft and cute, a very astute listener might've detected that its cuteness was somewhat self-aware and carried a hint of self-importance. The voice, belonging to Brandon Lee (who'd been put to bed by his father half an hour ago), said "Can I have a drink?"

All heads turned to look at Brandon and most of them smiled.

"What are you doing up, you little rascal," Amy said playfully. "You want some water?"

Brandon nodded and smiled as Jake jumped up, said "I'm on it!" and dashed toward the kitchen.

Then Amy, who'd had a bite of food during that moment, also stood up and said, "I just realized I know the perfect wine to go with this!"

She and her husband nearly collided with each other as one headed for the wine rack while the other loped toward the back part of the house, plastic cup of water in hand.

Briefly, nobody at the table spoke. Then Laura said, "I was watching this movie last night about different philosophies of self-actualization."

"Hmm, what movie was that?" asked Mike.

"You fell asleep five minutes into it."

"Oh, right. That one."

"Yeah. It was like a documentary. Well, not even really a documentary, more of like an educational film." She smiled and added, "Mike usually finds those pretty boring."

"Indeed I do."

Amy arrived back at the table carrying six wine glasses and a freshly opened bottle in a seemingly precarious fashion.

"Need a hand?" asked Bill.

"Nope, nope. Thank you, Bill. But I have got this." She set down the bottle in the center of the table and then began placing a glass in front of each person.

Laura continued, "Anyway, it got me thinking about what is the purpose of life. I mean, I know we should try to help other people, try to make the world a better place and whatnot. But what should be the, um, like the *internal* purpose. Like, what version of yourself are you striving to become."

"You have all *got* to try this," said Amy, smiling, as she went around the table a second time, pouring a little into each glass.

"And I was reminded," Laura said, "of this other movie, from way back, called 'Defending Your Life.' It came out, like, at least 30 years ago. Anybody remember it? It had Meryl Streep."

Everyone thought about this for a couple of seconds and a few small noises were made to indicate people's recollections.

"'Defending Your Life'? Yeah," said Jake as he strolled back into the room. "I think I remember that. Great movie!"

"I agree," said Laura. "It really stayed with me all these years."

Amy, having finished pouring and now standing next to her own seat, raised her glass and said, "Cheers, everyone!"

The others cheers'd in return and everybody took a sip. As Jake and Amy sat down again and Mike and the Smedes muttered about the wine being very good, Laura picked her thread back up.

"So in that movie the idea was, the whole purpose of life was to overcome fear. After you die, that's what they judge you on—how much did you manage to get rid of your fears throughout the course of your life."

The other five were all listening, apparently with interest. Amy and Jake, smiling and nodding, both looked as if they were on the brink of speaking. But Laura wasn't quite finished.

"I like that idea," she said. "I think it has a lot of validity, overcoming fear. But people don't think about it most of the time. We shouldn't be afraid of anything. Fear always leads to bad stuff."

"Definitely," said Amy. "I think, if it were me, I'd probably say we should eliminate waste. Wasting time, I mean. Life is short, you know? We should spend every minute of it having fun! Well, not necessarily having fun, but, you know, doing good stuff. Valuable stuff. Fear is an example, like you said. Not good. A waste of time!"

Yvonne thought of mentioning Jack Sutton, but hesitated for a microsecond and missed her window.

"Mmm-hmm," said Mike. "Totally agree. We shouldn't waste our time. That's why I'm outta here." He scooted his chair back and made as if he was about to stand up, then laughed.

"Nah, I'm just joking," he said. "No, actually, what I think is one of the great challenges of life is to, uh… I'll say to 'calibrate'… your, your self-confidence."

"What do you mean?" asked Yvonne.

"Well, the level of self-confidence we project is a big part of the impression we make on other people. And the impressions we make are hugely important."

"Yep, yep," said Jake, nodding vigorously.

"You know," Mike continued, "we want people to like us, to respect us, to trust us, all that good stuff. How confident we come across, it can make or break those things. Can't have too little of it. But, you can't have too much either. I mean, nobody likes a smug, self-righteous son-of-a-bitch."

He laughed. So did all the others except Laura, who just smiled.

"Speaking of smug and self-righteous," said Yvonne, "people are delusional. About many things, but especially about themselves. Their self-confidence is *way* too high, and it makes a *bad* impression."

Mike chuckled.

"They should work on not deluding themselves," Yvonne concluded.

"Yes!" said Jake. "Delusion is a problem. So many of the folks where I work are delusional. They just won't listen to common sense. I try to tell them. But they just won't listen. They just…" He trailed off, shaking his head, smiling, eyes darting from face to face around the table.

"Boredom is a big problem," said Mike. "I've always tried to eliminate boredom from my life. Seems like a worthy cause, heh…" Again he pretended for a second that he was leaving.

"Amen to that!" said Amy.

"Being bored isn't fun," Yvonne agreed. "But being boring—that's downright shameful. Now there's something everyone should strive for—to avoid being boring." Laughter all around. "And if they succeeded," she added, "then we wouldn't have to worry as much about being bored, either."

"Damn straight," said Amy, then, turning to Bill, "So what about you, Bill? You've been pretty quiet."

"Well, that's my main purpose in life," he replied. "Not to say anything."

Everyone laughed and Amy said, "You're pretty good at it!"

"Okay, here's something," he said. "You all know those cringe moments in life, right? Where something happens that is so awkward and unfortunate and uncomfortable... and, I guess, unexpected, usually. Anyway, whatever it is, it makes you cringe. Really hard."

"Yep, that sucks!" said Amy.

"Oh, god," said Jake. "Yep. It just... sucks."

"And the worst ones of all," said Bill, "which I think are frequently the self-created ones, are the ones that, any time you remember them later, you cringe again. No matter how far in the past it was. You *always* cringe when you think back to it. You can't help it. I call that a 'cringe memory.' You can never get rid of them. The best you can do is try not to add any more."

Laura's face was in her phone. The other four were still looking at Bill.

"So anyway," he said, "that's my main purpose in life. To stop creating new cringe memories. And so far I've sucked at it."

"Lame!" said Amy playfully.

"In fact, I may have just created a new one right here in front of you," said Bill, chuckling.

"Oh," Amy said, "I was telling you guys about trying to track down my adoption records."

"Hey Yvonne, what was that you were saying about being boring?" asked Mike with a sly grin.

Jake let out a huge guffaw at this. Yvonne and Bill responded with more reserved amusement. Laura's face was blank, but now pointing at Amy rather than down at a phone screen.

"Hah-hah, very funny," said Amy. "Okay, just quickly: I called the Michigan H.H.S. Department, but I couldn't get through to a live person. Tried like five times, left them multiple voicemails. Nothing. So anyways, I'm gonna see if I can visit them in person while I'm out there. Give 'em a piece of my mind!" She grinned and shook her fist in the air jokingly.

"Aren't they closed on weekends?" asked Bill.

"Yep. But not on..."—a deliberate pause for dramatic effect—"Mon-days! That's right, baby—three-day weekend in the Great Lakes State!"

There were general sounds of mild approval and mock disapproval from around the table.

"It's okay," said Laura. "I signed off on it."

"You going out there too, Jake?" asked Mike.

"Me? Nooo. No no no no no." He smiled and shook his head. "Somebody's gotta stay here and take care of the kids. So I am batching it this weekend!" He laughed, raised his glass toward the others, and took a gulp.

Yvonne, glancing down at her wrist, was sorely disappointed by both the step count and the current time. "Well, Bill and I should probably be heading out," she said.

"What?!" cried Amy. "You're crazy. It's not even ten yet."

"It's 10:06," said Laura.

"I have a really early start," said Bill apologetically. "You know, east coast hours..."

"New York, New York," said Jake, grinning.

Amy stood up and reached for another bottle of wine that had been hidden from view, already open, on a nearby hutch.

"One last round and then we'll call it a night," she said.

"Number two fifty-six!" shouted a scruffy, pimply-faced youth standing behind the counter, holding up a brown paper bag in his left hand.

"Right here!" Amy called out in response, waving her receipt in the air and stepping to the left and the right, alternately, attempting to find a way to move forward through the wall of bodies blocking her way.

When, after staring silently and blankly at some point very far away for 20 seconds, the lad yelled "Two fifty-six!" even louder than before and with a hint of annoyance, Amy stood two feet closer to the counter but still six feet away from it.

A few seconds later the bag was abandoned on the countertop. Eventually Amy reached the front of the crowd, retrieved it, and wormed her way back through the crowd again and out the other side into the (relatively) sparsely populated Terminal 3 main concourse.

It was pointless to search for a seat inside the "restaurant," or near her gate, or near any other gate. Only two options existed for a person who wished to sit down in this place: a toilet or the floor. Amy chose the latter, nestling herself against a mostly unoccupied eight-foot section of wall situated between the edge of a drinking fountain and the edge of a gift shop.

She took a sip of her Diet Coke and then, with a sigh, retrieved her Quarter Pounder and her fries from the bag and placed them in her lap. Despite being one of humanity's more positive-minded members, she felt a bit glum. Such was the power of LAX, generally acknowledged as the most horrible airport in America (and a solid contender worldwide).

Amy typically enjoyed the food proffered by McDonald's (she just wasn't accustomed to fighting so hard or waiting so long in order to acquire it) and as she chewed on a bite of rather tasty burger, a small smile formed on her face. Well, the worst is over, she thought to herself.

The ordeal had begun long before Amy had located the back end of the long, serpentine McDonald's line and placed herself there. When she'd ordered her Uber at 2:00 this afternoon, she'd been startled by the app's prediction that the ten-mile journey from office to airport would take a full hour. This estimate had turned out to be a tad on the low side—reaching the gridlock of the LAX internal loop road had in fact taken 75 minutes, and getting from there to the curb outside Terminal 3 an additional 20.

Once inside, Amy had spent quite a lot of time standing in non-McDonald's lines, first waiting 35 minutes to reach the front of one where she'd wrongly believed she could hand over her suitcase, then another half hour in the real bag-drop line, and finally 47 minutes at the security checkpoint (where she'd enjoyed three walks back and forth through the scanner, a bodily pat-down, and a search of her carry-on).

Fortunately, her flight had been delayed by an hour and a half, so after getting through security she'd not missed it, and had even had a little time to spare for grabbing a bite to eat. But not enough time for a sit-down restaurant (hence the fast food). Or so she'd thought. With her right hand now flicking through Phone World (while the left one covered burger and fry duty), Amy learned that her flight was postponed again, by another 90 minutes.

"Jeez Louise!" she said out loud. "Okay, that's it. Where's the bar?"

Half an hour later, Amy stood thirty feet from her former spot against the wall, her phone in one hand and, in the other, a Sunshine

Hurricane Indigo Tropical cocktail (purchased from the only vendor on the planet who sold them, for the relatively low price of $18), someone's giant handbag hanging on a high chair pressing into her abdomen and a "No Alcohol Beyond This Point" sign pressing into her lower back.

Although she'd yet to take the first sip of her drink (having surveyed both of the terminal's bars and chosen the less crowded one, then waited forever to get served, then waited forever again for the drink itself, then very gradually squeezed her way across the floor to her current cozy little spot), Amy felt pretty chipper. This was an adventure! And any time her surroundings failed to provide much fun, her trusty phone would substitute nicely—as it had already begun to do.

She finally took that first sip. "Mmm!" she exclaimed. "Damn, that is good."

Glancing up, she happened to catch the eye of another woman, packed in next to her, also clasping a cocktail and a phone.

"Where're ya headed?" Amy asked with a smile.

The other woman seemed slightly taken aback, and rather perplexed, by the question. She remained silent for a few seconds, face scrunched up as if thinking hard.

Then she said, "I don't remember."

Slowly stepping through the door of the aircraft, another slow stepper directly in front and another directly behind, feeling a bit like she belonged to a group of cattle filing into a slaughterhouse, and receiving a curt greeting from a flight attendant who bore a close resemblance to a theme park animatron, Amy discovered that the plane had just one aisle, running down the center.

"Uh-oh," she said.

Amy hadn't flown in years. Somehow, at some point in the past— she wasn't sure if it came from her own experience or from movies and T.V.—the notion had been planted in her mind that the standard configuration of the inside of an airplane was two aisles, with three seats in between them and pairs of seats on the sides. So, when she'd made this reservation and been assigned seat 27E, she'd assumed it was an aisle seat. She now realized her mistake.

After spending many minutes inching her way along, and many additional minutes standing still while people in front of her hoisted their enormous pieces of luggage (which somehow still met the carry-on maximum size requirement) into the overhead bins, Amy reached Row 27. Both her rowmates were already in their seats.

"Excuse me," said Amy to Samuel Anella, who occupied the aisle seat. He did not respond.

Samuel, a 35-year-old white man with shaggy brown hair around the sides and none on top, five-foot-nine and 310 pounds, had been working as a door-to-door salesman his entire adult life and was currently traveling home to Michigan after attending a sales seminar in L.A. He was rather unattractive-looking (by most people's standards), not terribly bright, and quite inarticulate, and was acutely aware of these facts. He sometimes felt perhaps he'd chosen the wrong career.

"Excuse me," Amy said again, this time gently putting a hand on Samuel's shoulder.

He looked up at her, clearly startled, and she realized he was wearing earphones. He hurriedly plucked them out and began rising from his seat.

"Oh, I'm so sorry," he said. "You need to get in here, don't you?"

"Don't worry about it!" Amy said, smiling cheerfully at him. "You're totally fine. It's not a problem."

Samuel grabbed ahold of the top of the seat in front of his (in which sat a miserable-looking man whose face now went even more miserable) and awkwardly wedged himself out into the aisle, his earphones dangling around his shins, attached to a wire that disappeared into his cardigan.

"Here, here you go," he stammered with a small arm gesture toward his seat and a nervous chuckle. "Please."

"Thank you, sir," said Amy, then wriggled her way into the row, slid snugly down into 27E, and began attempting, per crewmember instructions, to cram her big, bulky handbag into the tiny space underneath the seat in front of her, which otherwise would've made a really nice place for her feet.

Occupying the space between Amy and the window, as well as a little bit of Amy's space, was Hannah Conklin (age: 29, height: 5'3, weight: 226), who worked for a debt collection company in Los Angeles and was changing planes in Detroit on her way to visit her sisters in New York. Hannah disliked pretty much everybody she'd ever met but thought very highly of herself. She had no doubts at all about her career choice.

"Mmm, smells good!" said Amy, noticing that Hannah was cradling a large Taco Bell takeout bag and repeatedly moving her left hand back and forth between her lips and the inside of the bag, while emitting a continuous, quiet munching sound.

Although Hannah wasn't wearing any earpieces of any kind (and wasn't deaf), she didn't reply to Amy or react in any way whatsoever; she just continued to munch and stare out the window as if nobody had spoken.

"Okay," Amy finally said, and turned back to Samuel, who was still in the midst of getting re-settled into his seat and hadn't yet re-inserted his earphones (in fact he'd inadvertently sat on one of them).

"Hey there," she said to him.

Again he was startled and obviously on edge, but also pleased. He smiled and said, "Um, hi."

"They've got us packed in like sardines, eh?" Amy said with a laugh.

"Heh, yep."

Over the next few minutes, through Amy's persistence, their stunted dialogue evolved into a true conversation and Samuel became much more relaxed (though no more skilled at speaking). He introduced himself as Sam, even though he never went by that name.

The plane pushed back from the gate at 8:12, ten minutes after the latest announced departure time. (A third official delay, of 15 minutes, had taken place while Amy was waiting to board.) Then it sat perfectly still on the tarmac, right next to the terminal building, for 25 minutes; no reason was given for this. Then it taxied out to join the long line of planes intermittently creeping forward, awaiting their turn to take off. It finally reached the front of this line at 8:57.

Samuel and Amy had been chatting non-stop throughout this whole process, but they both fell silent as the jet engines roared and the plane began accelerating furiously. Before they knew it, they were airborne, both craning their necks for a view out a window and settling for the one next to 25A, as all closer ones (except for the one blocked by Hannah's head) had their shades down.

It was long past sunset, but still twilight, with a faint orange glow on the western horizon which provided just enough light to see the ocean ripples and the outline of the Palos Verdes Peninsula.

"Beautiful," Amy remarked.

"Yeah," said Samuel.

After a couple of minutes the plane went into clouds as it banked left, and the two travelers resumed their conversation, which continued for another hour unabated. The topics discussed would've bored everyone from the night before (except Jake) to tears, but Amy and Samuel were having a great time—she because she loved all interactions with all people, he because he was smitten with her. But eventually they ran out of steam and mutually agreed it was time for some shut-eye.

Their nap lasted until the wheels touched the ground at DTW, which jolted them and most of the other passengers awake (Hannah, still staring out the window and retrieving bites from her miraculous Taco Bell bag, being an exception).

One of the animatrons immediately came over the loudspeaker system to welcome everyone to Detroit and inform them that the local time was 3:26 A.M. He went on to semi-apologize (without actually accepting blame) for the fact that most people connecting here had missed their connections and would need to speak to a gate agent about making new arrangements. This announcement elicited no reaction from Hannah.

Samuel and Amy quickly and easily fell into a new conversation with each other, beginning with Amy commenting on a billboard visible through 25A's window which featured an image of a human infant and the message "Babies are a Gift from God." They chatted about this and other topics for half an hour, at which point all the rows in front of them had finally cleared out and they were able to move into the aisle and exit the plane.

They said goodbye to each other outside the restrooms near their arrival gate in the cavernous McNamara Terminal. Samuel had hoped to get Amy's phone number, but hadn't worked up the courage to ask. She would happily (and innocently) have given it to him, but the idea had never crossed her mind.

"Hello. What's your name?"

"My name's Amy."

Then a long silence. She didn't know what to say next. A few thoughts raced through her mind. My crazy mom sent me here. This is pretty exciting. You look exactly the same as in the photo, right down to your suit. I feel kinda stupid.

But she didn't really want to say any of these things out loud. She hoped he would speak again. And finally, he did.

"Uh, would you like me to sign that?" he asked, gesturing toward the book Amy held in her hand.

"Oh—yes, please," she replied and laid it down on the table in front of her.

The book, entitled "Revisiting the Hundred Flowers Campaign," had been published very recently and Arnold Chang was doing an academic's version of a promotional tour for it. Amy had been surprised to learn when she'd arrived at the Rackham building, on the main campus of the University of Michigan, that the lecture portion of this afternoon's event, which had the same title as the book, required a reservation and that every seat was already spoken for. So she'd caught her very first glimpse of Professor Chang when, after delivering his lecture, he'd entered the reception hall adjacent to the auditorium and taken his seat behind this table, where a formidable line had already formed. Reluctantly, she'd purchased a copy of his book from a smarmy-looking cashier and joined that line. 45 minutes had passed by the time she'd reached the front of it.

Why didn't I use that time to plan what I was going to say? she now thought.

Chang opened the front cover of Amy's new book, scrawled (with great speed and even greater illegibility) "To Amy – Kind regards, A.Chang" and smiled up at her, expectantly.

"You know, there are a lot of people waiting," said a nasal, self-righteous voice from behind Amy.

"Um... thanks so much, sir," said Amy, "for, um, signing that for me. I can't wait to read it. I'm sure it's a great book!" She let out a small laugh. "Hey, listen..."

He leaned forward, puzzled and ever so slightly intrigued. "Yes?" he said.

Amy's eyes darted around for a second, then came back to Chang's. She smiled warmly at him. "Is there somewhere we can talk?" she asked. "In private?"

Chang's face scrunched up in perplexity. "What?"

"Please, it won't take long. I'm sure all your… uh, fans, will…"—she turned and shot a quick glare at the complainer—"wait patiently for you."

Chang didn't make a move to stand up and his face suggested he was not buying this. He said, "But why—"

"Because I'm your daughter," Amy blurted out, then added, after a brief pause, "I mean, I think I might be."

Now Chang's expression was shock and his features were frozen.

"I mean," said Amy with another small nervous laugh, "somebody thinks that… My, uh, my mother—my adoptive mother—she thinks, she has reason to believe, that you could, might, possibly be… my father. My biological father." She smiled and gave a little nod of the head, pleased and relieved that she'd finished conveying her idea.

Chang caught his breath. A single tear had rolled halfway down his left cheek. Everybody was completely silent for a few seconds, even the people waiting in line.

Then he abruptly stood. "I'm sorry, everyone," he announced to the group. "I'll be right back. I just need a couple of minutes. Sorry."

He motioned for Amy to follow him, then launched into a brisk walk away from the table, toward a far corner of the massive room, which turned out to lead into a hallway.

A minute later, in the hallway, he stopped and turned to face Amy, who'd been right on his heels the whole time. They looked at each other for a moment, both on the verge of speaking but not quite knowing how to begin.

Amy found words first. "I'm really sorry about this," she said. "You know, you are not an easy fellow to track down!" She grinned and hoped the mood would lighten.

Chang smiled, not because he was amused or even remotely close to feeling happy, but as a token of good will. Thinking over her behavior these past few minutes, it seemed to him that she was earnest.

"I don't see any reason you'd be playing a cruel trick on me," he said. "Can I assume you're not?"

Amy was taken aback. "No!" she said. "God, no. Of course not."

"You're the spitting image of my daughter," said Chang, reaching into his back pocket. "How old are you?"

Amy felt bewildered. "I, um… I'm… 39."

Chang produced a wallet and opened it, displaying a photo of a woman who, in Amy's opinion, didn't look anything like her.

"Sarah," he said. "She would've been 39 next month."

"Oh my god, I'm so sorry," said Amy. "What happened?"

"Car accident," said Chang, then paused for a couple of seconds, staring off into space.

Amy, thinking he was done, was trying to figure out what she should say next. But he wasn't done.

"It was... stupid. Oh, Sarah. She hated using the auto headlights, insisted on doing it manually. I always told her she was being foolish."

"She forgot to turn on her lights when it got dark?"

"Yes, exactly. The other driver couldn't see her. Plowed right into her."

Amy grimaced. "I'm so sorry," she said again. "Was it recent?"

"Six weeks ago."

Amy grimaced again. "I'm so sorry," she said a third time. "Did she have children?"

"No."

"Well, that's good, anyways," said Amy with a faint smile, then thought, Wait, is it?

Chang looked at her and cocked an eyebrow. After a moment he said, "So, why did you think—"

"My mom thought."

"Your mom thought... that I was your father? Why would she—"

"Because she's loopy," Amy replied with a laugh. "No, here's the deal. She grew up in China, in this little village in Anhui Province called Kai-po."

Chang smiled. "My original home town. I wonder if she and I were there at the same time..."

"Oh yeah, you definitely were. She was a big fan of yours when she was a kid. Apparently you were like a legend there."

Chang looked a little embarrassed, chuckled softly and glanced down at the floor. "Well, I don't know about that," he said.

"Her name was Sue. Well, Shu. I guess she would've been called Lu Shu."

"Hmm..."

"She was just a kid. I think she was only like 18 when the village burned down."

"I think I do remember the Lu family..."

"Anyways, after the fire she ended up coming to America, started a new life here, blah blah blah. But she never forgot about you. She always wondered what happened to you. And—Oh! Jeez, I almost forgot—one of the reasons she wanted to find you is... oh my god, this is just, so silly..." She giggled.

"What?" asked Chang.

"She says there was this 'ancient text' "—Amy used a mocking tone and made air quotes with her fingers—"that was kept by the village elders, and it contained everybody's birth, death and marriage records, going back like hundreds of years..."

"Yes, it's true."

"Seriously? Damn! Well, get this: she also thinks you have a copy of it."

She paused, still smiling, and raised her eyebrows, almost expecting him to tell her that this was also true. And then he did.

"Yes, I do. The only surviving one, I think."

"Holy crap!" she exclaimed. "Wow. Unbelievable."

Chang was smiling now, too, amused by Amy's amusement and quite curious about her story.

"Well, Mom wants to know what's in that book," said Amy. "She doesn't actually know her own date of birth. So, that's one thing. And she wants some other info about her family. But also—here's another, sort of, zinger for ya—she thinks her family is related to yours."

"Really?"

"Yeah. She was raised believing it. All those wacky Lu folks, for whatever reason, had always believed it. For like, generations."

"Well, I suppose it's possible," said Chang. "And she's right—if it is true, the book will certainly confirm it. Or confirm it's false. And any other information she's looking for. The book knows all."

"Awesome," said Amy.

"So, *why* was it she thought you were my daughter?"

"Oh, yeah. Because of this." Amy held out her wrist, birthmark side up. "She thinks you have one too, exactly the same."

Chang extended his own wrist and held it next to Amy's for a few seconds while they both looked and evaluated.

"Hmm, well they're kinda the same," she said.

"Yes. Somewhat."

"Oh, and the other thing was: Mom joined some online group recently and she made friends with this other chick who's obsessed with the history of Kai-po. I think her parents were from there. But this chick was apparently really hard-core into it, did tons of research, traveled over there and everything.

"I mean, my mom had always hoped she could track you down, but, you know, she never really had the resources. Especially before the Internet. Hell, even *with* the Internet we could barely find out anything about you!"

"I do value my privacy," said Chang.

"*Yeah* you do," Amy said with a grin. "Anyways, Mom was lucky she got connected with this Kai-po detective chick, who, just FYI, has a detailed file on you, Mister Privacy Man. Just to warn ya. And she told Mom that you moved to the U.S. after the fire, that you came here, to Michigan, and that you had a daughter about the same time I was born, and gave her up for adoption."

"Well, that detective—"

"Also," Amy added, "I was adopted from Michigan. So that was my mom's train of thought. She put all these things together and decided—bam!—that's it, I'm your daughter."

"Right," said Chang, smiling. "Well, that detective has a few errors in her file. I settled in Minnesota after the fire, not Michigan. Twin Cities. Been there ever since. Wonderful area. And Sarah—although she was born near the time you were, as you know—was never given up for adoption. She was raised by her mother and me. She lived in Minnesota her whole life."

"Oh lordy," said Amy, laughing. "Well, I'm not surprised. That's Mom for ya."

Chang momentarily got a far-away look in his eyes, followed by a twinkle. Then he said, "It just occurred to me..." He shook his head and chuckled. "This is a bit ridiculous, but, I think you'll like it..."

"What?" Amy asked eagerly.

"Well, I *did* come to Michigan, much earlier, the first time I left China. Right here, to U. of M. I got my Ph.D. here, way back in the sixties."

"Oh wow, cool."

"And while I was here, I fell in love with a girl, and we were pretty serious. Her name was Anna. Anna Lee."

"Aw."

"But in the end, things didn't work out between us. We broke up, and I went back to China, and we lost contact with each other."

"Aw."

"Many, many years later, long after I'd returned to the States, I learned that Anna had been pregnant when we'd broken up, and that she'd given the baby up for adoption."

"Holy crap!"

"So," Chang said with a smile, "I suppose there is still a chance—granted, an extremely slim one—that you and I might be related to each other after all. I'm not your father. But I *could* be your *grand*father. Who knows?"

"Hah! I love it," said Amy, laughing.

Chang broke into a brief laugh, too.

"Anyway," he then said, "that ancient record book. It's funny, I actually brought it with me to Michigan. It's in the trunk of my car."

"Cool!" said Amy.

"But, unfortunately, my car is not here."

"Oh, is it at your hotel?"

"No. It's in Kalamazoo, I'm afraid."

"Where the heck is that?"

"It's another college town, about a hundred miles west of here. I did a lecture there yesterday. The car was having issues, and I left it to get serviced while I make a few stops over on this side of the state."

"Oh. Well, no biggie."

"So dumb of me, didn't even think to get the stuff out of the tr—"

"Hey, no—don't *even* worry about it. But, you wouldn't mind, like, sharing a scan with me, would you? We can do like an encryption thing with it... Or, you could even print it out and send me the paper copy. Don't worry, my mom and I are good at keeping secrets..."

Chang had been smiling and nodding. Finally he raised his hands, palms towards Amy, gesturing for her to stop.

"Yes, yes, it's fine," he said. "Secrecy is not a concern. For some reason, and I'm a bit embarrassed to admit this, I have never scanned the book. But I'll be happy to do that for you and your mother."

"Thanks!" Amy exclaimed with a big smile. "You rock, Professor Chang." She took out her phone. "Let me get your number..."

"There he is!" a voice behind Amy suddenly shouted.

It was followed by dozens of other voices, and hundreds of footsteps, and after a minute she and Chang were surrounded by a mob of frustrated people, all loudly complaining and waving around copies of Revisiting the Hundred Flowers Campaign.

Chapter 8

Bill Smede's ranking of the different ways of having a conversation with somebody were (in decreasing order of preference):

1. not at all
2. email
3. in person, face to face
4. text (or chat or other real-time written medium)
5. voice call
6. video call

Fortunately, he had, so far, largely succeeded in avoiding #6 (but suspected that, sooner or later, he would helplessly and irreversibly fall prey to its ever-growing prevalence). Unfortunately, some people in his life were very fond of #5. One such person was his sister Debbie.

As Bill sat at his "desk" on a Monday afternoon in late July, pondering whether to reply immediately to an email from Ted Bonar, or do it later, or never do it, or perhaps compose the reply right away but then save it and not send it out until first thing in the morning, his phone rang and he saw that it was her. He hesitated for a second, then decided to answer it.

"Hi Debbie," he said. "How's it going?"

"Heeey, little bro! What's going on?"

At some point in their childhood, Debbie had coined the term of (mainly) endearment "little bro" and had continued to use it frequently ever since. Bill wasn't truly offended, but couldn't help being ever so slightly perturbed over its technical inaccuracy: he was physically larger than her and three minutes older.

"Not much," he said. "How are you doing? How are Grace and the girls?"

"Good, good. We're all good."

"And I trust Fritz the Dog is doing well, too?"

Bill snickered. He'd started adding "the Dog" to the end of Fritz's name shortly after Debbie got Fritz, and had done it without fail ever since, finding it endlessly amusing. Nobody else had ever found it funny at all. Occasionally Bill would throw in a comment about Fritz starring in his own adult cartoon movie and, again, was alone in appreciating the humor of it.

"He's great," said Debbie. "Such a good boy. He's been learning patience and obedience."

"Oh, really?"

"Yeah, and some tricks, too. He did his first show a couple weeks ago and it was *so* fun. I'm gonna try to get him entered into this big national one next spring! Very exciting."

"Wow."

"So anyway, what about you? How are you doing?"

"Yeah, I'm okay," Bill said in a despairing tone. "You know how it is. Monday. Work."

He almost confessed, but then thought better of it, that he was slightly hung over. Without any assistance from the other Evils this time, he and Yvonne had stayed up far too late and consumed far too much wine (and had enjoyed themselves immensely) after jointly contracting Sunday Night Blues, an affliction, discovered and named by them, typically striking on a Sunday afternoon, whose primary symptoms were dread and depression regarding the impending work week.

"Right, gotcha," said Debbie.

"Hey, speaking of work," said Bill, "aren't you there now? Shouldn't be yacking on the phone in front of the little cherubs." (Debbie worked as an art and design teacher at John David Jackson High School in Norwalk.)

"Hah!" she shot back. "I'm already done for the day. Headin' home, sucker! One of the perks."

"Yeah, well…" Bill smiled. "I'm almost done, too. Just wrapping up a couple of things and then I'm free as a bird."

"Uh-huh. Says the man who has to be at his desk at 5 A.M. every day."

"Hey, some mornings I don't get there until nearly six."

"Ah. Slacker. So hey, have you talked to Mamsy in the last few days?"

"Mom? No. I think she wants to talk to me but we, uh, keep missing each other…"

Their mother was another person in Bill's orbit who loved old-fashioned phone conversations, and she had a habit of calling at very inconvenient times (which were most times). Their recent repeated missing of each other to which Bill was referring had largely happened as a side effect of him rejecting each of her calls, not listening to voicemail, and not calling her back.

"Well she's planning a Labor Day thing at her house—"

"Already? God."

"Yeah. Well, you know her. Fourth of July is over so she's obsessing about the next holiday. So anyway, I was thinking—"

"Ugh, she's probably fretting up a storm about it. Probably wants to ask me a bunch of questions I don't want to be asked and get detailed commitments out of me…"

"Oh yeah. Big time. You better talk to her. You know she's just going to keep climbing the wack ladder. The longer you wait, the worse it's gonna be for you!" Debbie laughed.

"Right. Yeah, I know," said Bill.

"Hey, have you heard about this guy she's been dating recently?"

"No. Do I want to?"

"So, he's a gynecologist. And, she says she's not so sure if she has any, you know, romantic feelings for him or whatever, but she says he's really good at his job and she's thinking of switching to him…"

"Enough, Deb. Please."

"To like, be her doctor! Oh, Mamsy…" Debbie laughed again.

"So anyway," she then said, "for that Labor Day thing, I was thinking maybe you could come to my place first and we could all hang out there for a few hours before we go down to Mamsy's."

Bill was starting to feel a little bit panicked. "Mmm, I don't know, Deb," he said. "I mean, I don't even know if I'm going to—wait a sec, what do you mean 'all'?"

"What?"

"You said we could *all* hang out. Who's all of us?"

Debbie laughed again. "Oh, you! I mean everyone, of course. You, me, Yvonne, Grace, all the kids, you know…"

The panic level was rising fast. "I don't know. I mean… I just don't know right now. Labor Day is so far off, and I don't know—"

"You're right, it's too far off. We should plan something sooner. You know, at my place."

"Uh..."

"We gotta get the girls together!"

"You mean you and Grace and Yvonne?"

"No, silly! We're the *women*. I mean the girls—Alice and Raylene and Anika."

"Uh..."

"Seems like the cousins hardly ever see each other nowadays. They used to have so much fun together!"

Bill thought about this for a second. Did they? He suspected his sister was inventing false memories to fit her fantasies.

"Mmm, uh," he stammered, "I don't know, Alice isn't really into little-girl things anymore..."

"Oh *really*," said Debbie with another laugh. "So what *is* she into now?"

"Well, she's... uh..." Bill laughed, too. "Honestly, I don't know. She's not exactly the most..."—he searched for the right word—"...communicative, of gals these days."

"You don't think she's on drugs, do you?"

Somewhat startled, Bill said, "Uh," then chuckled, then "*On* drugs? No... I doubt it. Probably not."

The entire complexion of Debbie's speech was rapidly transforming itself. Exceedingly playful and happy-go-lucky in most aspects of her approach to life, she took parenting very seriously indeed.

"William!" she now exclaimed. "You have to be *so* careful about these things. Teenagers are in constant danger, from all sides. They're naked out there. They need us, every minute of every day. They need us to be hyper-vigilant. You should be talking to Alice, all the time, every day..."

As Bill listened, his mind racing, searching unsuccessfully for a fast-yet-diplomatic way to end this, the front door opened and Alice came through it.

"Speak of the devil," he said.

Alice gave a casual wave of her hand and a lightning-quick glance in her father's direction as she made a beeline for the back of the condo.

"She's there?" asked Debbie.

"Yep, just came in. Looked clean and sober to me."

"Put her on the phone. I haven't talked to her in forever."

"Too late," said Bill as he thought about his surprise at Alice's arrival and what time it might be. "She's already gone to her room."

"Seriously? Wow. Bro, you really gotta—"

"Fuck! Shit!" Bill suddenly shouted.

"Whoa," said Debbie. "Chill out!"

"I forgot to set up the fucking slow cooker—"

"When did you start swearing so much? Was it college?"

"Sorry, gotta go, Deb," said Bill as he dashed into the kitchen.

"Nah, I think it was later than that," said Debbie. "Even when you were in your thirties I don't remember you swearing much. So where could you have picked it up from?"

Bill was now rummaging through cupboards, his head tilted to one side, the phone pinched between it and his shoulder.

"Deb I've been swearing my whole life. If you didn't hear it, you were just one of the lucky few that were... fucking spared."

"Ooh, so privileged!"

"Look, I really gotta go now. I'll talk to you later."

"Sure you will. Okay, bye little bro!"

"Bye."

Bill put the phone down and fully committed both of his hands to the task of food prep, and his entire mind to stressing about it.

"Fuck!" he said as he passed by the sink and noticed the precariously stacked collection of plates and bowls rising up from the center of it, surrounded by smaller stacks (which included glasses and mugs), some of them wedged in at an angle, and the entire great beast laced with randomly positioned (mainly metal) utensils of varying types and sizes. The sound of these kitchen objects striking against each other greatly unnerved Bill, almost unbearably so if it happened loudly or unexpectedly, which was always a danger with the Jenga Tower (Yvonne's term, which the rest of the family had adopted).

Bill sighed and momentarily stared out the window—where a couple of palm trees did almost nothing to prevent the Smedes and the people living in the building next door from looking into each other's homes—trying to weigh up the relative urgency of dinner prep versus the Jenga War. Then he hurriedly removed several items from the sink and rearranged several others for increased stability, then sighed again and wiped the sweat from his brow with his forearm. The war was waged 24-7, its tide frequently turning but with Bill on the losing end more often than not. After all, it was three against one.

The phone rang again. This time it was Irene Hoffman, yet another person in Bill's life who didn't hate phone calls as much as he did.

"Goddammit!" he said as he grabbed the phone. Then he swiped the green answer icon, put it up to his face and said, "Hey, uh, this isn't—"

"You stupid piece of shit," Irene said. "Where were you yesterday?"

"What?"

"You missed my prototype party."

"Oh, right. Sorry. I told you I couldn't make it."

"You were serious about that? Oh, William, William. What am I gonna do with you?"

"Uh, look, Irene, now's not really a good time. I'm in the middle of—"

"Your loss, my friend. You are missing out on history in the making, I'm telling you."

"Oh yeah? So the prototype turned out pretty good, huh?"

"It's the best. It's fucking awesome."

<hr>

"It's the worst. It fucking sucks."

Keith Hoffman looked at his son, aghast. "Language, Luke!" he snapped, then turned to Derek LeVay (who'd just asked Luke about his mother's new creation), smiled sheepishly and said, "I'm sorry."

The three of them were sitting in identical folding chairs, of which there were four others here, with LeVay's positioned at the center of a semi-circle formed by the rest. Everyone present except him had attended Irene's "prototype party" at her house two days ago, where they'd had an opportunity to experience the Soundtrack of Life (or S.O.L.) firsthand.

LeVay smiled warmly at Luke and his father. "It's no problem," he said. "Cursing is just one form of self-expression, no less valid than any other. And we are definitely here to express ourselves!"

The feedback LeVay had collected so far from this impromptu focus group, though generally not as linguistically harsh as Luke's, had mostly reflected the same sentiment. Irene's sister, Norma, had noted that the musical selections were, at times, odd, and the transitions choppy. Five minutes ago she'd related one experience that had particularly stood out to her: she'd been wandering through the rooms of partygoers, wearing the device and enjoying the 1990s dance hit "Macarena," when S.O.L. had inexplicably switched mid-song to "Who Let the Dogs Out," then switched again a minute later to a jazz track she didn't recognize. Norma agreed with the decision to give users access to music beyond their own personal library, but felt the software did a poor job of predicting which outside material someone would actually like.

Her brother, Daniel, had reported similar trouble, as well as forehead chafing from the plastic strap holding the camera. He'd also complained to LeVay that S.O.L. seemed to get confused when it was in a moving car: it had switched the music rapid-fire and not played any driving songs when he'd taken it with him for a quick beer run, mid-party.

Their mother, Margarita, had shared how she'd spent most of the afternoon trying to figure out how to control the phone app and, in the end, had never gotten any music at all piped to the headset.

"So," LeVay said, following a long silence from Luke after giving his initial appraisal, "can you tell me anything else about your experience?"

"No," said Luke, then stared at the ground with a pouting face.

"Well, perhaps your brother has additional thoughts he'd like to share?"

LeVay turned to Keith Junior, sitting on the other side of their father, who'd mentioned a few minutes ago, unsolicited, that none of the extremely boring situations in which he'd found himself during the party had inspired a wish for anything in his stellar music library, or indeed for any music at all.

But now he just shrugged and said, "Not really."

"Okay, that's fine," said LeVay.

Keith Senior, after initially claiming he'd loved his S.O.L. experience, had ultimately admitted (after being pressed about exactly what he loved so much) that he agreed with all the criticisms voiced by the others. Now he was smiling awkwardly and shifting his gaze around between the floor and the faces of LeVay, Luke, and Keith Junior.

"Thanks for including the boys in this," he mumbled.

"Of course," LeVay replied. "Thank *you*."

Meanwhile, 75 feet to the east, Irene was sitting in her minivan at the Del Taco drive-thru window, impatiently awaiting her breakfast burrito.

"What the fuck is taking so long?" she shouted, half-hoping that somebody behind the two little side-by-side electric-auto-open-close window panes would hear.

She glanced at the clock, then down to the pack of cigarettes lying in the plastic well between the seats, and started to reach for it with her right hand before realizing she already held a lit cigarette between the fingers of her left.

She pulled it to her lips, took a drag, extended it back out the car window, and looked at the clock again. It was still another 20 minutes until her appointment time with Derek LeVay, but she'd wanted to arrive early and huddle with her team first.

At last the panes slid open and a scrawny teen girl with an acne-riddled face held out a paper bag and said "Here you are, ma'am" with roughly the same degree of enthusiasm one might feel when contemplating watching paint dry.

"Thanks," said Irene, snatching the bag from her. "Did you have to wait for the hen to lay the eggs?"

The young employee responded to this by continuing to stare blankly straight ahead, but Irene did not know or care, stepping on the gas immediately and shooting out of the drive-thru lane and into the sprawling parking lot that served the strip mall sitting next to Del Taco.

This strip mall, called Grove Plaza (though nobody who shopped there knew its name, despite its being prominently displayed at the top of a sign near the street corner that conveniently listed all the businesses within), might have appeared nearly indistinguishable, to the untrained eye, from the dozens of others within a five-mile radius, but the discerning denizens of Orange County knew better. This one, for example, was anchored by a Stater Bros supermarket, whereas grocery shoppers who preferred Hank's had to visit the strip mall three blocks west and two blocks north of here. Like all the others, Grove

Plaza boasted a small, non-descript dry cleaner, and, like most of them, a space that had once been a Blockbuster Video and now occasionally housed seasonal businesses but was usually vacant.

Irene's office—sandwiched between a sandwich shop called Fat Larry's and a mailing/shipping place called Package World that was significantly larger, cleaner, and friendlier (but with even higher pricing) than Bill's old standby, Mail and Ship—had once belonged to a State Farm insurance agent (hers, in fact). Now the office was closed for business, its space and her time both 100% devoted to the S.O.L. project, so anyone urgently seeking the services of a one-person accounting firm had no choice but to visit the one located in the strip mall two blocks to the east and three blocks to the south (which happened to be right next door to a State Farm agent).

Pulling into a parking space, Irene sang quietly and mindlessly to herself: "Many is a word that only leaves you guessing—guessing 'bout a thing you really ought to know…"

She tossed her cigarette butt out the window, put the window up, cut the engine, and took off her seatbelt. Then, just as she was about to grab the Del Taco bag and her Starbucks cup (the obtaining of which had added 20 minutes to her journey, thanks to their long line and being the wrong direction from her house (in the strip mall five blocks east and one block south of this one)), she saw it: Keith's car, parked almost right in front of her office door.

"What the fuck?!" she said angrily.

Bursting into the reception area (so forcefully the bells fell off the door) 27 seconds later, missing her coffee and burrito but holding a fresh cigarette, Irene said "What the fuck?!" again, much louder this time.

She marched up to the closed door of Conference Room #1 and looked through its window. "Holy shit," she said.

She'd not expected to see any of these people, save Derek LeVay, here today. Even in her confused and enraged state, she noticed that his mullet had grown another two inches since she'd seen him in May. Keith turned his head and caught sight of her; their eyes locked for a moment, a look of panic exploding onto his face.

Glancing to her left, down the hallway, Irene saw that the door of her private office was open, with nobody inside, ditto for the restroom, and the kitchen area was empty too. But the door of Conference Room

#2 was shut. She took a quick puff on her cigarette and strode swiftly toward it, her face scrunched up into a tight scowl.

Inside the room, sitting around a table on which sat the S.O.L. headgear prototype and five smartphones, discussing the current state of the enterprise and the way forward, were Judy Goldstein, Stan Wojcik, Wanda Hagan, Donald Piper, and Marcia Vellay-LeVay. Also participating was Stacy Parabola, via one of the phones.

Owing to his startling ineptitude, as well as constantly getting distracted by other business ventures, Derek LeVay had in recent years, and especially in recent weeks, wielded far less "Say" at his V.C. firm than he or its name always suggested. Ten days ago the board of directors (whose very existence he hated to acknowledge) had asked Marcia, scion of the Vellay mayonnaise family and wife of Derek's older brother Gabe (who'd been disowned at the age of 21 after repeatedly stealing from his parents), to step in and unofficially take the helm. She'd reluctantly agreed.

Marcia showed no recognition of Irene's entering the room and approaching the table. She was mid-sentence when the door opened, and simply carried on speaking as if nothing had happened, enumerating potential enhancements (e.g. three cameras, A.I. software) from what was, for the moment, her own wish list, but would soon become the official requirements for the next round of funding. Even Irene's standing almost right next to her and saying "Who the hell are you?" elicited only a quick sideways glance accompanied by continuing to address the group as before.

"Who the hell is she?" Irene demanded to know again, this time looking at Judy.

Judy responded with furious stammering but only managed to produce the words "um," "Irene" and "she" in various combinations.

After a few seconds, Wanda intervened, standing up, raising her hands and addressing herself to everyone.

"Sorry to interrupt," she said. "Sorry, excuse me, please." The confident, assertive, and increasingly loud sound of her voice silenced Judy and, finally, Marcia too. "I believe an introduction is in order."

Wanda had been recruited by Judy to craft a detailed marketing and sales strategy for the S.O.L. product. They'd known each other since college, during which they'd planned/hoped to also become classmates at Harvard Law School. However, neither of them had ended up going there—Wanda had been admitted but ultimately had decided to pursue a Ph.D. in economics instead; Judy had attended Ventura College of Law. Unbeknownst to everybody on earth, including herself, Wanda was the most intelligent person in this room.

"Irene, this is Marcia. She's going to be heading up the LeVay Say team going forward."

As Irene frowned and cocked an eyebrow, Wanda paused very briefly and then continued, "Marcia, this is—"

"Aha, the notorious Irene Hoffman," said Marcia. "I thought you were with the caterers. Somehow I'd always imagined you looked… very different." She spoke with an odd accent which irritated Irene, clearly American but not standard or identifiably regional—it had a sort of mid-Atlantic, "I'm superior" style about it. Her appearance, also irritating, vividly reminded Irene of somebody, but she couldn't quite think whom (it was actor Susan Sullivan from about 25 years in the past).

"Anyway, pleased to meet you," Marcia added, extending her hand.

Irene grudgingly decided to reciprocate but then realized she was still holding her cigarette. Spotting a half-full cup of coffee nearby, she tossed it in.

"Hey, I was drinking that!" cried Judy.

Irene turned and glared at her. "Oh, I'm just getting started with you, Judy, Esquire," she said, precipitating the reversion of Judy's momentarily indignant facial expression to one of panic and fear.

As Wanda (who was still standing up) said "Listen" and Marcia simultaneously said "Ladies," they were both interrupted by Keith Hoffman coming through the door shouting "Irene! Let me explain!"

Irene spun around to face her husband and began shooting him the same daggers she'd delivered to Judy a moment ago.

"I'm sorry, sweetheart," Keith continued. "It's just… Judy told me I shouldn't tell you…"

Irene kept her eyes fixed on his, but said nothing. He'd left the house an hour ago with Keith Junior and Luke, claiming the three of them were going on a "donuts and hot chocolate run." It hadn't made much sense but she'd not bothered to give it any thought.

Keith chuckled nervously. "She, uh… she can be awfully persuasive when she wants to," he said.

Judy smiled with pride and gratitude.

"Don't you have a shift?" Irene asked Keith.

"Huh?" He paused for a couple of seconds, gears turning. "Oh, crap! You're right, I do!"

Recently, upon Irene's urging, he'd taken a part-time job waiting tables at The Orange Café to supplement what he made teaching summer school classes. The family finances were in dire straits and Irene was constantly wracking her brain for new ideas on how to forestall catastrophe. Keith had also started driving for Uber, and getting all the family's groceries from Sam's Club.

"Just get outta here," Irene said. "We'll talk about this later."

"Okay," said Keith. "Oh! The boys—"

"Just leave the boys here. I'll take care of them."

"Okay. Hey, where's Alex and Connor? Did you leave them at home alone?"

"Keith, just get out!"

"Okay, okay," he said, turning to go.

Irene carried on anyway. "Go make money! That's your job!" She steadily increased her volume as Keith went through the doorway and scurried off down the hall. "Thinking about stuff is my job! Alex is her mother's daughter! She'll be fine!"

Wanda had sat back down, looking a bit dejected and also a bit annoyed. Marcia was displaying a frustrated scowl and a look of perpetually being just about to speak, her narrowed eyes darting from face to face, arms folded across her chest. Stan's expression—a warm, mildly amused smile—hadn't changed throughout the whole time everything was unfolding. Neither had Donald's—extreme confusion with a hint of horror. The sound of Stacy sighing came out of a phone speaker on the table.

"Okay, here's what happened," said Judy once satisfied that Irene's tangle with Keith was complete and her attention could be recaptured. "Mr. LeVay called me about 23 days ago to talk about setting up this session."

"Yeah, I remember," said Irene. "He talked to both of us."

"Well, actually, that conversation was about 29 days ago. He called me again after that."

"What?! Why?"

"To tell me, um… to let me know that, he wanted to meet with the rest of us… without you. Just, you know, um… to get our complete, honest… unvarnished… input."

Irene was dumbstruck, but only for a second. "Un-fucking-believable," she then said. "Unvarnished?"

"That's what Mr. LeVay said," Judy replied, involuntarily cracking a smile.

"What about this one?" Irene asked, gesturing at Marcia. "What about all those people in the other conference room? My family, for Christ's sake! What the fuck?"

"Well, um," stammered Judy, "Mr. LeVay called me again, about 12 days ago, to check how things were going with the prototype, and I mentioned it was nearly done and, um, how we were going to have that thing at your house..."

Marcia, who'd been clearly unhappy and very restless, stood up.

"This is all standard procedure when we're working with small start-ups," she said. "We like to get independent perspectives from the key players."

Judy jumped back in. "So he said everybody from the party should also come here today to meet with him. So that's why I called Keith."

Irene, hands on her hips, glared angrily at Judy, then at Marcia, then at Judy again.

"Oh, and I didn't know about Ms. Vellay-LeVay until this morning," Judy concluded.

"Let's get back to work, shall we?" said Marcia, forcing a half-smile. "We have a lot to discuss." She looked expectantly at Irene.

For a split second, the words "Go fuck yourself" whizzed through Irene's brain and headed toward her lips, but an awareness of monetary realities swooped in to stop them and she simply sat down at the table without speaking.

Marcia's smile relaxed and she sat down, too.

"Now," she said, "let's find out what's become of the real caterers. Donald, would you be a dear and go check on that?"

Donald's face became even more confused-looking and he said, "Oh, uh... I don't think we, uh, ordered, any..." He trailed off.

"Well, perhaps you'd better tend to that, then."

He sat frozen for a moment, staring blankly back at her. Then he said "Oh!" and leapt to his feet. "Yes, ma'am. Right away."

Francisco Danilo Rosario, looking rather dapper in his Armani tuxedo (with not a single strand of hair out of place and perfectly manicured nails), reached awkwardly for the open bottle of wine standing at the edge of the table, just to his right, picked it up, and moved it toward the nearly empty glass of Yvonne Smede, who sat directly across from him wearing the nicest dress she owned, purchased several years ago to wear to an office Christmas party and now known as her "Francisco dress."

"Oh, no, thanks," she said, quickly covering the top of the glass with her hand. "I've had enough."

Francisco froze and shot her a look of uncertainty and worry. Most people would've smiled and/or said "Uh," but he did neither of these.

After a moment, Yvonne let him off the hook, smiling and moving her hand away. "Not really," she said.

Francisco's face relaxed into a warm smile and he briefly removed one hand from the bottle to wave an admonishing finger at her. "Yvonne! I must always keep an eye on you," he said with a chuckle.

After filling Yvonne's glass, he turned to Felaecia Berg-Weinberg, sitting to his left wearing a dress quite similar to Yvonne's (despite having recently received an evening gown as a gift from Francisco, which he'd chosen specially for tonight but which she'd forgotten about), and did the same for her.

Felaecia was a 36-year-old white woman of average size and shape, with brown eyes and shoulder-length brown hair. Her facial expression 99% of the time, including now, was one of simply existing—neither interested nor bored, processing everything around her but having no thoughts or feelings about any of it.

Next Francisco provided a top-up to Bill Smede, who was seated next to Yvonne and clad in the dressiest outfit he could put together (as he did not currently own a tie, a jacket, a pair of slacks, a proper shirt, or a real pair of shoes): his newest polo shirt tucked into his least faded pair of blue jeans (with a belt), black socks, and the kind of dark-colored athletic shoes that are poorly disguised as something more formal. He was also wearing a jacket the maître d' had provided him for the evening that was too large and color-clashed with everything else he had on.

"Thanks," he said.

Finally Francisco poured some wine into his own glass, set the bottle down, and spoke to the group.

"As I was saying, that communiqué was the final nail in the coffin, so to speak. The Earl of Gloucester began discreetly rescinding all the directives he had issued, and, in short order, what could potentially have grown into one of the most serious conflicts of the late eighteenth century simply fizzled into triviality."

"Interesting," lied Bill. The women said nothing.

It was Friday night and the four occupied a corner table in the richly but tastefully decorated dining room of Pastiche, located on a bustling block of Canon Drive in central Beverly Hills. This gathering had been on the calendar for the past seven weeks, and Francisco had counted down the days in eager anticipation.

Pastiche, which required a reservation (which could only be obtained far in advance) and featured prices so extortionate they weren't disclosed on the menu, was not a restaurant the Smedes would ever have considered patronizing except under duress. Founded by celebrity chef Rudy DeSapio decades ago (long before he became celebrated), it had operated continuously at the same address ever since, with ever-growing cachet. (It was exactly the sort of establishment for which Oleanna Arrandami aspired to one day work.)

Francisco smiled and shook his head for a moment, a thoughtful look on his face, then said, "That reminds me of a theory that I have been working on lately—developing it and writing about it."

Yvonne and Bill smiled politely across the table at him, waiting to hear what came next. Felaecia retained her standard face.

"It relates to the spectrum of political ideology," continued Francisco. "Conservatives are individualists. They believe in the opportunity, achievement and prosperity of Person X and Person Y—the individual citizens, rather than the whole of society. The systems and policies they favor, however, actually lead to a higher overall level of prosperity, but with a great many individuals sorely missing out."

He paused, and both Smedes supplied low-key nods and grunts to signal they roughly understood what was said and vaguely agreed.

"Liberals, on the other hand, see people as more tightly connected to each other, morally and spiritually. They want to take care of the whole society. However, the systems and policies that *they* support... in fact facilitate a lower level of progress and prosperity for the entire populace collectively."

Yvonne smiled and took a sip of wine. Bill gamely murmured a quick "Hmm" and lifted both eyebrows slightly.

"I have dubbed this phenomenon the 'prosperity paradox'..."

Francisco considered himself a writer these days, and currently had several projects underway, including half a dozen academic articles and two books (one on political philosophy, one on art history), none of which had yet seen any involvement from a publisher or a professional editor.

But this was a relatively recent segment of an ever-meandering career path. After initially obtaining a B.A. in biology, with a minor in classics, at the age of 22, he'd returned to school three separate times, adding an M.B.A., an M.A. in Latin American Studies, and a second bachelor's degree (this time in history) to his collection of credentials. In between these stints, he'd worked as a paralegal, an assistant in a physiology research lab, an apprentice on an archaeological excavation, a sales engineer for a software company (where he'd met Yvonne), a flight attendant, and a campaign manager for his childhood friend Lincoln Wacksworth, who'd run (unsuccessfully) for Mayor of Pasadena. He enjoyed telling people, with a curious air of pride, that he'd never stayed in any one job longer than 13 months.

Francisco had just opened his mouth to further expound his recent intellectual pursuits when he noticed that the waiter, George Roman, had arrived with everyone's food, and although it was being delivered silently, Francisco decided holding his tongue would be the respectful thing (plus he didn't want to compete for his audience's attention).

George, who'd been working at Pastiche for 37 years and had looked to be about age 65 the entire time, moved swiftly and gracefully. After setting each plate before its corresponding diner, he glanced briefly at all their faces to gauge the level of contentment, found it to be 100%, and departed.

"This looks positively exquisite," said Francisco with a big smile, then, turning to Felaecia, "Wouldn't you agree, darling?"

"Yes," she replied.

The Smedes smiled across the table at their counterparts. Everything did indeed look delicious. And they all tucked in.

Half an hour later, Bill was standing at a urinal, thinking about something hilarious he'd seen on T.V. many years back and enjoying the rapid decrease of his bladder's fullness. He heard the men's room door swing open and vaguely acknowledged in his mind that somebody had entered, but assumed this had no relevance to him. Then he heard the voice.

"Bill, I am so pleased that you are here," said Francisco.

"You already knew I was here," said Bill, still facing the wall. "Unless you thought I was lying when I said I was going to the bathroom."

"Bill, I must speak with you, man to man, about something of grave importance. Although I feel somewhat awkward, I must do it."

Instantly filled with dread, Bill tried to keep a cool head. "Uh, okay. Can I, uh, finish here, and zip up, first?"

"Of course, Bill. I apologize for the unorthodox circumstances."

After a few seconds of silence, Francisco launched into it anyway. "Bill," he said, "this may surprise you, but I possess an intense, expansive, and rather eclectic sexual appetite."

"Sorry, Francisco. Very flattering, but I'm just not attracted to guys at all."

Bill figured saying this would probably lighten the mood, or, just possibly, actually provide useful information. But it did neither of these.

"I am not propositioning you," said Francisco. "Please just listen, Bill."

"Okay."

"This may surprise you, but my relationship with Felaecia is, in fact, rather unconventional. Recently it has also been rather unsatisfactory."

Alone with Felaecia at the table, Yvonne had been repeatedly attempting to make conversation, with no success. She suspected Felaecia would be perfectly fine with the two just sitting there in silence, and wondered if she herself might be, too, but just couldn't quite give up the fight.

"So," she said, "you grew up in Oregon?"

"Yes," Felaecia replied.

A couple of seconds passed. Then Yvonne said, "I grew up in Washington State. So we were neighbors, sort of." She forced a smile. "The northwest is such a beautiful region."

Felaecia said nothing.

"Hey, want to look at the dessert menu?"

"Okay."

Yvonne signaled to George, who was standing a short distance away, scanning the room for any diners' needs he might service. He strode over immediately and, when Yvonne asked about a dessert menu, produced two of them as if by magic and handed one to each lady. Then he said, "I'll give you a few minutes," and returned to his lookout spot.

Yvonne perused the offerings. "See anything that looks good?" she asked.

"Yes," said Felaecia.

In the men's room, Bill had been making gradual progress on deciphering Francisco's rambling, while being treated to some stunningly graphic descriptions of sexual acts. He'd also managed to complete his business at the urinal and make himself more presentable. The two were now standing, facing each other, near the sinks.

"So, what you really want," said Bill, "is to have lots of sex, all the time, with different partners, and you want to just... get all kinky and crazy with it..."

"Yes, correct."

"...and you also really want to have a loving, close, intimate, serious long-term relationship with one special woman."

"Yes, correct."

"Hmm. I don't know, Francisco. That's a pretty tall order. And you say Felicia—"

"Felaecia."

"Right. You say she doesn't even fulfill *either* of these requirements?"

"Correct. Unfortunately, she does not."

"See, that's where I'm confused. She seems like just the ticket. I mean, you've been going out with her for years. And now you tell me that... that the two of you have this open relationship and that she's, uh, basically... up for anything in the bedroom..."

"The problem is her lack of passion, Bill, in every arena. Felaecia does not truly care about the romance, or the sex, or about me, or any of it. For her, it is all simply a matter of routine, of convenience, of... meeting some very basic human needs in the most expedient fashion... which is also the most monotonous, unimaginative, disengaged fashion conceivable!"

"Wow," said Bill.

The sound of a toilet flush came from one of the stalls. Then its door opened and a young, thin, white man emerged wearing a sports jacket, a very tight t-shirt and very tight jeans.

As he approached the sink area he said, "You guys sure are a couple of weird-ass freaks!" His tone seemed to imply disapproval and exasperation.

"I apologize for disturbing you," said Francisco.

Nobody spoke for a minute as the thin man washed his hands, then dried them using a towel offered by the somber attendant, who'd been sitting in a chair two feet away from the conversation, utterly ignoring it. After tossing the towel into a nearby basket, the thin man reached into his pocket and pulled out a small card.

"House party later tonight off Melrose," he said, handing the card to Francisco. "Hope you guys can come!"

Then, in an instant, he was gone.

"How strange," said Francisco as he glanced at the card before tucking it into his jacket.

"Well," said Bill, "we should probably be getting back to the table..."

"I have held numerous discussions with Felaecia about these fundamental difficulties," said Francisco, "and I have formulated and executed many strategies for improving the situation, but all to no avail."

"Well I don't think she's going to change," said Bill. "She is who she is."

"Yes, I believe you are correct, Bill."

"So you need to find somebody else. Or,"—he chuckled—"several somebody elses, I guess..."

"Ah, yes. Therein lies the biggest problem of all."

"What do you mean?"

"I am abysmally unskilled at approaching women, and terrified of trying."

"Shit. Really?"

"Yes. It has been a problem for me throughout my entire adult life."

"Well, what about the other women you've met recently? You know, as part of your open relationship with Felicia?"

"Felaecia. There have been none."

"What?"

"There have been no other women. I have not been able to bring myself to attempt to meet any."

"God. Hmm."

Bill puzzled over everything for a few seconds, then said, "Well, uh, seems like something you might want to talk about with a close friend. A close guy friend, I mean."

"Yes, precisely. That is why I felt compelled to raise this with you tonight, Bill."

"Oh. Right. Uh…"

Francisco smiled warmly at Bill, looking directly into his eyes. For once Bill desperately hoped that Francisco would begin speaking again, but he didn't.

"Uh…" Bill finally repeated, after what felt like an eternity. Suddenly a lightbulb came on. "Maybe I should introduce you to my friend Matt."

———

On Sunday, Yvonne was in a mood.

Bill and Yvonne were not much inclined to express their feelings verbally, especially their feelings about each other, and most especially *to* each other. The words "I love you" were seldom uttered; likewise the words "I'm so pissed off with you." Least common of all: "We need to talk." Though they both felt a perverse fondness and respect for this trait, in themselves and each other, they also recognized, somewhat dimly, that it could, at times, impede communication and understanding between them.

Bill had noticed Yvonne's sullen silence from the moment they got out of bed (or, more precisely, had noticed its persistence from the night before (when he'd thought perhaps he knew the cause but ignored it and hoped it was nothing)), and by the end of breakfast had deduced that she was indeed upset, and specifically with him, based on her curt and snide replies to the few small, innocuous verbal test balloons he'd floated (combined with her relatively friendly behavior toward Alice and Patrick).

When, mid-morning, he'd come out from a rather lengthy visit to the bathroom to discover that Yvonne had left the condo, his frustration and worry had mounted, and he'd decided he should go for a long walk. But not one involving the neighborhood loop route—too much risk of bumping into her.

As he strolled along Santa Monica Boulevard (the noisy, smelly mass of vehicular traffic crawling along next to him at about the same speed) underneath a billboard containing simply the headline "Breakneck," an image of a man's face, half in shadow, and, in the bottom right corner, "August 7th" (an advertisement for a movie or series, the further online investigation of which a passerby presumably would find irresistible based on this cryptic hook), his phone began to vibrate.

Glancing down at the screen, he frowned and began the quick mental calculation to determine which was likely worse—the total pain ultimately to be endured by answering, or by not answering. After a few hundred milliseconds, he paused his iPod, yanked out one earphone, swiped green on the phone, and put it to his head.

"Irene," he said. "This is becoming a habit. Not the good kind."

"Oh, is that right, Mister Tough Guy," she shot back. "Where the fuck were you last night? I called and texted like, a gazillion times."

"Yeah, I saw that. Sorry. I was out for the evening and forgot to take my phone with me."

"Hah. You stupid piece of shit."

There was a long pause, making Bill feel he was somehow expected to respond to this appraisal, either by refuting it or defending it.

Finally he said, "So what's going on? You've been having some issues with your new toy?"

"Toy?! William, my friend, that is insulting. The Soundtrack of Life is a powerful, sophisticated, and—mark my words—soon-to-be highly sought-after, electronic life-quality-enhancement product!"

Bill couldn't suppress his laughter. "Jesus. Okay. I meant no disrespect."

"Sure you didn't. So anyway, yeah, you might say I've been having some issues with it. Not so much with the product itself as with these V.C. assholes. They are a fucking nightmare."

"Oh yeah?"

"Oh yeah, big time. But anyway, I'm not calling to complain. I'm calling to recruit!"

"What?"

"I need you to join Team S.O.L., William. There's so much work to be done, and—"

"Whoa! No, no, I—"

"I need quality people I can trust. Smart people. And I hate to admit it, but you're actually pretty smart."

Bill waited a second.

Irene added, "For a dumbass."

He waited another second and she added nothing further.

"Irene," he said, "uh… I'm just a friend. These businesses you start… I offer support and encouragement from the sidelines, but I don't get involved."

"Well that needs to change. You *need* to get involved. And, hey, what the fuck—'these businesses you start.' You're on a roll this morning, dick!"

"Sorry."

"You need to get involved, William. *Because* you're my friend. But, for your own sake, too. You gotta… grab the bull by the horns. Stop being such a pussy all the time."

His mind racing, desperately trying to think of way to get out of this, Bill stayed quiet for several seconds, which made Irene think, mistakenly, that she'd offended him.

"Hey, it's okay," she said. "I understand. I used to be a pussy, too. You probably remember! But thankfully, I came out of my shell."

Whatever shell I might be in, thought Bill, I'd prefer to remain there permanently. "What could I even do for you?" he asked.

"What could you do? What *couldn't* you do! Just off the top of my head… Okay, we gotta figure out a marketing and sales strategy. Wanda is supposed to be handling it but, between you and me, she's not the sharpest tool in the shed, you know?"

"Marketing and sales? I—"

"And we gotta build a second prototype. Gotta make some improvements. But we gotta figure out *which* improvements will provide the most value. Like, I mean…" She paused, thinking.

"Uh… Listen, Irene. I don't—"

"I mean there are some complex things that have to be worked through. Design decisions, allocation of resources. You could help with that, William."

"No, I couldn't."

"Also, Stan. He's a fucking genius but he is swamped. And this software keeps getting trickier. I could use another brainiac computer geek on the case!"

"Irene, I'm not—"

"What else have you got going on that's so fucking important, huh? Walking around in a goddamn circle all day long?"

Bill sighed, and couldn't help smiling at this latest remark even though he still absolutely hated the idea Irene was pitching.

"Hey, seriously," she continued. "This *is* happening, you lazy, cowardly piece of shit. And we need to meet up and hash out all the details."

Bill sighed again. People who wouldn't take no for an answer had always fared pretty well with him.

"Okay," he said. "We can meet. I guess. Just to talk about it, okay? This doesn't mean I'm actually going to come on board."

Irene let out a hearty laugh. "Sure," she said.

"So when do you want to come up here?"

"What?! No, no, no. *You* come down to the O.C. That's how it works! Oh, William."

Chapter 9

"Um, excuse me, ma'am," said Bob Ashen, currently the next person in line at the Customer Service desk at Fedco (a big-box chain that had thrived in Southern California for half a century before going bankrupt and disappearing for over 20 years, recently resurrected (this time without membership) by a coalition of employees from the U.S. Bureau of Reclamation, the National Park Service, and the U.S. Bureau of Labor Statistics).

The woman being addressed, who'd completed her business with Customer Service but then gotten distracted by something on her phone, turned her head to glance quickly back at Bob, grunted, and shuffled away.

Bob stepped up to the counter to find that the employee behind it, Alexander "Woolly" Gitwood, was also totally engrossed in the contents of a phone.

"Criminy!" Bob exclaimed. "It's an epidemic!"

"Oh, sorry, sir," said Woolly, looking up and smiling sheepishly. "I was just checking out the highlights from the NSPL semi-finals..."

Bob's eyes widened and a smile began to grow across his face.

"It's, uh, it's this thing..." continued Woolly by way of explanation, but none was necessary.

"Oh, I know all about the NSPL," Bob said gleefully. "I'm their biggest fan!"

"Wow, cool," said Woolly with a little chuckle.

"I'm waiting 'til I get home to watch," said Bob. "I like to see it on the big screen, in all its glory!"

The National Strip Poker League was a professional poker organization that was structured and operated like a sports league, with players belonging to teams who competed against each other over the course of a defined season, at events staged in front of large audiences in arenas and stadiums, and each season concluding with a championship. The players were high caliber, drawn from the ranks of conventional professional poker; but in the NSPL, naturally, they did not play for money, instead receiving a pre-negotiated per-season salary, the same as athletes. A large, complex set of rules governed the matches, with monitoring and enforcement supplied by striped-shirted referees, who also signaled each new development to the spectators using both a microphone and arm gestures. Although the NSPL had a surprisingly large following, it was still extremely unusual for one enthusiast to bump into another in public by pure chance.

"Big screen *would* be pretty dope," Woolly said wistfully. "But my parents would be so pissed."

"Hey," said Bob, looking rather pleased with himself, "I'm having a little party on Sunday. We're gonna live-stream the Strip Bowl. You should come!"

At this point, Juice Hughes-Newton, who'd been standing in the line for six minutes and was three spots behind Bob, exploded with rage and disgust. "Oh my fucking god!" she screamed.

Woolly, Bob, everybody waiting in line, and a couple of shoppers passing nearby all went silent, froze, and turned their eyes her way.

Juice continued raving—"What... in the world... is *wrong*... with all you people?!"—as she left the line, marched up to the desk, and sidled right up next to Bob, her left elbow ultimately pushing against the right side of his sizeable spare tire.

Locking eyes with Woolly, she said, "Listen to me. I am returning these items." She plunked a plastic Fedco bag filled with clothing down on the counter. "The receipt is in the bag. Just put the money back onto the same credit card. Got it?"

After a couple of stunned seconds, Woolly nodded his head and mumbled "Okay," but by then Juice had already broken into a brisk walk toward the store exit.

"And don't you try to screw me over!" she called over her shoulder, attracting more gape-mouthed stares from patrons and a cart attendant. "I have detailed records! Including a photo of that receipt!"

Eight minutes later, Juice's silver BMW X5 came to an abrupt halt beside the red curb in front of the apartment building where Paul

Newton lived. Juice honked the horn—one loud, long blast—and put the car in Park, then took off her seatbelt and settled in for a phone browsing session.

The front door of the building opened and Juice's son, Henry Newton (age 14), emerged, carrying a duffel bag in each hand and wearing the same facial expression as always—a serious one. All his life he'd been respectful, obedient, and a diligent, conscientious worker—around the house, in school, at church—and Juice appreciated all of this, but felt like he went too far with it. Like he was actually *too* well behaved. Too buttoned-down. Too much of his father in him. Henry was about to start high school, and Juice harbored hopes that he would cut loose a bit once he got there.

Henry came to the back of the car, opened the liftgate, placed the two duffels (his and his sister's) inside, and closed it again. Then he came around to the street side of the vehicle and got in, taking the seat behind his mother's.

"Hi, Mama," he said flatly.

"Hi there, baby boy," said Juice, without looking up from her phone. "How are you?"

"Hot," he replied, again with almost no emotion. "Dad's air conditioning is broken."

"Hah," Juice laughed. "First week of August. Classic!" The high in the Valley that day had been 106.

The door of the building opened again and Lateesha Newton sprang out of it, energy almost visibly radiating from her, and began scampering toward the car. She was nearing her 10th birthday, and Juice was decidedly *not* looking forward to her starting high school.

Paul Newton, a tall, physically fit, exceedingly handsome, middle-aged black man, appeared in the doorway and watched his daughter as she made the crossing. As was usually the case (most exceptions being during conversations with his ex-wife), he wore a calm, easy smile. Juice regarded Paul as patently a good father and a good human being, but she couldn't stand him. They had so little in common, it seemed, and for years she'd felt a perpetual, low-level resentment toward him, for… what? She wasn't sure. Probably for stealing a period of her life, and for that moral superiority she felt certain he ascribed to himself.

Things had been great between them in the early days. Lots of chemistry. They'd met at the prestigious Health Institutes and Cancer Center at University of the Pacific, where Juice had done her residency in family practice and where Paul had started one in anesthesiology. But he'd eventually switched his specialty to ophthalmology, then given up on medicine and briefly pursued teaching before ultimately settling into a career as a social worker. Throughout this evolution, relations between him and Juice had grown ever rockier, and all her love and respect for him had withered away. The couple had limped on for a few more years, and had a second child, hoping it would help, but it didn't, and finally they'd called it quits.

Lateesha flung the car door open and hopped into the seat beside Henry, behind the passenger seat (which was occupied by Juice's bag and had been permanently reserved for that purpose). "Hi, Mama!" she shouted exuberantly.

"Hi there, baby girl," said Juice. "How are you?"

"Can we have McDonald's for dinner?"

"We sure can! We just gotta run a little errand first. Now, shut the door and put your seatbelt on, please!"

As Lateesha complied with this request, Henry remarked, "McDonald's isn't very healthy."

"Oh, Henry! It's fine," said Juice, pulling the car away from the curb. "You can get a Filet-O-Fish if it makes you feel better."

"We went swimming today," chirped Lateesha, "and I swam three lengths, underwater, holding my breath, and we played this game—"

"Now listen up," said Juice. "I've got something exciting to tell you both. You know I said we need to run a little errand? Well I'm meeting up with Nasty Nancy! You remember her, right?" She glanced in the rearview mirror. Henry's eyes met hers. Lateesha was looking out the window.

"The woman you knew a long time ago?" Henry asked.

"Yes, that's right! And now it's finally time for justice!"

"What did she do to you, again?"

"Oh my god—she did everything to me! Stole my necklace. Stole my boyfriend. Lied to me. Lied *about* me. Treated me like shit..."

"Mama, language!" shouted Lateesha.

"Basically cast me aside like garbage." Juice paused for a few seconds. "But we'll just see who's garbage now." She chuckled with gleeful anticipation.

Henry looked slightly puzzled. "I thought you said you couldn't find her," he said.

"Ah, yes, for a while that was true. But I persisted. I didn't give up.

And in the end, it paid off!" She chuckled again, this time marveling at her own cleverness and guile.

Never doubting for a moment that one of the four Shaylas simply *had* to be her old nemesis, Juice had meticulously retraced her steps in eliminating them, eventually zeroing in on Shayla #2—the one who allegedly lived in Hemet. She'd then concocted one new email ruse after another, each more elaborate than its predecessor, to try to trick "Shayla" into meeting face to face. At last she'd nailed it, persuading her prey (with the help of a phony website created by her geeky friend Sydney) to show up at a designated time and place to claim a fabulous prize (which happened to be a diamond necklace, an irony Juice felt enormously tickled with herself for crafting).

"I guess there's a good lesson in there," said Henry.

"Yes, indeed, my son. Oh—we're coming up on the place, I think."

The X5 was now cruising south on Topanga Canyon Boulevard, approaching a gigantic strip mall on the right. Juice slowed down and began scanning the addresses.

After a couple of seconds, she announced "Yep! This is it," pulled into the driveway, then performed a sort of S-curve maneuver around some parked cars, swung into a spot and put it in Park.

She checked the time. "Fifteen minutes early! Not a problem. Had to be sure."

"We could get McDonald's now," suggested Lateesha. She'd noticed one just across the street. "From the drive-thru. We could eat it in the car."

"Nobody eats in Mama's car," said Juice. "You know that. Now hush, child."

And she removed her seatbelt and settled in for a session of phone browsing.

Twenty-three minutes later, as the woman once known as Nancy Jane Parsons walked slowly along the concrete footpath that ran alongside the storefronts of the strip mall, glancing back and forth between her phone screen and the stores' signage, face scrunched up in concentration and puzzlement, a loud, sharp voice suddenly cracked through the air in front of her and blasted her consciousness.

"Hah! I knew it!" roared Juice, stepping out from where she'd been crouched behind a trash can about six feet farther along the path. Nancy was so startled that she dropped her phone, which hit the concrete with an unsettling smack.

"You bitch!" Juice continued, taking a couple of steps toward Nancy with a triumphant smirk on her face. "Surprised to see me?"

The other pedestrians occupying the path quickly and quietly organized a new flow for themselves which diverted them around the two women in both directions. Nancy stared at Juice, her mouth hanging slightly open. Her face registered a lot of confusion and no recognition.

Juice kept stepping. "What's the matter?" she taunted. "Cat got your tongue?" Now she was standing just a foot in front of Nancy, hands on her hips. Their eyes had been locked the whole time, and Juice's smirk ever-present. "I've waited a long time for this," she said with visceral relish.

"Do I know you?" asked Nancy meekly.

"Don't play dumb with me, Nancy. The jig is up!"

"I'm terribly sorry, but I'm afraid you have me confused with someone else. My name's not Nancy." Her tone was sweet and extremely innocent.

Juice could feel herself heating up. "Don't try to bullshit me, you bitch!" she snapped, pointing a finger in Nancy's face. "Obviously I know who you are! Now *you* need to admit who you are, too!" The volume of her voice, and the amount of rage it carried, were increasing. "Not just your name. Who you are in your soul. Rotten to the core!"

Some of the passersby were now stopping and watching the stand-off with curious and worried expressions.

Nancy, not losing an ounce of her composure, dropped her gaze from Juice's and bent down to retrieve her phone. "I'm so sorry about the confusion," she said in the same calm, sweet voice.

So far Juice had derived almost zero satisfaction from this confrontation, and she sensed that it was about to be over before it had really begun. Her frustration and anger were bursting the barometer, but what could she do? Already she'd attracted far too much attention.

"I really must be going," said Nancy, now standing and looking into Juice's eyes again, and smiling sweetly. "I do hope you find whoever you're looking for." Then she turned and began walking away.

Juice didn't speak or take a step. She just stood and watched, body quivering, teeth and both fists tightly clenched.

Exactly 48 hours later, Juice sat opposite Yvonne Smede at a small table on the terrace of The Crustacean, an extremely popular and even more extremely overpriced restaurant perched on a cliff above the Santa Monica pier. Juice had just finished telling Yvonne how furious she was with Nancy, before which she'd related an unfortunate recent incident involving Henry and a lawnmower which had nearly ended with him missing three fingers from his left hand but had actually ended with no injury at all. Prior to that, Juice had delivered a rant about Nancy, preceded by a rant about her mother (who, thankfully, had left Southern California and moved to Phoenix last year), preceded by a rant about Nancy. Before that, Juice had described a TV news segment she'd recently seen about a streaker at a Major League Soccer game who, when interviewed after the fact, claimed he'd worn a prosthetic "package" featuring a penis smaller than his real one. At the beginning of the meal, Juice had told Yvonne all about her confrontation with Nancy and how furious she was about it.

Now there was a moment of silence as they sat with their empty plates in front of them. Juice had been the one who suggested meeting up today, and suggested doing it on this side of the hill (i.e. not in the Valley) for once, which had impressed Yvonne. Juice had also selected the venue (with which Yvonne was far less impressed) as well as the timing—initially a late lunch, then switched, on very short notice, to an early dinner.

"It's beautiful, isn't it?" Juice said, gazing out at the pier, its base flanked by two improbably enormous patches of sand (Santa Monica's beach having the curious distinction of being the one public place in L.A. that always had plenty of space, though, cruelly, its parking lots and all routes leading to it never had any) dotted with Sunday afternoon revelers, its tip jutting out into the water with sunlight shimmering off its surface, and a bright blue, cloudless sky above.

Yvonne, who had her back to the ocean, wrenched herself around in her seat and craned her neck to quickly take in the scene, which was beautiful indeed. Not so much the pier itself—resembling a slab of totally flattened roadkill, completely covered in swarming flies, layered surreally underneath a lamer, tamer version of Coney Island—but the surrounding spread of (seemingly) serene sky, sea, and sand, the coastline curving gently outward in both directions, culminating in the Palos Verdes Peninsula far to the south and Malibu's Point Dume even farther to the north. Much closer, about a mile and a half up the shore, she could see, with a row of palm trees along its eastern boundary, the Annenberg Community Beach House complex, built on the spot where once had stood the mansion home of Marion Davies, Matt Spratt's movie star crush.

Turning back around to face Juice, Yvonne smiled and said "Yep."

"So, what's up with you, girl? You've hardly spoken the whole time we've been here."

Yvonne shrugged.

"How's everything going? How's Bill?"

Yvonne winced. "He's... He's fine."

Juice raised an eyebrow. "Really? You don't sound so sure."

Yvonne sighed, hesitated for a second, and then said, "Okay, okay. We, uh... We haven't really been speaking to each other."

"W-hoa!" Juice exclaimed with a short, booming laugh. "Since when?"

"Uh... About a week. A little over a week."

"What happened?"

"Nothing big."

"Did you have a fight?"

"No. I'm just... pissed off with him."

"Why? Come on, girl, dish it!"

"Well, it started... He was just rude to me. A couple of times. Rude and thoughtless, in his Bill way." She signaled exasperation and disgust by momentarily turning her head slightly down and to the side and rolling her eyes. "I guess, in itself, it's not that big of a deal. But, it's been happening more and more lately. And then, instead of apologizing when he's obviously upset me, he goes into Stupid Mode."

"What do you mean?"

"Awkward. Quiet. Serious. Always frowning, always looks like he's concentrating really hard on something..."

"Does he say anything to you?"

"Nope. Well, he does when he feels he has to—you know, in order to tell me or ask me about household operations, like cooking or whatever. But it's very short, very business-like... He uses this quiet, monotone, almost robotic voice. Mmmf. I hate it." The heat of anger was welling up inside her, just thinking about it.

"Oh, girl," said Juice, chuckling and shaking her head. "You gotta tell him what's up!"

"Yeah, maybe. But *he* should be the one who initiates. *He* should tell *me* what's up. What am *I* supposed to say? It's already obvious where I'm coming from."

"Well—"

"I mean, if I initiate, I'm just going to start screaming at him. I mean... Mmmf..." She trailed off, shaking her head and looking down at the corner of the tabletop.

"You should!" proclaimed Juice. "Go on, have a fight with Bill. You know what your problem is, the two of you? No fights. You never fight with each other. That is not a *good* thing! Fighting is the key to a healthy, successful relationship."

"Did you and Paul used to fight?"

"Hell, yes! All the time!"

"Hmm..."

"Speaking of fights: what am I gonna do about Nasty Nancy?"

Yvonne took a second to process this, then said, with a small laugh of disbelief, "What do you mean? Nothing, Juice. You do nothing. Just forget about her."

Juice shook her head. "Mmm-mmm, no way. Not an option. I must have justice. I need to find her again."

Yvonne was now shaking her head too, and laughing again. "Juice, Juice. No good will come of this."

"Come on, girl. Help me out here. How do I track her down? The email thing won't work anymore—she already shut down the account. Bitch. I guess it never *did* work all that well—heh. Not to mention being a huge pain in the ass. I need something better... I need to find out where she lives..."

Throughout this ramble, Yvonne had continued chuckling softly.

"Laughing at me isn't gonna help!" said Juice.

"Okay, okay," said Yvonne. "Let me think about this." She put her hand on her chin and pointed her eyes downward at nothing in particular, slowly moving them left and right.

Their server whisked past, depositing the bill on the corner of the table and cooing, "Whenever you're ready, no rush."

Juice glanced at the time on her phone.

"You could go back to that mutual friend, from Facebook," said Yvonne.

"Hmm," said Juice.

"Figure out who she is. Then figure out how she's linked with Nancy. Follow the trail." Yvonne shrugged. "That's all I can think of."

"Yeah, maybe. Listen, girl, I gotta run."

"You do?" Yvonne glanced at the unopened folder containing the bill.

"Yep." Juice had already stood up and was gathering her things. "Gotta get to the Kings Head before they close. I meant to go before meeting you, but I was running late."

Ye Olde Kings Head was a decades-old shop on Santa Monica Boulevard, near where it ended at Ocean Avenue, that sold imported British goods as well as homemade ready-to-bake meat pies (which were also served in the British pub/restaurant next door (also called Ye Olde Kings Head)). Juice absolutely loved these pies and endeavored to keep her freezer at home continuously stocked with them.

"So, what, you'll Venmo me for this?" Yvonne asked as Juice began walking away.

"No, I'm not on Venmo. I'll get you next time, girl. Bye!" Then she was gone.

Yvonne sighed, staring vacantly at the doorway through which her friend had just disappeared. After a moment she stood up, went around to the other side of the table, and sat down in Juice's chair.

She smiled. "Nice view," she said to herself.

Throughout his entire life (a period of 62 years so far), Lyum K. O'Peecia had never considered himself to be the slightest bit normal, and nobody who'd known him—those who liked him (few), those who disliked him (more), and those indifferent to him (by far the largest group)—had ever disagreed with that assessment.

He'd begun speaking in full sentences before his first birthday, and was completely toilet trained before his second, although he'd required assistance in actually using the toilet for three more years until he finally learned how to walk. He was reading at a 4th grade level when he was in kindergarten, but his abilities had only advanced to a 5th grade level by the time he entered high school.

He'd hated everything about school—academics, athletics, organized extracurricular activities, even socializing. He'd always received terrible grades in all his classes (except for one middle school art class in which he excelled greatly), and had never had any friends his own age.

But, strangely, Lyum's lifelong dream had been to advise high school students on their course selections, monitor their progress, and shepherd them toward graduation. Upon reaching adulthood, he'd begun pursuing this dream relentlessly, and within a few years had realized it. He'd also legally changed the spelling of his first name in an effort—which proved largely but not wholly successful—to stop people from constantly mispronouncing it (his parents, Betty and Al, had named him "Liam," but pronounced with a long 'I' sound).

In his mid-thirties, Lyum had developed, inexplicably and almost instantaneously, an intense fear of sunlight, which prompted him to trade in his car and make many lifestyle adjustments such as ending his leisurely picnic lunches in MacArthur Park. He'd briefly contemplated leaving Southern California for cloudier environs, or even residing in two different locations, spending half the year in, say, central Saskatchewan and the other half somewhere like Punta Arenas. But he couldn't quite bring himself to do it, having called this area home his entire life and having already served twelve years in a job he absolutely loved—guidance counselor at College High School.

So Lyum O'Peecia had stuck around, honed his sun-shielding skills, and remained in his dream job (though its name had changed slightly, to "guidance technician," after it was decided by the L.A.U.S.D. superintendent's office that the term "counselor" would signify being qualified to perform psychological evaluations, and that the district would employ only seven such people, roving around among the hundreds of school campuses as needed) for another 27 years and counting.

Currently he was sitting in his office, having just returned there from an unplanned trip to the parking lot to retrieve a pack of chewing gum he'd accidentally left in his truck. Sitting across the desk from him was Alice Smede, emotionlessly regarding the banner tacked up on the wall behind him which read, "Give It The Old College Try!"

"I'm sorry for keeping you waiting," he said to her as he began removing the various accoutrements he used to insulate himself from all that terrifying, obnoxious, health-degrading radiation that lay between the building and the truck.

Alice remained silent. She hadn't been able to decipher what Mr. O'Peecia had said because his mouth was still covered with a thick scarf. Had she known what he'd said, she would've remained silent.

The gloves were off. Next came the sunglasses and the scarf. Then the earmuffs. Then the hat.

"Now, let's see here," he said, scrutinizing the contents of his computer screen while fumbling around with his jacket zipper. "Your current cumulative GPA is... 2.0." He winced. "Honestly, Alice..."— he looked her in the face—"that isn't too good." He moved his eyes to his own upper body and the task of getting his arms out of his jacket sleeves. "I think you can do better."

Alice said nothing. She hadn't been asked a question, and felt no urge to offer Mr. O'Peecia any feedback about his opinions. He was somewhat surprised by this, but ignored it. Finally completely unencumbered by his protective outerwear, he returned his gaze to the computer screen.

"Now, let's see here," he said, clicking and scrolling. "You have got... Wow... You've got... Unbelievable, Alice." He looked at her again. "In the two years you've spent here so far, you've gotten a C in every single class you've taken."

For five seconds they just stared at each other.

Then, having concluded Mr. O'Peecia wanted a response this time, Alice said, "I do what is required of me."

Alice regarded passing her classes as an obligation, and she took obligations seriously. But she wasn't prepared to invest one ounce of unnecessary energy in the whole scholastic project, which had never brought her any feelings of excitement, or joy, or pride, or shame.

"Would you like a stick of gum?" asked Mr. O'Peecia.

"I'm good," said Alice.

Mr. O'Peecia pulled a stick of gum out of the pack, unwrapped it, popped it into his mouth, and turned his attention back to the computer screen.

"You scored very well on your PSAT, Alice," he said, then sat back, eyes still aimed at the screen, and chomped away on his gum for a few seconds, lips smacking. "And that," he went on, reaching for the mouse and scrolling a bit, "combined with the fact that you have never gotten a D or an F..." He looked at her again. "...leads me to believe that you are capable of so much more."

Another period of mutual staring occurred, briefer this time.

Then Mr. O'Peecia said, "Perhaps you're not being challenged enough."

Alice continued to hold his gaze, weighing up whether she should vocalize her disagreement.

He spoke again before she'd decided: "I think you should consider taking some honors classes this year."

"I would prefer not to," she replied.

Twenty-five minutes later, Alice was standing at the reception desk in the activities office (which had temporarily been converted into a combination photography studio and printing/lamination shop), awaiting the manufacture of her student ID card. Other students milled around on the same side of the desk where Alice stood; various staff and parent volunteers milled around on the other side of it.

Today's event had been officially named "Ready For Launch!" in a feeble and entirely unsuccessful attempt to get the kids excited about it, but really just amounted to conducting all the necessary administrative exercises to prepare for the start of the new academic year (slated for next Tuesday).

The students arrived on a staggered schedule and were funneled through a sequence of "Power Up" stations, each with a specific purpose. Prior to sitting for her photo, Alice had picked up her textbooks at the entrance to the book depot from a chap barely older than her, whom the administration had deemed sufficiently respectable to entrust with such a grave responsibility, standing on the opposite side of an L-shaped wooden panel that served as both a counter and the bottom half of a door. The young nerd had determined which books to hand over using the class list printout Alice had supplied him, which she'd obtained from Lyum O'Peecia near the end of their meeting.

Despite the somewhat tense moments between them, during which Alice had felt it was touch and go, she'd ultimately prevailed, leaving his office with precisely the classes she wanted: the four mandatory core subjects, all non-honors (and with history taught by the famously lenient Mr. Kant), and two electives (introduction to art and introduction to computers) that both promised to be an easy C.

"Alice Smede?" called out a bored-looking man from behind the activities office desk.

Alice received her ID card from him, walked out into the corridor and stood looking at the photo, frowning. She hated every photo taken of her within the past few years, and this one was no exception. Like all but the most egregiously narcissistic teenagers, she believed herself uglier than average, and like half of these, she was mistaken. In fact Alice was almost a spitting image of her rather striking mother. Her eyes and hair were both a shade darker (Yvonne's hair had been nearly white in childhood), and she'd always worn it quite long rather than shoulder-length, but her entire face was a carbon copy. A long-running Smede household joke contended that Bill didn't actually have any biological children; occasionally, when family members were in an especially wicked mood, they extended it to the notion that he was still a virgin.

Looking up, Alice noticed that her two best friends, Anita Guerrero and Tabitha Cole, were walking down the center of the long, cavernous hallway toward her. Both were clutching phones, with fingers working feverishly and eyes cast downward almost continuously. But every couple of seconds, their eyes flitted around in other directions—so briefly as to be all but imperceptible—and Alice knew from watching this that they'd spotted her and were coming to talk to her.

As they approached, she idly surveyed her surroundings. Each of the thousands of L.A.U.S.D. buildings boasted a unique exterior aesthetic, together ranging over the entire rainbow of possibilities; but on the inside, they all provided exactly the same vibe. Some hard-to-pin-down combination of elements—high ceilings with high windows, lines and shapes and surfaces comingling in a tightly regimented fashion, eerie acoustics, large quantities of brick and even larger quantities of concrete, and perhaps other mysterious factors too—evoked being in a penitentiary. A smattering of brightly-colored posters, flyers and banners adorned the walls—a deliberate effort to counteract this effect but one which only twisted it into something more macabre. Alice momentarily considered the nature of the school environment, with a moderate amount of philosophical interest but zero emotion.

The other two girls arrived in front of Alice and commenced fire. They had a rhythm so precise that it seemed planned and rehearsed, but was really just instinctual, whereby one would speak for three seconds while the other attended to Phone World and then they'd swap.

Anita: "Did you get your schedule? Did you get art history?"

Tabitha: "Heard anything else from Ryan? He wants to tap that sweet ass of yours!"

Anita: "So are we going for boba? I'm like so ready to get outta here."

Tabitha: "Hey, why didn't you hit me back, bitch?"

Alice reached into her backpack and retrieved her phone while trying to process all of this. Anita had been pushing the idea that they should all take art history together because the teacher, Ms. Geckens, was known to be flighty and hard of hearing, providing a great opportunity for chitchat or just doing whatever during class; but Geckens was also known to give copious homework and difficult tests, making this a losing proposition in Alice's mind.

Ryan Reynolds (who'd been miffed for the past several years about his parents' recklessness of many years before) was a boy from school who, just before the summer break, had taken a liking to Alice and begun trying to flirt with her (through texting only, never in person). He'd gone quiet for a couple of months but had resurfaced recently with more of the same. A straight-A student who also participated in badminton, lacrosse, orchestra, chess club and yearbook, Ryan was regarded by most other kids as smart and somewhat admirable, but not attractive-looking and just generally not cool. Alice, who couldn't have cared less about their opinions, hadn't yet decided what she thought of him.

"Boba" referred to a range of cold, sweet beverages made with tea and tapioca balls, originating in Taiwan, that in recent times had become very popular with Americans, particularly American high schoolers. Alice and her friends frequently, of an afternoon, stopped by one of the seven boba purveyors within half a mile of College High School, their favorite being Boba Fête! on Wilshire.

Sliding her thumb around on her phone screen, Alice scrolled through some previously unread texts from both Anita and Tabitha. Meanwhile, they had not paused for their friend to respond. In the preceding twelve seconds they'd fired off "Oh my god, I'm hungry. We should get some ramen too, right?" and "You should totally go out with Ryan! He's actually kinda cute." and "So what did O'Penis give you? That dude is sooo weird." and "But actually I dunno about Ryan. He is, like, kind of a major dork."

Alice shrugged and said, "Everybody's different."

Anita thought she meant Mr. O'Peecia. Tabitha assumed she was referring to Ryan. They were both partially right. But Alice was also talking about herself. She'd known these two forever, and she liked them well enough, even loved them a bit. They were her crew. But she never quite felt like she could fully relate to who they were, where they were coming from. All the drama, all the passion, all the fickleness, all the whimsy. All the talking! Alice sometimes wondered if she might be a sociopath. But she wasn't worried about it.

Bill Smede, sitting on a nearby bench against a wall, looked up from his phone and noticed his daughter. Like her, he was not, generally speaking, an avid phone user. But he'd had nothing better to do while waiting for her to go through all the Power Up stations, so he'd settled in for a session of browsing his favorite website, Wikipedia (which Gary Williams had turned him on to a couple of years back (prior to completely losing interest himself)). On the screen currently was an article about computer text adventure game pioneer Dave Lebling.

Bill got up and approached the trio.

"Hi, girls," he said awkwardly. "How's it going?" He tried to force a smile, and did an involuntary and slightly creepy wiggling of his eyebrows. He hated interacting with youngsters.

Anita and Tabitha were every bit as uncomfortable as Bill, and regarded him with barely concealed disdain. Alice felt no embarrassment about her father, but neither was she eager for him to converse with her friends. Different worlds, she thought, and members of both will be happier if they don't intermingle.

Correctly sensing that none of the girls intended to say anything, Bill spoke again. "So, done with all the stations?" he asked Alice.

"Yes," she replied. Technically two stations remained, one for joining clubs and one for signing up for sports, but she was skipping both.

"Got some papers for me to sign?" Bill asked.

"No." Alice did not roll her eyes or use an exasperated tone, as most kids (and indeed, many adults) would've done. "I told you before: the forms you signed at home and gave me were all there was. You didn't actually need to be here at all."

"Well, I couldn't just let you come out here all by yourself on the bus." He chuckled nervously and threw a quick glance at each of Alice's friends.

"I do that every day during the school year," she said.

"True," he conceded with a smile.

Bill occasionally still felt protective of his daughter, though he understood and respected the fact that these days she was perfectly capable of looking after herself. Today he'd also liked the idea of having a little father-daughter bonding time (which hadn't happened at all). Leaving the condo for a while had suited him well today, too: most of his New York colleagues were in all-day training so wouldn't miss him, and sharing a space with Yvonne (this was her weekly work-from-home day) had been weird and rough of late. But on top of all these things, he had genuinely believed the school would need him to sign some papers.

After another tense moment of silence between the four of them, Bill said, "Well, uh... Should we head out, then?"

"We were talking about getting a bite to eat," said Alice. "I'll just get the bus back."

"Oh!" Bill was startled by this but didn't have any issue with it. "Okay. Well, uh... I guess I'll... see you at home, then."

"Bye," Alice said, then immediately began walking away. Anita and Tabitha turned around and did the same.

"Have fun!" Bill called out as they disappeared down the corridor. There was no reaction from any of them.

Mulling over the notion that his decision-making this afternoon might well have been rather flawed, it occurred to Bill that he'd parked in a 15-minute zone, across the street in front of College High School Middle School, over an hour ago. Then it further occurred to him that trying to travel along Santa Monica Boulevard from here back to his own neighborhood (crossing under the 405) this time of day was always pure hell.

"Fuck," he said under his breath.

At 10:36 the following morning, Juice was sitting on her living room sofa, reviewing the day's agenda with her children.

"Make sure you get all the weeds," she said to Henry. "Don't forget that section over on the, like, side-back of the house. You know where I mean?"

"Yeah, I know it."

Henry was standing in the archway that separated the living room from the dining room, hands on his hips, looking attentively at his mother and organizing his thoughts in preparation for the yard work and other chores that lay ahead. He knew he'd find very few, if any, weeds on the entire property, as he'd conducted a meticulous weeding exercise just five days ago and the professional gardeners had been here the day before yesterday. He also knew that, most likely, Juice would never notice any weeds that were missed, unless they were at least three feet tall and in view of a window. But in spite of all this, Henry never remotely considered, even for a second, doing a halfhearted (or entirely imaginary) job. He would inspect every square inch of turf and would ensure a weed count of zero.

"Oh, and the laundry. Make sure you get all the laundry done," said Juice.

"Yes, Mama. I will."

"Okay, I'm gonna head out in a minute. Teesh! You ready, baby girl?"

Lateesha, who'd been a participant in this conversation a few minutes ago but had floated out of the room at some point, came dashing back in, an excited grin on her face.

"Ready!" she exclaimed. "We're going on a spy mission!"

"That's right, we sure are!"

"You two have fun," Henry said with a smile, then turned and headed toward the back of the house.

Juice pulled her car key out of her bag. "Go get the car warmed up for me, okay?" she said, holding the key out to Lateesha, who grabbed it and ran off toward the garage, giggling.

Picking up her phone and scrolling through the unread texts (most of which were auto-generated ads, notifications and appointment reminders), Juice noticed a new one from her least favorite and most texty colleague, Dr. Donna Marquez, who was the department head and, as such, tended to be very concerned with things that didn't concern Juice at all, like timesheets and waiver forms. This latest, rather sternly worded, text was Juice's third reminder that her semi-annual reports were overdue.

She groaned, rolled her eyes, and said "God! I'm a doctor, not a fucking report writer. Can't they get someone else to do this shit?"

She'd reply to the text on Monday, she decided. This was her weekend. She picked up her bag, dropped the phone into it and strolled across the room, down the hall and out into the garage, where a beaming Lateesha stood by the driver's door of the X5, waiting to usher her mother into the pre-chilled vehicle.

"Why thank you very much," Juice said, smiling, and climbed in.

"Can I sit up front?" asked Lateesha.

"No," Juice replied with a chuckle. "You know the rules. Get your cute little butt in the back, and buckle up!"

Lateesha didn't argue or even register any reaction. She simply sprang into action, closing her mother's door, opening the one behind it, clambering in, shutting it again, and putting on her seatbelt. Juice shifted into Reverse and the car rolled out of the garage into the 95-degree Tarzana morning.

They were headed for Moreno Valley, a town 60 miles east of downtown Los Angeles, still part of the continuous metropolitan sprawl but in the section informally known as the Inland Empire. For Juice and Lateesha, getting there involved taking the 101 to the 134 to the 5 to the 10 to the 71 to the 60—freeways with unpredictable traffic varying from quite bad to off-the-charts horrendous. But before that part of the journey could even begin, they had to make it to the freeway, which involved negotiating notoriously challenging thoroughfares like Tampa Avenue and Ventura Boulevard.

Five minutes from home, Juice found herself stopped at a light on Tampa, first in line in her lane to proceed through once it turned green. When it did, the driver of a car facing her from the opposite side of the intersection, who'd been waiting to turn left, immediately did so, rather than yielding to Juice and her fellow southbound travelers. This flagrant violation of other motorists' God-given rights was common on the streets of L.A., as was the behavior that accompanied it: the offending driver gave Juice and his other victims an L.A. Wave as he passed through the intersection in front of them.

The L.A. Wave was a quick flash of one's open palm (sometimes, but usually not, paired with a smile) directed at one or more total strangers in a traffic situation, either during or right after the execution of a rude and selfish maneuver. Ostensibly it expressed a combination of apology and gratitude, but the recipient almost never felt these sentiments were sincere, so in practice it served simply as assurance that the perpetrator was not merely oblivious or incompetent, but an actual, genuine asshole.

Following standard protocol, Juice and the drivers next to her all gave a very long, very loud blast of their car horns as the rule-breaker sped off down Topham Street. Then everybody continued on their way and a moment later had forgotten the whole incident.

Carole Culcoran was the founder, owner, manager, head chef, head server, and one of only three employees (the other two being her husband Wendell (generally known as "Ace"), the bookkeeper, and Nick Spitz, the part-time busboy/dishwasher/janitor) of a quirky little restaurant called Carole's Place.

The walls, scarcely a square inch of them bare, were adorned with: large photographs of Carole's face, along with numerous smaller photographs of other, unidentified people; prints of paintings widely varying in size, style, time period, and famousness; banners containing motivational slogans like "Don't sweat the small stuff—and it's all small stuff!"; informational posters like one saying "Breakfast served all day" with the words "all day" crossed out and replaced with "at night"; and different-colored balloons. These decorations also covered the door and all the windows, which had been blocked out with massive sheets of cardboard (meaning all the lighting was artificial, emanating from a dozen rows of bare bulbs protruding from the ceiling). Each meal of the day had its own menu of about ten items, none of which were normally associated with that particular meal (e.g. pancakes for dinner).

Carole greeted every customer with an extremely warm welcome the moment they entered, and meticulously attended to their every need from then until the moment they left. (She could manage this because there were only four tables and most of them were usually empty.)

Juice finally remembered the place as she came through its door just after 3 P.M. "Riiight!" she said to herself. (Stopping for a bite to eat on her way home from Palm Springs a few years back, she'd accidentally walked into Carole's Place intending to walk into Chili's (which occupied a much larger portion of the same building, with much larger signage, and had its entrance just six feet away from Carole's) and had ended up staying.)

But, seeing the proprietor in the flesh now, in the midst of wiping down a table with a wet cloth, Juice still didn't recognize her any more than in the pictures she'd found online. Carole was black, tall, and extraordinarily thin, her graying hair pulled back into a tight bun at the base of her skull. She wore a black t-shirt, blue jeans and white sneakers, with no jewelry and very little makeup. She was 67 years old but moved like a person half that age.

"Hello!" she shouted with a huge smile, abandoning her cloth and bounding toward Juice. "Welcome to Carole's Place! I'm Carole. It's so nice to see you! Please, sit anywhere you like."

"Actually, I'm not hungry," said Juice. "I'm trying to find my friend, Shayla Jennings. You know her?"

Carole looked perplexed. "Uh… I don't believe so, no," she said. "Who are you?"

"My name's Barbara Brown, and I desperately need to find my friend Shayla. She's run out of her medication and I've got the refill and I need to get it to her."

As Carole stammered, trying to absorb this, Juice produced a sheet of paper from her bag and thrust it forward.

"Here, this is her," she said. The image of Nancy snipped from Facebook three months ago occupied the entire page in extremely low resolution. "You know her, right? She's your friend, too. Right? Shayla!"

Carole looked back and forth between Juice's face and the one on the printout. She did not recognize either, and felt quite uneasy with the whole situation.

"No… sorry," she said. Her smile was gone. "I don't know anyone named Shayla. I don't know the woman in this picture."

"Listen," Juice said, now using a softer tone. "I know this is kinda freaky and weird. I get it. And I'm sorry about that. I just really, really need to find Shayla."

Carole shrugged. "I don't know what to tell you."

"You're friends with her on Facebook."

"Well, I'm friends with a lot of people on Facebook. Most of my customers, past and present!"

Carole gestured toward one of the photos of herself affixed to the wall, next to which a sign read, "Friend me on Facebook and get a coupon!" She was starting to cheer up again.

"Hmm," said Juice, looking over at the sign. "Right, of course. I mean, *I'm* Facebook friends with you, too, and we don't know each other…"

"Oh, have you been here before? Welcome back!" Carole grinned. "Are you sure you wouldn't like some food?"

Juice was lost in thought. After a long silence, she said, "Hey, do me a favor—go into your Facebook and look up how long you've been friends with Nancy."

"Nancy?"

"Shayla. I mean Shayla." She paused. "Sometimes people call her Nancy… just for fun."

"Well, uh…" Carole said hesitantly. "Okay."

She pulled her phone out of her back pocket and opened the Facebook app, then started meandering around within it, befuddled, repeatedly muttering "Um."

Juice snatched the phone out of her hand, saying "Here, let me."

After a few seconds of sliding her expertly trained fingers over the screen, she found it. "Okay, here we go: you and Shayla became friends… in May of this year. Hmm, not that long ago."

Carole, uncomfortable once again, said, "Okay…?"

"You probably still have credit card slips from May, right?"

Carole frowned and shook her head fiercely from side to side, her discomfort level skyrocketing.

"No, no, no," she said. "Absolutely not. That would be a huge violation of privacy."

"But this is important. She needs her meds, remember?"

Uncertainty flashed across Carole's face for a split second, but then the stern expression returned and she folded her arms across her chest.

"Nope. Can't do it," she said. "Sorry."

Juice forced a smile. "Okay," she said. "I understand." It was time for Plan B. "You know… maybe I will have some lunch after all."

"Oh! Um, okay..." Carole was taken aback but quickly realized she was pleased by this turn of events. "Sure!" She smiled and unfolded her arms. "Just sit anywhere you like. I'll go grab you a menu."

As Carole raced off toward the counter, Juice sat down at the nearest table, placed Carole's phone on it, then put her bag on top of the phone, then pulled out her own phone and fired off a quick text to Lateesha, who was waiting in the car and had been thoroughly prepped for her potential role here today.

Carole, who'd briefly vanished through a doorway behind the counter, reappeared carrying a menu in one hand and a glass of water in the other, hustled across the room and set these items down in front of Juice.

"Here you go, Barbara," she said with a big smile. "Just give me a shout when you've decided what you want."

"Okay," said Juice, flashing an artificial smile and sliding her phone back into her bag.

Carole walked over to the table she'd been wiping a few minutes ago. As she reached for her cloth, the door of the restaurant flew open and Lateesha came running in. Ignoring her mother completely, she aimed her eyes, voice, and highly kinetic body squarely at Carole.

"Lady, lady!" she shouted. "You gotta help me! My mama's stuck and I think she's hurt!"

Carole was dumbstruck as Lateesha came right up to her and grabbed her by the wrist, talking all the while. "Come on! You gotta help me! We gotta get my mama out!"

"Out of where?" Carole asked as Lateesha, tugging on her arm, did an about-face and began stepping back toward the entrance.

"She's stuck and I think she's hurt! She needs help! Come on!"

Carole, bewildered, allowed Lateesha to lead her by the wrist and the two of them moved briskly across the floor of the dining room and out the door.

Juice leapt from her chair and rushed to the door to check whether it had a simple bolt lock that could be turned from the inside without a key. She was in luck—it did. After locking it, she made her way, in the closest thing to a run that could be performed by a middle-aged overweight person who never exercised and was wearing high heels, to the opposite side of the room, behind the counter, through the doorway where Carole had previously gone, across the kitchen area, and into a small corridor.

She stopped for a second and glanced around, then spotted an open door nearby leading into what looked like a small office. She dashed for it but then abruptly halted again upon discovering, as more of the inside of the office came into view, that Ace Culcoran was there, sitting at a desk, working on the books.

Juice couldn't prevent herself from saying "Shit!" out loud, but simultaneously noticed that Ace, whose back was turned, was wearing headphones. Thankful he was unaware of her presence, but frustrated by his and desperate to figure out her next move, she instinctively began to slowly creep back down the corridor in the direction she'd come from, her mind and heart both racing.

Think, Juice, think. Maybe… maybe there's something behind the counter. A file box? A set of keys? Carole's purse? What would help? What do I need?

She hurried back through the kitchen area and through the doorway into the behind-the-counter area, then frantically began scanning the countertop and the shelves and drawers under it.

Next to the cash register sat a propped-up sign facing the other way and a fishbowl that appeared to contain a bunch of random business cards. She picked up the sign and looked at the front of it. "Leave your business card (with email) and get a coupon!" She looked back at the fishbowl. Pretty full, she thought. Probably hasn't been emptied for months… especially considering how few people must come into this place.

Juice knew this was a Hail Mary. She grabbed the fishbowl, turned it upside down, dumped all the cards onto the counter and started trying to go through them as fast as possible.

Two minutes into this process, she heard the front door of the restaurant vibrate violently, as if someone had tried to open it. Then a very brief silence. Then another, even more violent, vibration. Another brief silence. Then the pounding began. Initially it was casual, light, slow-paced—like a family member knocking on your bedroom door to check if you're awake. Then it got more serious, heavier, faster-paced. The intensity kept mounting and mounting, ultimately reaching a point where it sounded as if a team of sledge-hammer-wielding body builders were attacking the face of the building.

Throughout this, Juice remained laser-focused on the task at hand, and kept trying to work even faster than she had been (though she knew that wasn't really possible).

Then suddenly, there it was. She froze, almost unable to believe it was real. Shayla Jennings's business card. A triumphant, euphoric thrill ran through her body, just for an instant. Then the desperation and panic returned.

She snatched up the business card, then scrambled around to the other side of the counter and over to the table she'd sat at, grabbed her bag and dropped the card into it. All the while the fever-pitch pounding continued relentlessly. Juice stood for a moment, weighing up the situation. There must be a back door, she thought. Better to avoid another confrontation if possible.

And indeed there was a back door. Retracing her steps to the corridor beyond the kitchen and turning the opposite direction from the office where Ace still sat, blissfully oblivious to everything that had transpired, Juice found her exit and enthusiastically used it.

Though immensely relieved, she still didn't feel confident she was entirely out of the woods just yet, and kept looking over her shoulder for the next five minutes as she traversed the eerily quiet and deserted stretch of asphalt behind the gigantic retail building (which housed several other businesses in addition to Chili's and Carole's Place).

After rounding the corner and stepping up onto a strip of sidewalk in front of a small row of shops, Juice stopped, took a deep breath, and wiped the sweat from her forehead with the back of her hand. Then she got her phone out, dialed Lateesha, put it to her ear, and resumed walking, stepping off the curb into the parking area and beginning to weave her way between the cars.

"Hi, Mama!"

"Hey baby girl. Where are you?"

"I'm in the car, waiting for you!"

"Great. So—"

"Can we get McDonald's?"

"Maybe. Listen, what happened to that lady? She didn't follow you to the car, did she?"

Lateesha giggled. "Nope. She figured out it was a goof." Another giggle. "And then she just went back to her restaurant."

"You did great, baby girl. So great. I'm so proud of you."

A short silence, then: "Can we get McDonald's?"

"Maybe. I said maybe. Now listen—I'm almost back to the car. Make sure you have the engine running, and the A/C cranked up nice and high."

Chapter 10

"Buried treasure!"

Matthew Alan Rodney Spratt's eyes popped open as this utterance exploded from his lips, and he sat bolt upright in bed.

His name had been chosen by his father, Icarus "Prat" Spratt, an amateur astronomer and acronym enthusiast who'd simply loved the idea of having a son called M.A.R.S. His mother, Sue-Ellen Patricia Theresa Ingrid Spratt (née Charleston), an amateur physiologist who felt neutral about acronyms, had readily gone along with the idea. Like Matt himself, both Prat and Sue-Ellen had always been free spirits, for whom rules, responsibilities and careers meant very little. They'd never put much pressure on their son about anything, nor had anyone else in his life, including him. Even things that keenly interested Matt, or about which he felt passionate, never took on a sense of urgency. So it was perfectly natural that despite his enormous excitement eleven weeks ago about searching for the treasure chest Marion Davies had allegedly buried on the beach, right now was the first moment it had crossed his mind since then.

But oh, how it had crossed! He'd dozed off for a mere couple of minutes but had slipped into an astonishingly vivid dream—the most vivid, Matt felt certain, that any person on earth had ever experienced. Marion, that beguiling goddess, had spoken to him. "Find it!" she'd entreated him with her sweet, melodic voice (tragically absent from most of her films), smiling down on him from above, just out of reach, floating ethereally amidst swirling white vapors. A cosmic connection across vast stretches of time and space! This was his destiny.

Victoria Lumac, who was lying in the bed next to Matt, reached her hand over, beneath the thin white sheet that covered both of them up to their nipples, and squeezed his thigh affectionately. "You okay, baby?" she asked.

They'd known each other three weeks, having met after inadvertently locking eyes when she was walking through the bar area of Skip the Sandbrusher, a popular chain of tropical-themed restaurants which employed her as general counsel and routinely supplied him with drinks. Since then they'd engaged in many rounds of vivacious lovemaking (the most recent of which had concluded just before Matt's brief snooze) and had shared a few other activities as well.

Matt smiled, leaned over and kissed her. "Vickie, I am better than okay," he said. "I'm great!"

He rolled over, swung his legs off the side of the bed, and stood up, giving her a perfect view of his pasty white, barely existent buttocks. "I just remembered something so cool!"

"Oh yeah?" She smiled and sat up in the bed, pulling her knees up to her chest beneath the sheet and wrapping her arms around them. "What is it?"

"Well," said Matt, rummaging around in a massive pile of random objects in the corner of his extraordinarily messy bedroom, "you know how I love Marion, right?"

Victoria giggled. "The old-time movie actress?"

"Yeah. So it turns out…" Matt caught sight of an old pocket address book lying on a low shelf next to where he was crouching. "Hmm, could that be it?" He grabbed it and began flipping through.

Waiting for him to become undistracted, Victoria glanced around the room and started examining the various pennants Matt kept on his walls, which she'd never looked closely at before. Each bore the name and standard color(s) of some institution or franchise. A few included a little logo next to the name. Dodgers, Lakers, Kings, Rams. CuppaJoe, Barney's Beanery, LaBrea Bakery. UCLA, USC, Loyola Marymount. One banner puzzled her: "UPS" in gold lettering on a brown background.

"Wait, UPS?" she said.

Matt had discarded the little black book after determining it didn't contain what he sought, crawled to a different corner of the room and begun sifting through a different large pile of random objects.

"Yeah, my alma mater," he said. "A lot of good times." He stopped his search momentarily and stared into space, smiling and reminiscing.

"Alma mater?"

"Yep. Good old University of the Pacific Southwest. I went there after I finished at UCLA." He resumed sifting through the pile.

"Oh, right! So what'd you get your degree in?"

"Degree? Hey, here it is!"

Matt reached into a cardboard box containing various cleaning supplies including a bucket, inside of which were dozens of golf balls and billiard balls and one clay pot (of the very sort he'd once thought in passing he might like to create and sell on the boardwalk), inside of which were individually wrapped pieces of bubble gum, multi-colored mechanical pencils, a variety of coins, and a different little black book, this one technically a little blue book. He pulled it out and held it up triumphantly, letting out a small gleeful laugh.

Victoria laughed too. "What are you up to, you silly goose?"

As he thumbed through the book, Matt stood up and walked back toward the bed, all his bits dangling and swinging.

"My girlfriend Lonnie," he said, then, reaching the desired entry, "Yep! Found her."

He flopped back down onto the bed. "Can I borrow your phone?" he asked.

"Sure, baby."

She turned away, leaned over and retrieved it from the top of a cardboard box doubling as a nightstand, receiving a slap on the butt from Matt in the process, then turned back toward him, grinning, and handed it to him.

"Thanks, gorgeous."

Matt swiped the screen to discover that it was protected by a thumbprint lock. "Oh," he said, "uh, looks like I'm gonna need to borrow your thumb, too."

"Oh, really?" Victoria chuckled. "Well you're going to have to say the magic words, then."

Matt raised an eyebrow. "Magic words, eh? Hmm, let's see… Abracadabra?"

"Nope. Lame."

"Uh… Open sesame?"

"Better. But no."

He paused a couple of seconds, then, "I love your big, beautiful… brain?"

She laughed. "Good enough," she said, extending her thumb and unlocking the device.

"Much obliged, little lady!" said Matt, then brought up the telephone keypad and began transcribing the digits from the little book propped open in his other hand.

Victoria turned away again, slid out from under the sheet and stood up. "I'm going to take a shower," she said as she headed for the bedroom door.

"I hate to see you go, but I love to watch you leave!" Matt replied as he hit the dial button.

Lonnie Andersson was walking across a concrete courtyard just outside the observatory building in Griffith Park, where she worked as a tour guide and facilitator/greeter/usher, when her phone rang. If available to talk, she always answered every call immediately, without even looking at the screen to see if it was a known contact (or even a known area code or prefix).

"Hello, it's Lonnie!" she said, as always.

"Lonnie! It's so great to hear your voice, you sexy thing."

"Why thank you," she replied. "Uh, who is this?"

"This is Matt Spratt!"

"Oh my god—Matt! So awesome to hear from you! How long's it been?"

It had been just over 18 months. They'd met six months before that, when playing on adjacent lanes at Hollywood Bowl (the bowling alley, not the concert venue). Matt had abruptly struck up a conversation, causing Lonnie to throw a gutter ball. A torrid affair had ignited that very night and had blazed, full strength, for 9½ weeks, at which point it had entered an ever so gradual, but persistent, cooling-off phase. Nothing about the relationship had ever been made official (or even discussed), and the last time they'd seen each other, neither of them had realized it would be the last time.

"No kidding!" said Matt. "Too long, too long. Hey, what are you up to?"

"Well, right now I'm about to grab lunch. You're lucky you caught me, actually—I'm busy all day long except for this, like, 20-minute window when I dash out to the food truck."

"It's not luck, darling. I have a special, sort of psychic, connection with people. Like a sixth sense."

She laughed. "Oh Matt, you crack me up."

"What?" said Matt, chuckling himself. "I do. Seriously."

He'd been on the move during their conversation, the phone pinned between his tilted head and raised shoulder. After donning his paper-thin polyester bathrobe, he'd made his way into the kitchen, where he'd grabbed a joint, a lighter, and a package of Twinkies, then continued on through into the living room, where the T.V. was currently showing images of smiling Californians holding up Prop 65 warning placards, and playing the jingle "Get the signage you love at C-A-dot-gov!"

This was one of many commercials the state government had produced to promote a new online store—through which enthusiasts could purchase a specimen of absolutely any type of object the state owned—that had been launched recently in an effort to recover the revenue sacrificed when the gasoline tax had been reduced by 1% (five cents per gallon).

"So, what's on the menu?" Matt asked Lonnie as he plopped himself down on one of his disgusting couches.

"Either Mexican or Greek. I won't know until I get there. See, on the best stretch of curb there's only enough room for one truck. And they keep the area coned off until 11 every day." As she spoke she heard the flick of a lighter come through the phone line, then nothing for several seconds, then the sound of a long exhale.

"Then some park employee comes out and removes the cones, and there are these two food trucks who fight it out for the spot. I mean, they like, literally fight over it. Almost every single day."

"Hah! That's wild!" said Matt.

"Yeah. One time the Greek driver actually smashed his truck into the Mexican one."

"Holy Toledo." He took another drag on his joint.

"You can't make this stuff up."

"No, sir-ee. Hey, Lonnie, I need to get my hands on a super-old tape from CBS News. Doesn't your cousin work in the vault over there?"

Lonnie laughed. "My cousin Britt did work in their archive department. But she got fired a few months ago, for leaking copies of old T.V. footage."

"Aw, bummer!"

"Yeah. They take that stuff pretty seriously."

"Hey, maybe she still has her key or whatever and she could go back in for one more heist. They can't fire her twice!"

"No, their security is tight. I doubt she could get within ten yards of the front gate without them knowing it.”

“Hmm…” Another puff on the joint.

“Oh, but hey!” exclaimed Lonnie suddenly. “I just remembered. My other cousin, Tad—he's not Britt's brother, he's like, on the totally opposite side of my family, my mom's side—anyway, Tad has this friend, Chris…”

“And he works for CBS?”

“She. Chris is a girl. But no, Chris doesn't work there. But Chris has this cousin, Jamie…”

“And she works for CBS?”

“He. Jamie is a guy. But yeah, Jamie works for CBS.”

“Cool. In the archives?”

“Yeah, yeah, totally.”

“Sweet.”

“And I've heard Jamie is pretty nuts, so… he probably isn't worried about, you know… getting fired.”

“So you think you can hook me up?”

“Yeah, I think so. Just give me a day or two. Ah, it's Mexican.” Lonnie had just arrived in the food truck curb area. She took her place at the back of the rather long line.

Matt chuckled delightedly. “Aw, this is great. Thanks a million, Lonnie.”

“Sure thing. So what is this old footage you want, anyways?”

“Lonnie, I have discovered the most majestic creature who ever graced this earth. A human angel. Her name is Marion Davies. And I'm finding out all of her secrets!”

“The old-time movie star Marion Davies?”

“The very one.”

Lonnie laughed. “Oh, Matt. You always did know how to waste time.”

“One man's trash is another man's treasure,” Matt replied, then laughed at the unintentional extreme relevance of his word choice.

He continued: “I mean, the value of how we spend our time, it's… in the eye of the time spender, I think. If one person spends an hour reading great literature or studying science, and someone else spends an hour admiring and memorizing every sublime curve of Marion's lustrous face… Well, both of them are one hour more… enriched, you know? One hour more experienced in life. So there's really no such thing as wasting time, is there?”

"Yes there is, Matt."

Three mornings later at 8:48, Yvonne Smede, sitting behind the wheel of the ATS, turned off Jefferson Boulevard onto a long, winding driveway bounded on both sides by a sprawling, neatly manicured lawn. The driveway entrance was flanked by two large objects: on the right, a combination sign/logo/sculpture/fountain featuring the words "Shady Oaks" in huge letters, the words "Luxury Assisted Maturity Estate" in smaller letters underneath, and an artistic rendering of two oak trees bearing a peculiar resemblance to a giant pair of breasts draped in a giant piece of lingerie; on the left, an actual oak tree (just one, and in fact the only one on the entire property).

After passing by a few scattered palm trees, and crossing a tightly packed line of fir trees, the driveway opened up into a roughly square-shaped parking lot covering nine acres of land and containing 1,300 spaces (not including the special ones for buses), over a thousand of which were currently empty (which, though expected, brought a smile to Yvonne's face upon seeing it). On the far side of the lot, opposite the trees, stood a very wide, vaguely gothic-looking, sand-colored building with three-story sections on the sides and a ten-story tower in the middle, all levels of all sections covered with dozens of small windows. On the northern border of the lot (to Yvonne's left) was what amounted to a miniature train station but for golf carts. Lined up along the southern border were fifteen little bungalows, white with brown tile roofs.

Yvonne made her way toward the big gothic building, weaving a bit here and there but mainly just driving in a straight line over rows of empty spaces. As L.A. car journeys went, it didn't get much better than this one—traffic was relatively light between the condo (five miles to the northwest) and here at this hour on a Saturday, and Shady Oaks was her only destination in the entire county offering convenient, plentiful parking. Technically it was free, too, but Yvonne regarded it as simply rolled up into the exorbitant price tag of the whole residential package.

The Shady Oaks campus was located in Culver City, an actual city in its own right (unlike nearby poser Century City) belonging to a funky-shaped pocket of territory, measuring about nine square miles, surrounded on all sides by the city of Los Angeles, whose other members were a few small, unincorporated communities with names ending in "Hills" or "Heights" and a collection of sparsely populated mini-mountains littered with oil derricks. La Cienega Boulevard, one of L.A.'s major arteries, ran north-south through the pocket, linking the swanky neighborhoods above the 10 with the region adjacent to America's shittiest airport.

Pulling into a spot right at the edge of the lot, not far from the main entrance, Yvonne briefly flashed back to the thorny situation she'd masterfully negotiated seven years ago, maneuvering her father into an apartment here shortly after they'd opened their doors. Not only had she succeeded, through a series of cleverly crafted conversations, in convincing him that it was his own idea to move down to California and submit to a slightly assisted, but still largely independent, lifestyle. She'd also managed to wrangle a one-bedroom for the list price of a studio. Shady Oaks had been struggling to attract residents following their ill-advised grand opening ad campaign, which had targeted the other major senior community in Culver City—ritzy, full-of-itself, horrendously overpriced The Hill. The ads had described Shady Oaks as "a place for people who are over The Hill."

As Yvonne got out of her car and headed for the curb, she was dimly aware of another Cadillac ATS parked in the spot to her left, and an elderly white man with dark hair climbing into it. As she stepped up onto the concrete, she noticed a sign, posted in front of that space, reading "Reserved for Dr. Eckles."

Matthias Eckles was a physician, specializing in geriatric medicine, who both lived and worked at Shady Oaks. As a young man, he'd dreamed of being old, and he considered this current era the most glorious of his whole life. Eckles had never treated Albert Forrester, so Yvonne knew nothing about him, and accordingly proceeded toward the building without another thought.

Among those familiar with him, however, Dr. Eckles was univer-sally regarded as intelligent, caring, skilled, and very, very eccentric. One of his numerous oddities was an abhorrence of all personal security measures, and a firm belief that they were not just unnecessary, but a sinister and corrupting influence that bred mistrust, cynicism and paranoia. As such, he never password-protected anything that had the option of not doing so, never locked his bungalow, and had his car customized so the push-button start would always work, with or without the key fob that he'd thrown in a drawer long ago and forgotten about. The man Yvonne had just seen, who was now driving away as she strode diagonally across the stone quadrangle that lay between the curb and the building entrance, was not Matthias Eckles.

Out of the corner of her eye, Yvonne caught a glimpse of a bench-back ad she'd seen before (on bus stop benches all over the Westside) informing its audience that "sensory sensitivity is a sign of autism." The ad always reminded her of Bill, with his million different auditory and visual irritants that he could never seem to restrain himself from loudly reacting to and complaining about. She thought about how nice it would be not to share a bedroom with him. He'd always insisted on running various fans during the night, to drown out all the random little sounds that startled and annoyed him and disrupted his attempts to sleep, and in recent times he'd added an actual white noise machine to the mix. Yvonne hated it.

As she passed through the doorway into the main lobby of the building, she smiled and muttered to herself, "He's definitely on the spectrum."

Gramps was sitting in his easy chair, intently watching a 1962 episode of the long-running T.V. series "Gunsmoke," when he heard a knock on his door.

He hit the mute button on the remote he was already clutching in his hand, then shouted, "I told you folks before—I don't need any turn-down service. I get turned down all the time. Hah!"

"Dad, it's me," came Yvonne's voice from the hallway outside.

"Oh," he said, hopping out of the chair and making for the door. "Hello, darling. Coming. I wasn't expecting you just yet."

He opened the door and, as he'd done every time he'd seen his daughter throughout her entire life, placed his hands on her shoulders, leaned forward, and planted a quick kiss on her cheek. Then he spun around and headed back into the apartment, saying "Come on in."

Yvonne did come in, and shut the door with her right hand as she glanced at the time (and accompanying (disappointing) step count) displayed on her left wrist. "I thought we said nine?" she queried.

Gramps was settling back into his chair. "Yeah, that's right," he said, then paused and gave her a puzzled look. "Is it nine already? Wow. Doesn't feel like it at all."

Yvonne had followed her father into the main living area and was idly surveying her surroundings, unconsciously scanning for confirmations or warning signs regarding his day-to-day living habits, as well as choosing where to sit.

He continued, "You know how, on a weather thing, they have the real temperature, and then they have the 'feels like' temperature. You know, because it might be 80 degrees in reality, but the humidity makes it feel like 85."

"Uh-huh," Yvonne affirmed as she took a seat in the center of a small sofa, in between a stack of magazines and another stack of magazines. Gramps had always been a magazine lover, maintaining at least a dozen subscriptions at any given time. From a quick glance at these stacks and several similar ones on nearby tables and shelves, Yvonne surmised that Popular Science, Road & Track, Penthouse, Guns & Ammo, and Cigar Aficionado were (still) among his favorite titles. Behind his back she referred to them as "fantasy fuel."

"Well, they should have that same feature on a clock. The 'feels like' feature. See, right now, it's really nine o'clock but it feels like it's only half past seven. Hah! Get it?"

"Yeah, Dad." She smiled. "But on a clock that feature wouldn't be much use, because you already know what time it feels like, right?"

Gramps, uninterested in feedback on this, had already moved on. "So, Billy didn't come with you today..." he asked/stated.

"Uh, no," Yvonne replied, slightly unnerved. Could he possibly know? No, don't be silly. "He never comes here with me, Dad."

"Just as well," said Gramps, flashing a judgmental frown as he momentarily imagined his son-in-law standing there in the room with them. "What about my granddaughter? Sure would love to see that sweet little face of hers."

"She's... she and Patrick both, they're, uh, pretty busy today."

Gramps narrowed his eyes and cocked one brow, radiating suspicion in Yvonne's direction.

"They both send their love," she added.

"Come on, darling, who do you think you're talking to here? You don't have to blow smoke up my ass. I know they both think visiting Gramps is boring as hell."

She smiled. "It's nothing personal, Dad. They think everything is boring. Except their stupid kid stuff."

"Yep, you said it," he replied, chuckling. "So listen, how 'bout some breakfast? I'm starving."

"Sure, sounds good," said Yvonne with a tiny bit of hesitation. She'd noted, on her way in, the state of her father's kitchen—immaculate from lack of use, as always. They would definitely not be dining here in his apartment.

"Let's go to Howard's House. It's fantastic. You ever been there?"

"Yes, of course."

She'd been there many times, all of them with Gramps and all of them miserable experiences. Howard's House was an extremely popular (Yvonne couldn't fathom why) greasy spoon diner located in the heart of downtown Culver City, where parking was guaranteed to be a nightmare. In addition to the long wait time for a table, it featured terrible service, uncomfortable seats, high prices, and a menu containing nothing she liked to eat. The on-site Shady Oaks cafeteria, by contrast, was never crowded and offered semi-decent chairs and remarkably tasty food at astonishingly low prices.

"But what about the cafeteria?" she suggested. "It's pretty good."

"What?! No it's not. It's complete crap. Besides, I might run into Loretta there." Yvonne had never gotten it straight exactly what had happened between her father and Loretta, and never wanted to.

"Okay," she said with a sigh. "Let's go to Howard's House."

"Yep, you'll love it," said Gramps. "I think I'm going to get myself one of their bran muffins. I haven't taken a shit in four days."

———————

The next morning at 10:02, Lester Chiminsky, a 41-year-old white man with a wildly unkempt, dark red-brown beard and mustache and receding orange hair on top (pulled back into a foot-long ponytail), dressed in flip-flops, denim cut-offs, a size XXL black t-shirt with an image of famed Star Wars character Chewbacca on the front stretched taut over his belly, and a dark red satin cowboy vest, stood just inside the main door of County Line Comics, fumbling with his key, trying to unlock the deadbolt. He'd recently been named Senior Assistant Manager and entrusted with opening the store each day (as well as closing it each night). Although Lester prided himself on his punctuality, this morning he'd fallen prey to the nearly irresistible distraction of a stack of just-delivered "Duty Bound 8: Rogue State Armageddon" promotional posters, and was thus running a couple of minutes late.

Doesn't matter, he thought as the bolt finally slid back, unlinking the two halves of the door. Nobody ever shows up before noon. But he pushed it open anyway and took one step out into the slightly muggy late August heat for a quick left-right scan of the sidewalk, and got a huge start. Five feet away, immersed in Phone World, stood one of his oldest, dearest friends.

"Jacob T. Lee, as I live and breathe!" Lester exclaimed.

This nickname had been coined more than two decades ago and neither man could remember now the logic behind it. Jake's actual first name was just Jake, not Jacob, and his middle name didn't begin with T.

He looked up from his phone and flashed a huge grin at Lester. Then he looked back down at the phone for another 20 seconds, finishing up what he'd been doing. Then he looked up again, the same huge grin still on his face.

"Les, my main man!" he exclaimed, striding toward his buddy.

Jake wore white high-tops, dark blue track pants with red stripes down the sides, and a size XXXL black t-shirt with an image of a different Star Wars character on the front; no vest. The two men fist-bumped and then briefly embraced. Lester laughed with delight, slapping Jake on the back.

"Come on in, my friend. What a nice surprise! What brings you to my little neck of the woods this fine morning?"

As they went inside, Jake said "Aw, man, seeing you and just... being here, it's just so... the best. It's just so cool."

"Damn right it is," Lester replied, instinctively strolling across the sales floor, past bins and racks of merchandise, toward his standard perch behind the counter. "A celebration is always in order whenever the old S.C. posse is reunited!"

The two had founded Sex Club when Jake was 16 and Lester was 17. It had never had any other members. Ostensibly its initial purpose had been to facilitate and promote the sort of activities its name implied (which neither boy had ever engaged in outside of his imagination), but in practice it had mainly involved playing video games and griping about all the stuck-up bitches and jock douchebags who populated their school. Within two months of its inception, the club had been reduced to a meaningless acronym that simply symbolized their friendship, but it had stayed with them in that form ever since.

"This place is just..." said Jake, following behind, still grinning broadly, swinging his head left and right, taking in all the decorative items—plastic statues and cardboard cut-outs standing on the floor, posters pinned up on the walls, action toys dangling by threads from the ceiling. "Hey, do you guys sell any toys or models, or... or games?"

"Nah," said Lester as they reached the counter. "You'd think I'd have some say in all that. Been lobbying the old man since..." He assumed his position next to the register as Jake planted himself in the customer's spot, both leaning forward, forearms resting on the counter. "Hell, since forever! Since *his* old man was running the place way back in the day."

"Yeah!" said Jake, giggling.

County Line Comics, located on a section of Bloomfield Street forming the boundary between the cities of Hawaiian Gardens and Cypress, had existed much longer than Jake and Lester had. They'd enthusiastically patronized it throughout their teens and early twenties, all the while fantasizing about working here. But "Hotchner & Son" (Sammy and his ludicrously ancient father, Sam Senior) didn't hire just anyone. They maintained a very small, very elite staff, and never had any shortage of well-qualified applicants. The older you were, the better. They had a strict and vaguely suspicious 21+ rule (nobody had ever discovered the reasoning) but hadn't been known to take on anybody under 25, and very few under 30. By the time Lester had proudly joined these noble ranks at the age of 28, Jake was married and had moved up to L.A., following his wife in her high-flying I.T. career.

Lester continued, "Lord knows those folks would love to have our business. Always sending us flyers and posters and letters and..."

"Awesome!" said Jake.

"But the old man says those arrangements are too complicated, plus he doesn't have the right 'sales know-how' for it." (The words "sales know-how" were spoken in a special, mocking tone.) "He wants to keep it simple. Just comics."

Jake, shaking his head and chuckling, said, "Wow... just..."

"So anyway," said Lester, "how you been? How's Amy and..."

"Pretty good."

"Is it two kids now?"

"Yep. Pretty good, pretty good. Two kids. We're all doing good."

"That's cool. And how's work going?"

"Oh! Don't even get me started about work! That place..."

"You still at that same place?"

"Yep, Zoroft's. Still there. But, I'm tellin' ya... just... maybe not for much longer." He laughed.

Jake had been in his current job, as a Senior Assistant Manager on the factory floor of Zoroft's (a virtually unknown maker-for-hire of licensed plush toys, whose services were sought by the owners of many well known brands), for nine months. The last time he'd spoken with Lester (which was long after the birth of Brandon, Jake's younger child), he'd been employed in a similar capacity for It-Scrap, a supplier of sheet metal.

He went on, "Some of the jokers I have to deal with..."

"Tell me about it," said Lester. "Well, the other employees are cool, and the dealers are too, mostly. But some of our customers, holy crap..."

Jake laughed again. "Yep, I can, just... I can imagine..."

"You know, I'd love to believe that having a serious appreciation for comics was a guarantee of strong character, but sadly, it is not."

"Oh! You know what I do, to judge a person's character? I developed this thing I call the fart test." He smiled proudly and mischievously, and flexed his eyebrows.

Lester raised one of his own eyebrows and said "Okay..."

"See, how it works is, you fart when you're standing right next to them. You just... go for it, you know. Just, loud and, obvious and... You don't try to hide it. And you don't say anything. Like you don't say 'excuse me' or... just, nothing. You just fart and you just keep standing there, right next to them."

"Mmm-hmm..." Lester was nodding and grinning.

"And then you just... See, the hard part is over now. You just have to not get embarrassed about the fart. And then you just... observe, you know. Observe their reaction. You can learn *so* much about someone from how they react in a situation like that..."

"Yeah, definitely."

"I mean, just... You've just, put them in a very difficult situation." Still smiling, he reached up and tapped his temple with his finger. "Very clever."

Jake had never actually performed the fart test, yet, but he loved the idea of it and felt confident that one of these days, when the time and place (and test subject) were right, he would go for it.

Lester chuckled and shook his head, momentarily imagining the scenario his friend had just described. Then he moved on. "So, what brings you in here today, my man? Just visiting me, or...?"

"Yes, yes! Just visiting you, my man. But also... I am looking for... drumroll, please... Field Marshal Wield-Partial... Number Zero!"

"Seriously?"

"I'm dead serious. I want it. I gotta have it!" He laughed.

"Wow."

"So, you got it here?"

"Hell, no. You know how rare that thing is?"

"Yeah, I figured it was rare!"

"We hardly get any rarities here. I hate to say it, but you'd have a better chance looking in some of the shops up there by where you live, like downtown L.A. and stuff."

"Right!"

"But, you know, thinking about it... Even those places, the odds could be awfully slim..."

"Oh, really?" Jake smiled at this information even though it was bad news.

"Do you care what condition it's in?"

"Oh—mint. Definitely, just..."

"Okay, well—"

"It just has to be mint condition, man." He was chuckling as he spoke. "I just, don't accept any comics if they're not in mint condition."

"Okay, well—"

"Yeah... no... just..."

"Let me do some checking around for ya."

"Yeah, cool!"

"But, no promises. I mean, it might just not exist, for sale, anywhere."

"Right!"

"Hey," said Lester, "you remember 'The Matrix'? I mean the original."

"Yes! I love that movie," Jake replied eagerly.

"And there was also this other movie, came out around the same time, called 'Thirteenth Floor'..."

"Yeah!"

"The basic idea—"

"No, wait—actually I don't think I remember that one."

"Well the basic idea was the same—the world as we know it is just an illusion, you know, created by a computer."

"Right! Awesome!"

"So, just recently, I discovered this new graphic novel... I swear I've got it around here somewhere..." Lester quickly scanned the countertop and the shelves underneath but didn't spot it. "Anyway, it's like the same idea, too, but... taken to the next level."

"Cool!"

"It's just, so powerful. So powerful. And it has really, like, sparked my mind." He performed the same finger-to-temple gesture executed by his friend two minutes ago.

Jake was grinning and nodding enthusiastically.

"Got me doing some deep thinking. I mean, *deep* thinking. And I've realized something."

Jake waited excitedly as Lester paused for dramatic effect.

"It's all true! It has to be. Not with computers—it's much bigger than that. It includes all of time and all of space as we know it."

"Wow."

"Yeah, our entire universe was engineered... well, whatever 'was' even means outside of the concept of time... 'is' or 'was' or whatever. All of space-time is just an illusion. Just a simulation. Controlled by sentient beings the likes of which..." He directed his gaze toward the ceiling and moved his hands slowly back and forth in front of his chest in a vaguely mystical fashion. "...we could never possibly hope to comprehend."

Jake was impressed. "Wow," he said again. "It's so cool you were able to figure that out!"

Exactly four hours after this revelation, 26 miles to the northwest of County Line Comics, Bill Smede, whose butt had recently arrived on a couch in Matt Spratt's living room, snapped loudly at his friend: "Matt, Jesus! Could we *please* turn that thing off?"

Matt had been mid-sentence, but Bill couldn't stand it any longer, and anyway he had no idea what Matt had been saying because his brain was incapable of separating those sounds from the ones coming out of the always-on T.V. set (and, for the same reason, he had no idea what was on it, either).

Matt, seated next to Bill, laughed and said, "Oh, Bill," then took a bite from the very large, very old-looking slice of cold pizza he was holding, set it down on the couch armrest, stood up, and headed over to the T.V.

Bill's brain could now process the fact that the T.V. was playing an episode of the popular 1980s sitcom "Diff'rent Strokes." I think I saw this one when it first aired, he idly thought.

"I'll turn it down, but not off," said Matt, repeatedly pressing a little button on the side of the screen. As promised, the volume decreased significantly.

"You need this, dude," he continued. "Trust me. It's your... therapy."

"Thanks," said Bill in a tone that cast some doubt on just how grateful he actually felt.

Matt plopped back down on the sofa. "So anyway, how are things with you, man?" he asked.

"Mmm, pretty good."

"How's Vonnie doing?"

Bill hesitated, then began stammering. "Uh, well... she's... fine..."

Matt didn't speak because he'd just bitten off another mouthful of pizza, but his facial expression indicated that he could tell something was going on and wanted to know what it was.

"Uh," Bill went on, "see, she and I... We, uh... We're splitting up."

Matt went bug-eyed, hurriedly and prematurely swallowed his food, and cried out, "Holy Toledo! What?!? Dude, that's insane!"

"Yeah, I know," said Bill, slowly shaking his head, eyes aimed slightly downward at nothing as he searched his thoughts.

"Are you serious?"

"Yeah."

"Why? What happened?"

"Well, nothing, really." Bill clenched his teeth, wrinkled his forehead and rolled his eyes upward as he concentrated on untangling this subject in his mind. "We just… I just don't think Yvonne and I are very… compatible."

"Oh, come on, that's a bunch of B.S. You two are super compatible!"

"Yeah, I know we are, in some ways. But it's just… Maybe compatibility isn't the right word for it. But there's something not right between us. We have this way of… getting under each other's skin and paralyzing ourselves. Paralyzing our communication with each other."

Matt was listening intently. He'd completely lost interest in his pizza. "Hmm," he said. "I know you guys don't always talk to each other about stuff, but…"

"We've really devolved lately." Now Bill was looking down at the floor and shaking his head.

"How so? What's been going on?"

Bill looked up. "Well… It started a few weeks back. Maybe like a month ago. Yvonne was cold-shouldering me. It might've been… I think I remember, one night around that time, we had a small disagreement and I think I pissed her off. So, *maybe* that could've been what started it. But… I sort of… I started noticing that she wasn't speaking to me, and that she always seemed kind of sullen and angry whenever I was around her. And initially I thought… I don't know what I thought. Like, maybe it was nothing, or maybe she'd explain, or… maybe it was just, you know, temporary, and it'd just blow over and go away soon. But she just kept it up, day after day…"

Matt wore a slightly incredulous (and ever so mildly amused) face. "Why didn't you just ask her what it was?"

"I don't know. I hate that. I… I guess it's partly that I'm scared. You know—of how she'll respond. Scared she'll… bite my head off, or… tell me something I don't want to hear, or something I don't agree with… It's nerve-wracking."

Matt nodded.

Bill paused for a moment, then continued. "But the other part is, I get... sort of resentful, I guess? Like, I... don't really think it's... fair of her. You know, giving me the silent treatment with no explanation. And especially when, *probably*, what sparked it was just some tiny little thing I said or did. She gets offended really easily. And when she *gets* offended, she *stays* offended."

Another pause, then: "So I guess I felt like, it was on her, to say something. To get that dialogue going. Not on me."

Neither man spoke for a few seconds, as Matt nodded again and processed what he'd heard.

"Okay," he said then, "so what else happened? You didn't just say you guys were having some trouble. You said you were splitting up!" He reached for a lighter and joint lying in an ashtray on a side table.

"Well, I finally did say something to her. Or tried to, anyway. I—"

"Oh!" Matt suddenly said. "You should have some of this." He held out the lighter and joint toward Bill.

"No, thanks."

"Ya sure?" Matt smiled and raised both eyebrows. "It'll help." He winked.

"Yeah, yeah, I'm sure," said Bill. "That stuff just isn't my cup of tea. Thanks, though."

"Sure, man." Matt lit up and took a puff. "Anyway, you were saying, you talked to her...?"

"Right. So, after like a week and a half of this cold shoulder stuff, I finally got up the nerve to try to broach the whole thing with her."

Matt was taking a long drag but keeping his eyes fixed on Bill's.

"But... it did *not* go well."

Matt exhaled. "Why? What did you say?"

"I told her that I didn't like the way things had been... Well, actually I think I called it the way *she'd* been."

Subtle facial expressions were exchanged by the friends, Matt's conveying a tiny bit of judgment, Bill's ashamed acceptance of that judgment.

"And, uh, I told her that she had anger issues."

"Oh, Bill."

"No, but listen. I followed that by saying that we really should try to talk this stuff out."

"And what did she say?"

"Nothing. But she might not have heard me. She was already going out the front door by that time."

"Yikes."

"And I said I was sorry for everything. But she was long gone by then."

Matt smiled and shook his head, then took another drag.

Bill smiled, too. "Patrick might've heard me, though," he said. "He came out to get a snack right around that time."

"Okay," said Matt, "so she walked out. Then what happened?"

"Then..."—Bill sucked in air like he was in pain, and scrunched up his face—"things escalated."

"How so?"

"She was gone for a really long time. I'd assumed she was taking a long walk. Eventually I went down to use the car to go grab a few things from Hank's, and I discovered she'd taken the car. So then *I* went for a long walk. A *very* long walk. Like three hours. Finally I ended up at The Filthy Burro, sitting at the bar, drinking old fashioneds."

"All this time you never tried to call her?"

"No."

"Or even text her?"

"No."

"Oh, Bill."

"Anyway, by the time I got home, it was really late. Everyone had already gone to bed. And, Yvonne had put the chain lock on, so I couldn't open the front door of the condo. So I called Alice and she came and let me in. Then, Yvonne had also locked our bedroom door. So I crashed on the couch."

Matt was chuckling now. "Okay," he said. "What happened the next morning?"

"Nothing. Well, the next morning I discovered she'd also poured candle wax into my good bourbon decanter. But interactions-wise, nothing. I mean, truly nothing. Like, before that night it was next-to-nothing, but after that, absolutely nothing. We stopped coordinating on meals, or... anything. All communication ceased. We basically stopped ever being in the same room at the same time."

"So you're now a permanent couch-sleeper..."

"Actually, no. That's just not an option for me. I can't stand the couch. Can't sleep worth a shit on it."

Matt laughed. "So, what, Vonnie moved to the couch?"

"Nope. Still sharing a bed. There's just, like, an invisible wall going down the middle of it."

More chuckling, and another puff on the joint. "So what else? I thought you said you split up."

"Yeah, so, a few days ago, she suddenly called me. During the workday. I guess she was at the office. I couldn't believe it when I saw the call come in. Shocked the fuck out of me. I was scared. Scared of talking to her, of course, but also I thought, if she's calling, it must be something really serious, like something happened to one of the kids. But then I thought, how would she know about that before me?"

Matt laughed again, louder. "You're a trip, Bill. What did she say?"

"She said she'd been thinking about it and she thought we should separate."

"And what did you say?"

"I said, yeah, I agree. We should."

"Oh, Bill."

"Well I do agree! Things just aren't right with us, Matt. We're... I don't think we're right for each other."

Matt was momentarily silent. Then he lowered his eyes, shook his head and quietly said, almost to himself, "Jeez. This is the dumbest one yet."

Since they'd first begun dating each other in 1999 (after meeting in a software training class at the company Bill worked for at the time), Yvonne and Bill had broken up somewhere between four and eleven times (depending on the definition of "broken up"), including one that involved getting legally divorced (and, later, legally remarried). The official underlying causes (which Matt regarded as less dumb than the current one) had included: Bill's infidelity, Yvonne's infidelity, disputes over raising Patrick, disputes over raising Alice, disputes over money, and a dispute over whether to remain in L.A. or move to Seattle. (To Matt's immense relief, Bill had ultimately prevailed on that last one.)

"Anyway, enough about me," said Bill. "Let's talk about you. You and your big romantic quest. That's the whole reason you invited me over, right?"

Matt looked up, eyes sparkling, an excited grin on his face.

"Yes!" he cried, then stood, extinguished his joint in the ashtray, and speedily made for the opposite side of the room where, Bill noticed for the first time, sat a contraption consisting of a five-feet-long metallic cylinder perched horizontally atop a triangular set of legs about three feet tall.

Matt was talking the entire time as he prepared the contraption, which turned out to be a retractable screen, for use. "This guy Jamie—he works at CBS, Lonnie's cousin's friend's cousin—what a godsend! He kicks ass. He really came through for me. Fast, too!"

Having set up the screen, he was now heading over to the projector sitting on a big, industrial-looking wheely cart parked next to the couch (which Bill had noticed the moment he arrived but hadn't gotten around to asking about).

"You know how I wanted to get my hands on that old interview?"

"Yeah," Bill said.

"Well, Jamie got it for me! How awesome is that?"

Matt flipped a switch on the side of the projector and it came to life with lights and a low humming sound. Then he flipped another switch and both reels began spinning very quickly, rewinding the film they held from the rear one back to the front. "He could've just put it on a thumb drive for me—they've digitized everything up through like 1984. Pretty cool, eh?"

"Yeah."

Now Matt was flitting around the room, turning off lamps and shutting curtains (and turning the T.V. volume much further down, but still leaving it on).

"But this is even cooler! I was in luck—the original film was scheduled for destruction but they hadn't actually done it yet. Jamie found it stacked up in some, like big warehouse-type room, somewhere down in the catacombs, you know?"

He arrived back at his spot on the couch. "And he even offered to loan me the projector and the screen. Brought all the stuff right to my doorstep in the back of his pickup!"

"Wow," said Bill. "And he did all this for free?"

"Yep. Well, I did flow a little green his way, as a token of my appreciation."

The rewinding process ended with a loud click and Matt leapt up again. "And I don't mean money," he said, winking at Bill as he glided past.

"Now," he announced in a booming, officious voice as he took his place at the projector controls, "without any further ado, I give you... the interview!"

He flipped a switch, the reels began turning, much slower this time, and a beam of light shot out across the room onto the screen. Simultaneously, a speaker protruding from the front of the projector emitted some chaotic scratching noises. These subsided after a couple of seconds and an image appeared on the screen.

Two white men were sitting across from each other in easy chairs on a sound stage. Both had hair that seemed too big and long but had clearly been very precisely styled, and both wore plaid suits with extremely wide ties.

The younger man, whom Bill vaguely felt he recognized from long, long ago, turned toward the camera and said, "We're taking a look back at the Marion Davies Children's Clinic at UCLA, which began its life 25 years ago this week, when the former Hollywood actress made a two-million-dollar donation to the university for the purpose of creating it."

"She was the best," gushed Matt.

"Sadly, Miss Davies is no longer with us. But, sitting here with me now is a man who knew her very well, independent film producer Bart Holstedt. Mr. Holstedt, thank you for taking the time to join us here today."

"My pleasure," said the other man, who looked to be in his sixties.

"To start with," said the interviewer, "tell us about your relationship with Marion Davies. How did you meet?"

"We met through mutual acquaintances in the industry. I believe the first time we met was at a dinner party. This was a long time ago, probably in the late twenties or early thirties. I was a young man. I really hadn't done anything yet, but I knew some people through my father."

"Some would argue that you still haven't really done anything."

Bart gave a small, forced laugh and said, "Indeed."

"I'm only teasing," said the interviewer. "Please, go on."

"Well Marion and I, we really hit it off. There was a chemistry between us. Not romantic chemistry, but, we became close, very close, in a very quick but natural fashion. She was sort of like a big sister, or an aunt, to me."

"That's fananananananan"—the image froze for a couple of seconds, then was gradually erased from the screen by a curling ring that began in the center and grew outward to the edges as the film melted— "anananananananananan—"

"Crap!" exclaimed Matt, and turned off the projector.

Bill, who'd correctly surmised that this interview lasted well over an hour, felt relieved and thought, Maybe God does exist and he loves me.

"Well, no biggie," said Matt, heading for a nearby window to re-open its curtains. "I've pretty much memorized the whole thing anyway! I swear, I must've watched it, like, ten times. Hey, you want a beer?"

"No, thanks," Bill replied. "I'm good."

Matt opened another set of curtains on his way toward the kitchen, disappeared into it for thirty seconds, came back out holding two open beer bottles, and returned to the projector, where Bill was now standing, examining the damaged film with curiosity.

"So anyway," said Matt, "That interview. Holy smoke, it is *so* good. Bart reveals tons of great stuff about Marion. Some of it's pretty juicy, like she had this top-secret affair with some guy named Arch. Oh, hang on, this name is such a trip..."

Matt thrust one of the beers into Bill's hand, then spent a couple of seconds rummaging through a collection of tiny objects on the narrow ledge where the wheely cart was wider than the projector. He retrieved a crumpled scrap of paper from this collection, opened it up, and read from it.

"Archibald Teese Wailoverenson... or however you pronounce it. Hah! Check it out..."

He handed the scrap of paper to Bill, who glanced at it briefly, then started to hand it back but realized Matt had walked away, then stuffed it into his jeans pocket.

"So yeah," Matt said, hopping back onto the couch, "nobody except Bart knew about that affair. I mean he is just a gold mine of Marion info!"

"Great," said Bill.

"Oh! But, okay, here's the most fascinating part. For finding the buried treasure, I mean. So one time, Bart was having dinner with this other guy, Rick. This was like, ten years before the interview. But it was after Marion died. Anyway, Rick was an old friend of Marion's, and eventually he was her lover, actually, and he was also an old friend of William Randolph Hearst. You know, that newspaper tycoon guy, from Citizen Kane. And Marion, she was Hearst's mistress. That part is well known. She was his mistress for... decades. Everyone knew."

"This is awfully complicated, Matt."

"Yeah, I know. It's better if you actually see the interview."

"No doubt."

"But the point is: Marion confided in Rick that she'd taken some valuable artifacts from Hearst Castle, up north, put them inside a giant chest, and buried them under the beach by her house in Santa Monica. As like a secret insurance policy, in case… I guess in case everything ever went south somehow."

"Okay."

"And Rick, he got a huge kick out of this. And he wanted to dig the treasure up. By this time, Hearst was dead anyway. But Marion didn't want to dig it up. So Rick was like, 'Okay, but can I at least create an old-fashioned treasure map?' And she was okay with that. So he did."

"This is a very strange story."

"I know! It's so wild, isn't it? I love it!"

Bill, who'd abandoned his beer on the wheely cart ledge and returned to his spot on the couch, said, "So, we don't really *know* that any of what you've just described actually happened. All we really know is that Bart allegedly had dinner with Rick, and Rick allegedly told him all that shit."

"Correct! You're a pretty smart cookie, Bill. But personally, I think it's all true."

"Okay, maybe it is, but… so what? There are still a million obstacles to finding the buried treasure. I mean, take that map, for starters. It could be anywhere today. Or, more likely, nowhere."

"Aha, but there's one more thing you don't know about that interview!" Matt took a quick swig from his beer bottle. "Rick told Bart, when they had dinner, that he was going to mail Bart the treasure map."

"Why would he do that?"

"I don't know. Neither did Bart. In fact, Bart thought the whole thing was a bunch of nonsense."

"I like this Bart fellow."

"He couldn't care less about it. He never thought about it again, even once, from the time he left that dinner until he did this interview."

"A real stand-up guy. Really had his head screwed on straight."

Matt finally had to stop, breaking into soft laughter. "Oh, Bill," he said. "You crack me up. But listen, here's the kicker: Bart never thought about it again because he never received the map in the mail!"

"So?"

"Rick definitely sent it."

"How do you know?"

"Because. He's Rick. Think about it. Of course he sent it. He wouldn't just *not* send it." A short pause. "And Bart didn't receive it. Which means..." Matt waited for Bill to connect the dots.

"Uh... It got lost in the mail?" he said with a shrug.

"Yes! Exactly! It got lost in the mail. And eventually, it ended up in a dead letter office somewhere." He grinned and lifted his eyebrows as if to say "Ta-da!"

Bill just stared at Matt in silence for several seconds. Then he said, "God."

Matt chuckled, both amused by his friend's skepticism and delighted by the knowledge of what was to come.

"Mark my words, Bill," he said. "That map is still out there. And I *will* find it!" Then he took another swig of his beer.

Chapter 11

The steady clop-clop-clop of running shoes striking pavement filled the neighborhood air and the ears of the many denizens currently populating its sidewalks (though, in most cases, not their brains, which auto-filtered such sounds to help keep them in their own little world), as a glistening Gary Williams made his way along Utah Avenue, nearing his home and the completion of a 12-mile training circuit.

Back in April, when Gary had first started doing these neighborhood runs, he'd initially tried to make use of the sidewalks himself, but had abandoned this in short order after discovering it felt like a non-stop obstacle course. All humans and many dogs (those that didn't lunge, snarling, at you) failed even to acknowledge the existence of a runner approaching them, much less get out of the way, and their trajectories were highly unpredictable, with varying speeds and a tendency to suddenly move partially or entirely off the concrete in one direction or the other.

Gary had found the constant scanning and calculating for upcoming potential hazards, plus the acrobatics employed to avoid them (which sometimes carried a high risk of stepping on a "land mine" that lurked in the grass), far more exhausting than the running itself. And, as if the living, breathing obstacles weren't rough enough, he'd also labored under the perpetual specter of tripping on one of the pushed-up-by-tree-roots sidewalk slabs and winding up with a faceful of concrete.

So, he'd taken to the street, which, though not without its own set of risks (e.g. maniac drivers, folks lost in Phone World while getting into or out of parked cars), offered a generally more navigable course and a less frenetic experience.

Ahead on the sidewalk closest to him, on his left, Gary spotted Mrs.

Harris and Max strolling along, but did not recognize them. Lounging near them was Rufus Fletcher, engaged in an intense conversation with a squirrel named Sebastian.

Then, on the opposite sidewalk, Gary noticed a pair of power-walkers, nicknamed The Wonder Twins by the Smedes and frequently seen making their way around the neighborhood (though Gary did not recognize them). They were always side by side, barreling forward with great speed and purpose, engrossed in conversation with each other. Both were white women around 40 years old, of similar height but differing in weight by about 75 pounds. The lighter one always wore baggy sweats and a baggy fleece zipped all the way up, while the heavier one always wore a halter top and spandex shorts, a roll of belly fat hanging down over the top of them.

Then, on the left sidewalk, Gary saw somebody he did recognize: Yvonne. "Oh!" he said to himself with a smile.

She was alone, walking at a leisurely pace, and didn't appear to be wearing any earpieces or staring at a phone screen. So he decided to cut his run ever so slightly short and walk the remaining stretch with her.

"Hey guys! Good morning!" he exclaimed as he stepped onto the curb and sidled up next to her.

"Oh, hi Gary," Yvonne said, turning to smile at him and momentarily stopping as he joined her on the sidewalk. Then they carried on together.

"How are you doing?" asked Gary with a big, warm grin. He was always excited to connect with friends and catch up.

"Pretty good, I suppose," said Yvonne, also with genuine warmth but in her much lower-key style. "I was just thinking about some of the people I have to work with and the way they'll just state things as absolute fact, like they are totally, *totally* certain of it. And then later it turns out to be wrong, and it also turns out, they weren't really that sure about it to begin with."

Gary, still smiling, shook his head. "Heh. Aw, man…"

"I mean, why can't people just say 'I *believe* this is the case,' or 'It seems to me,' or 'I'm pretty sure'… You know, just, give you some indicator of how reliable is this supposed info they're about to deliver."

"Yep, yep." Gary was nodding now.

"Because, if they truly were certain about something, knowing that would be useful to me. I could probably, in most cases, trust what they said to be... almost definitely correct. But as it stands, I can never do that. Because they just say everything with that same supreme confidence. So I *always* feel like I can't take their word for it, I *have* to check it myself."

"I know exactly what you mean," said Gary. "It's the same at my work." He paused a moment, considering. "Actually, thinking about it, I still just take their word most of the time. And then I get burned!" He laughed.

Yvonne laughed too.

"Oh, hey, speaking of work," said Gary, "haven't you usually left by now?"

"Working from home today."

"Aha! Very cool, very cool."

"And every Thursday."

"Oh, yeah, I think I remember that. Well, super cool, then! So, just taking a lap to clear your head, huh?"

"Yeah, sort of. And, of course, trying to keep the step count up." She held up her left arm and tapped her wrist with her right index finger.

"Yes!" Gary chuckled as he held up his own left arm, on which was strapped an example of the rather bulky (and far too pricey for Yvonne's taste), top-of-the-line PaceTek model, the Mega-Ultra. "Technology! It's so great, isn't it?"

"Yeah."

"Of course, too much technology can ruin a sport. I sure am glad I got into marathon running and not Super-Sci-Cling! Woo, I tell you..."

A fiercely independent professional bicycle racing organization that, according to what Gary'd read, had sprung into existence virtually overnight in 2008, Super-Sci-Cling aimed to make the sport supremely fair, accurate, precise, measured, understood—in short, perfect—through the application of science. And, like science itself, throughout their history they'd been continuously refining and enhancing their approach.

They'd started with specially designed extra-wide courses (portions of which were constructed specifically for these races) riddled with sensors, on which they put groups of just five riders at a time (each with a dedicated lane, so as not to interfere with each other), one group per day, at the same time each day, over a period of two weeks, using identical customized bikes (which were also loaded with sensors), all connected to extremely powerful computer software.

But this arrangement had its "fairness flaws," such as daily weather variations and small differences in course length/curvature among the five lanes. So they'd brought the event indoors and put each rider and bike on a frictionless platform which rotated, tilted, bobbed and vibrated to replicate the forces that a real road would exert on them. The platform was synced up with 3-D photo-motion software that presented a continuous ultra-realistic image on a gigantic screen in front of the rider's face.

Eventually, to avoid injuries to the riders and cut down on the rather hefty mechanical maintenance costs, they'd gone full virtual: each rider donned an outfit that looked like a wetsuit but boasted astonishingly sophisticated electronic systems, literally woven in, and an accompanying "aural-visual-tactile-olfactory" V.R. helmet, and then completed the entire race perched on a specialized 3-foot-high pedestal called a "giga-seat," usually in their own home. For their muscles, nerves, and mind, the rider's experience was exactly the same as the real thing.

But the ambitious scientists of Super-Sci-Cling hadn't stopped there. Using quantum computing and A.I. technology developed in-house, along with the mountains of data collected from all the races over the years, they'd perfected a predictive model that determined who would win if the race took place, meaning it no longer needed to. The riders simply put on their suits and helmets at the designated time, submitted to an "F.B.B. Scan" (Full Body & Brain) which lasted about five minutes, and then the winner was announced later that same day, after the computers had crunched all the numbers. Ongoing refinements of the model had allowed for longer and longer spans of time prior to the race date during which registered riders could get scanned; once they'd all done it, the computers calculated forward to that date, accounting for all the training the riders would've undergone, and determined who would've won.

Currently the Super-Sci-Cling computers were in the midst of their biggest-ever number crunching endeavor, poised to announce in mid-September who, out of the many hundreds of riders who'd been scanned over the years, would ultimately decide to register for the 2053 race, and then, in early October, the winner.

One reason (though perhaps not the only one) Yvonne had never heard of Super-Sci-Cling was that it didn't actually exist; Gary had learned all about it by reading a short piece of satirical fiction which he mistook for a news article.

After Yvonne had decided that totally ignoring Gary's mysterious remark (which he did not seem to mind or even notice) was her preferred course, there was a short lull in the conversation. Then she said, "Your next marathon is coming up soon, right?"

"Yes!" Gary exclaimed excitedly. "Very soon! It's on Labor Day. Heading out Saturday morning. This was actually my final training run."

"Saturday morning? Are you doing another one of your cross-country drives?"

"Yep! All the way to Columbia, Missouri. The race is called 'Heart of America.' Going to check off my 'blue' requirement!"

Yvonne, having forgotten about the color-coded categories, didn't know what Gary meant, but she knew it wasn't important (like Super-Sci-Cling) and ignored it. "You're something else," she said, chuckling and shaking her head.

"Hey, at least I got myself a sensible, reliable car for this one!"

"Oh, yeah?"

"Yep! Just picked it up last week. Brand new!" He laughed with delight.

"Well, cool. Good for you."

"Yep, it was bye-bye Supra! I know I'll miss her. Actually, so will Scott, I think. Even though he'd never admit it..." He drifted off for a second, then came back. "But, you know. Times change. Onward and upward!" His big smile had reappeared.

"Yes," Yvonne replied, forcing a return smile.

After ten more seconds of walking together in silence, they stopped outside the entrance to Gary's building. "Welp, this is me," he said with a chuckle. "Hey, it was really nice talking with you!"

"Yeah, you too, Gary."

"We gotta get you guys over for dinner again soon, get caught up. Last time you guys canceled on us!" He laughed and wagged his finger in semi-mock admonishment.

"Oh, yeah... about that..." Yvonne paused, trying to figure out exactly what to say.

"Dang!" Gary suddenly exclaimed, looking at his watch. "Sorry guys, I gotta go! Early meeting about the new packaging proposal!"

He turned and began climbing the building's front steps.

"Bye, Gary," said Yvonne, then shook her head, smiling, and continued walking down Wexler toward her own building.

Gary, lost in thought and looking down at the ground, reached the top of the steps and almost crashed into Frank Barnes, who'd been standing there watching him approach.

"Whoa! Holy cow! Frank!" Gary was bewildered.

"Top of the morning to ya, Gare."

As Gary quickly re-oriented himself, a smile broke out on his face. "Top of the morning to you, too! It's great to see you again! It's been... months, I think. Hey, congratulations on your promotion!" (Frank had recently been made Principal Senior Associate, with Jim Jamb and several others reporting to him.)

"Enough gab, old buddy," he said. "We have some important business, you and me."

"Oh, um, okay. Well, I'm sorta pressed for time, but... come on in." Gary reached for the keypad mounted next to the door.

"Negative, my friend. No time. Let's talk about Missoula."

"Yeah, what happened to you that day? Did you finish? Boy, I tell you, I had a tough time. I mean, it was brutal!" He chuckled, thinking back on it. "Thought for sure I'd blown it. You know, for the big one."

Frank's face was blank.

"Took me nearly six hours to finish! But later, Scott looked up the rules, and it was fine! I got my 'yellow,' heh." He grinned widely.

"Forget the past, Gary," said Frank. "Think about the future. The race in Missoula three days from now."

"What? Oh—Miss*ouri*! You mean the Labor Day race in Missouri, right?"

"Exactly. It's going to be a tough one, man. You need to get your head in the game, you know what I'm saying?"

"Oh, absolutely! I am ready. I'm pumped! Hey, are you running that one? You wanna ride out there with me?"

"Pay attention, Gare. The air is different out there. The water is different. Everything is different."

"What do you mean?"

"Adaptation," Frank said, tapping his temple with his finger and smiling. Then he reached into his pocket and produced a small foil pouch, which he held out to Gary. "Here."

"What's this?" Gary asked.

"Take it," Frank commanded. "It's more valuable than gold, my friend."

Gary took it. "What are you talking about?" he said with a grin.

"Gary, have you ever heard of cortodiazone?"

"Um, nope, I don't think so."

"Trick question. Of course you haven't. Nobody has. Best kept secret in history."

"Frank, are you talking about performance-enhancing drugs? 'Cause, if you are, I, um... I'm not sure if I—"

"Not performance-enhancing. Disaster-averting. Cortodiazone helps runners. And I mean, helps them a lot. Under certain circumstances. Like the ones you're going to be in. Trust me, buddy, you don't want to do this race without it."

Gary was trying to keep an open mind. He looked down at the little packet in his hand. It had no markings of any kind on it.

"So, this is that stuff?" he asked.

"Use your head, Gare. No, no, no. What you hold in your hand is not cortodiazone. What you hold in your hand is your key. Guard it, my friend. Guard it with your life."

"Um, I'm not sure I really understand, Frank..."

"Don't worry, buddy. I've got your back."

After clapping Gary on the shoulder, Frank sprang into motion, darting down the steps and sprinting off up the sidewalk toward Utah.

Just as Yvonne reached the concrete footpath connecting the sidewalk to her condo's stairs, she received a phone call.

"Laura!" she said upon answering it. "Wasn't expecting to hear from you."

Laura was out of the office on vacation for a week and a half, starting today.

"Yeah, I wasn't expecting you to hear from me, either, but... unfortunately, Mike and I are in a bit of a bind."

"Oh yeah?"

"Yeah, turns out, somehow neither of us brought our wallets. Can you believe it? So stupid."

"So you can't get through security?"

"No, no, we're fine on that front. We have our passports. Actually we already flew the first leg."

"Already? Wow."

"Yeah, we had a really early flight this morning. It was when we were up in the air, and we wanted to order some drinks—that was when we realized we didn't have any money."

"Oh, wow. Not good."

"Yeah, so we're waiting for our connection, here at O'Hare, and Mike, um, he's got this… scheme, I guess you call it… this thing he calls 'The Bait and Switch' that he pulls on people that, um, basically… He's basically stealing from them."

Yvonne chuckled. "Sounds like him."

"Yeah. And, normally, I don't really have an issue with it—I mean, somebody who's gullible and greedy, arguably deserves to lose their money to somebody who needs it. But, you know, in an airport, or in a foreign country, I just… I don't feel comfortable with it, you know? I mean what if he got caught?"

"Right."

"So, I need you to go into my office…"

"I'm not at the office right now. I work from home on Thursdays."

"Oh, dammit, that's right!"

"What about Amy?"

"I already tried to call her but she didn't answer. I think she said she had a thing at Jennifer's school this morning."

"What about Mona?"

Laura hesitated and made a quick sucking sound, like people sometimes do when they're in a bit of pain. "The thing is, I really don't trust anyone else there except you and Amy."

For a moment there was total silence on the line. Then Yvonne sighed and said, "Okay. I'll go into the office."

"Thank you so much!"

"So what am I looking for?"

"There's a credit card in my top drawer. I need you to send me all the details."

"Okay."

"But not all together, that's too risky. Send me the first and third blocks of numbers on my work email, the second and fourth blocks on my personal email, and then text me the expiration and the 3-digit code."

Yvonne stifled a laugh. "Okay. Got it."

"Thanks, Yvonne! You are a lifesaver."

"So are you two headed for that extra special island, what's it called?"

"Het Juweel? No, not this time. We're saving the best for last!"

"But didn't you say that it's, like, heading underwater and it's going to be closed off soon?"

"Well, yeah, that's a possibility, but... We'll make it there before that happens. If it happens."

"So this time it's number nine, huh?"

"Well, sort of, but... It's our ninth trip but we actually decided to return to Kip van het Zee, which was number... um, number six, I think... because we just loved it so much."

"Hmm, okay. Well, hope you love it again."

"Hey, you're running the Titanium Ten for me while I'm gone, right?"

"Uh, what? No." Yvonne loathed this idea, which she was hearing about now for the very first time.

"Oh, I could've sworn I asked you. Anyway, you don't mind, do you?"

"Well, uh..."

In the background, Yvonne heard Mike's voice say gleefully, "Come on, babe. I've got the mark!"

"Shoot, I gotta go!" Laura said abruptly, sounding somewhat panicked. "Thank you thank you thank you, for everything!"

"But, wait, Laura..." said Yvonne, then realized the call had already dropped.

In nearly the exact same location 48 hours later, three Smedes—Bill, Patrick, and Alice—reluctantly and gloomily loaded themselves into the ATS and began the 32-mile, 75-minute journey to Cerritos.

For a brief time, Bill had enjoyed the delusion that he would not have to get together with extended family this weekend. He'd informed his mother, with feigned despair and regret, that appearing at her

Labor Day party would be quite impossible, owing to the fact that Yvonne would have the car and the kids that day for an outing with Gramps. But Mamsy had ultimately burst his bubble with the news that she was rescheduling her party for Saturday. His sister Debbie had then added insult to injury by coercing him into attending a "pre-party gathering" at her place.

Patrick, who'd not even remotely attempted to hide his disappointment when told about today, and had made several attempts to weasel out of it, rode in the passenger seat and engaged his father intermittently in pleasant conversation (staring down at his phone screen the rest of the time) as they made their way south on the 405, then east on the 105, then south on the 605.

Alice, in the back seat, spent the entire drive listening to music through her earbuds, staring out the window, and not speaking. When she'd learned of this trip, she'd simply asked whether her participation was mandatory and, after Bill had said yes, that it was, hadn't ever addressed the subject again.

As Bill brought the car to a stop curbside in front of Debbie's house, three figures burst from it and began charging across the lawn toward the street. Two of these, Raylene and Anika, were young female humans; the third, Fritz, was a middle-aged male dog of a somewhat German Shepherdish appearance. All three were emitting excited noises and wearing big smiles (or, in Fritz's case, something that wasn't really a smile but looked like one).

Patrick and Alice stepped out of the car and onto the grass just in time to nearly collide with the welcoming party. Patrick couldn't help grinning. He found his cousins' exuberance infectious, and, after hugging them, gave both a playful hair-ruffling on the tops of their heads. Alice provided a rather mechanical hug and a quiet "Hello" to each girl while trying, unsuccessfully, to smile.

As Bill got out of the car, he was greeted by Fritz, who'd already given both Smede children a quick sniff and was now coming around to the driver's side to complete his investigation.

"Fritz the Dog!" Bill exclaimed, then gave Fritz a quick pat on the head while laughing at his own rapier wit.

Turning around, he saw that the four cousins were making their way toward the house, with Fritz now galloping off to catch up with them, and that Grace Hogg had appeared in the doorway, standing with her hands on her hips, regarding the whole group with a smile.

She raised one arm and gave Bill a quick wave. He smiled and waved back.

Grace had a thin face with a thin nose, large light-brown eyes, and a long, thick, full mane of golden-brown hair. Her tan, slender yet curvy body rose five feet ten inches above the ground when it was standing up straight without shoes. One might have guessed that a woman with her looks could make a good living as a fashion model, and she'd proven such a guess correct by doing just that. It was immediately following one of her shows in New York that she'd first met Debbie, who'd shown up to the after-party by mistake and then been admitted to it by mistake.

As beautiful as ever, thought Bill as he closed his car door. Nobody who'd met Grace had ever disagreed with this sentiment, and on many occasions straight men who knew her, when talking amongst themselves (usually after a few drinks), had wholeheartedly agreed that Grace's orientation was a crying shame (and that Debbie had somehow managed to marry way out of her league). A few of these men had sometimes gone further, expressing opinions and wishes about Grace the articulation of which was unfit for most decent people's ears.

Half an hour after arriving, while chatting with his sister about dog shows over a cup of tea and a shortbread cookie, Bill unexpectedly and alarmedly recognized the voice of a particular straight man who, he happened to know, belonged to that more exclusive subset.

"Mister Roger's in the houuuuse!" the voice boomed, echoing through every room.

"What the fuck is he doing here?" Bill asked Debbie in a very quiet, very agitated voice.

"Mamsy invited him to the thing," she replied, "and then somehow he found out about us meeting up here before. I don't know how."

Roger Raderman, who'd many years back invented the nickname Mister Roger for himself (which he thought was exceedingly cute but all others thought was exceedingly stupid and annoying), had spent three years of his life as the domestic partner of Mamsy's brother's daughter, Philippa "Pippa" Goldstein (no relation to Judy), during which time they'd produced two children. These days Pippa was living in Papua New Guinea (where she'd abruptly headed for "a year, maybe longer" in order to find herself) and Roger was a single father to Jessica (age 4) and Rodger (age 2). He had always ranked very high on Bill's lengthy list of insufferable people, and even sunny, non-judgmental Debbie could barely stand him. But Mamsy loved him, frequently going on about how charming he was and referring to him as her "darling nephew."

"We're in here, Roger!" Debbie called out.

A moment later, Roger appeared in the doorway, leaned against it and said, "What up, homies," then let out a long, self-satisfied chuckle, then said, "Hey Deb, you got any beer?"

His dark brown, medium-length hair was slicked back but somewhat mussed (containing a fair amount of gel, but far less than Scott's) and his ever-varying mustache growth, which ranged all the way from shaved off to Hulk Hogan, was currently somewhere in between. He wore a black leather jacket, a solid white crew-neck t-shirt, a black leather belt, blue jeans, cowboy boots, and his son, who was attached to his left leg like a koala gripping a tree trunk.

"Uh..." said Debbie.

"Actually, scratch that. Toys! We need toys first, then beer. The little guy loves toys." He looked down at Rodger, who did not look up. "Dontcha, Rodger-Dodger?" Another long chuckle.

Debbie got off her chair and approached the doorway, crouching down and speaking in a soft, sweet voice.

"Hi there, Rodger! It sure is nice to see you. You know what?"

She had his attention, eyes taking her in with skepticism but interest, mouth curved ever so minutely into a tiny hint of a smile.

"I bet your cousins will be really happy to see you, too. And I bet they have some great toys for you to play with!"

She held out her hand. "Come on, I'll take you to them."

Rodger removed one of his own small hands from his father's jeans and placed it inside hers. As the two of them made their way out of the room, Roger chuckled yet again. Bill sat motionless, staring at the wall, hoping that he could somehow will himself invisible. For about ten seconds, it seemed to be working.

Then Roger said, "So, Bill Gates..."—another chuckle, short this time—"won't be long 'til we gotta start planning our next birthday bash."

"Right!" Bill couldn't manage to smile or infuse his tone with any positive emotion, so he just spoke very loudly to try to signal engagement.

"And this time we gotta make sure we get some gambling in there, am I right?"

As the fates would have it, Roger had been born on exactly the same day as Debbie and Bill. Every year he repeatedly brought up the notion of celebrating together (in fact, every single time he saw them, no matter what time of year), but so far it had never happened. Still, Bill lived in constant fear that eventually it would.

"Right!" he shouted again in response to Roger's latest remark.

"I actually gotta jet in a few minutes. Right after I have my beer. But don't worry, I'll be back. Just gotta go grab Jess. Give Dora a damn break already!" More chuckling.

Bill already knew exactly why Roger had to jet, because this was his standard operating procedure. His car, a 1986 convertible Corvette ("They never made a better 'Vette, before or since," he liked to say), had only two seats, meaning he could only transport one child at a time. Stubbornly refusing to let anyone else drive his kids around (for "safety reasons"), he made two trips whenever they both needed to go somewhere. Fortunately Dora was always at his house, ready to look after whichever child departed last or arrived home first. She'd originally been hired help, performing cooking, cleaning, and other domestic tasks. She still did all the tasks, as well as a fair bit of childcare, but Roger had stopped paying her as soon as he began sleeping with her.

Now Bill broke into a genuine laugh, because he'd just remembered the time (or was it multiple times?) Roger had explained to him, in a very serious fashion, why it was safer to own a car without a back seat: because no would-be assassin could hide there, waiting to garrote you the moment you got in.

Grace appeared, looking tense but smiling, carrying a bottle of Bud Light, covered in dust, which had been retrieved from her garage.

"Hey, my beer!" Roger exclaimed with a smile, moving in her direction. "And delivered to me by the most beautiful waitress nature could possibly conjure up!" He chuckled as he snatched the bottle from her outstretched hand.

For the next twenty seconds, the only sounds and movements in the room were those of Roger twisting the cap off the bottle, flicking it onto the table, taking a long gulp of beer, and loudly exhaling.

Then he said, "So! How ya been doing, Amazing Grace?" followed by a quick chuckle.

"Fine," she replied in a quiet voice with a wooden expression.

"*Yeah* you are. Heh. So how's the modeling going? Still burning up the runway?"

"Fine," she said again, same style.

"No doubt, no doubt," Roger said, then took another swig of his beer.

"Excuse me," said Grace, "I need to get back." She rapidly departed.

After several seconds of neither man speaking, Roger said, "You know, she's a Samara."

"What do you mean?" asked Bill.

"There was this girl in high school, Samara. She was totally gorgeous. I mean primo. But she didn't have much of a personality, you know? Really quiet. Never hardly had anything to say. And you know why?"

"Uh…"

"Because she was stupid! There really wasn't much going on up here." He tapped the side of his head with his finger.

"Well I don't think that Grace is, uh, stupid… or—"

"But I guess in a weird way she was wise. To be quiet, you know? What's that old saying? 'Better to keep your mouth shut and look like an idiot than to open it and look like even more of one.' Hah!" He chuckled again and took another swig.

"Good advice," said Bill.

"Mmm—oh, hey," Roger said as he swallowed his beer, "here's something I never knew before—people actually have *two* anal sphincters. One of them is voluntary and the other one is involuntary. Which means, you can always *stop* yourself from taking a crap… but you can't always *take* a crap, even if you want to!"

Two hours later, after Bill had endured further torturous interaction with Roger, and after Roger had driven back home and retrieved Jessica and brought her to Debbie's house, and after the four adults had gathered in the lounge to consume tea and shortbread and each other's speech while the six youngsters and Fritz tried to frolic together on the back patio, and after the ten humans had made their way to Mamsy's house in Orange County (the same house where Debbie and Bill had spent their childhood) using the ATS, the Corvette (twice), and a gigantic Toyota SUV helmed by Grace, everybody was standing in a big, awkward circle around the living room, Mamsy beaming with genuine excitement and cherishment while the rest beamed with the pretend kind.

"Oh, I just love it when the whole family can get together like this!" she exclaimed giddily. "Now I want you kids to just help yourselves, okay? We have snacks in the kitchen and games in the games cupboard, okay?"

"I like games!" announced Jessica loudly. Her brother wore a confused but hopeful expression.

Patrick smiled and nodded politely, as did both of his cousins, who also both muttered "Thanks, Mamsy."

Alice gave a small nod in her grandmother's direction; no smile.

Mamsy continued, "You ladies can help me out with the food prep, okay? I'm doing my world famous sausage potato chip casserole." She paused to savor this idea and to receive any sort of reaction the group might offer, but there was none.

"And you gentlemen can take some beers to the T.V. room and enjoy the basketball game!"

Roger let out a long guffaw, then said, "Football, Mamsy. But I like where you're going with this whole idea!" Then another guffaw.

"Well that's fabulous, Roger," she replied. "Oh, I just love it when the whole family can get together like this. It doesn't happen enough. I suppose the next time will probably be... well, I suppose it will probably be for my birthday."

"Oh!" said Debbie. She grabbed Bill and Patrick, standing on either side of her, by the wrists. "Excuse us just a sec..."

She tugged on their arms and all three retreated to the far side of the room for a private huddle. Roger joined them, unsolicited.

"I just wanted to let you L.A. Smedes know," Debbie continued in a hushed voice, "we're planning something really cool for Mamsy's 70th." She giggled.

Bill tried not to show his disappointment and dread on his face, but did anyway. Patrick smiled and raised his big, bushy eyebrows. Roger bellowed "Nice!" very loudly.

"Still working out all the details," said Debbie, "but we're thinking we're gonna rent a boat, you know, maybe—"

"Oh!" said Roger. He put his arms around Bill's and Debbie's shoulders and began pulling them away for a private huddle. "Excuse us just a sec," he said to Patrick.

"What's going on?" Debbie asked when they got around the corner into the hallway.

"I heard this great joke a couple days ago," said Roger. "But it's dirty, so, you know, not appropriate for the kid to hear." He chuckled. "Okay, so, these three guys get on a boat together—a priest, a rabbi, and a... What are they called? An imam. Yeah, an imam. And it turns out—"

"Oh!" said Bill, taking ahold of his sister's arm. "Excuse us just a sec."

He led her down the hallway and around another corner for a private huddle.

"What?" asked Debbie.

"I just can't stand that fucking guy," Bill whispered. "I had to get away from him. It was an emergency."

Debbie, feeling disoriented and annoyed, dropped her eyes and shook her head, but also couldn't help smiling. God—my family, she thought.

"I have a really bad feeling about this," said Scott to Gary. "Please reconsider."

It was 9:30 P.M. (Central Time) and the two men were sitting side by side in Gary's new Ford F-150 Raptor (in which they'd been traveling for two days), parked in front of a decrepit two-story apartment complex.

"Aw, come on, babe. You have a really bad feeling about everything." Gary laughed. "It'll be fine."

"Drug dealers are dangerous people."

"This guy's no drug dealer. He just happens to possess a very useful, very safe, perfectly legal... um... pharmaceutical product." He paused and grinned as Scott rolled his eyes. "It's not like he's selling crack or meth."

"You don't know—"

"In *fact*, he's not actually *selling* anything! Frank said no money will change hands."

Scott frowned and made a sound of exasperation, something like "Nnngh," in his throat. Then he resumed using words. "You don't know anything about this guy, really. Everything you know, you learned from Frank, who's an idiot."

Gary chuckled. "Aw, Frank's not—"

"He admitted he doesn't even know this guy personally. And he told you *that* thing"—Scott pointed to the tiny plastic bottle clutched in Gary's hand, containing a very generic-looking tan-colored tablet which had been inside the foil pouch Frank gave him—"was, uh, some kind of 'key' or something… What does that even mean?"

"Oh, he cleared that up later," Gary said with a smile. "He said I need to combine this first pill with the new one I'm getting tonight. And it turns out, they do know each other after all. Frank just got confused for a minute when he said they didn't."

"I still say this is insane," Scott replied. "I think we should just forget it and head to the hotel."

Gary smiled and patted Scott reassuringly on the thigh. "It'll be fine, babe. This isn't some dangerous drug deal. It's just a nice person helping out another nice person, to ensure he's able to bring his 'A' game tomorrow. It's all completely innocent and harmless."

He opened the car door and got out. Then, before shutting it, he leaned back in and said, "But, like you said before, if I'm not back in ten minutes, you call 9-1-1." He grinned.

Scott stared back at him, stone-faced.

Standing in what would've been the light from a fixture mounted on the wall next to the door of Apartment 2-G if its bulb hadn't been smashed, but was in fact pitch darkness, Gary looked down at a text he'd just received from Frank that said, "Exchange what youve got for what hes got."

"Dang," he muttered, then stood for a moment, reflecting on his situation, then timidly knocked on the door.

After what felt like two minutes but was really fifteen seconds, it was opened by James "Clubber" Peterson, a 35-year-old black man with a shaved head, a gold earring in each ear, a gold chain around his rather thick neck, and both arms loaded with tattoos and bulging muscles. As a teenager, he'd fashioned his own new nickname by tweaking the one that had been thrust upon him in early childhood, "Blubber" (which referred not to fatness but to the fact he cried a lot).

"May I help you?" Clubber asked.

Gary swallowed hard, then grinned widely. "Good evening, sir," he said. "Sorry to trouble you at this late hour. I was hoping I might have a quick word with Arvid Sloan?"

"Sure."

Clubber stepped to one side and ushered Gary into the rather large front room of the apartment, which was sparsely furnished, smelled vaguely of incense, and offered very few visual clues about the size or layout of the rest of the apartment—in one corner Gary saw a small doorway that appeared to lead into a corridor, and in another corner, the tip of a kitchen-type area that was mostly tucked away behind a wall.

Roughly halfway between these two, almost directly in front of Gary, a young, very thin, white man with thick-rimmed eyeglasses, a giant mop of dark brown hair on top and none on his face (possibly, but not definitely, because of shaving), wearing a baggy t-shirt and baggy sweats and a gold chain similar to Clubber's, sat in a very old recliner with green cloth upholstery that was fraying in several places.

"Mr. Sloan?" Gary asked as he approached the man.

"Who the fuck wants to know?" the man replied in a voice that attempted to project strength, aggression and ominousness, but failed to do any of this (owing to its high-pitched, nasal, whiny sound).

Gary, now standing right in front of the recliner, said, "My name is Gary Williams, sir. I was sent by Frank Barnes."

"Who the fuck is Frank Barnes? I don't know any fuckin' Frank Barnes."

Gary was having a hard time remaining scared, and in fact felt on the brink of having to stifle a laugh. But he was still trying to tell himself he should keep his wits about him, should keep his guard up.

"Um," he said, "I'm a runner. A marathon runner. And I was led to believe that you might be able to supply me with some, um, cortodiazone?"

"What the fuck? You mean carotodiazapene?"

At this point Gary did laugh. "Yeah, I probably do mean that, Mr. Sloan."

"Don't fuckin' call me Mr. Sloan," said Mr. Sloan, scowling.

"Oh, okay. Arvid?"

"No!" shouted Arvid, scrunching up his face in disgust. "Fuck! No. You call me... fuckin' Ass Man."

Gary grimaced, unsure how to interpret what he'd just heard and not pleased with any possible interpretation. "Um... Fucking Ass Man?"

"No! Just fuckin'... Just Ass Man."

Gary heard muffled laughter behind him as he said, "Okay. Um, Ass Man—"

"Because I fuckin' get so much fuckin' ass," explained Ass Man.

The laughter was no longer muffled, and Gary turned around to see Clubber emitting it, shoulders rising and falling, both hands on his abdomen.

"Oh, dear," he said, collecting himself. Then, "Don't worry about him, Mr. Williams. You probably know that positions of power tend to attract people who don't properly appreciate the gravity of those positions and are generally unfit to hold them. Well, our friend here is an innocuous example of that principle."

"Shut the fuck up!" shouted Ass Man. "You don't know what the fuck you're talkin' about, you big, stupid fuck!"

Gary, wearing a semi-smile of morbid bewilderment, turned back toward the recliner to see that Ass Man was now holding up a tiny plastic zip-lock baggie in his left hand. The baggie contained a very generic-looking tan-colored tablet.

"Do you want your fuckin' shit or not, cuck?"

"Yes, please," said Gary, extending his hand for the baggie. "That would be wonderful. Thank you."

Ass Man did not make a move to relinquish the baggie. "You fuckin' got somethin' for me, then?"

"Oh! Right! Yes, I sure do." Gary reached into his pocket, pulled out the little bottle containing the pill Frank had given him and held it out to Ass Man.

"What the fuck is that? No! Fuck!"

"Oh, sorry," said Gary.

"I think you got your fuckin' job description mixed up with mine. *I'm* the one who fuckin' sells the shit. *You're* the one who fuckin' buys the shit. Capiche?"

"Um, yeah, I think so." Gary put the bottle back in his pocket. "So, you want money?"

"What the fuck is wrong with you? Are you a fuckin' retard or somethin'? Yes, I want fuckin' money! I ain't runnin' no fuckin' charity here! Five hundred bucks."

Gary paused for a few seconds, almost physically cringing as he pictured Scott's face upon hearing of this latest development. Perhaps he should avoid that face by doing the "smart" thing and simply walking away from this deal? But he just couldn't shake the feeling that he was destined to fail miserably in tomorrow's race if his body didn't get some chemical assistance in adapting to its new environment.

"Okay," he finally said. "Hang on a minute. I gotta go back to my car."

Scott, feeling rather relaxed and happy, all things considered, flashed a smile across the tiny breakfast table at Gary.

"You're pumped, aren't you?" Gary asked excitedly.

"Yeah... Yeah, I guess I am."

"Hah! I love it! Me too. Ooh, so jazzed." He paused for a second. "Hey, I'm sorry about last night, babe."

"It's okay."

"I know I was... Wow, I guess I was out of my mind..."

"Really, it's okay."

At this point, Scott just felt relieved that Gary had ultimately decided against taking the carotodiazapene tablet, and that the whole ordeal was behind them. The potential danger to which they'd been subjected, and the $500 dent in their bank account, were, comparatively, small potatoes.

They finished the last few bites of tuna salad wrap and fruit (prepared last night using supplies obtained from a nearby supermarket, then stored in their little hotel mini-fridge) in comfortable, content silence, then got up from the table and launched into the remaining preparatory activities.

Everything was going swimmingly. They took turns brushing their teeth at the pathetic excuse for a bathroom sink. They packed a few final bits and pieces into Gary's race belt and Scott's satchel. Scott gave his hair one final shellacking in front of the bathroom mirror while Gary pinned on his race number bib in front of the bedroom mirror. At 4:55 A.M., exactly according to plan, they were nearly ready to go out the door and Scott was ordering their Uber. But then, calamity struck.

"Scott!" Gary cried, looking up with a panicked face from where he'd been fumbling with the contents of his belt.

"What?" Scott replied in an extra-calm fashion.

Gary then explained that he'd carelessly dumped the pill from Frank and the pill from Arvid "Ass Man" Sloan into the same container last night without realizing that they were indistinguishable from each other. Scott remained calm.

Next, Gary explained that half an hour ago he'd carelessly taken his multi-vitamin tablet, which had also been stored in that same container, without realizing that it, too, was indistinguishable from the other two. Scott began to panic a little.

After a few minutes of debating with Scott what to do, Gary made the command decision that he would go ahead and take both of the remaining pills, which he then did. After all, he reasoned, at least one of the three, probably two, and possibly all of them, were conducive to strong, healthy running. He also tried to reassure himself (successfully) and Scott (unsuccessfully) by mentioning that in the wee hours of the morning, he'd received a text from Frank explaining that the original pill was an "antidote" for the second one, to be taken at the end of the race to counteract any possible negative effects.

After this, they went downstairs, took their Uber to the starting line area, and said goodbye to each other. Then Gary made his way through the admission gate while Scott headed off to the bleachers in the spectator area.

In the starting pen, going through some lightweight mental and physical preparation exercises, Gary felt healthy, energized, and optimistic.

A few minutes after being released onto the race course, once he'd separated himself from the pack and gotten into a comfortable running groove, he was overcome by a feeling of serenity and oneness with his surroundings—a feeling of completely living in the moment. Soon he began to ponder, not for the first time, the notion that the present moment is always, in a sense, all there is. The past and the future aren't really real; they only exist in your mind, one as memories and the other as expectations. He stopped pondering this, and laughed out loud, upon realizing that he was no longer living in the moment.

Nevertheless, Gary's next five miles were joyous, filled with feelings of strength and giddiness and invincibility, and the occasional brief return of that pure serenity.

But then his fortunes changed drastically. First he was struck with repeated, increasingly strong waves of nausea, until eventually he ducked into a porta-potty to vomit. After that came waves of abdominal pain and chaos, in a similar pattern, culminating in another porta-potty pitstop for another furious expulsion (this time from the opposite end of his digestive tract). Next came an alternating sequence of fever and chills, followed by a series of severe leg cramps, followed by more fever and chills.

Gary spotted Scott, standing on the sidelines near the 15-mile marker, and went over to him for a bit of comfort and counsel, which Scott gladly gave. They spent five minutes talking, after which Gary, though immensely grateful, disregarded his husband's advice to quit the race.

By the time he'd covered another mile, during which he availed himself of the offerings of a Gatorade station and a beer station, all Gary's physical symptoms had subsided and he felt on top of the world once again. And to his great delight and relief, this state persisted for the remainder of the marathon and he tromped very forcefully and purposefully across the finish line at 1:24 P.M., enveloped in a dizzy cloud of euphoria.

A minute later, walking through the massive, dense crowd, just after spotting Scott, standing behind a rope twenty feet ahead, grinning excitedly, Gary was abruptly grabbed by a race official, informed he'd been selected for random drug screening, and ushered into a nearby tent. Despite feeling quite confident that taking carotodiazapene violated no rules (and that no test for it existed anyway), he couldn't help becoming slightly nervous about this unexpected turn of events.

Initially Gary was handed an empty plastic cup and instructed to go behind a curtain and fill it with his urine; he attempted to comply but found himself unable to produce any. Then he was directed to a chair with wide wooden armrests in another corner of the tent, where a person who did not look the least bit like a medical professional proceeded to tie a tourniquet around his bicep, thrust a needle into his vein, and extract a syringeful of blood. He protested vehemently during this process but was told that when he'd signed the release forms he'd given his consent, not only for this but for a whole host of other things the hearing of which made his skin crawl.

Dismissed from the tent immediately after the blood draw, Gary tried to calm down and pull himself together as he made his way through the crowd toward the rope. By the time he reached Scott, he'd succeeded in this effort and was wearing an ecstatic grin.

"I did it, babe!" he shouted, then gave his almost equally ecstatic husband a long hug and a quick kiss (the only kind Scott allowed in public).

As the two of them began pushing through a buzzing ocean of people in the direction of the Uber pick-up point, it crossed Gary's mind that he'd not seen or heard anything further from Frank, who may or may not have been planning (Gary couldn't remember for sure) to show up here and run this race. Then he had a strange, strong feeling that, somehow, he'd be seeing Frank very soon, and that they'd be taking their fantastic running collaboration to the next level. This brought a smile to his face.

Chapter 12

It was 11:30 on a Wednesday morning and Laura Johnson was sitting at a small circular table in the 17th floor break room, awaiting her friends and gazing out the window. The rather spectacular view offered subtle signals that mid-September was moving into late September, such as all the trees continuing to retain their leaves, the permanently gridlocked traffic, the bright green grass patch of Carthay Circle Park, dotted with the standard quantity of human and canine visitors, and the slightly pink hue of sunlight passing through smog.

She sighed, lamenting the hardships brought by her period, which had started two days ago. The cramps, thankfully, had been fairly minor this time around and were now nearly gone. But the flow was as heavy as ever, and as of this morning, she'd officially reached what she called the B.T.D. (bleeding to death) phase, during which, whenever away from home, she had to be sure that her purse was well-stocked with feminine products, that a restroom was always nearby, and, as an extra precaution, that she was wearing very dark-colored pants.

Of course, these were extremely private thoughts that Laura would never have dreamed of sharing with anyone. The only woman with whom she'd discussed menstruation in her entire life was her mother, Pat Johnson (née Webster). That lucky bitch had totally finished menopause before her 42nd birthday. Laura was currently 48—nearly 49—and still going strong. Not fair.

She sighed again, looking down at the Sum-Thin-Different! mail-order microwave meal sitting on the table in front of her. She and Mike had both been trying continuously over the past two years to lose thirty pounds, and during this time had both gained twenty. They hated to cook, and signing up for Sum-Thin-Different! was their latest attempt to reverse the weight trend. The meals, in spite of being quite small and invariably tasting similar to wet cardboard, cost them $10 a pop.

Yvonne Smede walked into the room looking a bit beleaguered, spotted Laura, came over to the table and set down on it her own microwave-ready lunch (a small plastic tub containing leftovers from Sunday's roast chicken dinner).

"Hmmf," she said. "Haggling with the Interface Team. Back and forth all morning, arguing the same stupid point." A groan and an eyeroll. "They drive me insane."

"Sorry," said Laura.

Yvonne glanced in the direction of the microwave. A couple of people were hovering near it. "Had your turn yet?" she asked.

"No, I was sort of waiting for you guys."

Yvonne sat down. "So, what tasty treat have you got today?"

"Um, I don't even know..." Laura examined the lettering on the little brown cardboard box. "Um... looks like it's officially called 'Scrumptious Prima Vera Medley with Rich Delectable All-White-Meat Ragout.' Wow."

Yvonne chuckled. "Maybe you can sue them."

"Yeah."

After a moment's silence, during which Yvonne stared into space, she said, "Do you think having a superior intellect—you know, being brighter and more educated and more thoughtful and, just, more aware—does it actually help a person make better decisions?"

"Yeah, of course!" Laura replied without hesitation. "Just look at yourself—very smart, which is why you always show up those interface folks."

The phrase "and my own teammates" leapt into Yvonne's mind but didn't make it to her lips. Instead she said, "Yeah, it probably helps with being right about stuff. I'm nearly always right." She smiled with amusement at how this remark sounded, but knew that, coming from her, it was not an exaggeration or even a boast. Being right—truly right, simply for its own sake, not for winning arguments or garnering glory—mattered hugely to her. "I make sure I am," she added.

Laura smiled too, and nodded.

"But," Yvonne continued, "that's not the same thing as making good decisions. I mean, I chose to go around in circles with those ding-a-lings. Was that the best choice? Maybe I could've argued my case more effectively somehow. Maybe I could've gone over their head. I *definitely* could've gone behind their back. Or just stepped away and let them fall on their face!"

Laura was laughing now. "An interesting point," she said.

"But it's not just work decisions. It's every part of life. Do smart people actually conduct their lives any more smartly than dumb people?"

"Yeah, I think so…"

"I don't. I think we make the same dumb decisions that dummies make, and for the same dumb reasons. We just do a lot more agonizing over them and mulling over them and rationalizing them. So who's really the dummy?" She grinned.

Laura was laughing again. "You're over-thinking this, Yvonne."

"Yes, exactly! There's a reason the term 'over-thinking' exists."

"Oh, dear," Laura said, shaking her head, still chuckling.

"You know I'm right," Yvonne added with a smirk.

"What's up, bitches!" called Amy Lee from across the room as she entered it. All twelve of the other human eyeballs present immediately turned toward her.

Striding rapidly over to the table where her two friends sat, she said, "Can you believe what an idiot Mona was during that meeting?"

Mona, who was just finishing making herself a Keurig tea, cast a hurt glance in Amy's direction, collected up her drink and other belongings, and scurried away into a corridor. Neither Laura nor Amy noticed her. Yvonne did, but decided to make her resulting cringe a purely internal one.

"Oh my god!" Laura exclaimed, pointing to the "personal" pan pizza (diameter: 12 inches) Amy was clutching in her hands. "I didn't know H.D. was here today!"

Humility Dough was a food truck that was occasionally parked at the curb in front of the building, but most days wasn't. Amy had been a fan for a long time, and Laura for nearly as long.

"Yeah, baby!" Amy said, plopping the pizza down on the table and taking a seat. "I was gonna run over to Rocco's, but when I came out the door I saw H.D. there and that was all she wrote!"

She laughed as she opened the box and all three women were hit by a wave of its contents' hot salty fatty deliciousness aroma. "Oh, you two are welcome to have some," she added.

Yvonne politely declined the offer and, seeing the microwave was available, stood up and headed for it with her little tub of leftovers. Laura thanked Amy and eagerly grabbed a slice out of the steaming box; Sum-Thin-Different! could wait until another day.

"Oh!" said Amy, her mouth full of her first bite. She paused momentarily to hurriedly finish chewing and swallow, then, "I'm going to Michigan again! Can you believe it?"

Laura, whose mouth was also full of first bite, raised her eyebrows and made a "Mmm?" sound.

"Yeah! So I was talking to my mom when I was downstairs, and she goes—god, she is a riot—she goes, 'Aim-ee, happy news, I have booked a fright for you'... Just, booked me a flight to Michigan, for Friday of next week. Didn't even consult me!" Though Amy's words seemed to be registering a complaint, her tone simply sounded amused.

"Wow," said Laura.

"So yeah, I'm going out there again, to meet this Lee couple in the flesh. Mom insists. Assuming I can even find them! So nuts." She laughed. "Kinda fun, though, I gotta admit."

"Your birth parents?"

"Yeah, did I tell you already? I can't remember. So last week I finally received this so-called 'dossier' that the H.H.S. people promised me when I went to see them back in July. It took, like... well, over two months to get to me. And, some dossier! It was one freakin' sheet of paper, with writing on like half of one side."

Laura was laughing. Amy *had* already told her all of this, but she enjoyed hearing it again anyway.

Yvonne slid back into her chair holding a piping-hot tub of bland-but-healthy food. She, too, had heard the dossier story previously.

Amy continued, "It just has basic info about the adoption, like dates and case numbers and stuff that's useless to me. And it has everyone's name, address and phone number, but from way back then—you know, like almost 40 years ago."

Yvonne and Laura were both looking at Amy, smiling, chewing, and shaking their heads.

"So, tried the phone number and it was out of service, no surprise there. Searched for them online but, you know, nada. Mom told me to write them a letter—like an actual, physical letter on paper, and mail it to that old address, but... I don't know, seems kinda weird and lame... A lot of effort and then you just put it out there and, probably never hear anything back..."

"So what are you going to do when you get to Michigan?" Laura asked.

"The only thing I *can* do—show up at that address and knock on the door!"

"That's crazy," said Yvonne.

"I know, right? But try telling my mom that! Lordy. Oh! She also wants me to try to track down this thing the professor came up with—you know, where it's conceivable I might possibly be his granddaughter? Shheeah, right, as if! Oh, dear..." She was shaking her head and laughing as she reached for another slice of H.D.

"Oh, hey," said Laura, "what about that ancient book he was going to send you a copy of? Did he ever do it?"

"Hmm, no. I tried calling him about it once but got voicemail. Then I sorta forgot about it. I'm surprised Mom hasn't been pestering me about that, too!" She laughed again. "Must be too distracted by this other stuff, I guess."

"What does your dad think of all this?" asked Yvonne.

"Oh, he doesn't care. My dad never has an opinion about anything. Oh, hey—don't forget, ladies-only happy hour tonight! We are going to paaar-tay! Six o'clock at The Seven."

"Oh, I thought it was seven o'clock at The Six," said Laura.

"Nah... I mean, I like The Six, it was fun last time I went but... The Seven is supposed to be, like, really happening..."

"Either of you ever been to The Five?" asked Yvonne.

"Yeah, years ago," said Laura. "I don't remember if—"

"Sorry, ladies," Amy said as she abruptly stood up. "I'll be back in a few."

Strolling away from the table, she added loudly, "Gotta change my freakin' tampon, *again*! I swear, I don't know how a person can lose this much blood and not die!"

She laughed heartily as she disappeared into the corridor at the other side of the break room.

At 10:35 A.M. the following day, Incel Haston, a tall, thin, 28-year-old white man employed with the Los Angeles Parking Violations Bureau, slapped a citation against the windshield of a Dodge Charger parked in front of the LaBrea Tar Pits on the 5800 block of Wilshire Boulevard, securing it with a wiper blade. He then stepped over to the electronic meter on the curb next to the car, inserted his key, and erased the remaining 17 minutes, setting it back to "Expired."

The fact that this particular Dodge Charger was an L.A.P.D. cruiser did not deter Incel in the least; rather, it motivated him immensely, for he recognized this car as belonging to his arch-nemesis, Officer Diane Seeste, a short, pudgy, 28-year-old black woman (who was currently getting donuts across the street with her partner).

The two had been mortal enemies for a long time. Neither of them could remember how long or, more crucially, why. But they both retained every ounce of passion they'd ever felt (and then some) for inflicting pain on each other. This mainly consisted of Incel giving Diane parking citations and her giving him tickets for speeding and running stop signs.

As Incel strolled back to his official parking enforcement vehicle, a self-satisfied grin on his face, he passed two palm trees, and also two men in their late thirties who were walking the opposite direction, headed from the tar pits' museum building, where they'd just had a brief visit, over to the Los Angeles County Museum of Art, which lay immediately to the west.

Both men were extremely well dressed, though one more formally than the other. The Latino man, wearing a dark blue Armani suit, light blue shirt, yellow tie, and black lace-ups, was Francisco Danilo Rosario. The white man, sporting very white skin indeed, blond hair, bright blue eyes, a white open-collar shirt, a navy blue Tommy Hilfiger sports jacket, tan slacks, and brown loafers, was Jefferson Lincoln Wentworth Wacksworth, known to everyone who knew him as Lincoln. The two had been good friends ever since attending 6th grade together at the prestigious Fairest Oaks Day School in Pasadena.

Their friendship was on Francisco's mind at the moment. Or rather, all of his very few close friendships were on his mind. He'd noticed that creating new, long-lasting friendships—real ones, strong and truly close—had been relatively easy in childhood but nearly impossible in adulthood. Was this a universal thing or was it peculiar to him? Thinking through the close friends he'd had in his life whom he still regarded as very close today, he realized there was only one he'd met in adulthood: Yvonne Smede. And, though he didn't really want to admit it to himself, deep down he suspected the only reason this particular friendship had been so close and so long-lasting was that he'd always been attracted to her and she'd never felt the same about him.

"Hey, Francisco," said Lincoln, "what's up? You're so quiet."

"Oh. Well..."

"Trying to rank all the women's asses you've turned around and looked at this morning?" teased Lincoln with a grin.

"What?" Francisco replied abruptly, a mild wave of panic crossing his face. He'd never known that Lincoln noticed this habit of his, even though he did it constantly and very indiscreetly. "No, no. No. I was merely thinking about... all of the splendid artwork we are about to enjoy together."

"Yeah, me too."

The companions crossed through the "Urban Light" exhibit (a collection of two hundred restored cast-iron streetlamps) in front of the main entrance, flashed their annual passes at the young chap manning the box office, and headed inside.

Francisco visited L.A.C.M.A. eagerly and frequently, and while inside always took copious notes on a little spiral-bound pad, but never actually enjoyed the experience (but would never have admitted to this). The people he occasionally persuaded to accompany him, Lincoln included, had no enthusiasm for it and generally said as much to Francisco, but after arriving there tended to derive quite a bit of pleasure from the art they observed (but would never have admitted to this).

"Hey, where'd you say Felicia was?" asked Lincoln as they entered the building.

"Felaecia. Felaecia."

"Right."

"She has no wish to patronize art museums, Lincoln. She does not harbor the same appreciation for art that I do."

Lincoln's eyebrows made a quick up-and-down motion as he muttered, "Hmm."

"And how about Mary?" asked Francisco. "Does she have a taste for art?"

Mary Wacksworth (née Lincoln), Lincoln's wife of 14 years and mother of three of his four children, had passionately pursued a career in aerospace engineering from a very young age, and continued to do so now (in spite of occasional, gently-delivered reminders from her husband that they were decamillionaires a few times over who had no financial need ever to work another day in their lives). Most weekdays she worked in the same El Segundo office building as Scott Portcullis, though neither of them knew of the other's existence.

"Oh, she's working," said Lincoln.

After this, they didn't speak again for over an hour as they slowly, methodically moved through several rooms of L.A.C.M.A., taking in its paintings, sculptures, photographs, and other, harder-to-classify works of art. When words were finally uttered, they were related to the only subject that both men felt strongly interested in: government and its attendant political processes.

"Lincoln," Francisco said as they were crossing a large corridor that lay between two painting galleries, "what would you say it takes to be a great president?"

"Hmm..." said Lincoln.

Francisco, not overly concerned about getting input from his friend, went on, "Certainly it does not require large amounts of, or specialized, knowledge or expertise. A president has supreme access to these in other people."

"True."

"Being a capable conversationalist or orator can probably help to a point, particularly in getting elected in the first place. It only indirectly bears on decisions, policies, and achievements, however, by bringing people around to one's viewpoint. Anyway, a great deal of one's communication can be scripted in advance by others."

"Well—"

"How about intelligence? It, too, is of limited value. As president, one has people who can explain any concept deeply and repeatedly until it is well understood. One even has people who can formulate solutions on one's behalf."

"Yeah."

"How about sound judgment? Again, one has people for that."

"You might need to judge which advisor's advice you should take," ventured Lincoln. "You know, if you're getting conflicting advice."

Francisco smiled. "Yes, but in theory one could even get someone else to do that part, if one gave this special surrogate sufficient inputs regarding guiding values, priorities, and desired outcomes."

"What about morality?" Lincoln suggested. "I think you need a strong moral compass."

"Well, it is true one's presidency would not be great if one behaved with malevolence, or took some kind of amoral approach, or embraced values generally deemed unsavory or morally wrong."

"Exactly."

"However, one need not obtain one's principles, values, and priorities from within. They can come from any source. One only needs to be willing to behave consistently with them. Such behavior can also be guided by others."

"Hmm."

"Additional qualities which might well be on the tip of your tongue are hard work and political prowess. Again, I assert that, while both offer immense value in one's attempt to get elected, they no longer do so when one is in power. Tasks, including strategizing, can be delegated to competent and savvy underlings."

"So what we're saying is, you need to be some things in order to *become* president, but once you do, you don't need to be anything." Lincoln laughed. "Absolutely anybody could be a great president!"

"Yes, anybody *could*, but not anybody *would*. What it really takes is simply to be committed to filling the role in whatever way serves the country best, according to a clear framework of values, principles, goals, and priorities that is established from the start."

At this point Lincoln excused himself to go to the men's room, but Francisco did not hear him (or notice his departure) and carried right on talking.

"In particular," he said, "one's ego must take a back seat, along with whatever other concerns, desires, interests, neuroses, worries, and beliefs one might possess. One must think of oneself as the office, not as a person. Everything one says, everything one does, every decision one makes, in one's presidential capacity—all of it must be solemnly undertaken *as* that noble office. To maintain utter respect for the office is... paramount."

Francisco paused and smiled, staring straight ahead at nothing, completely engrossed in the thesis he'd just formulated, reviewing it with satisfaction. "Yes," he muttered quietly to himself with a slight nod of the head.

Then he reached out with his left hand, placing it on the shoulder of Marissa Farmington, a total stranger who just happened to now be standing approximately where Lincoln had been a minute ago, and said, "I should write a book about this."

"About what?" Marissa asked cheerfully and with genuine curiosity.

"Oh," said Francisco, realizing his mistake.

Though he was instantly struck with a small amount of panic and a large amount of embarrassment, the physical manifestation of these feelings was the formation of a pleasant expression on the face and a brief, mild paralysis from the neck down, causing him to remove his hand from her shoulder only after a few more seconds, and then only slowly. Simultaneously he said, in an apparently calm voice, "I am developing a theory of governmental leadership."

"That sounds cool," said Marissa.

"Indeed it is," Francisco replied.

"I'd love to hear all about it... Maybe over coffee sometime?"

Francisco was stunned. "Oh. Well... Yes, absolutely!"

Observing that he did not seem to be holding a phone, but was clutching a pen and notepad in his right hand, Marissa snatched them from him, flipped the pad to a new sheet, quickly scrawled her name and number, and handed them back.

Francisco looked down at the pad. "Marissa," he said.

"That's me!"

"I am Francisco."

"Hi, Francisco. Nice to meet you."

"It has been a great pleasure meeting you as well."

They stared, smiling, at each other for a short while as Francisco desperately tried to think of something else to say, with no success.

"Well, bye!" said Marissa, then turned and walked away.

Francisco felt giddy. He would have to find Lincoln right away and share what had just happened. A moment's pause. Actually, no, on second thought, he would keep this to himself.

The next day at 3:50 P.M., Bill Smede stood in the lounge of the condo, preparing to depart to go sign a lease agreement on a nearby apartment he was planning to move into.

Relations between him and Yvonne had thawed (somewhat) almost immediately after they'd agreed to split up. But sharing a living space—including a bedroom—had been very difficult for either to abide, and they'd very soon begun discussions in earnest about who would move out, when, to where, and logistical details involving money, vehicles, and offspring.

As it happened, both of Bill's children were currently standing here in the room with him, aiming their vacant stares in two random directions, engaged in no apparent activity, their state of mind and intentions entirely unclear. Alice, as usual, wore her wireless earbuds. Patrick was fitted with a wired pair, one in his left ear and the other dangling over his right shoulder.

"So, Alice," said Bill, "I'm heading over to that apartment now to sign the papers."

"Okay," she replied flatly, one of her hands moving almost imperceptibly to pause the music playing from her phone.

"You wanna come with me?"

"I'm good."

"You sure? Thought you might be curious to see the place." He paused for a quick moment, then added, "I mean, it's where you'll be spending half your time," followed by a short, nervous laugh. He didn't know why he felt nervous.

"I'm good," Alice repeated, evincing no emotion.

"Okay," said Bill, then, turning to his son, "How 'bout you, Patrick?"

"What?" Patrick said, triggered by the sound of his name, prior to which he'd been paying no attention to the goings-on around him.

"You wanna come with me? To see my new apartment?"

"Oh, no thanks," Patrick replied with an awkward smile. "I'm, um... I'm pretty busy right now."

"Okay," said Bill again. "Well, I guess I'll see you two later."

He left the condo and went down the stairs and out to the sidewalk, and began heading south on Wexler, passing one of the building's tiny parking corrals where the ATS was wedged between two other vehicles. He and Yvonne had briefly entertained, but ultimately decided against, the idea of getting a second car, reasoning it wasn't worthwhile with money very tight and neither of them using the ATS to commute to work. Anyway Bill's new apartment did not include any parking spaces at all, and he would've been hard-pressed to choose between continually negotiating the cutthroat world of L.A. street parking or simply bringing all his groceries home in a Radio Flyer wagon.

Up ahead, standing on a small patch of grass near the southeast corner of the building, Bill could see Wally talking in a very animated fashion (including multiple complex hand-and-finger gestures that seemed intended to convey the sizes or shapes or relative locations of something) to Milton Kim, who lived alone in Number Six, was seldom seen by any of the other residents of the building, and about whom Bill knew almost nothing (including his name).

However, a few tidbits about Milton had been correctly guessed, by Bill and others, based on the artifacts perpetually littering the concrete, forming a three-stranded trail marker of sorts that connected his car, his condo door, and the dumpsters on the south side of the building: that he very much enjoyed cigarettes and lottery scratcher cards, and that he was a careless, unconscientious slob. As it happened, he was holding a lit cigarette currently, partially disassembling his scowl every few seconds as he brought it to his lips, all the while staring at Wally with narrowed, contemptuous eyes.

Bill also saw, coming toward him on the sidewalk, Faye, who lived in the building just north of his. He gave her a quick nod and smile as they neared each other. Her face registered no recognition and no interest; her eyes landed on him for a microsecond as she continued to maintain the same gait and to occupy the exact center of the sidewalk so that, when they passed each other a second later, Bill had to speedily step off onto the grass (and speedily judge which direction to step (he chose the right (toward the building), calculating unconsciously that it offered marginally better odds of not stepping in shit)).

As Bill reached the point in his trajectory closest to where Wally stood, he heard "Hey, Bill!" come from that direction. He turned his head but continued walking.

"You should come hear this too," Wally said. "It concerns the latest P.A.P. smear."

"Sorry, can't!" Bill called back, the distance between them steadily growing. "I'm late for something!"

"Roger that!" Wally replied. "I'll brief you later!"

The next two blocks of Bill's journey through his ever-irritating neighborhood were relatively uneventful, and even included the small treat of watching a middle-aged white man (whose face in reality looked very similar to Bill's but which Bill judged to be almost certainly that of a complete prick) try unsuccessfully several times to parallel park his BMW in a spot that was clearly too small for it, between a 1981 Toyota Corolla Tercel and a 1998 Chevy Cavalier, before driving off in disgust.

But then things really went south, and remained there for the final few blocks. This included four instances of noisy gardening equipment (always the high-powered, industrial kind used by professionals, as no Angeleno performed their own gardening) operating near the sidewalk, or, in one case, actually on the sidewalk (a man with a backpack-powered leaf blower). Also featured were three instances of pop-up sprinklers watering the concrete (and passersby's ankles) instead of the grass, two instances of commercial vehicles slowly reversing up the street with their warning alarm loudly beeping away, and one instance of a little Honda Civic del Sol, sporting a modified tailpipe the diameter of a manhole cover, blasting down the street at double the maximum legal speed, emitting a roaring engine sound that rivaled a freight train in decibels and handily bested it in obnoxiousness.

Then Bill stood outside the drab, 58-year-old apartment building at 2041 Dimvale Avenue, which he'd visited once before and would soon become his home, regarding it with skepticism and a wisp of trepidation. It looked astonishingly similar to the building that housed the Smedes' condo: same size, shape, and color; two driveways and cramped little carport areas in the same locations at the front; three narrow concrete paths leading from the sidewalk to three tiny pseudo-patios, each with a pair of mailboxes bolted onto the wall, a door leading into the ground floor unit and a wooden staircase going up to the unit above. And, oddly enough, the one Bill was going to rent occupied the same position—upper-right when facing the building from the street.

There was one major difference, however: this building contained twelve units in total, rather than six, with each of the apartments currently in view backing up against its counterpart on the rear half of the building. So anyone living here had windows on, at most, two sides of their (very small) home.

After a quick glance at his wrist, which revealed he'd done 5,639 steps so far today and was one minute late for his meeting with the landlord, Bill proceeded along the footpath and up the stairs, and hesitantly knocked on the door of Number Four. When there was no response after thirty seconds, he knocked again, more forcefully this time. Another thirty seconds went by, during which he became increasingly fretful and frustrated. Then he tried the knob and, to his mild surprise, found it was unlocked.

"Hello?" he called out as he slowly swung the door open and poked his head tentatively through.

The studio apartment, procured for the relatively low price of $1,900 per month, was dark, silent, and deserted. He stepped inside and shut the door.

Immediately to his right was the entrance to the bathroom. A few feet beyond that, ahead of him to the right, lay the seven-feet-square kitchen area, bounded on one side by a breakfast bar and on two other sides by walls, boasting appliances that looked to be about three decades old and a countertop that was probably original.

The remainder of the apartment—a single room, roughly a tenth the size of Francisco's main lounge area, stretching out in front of Bill and to his left—contained one large window covered with vertical blinds, a brown shag carpet that appeared to have been installed when shag carpets were fashionable, a matching set of two armchairs and a sofa in quite decent condition, a small wooden coffee table, and, against the far wall, a pair of bunk beds. It was Bill's plan that he would occupy the bottom one and Alice, when she stayed, would take the top one.

"Good times," he muttered to himself, hands on his hips, pacing around slowly and aimlessly near the front door.

He glanced at his PaceTek again, then promptly forgot what it said. He sighed. Then, with some alarm, he realized that he was feeling considerable pressure from his bladder.

"Fuck," he said, suddenly bombarded with serious regrets about the huge mug of coffee he'd poured himself at 3:30, which at the time had seemed like a splendid idea.

Once Bill had become aware of the potential impending toilet dilemma, he could not take his mind off it, and after a few minutes, during which, it seemed, his abdominal discomfort had increased continuously and exponentially, he'd whipped himself into a state of desperation and near-panic.

"Fuck," he said again. "Mmmf, *fine.*" The decision was made. He had no choice but to use this apartment's bathroom.

He opened the door, entered, shut it again, and turned the little circular locking switch in the center of the doorknob. Then he paused for a second. Best to sit down for this, he thought. Wouldn't want to risk any accidental splashing. Especially as there was no toilet paper with which to mop up those stray droplets. Okay, let's get on with it then. He lowered his pants, placed himself on the toilet and tried to relax. After a couple of seconds, the flow began. After several more seconds, his mood started to improve. He was almost out of the woods now. Everything would be fine, after all.

Then he heard the front door of the apartment fly open and, simultaneously, the booming voice of Joseph Tanur.

"Mr. Smede! Are you in here?" His accent, though differing only subtly from standard American, clearly originated from a country in which English was not the first language.

Bill felt it would *probably* be best to respond—to speak to Tanur through the bathroom door and simply explain the situation. But what a weird, awkward thing to do. He just couldn't quite bring himself to go through with it.

Seconds ticked by in slow motion. The stream continued its steady flow, softly striking the porcelain, giving the distinct sense that it was nowhere near reaching a natural end and that not even maximal exertion of all the muscles in Bill's body could bring it to a premature one.

The bathroom doorknob turned, quickly and easily like one that wasn't locked, and the door swung open, bashing into Bill's knees.

Tanur's face appeared from behind it. His skin resembled leather in both color and texture. His eyes were green and his swept-back hair silvery white.

"Ah, there you are," he said, neither smiling nor frowning. "You take liberties."

Bill grimaced. "Yeah, uh… Sorry. Just give me a minute, please."

"Hurry," Tanur replied. "I am busy man." Then he just stood there, staring.

Ten minutes later, the two were standing in the main room of the apartment, engaged in a handshake, their business concluded.

Bill had only one principle that he would actively defend: never actively defend your principles. In any potentially contentious conversation, just smile and nod. Even better, with a group of three or more, ignore the others and stare blankly into space (or, best of all, leave).

So, he'd chosen the first option when Tanur had informed him that, although he'd be responsible for rent payments from the 1st of October, the apartment would not actually be available for him to move into until after it had been painted on the 8th. And again when Tanur contradicted what they'd agreed on the first time they met by mentioning that all the furniture would be removed next week and Bill would have to re-furnish the apartment himself. And again when, contrary to all their prior discussions, Bill was told that none of the utilities were included. And again when told that the rent was in fact $1999, not $1900.

He even smiled at Tanur now, as their handshake ended, and said, "Thanks for everything," despite feeling the opposite of grateful and despite the fact that Tanur was not smiling.

Bill wasn't proud of being this way, but nor had he felt any shame about it in many, many years. He simply accepted it as an immutable, core piece of his character.

"Goodbye, Mr. Smede," Tanur said, then turned and began walking, it appeared, toward the kitchen.

Bill shrugged, left the apartment, went down the stairs and headed for the sidewalk, somewhat lost in thought as he tried to run through the particulars of the upcoming move. Then he heard the sound of a familiar voice. Two, in fact.

"Well, what a nice surprise," he remarked, stepping onto the sidewalk right in front of his children, who only then noticed him and stopped walking. Neither seemed at all embarrassed.

"Oh, hey, Dad," Patrick said. "Me and Alice were just heading over to this boba place I like."

"Great," said Bill.

"Um... Do you want us to bring you back anything?"

Amy Lee was cruising along US-10 in Midland County, Michigan in her rented Chevy Malibu, thinking back over her experiences of the past 18 hours.

Her husband Jake had gotten off work early yesterday and driven her to the airport, where they'd both thought it'd be nice for him to park and accompany her inside. Discovering at the entrance to the parking garage that he'd left his wallet at home, Jake had borrowed Amy's credit card for the little electronic device that lifted the barricade arm to let them in.

While collecting up her belongings at the far end of the security checkpoint conveyor belt, Amy'd received a call from Jake (who, for some reason, had spent a long time wandering around the airport grounds after they'd said goodbye), informing her that he couldn't get the car out without inserting the same credit card he'd used on the way in. So back out she'd gone to the public section of the terminal, met him, handed him the card, then made her way through the checkpoint for a second time.

Forty minutes later, waiting in the crazy-long McDonald's line, she'd realized she had no other credit cards and called Jake (who, by this time, was inching along Century Boulevard, a full half-mile outside the airport property) to bring the card back. So he'd turned the car around (eventually, after narrowly avoiding two collisions and failing to avoid seven loud, long horn blasts), made his way back into the labyrinthine hellscape of the LAX complex, parked at the curb this time (in the white zone, for immediate loading and unloading only), dashed inside, and handed the card back to his wife. After this, of course, she'd had to make her way through the security checkpoint for a third agonizingly slow time.

Amy laughed out loud remembering all this. "Oh dear," she said.

Fortunately, these delays had not caused her to miss her flight because, just like in July, its departure time had been drastically postponed, in increments, throughout the afternoon and evening. And just like then, she'd flown in a middle seat, wedged between two rather large fellow travelers.

As an added bonus not offered by the July trip, Amy's air journey hadn't ended in Detroit. Upon arriving there she'd sprinted frantically across the terminal to board another flight (which itself had been massively delayed) that would carry her a hundred miles north to Saginaw.

Scanning the landscape now as she rolled northwestward toward her mysterious destination, she noted how similar it looked to the other part of the state she'd visited: very flat, lots of trees, not much else.

She smiled. The travails of yesterday (and into the wee hours of today) hadn't dampened her spirits at all, and now, taking in the beautiful, peaceful autumn morning scene, she felt especially uplifted.

"I could get used to this," she said. "Michigan!"

A billboard, solid black with white lettering reading "HELL IS REAL," drifted past on the left side of the highway. A moment later, on the opposite side, a water tower with "Warren Township" stenciled across its top came into view and began floating toward Amy.

"Water tower. Check!" she said with a grin.

Upon first observing these structures, ubiquitous in Wayne and Washtenaw counties three months ago, she'd wondered if they could be a snazzy new form of advertising, or some kind of ultra-modern art. The front desk clerk at her hotel had set her straight. Now she was a seasoned expert.

So engrossed was Amy in the charm of her surroundings that she nearly missed her exit even though the voice coming out of her phone was currently discussing it.

"Whoops!" she said, slamming on the brakes. "Oh, dear." She chuckled as she turned the wheel and glided onto the off-ramp.

The remainder of her drive was brief and uneventful, and brought her to roughly the midpoint of a short road called Finchfeather Lane, lined on both sides with modest but well-kept houses that all looked rather alike. Having parked in front of one, Amy hopped out of the car, quickly traversed the short concrete driveway and even shorter brick footpath to the front stoop, feeling a bit nervous but mainly eager and giddy and curious, and knocked on the door.

Several seconds passed, and she was just raising her arm to knock again when the door abruptly swung wide open and she came within a few millimeters of slamming her knuckles into the face of the man now standing before her. He was white, roughly mid-fifties, with a giant unkempt mop of gray hair and a matching three-day beard growth, and clad only in a plain white t-shirt, pale blue boxer shorts, and dark brown socks.

"Yeah?" he said flatly, with a facial expression that conveyed no feelings, positive or negative.

"Um..." Amy stammered as she noticed that behind the man, on the far wall of his sitting room, a 50-inch television was playing an extremely explicit pornographic movie at quite a loud volume. "I'm, um... sorry to, to bother you, sir... but, um..."

The man wasn't going to help her out. He just stood and listened, meeting her gaze.

"This *is* 5231 Finchfeather, right?" she finally managed.

"No," he replied. "This is 5232."

"Oh! But I... um, I saw the number on the mailbox, there..." She half-turned her body and pointed vaguely.

The man smiled. "Across the street," he said.

"Oh, 5231 is across the street?"

"Yeah. They only put mailboxes on one side."

"Ah!"

"Lucky for me, it's this side." He chuckled.

The porn continued to rage on behind him. The actors had re-positioned themselves but hadn't lost any of their highly vocalized passion.

"Right!" said Amy. She chuckled too. "Well, okay... Thanks!" She took a step backward and turned to go.

"Have a nice day!" the man called out before closing the door.

"Thank God that was the wrong house," Amy muttered to herself as she made her way back to the road.

Looking across at the house opposite, she saw that it had the digits "5231" neatly affixed, in a diagonal pattern, to its wall, beside the garage door. "Yes," she said with a grin as she stepped off the curb.

A moment later, having knocked for the second time today on a stranger's front door, she found herself face to face with another white man, this time clean shaven and almost completely bald, fully dressed, and looking to be around 70 years old.

"How may I help you, ma'am?" he asked with a warm smile.

"Hi!" Amy said. "My name's Amy. And I'm, um... This is going to sound kinda weird, but I'm looking for some folks who lived in this house a long time ago. Like, 40 years ago."

"Well, you found 'em."

"Huh?"

"My wife and I have been living here for almost 50 years. Moved in right after it was built!"

Amy gasped, blurted out "Oh my god!" and attempted to process this information. "Unbelievable," she added as a grin broke out on her face. "So... you're... Mr. Lee?"

"Yep. Just call me Stan."

"Stan," she repeated, still reeling from the thought that at this moment she was looking into the eyes of her biological father, and the thought of how incredibly lucky she'd been to actually find him, and the thought that—holy cow!—her whole life she'd been half white.

"So, what can I do for you?" asked Stan.

"Oh! Right!" Amy chuckled. "Well… I'm the daughter you gave up for adoption way back then."

Stan's eyes bugged out and his eyebrows shot up. "Goodness gracious me!" he exclaimed. "Well, uh…" He began moving his shoulders and arms in an awkward fashion, clearly unsure whether a hug or merely a handshake was in order.

Just as Amy decided to opt for the hug and began to extend her own arms, she and Stan were startled by the noisy arrival of a car in the driveway.

"Oh," said Stan, "that's my son, Lil."

"Lil?" Amy queried. It sounded like a female name.

"Oh, yeah—short for Lillanoy. My wife's maiden name."

"Ah, gotcha." Odd name, thought Amy. Malaysian, maybe?

"Dad!" shouted Lil, who'd already gotten out of the car and was now retrieving what looked like a small aquarium from the back seat. "Great news!" He began walking toward them. "I've solved our mosquito problems."

Lil, who looked about the same age as Amy, was wearing a baggy blue hooded sweatshirt, baggy knee-length tan shorts, and a pair of black Converse All-Stars. He had a long, thick, shaggy head of dark hair, shooting out in all directions, and dark, bushy eyebrows. As he got close, Stan and Amy could see that his aquarium contained dozens of large spiders, all darting around wildly, crawling over each other and up and down the walls of their little prison.

"Yep," Lil continued, sidling up to the other two. "These suckers will eat 'em! They consider mosquitoes a delicacy! Hah!" He grinned, obviously proud and excited.

"Uh, yes," said Stan. "Well… please don't release them just yet. We can talk about this later. Right now, I'd like to introduce you to our guest, Amy."

Lil turned to Amy, seeming to notice her for the first time. "Nice to meet you," he said, still smiling widely.

"You too, Lil," said Amy cheerfully.

"Come on in," said Stan, stepping aside and making a "right this way" gesture with his arm and face.

"Thank you, sir," Amy said, stepping through.

Stan led the way past the front lounge, down a narrow, short hallway and into the combined kitchen/sitting area at the back of the house. Amy followed. Lil joined them after lingering in the entryway momentarily to get rid of his aquarium.

"Please, have a seat," said Stan. "Can I get you anything to drink?"

"Nah, I'm good, Dad," said Lil.

"I was talking to our guest. You can get your own drinks."

"Oh, I'm fine," said Amy, looking out the window at the rather spacious back yard. "But thank you... Hey, what's that thing?" She pointed at an object sitting in the middle of the lawn, about five feet tall, that appeared to be composed of three perfectly spherical rocks, their surfaces finely grooved, stacked on top of each other, each slightly smaller than the one beneath it.

"Oh, that? It's a snowman frame," said Stan, taking a seat across from the couch Amy was standing next to.

Seeing her puzzled face, he asked, "Do you live here in Michigan, Amy?"

"No," she said, turning away from the window and sitting down. "But I love it here! The seasons!"

"Hah! Seasons!" scoffed Lil, leaning against the kitchen counter. "All of 'em suck!" He chortled, amused by his own wit.

"Anyways, I'm from L.A.," Amy said.

"Awesome!" said Lil.

"Well, Amy," said Stan, "when the snow falls, it sticks onto the snowman frame and gives you the basic shape of your snowman without even lifting a finger. All you have to do is pop the extras in there, like twigs for arms, some kind of nose, maybe a hat or scarf, and... presto! Your snowman is done."

"Seems like that takes most of the fun out of it," said Amy.

"Rolling up those giant snowballs is not as fun as it looks on T.V.," offered Lil.

"Hmm," said Stan, "I do seem to recall the couple that adopted you lived in California."

"That's right!" said Amy. "And they still do. I'm a Cali girl, born and raised. Well, raised." She chuckled.

Stan sighed. "I suppose we should address the elephant in the room."

Amy flashed him raised eyebrows and a smile. She didn't know what he was talking about.

"You want to know... uh... why we gave you up. Right?"

"Oh, wow, holy crap!" Lil exclaimed. "That's *you*? Awesome."

"No, no," said Amy, smiling and shaking her head and moving her hands side to side, palms toward Stan. "It's totally fine. No worries. I understand, you had your reasons. Ancient history, ya know? But it's just so cool we found each other again!"

"We loved you," Stan continued. "We really did. You were wonderful. A blessing. But, you see, about a month after we brought you home, we found out Norma was pregnant. We'd never thought we could get pregnant. We'd, you know, tried... for years... We'd always wanted a child of our own, but, I had a low sperm count and..."

Amy was perplexed. What on earth was he talking about? She started to respond, but Stan wasn't finished.

"We just didn't think we... *could*, you know? Oh, Norma! There you are!"

A white woman about the same age as Stan had just entered the kitchen through a doorway on its far side. She smiled at the group as she made her way over to where they were.

"Come and meet Amy," Stan said. "She's, uh... she was our daughter, very briefly, long ago."

"Goodness gracious me!" exclaimed Norma, visibly taken aback. "Well, it's... It's so lovely to meet... to, uh, to see you..."

"Okay, wait a second!" cried Amy. "I think this is all starting to sink in. You two"—her eyes and pointing fingers darted back and forth between Norma and Stan—"are not my biological parents, are you?"

"No," said Stan. A short pause. "No," he repeated. Another short pause, then a chuckle. "Of course not. Is that what you thought?"

Norma giggled nervously. "We adopted you," she said.

Lil left his post at the kitchen counter and sauntered casually out of the room. "Awesome!" he called out as he disappeared down the hallway.

The other three were all silent for a moment. Then Amy burst out laughing.

"Un-freakin-believable!" she said. "I was *double* adopted. Oh, lordy. Wait'll my mom hears about this!"

Chapter 13

It was 5 P.M. on a Saturday in mid-October and Bill Smede was sitting alone at a conference table inside the Grove Plaza complex. On the table were his laptop (on which he was currently tapping away), three smartphones, and the third incarnation of the Soundtrack of Life hardware, which bore a strong resemblance to the other two and consisted of a plastic headband attached to which were three little cameras, a microphone, and a pair of earphones, with wires emanating from all six locations, then combining after a few inches into a single wire which continued on for another three feet, terminating with a USB-C plug.

"Fuck!" Bill screamed upon seeing, yet again, errors pop up during the computer's attempted compilation of his code.

"What the fuck..." was uttered slowly and at a much lower volume as he commenced troubleshooting the issue. He was putting the finishing touches on what would become version 0.3.27 of the S.O.L. software and, along with the headset lying a few feet away, would constitute the final "prototype" of the product prior to mass production and release to the public.

Wanda Hagan had advised against making a third prototype, because of the cost, when venture capital firm LeVay Say had completely dropped out of the project after being dissatisfied with the second one. As it was no longer a requirement at that point, Wanda had reasoned, the best course was simply to take LeVay's criticisms on board, conduct formal market research with professionally organized focus group sessions, and then concentrate all their attention and resources on finalizing the design and bringing it to market.

But Irene Hoffman had strongly disagreed with all this, citing the necessity of one more iteration of hardware manufacture to ensure it was just right, as well as the uselessness, tedium and inefficiency of focus groups. She'd overruled Wanda and eventually had fired her, declaring that keeping someone on who was a "poor fit" and refused to work for free would be irresponsible. At the time, she'd made a point of assuring Bill, who was also being paid (albeit rather nominally) for his efforts, that there was no danger of the same thing happening to him. He'd felt somewhat disappointed to hear this.

"Yes!" he exclaimed now, as at last his code compiled successfully.

Irene strolled into the room, singing quietly and mindlessly to herself: "Wish I didn't know now what I didn't know then..."

The S.O.L. all-hands "Phase 3 Wrap" meeting had concluded in this room ten minutes ago, after which Irene had left to accompany Judy, Stan, and Donald out to the parking lot (and to have a cigarette).

"How's it coming there, Mister Computer Genius?" she asked; then, without a pause, "Exciting times, huh?"

"Thrilling," said Bill. "Soon you're going to find out just how much of a computer genius I'm not."

"Don't be so hard on yourself, William. That's my job." She grinned.

"Anyway, it's done," Bill said. "I mean, it's built. We still need to test it."

"Mmm..." Hesitation and skepticism radiated from Irene. "We gotta ship this thing A.S.A.P. Let's keep the testing to just what's truly needed."

"Yeah, we always do. What's truly needed is a lot."

"Stan'll put it through its paces tomorrow."

"Well—"

"Hey, let's you and me give it a little preliminary test right now."

Bill raised an eyebrow. "*You* want to run through all these case trees in the harness?"

Methodical, formal software testing was a process that bored Bill to tears, and he actually understood it (mostly). The idea that someone like Irene would have any willingness to go that deep into the weeds he found completely unfathomable.

"What? No, dumbass," she replied. "I mean, push it out to the phones. Let's have a little fun. We'll take turns."

"Uh... Okay. Sure. Just a sec." He turned back to his laptop and launched into a furious stream of typing and clicking. "And... just... there and there and... there." He looked up again. "Okay, it's ready."

"Great," said Irene, reaching for her phone.

Bill picked up his phone too, opened the app, scrolled to "Settings," then selected "Advanced Tuning," where a user could, if so inclined, specify very complex prioritization and environment-dependent schemes for musical categories or individual tracks.

Irene was also busy scrolling and tapping away on her phone screen. "I'm feeling a rock-n-roll vibe," she said as she entered preferences for her imminent "Life Stroll."

Bill chuckled, eyes and fingers still fully occupied with the app. "Of course," he said. "When do you ever feel any other vibe?" He continued his screen-scrolling for another moment, then stopped, frowned and looked up. "Hey, do you have 'Bring Me Downtown' in your library?"

"What? Bring Me Downtown?" Irene kept her face in the phone.

"Yeah. From the nineties. It was by... Shit, who was it? It was part of that 'Jennifer' series."

Now she stopped and looked at him. "You are making zero sense, William," she said.

"You know, Eric Carmen did that song called 'Make Me Lose Control' where he said 'Jennifer's singing Stand By Me, and she knows every single word by heart'..."

"Uh, okay..."

"Well then somebody continued it with Bring Me Downtown. They had a line in there, 'Jennifer's singing Make Me Lose Control, and she knows every single word by heart'..."

Irene's face was blank.

"And then there was another one, a few years later, with, you know, Jennifer knows all the words to Bring Me Downtown. And, it just kept going. It's probably still going now. And they had contests where people would get on stage and try to prove they knew all the words to all these Jennifer songs by heart..."

Irene burst out laughing. "That's the stupidest thing I've ever heard," she said.

Bill laughed too, then said, "Well I think it's kind of cool."

"Oh!" said Irene suddenly, and put down her phone. "I've got a little treat for us." She walked a few steps over to a cabinet that stood up against the wall next to one end of the conference table. "To celebrate with!" She opened the cabinet and took out a bottle of wine, a corkscrew, and two glasses.

"Celebrate?" Bill queried. "What are we celebrating?"

"Being finished!" She was standing next to Bill's chair now, placing the pieces of her cabinet haul on the table one by one.

"Uh, Irene, we're not finished yet."

"In essence, we are," Irene proclaimed, scrunching up her face and staring at the corkscrew, the only item remaining in her hands, as if it were the Riddle of the Sphinx.

"Well, I don't—"

"Here, you do the honors," she said, thrusting the corkscrew in Bill's direction. "I don't know how to work this fucking thing."

Bill reluctantly accepted it, stood up, and started in on his new task. "You know," he said, "this A.I. stuff is pretty tricky. I know it makes the app more powerful but..." The cork came out with a quiet pop. "It's, you know, hard to get it right."

"Stan would never steer us wrong," said Irene, picking up the bottle and preparing to pour. "He's the best."

"Well, yeah, he's fantastic..." Bill laid the corkscrew and cork down. "But, he freely admits to having very little experience with A.I."

"Always the pessimist, William! You should try to see the glass half full for a change."

She picked up the two wine glasses, which were now half full (or half empty in Bill's mind), and handed one to him.

"It's not going to take A.I. very long to surpass us humans," he said, idly swirling his wine in the glass. "It doesn't have to get as smart as people *are*. It only has to get smarter than they *will be*. We're helping it all the time by getting dumber and dumber. Anyway, cheers."

"Cheers," said Irene. "To S.O.L.!"

They clinked.

"We did it!" she added.

"Mmm," said Bill after taking a sip. "This is excellent."

"It's been in there for years," said Irene. "Some client gave it to me way back."

One hour later—an hour they'd spent enjoying each other's company, talking and laughing, with plenty of philosophizing (mainly by Bill), plenty of speculating on the future (mainly by Irene), and absolutely no product testing—the two friends were sitting together at one corner of the conference table, experiencing a brief lull in the conversation, each momentarily in their own world. Bill came back first, noticing both glasses were empty and moving to remedy this situation.

"Irene," he said as he picked up the bottle she'd found in a cupboard in the kitchen (given to her long ago by another client) after the original bottle had run out, "you ever find yourself in a conversation with someone who you just have no respect for, and, just, feel totally superior to..."

"Of course," she replied.

"And maybe even," Bill continued, now moving the bottle over toward his own glass after filling hers, "some contempt, and... disgust, for the person. You kind of, uh, despise them a bit."

"Yes! Happens to me all the time." Irene was grinning.

"And yet, you humor them." He completed the pour and set the bottle back down. "You pretend to respect them, to have a real connection with them, to..."

"What? No, I don't do that. Not unless I have to. You know, like if I need something from them."

"Well, I totally do," Bill went on. "I behave as if I share in their beliefs and attitudes and concerns. And that I, uh, find their stuff amusing or interesting... when, in reality, I don't."

"Well, you *are* a total pussy," said Irene with a playful smile.

"Yes, true—some of it is to avoid awkwardness or backlash, or just for their sake, to boost them up. By the way: having compassion doesn't make one a pussy."

Irene rolled her eyes and muttered "Uh-huh."

"But anyway, that stuff is fine—I own that. Pussy or whatever. But that's not the whole story. I also do this... uh, pretending... for my own benefit. To, I guess, comfort myself, somehow. To make me feel superior, probably, and also to... sort of to explore the other person. To find their humanity. To reassure myself that they're made of something, and what they're made of is... imperfect, and vulnerable..."

"You're a funny man, William," said Irene, but her smile was soft now, and so were her wide brown eyes, looking directly into his.

Bill was suddenly struck by her beauty. He'd had a massive crush on her back in high school when they first became friends, and had eventually (after many, many months) worked up the courage to tell her how he felt, which she'd handled pretty well considering it came as a complete surprise to her and she had none of the same feelings whatsoever. Over the decades since then, he'd very occasionally, in passing, thought about her this way again, but never in a moment he was willing to seize upon. Until now.

He slowly leaned forward, holding Irene's gaze. Her smile remained. Their faces now two inches apart, he extended both hands and gently placed them on either side of her head, then closed his eyes, moved in that final little bit, and kissed her. He was somewhat startled and hugely thrilled to feel her kissing him back.

After a moment he pulled away ever so slightly and opened his eyes. "Is this... Is this okay?" he asked.

Irene's eyes turned upward and for a few seconds she didn't speak. Gears were turning inside her head.

"Yeah," she then said, looking back at him and smiling. "Fuck it."

Bill smiled too, then went in for another kiss. This one was longer and deeper, and before it had concluded, all four of their arms had sprung into action, grasping at the fabric of each other's shirts with a view to expeditious removal.

"Shit!" Irene suddenly exclaimed as she sat upright, ending a five-minute period of stillness and silence during which she and Bill had been lying on their backs on the conference table, side by side, both completely nude (except for Bill's socks), their legs dangling over the edge, enjoying the post-coital glow.

"What?" he asked.

"What time is it?" She jumped off the table and began scanning it and the surrounding floor for her phone.

"Uh, I don't know," said Bill, sitting up now and glancing around to see if his own phone was handy.

"Shit!" Irene said again, snapping hers up from the floor and seeing that it was 6:43. "I'm late. I gotta get home." She began scrambling for her clothing, which was strewn all over the place.

"Shit!" said Bill, spotting his laptop precariously perched at a strange angle, half open, three of its corners touching the wall, the floor, and the cabinet that had contained the first wine bottle, the other three touching just air. He leapt off the table and headed to retrieve it.

It took Irene 47 seconds to reach a state of being fully dressed and ready to depart.

"We'll touch base soon," she said, making for the conference room door. "Make sure Stan can access the build!" Then she was gone.

Bill was hunched over the conference table, still wearing nothing but socks, face aimed intently at his laptop screen, fingers tapping on the keyboard and sliding over the mousepad (the independent mouse he normally used still unlocated somewhere on the floor).

"Fuck... Come on..." he muttered, trying to confirm that nothing was lost, or corrupted, or malfunctioning.

Waiting for a seemingly eternal hourglass (or, technically, the little blue spinning circle that had long ago replaced the too-explicit hourglass) to finish, Bill's eyes wandered to the left and noticed a phone sitting on the conference table that wasn't his. Curious, he tapped its surface, upon which the screen lit up and appeared to show a phone call in progress, on speaker but with the speaker volume at zero.

He began to feel slightly mortified, and sensed that somewhere in the depths of his brain, he already knew what this was, but couldn't quite bring it to the fore. He also felt intuitively that what he really should do was press the red icon to end the call. But instead, somehow, compulsively, he unmuted the speaker. Noise immediately came through it, but a fairly quiet, steady noise. No voices.

"Hello?" he said.

"Hi there! Can you hear me now?" It was Stacy Parabola, who'd been conferenced in with the S.O.L. team during their meeting.

"Hi, Stacy," said Bill. "I, uh... I... didn't know you were still on the phone."

"Yeah. I'm driving, and... Something's wrong with my bluetooth. I can't do anything with it."

"Ah, right."

"Very, very frustrating."

"I'll bet." A long pause. "Hey, listen, Stacy, uh... Did you, uh... Did you hear..."

"Yes."

"Oh god. I'm so sorry. I, uh..."

"Forget it," said Stacy. "Just, could you do me a favor please?"

"Yeah, sure, of course."

"Could you hang up? Please!"

"Oh. Yeah, yes. Of course. Bye!" Bill pressed the red icon, his face now a similar color.

"Oh my god!" came Judy Goldstein's voice from behind.

Bill whirled around to see her standing in the doorway, eyes bugging, mouth agape, mid-step but paralyzed with shock.

"Judy! Holy shit!"

Casting around frantically for something to cover up with, the best Bill could do was his precious laptop, fresh from its last perilous adventure. He swiftly grabbed it by the lid with one hand, then positioned it, two-handed, in front of the least appropriately exposed portion of himself.

"Sorry," said Judy, still frozen in the doorway.

"No, no. *I'm* sorry. Judy. It's... I'm so sorry. What, uh... Can I..."

"Oh, I, um..." She stepped tentatively into the room. "I forgot my phone. So stupid. I almost got all the way home before I even realized!"

"Oh! Right!" Bill forced a laugh.

Judy began to laugh too, a quiet, nervous chuckling. "Why, it's been... at least 436 days," she said, "since I forgot my phone *anywhere*." Her eyes darted around for a second. "I... I think that's it, there," she said, pointing at the phone on the table next to where Bill stood.

"Ah, yes. Of course. Why don't you just come on over and get it? I'll, uh, get out of your way." He began backing very slowly away from the table.

After a moment, he spoke again. "Hey, uh, Judy? I've got a little problem."

"Yes, I noticed that."

"Oh, no... Not, uh... Not this problem. A different one."

"Oh?"

"Yeah. I need to get back to West L.A. Or, well, actually, my car needs to get back there." Bill had agreed with Yvonne that she would have the ATS tonight.

"I'm not really following you," said Judy.

"I can't drive myself home because I've had too much to drink."

"Oh. I see."

"Could you drive me?"

"Oh. Um, well..."

"I'd pay for your Uber back, of course. And, uh... something extra, you know, for your trouble."

"Okay."

"Really? Thank you! Oh, god... You're a lifesaver."

"My rate is $175 per hour."

Bill said nothing for a second as his eyelids and eyebrows involuntarily reacted. Then he said, "Okay."

"I'm an attorney," Judy said with a shrug and a mischievous, faintly proud smirk.

Almost exactly six days later, Sheila El Mallakh, a 39-year-old moderately obese woman with shoulder-length brown hair, parked her rollaboard bag on the concrete just outside of Terminal 5 baggage claim at LAX and took out her phone. Despite what one might've inferred from her current surname, both Sheila and her husband, Ron, came from a very long line of very white Americans. (Ron's father's father had been adopted as a newborn by a family of Egyptian heritage; he'd become permanently estranged from them at the age of 16 but kept their name.) Sheila and Ron both hailed originally from Moreno Valley, California (the same town where Carole's Place was located), where they'd met during high school and married soon after.

Sheila occasionally went by alternate names, calling herself Sheila Thompson (her maiden name) for "professional purposes" and, in some social situations, simply Sheila E, laughingly mentioning the pop music singer of the same name, who, she then asserted, without irony, was clearly the less talented of the two. She chuckled to herself now, thinking about this long-standing pseudonym, as she texted her location to the friend with whom, for no good reason, it had always been linked in her mind—Yvonne Smede.

Yvonne, sitting 100 feet to the west behind the wheel of the ATS, surrounded on all four sides by other motionless cars, glanced at the incoming text and frowned.

"A door number?" she said out loud, and began craning her neck to try to read the markings above the doors near her.

After a moment she managed to get a clear look at a door marked "1" and concluded she'd need to move forward substantially to reach door #13—no big surprise there, as she'd always believed Spirit Airlines came into Terminal 5 and had been puzzled by Sheila's previous text, 25 minutes ago, claiming to have come into Terminal 4.

Yvonne put on her left turn signal, started eyeing the line of cars next to her for any sign of movement, and let out a long sigh. Like most rational humans, Yvonne hated LAX, especially driving into it, and most especially trying to execute a curbside pick-up without suffering a nervous breakdown and/or a fender bender. Sheila had balked at the suggestion of getting an Uber to the condo, and then had also pushed back when Yvonne said she'd park and come inside. The reason cited was wishing to make the experience easier and cheaper for Yvonne, who suspected (correctly) that the real reason was Sheila's curiously strong aversion to walking any distance at all.

Idly scanning for an opportunity to pull out, Yvonne was suddenly struck by the similarities between Sheila El Mallakh and Juice Hughes-Newton. Both selfish and lazy, with a huge chip on their shoulder all the time. Arrogant, too. Hmm. But Sheila had some additional traits: always hungry for attention and seemingly semi-delusional about her own abilities and accomplishments. Yep, she was definitely the bigger pain in the ass of the two. Yvonne smiled and shook her head. With friends like these! It occurred to her that, as far as she could remember, they'd never met each other. She made a mental note to try to remedy that one day, but then thought, maybe two people with that personality wouldn't get along?

Sheila and Yvonne had met when both were members of the Beverly Hills chapter of Mom-Eaze (a club for mothers of young children that organized parenthood workshops, large-group play dates, and general mom support networks) when Alice was a toddler. In all their years of friendship, Yvonne had never gotten a clear explanation of why Sheila would've joined a club that was 75 miles from where she lived.

Ten years ago, Sheila had moved to Charleston, South Carolina, when Boeing, who employed Ron on one of their assembly lines in Long Beach, had informed him that he could choose between a cross-country transfer and being laid off. (This was actually quite a fortunate position for Ron to find himself in, under the circumstances—a year prior to that, he'd been busted for snorting cocaine on the line and selling it to his fellow workers.)

Since moving away, Sheila had come back to visit Yvonne every year in the fall. These visits typically began annoyingly, like this one, but the women gradually fell back into their old groove, re-connected on motherhood, and shared a lot of good laughs.

Spotting her (very narrow) opening, Yvonne cranked the wheel hard to the left and stomped on the gas, merged into the next lane, and began frantically watching the very-hard-to-see door numbers on the building and, simultaneously, the bumper of the car in front of her. Then she saw Sheila, standing near the curb, face in phone, outside the door marked "3."

"Typical," Yvonne muttered, correctly surmising that Sheila had fat-fingered the digit '1' and not noticed.

Then, to Yvonne's astonishment while surveying the two lanes of dense, stationary traffic between herself and the curb, trying to formulate a strategy for navigating through them, Sheila looked up, noticed the ATS, grabbed hold of her suitcase, and was on the move.

A moment later, she flung the passenger door open and shouted, "The glamorous life!"

"What?" Yvonne muttered, feeling quite irritable.

Sheila moved on. "Be a doll and pop the trunk," she said with a big grin.

"It was a little bit terrifying, frankly," said Mike Howell two hours later, describing the feeling of being strapped onto a toboggan-like vessel, but on rails, in a near-vertical orientation, head pointing downward, at the top of a cliff.

"Wow," said Jake Lee.

"I mean, it doesn't seem that bad," Mike continued, "when you're looking at it from a distance, or conceptualizing it in your mind. You know, 150 feet. Not a big deal."

Last weekend, Mike and his wife, Laura Johnson, had made an impromptu trip to Scream Resort, an extreme-thrill-ride park in Mono County, California (300 miles north of L.A.), whose attractions had been built on the slopes that weren't suitable for skiing so the owners of the surrounding resorts could make money year-round (and a little extra in winter).

"Totally!" said Jake. "It's so weird how… horizontal distance and vertical distance are just… just, so different!"

"Mmm-hmm," Mike said, nodding his head.

"I mean, just... Like, I remember one time, I was on the roof of this building on Wilshire, where they had this, like, restaurant... And I was, just, leaning over the rail, looking down at the street, and it seemed *so* far away! Like, just, *super* far away. But it was only six stories!"

"Right."

"I mean, maybe, what? 60 feet or something? If I was walking down the street, looking 60 feet in front of me, that would seem like nothing!"

"Mmm-hmm," Mike said again, taking a sip of his drink. "That ride scared the crap out of us, didn't it, dear?"

Laura looked up from her phone screen. "What? Oh, yeah. Yeah, definitely. The worst part is when you're suspended at the top, before the thing actually begins."

"Yep, exactly!" said Mike.

"Yep, yep," Jake said, smiling and rapidly nodding his head.

The three, sitting around a table inside Four Fifty-Nine, a "Whiskey Bar & Tapas Kitchen" in Brentwood, comprised half of the originally-planned group for this evening's happy hour gathering. The organizer, Amy Lee, had initially arranged a babysitter so she and Jake could both attend, then canceled the babysitter when both kids got sick, intending that Jake would stay home with them, then ultimately had stayed home herself instead when she got sick (by which time the kids had recovered).

"What did you have again?" Laura asked her husband, gesturing at his drink. They'd all ordered cocktails from the "Specialties of the House" section of the menu.

"Oh, uh... It's called 'Cold Comfort.' Made with Southern Comfort, I believe."

"Is it good?"

"Yeah, very good."

"Want to trade?"

"Uh, sure," Mike said, a bit warily, then chuckled. "What's yours again?"

"It's called a 'Cheesy Knob.' Made with Knob Creek and... cream cheese, I think, and... mmm, not sure what else. But, I don't really like it."

Mike shrugged. "Okay, whatever," he said, sliding his glass over toward Laura.

Jake piped up: "Mine is the 'Raging Stiffy.' I think it's almost pure alcohol!"

"Hi everyone!" said Sheila El Mallakh, now standing next to the table, smiling. They all looked up. "Great to see you all again!"

Yvonne, standing behind Sheila, was not smiling. While driving them from the airport to the condo, she'd been subjected to an ignorant rant about people on social media and their ignorant rants. At the condo, Sheila had taken forever to get changed and freshen up. On the way to Four Fifty-Nine (which was less than two miles from home— Yvonne would've walked there if she'd been alone (or with Bill)), Sheila had complained when the Uber driver, after stopping at a green light to let an ambulance go through, had remained stopped after it passed because the light had turned red; she'd claimed that cars were entitled to proceed through an intersection in the same order as they would've done pre-emergency-vehicle.

"Good to see *you*," Mike said to Sheila as Jake grinned, head bobbing, and Laura flashed a polite smile, then looked down at her phone. "It's, uh… Sheila, right?"

"Yes! Good memory. Sheila E, reporting for duty!" She continued talking as she pulled out one of the empty chairs and sat down. "Like the singer! Well, ex-singer. Hasn't had a record since, like 1985. Definitely a low-talent individual." She laughed.

Laura looked up from her phone briefly, smiling at Sheila again and then at Yvonne, who'd also just taken a seat. Jake was now fiddling with his phone, too.

"Hi," said Yvonne to the group.

"What do you do, Sheila?" Mike enquired.

"I do a lot! I've got my fingers in several pies."

"Literally," muttered Yvonne under her breath.

"I'm a business owner," Sheila continued. "I'm also a writer. And, some other stuff, too."

"That's great," said Mike.

Knowing she was being watched, Yvonne concentrated very hard on not allowing her eyes to roll. The "business" Sheila owned provided one-on-one fitness training in a person's home. It had only ever employed one trainer (Sheila herself) and, in its 15-year existence, had attracted a grand total of three customers. The writing to which she referred consisted of her rambling, utterly inane blog and a couple of poems she'd written hurriedly (and very poorly, in Yvonne's opinion) and submitted to a contest a few years back. The "other stuff," Yvonne suspected, was cake design/baking and motivational speaking; Sheila had talked frequently about both these endeavors for a very long time, but had never attempted either of them.

"It was 2020," said Laura. Everyone but Jake turned to her, puzzled. "When Sheila E last released an album," she continued. "It was 2020, not 1985."

Jake was shaking his head now, still looking down at his phone screen. "Nope, no," he said. "2019. Got it right here. 2019." He looked up and aimed a triumphant smirk in Laura's direction.

"What?" she said. "No. Um…"

Her face and fingers returned to the phone. Jake followed suit, mumbling unintelligibly to himself. Each of them believed they had exclusive access to the most authoritative version of the Internet, allowing them to cull indisputable facts and then generously share them with all the other folks who lacked such access.

"So, yeah," said Sheila, "I'm truly one of those pull-yourself-up-by-your-bootstraps people. If it weren't for me, I never would've ended up living the upper-middle-class life. I think it all comes down to my philosophy. Of course I'm a very hard worker, but it's more than just that…"

Yvonne, who happened to know that Sheila'd had a very comfortable upbringing, and had never worked hard at anything, said, "Sheila—maybe I should go grab us some drinks?"

"Hey," said Mike, a sly grin forming on his face, "I just read about this nifty trick you can pull on some stupid jerk. So you choose your mark—somebody greedy and gullible, you know—and, you follow him around in public. Discreetly. And you observe him, and you find out his name and what bank he uses."

Laura's eyes momentarily popped up from her phone screen and she smiled at Mike. Yvonne and Sheila were both listening intently. Jake was still deeply embedded in Phone World.

"Eventually," Mike continued, "you approach the guy, all casual-like, just, on the street. And you tell him something is wrong with your phone and ask him to call you. Then you've got his number. Heh.

"Now here's the good part. You call him later—from a different phone, of course—and you say you're from the bank. Meanwhile, you're on the bank's website, trying to log in as him, and you go to the 'forgot password' screen, you know, where they text you a code?

And so you tell the guy, like, there was a bank error in his favor, and, you're gonna credit his account, and… you're gonna send him a code, and he needs to read it back to you.

"Then, bang! You've got access. And then you reward yourself—and punish him—by withdrawing a nice, big, fat stack of cash."

Mike chuckled delightedly. Sheila laughed, too. Jake and Laura had their heads down, concentrating.

"These days when the bank sends the text," said Yvonne, "I think it usually includes something about how they'll never ask you for the code over the phone."

"Aw, this guy's not gonna pay any attention to that," said Mike. "He's too lazy and dumb. Heh."

"Ooh, that reminds me," said Sheila, "I'm supposed to face-time with my kids tonight."

"How many kids do you have?" asked Mike.

"Four living."

"Oh. I, uh… I'm sorry."

"Yeah, my youngest, little Ruthie, she's 15 now, she was a twin. Originally. In the womb. She was in there with her sister Emmalie. But… Emmalie died at 12 weeks."

"Sorry," said Mike again.

"One time, in kindergarten, Ruthie said she was a twin, and none of the kids believed her. They started laughing at her, and she—"

Sheila's face froze, mouth slightly open, eyes still pointing at Mike. He looked back at her silently for a second, not sure what to make of this. Suddenly a wailing sound burst from her throat and, simultaneously, water exploded out of her eyes like lawn sprinklers. Then she hung her head and began emitting quiet sobbing noises, her shoulders gently bobbing up and down.

Mike now wore a perplexed and worried face. Jake and Laura both looked up from their phones with similar expressions. Yvonne, who'd heard the story of Ruthie and Emmalie many times, was struggling to suppress a scowl.

Jake, sitting to Sheila's left, reached out his arm and placed it tentatively against her upper back. "Are you okay?" he asked.

"Yes, yes," she said, raising her head and wiping her cheeks with her wrists. "You must forgive me."

Yvonne had stood up. "Sheila," she said, "I'm going to bring you some wine, to drown your sorrows."

"Oh yeah! Drown everything!" boomed a voice from the direction of the main entrance. All heads turned to see Amy Lee rapidly approaching, beaming at them.

Jake laughed. "Hi honey!" he exclaimed. "Thought you weren't feeling good."

"Yeah, I wasn't," she said, arriving next to the group. "But then I felt better. And then I thought, 'I don't want to miss out!' And then I called the babysitter and told her to get her butt over to my house. And now here I am!"

"Cool!" Jake flashed a giant grin.

Mike chuckled. The other three women all smiled at Amy.

"Well okay then, peeps," she said. "Let's get this party started!"

On Sunday morning, Irene Hoffman took the S.O.L. headgear and her smartphone, containing the final, "release" version of the software, to downtown Huntington Beach, near where Stan Wojcik lived, for one final Life Stroll before unleashing her product on the world.

She brought her bike along, strapped to the roof of her minivan, and began with a cycling segment. It briefly crossed her mind that during this ride she'd have to forego wearing her standard safety helmet, but she shrugged it off, telling herself that one must take risks in life in order to move forward.

It was a gorgeous day—blue, cloudless sky and 72 degrees—and not many people were on the beach yet. Perfect. Irene began near the pier, rode one mile south on the asphalt path that cut through the giant swath of sand between Pacific Coast Highway and the water, then stopped, turned around, and rode north two miles, then reversed direction again and returned to her starting point.

S.O.L. filled nearly a third of this time with Led Zeppelin's "Kashmir"; other musical selections included Queen's "Bicycle Race," Don Henley's "Sunset Grill," two other rock tracks that Irene didn't recognize but liked, and several short pieces of generic orchestral music. Sounds from the real world around her that were deemed sufficiently noteworthy were also piped to the earphones, sometimes with artificial enhancements: she heard the roar of a jet engine as a plane flew overhead, and the furious revving of a motorcycle engine as another bike rider overtook her on the path.

She locked up the bike and continued the Life Stroll on foot, walking a serpentine route that took her up and down the pier, across the highway, and through several of the streets in the adjacent shopping/dining district. Musical transitions occurred more frequently during this segment, and more environmental sound effects were overlaid, some entirely artificial such as carnival game music and children laughing. Track selections included songs from The Beach Boys, Aerosmith, and Steve Miller, as well as half a dozen more orchestral offerings.

With the agreed-upon location and time for a meeting with Stan both rapidly approaching, Irene closed the phone app and removed the headset, feeling, overall, quite satisfied with her sojourn.

A group of unruly-looking teenage boys were coming toward her on the sidewalk, all abuzz, jaws flapping, and as they passed by she caught a brief snippet of their "conversation," consisting entirely of unimaginative smack-talk aimed, it seemed, at some folks who were present and some who weren't. She shook her head and let out a sneering nasal semi-laugh. Stupid punks.

It brought to mind a news story she'd seen last night about a recent amber alert in which a San Bernardino mother believed her estranged husband had abducted their 13-year-old son. It turned out the lad had stolen his sleeping father's car keys and gone for an extensive joyride, which ended quite dramatically in the desert outside Palm Springs when the cops pulled him over and ordered him out of the vehicle with multiple guns trained on him. Irene chuckled and shook her head again.

She thought about Junior and Luke, and wondered if they too were turning into (or had already turned into) examples of that abhorrent creature known as the Male Teenager. Then she thought about Keith, who'd been tired all the time lately because he'd taken a job working the graveyard shift as a janitor at the mall, and how fortunate he was to be married to someone with her strength and vision, who could gracefully guide them both through the challenges of parenthood and entrepreneurship. Then she arrived at the entrance to CuppaJoe, at the corner of Main and Olive.

Stan, who'd gotten there early, bought himself a coffee and taken the liberty of getting one for Irene too, saw her come in from where he was sitting at a little table by the window. He smiled and waved at her. She returned his smile, walked over and took a seat facing him.

"Stan the Man," she said, gingerly placing the S.O.L. equipment on the window sill. "Good morning, my friend."

"Hi," he said warmly.

"Thanks for the coffee, dude."

She picked up the cup, took a sip, set it down again, and sighed, then grinned. "Exciting times, huh?"

"Yes," Stan said, "very much so."

"Oh, hey—there's this old song I've been playing in my head, and I can't find it anywhere. 'Meet Me at the Bottom of the Charles River'…"

"Sounds pretty morbid."

"Yes. Brilliant. That may not be the title, but it's like one of the main lines from the song."

"I don't think I've ever heard it."

"Really? Shit. It's from the 80s, I think. Or maybe the 2000s…" She took another sip of her coffee.

Stan shrugged. "Sorry, no idea."

"So, anyway," said Irene, "I don't want to sound like an asshole or anything, but… I was kinda surprised you wanted to see me. I mean, your part is done! You can relax now, nerd. It's time for the Irene-and-Judy-and-Stacy show!"

"Right, well…"

"I've got everything all lined up, ready to pull the trigger. A block of Facebook ads, a sales and distribution, uh, platform, you know, thingie, with Amazon. And we are about to fire up the production line!"

She was working herself into a frenzy of enthusiasm. "Oh, yes, my friend! Stacy is going to order the cameras and mics and earphones and wires, and integrate them all in, right there on the line. Bam! We're gonna ship a thousand units."

Stan waited a few seconds, to be sure she was finished, still smiling. Then he said, in his standard sincere and mellow tone, "That's great, Irene."

Irene nodded her head and said "Mmm-hmm, mmm-hmm" quickly

as she swallowed another sip of coffee and lowered the cup from her mouth back down to the table. "Yep. It is great." She paused for a moment. "Christ, I need a cigarette." Another short pause. "So, anyway, what's up?"

In the most gentle fashion humanly possible, Stan said, "Do we have the money for this rollout? I thought we spent every remaining dime on the third prototype."

"What? Yes. Of course I've got the money. Come on, man—I may not be a super-genius like you but I'm not a fucking moron."

"Of course not," Stan replied, still smiling, still utterly calm.

"Hey, come on, let's continue this outside." Irene stood up.

"Sure," said Stan, also standing up.

No more words were spoken until they'd gathered up their coffees and other belongings and made their way out to a small patio wedged between the building and the sidewalk, and Irene had lit up a cigarette and taken a drag from it.

"Okay, listen," she then said. "Don't you worry your pretty little head over money, Stanley." (Stan's real first name was Stansted, a fact Irene had known long ago but had forgotten nearly as long ago.) "I'm all over it. I just met with my banker on Thursday and we signed a massive loan. Enough to cover the whole rollout. Plus more. It's a done deal! We're all good."

She grinned and took another drag. She'd conveniently neglected to mention that "her banker" was a person she'd never met before who happened to work at her local branch, that the interest rate on the loan was 20%, and that she'd had to secure it with some fairly unconventional collateral, including her life insurance policy and Keith's parents' luxury R.V. She'd also neglected to mention that her claim of "plus more" was a flat-out lie.

"Cool," said Stan, then coughed.

"So, is that what this was all about?" asked Irene. "The money?"

"Well, no, not really."

"Well then what then?" She took another drag.

"I..." Another cough. "Excuse me. I... I need you to know that I'm concerned about the software. About the robustness of the software."

"It seems solid to me. You gave William the easy parts, right?" She grinned.

"There were no easy parts. But yeah, I tried not to give him more than he could handle. And he did well. But..."

"What? Come on, we tested it. It's solid." Another quick drag. "You're worrying for nothing."

"Well, yes," said Stan, managing to stifle his cough this time, "we did some testing and it seems solid. But this A.I. stuff is very tricky..."

Irene rolled her eyes. "Yeah, so everyone keeps telling me."

"We can't really predict how it will behave as it spends longer periods of time with a user and 'learns' about them."

She took a final drag on her cigarette, then tossed it on the ground and stamped it out with her foot, all the while regarding Stan thoughtfully.

He let out a final cough, then continued. "From all the research I've done, I think there's a high probability that, over time, our software is going to exhibit more and more strange behavior. That it's going to become... unstable."

Irene looked at him silently, with a pensive face, for another three seconds. Then she reached up and patted his cheek with the palm of her hand.

"Don't you worry your pretty little head over it, Stan. Everything's gonna be fine. Trust me."

"Okay," he said with his usual warm smile, but he had every intention of continuing to worry about it.

Chapter 14

One Friday afternoon in late October, a short, thin, 43-year-old Hispanic man with close-cropped jet-black hair and a neatly manicured mustache was sitting on the sofa in the main lounge of the modest house he shared with his wife and his brother in Hemet, California (a small city located at the base of the San Jacinto mountains, an 88-mile road journey from downtown L.A.), reading a newspaper, when there was a knock on the front door. Or rather, a rapid-fire collection of knocks, loud and furious, combined with multiple ringings of the doorbell.

Puzzled, he folded and laid down the newspaper, rose, strode across the lounge to the door, unbolted it, and opened it. Standing before him was Juice Hughes-Newton, wearing a purple short-sleeve dress that hugged her figure, five-inch heels, various pieces of gold jewelry, and a big, friendly smile.

"Good morning, sir!" she bellowed.

"Can I help you?" he asked.

"Why yes, I'm betting you can," said Juice. "My name is Juice." She thrust out her hand. "Juice Hughes-Newton. *Doctor* Juice Hughes-Newton."

The man very tentatively took her hand and shook it, a confused and skeptical expression on his face.

"And you are?" Juice finally asked, when the handshake ended and the man hadn't spoken.

He continued his silence for another couple of seconds, then said, "Juan."

"Juan what?"

"Excuse me? What's this all about?"

"What's your last name, Juan?"

"Uh... That's none of your business—"

"Let me take a guess! Could it be..."—Juice raised her voice to a shout and switched her smile to an accusatory look—"Jennings!"

A hint of recognition flashed in Juan's eyes but he said, "No. What's this all about?"

"Aren't you going to invite me in, Juan Jennings?"

"My name's not Juan Jennings!"

"Oh, really? Why? Is it a *fake* name, like your wife, Shayla Jennings?"

"What? No. I don't know what you're... I don't know who that is. I ain't got no wife."

"Well what's your last name, then, Juan?" The smile was back now.

"It's Mena, okay?" he replied defensively. "My name's Juan Mena. Now what's this all about?"

"Aren't you going to invite me in, Juan Mena?"

"No," he said, frowning. "Can you just go away, please?"

"I'm afraid not, Juan," Juice said sweetly. "Now I don't know who taught you your manners, but you're being very rude: refusing to invite me in, and lying to me."

Juan raised one eyebrow.

"I know for a fact that the woman who calls herself Shayla Jennings lives here. Maybe you don't have a wife, but there is *no way* you could live in this little house, where 'Shayla' also lives, and not even know who she is."

They stared silently into each other's eyes for a second. Then Juan sighed, opened the door wider, stepped aside, and beckoned Juice inside with his arm.

"There, that's more like it," she said, stepping through. "Let us sit down together in your lovely home, like two civilized people, and have some truth." She headed for the sofa where Juan had been reading his newspaper.

Another man was passing through the room and glanced at Juice quizzically. Juan, as he was closing the front door, said, "My brother, Carlos."

"Carlos Sanchez," said Carlos Sanchez, abruptly changing his trajectory and moving toward Juice, his open hand thrust out in front of him.

"It's a pleasure, Carlos," she replied. "I'm Doctor Juice Hughes-Newton."

They shook hands. "Nice to meet you," said Carlos.

"Interesting," said Juice, "that you two have different last names."

Both men grimaced and Carlos made a hasty departure as Juan sighed and began trudging toward Juice and the sofa.

"Isn't it interesting?" she pressed him, smiling and attempting to look him in the eye (unsuccessfully, as he was looking down at the floor). "Your name's not really Juan Mena, is it?"

Another sigh as he arrived next to her and finally made eye contact. "No," he conceded.

Juice waited, staring expectantly at him.

"My real name is Jimmy Sanchez," he said eventually.

"Pleased to meet you, Jimmy Sanchez." Juice sat down on the sofa as she said, "Mind if I sit?"

"Uh... No, that's fine." Jimmy sat down too, about three feet from Juice, his folded newspaper lying halfway between them.

"Nice place you've got here, Jimmy," said Juice, surveying her surroundings. She noticed what appeared to be a wooden vacuum cleaner leaning against a wall, an entirely wooden clock (including its gears, which were exposed) hanging on another wall, and, in the kitchen, which was mostly visible from where she sat, a wooden refrigerator.

"What's with all the weird wooden shit?" she asked.

"Oh," said Jimmy, who seemed to be relaxing a bit now, "Carlos does a lot of woodworking. He loves it."

"Ah, wonderful. So, did he build this couch we're sitting on?"

"No."

"What about this coffee table here?"

"No."

"Don't woodworkers typically concentrate on furniture?"

"Yes, but... Carlos is different. He likes a challenge. He likes to, uh, use his imagination."

"I guess so! But then, so do you, in a way, Jimmy. You like to make up lies, don't you?"

Jimmy began to look slightly more wary and uncomfortable again, but Juice was still smiling and still speaking gently.

She went on, "As I said before, I'd like us to have some truth now."

"Yeah, listen, you know, uh... The reason I changed my name was... to protect myself. I got into some trouble, in L.A. That's why I moved out here to live with Carlos. See, I, uh… I used to be sort of a gangster."

Juice raised an eyebrow. "You don't look like much of a gangster, Jimmy. No wonder you didn't do very well at it."

Jimmy chuckled and said, "Well…"

"But I don't want to talk about you," Juice continued. "I want to talk about Shayla. She's using a fake name too. Her real name is Nancy Parsons. But you already knew that, didn't you, Jimmy?"

"Uh, no…"

"Come on, Jimmy. Truth!"

"Okay, fine, yes. Yes, of course I knew. Nancy was my wife. *Is* my wife. She's still my wife."

"Yet another thing you've lied to me about in the last five minutes. Oh dear, Jimmy."

"Yeah, okay, fine. But what do you want, anyway? What's this all about?"

"Are you playing dumb again, Jimmy?"

"What? No."

"Really? You don't know who I am? Nancy's never mentioned me to you?"

"No, I swear. Never. You say your name is Juice, like the drink?"

"Mmm, more like, 'Who's got the juice?' I do."

"Yeah I never heard of you before."

"Nothing about how I tricked your idiot wife into coming all the way out to the Valley to claim a special prize that didn't exist?"

"Uh, no…"

"Or, before that, an email inviting her to our supposed high school reunion?"

"That was *you*?" Jimmy exclaimed, his eyes lighting up. "I do remember that, because I wrote the reply. See, back at the beginning, when we were first—"

"So where is your wife right now, Jimmy?"

"Uh… She's at work right now."

"Oh *really*? You mean at Third Bank of the Far West in downtown Hemet?"

Jimmy looked surprised. "Uh, yeah, that's right. How do you—"

"She doesn't work there anymore."

"What?"

"That's right. Hasn't worked there in over a month. Suddenly quit one day."

Jimmy looked even more surprised now, and rather alarmed. "But," he stammered, "how... I don't... This..."

"Oh what a tangled web we weave—eh, Juan?" Juice chuckled delightedly. "Yeah, took me a long-ass time to learn that. I called that fucking bank dozens of times, and stopped by in person twice. Do you know how far away Hemet is from my house, Jimmy?"

She paused for a moment and Jimmy looked at her, wondering if he was actually expected to guess how far away Hemet was from her house. But then she started up again.

"What a pain in the ass. But *finally* I found someone useful in that damn place. Someone willing to spill the beans. Vanessa was her name, I believe. Or was it Valerie? Anyway, she was the best. She even gave me Nancy's home address. Heh. *Your* address." Juice, appearing to have said her piece, sat back and smiled smugly.

"So, what do you want with my wife, anyway? What's this all about?"

"It's about justice, dear Jimmy. Your wife and I, we go way back. And she wronged me. She wronged me hard, oh yes." A look of contempt had come over Juice's face. "And when I caught up with the little bitch recently, she had the nerve to—"

"Hey, whatever happened in the past, she ain't gonna remember it," Jimmy said.

"Oh, I will refresh her memory, don't you worry."

"No, I mean, truly. She can't. She's got total amnesia."

"What?"

"Yeah. From the accident. It was bad. I mean, baaad. We were in the hospital for, like—"

"Jimmy, you better not be lying to me again!"

"I'm not, I swear! The brakes failed on my car. This guy, Ned, he like, tampered with them. Me and Nancy were lucky to survive. That's when I knew—we needed to get some new identities. A friend of mine pulled some strings to make it look like we died. And then we—"

"Amnesia? Seriously?"

"Yes, I'm dead serious. She don't remember nothing from our old life. I mean, nothing. It's terrible. But I guess, in a way, it could be a good thing, you know? For... for safety."

"She remembers *nothing* from her *entire* life? Even childhood?"

Juice had been wearing the same incredulous, horrified expression continuously for nearly a minute now.

"No, nothing."

"God. . ."

"I swear it's true. I'm not lying. I can show you the medical papers. . ." He started to stand up but Juice raised her hand to signal that it wasn't necessary.

"That's okay," she said. "I believe you. Of course. Of course it's true." Now she was looking down and slowly shaking her head in despair.

After a moment, she lifted it again and screamed, "God, this is so *fucking* unfair!"

Twenty-four hours later, Bill Smede was standing at a decades-old sink, which sat across from a decades-old tub-shower and next to a somewhat newer toilet, in the tiny bathroom of his studio apartment, staring into the mirror.

Generally speaking, when looking at his reflection he saw the same college-age fellow he'd been seeing for the past 25 years. But occasionally, and this was one of those occasions, he managed to see past that illusion and objectively view his features. Hair that was starting to thin and recede on the top, and had turned almost entirely white at the sides. Skin riddled with frown lines, furrowed-brow lines, crow's feet, and numerous tiny inexplicable blemishes that appeared gradually through the years, always looking like something temporary but remaining permanently. Teeth forever becoming more yellow and more crooked.

Bill sighed, acutely aware that these were merely the indicators of aging located above his neck and on the outside of his body. Youth truly is wasted on the young, he thought. With their lightning-fast brains and their limber, resilient, healthy bodies and their utter lack of responsibility. They can do anything they want, easily. But what's the point, when you don't truly understand or appreciate anything yet? When you don't even know who you are. Hmmf. The universe isn't fair.

As if the universe had heard these sentiments and wished to slap him in the face, the first thing Bill saw upon opening the bathroom door was his teenage daughter Alice sitting on the opposite side of the room, cross-legged on her bed, earbuds in, eyes pointing vacantly in the direction of the front window.

When Alice was here (which seemed to be roughly half the time, but in an arbitrary pattern of her own choosing that didn't correspond with the sharing schedule agreed on by her parents), Bill frequently found the environment awkward and crowded. The one table he owned served as a makeshift workspace for both of them. He'd toyed with the idea of getting a real bed for her and a fold-out sofa for himself, but ultimately had decided there just wasn't enough space and reverted to the bunk beds concept suggested to him by the original furnishings that Joseph Tanur had removed. He'd intended for Alice to have the top bunk, but she'd annexed the bottom one immediately upon first arriving. So each night, Bill climbed up a little wooden ladder to get into his bed. He'd wondered if perhaps it'd be better for everyone if she just stayed at the condo full-time, and wondered if she'd wondered the same thing. But they hadn't spoken about it.

"Hey, Alice," he said, forcing a cheerful smile. "I'm about to go grocery shopping. Want to tag along?"

"I'm good," she replied, not looking up.

"That's 'No, thanks,' you rude child," Bill was tempted to say. Instead he said, "Okay, see you later."

He left the apartment, went down the stairs and out to the sidewalk, and began heading north on Dimvale. Coming toward him was a woman he recognized, a regular on the neighborhood walking circuit. Her name was Connie Slatt, but pronounced (by her, anyway) like "Coney Slot."

Connie was a connoisseur of old television programs. She passionately loved them—nearly all of them, but only from a specific interval of history she called "the golden age," which roughly comprised the 1960s, 70s, and 80s. Prior to this time, the airwaves had been filled with so-called "high culture" material—dramatic anthologies, largely featuring adaptations of novels and plays, performed live by experienced theater actors—which tended to be rather difficult to follow and very boring. During the 1990s, the rise of newer networks like Fox and Paramount, as well as the explosion of cable channels, had ushered in a watering-down of the quality of T.V. programming, and by the turn of the millennium, the entire industry was riding an unstoppable express train straight to Crap Town. Some of Connie's absolute favorites from the golden age were "Bay City Blues," "Detective School," "Sons and Daughters," "From a Bird's Eye View," "Kay O'Brien," and "The Dakotas."

Bill didn't know any of this about Connie. He didn't even know her name. All he knew about her was that a big, creepy grin was perpetually plastered on her face, and that she always greeted him (and, in the past, Yvonne and him) with an over-familiar, praising remark like "You're awesome." They were now face to face, a few feet apart, about to pass each other, and Bill's teeth were clenched in anticipation.

"You're awesome," said Connie as a tiny gust of air caused by her motion hit Bill's face.

"Hi," he said through pursed lips curled ever so slightly into a very weak smile. A split second later, she was behind him.

At the corner of Arkansas and Tappan, Bill passed by one of the ubiquitous yellow depositories that had started springing up four months ago, and shook his head at the pointlessness of them. He'd eventually learned from an L.A. Times article that they were intended for the collection and "recycling" (the meaning of which wasn't clearly explained) of "pet waste," as part of a beautification/conservation program City Hall had grudgingly cooperated with after heavy petitioning from various community groups. Regardless of any merits this scheme might have had in theory, Bill felt, dog owners were too lazy and apathetic to make the effort. His continued sightings, daily, of numerous examples of the yellow bins not being used seemed to bear out this belief. He chuckled as he stepped onto the curb after crossing Tappan, remembering that he'd recently read about a plan to expand the program so that people could begin submitting their own feces for recycling, too.

He chuckled again a minute later as an electric car drove past him making all the sounds (and then some) normally emitted from a gasoline-powered vehicle. These sounds were artificial, coming out of a set of tiny loudspeakers mounted discreetly at various points on the body of the car. Such a system was now mandated on all electric cars registered in California by a recently-passed law that was drawn up in response to several incidents in which a pedestrian who didn't hear a car approaching was struck and killed by it. In every case, both the driver and the walker had been texting at the time of the collision.

Coming along Wexler, Bill smiled and waved at a creature, lying next to a palm tree (and connected to it by a collar and piece of rope) in a front yard, that was in fact a dog but looked like a fictional species from a Dr. Seuss book. The creature, who'd been seen frequently in this location over the past few years and nicknamed "The Thing" by Yvonne and Bill, had become the subject of multiple elaborate scenarios they'd concocted involving its origins, the confusion/ignorance of its owners (who'd never been spotted in the yard), and its ultimate fate of being removed by county animal control personnel and/or shipped off to a top-secret government research lab.

Meanwhile, in another front yard across the street, a squirrel named Chester and another squirrel who'd never revealed its name to Rufus Fletcher were engaged in heated negotiations over an acorn lying on the ground between them that they both wanted. A few feet away, a sinister looking crow paced around ominously, eyeing them both.

As Bill neared his old building, he noticed that the ATS was missing from its parking spot. "Hmm," he said.

From the sidewalk he turned onto the concrete footpath leading to the stairs, then went up them to the little landing outside the front door of the condo. He knocked.

After what felt like two minutes but was really fifteen seconds, the door was opened by Albert Forrester.

"Ah, Billy," he said. "I've been expecting you. Unfortunately."

"Hi, Al," said Bill with an involuntary frown.

"I prefer Mr. Forrester."

"Right."

"You're looking for Yvonne's car, I suppose?"

"Uh, yeah. Our car. I was going to take it to Hank's. We—"

"The car's not here right now."

"Yeah, I noticed."

"Yvonne took it. She had to go back to some nightclub she was at last night."

"Nightclub?"

"She accidentally left her phone there. So she went back to get it."

Bill nodded his head and made a small "Mmm" sound of acknowledgment.

"She asked me, if you came over while she was out, which you did, to apologize to you."

"It's okay."

"But that's a load of horseshit."

"Sorry?"

"You're not entitled to any apology." Gramps spoke in a very matter-of-fact style, with no indication that he was joking, nor that he was angry.

"Okay," said Bill flatly. He could hardly have cared less what Gramps believed, or why. It was easy to stay focused on his priorities of minimizing interaction and, above all, minimizing controversy.

Abruptly the subject changed. "Where's that lovely granddaughter of mine?"

"She's at my apartment."

"Why didn't she come over to see me?"

"Uh, she probably didn't know you were here. Why don't you give her a call?"

Gramps let out a "Hmmf" sound that seemed to suggest that the idea of calling Alice on the phone had never before crossed his mind. Then, after a long silence, he reached into his jacket pocket, took out his phone, and began staring at it with a scrunched-up face.

Bill spent the next half hour waiting for Yvonne to return, standing on the doorstep of his former home, trying to teach his father-in-law how to operate a smartphone.

"You again!" Jimmy Sanchez exclaimed at 1:37 Wednesday afternoon, upon opening the front door of his house and seeing Juice standing before him.

"Yeah, well, I'm not thrilled about it either," she said. "Your fault, Jimbo. You wouldn't give me your phone number. So if I want to talk to you, I gotta drive my ass all the way out to this godforsaken place!"

"What do you want, Juice?"

"Can I have your phone number?"

"No!"

"Can I come in?"

"What's this all about?"

"Truth, Jimmy, dear boy. It's always about truth. Which I know, deep in your heart, you dig! I know that Jimmy Boy actually *loves* the truth!"

Jimmy paused momentarily, frowning, then ushered Juice into his front lounge, where they took a seat on the same sofa they'd sat together on five days ago.

"So, where's Nasty Nancy?" Juice asked. "Is she home?"

"Uh..." Jimmy cleared his throat. "*Shayla*... is at work right now."

"At the bank? I told you, she doesn't work there anymore."

"Well, *she* said she *does*."

"What else do you think your wife might be lying to you about, Jimmy?"

A look of discomfort seized Jimmy's face, but he said nothing.

"Like this whole amnesia thing. She could be faking it. Ever think of that?"

"What?!" he cried. "That's crazy. It's real. The doctors said. Plus, I would know if she was faking."

"Let's talk about something else: my necklace."

"What?"

"Nancy stole a necklace from me when we were in high school, and I want it back."

Jimmy shook his head incredulously. "You must be kidding! That was like, what? Thirty years ago or something? There's no way she's still got it."

"Oh, I disagree."

They stared at each other in silence for a moment before Juice continued, "Jimmy, I'm gonna need to take a look around your place."

"What? No way. Absolut—"

"Now, Jimmy." Juice didn't look at him as she spoke, her face instead engaged in getting out her phone and accessing her contacts. "I know you care about truth." She dialed.

Yvonne Smede picked up almost immediately with her "I'm at work" voice. "Hey, what's up?" she said.

"Hey, girl," said Juice. "You work in the lab. If I got you a sample of something, could you run some tests on it?"

"I don't work *in* the lab. I work in the I.T. department, supporting the lab."

"Fine. But you have lab access. You know how to run tests."

"Not really. I—"

"If I got you a piece of fabric, like from some clothing, or... like from the liner of a dresser drawer... If I get you it, could you test it for silver and diamond residue?"

"What?" Yvonne stifled a laugh. "Juice, you're a physician. You do know *something* about hospital labs, right?"

After several seconds of silence, Juice said, "Hey, do you know if there's a lab test for amnesia?"

"I need to go, Juice."

"Fine. To be continued. Hey, let's have drinks at Deep Blue again. That was fun!"

Deep Blue was a marine-themed bar/restaurant in Sherman Oaks where the two women had met last Friday evening so Juice could relate the story of her first visit to Jimmy's house.

"Sounds good," said Yvonne. "Just text me."

"You know it, girl!"

"Bye."

Yvonne hung up and turned her attention back to her computer screen, where she'd been trying to wade through a long chain of emails between Fred Nguyen and a lab technician named Mark Pinconning.

It had begun when Fred had wrongly believed he'd observed something amiss on the hospital registration system when he'd been logged in there to investigate an unrelated (and non-existent) issue. He also believed, incorrectly, that if the situation that wasn't occurring in registration were occurring, it could potentially have an impact on lab results, so he'd reached out to Mark (who, if Fred's beliefs had been correct, would've been the wrong lab person to reach out to about it) to give him a heads-up.

Mark, misunderstanding Fred's message, as well as many things about his own job, had replied with irrelevant utter nonsense. And so a (very friendly and enthusiastic) conversation had sprung up between the two, in which each of them repeatedly misinterpreted the other's worthless remarks and responded with his own, equally valuable, remarks.

All of Fred's teammates were copied on this thread, but so far, none had chimed in. Yvonne glanced over at Amy Lee, sitting at the next desk. She was engrossed in a celebrity gossip website.

A new email arrived, from Bill Smede. Yvonne raised her eyebrows in surprise, then opened it. The body simply consisted of "Reminded me of your childhood friend!" followed by a smiley-face emoticon. Below this Bill had pasted in a screen capture from a webpage describing an upcoming online training course on a new version of a statistical modeling software suite called SuperModel. He'd circled the name of the instructor, Chitra K. Navaneethakrishnan.

At Lakeside Elementary in Bellevue, Washington in the 1980s, teachers had always taken roll every morning from a computer print-out, calling out each name from the alphabetized list and awaiting a response of "Here" from that student. One of Yvonne's fourth grade classmates was a girl named Chitra Premachandran, whose name on the roll sheet appeared as "PREMACHANDRAN, CHIT" because the rather unsophisticated printing software allowed for exactly 19 characters per line and no more. The regular teacher, Mrs. Didwell, knew Chitra and said her name correctly when taking roll. But whenever there was a substitute, they would thoughtlessly pronounce the unfamiliar name as "Shit," which invariably drew howls of laughter from all but the most straitlaced kids in the class.

Yvonne smiled, thinking back on this classic story that had been retold many times over the years among various circles of friends. She clicked the Reply button.

Two hours later and half a mile down Wilshire, directly across the street from a billboard on which an advertisement for Porsche automobiles put forward the ludicrous proposition that being inside one of their powerful, precision-engineered vehicles could somehow improve the experience of negotiating totally congested L.A. roads, a 45-year-old non-descript white man named David Jisbourne sat nervously in the waiting room of the Outpatient Radiological Procedure Center located on the third floor of a medical building owned by Beth Universal Mount Zion. He was here today to have a tiny sub-dermal neurological monitoring device implanted near his pylorus, the latest procedure ordered by his gastroenterologist, Dr. Coleman Waxman, in an ongoing effort to diagnose the mysterious periodic gastric discomfort David had been experiencing for the past three years.

When they'd first begun working on this issue together, Waxman had prescribed David various drugs which had no effect, and then had performed an upper endoscopy on David which revealed nothing, after which Waxman got more creative and began outsourcing his endeavors to other departments (primarily radiology). David had taken a ride through various full-body scanners after being fed—or injected with—various "marker" substances. He'd swallowed multiple microelectronic sensors, and received one (featuring patented "spindle-powered upward nano-crawl" technology) in suppository form. A few weeks ago, he'd visited this very same center for an ultrasound-guided injection of bupivacaine into his abdominal wall using an extraordinarily long and thick needle. The physicians performing these procedures had invariably expressed their surprise that anyone would order them for a complaint like his.

David felt slightly frustrated now, sitting here, thinking of how all these non-standard treatments had cost him time, money, and stress, offering him an experience ranging from slightly unpleasant to extremely unpleasant, and how neither he nor Waxman had ever learned anything from any of it. Is the solution worse than the problem? he vaguely wondered. Waxman was already talking about the next step, should today's implant fail to uncover anything: removal of one of David's ribs, in a wildly experimental bid to give his stomach "a little more breathing room."

Glancing idly at the little window mounted in the door of the waiting room, David saw another white man pass by in the hallway outside, somewhat thinner and taller than himself, and somewhat younger (37), with wide, bright blue eyes and a rather stern facial expression. This other man was Scott Portcullis.

Scott continued to the end of the hall, where he entered a suite occupied by four general/family practice physicians including Dr. Leah Schwartz, with whom Scott had scheduled his first annual checkup—and indeed, first-ever visit—for this afternoon.

He approached the reception desk, where a slender, middle-aged Asian woman wearing a big plastic smile and a nametag reading "Joyce D" greeted him.

"Hello!" she said. "How may I help you?"

"I have a 4:00 appointment with Dr. Schwartz," Scott replied.

Joyce looked momentarily at a computer screen. "Mr. Portugals?"

"Yes."

"Great! I need you to fill out some forms." She produced a clipboard containing a formidable stack of papers (and a pen) and handed it to Scott. "Just bring it back to me when you're done!"

"Okay. Thanks."

Scott carried the clipboard to a nearby waiting-room-style chair, sat down, sighed, picked up the pen, and began the tedious work of form out-filling.

He'd been seeing a primary care physician near home, at UCLA Medical Center, when, a few years back, Lathrop Halliday had switched insurance carriers and suddenly his doctor was "out of network." So he'd selected a new P.C.P., this time near his office in El Segundo. When the company had pulled another switcheroo eight months ago and he'd found himself, yet again, in search of a new doctor, Yvonne Smede had suggested he try Beth Universal Mount Zion, whose providers "enjoy a sterling reputation in the healthcare community and among all Southern Californians" (the website's words, not hers). So, here he was.

Frequently seeing a new doctor, with its attendant redundancies, uncertainties, frustrations and discontinuities, was not ideal, to be sure. But Scott valued persistent, comprehensive healthcare, and, as with everything he valued in life, pursued its maintenance meticulously, methodically, relentlessly. He'd always tried to prod his husband, Gary Williams, in the same direction regarding healthcare, with minimal success. Understandable: Gary was not a Portcullis (and also, somehow, had never been injured or sick in his entire life (outside of Colorado earlier this year)).

Growing up as an only child in a modest working-class home in Riverside, Scott had always (through an unknown combination of nature and nurture) seen eye-to-eye with his parents on the basic principles of how to conduct oneself: focused, highly organized, clean, tidy, efficient, quiet, and, for the most part, serious. Since he'd departed their well-oiled three-person machine at the age of eighteen to live on campus at Cal Poly Pomona, there had occasionally been some fairly strong disagreements about certain topics, such as heterosexuality and church (both of which his parents were strongly in favor of), but he'd always remained pretty close with them.

Having mechanically, almost mindlessly, filled out the new patient information form up to this point, Scott stopped and pondered his next response upon encountering "17. What are your hobbies?" What a stupid question, he thought. Ordinarily, he would've—and probably had in the past, he couldn't remember—put "baseball" and perhaps "cooking." But for some reason, at this moment, Yvonne came back into his mind, as did her husband (or was it ex-husband?), and he smiled mischievously and decided to answer as he suspected they might. He wrote "filling out forms" and "lying about my hobbies."

After breezing through the remainder of the questionnaire and accompanying waivers and informational bulletins with a slightly amused new spring in his mental step, Scott delivered the clipboard (minus the sheets he was supposed to keep, which he carefully folded into perfect quarters and slid into his shirt pocket) back to Joyce, then returned to his seat, took out his phone and opened the Cooperstown Universe app.

He began by reading his newsfeed (which included another disappointing incident for shortstop Pete Wagoner, who suffered from a permanently numb left shin and often refused to accept that he'd been tagged out as he slid into second, third, or home), checking out the scoreboard, and making a few adjustments to his "profile," which was not a profile in the traditional sense but more of a highly finetuned configuration scheme used by the software to customize a user's "challenges" (the activities that earned points and, ultimately, greater status). Then he decided to launch a "speed challenge" for himself. This involved a rapid-fire sequence of questions designed to test the user's established knowledge, with no opportunity to seek assistance or perform research before answering. Scott had recently become a Blaster and was hugely proud of it, but keenly aware that precious few months remained in the season and he was still a very, very long way from MasterBlaster.

When he was about halfway through his challenge, a greeting popped up from work colleague and fellow baseball enthusiast Wendy Adams. They'd built a wonderful friendship very quickly after Wendy joined the company five years ago, and Scott deeply enjoyed chatting with her about their favorite topics or any other topic. But he'd always been gently nagged by a sense that Wendy had a bit of a crush on him, and that she might believe she could "turn" him. He absolutely did not in the least want to lead her on, but neither did he wish to give the false impression of having any lack of warmth and fondness for her and their interactions. Of course, there was always the option of just candidly telling her how he saw things. But that could come across so arrogant and presumptuous. Tricky. He decided he'd ignore her message for the time being. Unfortunately, his momentary hesitation ended up preventing him, just by a hair, from successfully completing his speed challenge.

A door opened on the far side of the room and a nurse appeared. "Scott?" he called out.

Scott, who was the only patient waiting, smiled, said "Yes," and stood up.

"You can come on back now."

As Scott strolled toward the door, he checked his watch, saw that it was 4:17, and did a nearly imperceptible eyeroll.

The nurse led him into an examining room, took his vitals and measured his height and weight, then assured him the doctor would be in shortly, and left.

Half an hour later (during which time Scott had managed to complete two Cooperstown Universe speed challenges), Dr. Schwartz arrived.

Eight minutes after that, Scott's checkup was over.

"You again!" Jimmy Sanchez exclaimed upon discovering that Juice Hughes-Newton was, once again, standing on his front doorstep.

"We have unfinished business, Jimmy," she replied. "May I come in?"

He sighed. "Yeah, sure."

"I brought an associate with me this time," said Juice as she stepped through the doorway. "She's going to help me get to the bottom of this."

Jimmy could now see that another woman had been standing directly behind Juice, as if intentionally hiding from view—a white woman with sandy blonde hair and bright blue eyes, probably about the same age as Juice and a few inches shorter. On her face was a rather apprehensive expression.

"Yvonne," she said, extending her hand.

"I'm Jimmy," said Jimmy, shaking Yvonne's hand. Then he ushered her inside and closed the door.

"Where's Nancy?" Juice, who was already making herself comfortable on the sofa, asked loudly.

"Uh, you mean Shayla," replied Jimmy.

"Christ! You can drop the charade already." Juice was scowling impatiently now. "Everyone here knows the truth, and everyone knows that everyone knows. Okay?"

"Hi, Carlos Sanchez," said Carlos, who was sitting at the dining table working on building a miter saw entirely out of wood.

"Nice to meet you," said Yvonne. "That's an impressive project you've got there."

"Thank you!" He beamed with pride. "It's going to be completely self-replicating!"

"Oh, come on!" shot Juice from her spot across the room on the sofa. "You're gonna cut wood with wood? Puh-lease!"

After hearing this, Carlos seemed to become lost in thought, a slightly hurt and confused look on his face.

Jimmy, who'd been standing awkwardly in the middle of the room and smiling uneasily, said, "Have a seat, ladies. Can I offer you a bite to eat?"

"No, thank you," Yvonne replied, making her way toward the sofa to join Juice.

"You can offer *me* one," said Juice. "I'm starving. What have you got?"

"Well," Jimmy said, "I was gonna make myself a sandwich with this new stuff we got…"

Realizing he'd laid the product down on the corner of the dining table on his way through from the kitchen to answer the front door, Jimmy picked it up again and read from the label. "It's called 'Fully Humane Protein Paste.' It's made from insects."

"Jesus!" Juice cried, scrunching up her face in disgust. "No. Fuck, no. I'm not eating that."

"Yeah," said Jimmy, not seeming at all offended and even smiling a bit, "it's kinda creepy, I know. Actually Shayla brought it home."

"Oh, really?" said Juice, speaking the word "really" in the long, drawn-out, sarcastic style.

"Yeah, she works at a health food store now."

"Or so she claims. How long did it take that lying sack of shit to come clean with you about losing her job at the bank?"

Now Jimmy did appear a tad offended. "Uh, well..."

Juice continued: "Anyway, where *is* the bitch?"

Yvonne was squirming in her seat now. She'd very much not wanted to come here, but after being pestered non-stop since Wednesday afternoon about the "Super Saturday Spy Spree" and told she was "indispensable" and "integral" and "invaluable," with "fantastic sleuthing skills" and "sharp analytical intuition" over and over, she'd finally relented.

During the long drive out to Hemet, she'd tried to imagine their conversation with Jimmy and had almost convinced herself that it probably wouldn't be that bad after all. And she'd enjoyed chatting with Juice in the car about topics other than Nasty Nancy— philosophical stuff like whether to boycott good music or movies or other art if you find the person who produced it abhorrent, whether to be completely honest with loved ones about absolutely everything regardless of their feelings, and whether it's appropriate for a couple to use the toilet in front of each other. She'd also been (secretly) quite tickled by the rather abrasive phone call Juice had received halfway through the journey from her boss, Dr. Marquez, about being mysteriously absent from work on Wednesday.

These past few minutes, though, Yvonne had been wondering why she'd ever agreed to participate in this batty mission, and feeling far more sympathetic toward a man she'd only just met for the very first time than her lifelong close friend.

"Look, Shayla's at work right now, okay?" said Jimmy, approaching the sofa.

"God," groaned Juice, rolling her eyes.

Jimmy sat down in the center of the sofa, between the two women, first moving a folded newspaper out of the way.

"So," he said, "what's this all about?"

"It's about truth, Jimmy," said an exasperated Juice. "And justice. You know that. It's always been about that."

"So, Jimmy," said Yvonne, "I understand you haven't been in Hemet very long. How do you like it?"

"Pretty good. I mean, the town is pretty nice. Sort of quiet and boring, I guess—you know, compared to L.A."

Yvonne nodded and smiled.

"But, maybe that's a good thing," Jimmy continued with a chuckle. "But, living with my brother has definitely been a big adjustment. No offense, man!"

"None taken!" Carlos called from the dining table.

"And… My wife not remembering nothing, I think that's the toughest part."

"I'm sure it's been very difficult," said Yvonne.

Juice let out another groan and rolled her eyes again.

"At least we're still alive," Jimmy went on. "I thank the Lord for that. And I'm completely out of the life now. Shoulda got out a long time ago."

"Gang-banging?"

"Yeah. It was stupid but, you know, I was mixed up in stuff ever since I was a kid. It was just… like, normal, you know? That was my world. And I got heavier into it when I was in my twenties, when I started working at Sid's garage. I was actually pretty good. I think I was sort of like… a natural leader, you know?"

Carlos laughed.

"What kind of stuff did you do?" asked Yvonne.

"Ah, you know… drugs, fake IDs, moving crap… some burglary, bootlegging, pimping…" He rattled off the list casually and indifferently. "Later we started promoting some underground fights. You know, bare-knuckle. And dog fights, too." Now a small smile, and a slightly wistful expression, had formed on his face.

"Wow."

"But nothing violent. Never violent. I'm, like, not a violent guy, you know? I don't want to hurt people."

"Right," said Yvonne.

"Not like Ned," Jimmy said. "He has no problem hurting people. And he's big and strong and… tough as hell. He's like, intimidating, you know?"

Yvonne nodded.

"So, in a way, he was a great partner for me. Kinda like the brains and the brawn, you know? He helped out with security, and he helped us... like, get into some riskier stuff. But, more risk, more reward!" He grinned.

"Okay, enough!" cried Juice. "Jimmy and Ned eventually had a big falling out, and Ned's a violent dude with a bad temper, and he tried to kill Jimmy and Nancy. Blah, blah, blah!"

Yvonne tried to conceal her amusement. Jimmy looked a little perturbed.

"You two don't need to know each other's life story," Juice continued. "My girl here just needs to get on with her detective work. I want my goddamn necklace back!"

"Ummf," Jimmy said in disgust. "You ain't going snooping around my house again. I told you, that necklace was gone a long time ago. You couldn't find it. I couldn't find it. Shayla couldn't find it. That necklace ain't—"

"Like she would even *try* to find it! Or admit if she *did* find it. God, like it's even missing! That bitch knows exactly where it is."

"Jimmy," said Yvonne, "is it possible you and your wife put some stuff into storage? Before you... uh, started your new life out here?"

"No. We didn't have no time for—" He stopped mid-sentence, gripped by a sudden thought, and stared silently into space for a couple of seconds. Then "Wait! Yes! There *was* a storage, like, shed, locker thing. You know, like at one of those self-storage places."

Juice's eyes had lit up.

"I remember now. We had it way back, me and Ned. And a couple times, like, a few years ago, me and Nancy took a bunch of our stuff over there. 'Cause the apartment was getting too, you know, filled up with junk..."

"Somehow the bill has always come to me!" commented Carlos from his spot at the dining table.

"This is great, Jimmy," said Juice. "We need to access that storage unit!"

"Well, I don't think your necklace is in there," he said.

"Yes it is," Juice retorted, standing up. "Yes it is." She laughed. "This is great!"

Turning to Yvonne, she shouted, "Girl, you are a goddamn genius!"

Chapter 15

Bill Smede was in a foul mood. Despite October having turned into November several days back, ridiculously warm weather had persisted and today was the worst yet, topping out at 80 degrees. He'd arrived back at his apartment five minutes ago from walking the new neighborhood loop he'd devised (which shared much of its length with the original, condo-based one) and his polo shirt was stuck to his back. Moreover, a glance at his wrist revealed an astonishingly low step count; he felt certain the PaceTek Nano was deliberately cheating him. And to top it all off, he'd had to endure four and a half hours of mind-numbingly useless meetings today. But now it was nearly 2:00 and the New Yorkers were wrapping things up. At least there's that, he thought. And tomorrow is Friday. A very small smile creased his face.

His phone, lying next to him on the only piece of furniture in the place that even remotely resembled a table or desk—and thus served all purposes requiring either of those—started ringing, and displayed a number Bill thought he recognized as the Cadillac dealer's service department. He'd been expecting to hear back from them about scheduling the ATS for maintenance.

He picked the phone up, swiped green, put it to his ear and said "Hello?"

"Bill! What's going on?"

It was Matt Spratt, and the question he'd posed wasn't really a question; it just meant "Hello."

"Hey, Matt."

"Feel like some company right now? Thought maybe I could check out your new place."

"Uh… Yeah. Sure. Where are you?"

"I'm on a pay phone at 7-Eleven. Near your old place. Corner of

Sepulveda and, uh..."

"Oh, yeah. I know where you mean. So, a pay phone? I didn't know there were any working ones left."

"Oh—no, not one of those old things. I just call it a pay phone because I paid to use it! Belongs to... What was your name again?"

In the background, Bill heard a woman's voice giggle and say "Elizabeth."

"Belongs to Lizzie here," Matt continued.

"Aha."

"Actually,"—he chuckled—"I didn't pay her for it. I offered to, but she's so decent and kind, she wouldn't allow it."

More giggling in the background.

"Good thing, too," said Matt. "I just realized, I don't have any money!"

More giggling. Bill couldn't help chuckling, too.

"So how do I get to you?" Matt asked.

"Hmm... Well... Probably easiest if I just come out and meet you."

"Okay."

"Just, uh, head east from where you are. Cross Sepulveda there and then just keep going east on Olympic. I'll meet you out on the sidewalk there."

"Great! See you soon."

"Oh, hey, Matt... Uh... Is your decent and kind friend coming over too?"

"Hah! You're a trip. No, she can't. She's got a thing. But I might try to catch up with her later, you know—"

"Cool. Okay, see you in a few."

"Okay, bye."

Bill hung up, tucked the phone into his back pocket, gathered his hat, sunglasses, wallet and keys (but not his iPod and earphones this time, although he hesitated briefly, considering it), went out the front door, down the stairs and out to the sidewalk, and began walking south on Dimvale.

"Fucking heat," he muttered. "Fuck."

Fifteen feet ahead in the center of the sidewalk, Bill noticed a shiny object roughly the size of a tennis ball but irregularly shaped. What could it be? he wondered as he approached. Some funky landscaping component that came loose? There wasn't any material under the sun, it seemed, that some Angeleno wouldn't want featured in their front yard.

Three steps shy of the mystery object, Bill realized its shimmering had been supplied by a layer of flies completely covering it, which were now scattering through the air. What remained was irregularly shaped, approximately half the size of a tennis ball, and had clearly originated from a dog's anus. Bill made a disgusted "Mmmf" utterance as he stepped over it and continued on his way.

The next couple of blocks were relatively uneventful, though they did offer up a small collection of irritants which included two noisy leaf blowers in action, one set of sidewalk-watering sprinklers, and one oblivious baby carriage pusher with her face in a phone.

Rounding the corner onto Olympic Boulevard, Bill immediately spotted a figure in the distance—only a silhouette against the bright sun that had already made its way to the western part of the sky, but clearly a grown man riding a bicycle intended for a youngster, thin, with wild, shaggy hair, a trail of smoke curling up from the point where his left hand gripped the handlebar.

Bill smiled. "Matt."

Half a minute later, Matt pulled up in front of Bill, hopped off the bike—which turned out to be a 20-year-old Schwinn girl's model, rust-colored (partly from its original paint job and partly from actual rust) and slightly misshapen, with a wire basket bolted onto the front—and discarded it on the strip of grass between the sidewalk and the street. Then he took a puff on his joint.

Bill glanced at the bike and back at Matt with a puzzled expression.

"Somebody else will use it," explained Matt, grinning. "Just like I did. Community bikes!"

"Okay," said Bill.

"Want some?" asked Matt, holding out his joint.

"No, thanks."

"Foolish," Matt said, then took another quick puff. "But understandable." He dropped it on the concrete and crushed it under his flip-flop.

The two men began walking, side by side, back the way Bill had come.

"So, what's new with you?" Matt asked.

"Mmm, not much."

"Been seeing anyone?"

"You mean like dating? No, no. Not yet. Not sure if I'm ready for that. Anyway I don't even know how I'd go about it."

" 'Go about it'," Matt repeated with a chuckle. "You're fun, Bill. So then what've you been doing with yourself? What's been floating your boat lately?"

"Well, there's my job, of course…"

Matt flashed Bill a skeptical smile that seemed to say "Oh, come on."

"And I was working on that thing with my old high school friend, Irene. Did I tell you about that?"

"Yeah, I think so. The musical toy thing?"

"Yeah. But that wrapped up like a month ago. Oh, that reminds me, I should check with her how it's going."

"I could try selling them on the boardwalk if she wants."

"I don't know if it's that kind of product…"

"It'd be fun! I wouldn't even ask for a cut."

"Thanks. I'll… mention it to her."

"So what else have you been up to?"

"Well… That's a really good question, actually. I've been doing some… I guess soul-searching, lately. Trying to figure out how I'd like to spend my free time. Which, you know, I have quite a bit of, now that the kids are older, and especially since Yvonne and I split up.

"I know it sounds weird but, it seems like… I don't really have any interests. Well, that's not quite true. Stuff does interest me. Tons of stuff, actually. But it's… I guess it's what I'd call a, a 'passive' interest: I like to watch and listen and learn. Read. Observe. I think that might be it—I'm more of an observer than a participant.

"Like if somebody suggests a real activity… like, I don't know… planting rose bushes or… attending a wine tasting or… playing a board game or… going hiking or… anything, really… I just think, 'Meh, I don't know.' It might sound kind of cool, but it never feels like it's worth… whatever—the time, the money, the aggravation, the… I don't know, all the inconveniences and irritations that inevitably come along with doing something.

"Unless they really push me to do it, I'll always pass. It's just not… interesting *enough*, you know? People are supposed to have hobbies. I don't have any hobbies. It's like… almost like I'm *incapable* of having hobbies."

Neither man spoke for the next twenty seconds. Then Bill started up again.

"I guess everything we do—all humans, I mean—can be classified as either production or consumption. And each category has its pros and cons. Production is, kind of by definition, work—requiring effort. And it seems like, except for very short spans of time doing just the right magical kind of work for your specific mentality or personality or whatever, there's a degree of unpleasantness that accompanies any productive activity.

"But consumption often includes a feeling of emptiness, or waste, or... foolishness, or shame... It doesn't generally feel very fulfilling for very long. And, of course, it can be costly... in financial and other ways.

"So everyone has to try to figure out what's their own personal right blend of production activities and consumption activities... And exactly which ones to pick. How do they make themselves feel maximally happy about both types? It's not easy. I think most people get it wrong. I think I get it wrong."

Another twenty seconds of silent walking.

Then Matt said, "Sorry, Bill—I kinda spaced out a while ago."

"That's okay. Probably a smart move!"

Matt laughed.

"So anyway," Bill continued, "*you* have tons of free time. Way more than I do. How do you spend it?"

"Me? I have adventures!"

Bill chuckled. "Yeah, I suppose you do. Oh, hey, speaking of: what's the latest with your hunt for buried treasure?"

"Ooh, glad you asked! I finally—finally!—figured out where the map is."

"You mean where it might possibly be, if it even still exists. If it ever *did* exist."

"Oh ye of little faith!" Matt grinned. "It definitely did exist and it definitely still does exist—though only through an amazing stroke of luck. So check this out. Normally letters are destroyed after a while if they can't be delivered or returned to the sender. But for some unknown reason, there was a glitch in the system, just for a short time, back in 1964, and a bunch of dead letters that were scheduled for destruction just ended up in permanent limbo, sitting in a warehouse."

"How about that," said Bill.

"They were all from Los Angeles, and all sent between February and April. Which fits perfectly with when Rick and Bart had dinner together! The map was definitely part of that batch.”

Bill couldn’t stop himself from smiling but did manage not to shake his head.

Matt went on, “And it gets even better! Eventually all the dead letter processing was moved to a single facility in Atlanta, but when they closed down the west coast office in San Francisco, the materials still in their possession were sent down here, not out there. So the map came home! It’s right under our nose. In a big USPS warehouse downtown. I’ve got the address!” He giggled gleefully.

“Wow,” said Bill. “And you really think this... 80-year-old, or whatever it is, treasure map... is sitting there in that warehouse.”

“Oh, I know it is!”

“This is my place, here,” Bill said, gesturing to the building now on their left.

“Nice!” said Matt.

After another few steps they left the sidewalk and traversed the concrete path and the stairway leading up to Bill’s apartment.

“Reminds me of your other place,” Matt commented as Bill was unlocking the door.

“Yeah. Except, as you’ll see in two seconds...” He swung the door open and motioned with his arm for his friend to enter. “It’s like half the size.”

“Oh yeah!” said Matt, surveying the entire apartment from one step inside. “Cozy!”

“Indeed,” said Bill, closing the door behind them.

“Hah! Bunk beds—I love it.”

“Yep. Fun times. Hey, have a seat, make yourself comfortable.”

“Thanks,” said Matt, sauntering toward the sofa.

Bill headed for his laptop. “Sorry,” he said, “I just gotta check on a few things here, for work.”

“No worries. So old Alice hangs with you here sometimes, eh?”

“Uh...” Bill was typing and clicking now. “Yeah. ‘Hangs with’ might be an exaggeration. But yeah.”

“How’s she doing? Seems like I haven’t seen her in forever.”

“Uh...” More typing and clicking. “She’s okay. I think. She’s quiet. Maybe a bit too serious. I don’t *think* she’s doing any drugs, but...”

“A little weed might be just what she needs. You know, to loosen up.”

Still focused on his computer screen, Bill let out a small chuckle. "Uh-huh."

"I could help with that."

Bill stopped and looked up, no longer smiling. "Matt, *please* don't sell weed to my kid."

"What kind of person do you think I am, Bill? This is your daughter we're talking about. I wouldn't charge her for it."

"Just, please..."

"Hey, you got anything to eat?"

"Uh, not sure. Just a sec." Bill's eyes were back on his screen now. He made one final mouse click, then stood up and headed for the kitchen.

"So," he said, "this treasure map thing..."

"Right!" Matt's eyes lit up as he remembered it.

"Supposing it really is there, in that warehouse... How are you going to get your hands on it?"

"Aha! Glad you asked, my friend. I have a foolproof plan. You remember my girlfriend Kellie?"

"Uh... maybe..." Bill was now rummaging around in his kitchen cupboards. "Was she the one who drove an old Trans Am?"

"No, that was Shellie."

"I've got some chips. You want some chips?"

"Yes, please! Anyway, Kellie drove a... Actually, I don't remember what she drove. But she worked at that hair salon."

"Hmm..."

"Anyway, her best friend has a cousin who works at the post office."

"At that special warehouse?" Bill asked, arriving at the sofa with a giant bag of potato chips.

"Thanks!" said Matt, taking the bag. "No. The cousin just works at some branch. In Alhambra, I think. But he knows somebody very high up in the organization, very powerful, but, like, super friendly and helpful. And that guy is going to arrange to sneak me into the warehouse."

He opened the bag, pulled out a chip, popped it in his mouth and began crunching away, all the while smiling excitedly. Bill, now sitting on the sofa next to him, said nothing.

Matt swallowed, then continued. "And then I'm going to search around in there and find the map!"

Bill spent a few seconds trying to think of a charitable way to phrase his next statement. "Uh, Matt... Keep in mind that no plan is ever perfect. Even when we put in a huge amount of thought and careful crafting, as I'm sure you have, we can never account for all the world's complexities and uncertainties. And therefore, no plan ever unfolds exactly as expected."

Matt was silent.

"So, just... you know, don't get your hopes up... too much..."

Matt laughed. "Oh, Bill. You're a trip. Some plans *are* perfect, and this is one of them!"

Bill smiled. "Okay..."

"Hey, you got any beer?" asked Matt.

The following evening at 8:30 P.M. Mountain Standard Time, one thousand miles away, Yvonne Smede was sitting at a bar in a hotel lounge. This was the only hotel in the tiny village of Pompey's Pillar, Montana, and in fact was not even really located there, but several miles east along the interstate and thus farther outside of the closest biggish city, Billings. The village, established in the early 20th century as part of the Huntley irrigation project, was named after a nearby 150-feet-tall slab of rock onto which egotistical William Clark (of Lewis & Clark fame) had scribbled his autograph a hundred years earlier.

The rather eccentric founder of Moonshot Systems (a maker of hospital laboratory software), Sienna Glouskinskance, had decided long ago, when building the too-large and weirdly styled "main campus" of her company, that it would officially be located in Pompey's Pillar, because she liked the name and the story, and because its true location wasn't *in* anywhere, but simply a nameless patch of earth on the banks of the Yellowstone River, surrounded on all sides by vast stretches of desolate nothingness.

Gazing out the window at snowflakes swirling in the very brisk night air, Yvonne marveled at the fact that M.U.G. (the Moonshot User Group annual convention) was always held here at this godforsaken spot, and always in November. Either somebody is a real moron or somebody is greasing somebody's palm, she thought to herself as she took a slow, leisurely sip from her glass of sauvignon blanc.

Each year, one member of the Lab Team was awarded an all-expenses-paid trip to M.U.G. following a great deal of jockeying all around for not being selected (exception: Fred loved going, but Laura felt it wouldn't be right to just send him every time). After drawing the short straw, Yvonne had booked her flight to Billings for today because, although the convention didn't get into full swing until Monday, the weekend was blocked off for somewhat nebulous "committee time" and she'd been persuaded by smarmy Tim Bates of Feggedah-Bowdett Hospital in Boston to join the Interfaces Committee. Some of it might even be interesting, she thought as she turned to the back page of the convention program lying on the bar in front of her, where the scant details of the weekend known before press time had been printed.

"Not again!" she exclaimed out loud upon reading the giant banner ("Gone Too Soon") and scanning the agenda underneath it— event after event, of every type imaginable, all day Saturday and all day Sunday, devoted entirely to memorializing T. Scott Erwenburlen, the original organizer of the Moonshot User Group and longtime former C.I.O. at Cancer Research Associates Pittsburgh, who'd died last month at the age of 98 after a long battle with Alzheimer's.

The last time Yvonne had attended M.U.G., five years ago, they'd been fixated on Melissa Porris, a woman who'd apparently been heavily involved with the group but with whom Yvonne had never crossed paths, who, at the time, had recently drowned in her neighbor's swimming pool after climbing over the fence from her own backyard into theirs late at night during a cocktail party she and her husband were hosting.

Throughout the week, all the convention-goers had been repeatedly herded into a large auditorium where, while munching and quaffing the complimentary refreshments, they watched slideshows about Melissa's life and listened to speakers up on the stage, a few of whom had actually known her, deliver lengthy testimonials about her that contained as much sniffling and sobbing as real words.

On the final night, while enjoying free wine and cheese, everyone had gathered to assemble care packages to be donated to a charity, in Melissa's home state of Arizona, dedicated to providing support for grieving widowers whose wives had been the victims of unsafe practices by pool owners. Most folks had left the auditorium that evening feeling rather pleased with themselves and sporting stickers on their shirts that read, "I made a difference!"

"I suppose this happens to you all the time," said a booming male voice with a southern drawl from Yvonne's left, startling her.

"Excuse me?" she said, turning to see, sitting on the next barstool a few feet away, a tall, heavy-set white man with brown hair and a mustache, about 40 years old, wearing dark dress slacks, a white shirt with the collar open, a sand-colored sports jacket, and a cowboy hat.

"Some big ugly bastard sitting next to you at a bar starts talking to you," said the man, then let out a booming laugh.

Yvonne smiled. "It is a bit of a problem," she said.

"Mind if I join you?"

"Sure."

The man stood up and began pushing his stool closer to Yvonne while speaking to the bartender. "Buddy, could you get the lady another of those, please?" He gestured toward Yvonne's wine. "Oh, and, get me another one too." A tall glass mug that appeared to contain some foamy remnants of a serving of beer sat on the bar in front of where the man had just been.

"Name's Tex," he said, extending his hand. "Well, really my name's Larry, but everyone calls me Tex."

"Yvonne," said Yvonne, shaking Tex's hand. Then, with a small smirk, she asked "Where are you from?"

"Houston."

"And people there call you Tex?"

"Yeah." He looked a bit puzzled.

"Cool." Smirk still present.

"How 'bout you? Where're you from?"

"L.A."

"No kidding? Wow. So, you been in any movies or T.V. shows?"

"None that I recall. Mainly I work in healthcare I.T. Don't you?"

"Huh? No, no. I'm a Senior Assistant Manager at an auto parts store."

"Interesting. What brings you to this particular hotel, then?"

"Well, my own stupidity, to be honest with you!" He laughed. "I'm in town for the big gun expo. But I waited so long to arrange my hotel room, by the time I did, there were no vacancies anywhere near the arena!"

"I'm surprised there were any here," Yvonne said sarcastically. Then, genuinely, "I am surprised they let you stay here without registering for M.U.G."

Their drinks arrived. Tex immediately picked up his beer and raised it in Yvonne's direction. "Cheers," he said.

"Mmm—" Realizing she hadn't quite finished her previous pour, Yvonne quickly downed that, then swapped it for the fresh one and clinked her glass against his. "Cheers."

"I'm glad I met you," Tex said after they'd both taken a swig.

"Yeah," Yvonne replied with a faint smile.

"Oh—so, yeah, I did have to register for M.U.G." He chuckled. "Had no idea what it was. Didn't care! On the form where it asked where you're from, I just put 'Houston.' They probably wanted a company name!" He chuckled again.

"I don't think they're too fussy," said Yvonne.

"Is that M.U.G., there?" Tex pointed at the program.

"Yep." She glanced down at it for a split second. "A veritable catalog of fun and frolic."

Tex had been idly gazing at it but suddenly moved his eyes back to Yvonne's face and said, "Sorry. Sorry. It's none of my business. Your papers are private."

She smiled amusedly and shrugged. "Most of my intimate secrets aren't in these particular papers."

"I know," Tex said with a chuckle. "It's just, I have kind of a hang-up about papers and privacy. I never leave any papers lying around—my home or my place of work. I wouldn't want anyone reading them. Doesn't matter what they are. They're private."

"Who's going to read them? The most scandalous thing imaginable could be written in huge letters right at the top and nobody would notice. Humans just aren't a reading species anymore. We've moved on to... more stimulating stuff, I guess. When a person today happens to catch a glimpse of some printed words, passing through their field of view, they don't care. They're not the least bit curious what those words say. They want music and flashy graphics and quick soundbites."

She paused momentarily, then added, "Most people, anyway. In my opinion."

They were both silent for a few seconds. Tex seemed to have been listening but not really absorbing what Yvonne had said.

Finally he bellowed, "You know what? Come to think of it, I don't even have any papers!" He laughed heartily.

Yvonne laughed too, much more softly. "Of course not," she said.

Tex finished off his beer with several giant gulps, then put down his glass and sighed contentedly. "You know, honestly," he said, "I'm tempted to have another!"

"I wouldn't think any less of you," said Yvonne with a smile. Then, after a very short pause, "How could I?"

"Hah!" Booming laughter. "You're a funny lady, Yvonne. I like you. Your sense of humor... I think they call it a 'dry' sense of humor..."

"I don't know or care what they call it."

"Heh-heh, nice! So, hey, you want another one too?"

"If you insist."

Tex ordered them another round and, over the course of an hour and a half, another, and another. They spent the time chatting about a wide range of topics, every exchange further cementing Yvonne's belief that they had almost nothing in common. They disagreed on politics, religion, and all of the less-controversial subjects that two people might disagree on. But it was very friendly and lighthearted and easy, and, at times, mildly interesting.

She hesitated for a moment when, after they'd polished off their latest round and agreed to call it quits, he invited her up to his room for a "nightcap." But then she thought, What the hell? Could be fun.

And indeed it was.

It was Sunday afternoon and Debbie Smede was standing in the Westside sunshine, perfectly manicured bright green grass under her feet, gazing at a very skinny 35-story tower rising up from behind the tree line half a mile to the east, strongly recognizing it but struggling to recall what it was.

The building, sitting on an eighth of an acre, was now the entire campus of Central Los Angeles College of Liberal Arts. Privately owned CLACLA (which had dubiously granted itself license to use the word "central" based on its map location exactly midway along a rather arbitrarily drawn, gently curving arc (dreamed up by nineteenth century cartographer Phineas L. Herfenberger) connecting the Civic Center to the Santa Monica pier) had begun its existence nearly 100 years ago as a well-endowed, well-respected institution that occupied a dozen city blocks near the Carthay neighborhood.

But over the decades, as various factors had necessitated belt-tightening and the value of their land had kept skyrocketing, they'd ended up, bit by bit, selling nearly all of it to developers. They'd had to accompany each round of sell-off with a round of new construction, in the upward direction, in order to maintain roughly the same total amount of square footage, but the cost of this construction was always tiny compared to the real estate windfall. Students had routinely complained about the ever-shrinking (now zero) supply of outdoor spaces and the tedium of constantly using elevators and stairwells; the college countered by reminding them of all the marvelous aerial views of the city.

"Hmm... Some kind of big tech company, maybe?" muttered Debbie to herself. "Girls, you know what that kinda needle-looking structure is over there?" She pointed at it.

"Nope," said Raylene and Anika, who were standing to her left, in unison. Neither of them had glanced at the tower.

To Debbie's right sat her dog, Fritz, silent and still but with ears standing straight up and a facial expression of apparent attentiveness. The four of them formed part of a large queue of humans and canines, surrounded by numerous orange traffic cones, all waiting to hear their names called so they could show their stuff for the judges of today's event, the Southwestern Autumn Classic, a dog show organized by the American Mixed Breed Presentation Society.

Grace Hogg had been here with the others, too, until a few minutes ago when Debbie had spotted Anna-Maria Schiaduffa moving around in the stands, greeting individual spectators and making exuberant facial and arm gestures to the whole crowd, and had quickly whipped a copy of Schiaduffa's latest advice/anecdote book, Dog Eat Dog, out of her bag, handed it to Grace and begged her to dash off and try to get it signed.

In addition to authoring, Schiaduffa was a highly regarded breeder and trainer, the founder and president of A.M.B.P.S., and one of Debbie's heroes. Today was the next small step, of many, in the quest to get Fritz entered in the ultimate contest, being held next spring in New York, named after and hosted by Schiaduffa, with the top prize a giant gold cup (also named after her) and a check for $25,000.

"The girls are both absolutely gorgeous," said a voice from behind Debbie. "Just like their mother."

She turned around to see a white woman about her own age with brown hair and brown eyes, heavily made up, of average height and build, standing next to a mixed breed dog.

"Thanks!" Debbie said with a big smile.

"Is she your sister?" the woman asked.

"Huh? Who?"

"The girls' mother. She was here a minute ago. I just thought maybe you were sisters."

"Oh! No..."

Debbie felt no anger toward the woman, but did feel a tiny sting from thinking of something she rarely thought about: that Grace was in fact the biological mother of both girls. They hadn't planned it that way; they were supposed to take turns. But when Raylene was two years old, with both women not getting any younger, they'd felt rather acutely the pressure to hurry up and get on with it. Some medical tests—she couldn't remember exactly what they were—had raised a little bit of concern about Debbie having a pregnancy just at that moment, and then... everything had moved so fast. She couldn't quite recall how the decision was made, but it was, and forward they all went. She shrugged mentally. Not a big deal.

"My goodness!" exclaimed Debbie's new conversation partner. "Are you her mother, then? You look fantastic for your age!"

Debbie laughed. "No. No. I'm not her mother. I'm... *their* mother." She gestured at Raylene and Anika. "We both are. They're our daughters. Together."

The woman looked blank for several seconds as she attempted to process this. Then a startled expression sprang onto her face and she said, "Oh!"

Debbie chuckled and nodded. "Yes!"

"Oh... Oh, my..." the woman stammered. "This is very, um... You see, I've never actually met... one of your kind... before."

"That's okay," Debbie said warmly, still chuckling, not offended in the slightest.

"Don't get me wrong—I don't have a problem with that lifestyle.

Not at all. I just… think it's kind of creepy and weird."

Now Debbie just smiled, unable to think of any response.

"Oh!" the woman suddenly exclaimed. "How rude of me not to introduce myself! I'm Tami. Tami Fleffren."

"Nice to meet you, Tami. I'm Debbie."

"I just love coming to these things with Princess, here." She glanced down momentarily at her dog. "They are so much fun!"

"Totally!" Debbie replied with a big grin.

"Do you live around here?"

"No. My brother actually lives just a few miles from here, by coincidence. But no, I live down in Cerritos."

"Oh, yeah? How do you like it?"

"I love it! A great blend of city and 'burbs."

"My friend almost bought a car there once," said Tami, "at the Cerritos Auto Square."

"Yep!" Debbie giggled. "So where do you live?"

"Oh, really close by. Walking distance. Just over there, in Crestview." She pointed vaguely.

"Cool!"

"Yeah, my whole world is walkable. It just became a habit. When I was interviewing for my first job out of college, and they were offering me the job—you know, it was a desk job in an office—and they were like, 'It's very important that you're never late. You need to be here at exactly 9 A.M. every single day. No exceptions.' And, I was…"

Debbie laughed.

"I know, right? And I was like, 'This is L.A.' I knew the only way I could guarantee I'd never be late for work was if I walk there."

Debbie laughed again. "Totally!"

"So, I got an apartment that was half a mile from work. And the rest is history!"

"I love it!" said Debbie with another laugh. "Oh, my phone!"

She retrieved the furiously vibrating device from her pocket and glanced at the screen. "Oh, sorry, Tami—I'd better take this. It's my mom."

"No problem!" said Tami.

"Hi, Mamsy! What's shakin'?"

"I'm at the salon! My girl and I are having the best time!"

"That's great!"

"Mmm, this cucumber water. So refreshing!"

"Yeah, I totally need to go with you sometime."

"Definitely! So, what are you doing right now? Are the girls with you?"

"Yep, they're here. We're at the dog show!"

"Oh, wonderful! Yes, you'll have to put them both on the phone. But first let's talk about Thanksgiving. Oh! Before I forget. You'll never guess who asked me out!"

"Who?"

"Albert Forrester!"

"Albert Forrester..." Debbie repeated, searching her memory. "Uh... Is that Yvonne's dad?"

"Yes, that's right!"

"Wow. That's pretty crazy."

"I know! He said he'd been interested in me for quite a long time, actually, but wasn't sure how to reach out to me. Isn't that sweet?"

Debbie laughed. "Yeah. That's... Wow."

"He's a very nice man, actually," said Mamsy. "He's very charming."

"Is he? I always kinda thought, uh..."

"Very smart, too!"

"So, are you gonna go out with him?"

"Well, yes—we're supposed to have brunch together next weekend. In Culver City."

"Wow."

"I'm excited about it!"

Debbie chuckled and shook her head. "That's... great. I'm so happy for you, Mamsy."

"Thank you!"

"Not sure how William would feel about it if he knew..."

"Yes, he did act kind of funny when I told him a few minutes ago."

Two days later Francisco Danilo Rosario was standing awkwardly on the Venice boardwalk, wearing a light brown Armani suit, no tie and his white shirt open at the neck, anxiously scanning his surroundings. He glanced quickly at his Rolex—3:06—then resumed scanning.

Then he spotted them: about ten feet away, next to a palm tree, stood a man and a woman engaged in cheerful, animated conversation. The woman was black, approximately forty years old, average height, very thin, hair sticking out wildly in all directions, dressed in a tank top, shorts, and flip-flops. The man was dressed similarly and also had wild hair, but he was white—pasty white—and even thinner than her, and quite tall; his age was indeterminable. The woman clutched an ice cream cone. The man held, by a stick, some kind of bread-surfaced elliptoid in his left hand, and in his right what appeared to be a lit marijuana cigarette, its almost majestic smoke curling slowly upward into the air.

"Matt?" said Francisco with a warm smile as he approached the pair. "I am Francisco." He extended his hand.

Matt had already been smiling excitedly and continued to do so as he turned to look at Francisco. "Hey!" he exclaimed, shaking Francisco's hand. "Fran! It's good to see you again."

"Francisco." The smile disappeared for a second but then returned. "I do not believe we have met before."

"Oh, really? Hmm. I could've sworn... Well, anyway, you look exactly the way I pictured you!" He laughed and clapped Francisco on the shoulder playfully. Then he took a final drag on his joint, dropped it on the ground and stepped on it.

"I'm Veronica," said Matt's companion, extending her hand.

Shaking it, Francisco replied, "I am pleased to meet you, Veronica."

"Ronnie and me were just talking about—"

"Ronnie and I," said Francisco.

"Huh?"

"Ronnie and *I* were just talking."

"Oh, you were?"

Veronica chuckled.

"No," Francisco said with a sigh. "I was simply pointing out that... Hmm, I suppose it is really of no consequence. Please, carry on, Matt."

Matt shrugged. "So anyway," he said, "we were talking about our favorite foods. She's into sweet treats—as you can see! Whereas I'm more into the salty stuff." He held up his snack for Francisco's viewing, then bit off a piece of it.

"Indeed," said Francisco with a smile. "Savory foods."

"Oh, hey—you want a bite?" Matt held out the half-eaten bread-and-meat skewer.

"Thank you, no. I... had a late lunch."

"Well, sorry, I gotta run," said Veronica.

"No problem, little lady," said Matt. "I will look forward to seeing you again soon!"

"Bye, nice meeting you," she said to Francisco, and turned to go. Matt managed to smack her on the butt with his hand as she departed, which elicited a giggle from her.

Francisco was smiling and shaking his head, marveling at what he'd just witnessed. "How do you do it?" he asked.

"Do what?"

"Your abilities with women are astounding. Do they ever reject your advances?"

"Advances?" Matt chuckled. "Uh... I mean, sometimes a lady isn't really feeling it, you know? Doesn't really want to hang with me. If that's what you mean."

Francisco looked at Matt skeptically for a moment, doubting the truth of what he'd just been told. Then he said, "You certainly are an ideal instructor."

"Instructor?"

Matt, who'd just swallowed the final bite of his snack, flung the stick toward a trash can several feet away. He didn't see it hit the rim and fall on the ground (though Francisco did, and winced).

"Yes, that was the whole..." Francisco paused briefly, suddenly feeling a little embarrassed. "The whole point of our convening today was for you to... teach me."

Matt looked at him blankly.

"To teach me how to... pick up women." It sounded a little silly when he said it out loud.

Matt laughed. "Seriously?"

"Yes. Did Bill not mention this to you?"

"No..."

Francisco's face felt hot. He tugged at his collar, which, although it was unbuttoned, seemed to be squeezing his throat. "Where *is* Bill, anyway?" he asked in a more flustered-sounding voice than he would've liked.

"I don't know," Matt said with a shrug. "Come on, let's walk. Bill can find us if he needs to. You have a phone, right?"

Francisco followed Matt's lead and broke into a stride. "Yes, I have a phone," he said.

By the time the two men had taken a dozen steps down the boardwalk side by side, he'd relaxed considerably and his current situation had begun to feel like the leisurely, pleasant stroll it was intended to be.

Eventually he said, "So, Bill did not mention anything to you about my troubles with women?"

"Well, he did say you'd been having a tough time with what's-her-name..."

"Felaecia. Yes, I recently ended our relationship, after seven years and four months. I believe it was the correct decision, but these matters are fiendishly difficult to evaluate." He sighed. "I have experienced mixed emotions after the fact."

"Yep, the heart's a funny thing..."

"What else did Bill say about me? Did he discuss my wishes with you?"

"Your wishes? Well... He did say you were sort of a major horndog..."

"That is not a term I would—"

"And into a lot of kinky stuff. You know, there are websites out there to help folks hook up for every kinky thing you can dream of..."

"Alas, no—such an approach does not suit me. I do not seek meaningless encounters; I require a true connection with my sexual partners. Additionally, I find these electronic means of communicating rather distasteful... I suppose I might be somewhat old-fashioned in that respect, but I prefer real conversation, face to face."

Matt was chuckling and shaking his head. "You're a trip, Fran."

Francisco almost couldn't, but did, resist issuing another correction. Instead he chuckled himself and said, "I suppose it is perhaps paradoxical, and certainly a tragic inconvenience, that I possess the powerful and varied sexual appetites that I do, while at the same time, effortlessly, inevitably—and, mind you, in most cases very agreeably—becoming deeply emotionally invested in every woman I encounter!"

Matt smiled and glanced over at Francisco, not understanding this utterance very well and hoping he wouldn't need to.

"For example, just yesterday I was viewing a pornographic film, and—" Francisco stopped himself, realizing this was not the sort of thing he would normally freely discuss or even admit to. But, curiously, he felt quite at ease in this moment, bringing it up with Matt. "Do you ever view pornography?"

"Yeah, sometimes. I mean, if a lady is into watching dirty movies I'll watch 'em with her. It can be pretty fun."

"Yes, I find them quite stimulating. As I was saying, yesterday I was viewing one—alone—and found myself becoming extremely interested in one of the performers. I am not referring to her body or the acts in which she was engaging. Of course, those things are highly exciting, and my intent had been to focus on them exclusively. Instead, I found myself thinking about what sort of person she might be, wondering about her life, wishing I could meet her..."

"Heh. Yeah, that is kinda wild. But I guess it happens though, sometimes..."

"It happens to me all of the time."

"Really?" Matt laughed. "Huh. Well... I don't know... Maybe you *could* meet some of them! I mean, they have conventions and stuff..."

Francisco, frowning, went pensive for a long moment. Then he said, "Anyway, I must learn better how to approach women and develop a favorable rapport with them... by which I mean the sort of rapport that leads to romantic and sexual interactions."

Matt looked over at him, half-smiling, one eyebrow cocked.

"Please share with me your strategies and techniques, Matt."

Matt chuckled. "Sorry, Fran—I don't have any strategies. Or any techniques."

"Surely that cannot be the case!"

"But I do have some advice for you. I know it's kind of a cliché, but just be yourself. Just relax. And don't try so hard—just let things happen naturally, you know?"

"Interesting. I did meet a woman quite accidentally, several weeks ago, at the museum. We had a brief, but very pleasant, conversation, and she gave me her telephone number."

"See? There ya go!"

"Unfortunately, when I made use of the number later that day, I horribly bungled the effort and have not spoken with her again since."

"Crap! Well you probably got too uptight about it..."

"Indeed."

"Started acting the way you usually do, instead of relaxed and natural like when you were at the museum."

"Yes."

"Our minds can play tricks on us, Fran."

"Please—Francisco. You are, however, absolutely correct. The unconscious mind guides human behavior far more than most realize. Our brains are constantly working to process all the information we have taken in, to make sense of it and to help move us in the direction of our wants and needs—many of which we may not even realize we have.

"This 'behind the scenes' brain activity influences our thoughts, our emotions, even our physical sensations to some degree, in ways of which we are dimly, if at all, aware. Quite often, an individual does not truly know why he or she is saying or doing a given thing, in the moment; people *decide* why, after the fact, based on what they believe makes sense or what they hope is true. I use the word 'decide'—as opposed to 'determine' or 'discover'—very deliberately here, because the *real* reason for the behavior remains hidden."

Again Matt was looking over at his companion with a bemused face.

Francisco, now grinning delightedly, went on: "Moreover, it has been argued rather convincingly that an analogous phenomenon—probably linked in some ways to its personal counterpart—exists on a much larger scale, at the level of systems—groups, corporations, governments, society. The contention is that the forces truly driving actions, decisions, trends, policies, and so forth are not the obvious ones related to official titles and statements and established hierarchies, nor even the private motivations of the people involved. Rather, they are a product of the system as a whole, in all its complexity, and are, as such, nearly inscrutable."

"Holy Toledo," said Matt with a chuckle.

Looking over at him, Francisco nodded.

"Hey, listen," Matt said, "I'm not book-smart, like you and Bill..."

"Bill?"

"I just, you know, follow my instincts most of the time."

"The unconscious mind!" Francisco grinned again.

"Right. I guess. Anyway, I think maybe sometimes being smart in life is the opposite of being book-smart. You actually have to *not* think about stuff, in order to be smart about it. You know?"

"Yes, I believe I take your point."

Matt's face suddenly lit up. "But you know, sometimes,"—he reached into the pocket of his shorts—"when the situation calls for it,"—out came two folded-up, ancient-looking sheets of paper—"I can do my fair share of hardcore thinking, too…"

Francisco was intrigued, and became more so as the papers were unfolded and he saw that one of them contained an intricate, hand-drawn map that included dashed lines, arrows, numerous little notations, and one giant letter X.

"Check it out!" Matt exclaimed with a huge smile.

Francisco was smiling too. "Bill mentioned to me your ridiculous hunt for buried pirate treasure. This is related to it, correct?"

"Hah! Bill. I love it. Not ridiculous, and not pirate. But yeah, it's related. Big time! This is my ticket, Fran."

"Francisco."

"This map"—he was staring at it gleefully—"shows me *exactly* where the treasure chest is buried. Right there on the beach in Santa Monica! All those people, for all those years, walking on top of it all the time. And they never knew!"

"How did you manage to obtain the map?"

"Swiped it this morning, from the dead letter office. I have to say, my plan was brilliant. Everything went off without a hitch!"

Francisco, beaming now, both pleased for Matt and impressed by his achievement, enquired, "What does the other sheet contain?"

"Oh, glad you asked! This letter was in there with the map. I wasn't expecting it. Gives more insight into Marion's life… which is always great!"

Matt handed the letter to Francisco, who read it silently and very quickly.

> *Dear Bart,*
>
> > *I'm enclosing the map, as we discussed. I must confess, I feel a bit silly, for drawing it in the first place and for how dear it still is to me.*
> >
> > *When Marion first revealed to me what she'd done, I could tell she didn't want to.　We were just casual acquaintances then, through Mr. Hearst.　I felt hesitant, myself, asking her about what I'd happened to witness that morning, but it was just so peculiar, seeing her there talking with that man in the hard hat, the one she later informed me was a digger.　I was overcome with curiosity!　She was clearly embarrassed, and somewhat*

*guilt-ridden, about the theft, and also surely must've
been frightened that I would inform Mr. Hearst.   Yet,
she told me the truth anyway.*

*As I believe I mentioned at dinner, the map didn't
even exist until many years later.   We happened to be
walking on the beach one day, past her old property, and
I remembered the buried chest and began teasing her about
it, and eventually forced her to show me the precise spot
underneath which it lay.   I suggested we could probably
get the necessary permissions from the city, or whomever,
to unearth the chest, but she simply wouldn't hear of it.
Creating the map was actually her idea, which I think she
meant as a joke, but I thought it positively smashing,
and carried out the task meticulously, thinking ever so
lovingly of Marion the entire time.*

*Not long after that, however, possibly because she
never seemed nearly as fond of it as I was, the map found
its way into a stack of papers at the bottom of a drawer,
and I forgot all about it, for years.*

*When I discovered it again recently, the emotions it
brought on were shockingly powerful!   I felt I could bear
neither the pain of keeping it, nor the pain of throwing
it away.   Luckily, I ended up seeing you and was able to
avoid both!*

*Thank you, so very much, for agreeing to be the
custodian of this silly old scrap of paper that maintains
such an irrational grip on my heart.*

Yours,

"Rick" appeared at the bottom, handwritten in blue ink.

"This letter is quite odd," said Francisco.

"I know!" said Matt. "This guy, Rick—the guy who wrote the
letter, and drew the map—he was a trip. Rick Rhineston. From what
I've read, really uptight and conservative—so different from Marion!
Oh, and he had this huge hang-up about what he called 'the sanctity of
marriage.' Thought adultery was like the most horrible, unforgivable
thing a person could possibly do. He didn't mean legal marriage.
He meant, like, spiritual marriage. He was never legally married to
Marion. Neither was Hearst, actually..."

"Fascinating," said Francisco.

"Yeah, the only man she was ever legally married to was this crappy guy named Horace Brown. Funny! But anyway, yeah, I guess Rick didn't think it was too much of a problem once, uh, you know—death did them part. Sly devil eventually hooked up with his friend's wife!"

"I must confess," said Francisco, "I am still rather confused."

They were just coming up on The Sidewalk Cafe.

"Hey," said Matt, grinning and gesturing toward it with his thumb. "Let's take a little break in there. I'll explain everything to you over a beer."

Chapter 16

Gary Williams was flitting anxiously around the breakfast table, unable even to stand still, much less sit, almost coming out of his skin.

"I have no choice!" he cried. "I gotta try for it!"

His husband, Scott, sitting at the table in front of a half-eaten plate of food and an open laptop (slid over to his side by Gary), was considerably calmer, though still somewhat agitated owing to the preposterous suggestion he'd heard a moment ago.

"Let's not be rash," he said, glancing at the laptop screen, which showed a webpage about a marathon taking place the last Sunday of November in Willemstad, capital of the tiny island nation of Curaçao (located 40 miles north of the Venezuelan coast). "Let's carefully consider all options."

"There are no options, babe! This place—Williamstan, or whatever—it's very, very far away... in another country..."

"True."

"Several countries away, in fact..."

"Well—"

"And it's the only 'green' race left, before the deadline, right?"

Scott clicked over to a different browser tab, on the Golden Road Championship Classic site, and gave it a quick skim. "Looks that way, yes."

"So I need to start driving *now*. I have no idea how long it'll take to get there."

"You have no idea *if* you can get there," Scott said, switching tabs again, this time to Google Maps. "Remember, like two minutes ago, when you read this out to me? 'Sorry, we could not calculate driving directions'..."

"Well I gotta try! I can't just give up. 'Specially after everything I've been through... Everything I've... survived. The altitude training! And... Montana, when I almost showed up too late to register. And, and... Missouri, that drug screening thing—getting off on a technicality... I mean—whoa!"

"Yes," said Scott, "and every scrape you got yourself into was because you ignored *my* advice."

"Okay, so what do you advise now?"

"Fly there. Of course."

"No!" A look of terror broke out on Gary's face. "No, no, no. I can't do that again. I just... can't. I just can't."

Scott was shaking his head in bewilderment and frustration, eyes closed momentarily. Then he opened them and said, "Gary, what you're proposing is much, *much* more frightening than flying on a plane—and with a much lower chance of success."

Gary's phone, lying on the table, started vibrating and ringing. He reached down and answered it on speaker.

"Jim! Good morning! How are you?"

"Pretty good," said the voice of Jim Jamb. "Or, well, I was until I saw your text. You might not be coming in today?"

"Right, well, I've got a major crisis going on here."

"Imaginary major crisis," said Scott.

"Oh—hi, Scott," said Jim.

"Hi, Jim."

"It's my marathon stuff," said Gary. "It turns out I need to get my butt out to the Caribbean, stat. Or else I'll be disqualified. I don't know how I didn't realize it before!"

"Well, you know we've got that thing today, about the new packaging proposal..."

"Yeah, I know..."

"Well, it's really important. Couldn't you—"

"Yeah, I'm sorry, I know it is, but, well, you know, honestly, this is *more* important. This is huge. And I can't wait. I gotta go *now*. I should really already be out there on the road, not standing here talking to you..." He suddenly chuckled, hearing his own words.

"What? Oh, wait, no..." A long sigh came through the speaker. "Oh, Gary. You're planning to *drive* to the Caribbean, aren't you?"

"Well, I know I'll have to get on a boat at some point." He grinned awkwardly. "That's not a problem."

"Gary, you're insane."

"Yep!" shouted Scott.

"Gary," said Jim, "I'm telling you this not just as your friend, but as your boss: Don't do this."

(There'd been recent reorganizing, including some downsizing, at CuppaJoe. Jim had been promoted to fill the position vacated by the firing of Frank Barnes for gross incompetence, and Gary had been moved directly underneath him.)

"I'm really sorry, Jim," said Gary. "I gotta go. We'll talk more later. I'll call you from the road."

Another long sigh came over the line as Gary reached down and touched the red icon to end the call.

"I'm late for work," said Scott, standing up. "Please, just, go do your job, come back home tonight, and we'll work on this some more. We'll figure it out."

The two stared at each other in silence for a moment.

"Trust me," Scott added, forcing himself to smile. "We'll figure it out."

The next time Gary and Scott would've spoken to each other, if only there'd been sufficient cell reception and the call Gary tried to place had actually connected, was seven hours later as he zoomed along on I-10 in his Raptor, crossing the empty patch of desert between Phoenix and Tucson.

"Dang!" he exclaimed in frustration as his second attempt also failed. "Guess I'll have to wait 'til I've got a stronger signal."

He'd hoped to tell his husband how excited he felt about his impending travel through Latin America, and not to worry because he had a really good feeling about it, and that he'd managed to get directions most of the way there from his truck's navigation system, and also about his astonishing good luck in finding a 16-CD "Learn Spanish Fast!" box set for sale inside a truck stop shop a few miles back.

On the negative side, he'd also wanted to share with Scott his disappointment and trepidation regarding his job—he'd taken an unsuccessful crack at joining this morning's meeting by phone (the system had repeatedly refused to accept his PIN), and hadn't yet mustered up the courage to try calling Jim, who, he felt certain, was quite angry with him.

Shaking off these thoughts and breaking into a big grin, Gary said, "Well, let's give this puppy a whirl," then reached across to the passenger seat and pulled the first disc out of the giant box. He'd been puzzled that day at the Ford dealer a few months ago when he'd inspected this cab for the very first time and discovered that it featured a CD player ("When we say 'all the bells and whistles,' we really mean all of them," extremely helpful sales rep Lisa Shortler had explained), but today felt enormously grateful for it. Fate was on his side! He popped in the disc.

A few seconds of silence. Then a cheerful voice shouted "¡Hola!"

Gary was mesmerized.

The next time Gary and Scott would've spoken to each other, if only Gary'd still had his phone with him, was another three hours later, shortly after Scott got into his car in the parking garage at Lathrop Halliday to begin his journey home. He buckled up, started the engine, initiated the call from his dashboard touch screen, then put the car in gear. He was slightly surprised when the call went straight to voicemail.

After the beep he said, "Hi, it's me. Hoping... *Trusting* that you did the smart thing and stayed in town and went to work. My day was horrendous. Just nuts. So, wasn't able to do much research on the whole marathon situation... But, I did look at their website again, just for a quick minute, and, looks like there's another 'green' race you can still do, right here in the good old U.S. of A. Anyway, we'll work on it tonight. Bye."

As Scott was moving his finger over to press the red hang-up icon, Gary was flashing a huge grin at the Mexican border guard who'd just given him back his passport and raised the metal barrier arm that had been hovering a few inches from the nose of his truck.

"Gracias," he said for the fourth time, then chuckled delightedly as he pulled forward, entering the town of Agua Prieta, in the state of Sonora, just south of Douglas, Arizona.

He still hadn't noticed his phone was missing, or much of anything, for that matter. He'd been completely wrapped up in the thrilling world of Spanish, listening to his training discs virtually non-stop until the point when he'd had to roll down the window and speak to the guard (an opportunity to practice his new skills on which he'd seized with great enthusiasm and pride (and felt he must've done a pretty good job at, as the guard had immediately responded to him in perfect English)). And now, entering this new, exotic, Spanish-speaking country, he was even more preoccupied. What a majestic land!

He proceeded slowly along Avenida Panamericana, then turned left onto Calle 1, the whole while gazing side to side and all around, taking it all in. The rapture continued for the next ten minutes on the streets of Agua Prieta, and then for another two hours on Carretera Federal 2 (despite this segment offering almost nothing in the way of scenery), finally ending when Gary was jolted back to reality by his "low fuel" light coming on and the accompanying pinging sound.

"Dang!" he shouted, realizing that, given the extremely desolate landscape (not to mention the rather late hour), it was possible he could soon find himself in a fairly serious pickle. He turned off the stereo and tried to concentrate on what to do next.

The loss of the phone had occurred in conjunction with the previous time Gary'd determined he needed to gas up his vehicle. He'd kept his language lessons playing, quite loudly, throughout the entire stop, and had remained so thoroughly enthralled that he'd neglected to remove the pump nozzle from his tank before driving away, and had also, absentmindedly and for no reason, placed his phone on the roof of the car during the pumping, then completely forgotten it was there.

"Dang!" Gary shouted again as he fumbled around futilely for the phone. After a moment of this, when it began to dawn on him that it was probably not in the truck at all (else the bluetooth would've connected), he cried "Shit!" (an expletive Gary used only in the most dire of situations). Highly unusual feelings of fear, embarrassment, and despair began to flood him. "What am I gonna do?" he whimpered.

Fortunately, thirty seconds later he came upon the town of Janos, where he quite easily found a gas station at which he quite easily filled his tank and paid for it with a credit card. Communicating with the sole employee, however, about whether a public phone existed, or whether he might borrow a cell phone for an emergency call, or about nearby shops that sold phones, or about any topic at all, proved not nearly as easy (or even possible).

Two hours later, Scott made another attempt, before heading off to bed, to call his husband. He felt disappointed but not surprised when it went straight to voicemail again. He'd surmised that Gary, against all advice, had gone ahead with his ridiculous plan of trying to drive thousands of miles through several foreign countries, and that something had gone wrong with phone communication, probably an issue with either reception or international roaming. (He bitterly lamented the fact that, in all their years together, they'd never gotten around to consolidating their wireless accounts and he had no way of accessing Gary's online.) He tried his best to keep the anger and the worry—natural as both were—at bay. Gary is Gary, he told himself. Everything will be fine in the end.

At that moment, Gary, who'd managed to recover most of his good cheer and optimism after his pitstop in Janos, and since then had carried on driving through the dark, empty countryside of Chihuahua, listening intently to his CDs, suddenly realized he was feeling very sleepy.

As luck would have it, a light immediately appeared on the horizon which, as it drew nearer, turned out to be a sizeable building just off the righthand side of the highway. Gary pulled off and parked in front of it. It looked like it might be a hotel of some kind.

The next morning, he woke up feeling wonderful. He'd had such a fantastic evening getting to know his great new Mexican friends, and the excitement of it was still with him. The building he'd stopped at had not been a hotel, after all, but a private house occupied by an extremely kind and generous couple—Pedro and Marta—who also happened to speak perfect English. Despite his showing up unexpectedly quite late at night, they'd welcomed Gary warmly, fed him, sat around the fireplace with him, chitchatting, asking him all about his life in California, and had unhesitatingly offered him one of their spare bedrooms.

Perhaps even more charming than these people was their dog, Arturo, who looked a bit like 1980s T.V. beer mascot Spuds MacKenzie and greatly enjoyed smoking. Though his owners tried relentlessly to keep the cigarettes away from him, he was constantly thwarting their efforts. He routinely created distractions, immediately after Pedro or Marta lit up, causing them to momentarily abandon their cigarette, which Arturo would then steal from the rim of their ashtray. And sometimes, if a pack had been inadvertently left lying around, Arturo would later be seen puffing away, his method of lighting up remaining an utter mystery.

But, unfortunately for Gary, this household did not possess a single phone of any kind, land line or cellular.

As Bill Smede climbed the stairs to the front door of Number Four, he felt a little pang of excitement mixed with fear, like the feeling you get before going on a date. But he was not going on a date; he was simply going for coffee with a friend. Granted, this particular friend was the mother of his children, and for a very long time had been his partner. And then for a very short time had been almost like an enemy of sorts. And then recently had become just a friend. But regardless, this was still simply coffee with a friend. He'd called her half an hour ago, on a whim, feeling bored and restless, to pitch the idea, expecting she'd probably politely decline. Now he was standing on the doorstep of his former home. He wasn't sure whether it seemed odd to him that having that little pang didn't really seem odd to him. He knocked.

Yvonne opened the door almost immediately, smiling pleasantly but not exuberantly. "Hey," she said.

"Hey," said Bill. He compulsively looked at his wrist.

"Ah, yes," said Yvonne. "My count is terrible. I need this coffee walk."

"Heh, right." He started to look at his wrist again because he couldn't remember what it said two seconds ago, then realized that Yvonne was stepping out onto the landing.

"Oh," he said, "uh... Would you mind if I came in quickly and, uh..."—he smiled embarrassedly—"took a spoon from your kitchen drawer?"

"Of course," she replied, smirking and stepping aside so Bill could enter.

Passing through the main room of the condo, he said, "There's this one spoon..." He noticed that Alice was standing a few feet away, gazing disinterestedly into space. "Oh! Hey, Alice."

She glanced at him.

"What are you... Uh... How did you get here? I thought you were in bed when I left the apartment."

"I took a different route," she said in a flat tone, with a blank facial expression and a small shoulder shrug.

After a second, seeing that her father was still looking at her and still seemed perplexed, she added, "I walk faster than you."

"Hmm, okay," said Bill, still feeling slightly disoriented, then proceeded into the kitchen.

Yvonne followed him. "So, are you short on spoons at your place?" she queried.

"No, it's just..." He was rifling through the silverware drawer now. "There's this one perfect size spoon... Ah, here it is!" He held it up triumphantly for her to see.

"Perfect size?"

"Yeah. It seems like, every set of spoons, including the ones I got for the apartment, they're always either these teeny tiny ones that are only good for stirring tea, or else they're these big whopping ones for, like, eating soup. This one, though,"—he held it up once more before sliding it into his jeans pocket—"is right in between. It's perfect."

"Cool." The smirk again.

As they exited the kitchen together, Bill added, "It used to be part of a set, that we got way back, a long, long time ago... I don't know where... But, you know, over time, they got lost or chewed up in the garbage disposal, and now there's only one left." He smiled. "Maybe in the entire world, it seems!"

He now noticed that Alice had vanished from the room, and standing in the spot where she'd been a minute ago was Patrick, staring at his phone.

"Oh! Hey, Patrick."

"Hey, Dad," he said, not looking up.

"Oh," said Yvonne, "Patrick has some exciting news."

Now he did look up, grinning at his parents. "I'm getting my own place," he said. "Well, with Len. Me and him are gonna get an apartment together."

"Wow," said Bill. "Cool. So... you can afford that?"

"Yeah, we should be able to. We've got a few things we're working on, to get a few revenue streams going. So, yep, should be all good."

"Okay. Cool."

Bill and Yvonne left the condo, made their way to the sidewalk and began heading north on Wexler.

"So what do you think are the odds he'll actually move out?" asked Bill.

"Five percent," said Yvonne.

"Ooh, you're quite the optimist."

She chuckled.

After a moment, Bill asked, "Seen anything that makes you think Alice is doing any drugs?"

"No, I don't think so..."

"Cool."

"Why? Have you?"

"No."

"Okay, good. Yeah, maybe I'm being naive but, I don't really... What is it?"

Bill was distracted, looking at the cars parked on the curb, almost all of which bore, pinned between a wiper blade and the windshield, the trademark little rectangular pink sheet of paper containing a parking citation from the city.

"They had a field day," he said, pointing.

Parking tickets were notoriously easy to come by in L.A. (even for folks who weren't sworn enemies of Officer Haston). Curb parking was governed by an enormous tangled mass of rules, many of them difficult to decipher, or even seemingly contradictory, and all of them subject to change at any time.

"Oh, yeah," said Yvonne. "I think they switched the street-sweeping day for some unknown reason."

Every strip of L.A. curb had a designated 3-hour period each week for sweeping, during which parking was prohibited. The days and times were different depending on the neighborhood, and also different for the two sides of any given street. Occasionally, the day and time for a particular set of curbs would temporarily change, with the new schedule typically, but not always, announced on a sheet of paper that was placed over the metallic sign providing the standard one.

"Bastards," said Bill. "I think they intentionally engineer it to maximize their revenue."

"Those are another example," said Yvonne, pointing to a nearby instance of a slightly different breed of curbside sign, which read: 2HR PARKING M-F 9AM-5PM. PERMIT #4321 EXEMPT.

"Right," said Bill with a chuckle.

"The only truly safe strategy for L.A. street parking is not to do it at all."

"Yes!"

They walked in silence for the next couple of minutes, passing by three palm trees. Then Bill spoke again.

"Hey, you talked to Francisco lately?"

"No, not in the last few weeks. Why?"

"I, uh... I sort of stood him up, about two weeks ago. Him and Matt both, actually."

"Ooh, this sounds interesting."

"Yeah, I was supposed to meet up with them in Venice, after I finished work for the day, but I got roped into this thing with fucking Ted Bonar and... Well, honestly, I figured it'd be awkward and... I mean, they didn't really need me anyway. The whole point of it was for those two to get together..."

"God," said Yvonne, laughing.

"Yeah, it was pretty lame of me. I did eventually text Francisco an apology, and he replied that it was fine, but, I can't tell if it's *really* fine..."

"I'm sure it is," said Yvonne. "But you're right, it was pretty lame of you."

Bill chuckled, then said, "Oh—on a different subject: your dad asked my mom out on a date!"

"Yeah! Crazy, isn't it?"

"Very crazy. I was blown away when she told me. And kind of annoyed with her, actually, for multiple... I mean, it was just... Well, she should know better..."

Yvonne was looking over at Bill, half-smiling, one eyebrow cocked.

He went on, "But then I thought, well, maybe those two deserve each other." He laughed.

"Oh, come on. They're both nice people, really."

They glanced at each other and Yvonne amended her remark: "Well, your mother is a nice person, anyway."

Bill laughed again. Then, after a short, contemplative pause, he said, "I suppose it's all relative... uh, no pun intended. Anyway, your dad's not the least nice person in the world. I'll give him that much." Another pause. "He's probably a nicer person than *my* dad, for instance."

For half of Bill's adult life, Richard "Dick" Smede had lived in Milwaukee with his second wife and second set of kids. For the other half, he'd lived in Dallas with his third wife and third set of kids (an arrangement that, according to some rumors, was now potentially on the brink of ending). For all of it, their relationship had consisted of brief, cordial phone conversations four times a year—their birthdays, Christmas, and Father's Day. It had been somewhat more substantial during Bill's childhood, including Dick occasionally arriving home from work in time to eat with the family and the annual father-son outing to browse around Acres of Books in Long Beach. Though he'd always considered Dick's overall performance as both a husband and a father to be significantly sub-par, Bill felt at peace with who the man was and didn't harbor any resentment (unlike his twin sister, Debbie).

After a moment of mutual silence during which Bill surmised that Yvonne wasn't planning to weigh in on the matter of which of their fathers was a less decent human being, he asked, "So do you know how it went?"

"Their date? No, haven't heard anything. How 'bout you?"

"No! No. Not sure if I want to. Not from her, anyway. God. I usually don't take her calls but, somehow, a few weeks ago, she tricked me into answering. That was when I found out about the date."

Yvonne was laughing.

"So how's work been?" Bill asked. "Just as irritating as ever?" He grinned.

"God, don't get me started."

"Yeah, you're right. Forget I asked."

"Too late. Yeah, the irritations are always evolving, but they're always there. Lately… Ugh… People and their stupid assumptions, always causing issues. I mean, it's okay to make assumptions. It's impossible not to, in fact. We all have to do it, all the time, in order to function. The bad part is when you're unwilling to adjust assumptions you've made, in light of new information… Or, worse yet, you don't even realize you're making them. Happens all the time…"

"Mmm-hmm…" Bill was nodding his head and smiling.

As they rounded the corner onto Santa Monica Boulevard, the volume of the ambient noise (which was already quite high) went up a few notches. In addition to the standard vast army of vehicles completely filling three lanes in each direction, emitting sounds generated from engines, tailpipes, tires, stereos, horns, and a few drivers' mouths, and the standard collection of street and sidewalk dwellers on foot (or, in some cases, butt) and on bicycles, throwing in their two cents, at the moment there was also a helicopter floating around overhead, its purpose unclear. This was actually fairly standard, too.

"Wow, so loud," said Bill.

"What?" said Yvonne, unable to hear him.

They adapted their own volume to the new circumstances.

"I just said, it's so loud out here."

"Yes. We should've stayed in the neighborhood longer, gone along Utah."

"Yeah."

"So I guess this isn't your routine—Sunday morning coffee run?"

"No, no... Actually... I don't think I really have any routines. I kind of like the idea of not having them, because, I don't know, it kind of seems like, if you're a creature of routine, you're surrendering a little bit of your mind. It's like you're just a robot... And, also, just trying to determine and establish the routine in the first place seems daunting to me... So does trying to maintain it... Also seems like maybe a waste of effort..."

"Hmm..."

"But, you know, I have to admit, figuring out my non-routine all the time takes a lot of energy too, and brings its own kind of stress..."

Yvonne started laughing after looking over at Bill and seeing that he wasn't. "Oh, Bill," she said.

They arrived at the CuppaJoe on Westwood Boulevard ten minutes later, time they'd both enjoyed, the auditory challenges of Santa Monica (where they'd spent nine of the ten) notwithstanding.

Another twenty minutes after that (a somewhat less enjoyable period that had involved gradually inching forward to the front of the long, twisty line, packed in tightly with scores of folks who were in Phone World (excluding the two bratty little kids just ahead in the line (but not excluding their mother)), then telling the cashier their very simple order—two large coffees—three times before he understood it, then paying eight dollars for those coffees, then pressing their way, steaming cups in hand, through the clutch of people planted at the end of the bar, awaiting Foaming Macchiato Supremes and Power Cappuccino Delights, then stopping by the crowded, chaotic, disgustingly messy and filthy cream & sugar station to add milk to their drinks, and finally squeezing back out through the door onto the sidewalk), they stood near the corner of Westwood and Utah, underneath a billboard advertising a pseudo-medical service for women called Re-Vaginate, smiling at each other and sipping.

They exchanged comments about how tremendous the coffee was, enthusiastically agreeing that it tasted far better than anything they could've produced at home. But privately, they both wondered if this belief was merely a delusion conjured up by their brains to rationalize all that money and all that aggravation.

"Woo!" exclaimed Gary. "It. Is. Hot." He wiped his forehead with a rag he'd just retrieved from a makeshift utility belt, both provided to him by his traveling companion.

"I mean, wow! I thought maybe when we got out here on the water, you know, and out from under all that lush growth—that, like, jungle kinda thing... I thought, it might be a little cooler... But, I think it's even hotter out here... That sun, it's cooking me!" He chuckled.

Gary was sitting at the front end of a six-feet-long canoe-like vessel which, until a few minutes ago, he'd been helping to carry through what was, in essence, as he'd just noted, a jungle. Now the boat was steadily moving forward through the murky, weed-ridden, quite shallow water of a rather narrow, winding river. The man sitting in the rear of the craft, operating a small outboard motor, whose real name was Hector Medina but whom Gary knew simply as "John," and to whom all of Gary's comments were addressed, continued to not provide any response to any of them.

John was dressed like Bill Smede: baseball-style hat, sunglasses, polo shirt, jeans, sneakers. He was also about the same age as Bill, and about the same height. But the similarities ended there. John's skin was many shades darker, his physique far more muscular, and his never-changing, expressionless face far more reminiscent of an ancient stone statue. He was also far more likely than Bill to have ever been caught dead within a hundred miles of this location.

"But, you know, I can't really complain," continued Gary. "Maybe it feels like I'm in a broiler, but I'm alive, I'm healthy, I'm making progress... all thanks to you!"

Gary wasn't sure whether John's taciturn style stemmed from some combination of not knowing English very well and just plain being anti-social, or if it was more a case of him being a very good listener but shy about expressing himself. Gary chose to believe the latter.

"Yep, your kindness is *so* appreciated. I try to be a kind person, myself. I think mostly I am...

"It can backfire sometimes, though. Ooh, boy—one time, maybe three or four years ago, there was this gal at my office who was really down on her luck... Well, I should say, I knew her from the office, but she didn't work there anymore, but she still had my phone number... So anyway, she needed a place to stay. She was getting evicted from her apartment, and she was broke, and she didn't have anywhere to go. So I said she could stay with me for a while. You know, just a little while, 'til she got back on her feet.

"My husband, Scott—did I tell you about Scott?—anyway, he didn't like the idea. Hah! He hated it, actually. He warned me not to do it. And he was right... He was right...

"So, yeah... I mean, you can probably imagine what happened. She stayed for-*ever*! And she was like, never looking for a job, never helping out around the house. Just, sitting on the couch, watching T.V., all the time. It was bad!" He paused and chuckled, thinking back.

"Eventually Scott told her she had to leave. I mean, I was on board with it and everything, but... I just couldn't do it myself. Couldn't bring myself to do it. I cried, actually, the day she left. Felt so bad for her. But it was fine. She was fine. She got back on her feet. Might've been exactly what she needed, you know? A little kick in the behind!

"But yeah, I can't give up on kindness. Nobody can. We need it, in the world. We need so much more of it! And you sure did step up. I can't thank you enough. I don't know what would've become of me, without your kindness. . . "

John had discovered Gary late Wednesday afternoon, wandering around, utterly lost and scared, having abandoned his truck and continued on foot after his attempt to off-road through a larger-and-denser-than-it-initially-appeared wilderness had ended with getting irreversibly stuck in what he felt must have been the world's deepest and thickest mud. ("Hmmf, 'Raptor,' my ass," he'd muttered at the time.)

This wild drive had been undertaken in desperation after gradually realizing there were no roads out of the small Panamanian town of Yaviza except the one he'd come in on—it was truly, absolutely the end of the line (a mind-bogglingly long line that had taken him (from Pedro and Marta's home) over four days and across the borders of Guatemala, Honduras, Nicaragua, Costa Rica, and Panama (at all of which he'd been threatened with being denied entry but ultimately (sometimes through the use of a bribe) had always prevailed)).

Speaking to each other in a mix of Spanish and English, with a fair amount of trial and error on the mutual understanding front, John and Gary had ultimately crafted an arrangement they were both content with: John—who was astoundingly well-prepared, dragging the canoe by a rope and wearing a small, efficiently packed rucksack from which he produced the utility belt and a water-proof plastic bag for Gary to carry his valuables in—would guide them both through this roadless patch of swamp/mountain/marsh, a journey of "fifty kilometers south," ending at a coastline of some kind, where he'd secure ferry boat passage for Gary to the Colombian port city of Turbo; in exchange, at the conclusion of the walk-and-canoe portion of the trek, Gary would pay John nine hundred American dollars in cash.

Now it was Friday and Gary was, privately, a little bit worried—mainly because his marathon was the day after tomorrow and he undoubtedly still had hundreds of miles to cover after reaching Turbo. But also because it seemed they'd already traveled considerably more than 50 kilometers, much of it not in a southward direction, and on several occasions they'd crossed paths with other travelers, always of a shifty appearance, who'd always spoken with John entirely in Spanish, and to whom John had always instructed Gary to hand a stack of cash before they went on their way.

"Hey, what time is it?" Gary asked. (His phone was tucked away in the plastic bag and John was holding onto the PaceTek Mega-Ultra as collateral.)

John didn't answer, which didn't really surprise Gary. He craned his neck for a moment and took a guess, from the position of the sun in the sky, that it was probably between noon and 2 P.M. But he was lousy at guessing such things.

"Woo!" he exclaimed. "Hot!"

After wiping his forehead with the rag again, and spending a few seconds gazing out over the lush landscape in front of him, Gary began to regain his normal, cheery outlook.

"You know, it's actually really beautiful out here," he said, smiling and re-orienting himself in the boat, to face John. "In its own way. Don't you think?"

No answer.

"You're the analytical type. I can tell." Gary chuckled. "Smart. Analytical. A man of few words! Hah. But you know exactly what you're doing. My husband, Scott, he's the same way. He's analytical."

Gary's analytical husband had been extremely relieved initially, but had then become extremely frustrated and incredulous, when they'd finally spoken to each other Saturday evening after Gary had managed to acquire an old-style flip phone (and a new Mexican cellular account) at a wireless shop in Gómez Palacio. The conversation had begun with very positive emotions being shared in both directions, but had deteriorated rapidly and severely when Gary, having been told that the Willemstad race was not necessary and he could turn around and come home, had refused to do so.

He chuckled now, recalling Scott's exasperation and total lack of sympathy. "Maybe a little *too* analytical, you know? He just doesn't always… Sometimes he just doesn't seem to understand *passion*. Well, no, that's not quite it. He's passionate about things but… I don't know… being impulsive… being spontaneous… going with your gut… Those aren't really his thing…"

The next chuckle was slightly hollow, as Gary began to realize that he missed analysis-prone, non-impulsive Scott, and lamented how angry they'd gotten with each other, and the sour note on which they'd left things.

"But don't get me wrong—he's a great guy. A really great guy. I love him to pieces."

By some combination of residual anger/hurt and the fact that Gary'd been moving through six different countries with various cellular carriers and numerous pockets of no reception, the husbands hadn't spoken again throughout Sunday, Monday, and Tuesday, after which Gary had entered the beyond-civilization region he was still currently struggling to traverse, which, not surprisingly, was a total cell service dead zone.

I really need to call him when I get to Turbo, he thought. Ooh, and Jim too.

"Oh, hey," he then said to John, beginning to chuckle again, "I gotta tell you about this guy I knew at work, years ago. Funny guy. Very young. Heh, well, I guess we all were back then... Anyway, he was a nice guy, and not stupid, but just a little... In some ways, he was just a little... quirky, I guess. Like, the main thing I remember about him was: he couldn't check his voicemail to save his life! He tried but, he was, like, impaired that way, or something. Just could never get it. So if you called him and he didn't answer, there was no point in leaving a message. 'Cause he'd never hear it!

"But anyway, there was this hilarious incident with him one time. We'd been working like crazy, around the clock, for weeks, preparing this huge presentation for a prospective client, right? And we were all totally exhausted. I mean totally, *totally* exhausted. We were pooped!" He laughed.

"So, the big day arrived. And we were all gathered around this huge table in this huge conference room—us and the client. Probably like, thirty people were sitting around that table. And, about 10 minutes into it, I noticed that guy was asleep. He was sitting up straight, but his eyes were shut. And everyone noticed it, eventually—it was so obvious. Especially when it was his turn to present something and he just sat there with his eyes closed!

"But everyone was understanding about it. The client, too. We all thought, poor guy, he's just, you know, he's just totally exhausted. He's literally at the limit of what he can handle, physically. So we just continued on with the meeting and didn't try to wake him up."

Gary deliberately paused for dramatic effect, then laughed again, thinking about what came next.

"But get this: all of a sudden, like, maybe 40 minutes into this meeting, this guy opens his eyes, and he has this look of panic on his face, and he says—really loud, to the whole group—he says, 'Oh my god, was I masturbating?'..."

For the very first time since they'd met, a tiny, almost imperceptible hint of a smile appeared on John's face.

"He wasn't, by the way," Gary added amidst laughing heartily, hugely tickled by his own story. "In case you were wondering."

Twenty-four hours later, Gary was sitting in the driver's seat of a rental car, parked on the shoulder of the Montería-Arboletes highway near the coastal Colombian town of Puerto Rey, where he'd pulled over after observing that his little flip phone finally had bars.

"This dang thing!" he shouted as he fiddled with the phone, attempting to access his voicemail. "How can anybody possibly work it?"

The rest of his time with John had gone smoothly, all things considered, and he'd been delivered, as promised, with his PaceTek, onto a ferry that took him on a slightly curvy, 15-mile crossing of the Gulf of Urabá (though the price had mysteriously gone up to a thousand dollars, which, coincidentally, was all of his remaining cash).

He'd been a bit disturbed to see, as the dock from which they'd launched receded into the distance, what appeared to be John getting arrested, and far more disturbed when, upon landing in Turbo, he'd been arrested himself. But after questioning him for an hour, they'd let him go, and had even described, in great detail (and in English!), how he could go about obtaining a vehicle.

So now, here he was—alive, healthy, in possession of wallet, passport, phone and car, working on the final—fast, easy, and safe, he hoped—leg of his journey. It seemed fate was on his side, after all (except for the little matter of getting in touch with Scott, where he'd continued to be thwarted, until a few minutes ago, by a lack of cell reception).

"Aha! Finally!" A big smile broke out on Gary's face. He couldn't quite make out everything the voice coming through the earpiece was saying, but he could tell he'd successfully connected to his mailbox and felt fairly confident, when he heard "marqe número uno," that if he pressed '1' he could listen to his messages.

The first one was indeed from his husband.

"Hi, it's me. Listen, I know you made it very clear how you feel about this trip, but I've just found out something new: it's literally impossible to drive there, because there's this giant void called the Darién Gap, on the boundary between Central and South America.

So, please, *please* turn around and come home. And call me, okay? Bye."

The Spanish-speaking voice came back on and rattled off several mysterious menu options. Gary pressed a random key. The voice made a few more remarks that he couldn't understand, then played his second message.

"Gary!" It was Jim Jamb. "I hope you're doing okay. Look, I just need you to know that things are really heating up here at the office. So, if you're not locked in a prison cell somewhere, I highly recommend that you get your ass back here A.S.A.P. Frankly, your job might depend on it. Call me when you get this."

Gary listened to another stream of indecipherable Spanish, pressing another random key in the midst of it. His third and final message was another one from Scott.

"Hi, me again. Uh... Just in the *highly unlikely* event that you ignore my advice and insist on trying to cross the gap... Apparently the way to do it is not to cut straight through, which is like, a recipe for death. Instead what you do is, leave the Pan-American Highway before it ends, head north to the coast, and then you can hike over the border into Colombia and get a boat from Sapzurro to Turbo. The whole thing only takes a few hours and it's supposed to be, uh, pretty safe...

"But, don't do that. Just come home. Please. Oh, and, uh... Happy Thanksgiving, Gary. Okay, bye."

At the very same moment, back in Los Angeles, Alice Smede was thinking to herself: All the enjoyment has left this. Time to end it.

"You both need to go now," she said matter-of-factly to Tabitha Cole and Anita Guerrero, who were sitting cross-legged on the floor of the den, faces in their phones, cans of soda perched precariously on the carpet next to them.

The final straw had been when Tabitha'd returned from the kitchen a minute ago, holding a fresh can of Dr. Pepper she'd helped herself to (even though the original can Alice had given her was still sitting here, only half-consumed), and, while clumsily sitting down had, apparently without noticing, sloshed some of the contents onto the floor.

Prior to that had been a series of other offenses, a partial list of which was now streaming through Alice's mind. Both friends failing to remove their shoes or even wipe their feet upon entering the condo, and tracking mud across the lounge, the corridor, and into the den. Anita wandering into Patrick's bedroom (which was unoccupied, but with closed door), rummaging through his belongings, finding a vaping device and asking if she could use it. Tabitha following her in there and carefully examining everything that was lying on his desk or tacked up on his walls while asking lots of questions about him like whether he was dating anyone and whether Alice had seen his penis. Anita grabbing Alice's laptop without permission, briefly reading the beginning of something Alice had been writing, then, bored with that, launching a video game and briefly playing it, then, bored with that, literally casting the laptop aside so it ended up lying upside-down in a location where it could easily get stepped on. Tabitha suggesting that maybe they could fix up her mom with Alice's dad. One of the girls—unclear which one—at some point making a rather disgusting deposit in the toilet and not bothering to flush it.

"Did you not hear me?" Alice asked calmly, observing that neither Anita nor Tabitha had budged, or even glanced up. "Or are you just ignoring me?"

The morning had started off pleasantly enough. The three had met each other at a bus stop near their school, then walked up to Wilshire Boulevard, cutting through the empty plot of land allocated for the campus of a new community college called High School College, and stopped in at Boba Fête! for some refreshment. After that they'd zig-zagged their way back down to Santa Monica Boulevard, passing by the basketball courts where the boys their age could reliably be found milling around and talking smack, and had stopped in at the 99 Cents Only store to browse. The entire time, though she'd had to endure a certain inevitable amount of inane chatter from the other two, Alice had generally enjoyed their company and had remained in good spirits.

Things had started to go downhill after Anita had suggested they all hang out at Alice's place, a proposition Alice had always rejected in the past because the condo was small, and she felt self-conscious about her home, and she wasn't confident how her friends might behave there.

But today, under considerable pressure from both of them, she'd finally relented. Regrets had begun to form even prior to arriving here, when they were completely ignoring her, while playing loud music, during the bus ride.

"Please, you two—it's time to go," said Alice now, still having received no response whatsoever from either of her guests, a small hint of agitation finally creeping into her voice.

Her phone, lying on her desk, made an alert sound, and she reached for it.

Tabitha looked up, grinning. "Is it Ryan?" she asked.

Anita looked up, grinning. "Is it Ryan?" she asked.

It was indeed Ryan, with a message very similar to all the others he'd sent, at a rate of approximately one per day, over the past three and a half weeks. Alice read it quickly and set the phone back down again. She'd decide later how—and whether—to reply.

For most of September and October, she and Ryan had officially been a couple, but he'd abruptly ended it, providing a reason that was stated in vague, disorganized terms but seemed to amount to his finding all of her physical and mental traits utterly unappealing. Alice had taken this in stride and promptly moved on with her life. But a few days later, he'd started with the texts, which, though varying in tone from groveling to philosophical to angry, always suggested they should get back together. She had no interest in doing this.

"You should just block his sorry ass," said Tabitha.

"Oh!" exclaimed Anita. "That reminds me..."

She leapt up, tipping over a can of Dr. Pepper in the process, and headed for her backpack, which she'd flung down in an arbitrary location upon arriving. "I gotta show you what Andy drew in Spanish today..."

Alice quickly scooped up the knocked-over can, returned it to a vertical orientation and placed it gently on her desk, then began staring at the puddle-shaped dark spot on the carpet, pondering what, if anything, she should do about it.

"Here, look," said Anita, holding out a sheet of notebook paper that garnered a momentary glance from both of her companions, after which each returned their gaze to its previous target.

Tabitha reacted to what she'd seen with a loud "Hah! Love it!" while Alice gave no reaction.

On the paper was an extremely detailed pencil drawing of a human vulva and the area immediately surrounding it, closely resembling a diagram one might find in an anatomy textbook except with none of the parts labeled.

"Like he's ever seen one in real life!" Anita said, laughing. "He wishes!"

Alice was now making eye contact, her face expressionless. Tabitha was staring at her phone but joining in the laughter.

"He sits right in front of me in Spanish," Anita continued, "and he, like, draws this exact same thing, literally every single day. And this guy Sean, his friend who sits next to him... Like, they both think it's so hilarious...

"I always know when he starts drawing it because they both start going, 'Fff-fff-fff'—like, these stupid, quiet laughing sounds—and I can hear the shhhnk, shhhnk, shhhnk, shhhnk"—she mimed four line-drawing motions—"of the pencil. He always draws the thighs first, then he fills in the middle. What a loser!"

"Totally!" echoed Tabitha, looking up for a quick moment. More laughter from both of them.

"So today I finally, just as he was finishing it, I grabbed it from him! God, he was so pissed!"

"That's so middle school," said Alice.

"I know, right?" More laughter.

"Oh!" said Tabitha, looking up from her phone again. "So, okay, so there's this cool thing on the group chat right now, about, like, if someone dares you to do something really gross, like, how much money would they have to pay you to do it. So, like, for example, to eat a piece of shit. Would you do it for a million dollars? I totally would."

"Me too," agreed Anita. "I always do a dare. Even if there's no money. You gotta do it. It's a dare! I mean, if you don't do it then, you're like, a coward..."

"What about you, Alice?"

"What?"

"Would you eat a piece of shit for a million dollars?"

"I don't know. Probably not."

"Yes you would! You're such a liar. Of course you would."

There was a soft rap on the shoji door and, a second later, it slid open about a foot and Yvonne Smede poked her head in.

"Hi, girls," she said.

"Good morning, Mrs. Smede," said Anita and Tabitha in unison, both looking at Yvonne with smiling, angelic faces.

"How are you?" added Tabitha.

"Uh... I'm fine. Thank you."

All three girls continued to regard Yvonne attentively, two of them with big smiles.

"So, I was just about to go to the grocery store, and I was wondering if there's anything you'd like? Drinks, or snacks?"

"No, thank you, ma'am."

"No, thank you, ma'am."

Alice's previously emotionless facial expression had changed ever so slightly in the direction of annoyance.

"You look sleepy," said a female voice with an American accent coming from Gary's left, startling him.

He turned to see a white woman of average height and build, probably in her forties, with brown hair and brown eyes, smiling at him from a couple of feet away. Her arms and legs were covered in little red welts that looked like bug bites of some kind.

Gary smiled back. "I sure am," he said. "Haven't slept in over 24 hours!" A short pause. "And you know, come to think of it, the last time I slept in an actual *bed* was, like, five days ago."

He drifted away momentarily, recalling the most recent episodes of his Latin American adventure—the ones that had happened *since* Turbo, happened *after* he'd thought the most harrowing part surely must've been behind him. These had included being turned away at the Venezuelan border for not having a visa, then ambushed two minutes later by a team of official-looking men who'd stuffed him into his own trunk, driven him across, then pulled him out and disappeared again, without requesting or stealing anything from him.

The next major bit of drama had been involuntarily picking up a man who'd blocked the car's path, then lunged at the driver's door, smashed the window, and put a knife to Gary's throat. Later, at a traffic light in central San Rafael de El Moján, the hitchhiker had protected Gary from a pair of would-be carjackers, stabbing both of them in a fashion that looked most likely lethal. After riding along for another 25 miles, he'd peacefully, cheerfully, and very unexpectedly jumped out of the car at a traffic light in central Maracaibo and wandered off.

Finally, after arriving in the coastal town of La Vela de Coro at four o'clock in the morning and milling around near the docks for half an hour, fretting, Gary had bumped into a shifty-looking fellow who'd informed him that ferries only operated during daylight hours and that, furthermore, the crossing to Curaçao took about five hours to complete and that, furthermore, the ferry service to Curaçao had been out of operation for several years.

But a few minutes later, he'd bumped into an even shiftier-looking fellow who'd offered, for the relatively modest price of his PaceTek Mega-Ultra, to take Gary over to Willemstad in a little speedboat. They'd done precisely that and he'd presented himself at the marathon entrance gate twenty minutes ago—which was ten minutes past the arrival deadline—where the race officials had expressed enormous amounts of hesitation before ultimately agreeing to let him through.

Gary grinned. Fate really seemed to be on his side, after all. As he came back to the here and now, he realized that his race companion was holding out her hand, which contained a small, unmarked foil pouch.

"Here," she said. "Take this."

"Oh, no, thank you," said Gary.

"It'll help you wake up."

"That's okay," Gary said. "I'll be fine. Thank you, though."

"You look familiar. Have you ever been on a T.V. show?"

"No." Gary chuckled. "No, never."

The woman extended her hand again, palm vertical this time. The foil packet had vanished. "Patty Barnes," she said.

Gary shook her hand, smiling. "Gary Williams," he said.

"Pleased to meet you. Where are you from, Gary?"

"Los Angeles."

"Really? Me too!"

"Wow, small world! That's great... Hey, wait a second... Your last name is Barnes? Are you related to Frank Barnes, by any chance?"

"Nope, don't think so. Never heard of any Frank Barnes. I am related to Solomon Barnes. And I have a cousin named Barnes Barnes. Heh. Isn't that ridiculous?"

"Um... Yeah..."

"Beautiful island, isn't it?"

"Yes, it sure is."

"Done much sightseeing since you got here?"

"Um, no... not really..."

Gary's mind suddenly flashed to his regular life, waiting for him back in California after this whole crazy thing was over. He'd had a few conversations on his little Mexican flip phone yesterday, with Scott Portcullis and Jim Jamb, none of which had gone well. He frowned.

"Lots of mosquitoes!" Patty exclaimed.

"Oh... Well, I suppose we are in the tropics. I hadn't really—"

"I love 'em! They are just so darling."

"Really? You think?"

"You don't find many—in the wild, I mean—back in L.A. That's why I keep a private collection."

"You do? Wow."

"But here they're all over the place, all the time!"

Gary compulsively glanced down at his forearms to see if one had landed on him.

"People complain about the bites, but I think I must be immune or something. They never bite me! Or maybe the little critters just know how much I love 'em..." She laughed.

"Hmm," said Gary, but he was smiling again now.

"My friend, Peshwar, he hates them! Hates all insects, actually. He's always saving these spiders' lives, trapping them and moving them to a different location, near more insects. And he talks to the spiders, too! He says, 'Now listen, spider, I'm sparing your life conditionally. You have to repay me by eating tons of insects, okay?' Isn't that ridiculous?"

"Um... Yeah..."

"Me, I hate spiders. So disgusting! I always kill 'em right away."

Gary continued smiling but couldn't think of anything to say.

"So what are you doing after the race?" Patty asked.

"Oh, um... Well..." Gary had no idea what he was doing after the race. His mind went back to Scott and Jim.

"I thought I might check out that 'Mirage' place—you know, that bordello, near the airport?"

Gary raised his eyebrows, wondering if (and hoping that) he was misunderstanding her.

"Yeah, it's legal for foreign women to work there. In fact, it's *illegal* for local women! Can you believe that? Ridiculous. So anyway, yeah, I figured I could make myself a little money before I head home!"

There was a moment of very awkward silence. Then, to Gary's immense relief, the starting gun for his group fired, the ribbon across the pen came down, and people began filing out onto the course.

Five and a half hours later, he crossed the finish line, feeling energized and grinning ear to ear. Despite everything he'd endured leading up to this race, the running itself had gone very smoothly and he'd completed it in record time. What a triumph!

After a couple of minutes of savoring this monumental achievement, Gary's mind turned again to the matter of trying to put his life back together. He didn't ponder it long before taking a taxi to the airport and buying a one-way ticket to L.A. Not only did he feel he couldn't handle, physically or emotionally, putting himself through that 4,900-mile overland journey again. He also suspected that, if he did, he'd have no job, and possibly even no marriage, by the time he got back. No, there was really no other option but to bite the bullet and get on a plane.

Besides, he told himself as he sat by the gate, this flight couldn't possibly be as horrible as the one back in June, and being so exhausted meant he'd probably sleep the entire time.

Both of these beliefs proved to be utterly incorrect.

Chapter 17

"Hey there, Bill!"

Bill Smede, who was already feeling rather anxious (despite having sucked down his first old fashioned in record time and started on his second, delivered to him a moment ago), physically shuddered when hit by this cheery vocal torpedo, his eyes shooting up from where he'd been casually scrolling through a Wikipedia article about George P. Schultz (who'd held cabinet-level posts in the Nixon and Reagan presidential administrations) to see that the speaker was Amy Lee and that she was rapidly approaching, followed closely by her husband Jake, huge grins on both their faces.

"Hi," he said to them, smiling.

"Thought we'd be the first ones here," said Amy as she slid into the booth and Jake simultaneously slid in from the other side (so that Bill was now trapped).

"Yes!" cried Jake, breaking into a laugh. "We just… We're never early for anything!"

"Right," said Amy. "But, for some reason, the babysitter showed up early. So we thought, what the heck. Actually we thought, we have enough extra time to stop by Hank's, to, um…"

"Can I get you anything to drink?" asked the server, an extremely thin, white, male person (whether the applicable term would be "boy" or "man" was unclear from his appearance), who'd noticed the arrival of the Lees after dropping off Bill's drink and had circled back.

"Yes!" cried Jake. "I am in the mood for… a beer! Mmm, yes, that sounds delicious. Something, uh…"

"Negroni, please!" said Amy.

"Negroni, okay," said the server.

"Thank you very much, sir!"

"I want something hoppy," said Jake. "I'm feeling the hops tonight. But, it can't be overly hopped. No, no. You don't want too much hops... because that just... That will ruin it..."

"Would you like me to bring a beer list?" asked the server.

"Yes, that would great! That would be, just..."

"Okay, I'll be right back with that."

"So, Bill," said Amy, "it's been a while! Good to see ya again!"

"Yeah, good to see you too. Thanks for inviting me."

"Oh, that was all Yvonne. She gave the go-ahead." A short pause, during which Amy adopted a sly, conspiratorial face. "So—you two, are you... ya know..." She grinned and moved her eyebrows up and down.

"Yes! Boom-chicka-chicka," said Jake, chortling.

Bill felt his face heat up as he smiled and shook his head. "No, no," he said. "We're just friends."

"Aw, we're just givin' you a hard time," said Amy, playfully shoving Bill's shoulder. "But seriously—glad you two are friends again."

"Well, we never really *weren't* friends..."

"Oh!" said Amy. "Yeah, so, I was explaining why we were early... Speaking of which—never thought I'd see *you* here so early. You're always the guy who shows up last!"

"Well, I tried to do that this time but failed miserably. I assumed it was happening at five. Got here at 5:30."

"Nope—I made it for six 'cause I wanted to go home and change first. My shoes were killing me! They're new, and, ugh, I don't know if I'll ever wear them again. Lordy! But then, it's funny, I left work early anyways. *And* the babysitter was early..." She laughed.

Jake laughed, too. "Yes!" he cried. "Just, so funny... Just..."

"So anyways, yeah, we stopped by Hank's to pick up some stuff for Jennifer's birthday..."

"Here's that beer list," said the server, setting down a large, laminated card in front of Jake.

"Awesome!" he exclaimed. "Yeah, this is just... perfect. Just, perfect. Oh, let's see what we've got here..."

"And, are you expecting anyone else to join?" the server asked as he placed a Negroni in front of Amy. "The gentleman said he wasn't sure how many in your party..."

"Six," said Amy with a big grin. "We've got six people altogether for our"—she switched to a sing-songy voice—"Fer-iday eve-ening paar-tay!" Then, switching back: "So we've still got three more coming."

"Six? Okay, great. I'll bring menus after everyone is here. Unless you wanted to order some food now?"

"Um..." Amy quickly mulled this over. "No, I think just drinks for now. We'll probably want to get some appetizers at some point, but... I think we'll wait on that..."

"Okay, sounds good. Sir, did you decide on a beer?"

"Uh... hmm... uh... No, not really. I just... uh... Could you pick one for me?"

The lad seemed taken aback and a bit panicked, but said, "Sure. Okay," but then said, "I mean, I guess. I mean, I don't really know very much... about beer..."

"That's okay," said Jake. "Just... uh... hmm... Just, uh... Just bring me... a Bud Light."

"Sure. Okay." He hurried off.

"Mmm," said Jake, smiling, eyes darting back and forth between his wife's face and Bill's. "I just... can't wait to taste that beer... Just... Mmm, so good..."

"Oh!" said Amy. "Yeah, so, we went to Hank's... I swear—I'm never gonna finish telling this story!" She laughed. "So anyways, Jennifer wants all these decorations for her birthday, even though it's just the family. Little brat! So we went to Hank's, to try and get some of them, and we went to the floral counter for, you know how they have those helium balloons there?"

Bill nodded and smiled, though he didn't actually know (and couldn't have cared less).

"And I say to the chick behind the counter that we're going to pick out some balloons, and she's like, 'Sorry, I can't fill them up, we ran out of helium, there's a shortage.' A freakin' *helium* shortage? I mean, who ever heard of such a thing?"

Bill chuckled. He genuinely was now finding Amy's tale mildly amusing.

"I don't think there's a shortage. I bet her and her friends all took turns sucking in the helium so they could talk in a cartoon voice!"

Jake burst into big waves of hearty laughter. The other two also laughed, in a far milder fashion.

After everyone had gone quiet, Amy said, "Ah, kids—gotta love 'em. Brandon's been acting like a major brat, too. I told him to stay away from the paints, but did he listen? Oh—hey, guys!"

Laura Johnson and Mike Howell had just arrived at the booth and were sliding in, both on Jake's side, Mike first.

"Sorry we're late," said Laura.

Bill looked at his wrist and saw that it was 6:01.

"Hey," said Jake to Mike, "I need you to recommend me a beer!"

"A beer?"

"Yeah. I ordered one already, but—oh, here it is!"

"Bud Light," said the server, setting the glass down in front of Jake.

"But, I could, uh... send it back. If you know a better one?"

The server, who'd still been in the process of returning to an upright position after leaning over the table, froze, a worried/confused look on his face.

Mike shrugged. "I don't really know anything about beer."

"Oh, okay, uh... Uh, hmm... Just... Uh... I'll just keep this." Jake put his hand around the glass and smiled.

The server relaxed his face and finished standing up. Then he asked the newcomers what they'd like to drink. Mike ordered a bourbon; Laura, after being prodded by her husband to look up from her phone and supply information, ordered a glass of pinot grigio. The server departed.

Realizing he was no longer there, Amy, who'd been distracted by something on her phone, said, "Aw, we should've ordered some appetizers!"

"Bill," said Mike, extending his arm across Jake (who definitely didn't mind and possibly didn't even notice, continuing to smile and slowly nod his head with a far-away look in his eyes). "Good to see you again, my man."

"Good to see you, too," said Bill, shaking Mike's hand. "How've you been?"

"Yeah, I've been alright. Can't complain... Oh, hey—I don't know why... Anyway, the other day, I was talking with Chazz while we were working on this old guy... And, we knew he wasn't gonna make it, and I said something like, 'Everyone has to die eventually.' And Chazz challenged me on that! He said only half of all the humans who've ever been born have died so far. But of course we assume that, you know, all the rest of them are going to, someday. But, it's really just that—an assumption."

All eyes were on Mike now, all faces thoughtful looking. Laura muttered "Really?"

"Interesting idea," Mike continued. "And it reminded me of you, Bill. I don't know why."

"Because I'm afraid of death?" Bill offered with a grin.

Mike chuckled. "I think it's because you're intelligent," he replied, winking.

There was a quiet laughing sound from Yvonne Smede, whom nobody had noticed approaching, as she slid into the booth next to Amy, who turned and shouted "What's up, girlfriend!"

"Hi," said Yvonne to the group, clearly uncomfortable with the spotlight.

"Okay," said Amy, "let's get this party started. Where's that little waiter kid?"

"Right here," he replied with a frown, arriving tableside, holding a stack of menus, which he then began distributing.

"Oh!" Amy exclaimed, laughing. "Great timing!"

"My name's Drew and I'll be your server—"

"Drew," said Jake with an excited grin and gleaming eyes, "let me just... just stop you for a second. I just want to say... We kinda got off on the wrong foot, with, you know... just, with that beer thing. But I would've said this anyway, irregardless... I just... I wanted to say it anyway.

"See, we're all human beings here—you are, I am, my friends are..."—a quick arm gesture toward his tablemates—"And, it's important that we just... just, relate to each other, as human beings. Don't focus on being 'the waiter,' or, 'the customer,' you know? Just focus on... just, being human beings.

"And we shouldn't judge each other, you know? When you look at me, try not to see... a big fat jolly Asian dude." His grin momentarily got wider and he quickly glanced around the table for a reaction but got none.

"Just like, when I look at you, I don't see a scrawny, wimpy, ugly kid. Right? I just see you as a person. No judgment." Deep down, Jake dimly suspected that he wouldn't have had the guts to deliver this speech to a restaurant server whom he hadn't already judged as matching the description just given.

"So," he went on, "total honesty. Just... total. And I'm gonna start, by telling you, Don, that I think you are a wonderful person... We all do, actually... And, we are going to give you a nice, big tip! You know, at the end of the meal. It's gonna be... uh... big. Just, very big. You will be happy! And it doesn't matter whether you do a good job as a waiter, and it doesn't matter... uh... how much we order, you know, and stuff... None of that matters."

Drew's face was projecting a mix of pain and bewilderment, as were the faces of the others in the booth, except Amy, who just looked amused, and Laura, who was in Phone World.

"So, I want you to just... relax, and... just... be honest with us, you know? Don't worry about anything. We're all just human beings here, and we're all just... just..."

Still smiling, Jake glanced around the table again, wiggled his eyebrows a bit, and made a meaningless gesture with his hands, seeming to suggest that everyone here already understood the conclusion of what he'd been saying, and that perhaps one of them might even finish his sentence for him. But none of this was the case.

"That's wrong," said Laura, finally looking up from her phone, and at Mike.

"Excuse me?" he said.

"It's not true that half the people who've ever lived are still alive. There have been over a hundred billion people."

"Whoa!" said Jake, then grabbed his phone off the table and began tapping away on it.

"Um," said Drew, "unless you have any questions about the menu, I'll let you—"

"Jeez Louise!" exclaimed Amy, the only one who'd looked at the menu, as she looked up from it. "Yeah, I have a question about the menu: is this really the freakin' menu?" She laughed.

"Um..." Drew didn't know how to respond. "I don't... Well, yes... It... is..."

"I thought this was a barbecue place!"

"Um... No, ma'am... It isn't..."

"But all I see on here is..."—she looked back down at the menu—"fried fish, and... breaded, fried... I guess that's fish, too... and, um, looks like french fries... Oh, and, listen to this." She glanced up for a split second, grinning. "It says, 'mix and match your favorite remoulades'... What the heck is that? Oh, and everything comes with a piece of lemon..."

"You're right!" Jake suddenly exclaimed, looking up from his phone at Laura. "Over one hundred billion humans. It's true."

Amy said, "I think we're gonna need a few minutes to talk amongst ourselves, Drew."

"Sure thing," he said before hastily departing.

Amy's misconception about the restaurant (which had been selected for tonight's outing by her) was somewhat understandable. But in fact its name, BBQ Plaice, referred to the type of fish in which it specialized and to the name of its founder, Benito Berto Quiñónez, who'd grown up in a wealthy Spanish family, lived in Denmark for several years, where he'd become very fond of some of their cuisine, and finally had moved to L.A. twenty years ago to launch what he'd intended to be a culinary empire but had in fact always been simply a pet project that consistently lost money.

"Okay guys," said Amy, "let's talk about this."

She then pitched the idea of leaving BBQ Plaice after drinks and heading somewhere else for dinner, which the group decided to do after a few minutes of discussion that included the other five advocating staying put.

"Ah, now this is more like it," Amy enthused two hours later as she stood in the reception/bar area of Four Corners (located two miles west of BBQ Plaice on the ground floor of a very swanky apartment building at the intersection where Le Doux Road, Burton Way, Fourth Street, La Cienega and San Vicente all met), examining the options for burgers and tacos presented on the menu Jake had handed her a moment ago.

"Yes!" he agreed emphatically, not actually looking at the menu, and let out a hearty laugh.

"Whoa, is this place crowded," Mike commented.

The three of them, and the many other patrons waiting for a table, were indeed packed in like sardines, with an accompanying rather high level of background noise from all the flapping jaws. This, the second and, so far, last instance of the Four Corners chain to open its doors, had been immensely popular ever since doing so five years ago. By contrast, the original, which sat on the grounds of the Four Corners Monument, had always struggled to attract an adequate amount of business (particularly after it stopped serving breakfast and lunch) and had recently closed down permanently.

Squeezing through the nearest layer of the human wall to occupy a little patch of floor next to her husband, Laura said, "I put our names in. It's a 90-minute wait."

"Well that sucks!" said Amy.

"She said she could seat us right away at one of those high tables in the bar…"

"Oh, awesome!"

"But she said those tables only seat four."

"Oh…"

"And she said there are no servers working those tables right now."

"Of course," said Mike with a chuckle.

"Of course," echoed Jake, grinning and nodding.

"Where are those darn Smedes, anyways?" asked Amy. "Shouldn't they have been here by now?"

The four present, who'd arrived at BBQ Plaice in their own cars, had offered the other two a lift over to Four Corners, but Bill and Yvonne had both declined, opting for some exercise and fresh air. And indeed they had enjoyed the walking and the brisk, 67-degree December air, as well as each other's company—so much so, in fact, that upon reaching the restaurant entrance they'd decided to carry on a while longer, traversing La Cienega, Clifton Way, Arnaz Drive, and Burton Way in a big circuit that would bring them back here. The rest would just be waiting around for a table anyway, they'd reasoned.

Meanwhile, the rest had reformulated their plan slightly after encountering the extreme scarcity of parking anywhere near Four Corners, all of them driving over to the Lee residence where Amy and Jake had left their car and climbed into Mike's ambulance, then returning to the vicinity of the restaurant and driving around in steadily larger circles for 20 minutes before ultimately parking half a mile away.

Now, as everyone shrugged their shoulders and made a token effort at looking around to check that the two Smedes hadn't already stealthily shown up, Mike muttered, "What we need is some drinks."

"Yes, Mike!" said Amy. "I like the way you think!"

"I'm on it!" Jake shouted, turning himself in the direction of the bar.

"I'll come with you," said Mike, and the two began squeezing their way into the crowd.

After a few seconds of silence between the women, Laura said, "Hey, so what's the latest with tracking down all that family stuff?"

"Oh—right!" said Amy. "Yes. Making some progress, actually…" She paused very briefly and her face fell. "Well, actually, got some really sad news... Professor Chang died."

"What?! How?"

"Car accident. Yeah. His wife finally called me back and told me. So sad..."

"That's terrible."

"Yeah. It actually happened back, months ago, whenever that was, when I went to Michigan and met him?"

"Uh-huh..."

"Yeah, he was on his way back home from that same trip!"

"Wow."

"I know—so creepy! God. And... apparently it was really bad... Like his whole car went up in flames, a giant fireball..."

"Oh my god."

"I know. I know. Mmmf..." She grimaced and shuddered.

"Do you know how it happened?" Laura asked.

"Apparently a big truck plowed right into him. Chang didn't have his headlights on for some reason, so... you know, the truck driver couldn't see him..."

"Wow," said Yvonne, appearing from between the shoulders of two strangers whose backs were turned, "I didn't think anyone could have a more miserable face than Bill in this place. But you two are giving him some competition."

"There you are!" said Amy, her smile instantly returning.

"Hi," said Bill as he pushed into view from the same pair of shoulders.

"Mike and Jake went to get drinks," said Laura. "But, they didn't know you were here..."

"That's okay," said Bill. "I'll, uh..." He began scanning the landscape, trying to size up just how torturous it was going to be to make his way to the bar.

Laura was already tapping on her phone. "I'll just text Mike, let him know," she said.

"Oh—yeah, thanks, that'd be great. Uh... Old fashioned for me, please..."

"Yvonne?" Laura asked.

"White wine, please."

"So," said Amy, "I was just telling Laura the latest in my little, um, ancestry... quest." She paused to laugh. "Anyways, um... Well I'll skip the sad stuff for now. God. But, there's some cool stuff, too!"

Both Smedes were making eye contact with Amy, Yvonne smiling and Bill not frowning. Laura was still face-in-phone.

"So get this—I did some detective work and…"—Amy's grin now carried a hint of pride—"I discovered this old college yearbook online, in a PDF. I mean like, a *searchable* PDF document. Not just scanned images. The entire freakin' yearbook was made into an actual document. So random!"

Laura was now visibly attentive.

"And so I searched for that chick who hooked up with Chang way back then. Anna Lee was her name. And I found her, in a couple of places in the yearbook, and, one of these was called, like, the Young Women Historians Club or something, and… Anna was the co-president of the club, along with this *other* chick named Winnie Kesterbaum…"

"We come bearing gifts!" shouted Jake, bursting through the wall of people into the little space staked out by the friends, holding a glass in each hand, grinning widely.

"Yay!" said Amy. "So anyways, I've had no luck at all tracking down Anna, but I *did* track down Winnie. She lives in Hawaii now, of all places. So I tried to call her but she didn't answer. Left her a message. So, fingers crossed!"

Mike had now also poked through, also holding two drinks, and he and Jake had begun distributing their haul.

"Where's Yvonne's drink?" Laura asked Mike. "And Bill's?"

"Sorry, guys," said Mike. "Didn't know you were here…"

"Don't worry, I'll hook you guys up," announced Jake, and he aimed himself in the direction of the bar again and began the pushing process.

"Well, I'm not waiting," said Amy. "Sorry, guys. Cheers!"

"It's okay," said both Yvonne and Bill as their friend took a sip.

"Mike, I sent you a text," said Laura, looking disproportionately alarmed (though not angry). "My phone said you read it."

Mike performed a one-armed shrug as his other arm was retrieving his phone from his pocket.

"Ah, yes," he said, looking at the screen. "There it is."

An hour later, after the group had commandeered one of the high tables in the bar by informing the folks who'd been sitting there that they'd never get served, and after everyone had gone to the bar, one by one, to order their food, and after a second round of drinks had been handed out, and after Jake had stolen chairs from another table for himself and Bill (both of whom had initially agreed to just stand at the two ends of the table while the other four sat), and after all the food had arrived, along with a third round of drinks, and everyone was eagerly tucking in, the topic of Amy's "ancestry quest" was brought up again.

"Oh, hey," Laura said to her, "what about your adoption? Your original one, I mean..."

"Oh, right! Yeah, Stan and Norma... God, they are the sweetest people... I almost, just *almost* wish I'd grown up with them. No, I totally love my mom and dad. They're the best. But, Michigan rocks! Stan rocks and Norma rocks!

"But yeah, anyways, they gave me all the info they had—which was practically nothing, of course! But I was able to get in contact with the adoption agency... Oh, and, get this—it's in England!"

"Really?" said Bill, the only person here who hadn't already been told about this at a previous happy hour gathering.

"Yep. I know, crazy, right?" Now she affected a British accent: "I was born in jolly old England... Tea and crumpets, anyone?"

This elicited huge guffaws from Jake, highly amused chuckles from Laura and Mike, and mildly amused smiles from Yvonne and Bill.

"So, anyways," Amy went on, "they said they *could* provide me some info about my birth parents..."—a deliberate dramatic pause—"but only if I show up there in person!"

"Wow," said Bill, again the only one who didn't already know.

"So, nothing new on that front?" Laura enquired.

"Nah," said Amy. "It's kind of a dead end. I mean, I tried a little bit to negotiate with them but they totally shut me down. Unless I want to fly thousands of miles to another country to try and chase up this silly mystery, you know?" She laughed. "Of course, Mom wants me to do it. But she's not willing to go with me, hah! Says she's too old for that kind of travel..."

Mike and both Smedes were making low-key nodding and shrugging motions, with a bit of mildly reactive eyebrow movement. Jake was nodding and grinning, eyes darting around the table. Laura looked thoughtful, and like she might be about to speak.

Then she did: "I mean, if you were going to take a trip over there anyway, you know, for like a vacation and sightseeing and stuff…"

"Right, exactly," said Amy. "Then it would seem more… you know… reasonable…"

"You should do it!" Laura said. "You and Jake and the kids, you could do a whole Europe thing…"

"Yes!" Jake shouted.

"Oh, speaking of travel," said Amy, "when's your next trip to the SDI islands?"

"Pretty soon!" Mike excitedly replied.

"S*G*I," said Laura. "Not D. But yeah, we're going next month. It's—"

"We like to go in the winter," said Mike with a chuckle, "to get away from the cold weather."

"It's Groot Bot this time," said Laura. "A brand new one."

"Second to last," said Mike.

"We're excited," said Laura.

"Well, cool!" said Amy. "Very cool."

"Yes!" Jake shouted again.

"Oh, on our last trip," said Laura, "we met this girl, Greta… See, normally when we're there, everyone we meet is a tourist like us, or else works in the, you know, hospitality industry…"

"Greta was so sweet," Mike said.

"Yeah," Laura went on, "she was just this ordinary girl, who's lived there all her life. We got lost during one of our walking tours, and we bumped into her. She was on her way to… somewhere, I can't remember… Anyway, she walked with us for a while and helped us find our tour group, and, we kind of, got to know each other a little…"

"Aw, that's sweet," said Amy.

"Sweet," Jake repeated, nodding and grinning.

"But here's the thing," Laura said. "She had a tough life. She was missing half of one of her arms… We didn't ask her about that. And, she mentioned her father had died in a motorcycle crash. And, one of her brothers had also died, I'm not sure how. And the whole family lived in like a… a little… What did she call it?"

"Uh," said Mike, "I think she called it a 'straw thatch'… whatever that is."

"Yeah, so, tough life, but, she didn't seem the least bit sad, or… bitter, or resentful, or *anything.* She was so smiley and cheerful and… talkative… Just, happy as could be."

"I think every person is born with a default level of happiness," said Yvonne. "And, when things happen to them, good or bad, they move away from that default level for a while, but then they adjust and come back to it."

"I think you're right," said Mike.

"I mean, I don't want to take anything away from this Greta girl," said Yvonne. "No doubt she's seen hardship, which is a shame, and no doubt she's suffered, and no doubt she's shown a lot of bravery in the face of that suffering..."

All five of the others were looking at Yvonne, apparently listening with interest.

"It was just, your story reminded me of this, kind of, theory of human happiness automatic recalibration... that I've been turning over in my mind for a while now..."

"Some people, like Greta, are just happy people, no matter what crap life gives them. And others are miserable and grumpy all the time, even though they have a perfect life." She made a subtle motion with her head and eyes in Bill's direction.

"It's true," he said.

"Well check out Yvonne, laying the philosophy on us!" said Amy with a big smile, a reaction that clearly showed how pleased she was by her friend's unusual outspokenness and made Yvonne feel inclined to keep it very unusual indeed.

"Oh!" said Jake. "Remember that speech I gave to that kid, at the other restaurant? The one who waited on us?"

Everyone nodded and Bill said "Of course."

"Well, I was inspired by this book I've been reading. It's just, so... just..."

"What book is it?" asked Laura.

"It's called 'Soothsayer: The Reckoning'... It's a limited series, and it's just so... Aw, it's just so, amazing..."

Seeing Laura's puzzled face, Mike quietly said to her, "It's a comic book."

Amy overheard and, grinning amusedly, corrected him: "Graphic novel!"

"Yeah," said Jake, "it's this graphic novel I discovered and, just... It's about this guy who's... Well, it's about *omniscience*..."—he deliberately spoke more slowly here—"and... *omnipotence.* See, they're very different things. God has both. And, of course, ordinary people don't have either one. But this guy—his name is Kaareth, he's from the future—he has omniscience. Only omniscience. Which means, he knows everything. He just... knows absolutely everything there is to know! Think about that. He just, *knows everything* that's going on... with anyone, any time, any place."

Jake paused to let this sink in. Laura was now looking at her phone but everyone else was still looking at him, smiling pleasantly.

"So, he's always just, fascinated, by everything he knows. And, he can totally relate to people, you know? He can connect with them because he just... He knows what they're going through. It's just, *so* good. Just..."

"Hey, how's it going with your hunt for that super-rare comic?" asked Bill. "What was it? The field marshal, or...?"

"Yes, yes!" said Jake, enthusiasm and smile growing even larger. "Good memory, my friend! The elusive Field Marshal Wield-Partial Number Zero! Aw, I'm tellin' you... If I could lay my hands on that book... Oh, just..."

"So, any luck?"

"Well, my friend Les really dug into it for me. He's just, the best. So, and, it turns out... You see, there were only ever 500 copies printed in the first place. It was an *extremely* limited... uh, thing.

"And then, a lot of them were destroyed, on purpose, like, a couple years later. They *burned* them at this protest thing, 'cause... 'cause they just, they were upset because, they thought it just didn't stay true to the... just, the... They thought it was a sell-out, you know, by Ralston Comics... That it was all just like a cynical marketing ploy. And so, they were angry about it, you know?"

"And most of the others were bought up by collectors," said Amy.

"Right," said Jake. "But not just ordinary collectors—it's these special Collection and Preservation Collectives... The C.P.C. gang!" He paused to laugh. "And they're just... They're never gonna get rid of them. They're basically like a museum."

Amy jumped in again. "And it turns out, the remaining few copies, that were, you know, in the hands of just regular people—all of those, or, almost all of them...?"

"All of them! Yep, it's just... Whoa. So, yeah, all the other copies that were out there were donated to this big charity auction. Yep, they're all accounted for. So... yeah, so, that's my only shot at getting one, that auction..."

"You gotta make sure you register for that, honey."

"I gotta make sure I register for that. Yep."

"Excuse me, sir," said a voice from behind a glassy-eyed Bill, jarring him back into the moment.

He turned to see a muscular, middle-aged white man who wasn't wearing a Four Corners uniform but had an official air about him.

"We're going to need this chair back from you," said the man. "We're going to need to return it to the table you stole it from."

A sly smile came over Mike's face two hours later as he sat, nestled into a beanbag in the corner of the living room of his apartment, holding a glass of whiskey. "I'm gonna tell you guys about something kinda wild," he said.

Facing him were Jake, in the only other beanbag, and Bill, butt pressed awkwardly against a window sill, both of whom were also holding whiskeys.

"But," Mike continued, "you gotta promise not to tell your wives about this."

"Ooh!" said Jake, eyebrows pumping up and down.

Fuck, thought Bill.

They'd split off from the women shortly after arriving here, on Jake's suggestion (because the women started "talking shop"), and since then had been conversing on a range of masculine topics, most of them linked somehow to comic books, tropical vacations, or whiskey.

"And *most* important," Mike added, "don't let Laura know you know."

He glanced across the room at his wife. She was on the sofa, deeply engaged with Amy and Yvonne, all of them trading ideas about how to handle the latest round of nonsense communication they'd received from the Interface Team.

"What is it, Mike?" Jake asked loudly, leaning forward, eyes gleaming, smile wide.

Mike's own smile disappeared momentarily as he said "Hey, keep your voice down" and looked over at the women again. Then it was back.

"Okay, listen," he said. "You know how Laura and I like to... have adventures, and, explore and... try new things..."

"Yeah, totally," said Jake, taking care to keep his voice down.

"Well, recently we decided to try... swinging."

"Wow," said Bill. The thought of maybe trying to get Francisco Rosario connected with Mike and Laura flashed through his mind. No—too awkward, too complicated, too risky.

"You mean like wife swapping and stuff?" Jake asked.

"Yes, exactly. Well, not swapping, like for the whole night or anything, but... We were all in the same room together and it was just like... Anybody could do anybody." He chuckled. "Like a free-for-all."

"Awesome!" said Jake.

"Yeah."

"Reminds me of my college days... But wait, so... Another man was... Another man was,"—he lowered his voice even further—"was having sex with your wife?"

"Well, yeah..." Mike looked a bit sheepish.

"And you were okay with it?"

"Well, pretty much, yeah... I mean, mentally, I was cool with it, but, emotionally... Well, I'd be lying if I said I didn't feel jealous. You know—that, that *heat* that wells up inside you..."

"Right!" said Jake.

"But, the thing is... I believe, and so does Laura, that... you gotta push past that. Because, there are thrilling, wonderful experiences on the other side of it. Jealousy is... a very natural human emotion. We have to accept it. But we don't have to be controlled by it."

"Aw, yeah, jealousy... I would just... I just, I don't think I could stand it if my wife was with another man... Especially if I had to watch!"

"Mmm-hmm, I understand," Mike said.

"And, Amy would be jealous too, if I did that. *So* jealous..."

"So, everyone enjoyed it?" asked Bill.

"Well, heh... Yeah... We did, but... Okay, so here's maybe the best part of the story. It's embarrassing for me, but... What the hell. You guys are my friends." He made a small gesture with his glass, toward the other two.

"So, we've done it twice so far. Met up with this other couple, at a hotel."

"Same couple both times?" asked Bill.

"Yeah. They're nice. We met them online. Anyway, so, both times we've met up so far... I, uh, I couldn't get hard."

"Whoa, seriously?" said Jake.

"You mean, not at all, the whole time?" asked Bill.

"Yep. I hate to say it, but, yes—soft as a well-cooked noodle. The *whole* damn night. Both times!"

Bill started laughing involuntarily. "Sorry," he said.

"That's okay," said Mike. "Laugh it up. I deserve it!"

"So, what happened?" Jake asked. "You drank too much?"

"No, no... barely drank anything. I guess I must've just been... nervous or something. All the, uh... anticipation, and... the pressure... I guess it got to me..."

"Right, yes..."

"What about the other guy?" asked Bill. "Did he have any trouble?"

"Not at all," said Mike. "He was standing at attention right from the get-go..."

Bill was laughing again, and Mike began laughing, too, as he carried on with his story.

"Yeah, he was unstoppable! Going great guns—all night, both nights!"

Jake started laughing now too. The other two were doubled over, barely keeping their drinks balanced in their hands.

Mike pulled himself together a bit to say, "All three of them, just going at it, having a fantastic time... And I'm just there, like..." Then he broke down laughing again.

"Third time's the charm, maybe?" suggested Bill.

"What's so funny over there, gentlemen?" called out Amy, just as her phone, sitting next to her on the coffee table, started ringing.

"Oh my god!" she said, looking down at it. "Hawaii number! I better take this." She jumped off the sofa and snatched up the phone.

"I'm just gonna take it in your bedroom," she said to Laura, hurriedly striding off in that direction. "So I can hear better."

"Oh, I don't know..." Laura said, but then realized it was futile.

If she'd had her way, there wouldn't have been any guests in her apartment tonight—as usual the place was a total mess, especially the bedroom and bathroom. The group's original plan, after finishing their meal at Four Corners, had been to call it a night. But Amy had intervened at the last minute, almost physically stopping both Smedes from ordering Ubers and informing everyone that she and Jake would be hosting them for drinks. So all six had piled into the ambulance, some more enthused than others, and headed off. Then, while stopped at a light on Wilshire, Mike had spontaneously suggested they switch the destination to his and Laura's place (which was only a few blocks from the Lees'), which was met with highly vocal approval from both Amy and Jake, and before Laura knew what was happening, the decision had been made.

"Hello?" said Amy, inside the bedroom, as she nearly tripped over a basket of laundry sitting on the floor.

"Yes, hello," said a woman's voice on the other end. "I'm trying to reach… Amy Lee?"

"Yes! You've reached her! Is this Winnie Kesterbaum?"

"Yes, it is… Well, Winnie Sumloozeessum now… I got married."

"Gotcha. Well, thanks so much for calling me back, Winnie!"

"Sure, no problem. But, unfortunately, I don't think I can help you in locating Anna. She and I lost touch decades ago, I'm afraid."

"Aw, bummer. Did you have a falling out?"

"No, no… It was just, we just drifted apart over time. I mean, we did stay in touch for many years after college, but eventually, you know how it goes… "

"Sure, of course. So, hey, is there any chance you could tell me anything about, um, Anna's daughter? Who would've been born maybe when you guys were still there at U of M?"

"Yes! Oh wow, that brings back memories. Essie. Her name was Essie. Well, Estuary on her birth certificate, but nobody except her mother ever called her that."

"Cool, cool," said Amy with a small chuckle. "And her last name would've been… Lee?"

"Yep, yeah… Anna was a single mom, and, there wasn't… Anyway, yeah, she gave her baby the same last name as her."

"Gotcha."

"That Essie, she was always a little hellion," said Winnie. "A rebel to the core, right from an early age."

"Oh, yeah?"

"Yeah, poor Anna. Not an easy child to raise. And as a teenager, apparently, really went off the deep end."

"What happened to her?"

"Well, nothing too terrible. At least, not that I know of. But, she got pregnant, at 18, and then… By this time, she and her mother were barely speaking to each other… And then she moved to England. Her boyfriend was British."

"Oh my god!" Amy exclaimed. "Do you know what happened with the pregnancy?"

"Yeah, she gave birth—over there, in England. And then she gave the baby up for adoption."

"Oh my god!" Amy exclaimed again. "Do you know if the baby was a boy or a girl?"

"It was a girl."

Amy gasped and silently mouthed the words "Oh my god" as Winnie continued.

"Yeah, Anna wanted to adopt the baby, actually, and raise her as her own—you know, back here in the States. But, Essie. Yikes. Gave the baby to a complete stranger instead, just out of spite."

"Holy crap!"

"I know, I know. That was the last straw for their relationship. They didn't speak at all after that."

"Well, that's a shame."

"Yeah."

After a long silence on the line, Amy said, "Well, listen, Winnie, thank you so, *so* much for calling me back. I really appreciate it."

"Not a problem. Good luck with your research."

"Thanks! Bye!"

Amy hung up and scurried back into the living room. The sexes had rejoined each other during her absence: Yvonne and Laura still occupied their same spots on the sofa, but Mike was now seated next to Laura (where Amy had been previously), Jake was in a nearby recliner, and Bill was leaning awkwardly against a nearby bookcase. They were all in the midst of a discussion about their departure from BBQ Plaice.

"Really?" said Laura. "I could've sworn I saw you..."

"Nope," said Bill. "For some reason I thought Jake was taking care of it."

"Well I certainly didn't," said Yvonne.

Jake turned to his wife with a big, amused grin. "Honey—we don't think anyone actually paid the bill at that first restaurant!"

"Holy cow, really?" she said.

Noticing that his glass was empty, and that it was nearly midnight, Bill said, "Uh, sorry everyone, I think I'm going to have to get going..."

"Yeah," Yvonne chimed in, "I'm pretty wiped at this point, to be honest."

"Aw, come on, guys!" Amy chided.

"I gotta admit," said Mike, "I don't know if it's the whiskey or just gettin' old, but… sleep does sound pretty nice right about now."

"Mr. Sandman!" shouted Jake, then laughed.

Laura was now in Phone World.

"Listen up, guys," said Amy. "I just found out something that is un-freakin-believable! So, one last round and then we'll call it a night."

Chapter 18

Along the curbs of Orange Grove Avenue and Hayvenhurst Street, attached to wires draped across the branches of trees sporting great masses of bright green leaves, thousands of holiday lights twinkled very brightly, though they were barely visible bathed in the even-brighter mid-morning sunlight. On a patch of grass on one of the corners where these two roads intersected, underneath a giant sign listing the businesses that occupied the building behind the parking lot behind the patch of grass, sat a collection of "life size" plastic models representing Santa Claus, a sleigh, and nine reindeer. A middle-aged man walking past in shorts, tank top and flip-flops glanced over indifferently.

Inside the building, Irene Hoffman sat at a circular conference table in one of four identical chairs that were spaced evenly around its perimeter. The other chairs were currently occupied by (proceeding clockwise from Irene): Judy Goldstein, nobody, and Stan Wojcik.

"Once upon a time," said Irene, grinning, "there was this eye doctor named Tom. And he was… He wasn't just one of those eye doctors who checks people's vision and, prescribes them glasses, or whatever. He was a *real* eye doctor, an ophthalmologist. Went to med school and got an M.D. and everything. Although, I guess that doesn't actually matter…"

Judy and Stan were both listening intently.

"The point is, he opened up an eye clinic and, his patients, they fucking loved him. I mean, he was friendly and charming and… He knew his shit, too, of course, but, his bedside manner was off the charts. So business was booming, and it kept getting better and better. But eventually, it reached a plateau because, you know, there are only so many people who live near the clinic who need an eye doctor."

"Right!" said Judy.

"But here's the thing. Making patients happy and loyal wasn't his only talent. He also kicked ass at training other eye doctors to be the same way... and then, really super-smoothly, almost like a... like a fucking magician... he could *transition* their care... over to some other doctor. He could get the patients *loving* the hell out of that other doctor, the same way they loved him."

Irene's eyes were gleaming as she added a sort of "Unnhh?" utterance to convey the idea of "Pretty impressive and valuable, right?"

Her audience responded with nods and smiles.

"So, after seven years of working his magic, and hiring a few doctors, the place was making a shitload of money, and it was on auto-pilot! Tom was still the owner, but he was able to reduce his day-to-day job duties down to zero... which freed him up to start the whole process over again! He opened a second clinic, in a different part of town."

"Wonderful," said Judy.

"And he kept repeating it. With the same success every time—of course. Six times altogether. Six eye clinics, spread out all over town. An eye clinic empire! And, it was hard work—each cycle took him seven years. But after those 42 years of building up his empire, he retired. And just watched the money roll in! He still owned all the clinics. And altogether, he was clearing four million dollars a year..."

"Wow," said Judy.

"Impressive," said the voice of Stacy Parabola from a phone lying on the table.

"Just think about that," Irene continued. "Four million a year. Every fucking year. Forever!" Her grin was so huge now that it almost seemed to be leaping off her face.

Judy chuckled delightedly. Then nobody spoke for a moment.

Then Stan asked, "Is that a true story, Irene?"

"Yep," she replied. "My friend Tom Waters, from college. Now he's my eye doctor."

"So he's not retired?" asked Judy.

"No! He's my age. Okay, so, listen... Part of the story hasn't happened yet. Probably never will, actually—but only because Tom's a big pussy! But it *could* be a true story, so easily. It *should* be. I've told him, over and over. He just needs to seize the opportunity..."

"How many eye clinics does he have so far?" asked Judy.

"God, Judy!" Irene snapped. "One. Just one, of course.

Because that's all he has the balls for. But, I'm tellin' you... Massive opportunity. He's a great fucking eye doctor. His patients fucking love him..."

A tall, thin, white man of about 60 named Ty Luddington, wearing a three-piece navy blue pinstriped suit, who'd just strode into the room from the hallway and was now in the midst of seating himself in the previously unoccupied chair, said, "I have found that vulgarity during business meetings lowers the tone and hinders progress."

"What?" said Irene, making no attempt to hide her annoyance.

She'd only met Luddington for the first time 15 minutes ago, when they'd convened this meeting, but had already disliked him prior to that, based on his emails: long-winded, pretentious, condescending gibberish in the body and a string of unrecognized acronyms appended to his name in the many-lines-long signature. When her assistant, Donald Piper (who'd been friends since middle school with Ty's son Carnick), had suggested bringing him on board to advise on financial matters, Irene had initially sneered at the idea, but had eventually, with the strong encouragement of the other team members, very grudgingly relented.

"Now, where were we?" Luddington asked, fiddling with and staring at a small stack of papers on the table in front of him.

"Nowhere," said Irene. "As soon as we started, you excused yourself to go to the restroom."

"As I understand it," said Luddington, "the artificial intelligence capabilities within your software product are experiencing some difficulties."

"Right. The shit isn't working properly. *Very* frustrating! I mean, it *was* working, and now it's not. You're gonna say 'I told ya so,' right, Stan the Man?"

"Not at all," Stan replied in a gentle, sincere voice, smiling.

"As I understand it," said Luddington, "fixing this problem will require the purchase of third-party services, and the General Fund has been largely depleted."

"Well, I don't know what the fuck the 'General Fund' even is, but... If you mean we're broke, then yes, we are. To say that sales have slumped would be the understatement of the fucking year! And yeah, I think to reverse that we're gonna need to fix the A.I. somehow."

"Indeed."

"But, as for services... Well... Yes, probably. I mean, brainiac over here,"—she made a quick head-and-eyes motion in Stan's direction—"he designed—and built, in his own private little home microelectronics lab, holy shit!—this little plug-in piece, you know, that snaps into the phone jack, that's supposed to, like, give the A.I. a shot in the arm, or whatever."

"So, fixing this problem will require the purchase of third-party services."

Irene only spoke after a moment of simply looking at Luddington with a face of mild confusion and contempt. "Like I said: yeah, probably. I mean the plug-in thingie is brilliant, and it does seem to help quite a bit, from what we can tell... But, you know, it's still kind of a roll of the dice... plus, cumbersome, awkward... increases hardware production costs..."

"In essence there are three ways to grow the General Fund," said Luddington. "The first way is to boost sales."

"Yeah, sort of a catch-22 situation there, as I was saying."

"Not necessarily. Sales can be boosted through a number of methods, such as increased advertising—"

"Again... More advertising costs more money. Facebook and Amazon—"

"I recommend canceling your contracts with Facebook and Amazon. There are—"

"I can't just cancel them on the spot. I'm locked in for six months."

"The second way to grow the General Fund is to cut costs," said Luddington. "Where do you feel your business might stand a bit of trimming?"

"Nowhere," said Irene. "We're already cut right down to the bone."

"As I understand it, most of your marketing, sales, packaging and distribution is being handled by Amazon."

Irene sighed and rolled her eyes. "Yes, correct. And Facebook."

"I recommend canceling your contracts with Facebook and Amazon. There are less costly alternatives for handling your marketing, sales, packaging and distribution."

"Yeah, I know there are. We looked into some of those, back in the summer. But the thing is—"

"Sorry I'm late, everyone," said Donald Piper, briskly entering the room.

"You weren't invited," said Irene.

"Oh—hi, Uncle Ty!" Donald said to Luddington with a big smile.

"I've told you repeatedly not to call me that!" snapped Luddington.

"Donald," said Irene, "why don't you make yourself useful and order us some pizza?"

"Uh... Okay." Donald looked nervous. "Can I put it on the company card?"

"Yes."

"Okay." He smiled, then turned and dashed out of the room.

"The third way to grow the General Fund is to attract new investment," said Luddington.

"It's a nice idea," said Irene. "I would love it if we could! But I think we've already exhausted all the options."

"Venture capital comes in all shapes and sizes," Luddington offered, attempting a smile for the first time today with a result that illustrated why he so seldom attempted.

"Yeah!" scoffed Irene. "Not *our* shape and size."

"Organizations exist," said Luddington, "operating through the World Wide Web, which act as a brokerage of sorts for obtaining investment streams from ordinary citizens of all stripes."

"What?"

"I believe they have names like 'Kick-Starter,' or, 'Go-And-Fund-Me'..."

"Oh, right." Another eyeroll. "Yeah, we tried that already. No fucker wanted to kick-start us or go fund us."

"You might wish to consider..." He paused deliberately, eyes twinkling, cracking another pseudo-smile. "Investing. In. Yourself!"

"What?" Irene was near the end of her rope.

"A monetary infusion from your own personal funds."

"I ain't got no 'personal funds' left, dude. That ship sailed a while ago."

"Well, how about your home equity?"

"Nope! Already leveraged it to the max a few years ago when we remodeled the bathroom."

"Well, though it carries significant risk, you could consider making use of credit cards."

Irene stood up. "I maxed out my last one to pay you your gigantic up-front fee, Mister Expert Consultant!"

Luddington looked somewhat taken aback.

Now halfway to the door of the conference room and heading for it fast, Irene called out over her shoulder, "Which I'm guessing is nonrefundable, right? Christ!"

Darrell Barry-Straw, age 15, standing on the sidewalk running alongside all the strip mall storefronts, was deeply engrossed in his phone activities and didn't notice a middle-aged woman bursting through one of the nearby doors, sighing, quickly surveying the parking lot sprawled out in front of her, and lighting up a cigarette.

Irene didn't truly notice him, either, initially. But then, after a few drags and several fretful thoughts about her current business predicament, she realized, out of the corner of her eye, that a few feet from her stood not just a kid with a phone, but a kid with a phone with a contraption on his head. As she turned her own head to get a proper look, a surge of emotion shot through her—a mix of shock, thrill and fear.

"Fuck me," she muttered to herself; then, louder, to him, "Hey, kid!"

Darrell looked up at her with a blank expression.

"Take that thing off for a sec," she said, stepping toward him and miming the requested action with her own arms, lit cigarette still pinched between two fingers of her right hand, its smoke curling slowly upward.

Darrell complied, though his face had shifted from blank to mildly confused and irritated.

Irene took a drag, then said, cigarette hand stabbing the air in the direction of the S.O.L. headset Darrell was now holding against his torso, "Where'd you get that?"

"My parents got it for me. For my birthday. No idea why. I asked for—"

"How do you like it so far?"

"Hey,"—he pointed at the cigarette—"think I could get one of those?"

"What? No! Jesus. Tell me what you think of your birthday present."

"Shit."

"Excuse me?"

"It's a piece of shit. It doesn't fucking work right."

Irene could feel the rage welling up inside her. "You kiss your mother with that mouth?" she snapped.

"What?"

Try to keep your cool, she thought. This is a learning opportunity. "What's so shitty about it?" Her voice was still a bit edgy.

"The track choices are pretty gay," said Darrell. "Everywhere I go, it always plays these, like, sad love songs that I've never even heard of before. Like, oh boo-hoo, I'm so sad, my partner left me, or whatever. With like, slow, sad music and shit. And the controls don't make any sense..."

"The controls are made for smart people," said Irene. "Sounds like user error to me."

Darrell's blank face had returned. He seemed to have been neither offended nor enlightened by her words.

"Sorry," Irene said after a second. She took a final drag, then dropped the cigarette and stepped on it.

"I'm not always this much of a bitch. Just..." A long pause and a deep sigh. "Some bad crap has been happening to me lately."

Though not visibly sympathetic at all, Darrell said, "Yeah. I know how that goes."

"Oh, really?" Irene asked with a smirk. "What's the worst thing that ever happened to you in your whole life?"

Darrell made a thinking face for a moment, then said, "Probably my birthday party when I turned 13. I had my friends over for swimming and a sleepover, and, first my friend Jeremy cut his foot on some broken glass by the pool, because my sister had like a temper tantrum and threw a cup out the window. And then, my friend Zack tried to a do a cannonball and he knocked out one of his teeth and he was, like, screaming and bleeding all over the place, and my parents had to call his parents to come pick him up. And then, when we were having cake and ice cream, my friend Jason suddenly puked all over the floor for no reason. And then—"

"Okay, that's enough," Irene said with equal parts amusement and annoyance. "Trust me, kid—that event was something that happened to your parents, not you."

The blank stare was back again.

"So... Too many sad breakup songs, huh?"

"Yeah."

"I happen to think some of those songs are pretty good." She paused, thinking of Phil Collins's early 1980s hit "Against All Odds," which S.O.L. had selected for her during a recent Life Stroll.

"Usually when I hear them, though... You know how, you're supposed to identify with the singer, who's been dumped and they're all desperate and heartbroken. But I always... Instead I always identify with the other person. The one who did the dumping." She grinned. "I mean, I do feel sad, for the pain the singer is going through, but I don't feel like it's my own pain. I feel like, I'm the one who caused the pain. Isn't that weird?"

"I guess."

After a long silence that would've felt awkward to many people but didn't to either of these two, Irene said "Oh!" and reached into her pocket. "I have something for you."

She brought out Stan's recent invention, which resembled a very small thumb drive or the receiver component for a wireless keyboard or mouse, and held it out toward Darrell in the palm of her hand.

"Just to borrow," she added. "You bring it back to me tomorrow."

He looked at the tiny device, then at her. "What is it?" he asked.

"Plug it into your phone. It'll improve the performance of S.O.L."

"What?"

"This!" she said, jabbing the headset with the index finger of her other hand. Her mood was starting to swing back the other way again. "It'll make *this*"—another jab—"work better."

"Oh. Okay." Darrell rather tentatively reached out and took the piece.

"And as for the settings, just use all the defaults. To begin with."

"What?"

A sudden, calamitous burst of sound from behind her prompted Irene to whirl around. Upon doing so, she saw Donald, having just emerged from the office, glance over at her as he crossed the sidewalk in a rapid stride toward the parking lot.

"Uncle Ty said he doesn't like pizza," Donald announced without slowing down. "I'm going to pick up his order from La Trattoria Costosa..."

Forty-eight hours later, Yvonne Smede was walking west on Arkansas Avenue, having said goodbye to Bill Smede at his apartment five minutes ago after they'd gone for coffee and a few neighborhood loops together. It was a gorgeous day, and Yvonne smiled, thinking of how nice life was (a thought she didn't have very often), and in particular the people she had the pleasure of sharing it with, and in particular Bill, who'd been delightful company this morning. (Well, mostly delightful. She couldn't deny that experiencing the attendant irritants of these sidewalks—dogs and Phone World dwellers and gardening noises and vehicular noises and construction noises—was rendered additionally irritating by hearing someone constantly complain about them.)

Lately things between Bill and Yvonne had taken a romantic turn, starting late last Saturday night when he'd abruptly kissed her while they were sitting together on the front steps of the condo, enjoying the cloudless sky and a sneaky (and very unusual, for both of them) cigarette. Over the past six and a half days, that kiss had been followed by several others, as well as a bit of sex, and no discussion at all of where things stood between them—which suited Yvonne just fine and, she suspected, suited Bill even better.

In the days leading up to the kiss, she'd half-expected it, and had felt mildly curious about if and when it would happen. Her entire history with Bill had been somewhat of a love rollercoaster, and although it had brought many very powerful emotions, both positive and negative, she'd never fretted over the course of things or nursed any strong wishes about where they'd go next. And these recent days were no exception. But she was glad he'd kissed her.

Rounding the corner onto Wexler Avenue, Yvonne nearly collided with a young man on an electric scooter as he whizzed past. Already being subjected to harsh judgment for this, the man fell even further in her estimation a split second later when she noticed the eight-foot leash connecting his hand to the collar of a small dog, who was frantically racing along behind the scooter, struggling desperately and almost unsuccessfully to keep up. She shook her head incredulously and momentarily considered yelling at the man or even attempting to give chase, reach down, and detach the leash from the collar, but instead carried on walking the opposite way.

She saw a homeless man across the street, lounging on the sidewalk near a palm tree, who seemed vaguely familiar—not just like she'd seen him before, but perhaps actually met him. Could it be? He appeared to be speaking to somebody, in a rather cheerful, animated fashion, but nobody was with him. Rufus glanced over and saw Yvonne, too.

And he too felt maybe they'd met, but couldn't quite place her.

A car cruised past with all its windows open and music playing at a volume seemingly almost guaranteed to cause the driver hearing loss, a very common practice in L.A. and one that normally annoyed Yvonne but not this time, because the song was one she recognized, a favorite from her youth. She was immediately back in that world (despite not having thought about it at all for many, many years), adoring her boyfriend Bobby Hinton and frolicking in Lake Sammamish with him, his buddy Troy, Troy's girlfriend Angie, four inner tubes, and a case of beer.

Funny, Yvonne thought, how a song gets sentimentally linked in your mind with a person or an event simply because of the time in your life when you heard the song—nothing to do with what the song is actually about. She realized she'd never known (or particularly cared) what this song was about, even though she could probably recite all the lyrics. And who was it by? Spin Doctors? She smiled and shook her head. The car was gone now, but the song played on inside her mind. In fact its subject was the fleeting nature of an epiphanic moment, and it was performed by Toad the Wet Sprocket.

As she approached her building, Yvonne saw a yellow taxi pull up outside it. She already knew the identity of the passenger before he climbed out of the back and stood by the driver's window, thrusting a fistful of cash through it: her father, Al Forrester, a.k.a. Gramps.

His visits were always announced in advance, but always with a vague timetable like "this weekend," and he insisted on having his own key and arranging his own transportation (in one direction, that is—he was perfectly happy to abruptly request a lift home from his daughter, usually at an inconvenient and high-traffic time). She'd warned Bill this morning about the probable impending arrival of Gramps, which had precipitated Bill's returning to his apartment after their walk rather than coming to hang out at the condo with her.

"Hi, Dad," Yvonne called out as she came up the sidewalk behind where he was now also walking along, his business with the driver concluded.

He stopped and turned around just as she caught up with him. "Ah, hello, darling," he said. "Perfect timing."

Placing his bag on the ground momentarily, he put his hands on her shoulders, leaned forward, and planted a quick kiss on her cheek. Yvonne smiled a genuine smile—she truly felt pleased to see her dad.

For now, at least.

They went side by side along the concrete footpath, up the stairs, and into the condo.

"Hi, Gramps," said Patrick Smede, standing in the middle of the living room amidst a sea of cardboard boxes.

At the far end of that sea stood Patrick's best friend, Leonard "Len" Park, who did not react to their arrival. His body was entirely still, as was his face, which was aimed toward the front window. It was unclear whether he was gazing at something outside, listening to something on his wireless earbuds, both, or neither.

"Well hello there, Patrick," said Gramps. "How's the main man?"

Patrick grinned. "Good," he replied. "I'm moving!"

Gramps turned to Yvonne. "What's with all the boxes?" he asked.

"Patrick is moving out, Dad. He and Len are getting an apartment together." She tried to indicate with her tone and facial expression that this was kind of a big deal.

Gramps paused for a second, possibly or possibly not digesting the new information, then said, "And where's my favorite granddaughter?"

"Oh, I think she's probably in her room," said Yvonne, starting to head in that direction. "Why don't you have a seat, Dad?"

"Where? On top of a box?"

Patrick laughed, then said, "Alice isn't here."

"Oh," Yvonne said, stopping halfway to the back of the condo and turning around again. "She went out somewhere?"

"Yeah."

"Heh, that sweet, crafty little scamp," Gramps muttered, sitting down on one of the dining chairs. "Always out and about, doing her thing."

"Do you know where she went?" Yvonne asked her son.

"No," he said. "She was moving her stuff into my room... I mean, um, the room that *was* mine..."

"Yeah?"

"Yeah, so I told her that room was going to become your office. Then she left."

Yvonne rolled her eyes as she joined her father at the dining table. "Nothing's been decided for sure yet," she said. "Most likely the den will be my office."

"Seemed like she might've been angry," Patrick added, shrugging his shoulders.

"Yeah, *okay*, Patrick. Thank you."

Yvonne turned to Gramps, who was now staring across the room at Len, seeming to have just noticed him for the first time.

"Can I get you anything, Dad?"

He shifted his gaze to her and smiled. "No thanks, darling. I'm fine."

"So..." She wracked her brain for conversation fuel. "How've you been?"

He made a sound that was half "Meh," half grunt. "The same as always. My back hurts like the dickens."

"Oh! So tell me about you and... uh..." She wanted to use Bill's mother's first name, but couldn't think of it. She really didn't want to say "Bill's mother"... Come on, what's her name? "Uh..." Why is he just raising his eyebrows at me? He knows who I mean. "Uh..." This is insane. "Mamsy! You and Mamsy."

"Who?"

"Oh, come on, Dad! Bill's mother. You went out with her."

"Oh, Cathy. Yes. What a delightful lady."

"So, you had a good time?"

"Such a tragedy, having those two as her children."

"Dad! Please focus. And try not to be so rude. For once."

"What, darling? What?" His face, voice, shoulders and hands worked in concert to beam intense innocence and ignorance at Yvonne.

"Did you have a good time with Cathy?"

"Well, yes. Yes, of course. We had a marvelous time."

"So you're going to see her again?"

"Where is Billy, anyway? He's not lurking around here somewhere, is he?"

Yvonne sighed. "No, Dad. He's not here right now."

"I hope you've finally stopped wasting your time with him."

Yvonne just stared at Gramps.

"So you can finally meet someone worthwhile."

The silent staring continued.

"You know—a real man."

"Dad, I..."

"What?"

"Nnnf... Forget it. Just... Are you going to see Cathy again?"

"No, I doubt it."

"Why? Did something go wrong?"

"Not at all. Everything went great."

"Well why, then?"

Gramps made a sort of "Ennh" sound, accompanied by a dismissive wave of the hand. "She doesn't want to go with a man like me."

"How do you know?"

"I can tell. I can read people, darling. Now don't get me wrong—she likes me. She likes me a *lot*. But, she thinks I'm too good for her."

Yvonne gave her father one of the most skeptical faces in the history of faces.

"She *does*. Trust me."

They stared at each other.

"I'm not saying that I *am* too good for her. Because I'm not. Obviously. But that's what she believes."

Another brief moment of mutual staring.

"So it could never work between us."

"God, Dad," said Yvonne, rolling her eyes and involuntarily cracking a very small smile. But his attention was elsewhere now.

"Hey," he said to Len, who'd come over to the near side of the room to mumble something to Patrick and was now standing very close to the table, his hands meandering around over the top of one of the boxes. "What's your name, young man? Is it Ling?"

Len looked startled, then smiled, took a step closer and extended his hand.

"Len," he said. "My name's Len. It's a pleasure to meet you, sir."

Gramps stared at Len's hand for a second as if he were trying to solve a complex math problem, then stood up, shook hands and said, "Al Forrester."

Len smiled. "Cool. Nice to meet you, Mr. Forrester."

Gramps smiled too.

Despite the benign and hope-inspiring start of this interaction, Yvonne was monitoring the situation closely from her seat, with her internal cringe-ometer, fight-or-flight tactical command center, and damage control resources management authority all on high alert.

"You talk just like an American," said Gramps.

Yvonne braced. Mayday, we're going down.

"Um..." stammered Len. "I *am* an American."

"Where are you from?" Gramps asked.

"Um... I'm from... Downey."

"No, no… I mean originally. Are you Chinese or Japanese?"

"Um… Neither one. I'm Korean."

"Can you tell the difference between Chinese people and Japanese people just by looking at them?"

"What?"

Gramps was reaching into his back pocket. "Some orientals say they can tell the difference." He pulled out a bulging black leather wallet, packed far beyond its intended capacity. "But I don't believe them."

"Dad," said Yvonne, "leave poor Len alone."

"It's okay, Ms. Smede," said Len.

Gramps was rifling through the wallet. "So Ling," he said, "can you tell the difference between Chinese and Japanese just by looking at them?"

"Um, I don't know… I mean… probably, sometimes, I might, um…"

Yvonne glanced over at Patrick. He was rummaging through a box, seemingly totally unaware of this conversation.

Gramps had produced a small photo and was holding it up for Len to see. "Is this man Chinese or Japanese?"

"Um, that's the Japanese prime minister," said Len.

"So what's your answer? That he's Japanese? If so, you are correct."

"Yeah, but… I already knew who he was, so, um…"

"But if you didn't already know who he was, would you still know, just from this picture, that he's Japanese?"

"Um… Yes. I think so."

Gramps was shaking his head and thumbing through the wallet again. "No, no," he muttered. "You're just saying that because you already knew who he was…"

"Come on, Dad," Yvonne entreated. "That's enough. Hey, why don't we go for lunch somewhere?"

"Hang on, darling," he replied. Then, showing Len another photo, "Okay, how about this one? Chinese or Japanese?"

"That guy is white," said Len.

"So?"

"So, um… He isn't Chinese or Japanese."

"Wrong!" Gramps exclaimed triumphantly. "This is my lifelong friend, Sheldon."

Len smiled in bewilderment.

Gramps continued, "He lives in Japan with his Japanese wife, Nashko."

"Oh, um... Okay."

"Dad," said Yvonne, standing up.

"And he is a Japanese citizen," Gramps added with a smirk and a flick of the eyebrows.

"Cool," said Len, followed by a nervous chuckle.

"Pretty impressive, eh, darling?"

"What? Your friend Sheldon?"

"No. Me. For having a friend who's an oriental. You always accuse me of being a racist. Hmmf."

"Why don't we just go for lunch, Dad..."

"Hang on." Gramps was digging in the wallet again. "I've got another one for Ling, here..."

Yvonne brought out the big guns. "Hey, how about we have lunch at Howard's House?"

"Ooh," said Gramps, eyes lighting up. "Great idea, darling."

He hurriedly closed the wallet and stuffed it back into his pocket. "I love Howard's House. You're going to love it, too. Come on, let's go."

————————————

At 10:00 the following morning, a huge family-style vehicle rolled into the identical-to-thousands-of-others-nearby driveway of an identical-to-thousands-of-others-nearby house in Orange County, paused briefly as the garage door went up, then proceeded in, came to a stop, and cut its engine.

Inside were two people, both with full stomachs and in relatively good spirits after having completed one of their traditional periodic breakfast outings together. In the driver's seat was Irene Hoffman, co-owner (or, in her mind, owner) of the vehicle and the house; in the passenger seat was her longtime friend (who felt wary of owning (or driving) anything), Bill Smede.

They both hopped out and sauntered toward the back of the vehicle, Irene singing quietly and mindlessly to herself, "Yeah life is such a drag when you're living in the past..." Their paths converged a couple of steps outside the garage in the mid-December sunshine.

"Well," said Bill, "great seeing you, as always."

"It was good to see you too, dumbass," Irene replied.

Then they moved in for a lightweight, token hug, which Bill couldn't help feeling a bit awkward about, owing to their having spontaneously had sex in Irene's office two months ago (though he was pleased the topic hadn't been brought up at all this morning or any other time since then).

In occasional moments of complete self-honesty, Bill recognized that he'd briefly, in the days following that thrilling encounter, entertained the notion that, conceivably maybe, it might possibly lead to something developing between the two of them. But he'd quickly dismissed this as silly, impractical, and not really desirable anyway. Ultimately he'd filed away the incident in his mind as one that didn't really "mean" anything to him (and certainly not to her!), and which definitely shouldn't ever be repeated.

"Alright, take care," he said as he began marching down the driveway toward the ATS, parked at the curb.

"Hey!" Irene called out after glancing at her phone.

Bill stopped and turned. "Yeah?"

"I've still got some time," she said. "You should come in and check out the latest, greatest S.O.L."

This was another topic Bill had hoped to avoid during today's interactions (though for a completely different reason—it was boring to him and the polar opposite of boring to her), and so far had largely, though not entirely, succeeded. Their conversation at the restaurant had included discussion of the Delicious Hot Food Paradox (in which an eater wishes to consume their delicious hot food quickly so it maintains its heat, but simultaneously wishes to consume it slowly so as to properly savor it), the phenomenon of judging somebody upon first meeting them and then later having to amend that judgment—sometimes negatively, sometimes positively—after learning more about them (Bill had experienced numerous examples of both versions, while Irene had experienced only the latter, and only very rarely), and their respective plans for Christmas.

Irene had unintentionally had Bill in stitches describing her standard approach to gifting her children, nieces, and nephews (and even a few adults), which involved forcing them to read the entirety of her lengthy, highly opinionated greeting card inscriptions by lacing them with small, cryptic clues used to deduce a PIN that could then be entered into a phone app (written by Stan Wojcik) to unlock the money that conventionally would've been enclosed with the card in paper or plastic form.

They'd also shared a chuckle over the ancient art, practiced by both of them during their teens and twenties, of recycling love songs—linking a given sappy, sentimental, heart-tugging recording very tightly with a particular person, the object of one's intense love (unrequited or otherwise), and then, at some later point in time, linking the very same tune, just as closely and for the same reason, with a completely different person. Bill had cleverly managed to segue into this subject, using the commonality of music, after being subjected to S.O.L. talk for a couple of minutes.

"Come on, you piece of shit!" Irene finally shouted now, fed up with Bill standing still in the middle of her driveway, making a continuous quiet moaning/grunting sound, eyes flicking back and forth between his wrist and her. "It's not like you've got some place you need to be! Don't think for a second I don't know you're just looking at your fuckin' step count."

Bill grinned, shrugged, and began walking back toward her. "Yeah, okay—you got me," he said.

Five minutes later, they were standing in Irene's kitchen, clutching glasses of lemonade ("Fresh from my extremely tiny harvest, except frozen for six weeks," she'd quipped), following an introduction between Bill and the younger half of Irene's offspring, which had occurred perhaps three or four other times since they'd been delivered into the world. Each time, they'd had no recollection whatsoever of his existence and he'd fared only marginally better at remembering theirs. Alex was sitting at the informal dining table (the only dining table in this house) in the "breakfast nook" area adjacent to the kitchen, calmly perusing an issue of Newport Lifestyle magazine. Connor was flitting around in a frenetic fashion that stunned Bill and put him on edge; the boy was seemingly both in the kitchen and not in the kitchen simultaneously, continuously.

"Mommy," he whined, "Luke and Keith aren't watching me!"

"What are you talking about?" Irene asked in a slightly exasperated tone.

"They were supposed to be watching me, but they went out back to throw the football around."

"Well, your sister is here."

"I wanted to throw the football around!"

Irene's voice grew more stern. "Settle down, Connor Jeffrey. Why don't you read a magazine, like Alex."

"I don't like magazines."

Even more sternly, bordering on angry barking: "Look, I don't care what you do. Just park your butt and shut your mouth!"

Connor stopped flitting, scuttled silently over to the living room and began fiddling with the T.V. and the Xbox.

"Gotta be careful with these boys," Irene said to Bill. "Gotta try to stop them from living in their bubbles."

"You mean like social media?"

"Yeah, that and... really everything on the Internet. The way stuff can shape their beliefs about what's true and false, what's right and wrong... And, you know, which ideas and opinions are stupid, or immoral..."

"Mmm-hmm," Bill said, nodding. "I think there's also a broader, more universal kind of bubble that's just part of human nature. It's always been with us, and always will be, regardless of, you know... how we get our news, or how we use technology, or what kinds of people we interact with..."

Irene was nodding her head and meeting his gaze, but her eyes were beginning to glaze over just a bit.

He went on: "It's this basic, unconscious assumption that the way we experience the world is the way everybody experiences it, that our own thought processes are the only reasonable kind, that our emotional reactions to things are the natural, normal, correct ones. And that... anything we feel certain about, of course we must be right, and anyone who disagrees—if there even are any such folks—is messed up somehow. That our personal values are universal values, that the stuff occupying our minds is the stuff occupying everyone's minds..."

Bill's phone began ringing. He took it out, saw that it was a 310 number he didn't recognize, silenced it, and put it back in his pocket.

"Probably my friend Matt," he said.

Irene was now looking at her own phone and couldn't have cared less who was calling Bill or why.

He went on, "Doesn't want to try digging where his 'treasure map' says to dig until we've made some ridiculous road trip… Ugh. I know I can't keep avoiding him forever, but…"

Irene looked up from her phone and sighed. "I have too many advisers," she said.

"Well, you won't get any advice from me," Bill replied with a smirk.

"Well, too many shitty ones, anyway." She looked down again, gave the screen a little scroll, and let out another sigh. "I'm looking at these Ass-Backward folks, trying to figure out if I should approach them again…"

"Ass-backward? Doesn't sound like—"

"Oh, that's just what I call them. Their real name is Abst Blackboard, or just A.B. for short. Stupid name! Founded by this young punk, Seymour Abst—comes from a long line of mega-rich east coast fuckers going all the way back to… like, the robber barons…"

"Fuckers!" shouted Connor from the T.V. area, then giggled.

Bill's phone made a pinging sound, indicating a voicemail had been left.

"So anyway," Irene went on, "pondering looking at them for the next round of funding—if I even need another round, that is. Probably never will, actually. Anyway, Luddington the Luddite recommended them. That should be reason enough for me to forget it, right?" She chuckled.

Bill smiled and concentrated hard on maintaining his "I'm interested" face.

"I mean, we looked at them before, back at the beginning, but, they only work with businesses that are already up and running, which we weren't at the time. But now it's a different story. But, I don't know, they seem like their thing is more like being a partner than an investor. They provide all this guidance and they work with you on 'brand building'…"—she used a mocking tone and made air quotes with her fingers—"Just seems like, too many strings attached, you know?"

Bill made a "Mmm" sound to indicate acknowledgment and passive agreement. Then many seconds passed during which Irene continued mulling over the A.B. question while Bill attempted to cut through the fog that had filled his brain and formulate some kind of plan for getting the conversation moving again, ideally in a different direction.

Finally, unable to come up with anything better, he said, "So the business is going pretty well, huh?"

"*Yeah* it is! Well, it's about to be. We hit a little snag recently..."

"Oh yeah?"

"Yeah, no biggie. You know that A.I. stuff we did, back in the summer. It, uh... well it kind of started getting all funky on us."

"Told you so."

"Hah-hah, Mister Comedian. Well it's not a problem anymore, okay? It's all taken care of."

"Oh yeah?"

"Yep. Bringing in an outside A.I. firm. They're gonna fix the problem, lickety-split. Not the place that three-piece-suit-wearing *moron* recommended. Stan knew a better one. More expensive, but, you get what you pay for. They're solid. They'll get it done right."

"I thought you were having money trouble."

"Ah—yes, we *were*. Not anymore. Got the A.I. development covered. Plus the rollout of the patch. *And* another round of manufacturing. Plus more. We're flush now, William."

"Wow, cool."

"Yes, very cool. Keith hooked me up—Keith, of all people, can you believe it? Knew this guy from work who knew this dude over in Santa Ana, Chuck Jones. And he knows how to get his hands on money. And I mean *serious* stacks of cash. Literally—he handed me a briefcase full of cash. Incredible."

Bill raised an eyebrow. "Seriously?"

"Yeah. He said it was better that way. You know, simpler. Less paperwork and... accounting..."

"You do accounting for a living."

"Not because I enjoy it! This way I got the best possible interest rate, and we cut out all the skimmers, and just... the bullshit."

"Bullshit!" exclaimed Connor.

"Watch your mouth, kid. But yes, it's true. We do away with the bullshit and just get on with our business. There are no strings attached. It's so... liberating!"

"This guy sounds like some kind of loan shark," said Bill.

"What? No! He's totally legit, dude. He just happens to be man a who recognizes a great business idea and isn't afraid to put complete trust in the fucking *genius* who came up with it."

"Fucking!" yelled Connor.

Bill's phone started ringing again. He took it out, saw that it was his mother, silenced it, and put it back in his pocket.

"Ugh," he said.

"So, yeah—trust," Irene continued. "It's all about trust, William, my friend. I feel good. I think this thing is about to really take off."

"So what does Judy think about this Chuck Jones guy?" Bill asked.

"Oh, Judy's out. I fired her."

"What?!"

"Yeah. On Friday, actually."

"Why?"

"I told you, too many shitty advisers..."

"But, she's your friend..."

"Yes, and she's a wonderful person. But I gotta keep that separate from business. And when it comes to business, she blows. She blew it, again and again."

"Wow..."

"I mean, she's the one who brought in that fuckhead, Luddington."

From the T.V. area: "Fuckhead!"

"Is she?" Bill queried. "I thought you said it was Donald."

"Oh, right," said Irene. "Yeah, you're right—it was Donald who found him. But Judy's the one who drew up his contract, which was what really screwed us over."

"Uh, didn't you say *you* wrote the contract? Because you couldn't trust Judy to do it?"

"Exactly. She can't be trusted."

"Irene!" a voice shouted unexpectedly from somewhere out of view, accompanied by the sound of a door slamming. It was Keith Hoffman, Irene's husband.

"Hi, Daddy," said both Connor and Alex, nearly in unison.

"Keith," Irene said, moving toward the breakfast nook, as he appeared from around the corner and walked right up to her, a very strange look on his face, like madness. His eyes were wide; his cheeks were bright red.

"Irene," he said loudly, "I need to talk to you."

"Keith, what are you doing here? You're supposed to be working."

"I quit!" he replied angrily.

"What?! You can't quit. We need—"

"I'm leaving you, Irene," Keith said in a deliberately dramatic voice. "This marriage is over."

A few milliseconds went by before she responded, during which her eyes narrowed and her jaw tightened, both minutely. Then: "Alex, take your brother outside right now and play football with your other brothers."

"Okay, Mommy," replied Alex, leaping into action with astonishing swiftness and precision.

It was extremely quiet for the next 15 seconds as she deftly collected up Connor and made herself and him scarce through the sliding glass door leading out to the back patio.

"Keith," said Irene once the slider had closed, "what the fuck is wrong with you?"

Tears had begun streaming down his cheeks. "This isn't because you cheated on me," he said. "It's because of the way you've treated me. For months and months and months. You've treated me like *shit*!"

Unmoved, Irene said, "Jesus. Pull yourself together, you stupid piece of—"

"You see?" he yelled, wagging a finger in her face. "That's what I'm talking about. No respect! You don't respect me."

"Respect has to be earned, Keith." She remained quite calm.

"Making me work all these... *fucking* jobs..." Keith was trembling, apparently on the verge of either violence or collapse. "Just to... to get *money*... so you can have your... your fucking *business*..." He waved his hands and arms around now, to emphasize the lunacy of Irene's priorities.

She stared at him, thinking hard, trying to figure out how to handle this.

"And as if the jobs weren't enough," he continued, "you've got me taking care of the kids, and taking care of the home, and... I even *saved* your damn business by putting you in touch with Chuck Jones..."

"Come on," said Irene, "that guy's nothing but a loan shark and you know it."

Bill's phone started ringing yet again. "Sorry," he muttered, hurriedly pulling it out and silencing it. The only reason he was still here was that the Hoffmans (neither of whom noticed the phone or the apology) were physically blocking the way out of the kitchen.

"But do I get *any* appreciation at all," Keith said, "for *any* of this? No! In fact, I get the *opposite* of appreciation from you..."

"Keith," Irene said, "let's just—"

"You treat me like shit. Like worthless... shit. But that's not why

I'm leaving you. I'm leaving you because you cheated on me. When I think about you with... with him... I just..." He clenched his fists and his face went a slightly brighter shade of red than it'd already been. "It makes me want to... smash his face in!"

"Just take a deep breath, Keith," said Irene.

"No! I don't want to take a deep breath. I don't want to do *anything* you tell me to do *anymore*."

He paused and took a deep breath, after which he seemed considerably calmer.

"Fuck you, Irene," he then said in a level voice, before turning and striding quickly and purposefully away.

A moment later came the sound of a door slamming.

"Wow," said Irene, turning toward Bill. "Well I don't know what brought *that* on... but it's not good."

"Irene..."

"Bad for the family, bad for the business. This can't stand. This needs to be fixed."

"Irene! Why did you tell him what happened with us?" Bill was as openly incensed as Bill ever got with another person. (Inanimate objects, environmental elements, and his own inconsequential blunders were a different story entirely.)

Irene made a dismissive noise with her mouth, similar to a pretend fart sound. "Don't worry about it," she said. "I didn't tell him it was you."

"Well why did you tell him about it at all?"

She shrugged. "I don't know... Seemed like I should. 'Cause, you know, he's my husband and shit. But... Mmmf..." She rolled her eyes. "Yeah. *Clearly* that was a mistake..."

Bill's phone, which was still in his hand, emitted a text sound. He glanced down and saw that the message consisted of just "911!!"

"Mom, are you okay?" he said two minutes later, standing in Irene's driveway, holding his phone to his ear.

"Yes, yes, I'm fine."

"Well why did you text me 9-1-1?"

"Because it's the only way to get your attention! You always ignore me."

"Mom, have you ever heard the story of the boy who cried wolf?"

"Of course I have! I used to read it to you when you were a little boy."

Bill sighed. "Well, anyway… You've got me now, so… What would you like to talk about?"

A silence on the line. Then, "How have you been doing lately?"

Bill sighed again. "Fine, Mom. I've been doing fine. Uh… How about you?" He began to regret his next words—born mysteriously and very spontaneously from the deep recesses of his overloaded, muddled, agitated brain—even as he was speaking them. "How was your date with Yvonne's dad?"

"Oh, it was wonderful! Such a sweet, charming man."

"Are you sure you're not confusing Yvonne's dad with some other man?"

"What do you mean?" Mamsy asked, confused.

"Never mind. So you're going to see him again?"

"Oh, no, probably not."

"Why?"

"Al doesn't want to go with a gal like me."

"Why not? He doesn't like you?"

"No, he likes me. He likes me a *lot*. I can tell. But, unfortunately, he has his hang-ups and, well…"

"What?"

"He thinks he's too good for me."

"Well, don't take it personally, Mom. That's just the way he is."

"He's *not* too good for me. Obviously. But *he* thinks he is. So it's just not going to work, I'm afraid."

"Hmm, okay, well… Sorry to hear that."

"We still need to plan Christmas Day," said Mamsy.

"Aha," said Bill. "The real reason for the 9-1-1."

"What time will you be arriving?"

"Well, Mom, a lot of things are up in the air. I don't even know if—"

"Oh, it's going to be so wonderful! I just can't wait. Did I tell you my darling nephew Roger is coming?"

Chapter 19

It was a Thursday in early January, and for several hours there'd been thick clouds floating overhead and intermittent light rain—fairly typical Southern California weather in January (on Thursdays and other days, too).

In the parking lot of a UShopQuik convenience store in the northwestern part of the city of Gardena, 27-year-old Calliope Waxxon emerged from a white 2009 Dodge Caliber wearing a nervous facial expression and glancing down at the time on her phone—a few minutes past 11 A.M.

Striding purposefully toward the store entrance, she swallowed hard and tucked the phone into the front pouch of her bright red hoodie, where it bumped gently against the other object being carried there, a Glock 26.

An electronic bell sound radiated out from somewhere as Calliope came through the door, and the cashier, a middle-aged white man with thinning, sandy hair and a mustache, gave her an extremely brief, detached look. She turned right, headed toward the coolers, and began scoping the place out. Already she could see that several customers were milling around—not good.

Since early childhood, Calliope had desperately longed to become a successful robber. She'd not been at all lazy or unfocused in pursuing this dream, but nevertheless had made very slow progress on it as she'd contended with some of her (under the circumstances, rather unfortunate) fundamental traits: cautious, fearful, indecisive, and easily intimidated by almost every other human being.

Her current visit to this particular UShopQuik was not her first, nor was it her first while carrying a gun, nor her first while fully intending to aim that gun at somebody and demand money from them. But all previous visits had either been officially classified as fact-finding missions or training exercises, or had ended with "chickening out" (a term she frequently used when self-coaching in the bathroom mirror). Meandering around the shop floor now, going over the plan in her mind and waiting for the customer count to tick down, this time felt... different.

After a couple of minutes, as far as she could tell, the only one remaining was an elderly Hispanic woman who'd been hovering around the hot dog warmer for an eternity. Oh, well. Good enough.

Calliope speedily approached the counter, brought out her weapon, aimed it squarely at the cashier and said, "Empty the register! Uh, into one of your plastic bags."

The elderly Hispanic customer, Maria Torres, did not seem to notice (or perhaps simply didn't care) what was going on, and continued her stoic inspection of the pork products on offer.

Another customer, however, who'd been perusing stacks of boxed donuts in a spot near the back of the store that wasn't visible from any of the security mirrors, or from the front, or from almost any vantage point, reacted quite furiously to this latest turn of events. His name was Kip Smyrna, and he was an off-duty (but armed) Gardena cop.

"Holy shit!" screamed Officer Smyrna, then bolted through the nearby "Employees Only" door, across the storage room, and out the back of the building.

Meanwhile, Calliope and the cashier were staring at each other, both silent.

Calliope concentrated hard on the task at hand: don't blink, don't waver, don't tremble, keep aiming straight for the dude's chest. She knew if she looked sufficiently confident and serious, he would never suspect that the gun wasn't loaded. This was a tricky issue with which she was still wrestling—whether she truly felt okay with the notion of shooting someone. Unless and until she'd come to grips with it, best to leave the bullets at home.

The cashier, not moving a muscle (facial or otherwise), was turning the situation over in his mind, struggling to decide what to do. He felt no fear of, nor sympathy for, this young woman standing in front of him, and did feel strongly tempted to reach for his own gun, which was currently sitting under the counter, loaded, a few inches from his right hand, and which he knew very well how to use. Another option would be to attempt to alert the police and then perhaps stall her until they arrived. But neither of these "hero-style" approaches, as they were called by the store owners in numerous policy lectures he'd been on the receiving end of, were the prescribed course of action. No, they'd instructed him to cooperate fully with any would-be criminals on the premises. Get their status changed to "off the premises" A.S.A.P. Then, and only then, report what had happened.

So, he mentally sighed and mentally shrugged and began to reach for the drawer to comply with Calliope's request.

At that moment, she lost her nerve. Quick as a flash, the gun was back inside the hoodie, the door was practically flying off its hinges (with accompanying fake bell sound), and she was tearing across the parking lot, eyes welling up with tears. Not so different after all, she thought angrily. You're pathetic!

Making a snap decision to leave her car for now and return inconspicuously for it later, Calliope executed a sharp left turn and continued her breakneck sprint, not letting up at all as she crossed the remainder of the UShopQuik lot, leapt over a small brick wall, and traversed the entirety of the next parking lot, belonging to a UStoreIt facility.

As Calliope, a shooting streak of red, disappeared behind one of the long, low buildings, a car rolled languidly into the lot—a dark green 2005 Buick LeSabre. It parked in one of the many available spaces, its engine was cut, its driver's door opened, and its sole occupant, Jimmy Sanchez, got out. He placed a bundle of keys into the left pocket of his black leather jacket, then removed a single key, attached to a little circle of thin plastic, from the right pocket, stared at it for a second, and replaced it. Then he took a quick look around himself, shut the car door, and began walking toward the storage units.

A brand-new silver BMW X5 pulled into the lot and speedily made its way to the parking space farthest from Jimmy's car. The engine turned off, the driver's door flew open, and Juice Hughes-Newton sprang out, eyes trained on Jimmy's back as it receded, getting close now to vanishing behind a wall.

"Dammit," she muttered, scowling, as she felt the drizzling rain on her face and head. She only paused a moment, though, then shrugged, shut her car door, and launched herself quite briskly in Jimmy's direction, with the aim of significantly closing the gap between them but still remaining undetected.

Jimmy had warmed up to Juice considerably (and had, she thought she sensed, cooled off considerably toward his wholly untrustworthy wife) since their initial meetings with each other back in late October, during the third of which he'd finally, with some prodding from Yvonne Smede, agreed to give Juice his phone number, alleviating the need for her to make a 2-hours-each-way drive every time she wanted to speak to him. And indeed, they'd had several phone conversations throughout the holiday season, in which Jimmy'd always seemed genuinely interested in trying to help Juice in any way he could.

Yet he'd been of absolutely zero help so far. Whenever she'd asked if he'd gone to the self-storage unit, the answer was always no—with excuses running the gamut, from being too busy, to temporarily forgetting about it, to not knowing where he'd put his key, to not even remembering the location of the facility. And likewise, whenever she'd asked him for alternative theories on the fate of her necklace, the answer had always been the same—he had no idea, and neither did amnesia-ridden Shayla/Nancy. He'd also made it clear, on multiple occasions, that he believed the necklace to be hopelessly lost, very long ago, and not worth fretting about. But he'd never tried to avoid her calls or hurry them to conclusion; on the contrary, he often eagerly chattered away at her on virtually every topic under the sun that didn't interest her.

Finally, yesterday, Juice had extracted a promise from Jimmy that today he absolutely positively definitely would take his key (which he'd finally located) and drive to the storage facility (which he'd also finally located) and search his unit from top to bottom. He'd solemnly sworn to her that if the necklace was in there—he was confident it wasn't, but if it was—then today would be the day when it'd be found and retrieved, and then, at some point in the near future, safely returned to its rightful owner after all these years, perhaps over lunch somewhere.

While Juice had been very pleased to hear this, she'd not entirely trusted Jimmy to get the job done, and had also felt she'd reached a frustration threshold with only being able to pressure and intimidate him over a phone line. Another trip to Hemet was in order. But a more meticulously methodical, less in-your-face one this time. She wouldn't have wanted to risk ruining a smooth operation by interfering with it prematurely. So she'd opted for stealthy monitoring of Jimmy, for the time being, anyway.

True to his word, he'd emerged from his house this morning, gotten into his car, and made the nearly-100-miles journey directly to this

UStoreIt. A small thrill surged through Juice now as she plodded along over the wet asphalt in very high heels, her hairdo being gradually destroyed by the relentless misty rain.

A moment ago he'd stopped walking, outside one of the hundreds of identical-looking giant orange metallic roll-up doors, and had grabbed hold of the padlock that secured it shut. Luckily for Juice, he was about thirty feet from—and she was just passing by—the corner of the massive building. She ducked behind it, waited several seconds, then slowly poked her head out a few inches and took a peek.

He'd removed the padlock and was now hunched over, gripping the handle of the big door, about to raise it.

Juice pulled her head back behind the wall and listened to the long, chaotic, clanging noise of the storage unit being opened up. She grinned.

What now? Maybe head back to the car for a bit, get out of the rain? It might take him a while to look through all his crap. But could he be trusted, to do a thorough job and give an honest report? Maybe just walk in there and offer to help him. But that could freak him out, and then no telling what he might do. Hmm...

She decided she couldn't resist taking a quick look inside the unit. She'd just creep quietly along that 30-foot stretch of wall-and-doors, have herself a slow, subtle gander, and evaluate. He wouldn't know she was here if she didn't want him to.

Juice stepped out from behind the wall, gasped in shock, and lunged back into her hiding place. She'd just seen, apparently about to walk into the storage unit, Nancy Parsons.

"Holy shit," she muttered out loud. The question of how to play this, already a complex one, had just become vastly more so.

Without formulating any strategy, she stepped out again, saw nobody this time, and began a rather hasty tiptoeing toward the unit. *If they see me then they see me. Whatever.*

Easing up to the edge of the big doorway, hugging the wall, she could hear Jimmy speaking in a harsh tone.

"...lying to me about stuff," he was saying, "and, and... staying out all hours... staying away... It's not cool. So don't ask me what I'm doing here. I should be asking *you*, what are *you* doing here. In fact..."

During his long pause Juice became aware of continuous sounds of objects bumping softly against each other, like somebody was shuffling through them.

"How *can* you even be here?" he continued. "How do you even know about this place?"

"My memory's coming back to me, Jimmy." Nancy sounded slightly annoyed, slightly bored.

"It is? Hey, you called me Jimmy!"

"Anyway I'm here to get some of my shit." More shuffling.

"You called me Jimmy. Not Juan."

"Yeah, 'cause it's your fucking name. I'm tired of calling you Juan."

"Tired of it? What's this all about?"

The noises stopped. "I've got *all* my memory back, okay?" Nancy snapped. "I've had it back for a long time."

"I knew it!" Juice whispered to herself.

"You have?" Jimmy asked in bewilderment. "Uh, how long? Since when?"

"Since always, dipshit. Since, like, practically since the day we left the hospital." The shuffling noises resumed.

"But... that's crazy! Why didn't you tell me?"

"Because... I don't know, it would've been a hassle. You would've just been asking me a bunch of damn questions all the time."

"Jesus Lord..." Jimmy sounded like he was really reeling from this revelation.

"Plus it was fun," added Nancy with a small chuckle. "It was fun fucking with you."

"I can't believe this..."

"But it's not fun anymore. I'm sick of it. I'm sick of Hemet. Sick of the double life. Honestly, Jimmy, I'm sick of *you*."

"I've only been trying to protect you..."

A scoffing "Hah!" followed by another chuckle.

"So, you remember everything?"

"Of course I do."

"So, you remember Ned?"

"Of course." More chuckling. "Oh, Jimmy, Jimmy."

"Well I'm glad you find the whole thing so funny!"

For a moment there were no voices, only the shuffling sounds. Then Jimmy spoke again.

"So, then, you *do* remember your old friend Juice..."

"Friend—hah! Of course I remember her. Used to be a sniveling little piece of shit, now a total raving psycho!"

"That's *it*!" roared Juice, stepping out from behind the edge of the storage unit doorway.

Nancy, facing Juice, about six feet inside the unit, was so startled that she dropped both the items she'd been holding, a small metal box and a small wooden box; they hit the concrete floor simultaneously with a loud combo-smack. Jimmy, equally startled (but not holding anything), standing two feet in front of Juice with his back turned, whirled around to face her.

"You bitch!" Juice continued, taking a couple of steps toward Nancy with a triumphant smirk on her face. "Surprised to see me?"

Nancy had regained her composure. "What the hell are you doing here, psycho?" she barked back.

"Yeah," said Jimmy as the two women glared at each other. "What are you doing here, Juice?"

"Justice!" shouted Juice. "I want an apology, for starters. And I want my goddamn necklace back!"

"Get the hell out of here!" yelled Nancy.

"No!" snapped Juice, taking two more steps toward her nemesis and pointing a finger in her face. "Not 'til I get what I came for!"

"Ladies, please..."

"This is private property," said Nancy, her gaze meeting Juice's and carrying a similar amount of contempt. "Don't make me call security."

"Go ahead! While you're whining to the rent-a-cops I'll go through this shit and find what's rightfully mine."

"Nothing here is rightfully yours, psycho!"

"Oh yes it is, you evil bitch. Along with revenge!"

There was a short lull in their verbal exchange, but the hostile glare-off continued. Watching them, Jimmy was grimacing, shaking his head and literally wringing his hands.

Then Nancy said, "I know the guy who owns this place. Trust me, you do *not* want to mess with him."

"Yeah, right!" Juice responded defiantly, but her eyes finally left Nancy's and pointed in Jimmy's direction.

"It's true," he said. "You really shouldn't be here, Juice. You should leave now. I'll call you later."

She looked back at Nancy, who still appeared angry but was now smirking rather than scowling.

Juice felt on the brink of exploding with rage. She narrowed her eyes and stared deep into Nancy's for a full three seconds, teeth clenched and bared, lips curled into an almost grotesque shape. She nearly screamed "Fuuuck!" at the top of her lungs, but managed to hold back, knowing Nancy would enjoy it if she did.

Instead, she raised one finger in front of Nancy's face and said, "This isn't over!"

Then she turned on her heel and strode quickly out of the unit and away, back down the long strip of asphalt toward the parking lot.

Three minutes later, still seething, she yanked open her car door, climbed in, and slammed it shut.

"How'd it go?" asked Yvonne, sitting in the passenger seat with a laptop atop her lap. (After a considerable amount of arm twisting, Yvonne had very grudgingly agreed to come along on today's spy mission, to lend her "super-sleuthing skills" to any potential situation that might benefit from them. But this was still a workday, and she'd been keeping very busy indeed from her mobile office, using her (now scorching hot to the touch) phone as a Wi-Fi hotspot.)

"Nasty Nancy showed up!" Juice exclaimed. "Ruined everything. Started threatening me..."

"Wow."

"Fuuuck!"

Yvonne winced outwardly and rolled her eyes mentally.

"What the fuck am I gonna do now?" said Juice in a quieter, but still too loud, voice.

"I don't know," said Yvonne. "Maybe just give up the whole thing and forget about it?"

Juice was lost in thought and didn't respond.

"Anyway," Yvonne said after a moment, "you might have more pressing problems. You left your phone here..."

Juice glanced over at her friend, only half-registering what was coming into her ears.

"...and, your boss called. Twice."

"What? I don't have a boss."

"Dr. Marquez?"

"Oh..." Juice had almost fully returned to the here and now. "*She* called me?"

"Yeah. Twice in the space of five minutes."

"What did that bitch want?"

"I don't know, Juice. I didn't answer."

"That's okay, I know exactly what she wanted." She sighed. "She is such a pain in my ass. She was complaining last night about me taking a sick day today. Said maybe I could work tomorrow to make up for it. Fuck off, bitch! I'm not working tomorrow. Tomorrow's my day off! Right?"

"Right."

Juice sighed again, said "Shit," shook her head, and sighed a third time. "You know what? I'm tired of South Valley. That place sucks ass. I've had enough of it. You got any openings over at your place?"

"For physicians? I have no idea."

"But you could put in a good word for me, right?"

"I don't know, Juice… I really don't have much to do with the clinical side…"

"This is going to be so cool," said Juice, grinning at her friend. "We're gonna be working together, girl!"

Yvonne managed a weak smile.

"Now come on, let's go grab some lunch."

Thirty-two hours later, Yvonne was taking a sip of wine at a cozy table in Pastiche, wearing her Francisco dress, its namesake sitting across from her, immaculately clothed and groomed, eyes twinkling with warmth and delight as he spoke, and Bill Smede sitting on her right, also taking a sip of wine. The fourth chair at the table was unoccupied. It had been intended for Samantha Weber, Francisco's intended date for this evening, but she'd not shown up, and hadn't answered any of the six times he'd called her.

"So, as can be inferred from these examples," he was currently saying, "receiving compliments, praise, or any sort of positive feedback, generally—exceptions do exist, of course—but, generally, does not directly stroke the ego, in the sense of making one feel proud, or adored, or powerful. Rather, it nourishes the ego indirectly, by providing a form of reassurance—by confirming the validity of one's worldview, or a portion thereof, anyway. It affords one the opportunity to feel that one is doing things 'right,' presenting oneself in a reasonable fashion, perceiving and accounting for the things around one in a way that fits well with other, presumed 'normal,' healthy, aware, individuals."

Yvonne smiled across the table at Francisco but did not give any vocal response or even nod her head.

Bill supplied a slight nod and a "Mmm-hmm" sound. He wasn't sure if he agreed with what had been said or not, and didn't find it interesting enough to try to decide.

Swallowing some of his wine, Francisco noticed that both of the Smedes had nearly run out of theirs and moved hastily to remedy the situation.

As he maneuvered the neck of the bottle toward Yvonne's glass, she covered it with her hand and said, "No, thanks. I've had enough."

His arm froze on the brink of pouring and he looked at her with a face of uncertainty and worry. She looked back at him, expressionless. Bill suppressed a smirk.

After a moment she broke into a smile and said, "Not really," moving her hand away.

Francisco's face relaxed. He chuckled as he filled her glass, then, after setting the bottle down, waved an admonishing finger at her and said, "Yvonne! I must always keep an eye on you."

"Uh, Francisco," said Bill, "I've also not really had enough."

"Oh! Yes," he replied with an embarrassed smile, and reached for the bottle again. "Forgive me, Bill. Yes, of course." He began filling Bill's glass.

"So," said Yvonne to Francisco, "you're back in the game, huh?"

"Pardon me?"

"The dating game. You and Felicia finally called it quits, and..."

"Felaecia. Yes. That was..." He sighed and stared off into space for a moment. "That was... unfortunate, I suppose, in some ways..."

"So tell us about some of your adventures," said Yvonne. "I assume you don't get stood up *every* time?"

Francisco smiled and delivered another finger-wagging, then said, "No, not every time. It does seem, however, that each new effort goes wrong somehow, if not immediately upon undertaking it, then soon afterward."

"Bummer," said Bill.

"Yes, indeed. Recently I have been entertaining the prospect of acquiring a pet dog. As I understand it, the presence of a canine companion can sometimes soften a woman's heart, as well as serving as a catalyst for conversation."

Both Smedes performed the small-nod-with-raised-eyebrows-and-semi-frowning-mouth that signifies the sentiment of "Hmm, yeah, might be worth considering."

"Anyway, that is quite enough about me," Francisco said with a dismissive wave of his hand. "Let us talk about the two of you. It seems you have rekindled your... fire, as it were."

"We may have started to take a passing interest in each other again," Yvonne conceded.

"That is marvelous. Bill, you impress me. In spite of appearances, you are, in fact, quite the Casanova."

"Thanks," said Bill.

"Oh, speaking of which," Francisco continued, "I must relate a humorous incident from last weekend. First, a little background. I recently registered for a service called 'Technical Casanova,' consisting of a collection of written materials, seminars, practical exercises, and mentoring, all related to... to the endeavor of... of meeting and attracting women."

Bill and Yvonne were both smiling, intrigued and already starting to judge. Francisco's face now held a hint of hesitation, but he carried on anyway.

"The concept is that anyone can learn how to succeed in this endeavor—regardless of natural levels of charm, social facility, extroversion, good looks, charisma, and so forth—by simply mastering an expertly formulated system of strategies, techniques and behaviors. I attended the first seminar last Saturday morning, at the Saban Theatre, on Wilshire Boulevard."

"Near my office," said Yvonne.

"Yes, indeed. It would seem that T.C. is, in fact, a one-man operation—a fellow named Chet Whittaker—but he was quite compelling on the stage. He went through several fascinating scenarios in great detail, providing explanations of the relevant underlying principles every step of the way, the entire time energetic and animated. It was rather inspiring."

"I'll bet," said Bill.

"Following the seminar, we went out, 'into the field,' as Mr.

Whittaker calls it, to a nearby park, for a practical demonstration. This was the humorous part to which I referred." He chuckled amusedly.

"I take it he bombed?" Yvonne conjectured.

"He did not fare very well, Yvonne, no." Another chuckle. "The first woman expressed disgust, non-verbally, and walked away. The second woman did not even realize he was speaking to her. The third woman threw a drink into his face. A cold drink, mind you—he was not harmed."

"But he seduced the fourth woman, right?" asked Bill.

"There was no fourth woman," Francisco replied. "He ceased his efforts after the third, as our allotted time had nearly expired and he needed the few remaining minutes to explain that these three attempts were not failures."

"They weren't?" Yvonne queried.

"No. He explained to us why those particular women were categorically unattainable, and undesirable anyway, and also how the experience had brought valuable new data into what he calls our 'awareness cache.' I found his resilience very admirable, and his insightfulness even more so."

Seeing that Yvonne was quietly snickering, he chuckled again and added, "Indeed it was a humorous incident."

"Uh, Francisco," said Bill, "I don't know... Honestly, I kind of think your doing this Technical Casanova program might not be such a great idea..."

"Matt said the same thing," Francisco replied.

"Oh, right—Matt! Of course!" Bill smiled. "Forgot you two had met up with each other. Yeah, he's got to be a much better... uh, coach... than this Whittaker clown. You guys should hang out again."

"Oh, Matt and I *have* gotten together again, several times, and have enjoyed one another's company immensely. He is a wonderful man. Alas, though, what Matt has cannot be taught. He is a born virtuoso. What I require is systematic, practical advice, from a technical expert, such as Mr. Whittaker."

Yvonne made a "Hmm" sound.

"Wow, so you and Matt have become bosom buddies," said Bill. "Cool. Weird, but cool."

"Yes, indeed. It is interesting: in my friendships—with male friends, that is—I have seldom attained a high comfort level with completely opening up... with 'being my whole self,' one perhaps might say. A curious exception to this rule is you, Bill."

"Nobody's more puzzled than I am."

"Moreover, as it turns out, quite surprisingly, Matt is another."

"Wow," Yvonne said, though she felt bored.

"Oh, that reminds me," said Bill. "You know all those little apartment buildings along the boardwalk in Venice?"

Both of his companions nodded.

"Well Mike was telling me, last time we saw them, about this plan he's concocted, because he noticed one of those places has been advertising an available unit for a couple of weeks. He says he's going to sneakily paste his own phone number on top of the real one, you know, on the sign out front. Then he's going to pick the most obnoxious, rude, unpleasant applicant, and do a fake lease agreement with them. And then, just, make off with their security deposit."

"That is a devious scheme," said Francisco.

"Wow," said Yvonne, and meant it this time. "So, how is he going to show them the unit? Or provide them with the keys to their new home?"

"Good questions," Bill conceded with a smile and a shrug. "He was a little light on details. I don't even know if he's serious at all... I doubt it. I hope not. But, anyway, amusing idea."

George Roman, the waiter, appeared with the coffees everyone had ordered and began dispensing them.

"Forgive me, Yvonne," said Francisco, "but I do not recall—is Mike a work colleague of yours?"

"No. Well, sort of, I guess. He's my boss's husband, so I do know him kind of through work. But, he's part of this group of friends we have. Six people—three couples. And, we hang out a lot, you know, drinking and... mainly drinking."

Francisco smiled warmly. "That sounds nice," he said.

Bill, setting down his coffee cup after taking his first sip, said, "I don't know why I ever order coffee at the end of a meal. I mean, I know it's traditional but... And, don't get me wrong, I love coffee... But, honestly, I've just realized, I don't want it after dinner. I want it in the morning. I mean, I still have a glass of wine here!" He picked up the wine.

"Well said," Yvonne, who hadn't touched her coffee, replied as she reached for her own wine.

"It is interesting that you call it 'traditional,' Bill," said Francisco.

"Recently, I have been exploring the notion of tradition as we hold it in our collective, societal mind, and also, to some degree, the reality of traditions."

Bill and Yvonne looked quickly at each other, smiling, then back at their friend.

"Traditions are always in a state of flux," Francisco continued, "and, in fact, no human cultural practice is nearly as permanent as people imagine many are. I have been working on devising a system whereby we might eventually replace the sloppy term 'traditional' in our everyday discourse—no offense intended, Bill..."

"None taken."

"...with a more nuanced, precise, and accurate indication of the true traditional complexion of... whatever the object of discussion."

"Wow," said Yvonne.

"Cool," said Bill.

For a full minute nobody spoke, Francisco thoughtfully sipping his coffee and both Smedes (somewhat less) thoughtfully sipping their wine.

Then Francisco said, "The idea has crossed my mind, I must confess, of deliberately allowing my car to gently slide forward into a crosswalk, when I am stopped at a traffic light, and to gently strike a woman who is in the midst of crossing, so that I might have the pleasure of making her acquaintance."

After a few seconds of silence and everyone exchanging glances around the table, Bill said, "Uh... Honestly, I kind of think that might not be such a great idea..."

"Matt said the same thing," Francisco replied.

The following day at 3 P.M., Yvonne and Bill were walking past the building on Wexler Avenue where Gary and Scott lived, nearing completion of a classic condo-based neighborhood loop, each with around 12,000 steps on the clock and rather pleased about it.

Bill was most displeased, however, with the drizzling rain that had appeared one minute after they'd begun the loop and had continued ever since, and he'd been issuing a stream of bitter whining about it which Yvonne found far more annoying than the rain.

Now, with a big blue garbage truck (that had crossed Utah just as they'd turned left off it) rumbling along beside them and going about the very noisy business of mechanically lifting the bins that sat by the curb high into the air and tipping and shaking them so their contents (apparently consisting primarily of metal and stone and glass) fell into its massive mobile receptacle, progressing at exactly the same pace as Yvonne and Bill, he switched the object of his complaints.

"God, these fucking trash trucks!" he said. "I want a copy of their goddamn schedule!"

"They must be picking up from some places far more often than they do from ours," said Yvonne.

It was a very well known but very poorly understood fact that the garbage trucks, which carried at least a dozen different color schemes and company names on their sides, could be found roaming the neighborhood seven days a week for several hours each day, with no discernible pattern to their routes.

"And the fucking squeaky brakes!" exclaimed Bill as the truck inching along beside them obligingly furnished a demonstration. "I mean, *all* of them? Is there some kind of law about it?"

"They're part of the team," Yvonne replied, smiling. (Bill had informed her long ago of the existence of Team Kill Bill.)

"Ah. Yes, of course."

A truck of a different variety, not nearly as much of a nuisance but just as frequently seen on these streets, approached from behind them, went around the garbage truck and zipped away down Wexler. This was an ordinary pickup, except that a homemade camper shell, composed entirely of plywood, had been attached to the bed. Bill watched it turn right on Arkansas and disappear. He'd long been curious about the motivation behind the construction of these shells and about what was inside of them. I'm going to research that, he thought now, just as he'd thought many times before.

Glancing to his right, he noticed the building they were currently walking past had been tented for fumigation. He wondered what sort of critters were being battled, and whether there was any danger to the other buildings nearby. Cockroaches were, sadly, a fact of life on the Westside, but Bill had always encountered them on driveways, sidewalks, and—the creepiest situation—climbing up the trunks of trees (which he compulsively checked for now, on the palm tree he was passing); never indoors. He suspected some degree of chemical intervention was owed the credit for this, but doubted that anything as drastic as tenting was ever necessary.

"Hey, check it out," he said to Yvonne, pointing.

"Yeah. A bit ominous. Oh, Juice was telling me on Thursday about somebody she knew… well, not truly knew—a patient of hers. Anyway, this poor guy woke up one morning and his house had been tented and he was alone inside the house, and they were getting ready to start pumping in the poison. Allegedly."

Bill smiled. "Do you think it's true?"

Yvonne shrugged. "I don't think Juice deliberately lied about it. But she could've been confused. Or *she* could've been lied to."

"Right."

"Anyway, the guy managed to get out before they gassed him. But he tripped and fell and fractured his tibia."

"Allegedly."

"Yes."

Bill and Yvonne, who lately had been behaving pretty much like a long-term committed couple, had not talked at all about feelings, or expectations, or what went wrong last summer—nor did either of them have any intention of ever doing so. They had talked, however, about the possibility of Bill moving back into the condo, perhaps into the bedroom that had belonged to Patrick, which had gone through a brief limbo period after his departure, then had housed Gramps for an extended visit, and now was being re-painted and re-carpeted in preparation for becoming Alice's. (Yvonne's use of the word "ours" two minutes ago in reference to curbside garbage collection, which neither she nor Bill had consciously noticed, had not been directly inspired by these discussions.)

As they neared her/their building, they saw what looked like a woman and a dog on the sidewalk, coming toward them but still a fair distance away.

"We'll make it," Bill muttered.

"Yeah," agreed Yvonne.

Then their attention was drawn to Gene Shaheen, who lived in Number Five with his sister, Jean, and was currently strolling diagonally across the ground in front of the building (having just gotten out of his car), smiling and waving at them.

"Well, hello there!" he called out. "Haven't seen you two in a long time."

"No," both Smedes replied in unison. Bill wasn't sure whether he'd ever spoken with Gene before. Yvonne knew for certain that she never had. Neither of them knew his name was Gene.

"Well it's great to see you again," said Gene as the three converged at the spot where the sidewalk met the footpath leading to the stairs up to Number Four.

"Yeah, you too," said Bill.

Yvonne smiled.

"Walking," Gene continued. "Mmm-mmm, *so* good for the body. You guys are champs, you know? Me, I could never bring myself to go for a walk."

"It can be tough to get motivated sometimes," said Bill. Then, beginning to feel very awkward after two seconds of nobody saying anything, "Bringing coffee along can help."

"You two don't have any coffee," observed Gene.

"Sometimes we do," said Yvonne.

"I never touch the stuff," said Gene. "Or cigarettes, either."

"Smart," said Bill.

"Yeah—my dad, he dropped dead at the age of 53. Every single time I ever saw the man, he had a cup of coffee in one hand and a cigarette in the other."

"Wow," said Yvonne.

"How did your dad die?" asked Debbie Smede, severely startling all three of them. Then she added, thrusting out her hand toward Gene, "Debbie. Nice to meet you."

"Fritz the Dog!" Bill exclaimed as he turned and attempted to absorb all the new information. Then he bent down and gave Fritz, who was sitting on the sidewalk next to the four humans, a brisk rubbing of the head and ears.

Gene, having shaken Debbie's hand and told her his name, said, "Got hit by a bus. Dumb bastard."

"Hey, little bro! Surprise!" Debbie said, grabbing hold of Bill and hugging him.

"It sure is," he replied.

"Parking around here is a real bitch," she commented. "I'm like, three blocks from here, and it took me five minutes to wedge myself into the spot."

"You were lucky," said Bill.

"Well, we'd better get going, Gene," said Yvonne. "Nice to see you."

Ten minutes later, inside the condo, Bill set down three cups of tea and a platter of cut-up slices of buttered toast (he'd been unable to find any cookies or crackers of any sort in the pantry) on the dining table where Debbie had been explaining to Yvonne how she'd decided to stop by unannounced after unexpectedly departing early from a dog show in Santa Monica.

"Thanks," said Yvonne to Bill.

"So, yeah," said Debbie, "the guy—this so-called adjudicator or whatever, god!—he gets all up in my face about it, all bent out of shape, and tells me I'm in the wrong line, when I was only following the written instructions that *he* gave me in the first place!"

"Wow," said Yvonne.

"So, I didn't stoop to his level, you know? I was calm and polite, and I said, 'Sir, with all due respect,'..."

"Which is hardly any," Yvonne interjected.

"Yes!" Caught off guard, Debbie laughed. "Exactly! So, yeah, the stuff he was saying just kept getting dumber, and, finally, I realized, you know, thus far I am not enjoying this event. It's raining, and, this jerk is in my face, and... Fritz doesn't actually need this one in order to qualify for the big one—you know, the one in New York that Anna-Maria Schiaduffa is hosting."

Bill (now sitting at the table with them) and Yvonne both smiled and nodded, but neither of them knew what Debbie meant.

"So, yeah, I left! Catching up with you guys is a way better way to spend my afternoon!" She smiled and put her hand affectionately on top of Yvonne's.

"So Grace and the girls didn't join you on this one?" asked Bill.

"Nah... It *is* more fun when they come along, but... Well, honestly, Raylene... Well, actually, both of them lately... They just aren't very interested in the shows."

"Understandable."

"Kids!" Debbie laughed again. "I swear, they can be so tricky."

"We're nearly done," Yvonne said.

"I mean, the natural thing is to, like, think of your kid as another copy of you. But they totally aren't. They are one hundred percent their own person!"

"I'm thankful for that," said Bill.

"I mean… What do we want for our kids? Of course we want them to be safe, and healthy… and happy… But, beyond that…"

"Out?" suggested Yvonne.

Another laugh from Debbie. "No, what I mean is, *who* do we want them to become? You know, ideally. The fantasy scenario. I guess I kind of do like the idea of a daughter of mine being just like me. Well, not *exactly* like me—I wouldn't want her to have all my flaws. I guess… I'd want her to be just like me, but better."

Bill and Yvonne both nodded slowly and tried to make their faces look as if they too were pondering this matter.

Suddenly Debbie jumped up and shouted "Oh my god, I'm so sorry," having noticed that Fritz had just relieved himself on the floor.

"It's okay," Yvonne said after a moment, when she finally realized what Debbie—who was already returning from the kitchen holding a big wad of paper towels—was talking about.

"I guess he got nervous or something," she said fretfully, her face slightly red. "Again I am *so* sorry."

"Really, Deb, it's cool," said Bill. "Don't worry about it."

"It definitely won't be an issue for his performances," Debbie said as she conducted a frantic clean-up. "I'm positive he would never do it in that environment… And even if he did, I don't think they would take away points for that…"

Yvonne and Bill exchanged glances. Both were looking forward to chatting during their next neighborhood loop.

"So, it's really critical to get that finished, and submitted, before noon on Wednesday," said Donna Marquez.

"Yeah, okay," Juice Hughes-Newton replied. "But, listen—was this really so important that you had to interrupt my weekend for it?"

It was Sunday afternoon and Juice was slouched on her sofa, a potato chip in her right hand and her phone, pressed to the side of her head, in her left. In front of her, with the volume turned very low, the T.V. was showing live coverage of a professional golf tournament in Massachusetts. The perpetual, muted sound of a lawnmower being pushed around (which Juice had instructed her son, Henry, to do, despite the fact the grass hadn't grown at all since the last time it was done) came faintly through the windows of the house into the room.

"Well, Juice, you know, this is my weekend too, and, you never reply to email and, frankly, you almost never answer your phone, either."

"I've always liked you and respected you, Donna," Juice said in a slightly-too-sweet voice. "And I know you respect me too, and I appreciate that."

She paused for a second but there was just silence on the line.

"So, I'm telling you the following as a courtesy: other hospitals are interested in me, and if I'm not feeling the love at South Valley then I'm going to have no choice but to consider what they might have to offer. Ooh, nice shot!"

On the T.V., Bruce Rehnquist had just sunk a difficult putt.

Dr. Marquez said, "I've also been trying to talk to you about the Val-Square."

Val-Square was shorthand for Evaluation Squared, a program at South Valley General Hospital that involved the Quality of Quality Panel (self-assembled from the ranks of the willing within the H.R. department, the executive team and the board of directors) annually performing an evaluation of all the evaluations of physicians submitted by their patients.

"I hope we understand each other," said Juice as she crunched away on her chip and began moving her hand toward the bag to grab the next one.

"So do I," said Dr. Marquez.

"You know, there's a rumor going around the hospital about you, Donna..."

Silence.

"They say you lose your patience a lot!" Juice let out a huge guffaw.

"So, anyway," said Dr. Marquez, "I've reviewed your Val-Square, and—"

"I'm going to have to let you go, Donna."

"But—"

"You think about everything we discussed. Bye!"

Juice tapped the red hang-up icon, said "Stupid bitch," popped a chip into her mouth and crunched away on it thoughtfully.

"Mmmf," she said, focusing on the T.V. again. "This guy is good." Her mouth was still full of chip.

Approaching the tee now was golf superstar Wolf Lake, who'd just emerged from a special "mobile sensory deprivation tent" in which the upper half of his body spent most of its time whenever he was on the green. Wolf suffered from a severe case of sex addiction, and even the tiniest, most seemingly innocuous stimulus—primarily visual, but occasionally auditory or olfactory—from a spectator, referee or fellow player would trigger his illness and hopelessly distract him from the game.

"Oh!" said Juice, turning her attention back to her phone and launching into a flurry of tapping and scrolling which culminated, after two seconds, in again bringing it up to her left ear.

"Hello?" said the voice of Paul Newton.

"Hello yourself," said Juice. "Why do you always do that?"

"Do what?"

"Answer the phone like such a doofus. 'Hello?' you say,"—she spoke the word "hello" in a deliberately dopey tone—"as if you've got no clue who might be calling. You know it's me—your phone just told you it was me!"

"I'm kind of busy right now, Juice."

"Oh, *really*?"

"Yes. I'm in a meeting with the other deacons. Is there something I can help you with?"

"As a matter of fact, there is. I need you to pick up Lateesha from Regina's house at four o'clock."

"From Regina's house?"

"Yeah, she's over there for like a play date thing or whatever. I would pick her up myself but I've been detained with an unforeseen medical emergency. One of my patients, you know..."

"I thought we agreed she wasn't allowed to see Regina for a month, as punishment for—"

"Oh! That must be what she was babbling about this morning."

"Who? Lateesha?"

"Yeah. Regina's mom stopped by, out of the blue, with Regina, and they invited Teesh over to their—holy shit!"

"What is it?"

"Oh, nothing—just watching the golf."

Wolf Lake had just dropped his driver and run frantically away, quivering, after one of the spectators had removed their jacket, exposing their bare forearms.

"So," Paul said, "you still let her go to Regina's house even though she reminded you about her own punishment?"

"I need to get back to my patient, Paul. Just pick her up at four, please."

Paul sighed. "Okay, I suppose I can rearrange—"

"Bye!"

The moment Juice hung up, the phone began ringing. A glance at the screen revealed it was Jimmy Sanchez. She answered excitedly.

"Jimmy! It's about time, dear boy. When I call, I expect you to pick up."

"I had to go to the bathroom," he replied. "So, uh… did you get the picture I sent?"

"Yes, I sure did. And that is indeed my necklace around her worthless neck in that photo."

"I knew it!" he exclaimed. "I knew it must be your necklace. And she was, like, taunting you, too, when I took the picture. Taunting both of us—"

"So did you get it from her?"

"What? The necklace?"

Juice let out an exasperated sigh. "Yes! Yes. *My* necklace. Did you get it?"

"No."

"God! Why not?"

"Well, I asked her if I could borrow it—"

"Okay, listen, you need to give me *all* the details on her. Daily schedule. Where she likes to hang out. Who she's hanging out *with*. Oh, and her latest job! I am *definitely* going to fuck with her job…"

"Hey, how 'bout we meet up for a cup of coffee?" Jimmy asked. "Or, uh… dinner. How 'bout we have dinner together?"

"Slow your roll there, Jimbo," said Juice. "Focus on Nancy. Tell me about Nancy."

Jimmy was flustered now and struggling to articulate his thoughts. "Nnngh, forget about Nancy, that crazy bitch. I don't know nothing about her anymore. Maybe I never did..."

"Okay, now just calm down," said Juice. "What the hell are you talking about?"

"She's gone, okay? She said it's over between us."

"Christ."

"She's gone and I don't think she's ever coming back. Which is fine. She don't love me."

Juice was silent, absorbing the information, processing it.

Jimmy continued, "She told me she was carrying on with Ned! Since, like, forever! Can you believe it? Nancy and Ned. That whole time. He didn't know she was gonna be in the car that night!"

"Christ," Juice said again.

"She went back to him, I think," said Jimmy. "I mean, that's what she said she was gonna do..."

"Well, I gotta go now, Jimmy. Good luck to you."

"Uh," he said, "well maybe we could—"

"Bye!"

Juice tapped the red hang-up icon, then immediately performed the additional taps to block calls from Jimmy. Then she sat back and mulled over the situation.

"Hmm, interesting development," she said, reaching for another chip. "Nasty Nancy is quite the adversary, after all..."

She glanced over at Yvonne Smede, sitting two feet away on the sofa, currently looking at a phone screen.

"Hey," Juice snapped. "Stop ignoring me, girl. Rude."

Chapter 20

Gazing idly at a sheet of paper on the table in front of her, on which her own last name had been misspelled as "S'meed," Yvonne thought of Rhianna "Rhee" Pwacciusso, a so-called analyst on the Ambulatory Team who was dumber than a bag of rocks and whom Yvonne had, on multiple occasions, had the distinct displeasure of visiting at her desk down on the fourth floor (because Rhee never responded to phone calls, emails, or instant messages). On one such visit, Yvonne had noticed a check lying there for quite a large amount, made out to Rhee with her last name misspelled, from a company called ABC Construction, and had foolishly made a small reactive sound of mild curiosity, prompting Rhee to supply an explanation that featured quite an elaborate backstory.

As it turned out, prior to launching a second (and shockingly successful) career in I.T., Rhee had spent many years working as a crane operator on high-rise building projects; or rather, not truly an operator but a "specialist technician" who would ride along, perched in a little seat at the tip of the crane, to assist with any delicate or complex manipulation of materials that necessitated human hands.

Many safety mechanisms and protocols existed for the person performing this job, but Rhee ignored them all, being lazy (both mentally and physically) and having no real fear of heights or death. One day she'd slipped and ended up dangling perilously, two hundred feet above the street, for nearly half an hour while the hapless members of both her own crew and the fire department fretted and scrambled around. Ultimately she'd managed to climb back into her seat, where she'd waited for an additional half hour before they finally restored power to the crane.

After the incident, Rhee's father, who'd become chummy with a couple of partners in a law firm whose offices were housed in the building where he worked as a janitor, had persuaded them to represent Rhee in a suit against her employer. They'd settled for a sum so exorbitant that she and her father were both able to retire (temporarily in her case, until she developed a keen interest in computers).

"Oh!" exclaimed Matt Spratt (who'd been sitting at the table for several minutes, relating factoids about Marion Davies) suddenly, jolting Yvonne back to her present environment.

"The funniest thing happened this morning," he went on. "I'm walking past the 7-Eleven there on Lincoln, and I see this little red convertible Mazda just like my girlfriend Ily used to drive. And the license plate—so cool!—it says, T-G... You see, Ily—I think her real name is Ilene, but everyone calls her Ily—she—well, I guess not her *original* real name. Anyway, she used to be a man. So anyway, this license plate, it says T-G-R-L-1-L-Y. So I'm like, holy crap—it's her! What an amazing coincidence!"

"Wow," said Yvonne.

"But then the girl came out of the store and got in the car, and she wasn't Ily, she was some other girl."

"Wow," Yvonne said again.

"Really sweet, though," said Matt, momentarily sporting a far-away look in his eyes. "I might be seeing her later. You know, when we get back."

"Cool."

Matt and Bill had arranged a day trip up to Hearst Castle (4 hours each way (in a fantasy world with no traffic)) for tomorrow, to try to retrieve a key that supposedly would open a buried treasure chest. Yvonne thought it was silly, and she knew Bill thought the same, and that he knew she did too. But he was Bill—he couldn't say no to his friend. To further twist the knife, they were using her car to get there. And to twist it further still, Matt was crashing at the condo tonight (where Bill had been sleeping every night in recent times), so they could get a nice, early start.

"So what do you think of this landlord guy?" Matt asked. "He's a trip."

"Yes," Yvonne agreed.

They were sitting in Bill's apartment, where Yvonne had arrived two hours ago to help Bill with boxing up his belongings in preparation for moving. Matt's arrival, one hour ago, had slowed their efforts, and things had ground completely to a halt when Joseph Tanur had shown up 20 minutes ago.

"You ever met him before?" asked Matt.

"No," said Yvonne. Then, more quietly, "Hope I never do again."

Matt chuckled and glanced over his shoulder. "What are they doing now, anyway?"

The two men were slowly meandering around the perimeter of the one-room apartment, Tanur muttering every few seconds and making notations on a clipboard, Bill nodding and grunting, wearing a face of feigned solemnity layered on top of heartfelt frustration and pain.

"Not sure," said Yvonne. "I think this is sort of like a move-out inspection... except Bill's still on the hook for everything, until he finds a new tenant to take over."

"Wild! So for how long?"

"Well, he signed a year lease. So I guess there's still like... over eight months left on it. God."

"And what was *that* all about?" Matt queried, gesturing at the sheet of paper on the table. Tanur had spent ten minutes sitting here scrawling on it as Bill stood behind him, observing and providing periodic input.

"I think it's an application form, to lease the apartment," said Yvonne. "He wanted to show Bill how it should be filled out, so Bill could show a prospective new tenant how to do it." She involuntarily cracked up.

Matt laughed, too.

"And he used all of Bill's info," she continued, still laughing, "for the example."

"Love it," said Matt, getting up from the table. "I'm gonna step outside for a few."

Yvonne stood up too, saying "I'll walk out with you. I should probably get back to the condo and start on dinner."

As she made for the exit she managed to exchange a glance with Bill, who wordlessly conveyed that he understood her departure and that (unrelated) he was miserable.

Three minutes later, as Yvonne rounded the corner from Dimvale onto Arkansas and noticed the Wonder Twins frenetically power-walking on the other side of the street, her phone started exploding.

Looking at the screen, it appeared she was simultaneously receiving from Laura Johnson, her friend and boss, an e-postcard and a call. And indeed this was exactly what was happening, but only because Yvonne's cell carrier and her eJackal app (which had been pestering her recently to update to the next version) had mysteriously conspired to prevent the delivery of the postcard until 48 hours after it was sent.

"Hi, Laura. Everything okay?"

"Yvonne, hey. I... Yeah, everything's fine, why wouldn't it be?"

"Well you're not generally in the habit of calling me while vacationing halfway around the world."

"Oh, no we're back now. Got back last night. Flew all day yesterday."

"Wow."

"Yeah. I guess I am kind of tired and jetlagged, but, I actually feel pretty good. We had a great time. Did you get my postcard?"

"Uh, yes... It..."

"Yeah, it was gorgeous there. A really nice island. Well, all of them are really nice, but..."

"So, you came home on a Friday? You didn't want to, you know, take advantage of the weekend and stay a bit longer?"

"Well, Mike has this scheme where, in order to save money on our plane tickets to SGI, he buys two trips at a time, with the dates mixed up."

Yvonne chuckled. "That sounds like Mike."

"Yeah, so, the flight we came home on yesterday, technically speaking, it was actually the *outbound* leg of a different roundtrip ticket."

"Right..."

"Yeah, so, then the return leg of that one is when we go back in May. It's kind of goofy." Laura chuckled too.

"But... Don't you go to a different island every time?"

"Oh, yeah but, we always fly into the same big, like, international airport. On the big island. Then we take a hopper flight to whichever little island."

"Ah, right."

"One time we flew in one of those planes that has, like, skis on the bottom instead of wheels, and it can land on the water..."

"So, how does Mike's scheme save money?" asked Yvonne. "Are flights cheaper for SGI residents vacationing in California?"

"No, I don't think it's that. He said it's about staying over a weekend. If you book travel that involves staying over a weekend, for some reason the airline charges less for that."

"But there are plenty of weekends between now and May. So it wouldn't have mattered whether *this* weekend was included..."

After a long silence, Laura said, "I don't know. Mike says we save money. Maybe he's wrong!" She chuckled again. "Anyway, I was wading through my emails, you know, trying to get caught up for Monday, and I saw there were quite a few flying around about this bug fix in Moonshot?"

Yvonne sighed. "The people calling it a bug fix have no clue what's going on. See, the Interface Team is asking us to populate the Marital Status field in the lab orders going to the state for newborn screening."

"Which it doesn't do currently?"

"Right, and there's no reason it should. Ever heard of a newborn baby that was married? Anyway, there's no bug. This would be an enhancement. A pointless one."

"So why do they say they need it?"

"Because they're brainlessly checking all the boxes on their testing checklist. Even if the state cares about that field, which I highly doubt, the Interface Team can populate it themselves in their engine, in like two seconds."

"Hmm..." said Laura. "Just looking through some of these emails... Seems like there are a lot of different opinions flying around."

Yvonne sighed again and rolled her eyes. "Well, Amy and Jack and Rob all agree with me. This isn't needed. We should push back."

When Yvonne needed to build an alliance for making contentious team decisions, her main recruiting criterion was whether the correct way forward involved doing work or refraining from doing work. Fred and Mona were always eager to expend energy on any type of endeavor, no matter how useless (or even harmful). Rob and Jack were just the opposite—they'd never lift a finger if there were any way to avoid doing so. Yvonne could always count on easily lining up the support of whichever pair was relevant to any given situation. And she could usually persuade Amy to agree with her position based on its true merits.

"Hmm..." said Laura. "Okay, we'll discuss it on Monday as a team. Oh, hey, I guess I'll be seeing you tomorrow night?"

"You will?"

"Yeah, the thing at Amy's."

"What thing?"

"It's a potluck happy hour thing. You're definitely invited—Amy was talking about you being there… about, you know, all six of us…"

"On a Sunday?"

"Um… Yeah, pretty sure…"

"We should do it tonight instead. Bill wouldn't go because he has a friend staying over. Everybody wins."

"Yeah…" Laura replied vaguely.

"Check this out, babe," came the voice of Mike Howell in the background.

"Hey, um," said Laura, "I'd better let you go…"

Passing by a couple of palm trees and amusedly watching a property across the street where workers from LADWP, a gardening service and a tree service—none of whom had expected the others to be there— were struggling to get their jobs done, Yvonne turned her eyes back to the way in front of her and realized that Scott Portcullis was walking toward her, approaching Wexler Avenue from the opposite side.

Their eyes met and he acknowledged her with a small smile and an even smaller, very quick nod of the head. She raised one hand in salutation.

When he reached the corner, he stopped and waited for her to cross over and join him; then they proceeded up Wexler together.

"Don't usually find you out and about," said Yvonne.

"No," Scott replied with a grimace. "And I wouldn't be now if it were up to me. The H.O.A. brought in this company to do seismic retrofitting—which, incidentally, I don't think is actually necessary because our building is a newer one, but nobody listens to me—and so, now, the parking garage is filled with their people and materials and equipment, so everybody has to find parking on the street…"

"Lovely," said Yvonne, smiling and shaking her head.

"…which, if you didn't already know, can be very difficult."

"Yes."

"How have you been doing?"

"Pretty good, I suppose. The standard joys, the standard frustrations."

"I think I understand," Scott said with another small smile.

"We should get together soon, the four us. Seems like it's been forever."

"Yeah, that'd be fun," said Scott, though he wasn't sure if he meant it. "Actually, Gary's been talking about having you guys over for dinner. I'm sure he'll reach out to you soon about it."

"Oh, how's it going with his marathon stuff?"

"Don't get me started," said Scott. "No, it's okay. But I'll let *him* tell you all about it."

"Okay," said Yvonne with a chuckle. "Well, how about your stuff? The baseball thing?"

"Oh, C.U.? It's not going great, I'm sorry to say. Turns out reaching MasterBlaster is a little more complicated than I thought. And the competition is tougher than I thought—you know, in the head-to-head challenges."

"Sorry to hear."

"Yeah, and I'm running out of time. The season ends in three weeks."

"Wow."

At this point began a lull in the conversation that for two minutes both their minds were racing to try to fill, but with no success at all. Then, for another two minutes, they both tried halfheartedly, again with zero success, repeatedly distracted by other concerns. Then they both stopped trying and just walked side by side in resigned silence, each in their own world.

Climbing the stairs to her front door, Yvonne saw that someone she didn't recognize was standing at it: a young, thin, white man in dress slacks, short-sleeved shirt and tie, with a close-cropped, 1950s-style haircut.

"Don't admit to anything," came the hushed voice of Wally from somewhere below. "Operation 64 has been green-lit."

Turning to Yvonne as she reached the top of the stairs, the visitor smiled widely and said, "Good afternoon, ma'am!"

"Hi," she replied warily.

The door opened and Alice Smede was standing there, wearing earbuds and a blank expression, one hand clutching a phone.

"Oh," said the man, turning back to look at her. "Why hello there, young lady!"

He continued talking as he tried to re-orient himself to face both members of his audience at the same time (a somewhat elusive aim, as Yvonne was in motion, trying to push past him to the door). "I'm so pleased I caught both of you today. Tell me, have you heard the good news?"

Mother and daughter, now standing side by side in the doorway, both stared at him silently, unsmiling.

"About Jesus Christ?" he added.

Now Yvonne did produce a smile—a tight one—as she said, "Sorry, we're not interested."

The man began speaking again as both Smedes stepped back and Yvonne closed the door on him.

Alice's music trigger finger was in motion, two millimeters from its button, when she noticed she was about to be spoken to.

"I feel bad being so curt with them," said Yvonne, "but... I just don't want to waste my time. Or theirs, for that matter."

Alice, not having been asked a question, said nothing. But she also kept her finger stationary, sensing correctly that her mother wasn't finished.

"I mean, spirituality is one thing. I'm fine with that. Some kind of higher power, out there in the universe somewhere? Maybe. But, organized religion—that's just... too much. I think it probably does more harm than good, honestly."

Another moment of shared silence.

"I don't know," said Yvonne. "What do you think about religion?"

"I think religion used to work for people a long time ago because they were so vulnerable and so ignorant. I think these days it works for sort of the opposite reason—their worlds are so secure and comfortable and orderly, it's easy to believe that God is looking after everything, and preventing chaos and senseless suffering and woeful injustice."

"Interesting," was all Yvonne could manage to say in response. She was a little stunned to hear commentary so thoughtful and articulate—and lengthy!—from her daughter. Could Alice be high on drugs right now?

After several seconds had gone by, and Alice was once more on the brink of starting up her music, Yvonne spoke again.

"So, what are you up to now?"

"I'm going to move the rest of my stuff into my new room."

"Oh, could you hold off on that? Dad's friend Matt is staying here tonight and we're going to put him in there."

Yvonne's phone began ringing and, looking at the screen, she saw it was her son Patrick calling. She answered it on speaker.

"Hi, Patrick."

"Um... Hey, Mom."

"I'm here at the condo with Alice. How are you doing?"

"Um... Good. Good."

"So what's up?"

"Um, I have some good news. I'm moving back in with you guys."

"Oh," said Yvonne, scrambling to modulate her tone and choose the right next words.

"Yeah," he said.

"Did something go wrong with your apartment?"

"No, the apartment is fine. It's just, um... Len's girlfriend is moving in."

"Oh. I didn't know he had a girlfriend."

"Yeah, he didn't, but... now he does. And... um... well, the rent is kind of expensive..."

"Rent certainly has a way of being like that."

"Yeah."

"So, hey, you want to come over for dinner tonight? We can chat some more about your plans, and, hang out..."

"Um... Um... Maybe... Yeah... Maybe... Um, I'd better get going now, Mom. I'm kinda busy with... some stuff."

"Okay. Bye!"

The call dropped. Yvonne shrugged, smiled, and shook her head.

"He's going to move into the den, right?" Alice asked.

"I don't know," Yvonne said with a sigh. "We'll figure it out."

The sound of Bill's 5:30 A.M. alarm jolted him out of a dream.

He was participating, along with about a dozen other people (none of whom he recognized), in an event that seemed like a combination of an auction and a card game. Until a moment ago, one member of this group, a middle-aged white man, had been delivering a rapid-fire, hype-it-up, auctioneer-style pitch to try to sell—or was it trade?—a playing card which was a 12 of Clubs, somehow universally known to be the least valuable card in the deck. Then someone else, also a middle-aged white man, had unexpectedly launched into a counter-pitch of sorts, urging the group to switch their focus to a 13 of Clubs instead, because it's worth even less. A third middle-aged white man had helpfully pointed out that a 13 of Clubs does not exist, and a fourth one was in the midst of suggesting they could just pretend it does for the time being (this being merely a practice exercise, after all) when the alarm put an abrupt end to the whole affair.

Fumbling around for his phone on the nightstand, Bill felt some relief at having escaped from a situation so bizarre (though no more so than most of his dreams and, he imagined, most other people's too), but more strongly felt disappointment and dread at being awake but very tired and about to embark on a long road journey for the purpose of performing some potentially risky and definitely pointless antics.

"Fuck," he muttered.

"Rise and shine, treasure hunter!" said Yvonne, already standing next to his side of the bed, silencing his alarm, despite having been awakened by it at the same moment he was.

She turned off his bedside white noise machine next, then began a quick circuit of the room to do the same to his fans and air filter machines. There was a slight, giddy spring in her step—she was eagerly anticipating returning to bed for a few more hours of delicious sleep in a spacious, still, solitary, utterly silent environment.

"Better get a move on," she added as she slid back under the covers.

"Fuck," Bill muttered again, head still on the pillow, arm still protruding from the bed, hand resting on the nightstand near his phone.

Ten minutes later, he emerged from the "master suite," bladder empty, dressed but not showered (he preferred to shower in the afternoon or evening, unless (and this very rarely happened) there was a morning event on his calendar that absolutely, positively required him not to smell faintly of sweat), hair slightly less messy than it had been when he woke up, miserable scowl still intact.

Proceeding down the corridor, he cursorily examined the bedroom door at the other end of it and the sliding shoji door on the left. Both were fully closed with no sound coming through them and no light underneath. Behind the latter, his daughter presumably slept peacefully, and he had no issue with that. Regarding the former, he said (mentally): "Come on, Matt—if I have to drag my ass out of bed for this stupid thing then you sure as hell do too."

He made his way to the kitchen and began scanning the contents of the cupboards and the fridge, pondering what to have for breakfast and whether it might be wise to take something along for lunch. Otherwise, he reasoned, they'd end up stopping somewhere, wasting a bunch of time, spending a bunch of money, and eating something insanely unhealthy (which they'd undoubtedly be doing for dinner regardless— better just once than twice).

Stacked up on the middle shelf of the fridge were several Tupperware-style tubs inside of which, Bill knew, were the copious leftovers from last night's roast chicken dinner (which had been attended by only three people (though, granted, Matt always ate enough for at least two)). Could be a great thing to bring along for lunch, he thought. But what would be the exact logistics of that? Bring it all, or transfer some of it to smaller containers? Bring a little of everything, or just focus on the meat and potatoes? Plates? Real ones or paper ones? Forks, knives. . .

He turned his attention to breakfast. Something hot? No, too much trouble. Keep it quick and simple.

Ten minutes later, having prepared and eaten a serving of bite-sized shredded wheat cereal with soy milk, taken the bowl and (too large) spoon back to the kitchen, made some danger-mitigating adjustments to the Jenga Tower, and returned to the corridor in the back of the condo (from which he'd heard not a peep the entire time), Bill gently knocked on the door of the bedroom that had once belonged to his son.

"Matt?"

Silence.

Bill knocked again, called out again, waited a few more seconds, then gingerly turned the doorknob, slowly pushed the door open and tentatively poked his head inside.

"Matt?"

Still no answer. Taking a step forward so he could see the entirety of the bedroom, Bill confirmed that, as he'd begun to suspect, it didn't contain anyone (and in particular, not Matt).

"Fuck," he said.

Coming up Wexler Avenue, nearing completion of a solo neighborhood loop (which had been relatively pleasant overall but had featured a surprisingly high number of encounters with dog walkers (including a record-tying two with Mrs. Harris and Max)), Bill spotted a tall, shaggy-haired figure in the distance, speeding toward him on a skateboard, one hand clutching some kind of parcel, a trail of smoke rising up from the other hand.

Bill waved, Matt waved back, and a moment later they were standing face to face on the sidewalk in front of the condo building.

"Where've you been?" Bill asked, trying, almost successfully, to hide the frustration and fretfulness he'd felt for the past half hour.

"Had to get some supplies for the trip," said Matt, grinning.

He took a final puff on his joint, dropped it, stepped on it, then used his newly freed hand to assist in pulling apart the sides of the plastic bag he was carrying, revealing its contents.

Glancing down, Bill saw several examples of beef jerky and other "meat snacks," a canister of mixed nuts, and a few single-serving pouches of corn chips.

"Cool," he said. "So, what's with the skateboard?"

"Oh, yeah," said Matt, eyes briefly darting to where he'd discarded it on the strip of grass between the sidewalk and the street. "Pretty wild! I hadn't ridden one of those in... a lot of years. It's true what they say, though: you never forget how."

"Where'd you get it?"

"Outside the store, leaning against the wall there. Community skateboards!" He chuckled delightedly.

"Right," said Bill.

"So, what've you been up to, man?"

"Well, I woke up pretty damn early for this crazy road trip we're doing..."

Matt chuckled again. "You're fun, Bill. Well, great then—let's head out!"

In the midst of the arduous, twenty-minutes-long process of getting the ATS to the 405 on-ramp (located an as-the-evil-crow-flies distance of one thousand feet from the condo), stopped at a red light across from a pair of billboards advertising the big-budget live-action comic book superhero movie coming out next weekend and the one coming out next month, Bill noticed that the car in front of him, a yellow 2014 Dodge Charger, was very slowly rolling backward. There was still a space of about five feet between them, but he began to feel nervous.

"Check this out," he said to Matt as he glanced in the rearview mirror, confirming his suspicion that another car—a black BMW sedan—was directly behind him. "This guy in front of us."

"Holy Toledo," said Matt with a grin. "What's he thinkin'?"

The Charger's brake lights came on and its gradual roll halted.

"Phew," said Bill, exchanging a pleased look with his friend.

The brake lights went off and the rolling resumed.

"Fuckin' L.A. driving," said Bill. "Believe it or not, this has happened to me before."

"Hah! I love it," said Matt.

Now the Charger was only about two feet in front of the ATS.

Bill honked the horn. He could see the driver—who appeared to be young and male, with extremely short hair—glance in the rearview mirror, but the rolling continued.

"Fuck," said Bill, now in a state of near-panic.

The collision was quite soft, but still lightly jolted the pair in their seats. Bill swallowed hard. What now?

The Charger's brake lights came on again momentarily. Then the driver's door flew open and a very tall, slender young man with extremely short hair leapt out and began glaring at Bill.

Bill opened his door and got out. The young man was approaching.

"What the fuck are you doing?" he shouted angrily.

"Uh..." said Bill. "Excuse me?"

"Why'd you hit me?"

"Uh... I didn't. You rolled backwards into me."

"That's the stupidest thing I ever heard. Why the fuck would I do that?" The man was now standing, hands on his hips, right in front of Bill, glaring down at him contemptuously.

The light turned green and bedlam immediately ensued, with all the drivers lined up behind the ATS laying on their horns and trying to pull out into the next lane, while the cars already in that lane began whizzing past, just a few inches from where Bill was having his tense standoff. He'd managed to make eye contact with his young adversary but was unsuccessful in developing a retaliatory angry glare and just stared up with a blank face.

"Hey guys," said Matt, who'd emerged from the passenger side and lit up a joint. "It doesn't really matter who hit who, right?"

The other two looked over at him as he took a long drag.

"I mean, both cars are fine," Matt continued, smiling and waving his jointless hand vaguely in the direction of the point at which the two bumpers rested against each other (which was not visible from his vantage point). "There's no damage."

Bill looked back at the young man, who now seemed to be staring off into space, perhaps attempting to think.

"Why don't we all just... go on our merry way?" Matt added before taking another puff.

"Sounds good to me," said Bill.

The young man was now moving his gaze back and forth between Matt and Bill, still looking unhappy but no longer enraged.

"Asshole!" shouted somebody through the open window of a car going past them.

"Okay, fine." said the young man. "Whatever."

"Cool," said Bill.

"Hey man," said Matt, leaning across the hood of the ATS and extending his joint toward the young man. "You want some of this?"

The young man looked slightly taken aback.

"I know Bill doesn't want any," Matt added with a laugh, and then, in a quieter, mock-conspiratorial voice, with his other hand up against the side of his mouth, "It's 'cause he's a square."

The young man reached out and accepted the joint, then brought it to his lips and began to take a drag.

"God," said Bill, rolling his eyes and maneuvering around his open car door to get back in.

"Hey, you know what," said Matt, curling himself up from the hood, "just keep it."

Chuckling and heading for the passenger door, he added, "My peace offering!"

The driver of the BMW sedan, who hadn't managed to pull out and go around, leaned out his window and shouted at Bill, "Move it, fuckface!"

"You know, Matt," said Bill as the ATS, moving along the 101 freeway at the relatively respectable rate of 35 miles per hour, crossed from Los Angeles County into Ventura County and he noticed it needed fuel, "I know I've said this before but... I'm really uncomfortable with the idea of stealing something from Hearst Castle. I mean, that's pretty serious."

"Don't worry," said Matt. "We're not actually stealing it, because it's not theirs. It's hers!"

"Well, I'm not sure they'll see it that way..."

"She just hid it there sneakily, you know? It's not part of their official collection. They probably don't even know about it!"

"Hmm," Bill said, steering the car onto the off-ramp for Hampshire Road.

"Anyway, they're not going to know I took it, because I'm gonna do it when nobody's watching."

"And, uh, what do you need *me* there for, again?"

"For the distraction, dude—of course!"

"Aren't they going to have a bunch of security cameras?"

"Oh, Bill. You worry too much."

They pulled into a gas station.

"Also I need you because I don't have a car," Matt added with a chuckle.

Bill parked next to a pump, cut the engine, sighed, and turned to his friend. "So... How do you even know this key exists? You said there was something written on the map?"

"Right!" Matt replied excitedly, reaching into the back seat. "She added some notes on there... or Rick did..." He retrieved the treasure map from within a small leather satchel.

"Look!" he said, shoving the ancient sheet into Bill's hands.

Bill slowly rotated the map and moved it closer to his face, squinting at it. He spotted a few lines of text, scrawled in pencil near one corner of the page, badly smudged, looking almost as if they'd been hastily jotted down on whatever scrap of paper was handy and had no connection with the map or the treasure.

"This is barely legible," he muttered, attempting to decipher it.

"I know!" said Matt. "Took me a while to figure out what it meant. But I did!"

The first line, smudgy in the middle, appeared to be "pad lock!" The next line, containing nearly no clear text at all, consisted of a smudge, then "old," then another smudge, then "key." The third line, similarly obscured, was: smudge, "ectory," smudge. The last two lines, though also badly smudged, obviously had once consisted of "Hearst Castle" and "San Simeon, CA."

Bill looked up at Matt with a very skeptical face. "This could mean anything, Matt. Or, more likely, nothing."

Matt laughed. "You're a trip, Bill. It definitely *does* mean something, and I know what that something is. You see, I did my homework. I'm not just a pretty face." He grinned.

Bill smiled.

"Clearly," Matt went on, "the treasure chest has a lock on it, and the key that opens that lock is hidden in Hearst Castle, in the..."—he pointed to "ectory" on the third line of smudged pencil scribblings—"refectory! It's like this giant dining room where Hearst would entertain his guests."

"And specifically it's this 'old key'...?" Bill ventured with a smirk.

"Hah! Yeah, maybe. I think it's actually a *gold* key, and the 'g' got rubbed off. But, I'll be able to figure it out when I'm in there."

"Of course."

Bill handed the map back to Matt, opened his door, and got out.

Matt gazed at the map for several seconds, gleefully anticipating his great discoveries at the castle and, ultimately, on the beach. Then he returned it to its place inside the satchel.

"Goddammit!" came Bill's voice from outside, near the pump.

Matt opened his door, poked his head out and said, "What's up?"

"Their pump-mounted card readers are on the fritz," Bill said gloomily, gesturing with his face toward a little handwritten notice taped onto the machine. "I have to go inside to pay."

"I'll come with ya," Matt said cheerfully.

Standing next to Matt inside of the surprisingly—and disorientingly—cavernous, crowded, chaotic gas station shop, which bore a gigantic sign on its roof reading "Thousand Oaks Sundry, Novelty & Entertainment Emporium," Bill realized, amplifying his sense of bewilderment, that the man standing nearby, about fifteen feet to his right, talking and gesticulating excitedly to an unknown male companion, was none other than Jake Lee, Yvonne's work colleague's husband and one sixth of the notorious middle-aged party gang known as The Evils.

"Jake!" he called out, waving his hand.

Jake immediately looked over, recognized Bill, and began galloping toward him, sporting a huge grin and saying "Bill Smede, as I live and breathe!"

His friend, looking both confused and amused, followed.

"Small world," said Bill. "Uh, this is my friend, Matt."

"What's up," Matt said, smiling and extending his hand.

Jake, taking it and shaking it vigorously, eyes darting back and forth between Matt and Bill, said, "Aw, wow, just... This is just so... I mean, you're the last person I would've expected..."

"I'm Les," said the man standing next to Jake.

"Nice to meet you," said Bill.

"What's up," Matt, still smiling, said, and shook hands with Lester.

"So, what brings you to this neck of the woods this fine morning?" asked Jake.

"We're on our way up to Hearst Castle," said Bill.

"Oh! Yes! I've heard of that place! It's like a... just, like a medieval castle, right?"

"Not really. It's this gigantic dream home this newspaper tycoon built for himself."

"Oh yeah, I've heard of that place," said Lester.

"It's supposed to be pretty bad-ass," remarked Matt.

"We're going there to retrieve a key," Bill said, struggling to keep a straight face. "To unlock a buried treasure chest."

"Oh!" exclaimed Jake. "You're that buried treasure guy!"

"Yep, that's me," Matt happily confirmed.

"Bill's talked about what you're doing. That is just... *so* cool. Just... *so* cool."

Matt's eyes were twinkling now. "The coolest part about it is the woman who buried it, Marion. She's a movie goddess from the days of old..."

"Awesome!" said Jake.

"Marion," said Lester. "Like from Indiana Jones!"

"Right," said Bill.

After a few seconds of nobody speaking, Matt said, "Well, I'm gonna go rustle up some snacks for the road."

"Ooh," said Jake, "see if they have any Chocodiles! I love those."

"Right-O," Matt called over his shoulder as he headed off into the aisles.

"So what are you doing here, Jake?" Bill asked. "You on a road trip too?"

"No, we're doing some specialty comics shopping. Turns out, they've got a great collection here! Just... who would've thought, right? But Les, he knew about it!" Jake flashed an appreciative grin at Lester.

"Amy and the kids come with you?"

"Nah. Les hates them!" A big guffaw.

"No I don't!" said Lester, looking alarmed.

"Nah, I'm just joking," Jake said, clapping his friend on the shoulder. "No, Amy just had some of her own shopping she needed to do..."

The statement Jake had classified as a joke was in fact true, and always had been, though he'd never (consciously) realized it. Jake and Amy had first met during their freshman year at Cal State Fullerton (despite having grown up just a few miles from each other, in the neighboring (though on opposite sides of the Orange Curtain), and often confused in people's minds, cities of Cypress and Cerritos, respectively). He'd fallen pretty hard, having never had a girlfriend (or even a date) prior to that, and she'd almost instantly become a huge part of his life, jumping ahead of longtime bosom buddy Lester, who'd reacted to this shocking shift—understandably, having himself been entirely girlfriendless and mostly friendless—with strong feelings of jealousy and resentment, which, though he'd learned to manage them very well over the years, had never gone away.

"Oh," said Bill, "are you looking for that super-rare comic? The field marshal?"

"No, no..." Jake shook his head glumly. "They don't have that here..." His smile returned. "Or anywhere! The only way to get your hands on one of those now is to get it from the auction, next month."

"Which *this* dumbass forgot to register for!" Lester added.

"Yep," Jake affirmed. "That's me! Just... But, I think I can still, like, get my foot in the door, just... somehow. Yeah, so, anyway, no, we're just... We're here looking for some other cool stuff..."

"I'm gonna show him what's what," said Lester with a proud and excited grin.

"Cool," said Bill, smiling. "Well, I'd better go pay for my gas…"

"Okay, well, great seeing you," said Jake. "Oh! I guess I'll be seeing you tonight, right?"

"You will?"

"Happy hour at your place!"

This was the first Bill had heard of this.

"This is the first I've heard of it," he said.

Jake shrugged and smiled widely. "That's what Amy told me."

Sitting at a picnic table on the back patio of Chapwick's Grill-n-Chill, located on Highway 1 near the town of Cayucos, Bill gazed out, past his half-finished Super Macho Chili Cheese Dog (which Matt had insisted he order) and Bud Light (which Matt had also insisted on), at a group of young surfers currently paddling out from a small beach at the bottom of the cliff the restaurant was perched atop.

"You still surfing?" he asked.

"Oh yeah," Matt, seated next to him, replied. "Every chance I get. Well, sometimes I just go for a swim. Oh! I saw this documentary a couple weeks ago, about, like, all the microscopic details of human reproduction, right? And, one of the things they covered was how far a sperm has to swim in order to fertilize an egg…"

"Okay…"

"And, I mean, the distance varies all over the place, of course, but they said, in some cases, it can be as much as 30 centimeters…"

"Mmm-hmm…"

"Which is the equivalent of a person swimming *six miles*! I mean, holy cow! Imagine yourself swimming six miles, in the dark, not knowing where you're supposed to go or if you'll ever get there…"

"Certainly hard to imagine."

"Those little guys sure are brave."

"Mmm. They don't really have much of a choice, though."

"Hah! Right."

"Oh, hey—speaking of sex: how's Francisco been doing?"

"Fran!" Matt exclaimed. "Yeah, Fran's a great guy. I love him."

"Yeah."

"But he *is* a total trip, I gotta admit. The other day we were on the boardwalk together and he goes... You know how there are all those little apartment buildings?"

"Yeah."

"So we're walking past some of those, and he goes,"—Matt affected a stiff, formal style and a lower pitch—"'Just think about it, Matt—people are *having sex*, right *now*, as we *speak*, inside that building there.'" He chuckled, then resumed the impression. "'They're only a few feet away from us. Just *think* about it.'" More chuckling. "Aw, Fran is funny."

Bill was laughing too. "Yeah, definitely," he said. "So, has he had any luck?"

"No, not that he's mentioned. Poor guy, he psychs himself out."

"Yeah."

Bill looked out at the young surfers again, who were all now trying to ride in on a wave, with varying degrees of success.

"It's weird to think," he said, "that back in the early days when we were surfing in Santa Monica... well, when *you* were surfing and I was just making a total ass of myself..."

"Hah!"

"When we were doing that, none of those people down there had even been born yet."

"Yeah, wild..."

"It doesn't seem that long ago."

"No, it really doesn't."

"Isn't it strange how... two periods of time that, in reality, are the same length—like, say, a period of ten years—can *seem* so different..."

Matt was taking a swig of beer and looking at Bill, eyebrows raised, waiting for more.

"Like, for example, the 1980s lasted forever. It was like an eternity, like a whole lifetime. The 90s were... well, they went on for a really long time, but not as long as the 80s. I think, maybe, time just keeps getting faster and faster..."

Matt made a quick "Hmm" sound of acknowledgment while lighting a joint he'd just stuck between his lips.

"Like take that boat ride we did out to Catalina. Remember that?"

Matt exhaled a cloud of smoke. "Yeah, of course! That was awesome!"

"Well, this summer it'll be nine years since we did that."

"No way! Seriously?"

"Yep."

"That trip seems like it was just a couple years ago."

"I know. It's crazy. Sometimes, I think about an event in the past that doesn't feel like it happened a *long*, long time ago, and then, I calculate it and realize the event was closer in time to when I was born than to the present."

Matt chuckled, shaking his head, then took another drag.

"And that *really* weirds me out," Bill added. Then, after a short pause, "Periodically, just, out of curiosity, I calculate exactly when was the halfway point between my birth and now. And when I do, I'm always stunned by how *recent* it is. You know, by realizing that all these various experiences and ages all happened *before* that halfway point."

"Oh, Bill," said Matt, glancing over at his friend and chuckling again.

After several seconds, Bill said, "So what else have you been doing for fun lately? Besides this buried treasure thing."

"Hmm, let's see..." Matt took another drag while pondering this. "Oh! There's this new T.V. show that I'm totally hooked on."

"Oh yeah?"

"Yeah, so, you know how I usually just watch older shows?"

"I guess."

"Well, my cousin Trey was in town recently and he upgraded my computer. Great guy. But anyway, now I can watch shows online, and there's this new one that is so cool. It's called 'Chula Vista.'"

"Oh, yeah—I think I read about that show. It's supposed to be revolutionary or groundbreaking in some way?"

"Right! It's on 24 hours a day, in real time, and it's got five different channels that follow five different people, all the time."

"Okay, like a reality show?"

"No! That's the thing—it's all scripted. It's all fictional! Isn't that wild?"

"Yeah."

"Yeah, so you're following these five characters all the time, 24-7. Every minute of their lives. But they're just made-up characters, played by actors."

"I imagine some of the five interact with each other sometimes?"

"Yeah, totally! All the time. Their lives are all entangled with each other. It's kind of like a soap opera."

"So, when they're together, their channels are combined?"

"Yeah. Sometimes it shows exactly the same footage on multiple channels, or sometimes it's slightly different, like you get the same scene from different people's perspectives."

"Hmm, cool. So, it's literally impossible to watch the entire show. Even for someone like you who never has anything better to do."

"Hah! Right. Yeah technically it's impossible, but you can fast-search through a lot of it, like when they're asleep or when they're just driving somewhere."

"Right."

"And they write summaries of what happened on each channel during, you know, whatever time period, and all the footage is indexed, so you can jump to the important parts, or the parts you want to actually watch instead of just reading about..."

"I see. Fascinating."

"Yeah it really is. And the story is awesome. It just... sucks me in."

"This show must be astronomically expensive to produce."

"I know, right? But, it is *so* popular. I was reading about the ratings the other day and they're just through the roof. I think they're making a healthy profit."

Bill chuckled, then thought for a moment, then said, "What about those poor actors? How can they possibly handle this thing?"

"Yeah, good question! I think they use a lot of body doubles and a lot of C.G.I., so the actors can have a break. But, yeah, it's gotta be rough..."

Bill chuckled again, then looked back out at the young surfers. Today was a gorgeous day, he suddenly realized. A peaceful contentedness came over him, and for the very first time, he felt pretty much okay with the whole accompanying-Matt-on-a-thievery-mission thing.

Bill dimly recognized that, although he never felt inclined to visit a museum, perhaps it was foolish of him not to push himself to visit them anyway, because whenever presented with pictures or words on a wall—regardless of their content—he always immediately became deeply engrossed. This phenomenon was happening currently, as he stood before a wall inside the Hearst Castle Visitor Center, absorbing all that it had to offer.

The castle itself sat on a nearby hilltop, and the only way to reach it was to ride up there aboard an official tour bus, which followed a winding 5-mile road and featured a recording of former game show host Alex Trebek describing some of the history of the property and pointing out areas along the way where William Randolph Hearst had once kept animals or engaged in outdoor sporting activities with his many esteemed guests. Bill and Matt had purchased tickets for the "Grand Rooms Tour" and then found themselves with 45 minutes to kill before the departure of the next bus.

Bill was now carefully examining a display of the names, years of service, and official portraits of all the presidents of the Hearst Castle Management Bureau, from Harold W. Flankey, who took the job in June 1958 when the Hearst Corporation donated the property to the State of California, all the way through to current president Saxon Jackson.

Next to the display was an old-style cork bulletin board to which various paper notices had been affixed with pushpins. One of these showed a more recent, less formal photo of Mr. Jackson, smiling and giving a thumbs-up, above a block of text reading, "To members of the Preservation Society: Our president upped his contribution. Up yours!"

Beyond the bulletin board lay a window, with a gold-colored plaque underneath it describing the original visitor's center and mentioning that the building which had housed it was still standing today and could be seen from this window.

Bill looked out at the rather dilapidated little structure, its windows boarded up, sitting in a field of weeds about fifty yards away. Above what looked like it had once been a doorway, he could just make out badly faded lettering that had been painted onto the wall, reading "Directory Services."

"Interesting stuff," he said, believing he was speaking to Matt, but, looking around, discovered that his friend was nowhere to be seen.

"Fuck," he muttered.

Precisely three hours later, Bill was standing in the same spot, staring out the same window, but focused on nothing in particular this time and in a far worse mood.

He'd gone up to the castle on the tour bus at the appointed time, without having located Matt, figuring they'd probably find each other up there. Then, less than ten minutes after the tour had begun, he'd been escorted out and placed back on the bus for immediate transport back down to the Visitor Center.

This was not because of any attempt to commit (or distract people from) a theft. Rather, it resulted from a completely innocent, one-man comedy of errors. Bill had left the tour group in search of a restroom and unknowingly entered a restricted area, where he'd accidentally knocked an antique porcelain statue off a shelf, shattering it, while making his way through a corridor at the end of which was one of the original bathrooms of the residence; this was where security had found him, roughly midway through urinating into an unplumbed, hundred-year-old toilet.

Upon returning to the Visitor Center, Bill had resumed wandering around it, exploring the contents of its walls. But now there was nothing left to look at, and his feelings of frustration—with himself, Matt, and especially those silly castle security folks—and boredom were welling up, joined by a sense of hopelessness, and threatening to envelop him.

He let out a long sigh and said quietly, "Matt will find me eventually... right?"

Just as it was occurring to him that he could sit on a bench somewhere and browse Wikipedia on his phone, he heard his friend's voice call out.

"Bill!"

He turned to see Matt strolling rapidly toward him, grinning exuberantly, accompanied by an Asian woman of average height and build, with long, straight hair, maybe 40ish years old.

"Where've you been, my friend?" Matt asked, sidling up to Bill.

"Where've *I* been?" Bill replied.

"Aw, wow," said Matt giddily. "What a world! What a life!"

"Who's your friend?"

"Oh, right! Mandy, meet Bill. Bill, Mandy."

"Amanda," said the woman. "It's nice to meet you."

"You too," said Bill.

"I'm tellin' ya, Bill," Matt enthused, "we have just been having the *best* time. This Hearst Castle place is the bomb. And! The best part of all..."

He reached into the pocket of his shorts and drew out a surprisingly large, long, old-fashioned, gold-colored key. Then he laughed joyously and cried, "I got it!"

"That's great," Bill said, forcing a smile. It struck him that this key would not fit any padlock he'd ever seen. "So, you didn't need me after all."

"Well," said Matt, "I mainly needed you for moral support, dude." He gave Bill an affectionate slap on the upper arm. "Which you did a great job of providing!"

"Glad to be of service."

"So, you two crazy kids, what should we do to celebrate? Oh—Bill! Great news, by the way: Mandy's going to ride with us back down to L.A.!"

Chapter 21

It was 12 noon Eastern Standard Time on a Saturday in early February, and a 38-year-old black woman with long frizzy hair and a thin but curvaceous body, wearing a red dress and matching lipstick that outlined her big, gleaming smile, was sitting at a table in Doll\Fin (a restaurant considered rather swanky by those who were willing to eat there, located on the ground floor of a high-rise "luxury" apartment complex in downtown Miami), eagerly monitoring the entrance, which lay about twenty feet away, almost directly facing her.

Then she saw him—her old, dear friend, seemingly bursting into the room from the street, radiating the same optimism, confidence, and joy that he always had: Gary Williams.

He spotted her immediately and rushed over, his grin perhaps even wider than hers. She stood up. They both flung their arms open wide, screamed delightedly and cried "Oh my god!" in unison. Then they embraced, warm and tight and long.

"Andrea, I can't believe it," said Gary. "How long has it been?"

"Oh, ages and ages," she said. "Too long!"

It had been nearly six years since they'd met face to face, though there'd been periodic phone calls and emails in the interim that had allowed them to remain loosely connected and vaguely up to date on each other's lives. There had been a time, much longer ago, when Andrea Ritenour was Gary's best friend in the world and the two were inseparable. They'd lived on the same floor of a dorm at Cal Poly Pomona their freshman year and had instantly formed a deep bond. Both sporting model-level good looks, when seen strolling around campus together they'd often been taken for some kind of power-super-couple rather than astonishingly perfectly matched straight-girl-gay-guy besties. It was Andrea who'd introduced Gary to Scott Portcullis; she'd met Scott in a math class and hadn't really liked him very much herself, but somehow felt in her gut the chemistry would be right.

After the two old pals were seated across from each other, Gary said, "So what's new with you? Tell me everything!"

"Oh, there's nothing to tell," said Andrea. "My life is just so plain and ordinary. Let's talk about you and this marathon thing. So exciting!"

"Yes indeedy-doo, it sure is, I have to admit," Gary said with a gleeful giggle. "So, the big one, the Golden Road Championship Classic, is coming up pretty soon now—it's in Albuquerque, in April. Ooh, so exciting! But, people have to qualify to run that one, by running a few others first..."

"Right, you were saying on the phone. You've been crisscrossing the country... well, even beyond this country!"

Gary chuckled. "Yeah. Turns out, though—we just discovered this Thursday night—you don't actually need to have a 'green' and a 'red' in order to qualify for the G.R.C.C., as long as you have at least one of them. Doesn't matter, though, 'cause after tomorrow, I'll have both anyway!"

Andrea was smiling but couldn't conceal that she didn't really understand.

Gary chuckled again. "Never mind," he said. "Doesn't matter. The main thing is, I am super jazzed! The big one's gonna be great, and tomorrow is gonna be great, too. I've been preparing like crazy—not just running but, also, really studying the course, and... I even did a virtual video tour of the whole thing... And, just, everything. Woo! I'm ready! Let's do this!" His grin was practically leaping off his face.

Now Andrea chuckled, too. "Well, good for you, Gary. I'm so happy for you."

"Thanks! So, what about you? 'Plain and ordinary'—hah! I don't believe that for a second. I know you, babe!"

"Hi, I'm Seth," said their server, Seth, arriving tableside. "I'll be your server today."

"Oh, we haven't had a chance to look at the menu yet," said Gary.

"Okay, I'll give you a few minutes, then. Unless you'd like to order any drinks?"

"No, thanks, not right now," Andrea and Gary both said, smiling up at Seth, who smiled back at them for a microsecond before speedily departing.

"So," said Gary, grinning, "bright lights, big city. You been partying your tail off?"

"Well, yeah," Andrea conceded with a small giggle. "I really love it here, actually."

"I knew you would!"

Andrea had moved here just a few months ago, after nearly three years of what she considered a rather humdrum existence in Cumming, Georgia, a quiet, far-northern suburb of Atlanta where she'd landed primarily because of a boyfriend whom she'd ended up dumping in fairly short order.

"Yeah, I really think I'm a city girl at heart..."

"*Yeah* you are!" Gary exclaimed with a laugh.

"And a hot weather girl, too!" she added. "Looking back now, I don't know why I dragged my feet for so long..."

(She'd ultimately been prompted to move by a hefty local tax hike, following the shutdown of a huge volunteer-organized program aiming to increase civic responsibility among current residents, attract new ones, and boost tourism, which had failed utterly to achieve any of these. The program, whose slogan was "You ARE Your City," had never truly gotten off the ground, making one foolish misstep after another throughout its whole existence. Perhaps the most embarrassing of these was encouraging people to walk around in public wearing a colorful sticker on their chest that read, "I'm Cumming!")

"So, got yourself a cool sports car yet?" Gary asked.

"Mmm, no, not yet..."

"Come on, babe! You love yourself a cool car, to go with your hot weather!"

"Yeah, but... it's a big responsibility, owning a car. You gotta pay for it. You gotta keep it insured. You gotta maintain it. You gotta have some place to park it!"

Gary chuckled. "Well listen to you, Miss Mature-and-Responsible. True, true. All of that is true but... I know you. I know how a cool sports car makes your pulse race..."

"Well, yeah..."

"You love it! You can't resist it! You gotta gotta gotta have it!" A hearty laugh.

Andrea laughed, too. "You're right. Of course you're right. But, well... I was talking to my mom about this, actually. It's funny, that woman is smarter than I ever knew! Anyway, say I do get myself that cool sports car. What happens next?"

"Then you drive it!" Gary exclaimed. "And you're lovin' it!"

Seth had reappeared next to them. "Any questions about the menu?" he asked.

"Uh, no," said Andrea.

"I think we need a few more minutes," said Gary.

Seth smiled and left again.

"Okay, here's the thing," said Andrea. "What you just described, that's the fantasy. That's what you *think* is gonna happen. But it's not the reality."

"It's not?"

"No. Once you've actually got the cool sports car, you get used to it, and you become aware of all its flaws. And the whole idea of... possessing that car, it's no longer magical. It's real and normal and ordinary now, because you've done it."

"Hmm..."

She was on a roll. "And it turns out your specific car is only one example of that model, and probably not the very best example. You see others on the road and they seem better than yours. Plus, it was never the only really exciting model out there. There were others, and now *they* have a special appeal, because you don't own them. And new cool cars are coming out all the time, while the existing ones, including yours, just keep getting older and older."

Gary was grinning widely and shaking his head.

"So," Andrea said in conclusion, "now you've got this car that's, meh, pretty cool, but you haven't actually quelled that feeling—the super-desire feeling that made you buy it in the first place. You still get that feeling, all the time, about other cars. So what have you really accomplished?"

"Wow," Gary marveled.

Andrea burst out laughing, mentally listening to everything she'd just said. "It's a trap!" she exclaimed, mid-laughter. "The cool sports car is a trap."

Gary laughed, too. "When you put it that way, I can't argue! Woo! You should be an attorney or something."

After a short silence, Andrea asked, "So, how's Scott doing? He didn't tag along on this one?"

"Nah, not this time. He had a thing with his parents this weekend anyway, and... you know, there's a lot going on... But, yeah, he's doing great! Thanks for asking!"

"And the two of you are doing okay?"

"Oh, yeah, we're doing great," Gary replied with a big grin. Then, switching to a puzzled face, "Why?"

"Well, you said... when we talked on the phone, a couple months ago or whenever it was, you said you guys were sort of going through a rough patch."

"Oh, right! That. Wow, that seems like a million years ago. Yeah, we had some... uh, friction, I guess... around that whole South America thing." He chuckled and shook his head, thinking back on it. "But Scott—I know he doesn't seem like it, on the surface, all stern and uptight about everything—but, he's got the biggest heart of anyone I ever knew. So loving, and caring..."

"I'm really glad to hear," said Andrea, smiling warmly.

"Yep. He's the best. He even helped me keep my job. Really smoothed things over with Jim. I've told you about Jim, right? My old buddy from work? Ended up being my boss for a while. But, now, we're both back where we were a year ago... Yep, lots of changes around that place..."

"Have you folks made any decisions?" asked Seth, who was back with them again, in as cheerful a tone as he could manage.

"Uh, no," said Andrea.

"I think we need a few more minutes," Gary said to Seth, who promptly left.

Then, turning back to Andrea, he asked, "Uh, what was I saying?" and then laughed at his own absentmindedness.

"The wild world of CuppaJoe," she replied, grinning.

"Oh yeah! CuppaJoe, woo! Never a dull moment. But seems like things are settling down now—Oh my goodness! Who's this?"

A small canine face, covered in long, shaggy, white hair, had suddenly emerged from the top of Andrea's bag, which was sitting on the chair next to hers. Two dark, beady eyes were fixed on Gary.

"Oh!" said Andrea, glancing down. "There you are, you little cutie! Did you have a nice nap?"

Gary was happy but still reeling a bit from the surprise. "Wow," he said. "I, I had no idea..."

"Gary, this is Winston," said Andrea. "Winston, Gary."

"Pleased to meet you, Winston!"

Winston continued to stare. His tongue made a lightning-quick appearance, flicking up to touch his nose before vanishing again.

"Yeah," said Andrea, "I decided, new life in Miami, let's shake things up a little. I'd been thinking for a long time about getting a dog..."

"He's adorable," Gary said with a huge smile. "Big responsibility, though, dog ownership. 'Specially living in an apartment."

"You're so right. It really is. A lot of dog owners don't appreciate that. I talked to my mom about this—about the burden I've taken on. I mean, it's a labor of love, but it's still a burden. Simple fact."

"Yep, yep... It's funny, actually—Scott was just talking about dogs the other night. About the strange place they occupy in our... I guess in our collective consciousness?"

"Oh yeah?"

"Yeah. Scott can explain it better than me, but, basically, we always love dogs unconditionally. We never judge them. Their... um, their... total innocence, it appeals to us. They have no bad intentions. Heck, they have no intentions at all! They've got—"

"Excuse me, ma'am," Seth suddenly said from several feet away, pointing at Winston's head. "Dogs aren't allowed in here."

"Oh, come on," Andrea said in a rather sweet, pathetic voice. "He's just an itsy bitsy little guy. And quiet as a mouse."

"He *is* so well behaved!" remarked Gary, smiling enthusiastically.

"Um..." said Seth. "Um... I guess I could go, check with my manager."

"Oh, it would mean so much to me," said Andrea.

Seth hurried away, a pained expression on his face.

Gary chuckled and shook his head.

"Hope they don't kick us out," said Andrea, though she didn't seem too worried about it.

"Nah, they won't," said Gary. "It'll be fine. So anyway, what were we talking about?"

"Dogs."

"Oh, right! Yeah, so, dogs, we give 'em this 'free pass,' you know, that no human could possibly get. Total acceptance, love, affection, kindness... with zero expectations."

"Mmm-hmm..."

"But, on the other hand, what would happen if there was any sort of, like, crisis situation? The dog would be lowest priority. Compared to people, I mean. We'd abandon a dog in a heartbeat, you know, if it came down to it."

"Yeah, true."

"So, there's kind of like, this, paradox going on... where these traits a dog has—or, doesn't have—you know, lack of awareness, lack of contribution, lack of opinion... It endears the dog to us, but at the same time, sort of, un-endears the dog to us, too, you know? Really interesting."

Andrea nodded, then said, "Oh! So, tell me—did you drive all the way out here? Or did you brave the scary world of flight again?"

Gary chuckled. "I flew."

"Good for you!"

"Didn't have much of a choice. And guess what? It was the worst flight I've ever had."

"No! You're kidding!"

"Serious. Every flight I have is the worst one yet. They just keep getting worse! And I have to fly home from this, too!"

Andrea was laughing now.

"But that's the last time," Gary went on. "When I go to Albuquerque for the big one, I am *driving*!"

They noticed Seth was once again standing next to them.

"Okay," he said. "You guys can stay. With your dog. Your dog can stay."

"Yay!" said Andrea. "Thank you!"

For a moment the three (or four, including Winston) looked at each other, smiling (except for Winston) but not speaking.

Then Seth said, "So, um... have you decided on anything you'd like to order?"

"Uh, no," said Andrea.

"I think we need a few more minutes," said Gary.

At that very moment, in the southern part of Santa Monica, near its border with Venice, Bill and Yvonne Smede were also informing a server they needed a few more minutes, who also strode away rapidly, making a mental shrug along with a mental note to wait longer before returning again.

"So, Patrick said he had a thing with Len this morning?" Bill queried.

"Yes," Yvonne replied, rolling her eyes. "Last night at dinner. You were sitting right there next to him."

"But, we planned this like a week ago."

This breakfast had originally been conceived as a Smede family event, to celebrate the (somewhat dubious) milestone of all four of them being reunited under one roof.

"Right," said Yvonne. "That was also mentioned at dinner. He pleaded 'unforeseen circumstances' and 'high importance'... with his usual extreme awkwardness, of course."

Bill smiled. "Right. Hmm. Okay. And... I should probably remember this too, but, what about Alice? What was her excuse?"

"Didn't need one." Yvonne smiled too. "When we first mentioned it to her, she asked if she 'had to.' And we said no, she didn't have to."

Bill chuckled. "Alice." He sighed and shook his head. "Yep, they're both in character."

"As are you."

"Indeed. And you as well." Another chuckle and a short, thoughtful pause. "Yeah, memory is a funny thing... How do we store our memories? Why are certain things very easy to access later on, while others are so difficult?"

"In your case I think it's linked to whether that thing actually matters at all," Yvonne said with a smirk. "No, I know what you mean. Memory is strange, for sure."

"And sometimes, I can remember stuff only in an abstract, factual way. Like, I remember that something happened... and, *maybe* I might even have some mental notation that, you know, at the time I felt this specific emotion, labeled X, Y, or Z. But I can't truly recall what it felt like for me, to be in that moment. Or what it looked like, or sounded like, or... anything. So, it's as if I don't truly have a memory of an experience—I only have an entry in a database telling me that such-and-such took place. Like it could've happened to someone else and just been told to me—no difference."

"Mmm-hmm, yeah, I think I know what you mean..."

"But anyway, I digress... The point is, screw Patrick and Alice.

This is more fun without them anyway."

"Agreed," Yvonne said with a laugh. "Oh, so, forgot to ask you yesterday: any more progress on finding your own replacement?"

"Ugh. No."

"Even now that the place is totally empty and clean and... you know, move-in ready?"

"No. Never had any trouble finding people who want to rent the place. They're lining up around the block! They can't wait to pay through the nose for a shitty little... piece-of-shit place. With an asshole landlord."

Yvonne was cracking up.

Bill went on, "No, the problem is—and always has been—*him*. That old, persnickety prick. Won't accept anyone I bring to him. Always finds something wrong with them, why they would be 'not good tenant'..."

"God." Yvonne was still laughing.

"He wasn't nearly so fussy when *I* applied. Signed me right up. 'Cause it was vacant and he wasn't getting paid for it!"

"Yep."

Their phones pinged simultaneously.

"Cherub Channel," said Bill, using a term Yvonne had coined a few years back to refer to the group chat that included all four Smedes.

"Yeah... Oh..." Looking down at her phone screen, she realized they'd assumed wrong. "Who's yours from?"

"Uh, let's see... Oh, just Bedwetter again." He snickered. (Bill was eternally tickled by—and couldn't help physically reacting every time he used—his nickname for Steve Ledbetter, an extremely kind, friendly, easygoing man and by far the most boring friend Bill had ever had.)

Yvonne was tapping out a quick reply.

"How about yours?" Bill asked.

"It's, uh..." She finished her texting and looked up. "It's Horton again. Just asking me if I've spoken to them yet."

"Mmm..." Bill nodded gravely.

Horton Bannaker, who'd worked for twenty years on the Interface Team but was now about to get downsized out of the entire organization if he couldn't manage to secure a transfer to the Inpatient Team, and whom Yvonne regarded as a fairly close friend and quite a decent human being, had asked her to officially vouch for him as part of the interdepartmental vetting process. This presented her with a dilemma, because she knew Horton to be grossly incompetent in his current position, and had no doubt he would be even more so in his new one, were he accepted for it.

"Luckily, they sent me a questionnaire. So, at least I don't have to literally *talk* to them. But, it's still tough. You know, I don't want to lie... but I also don't want to do anything to hurt his chances."

"Right. Loyalty to your friend is important to you, but so is your integrity."

"Yeah, and just, the quality of the work we do for the hospital..."

"Conflicting values."

"Exactly. It's funny, actually—Francisco was going on about this very thing when I saw him last weekend."

"Oh yeah?"

"Yeah. You know, one of his... pseudo-academic rambling monologues..."

Bill chuckled.

"He was saying that most stress and anxiety can be traced to a conflict of personal values. That you're in a position where you have to choose between two particular values, that you hold, you know, equally strongly."

"Hmm, interesting." (Bill had uttered this same phrase disingenuously hundreds of times, but not this time.)

They both suddenly noticed their server had returned.

"How're you guys doing?" she asked.

"Uh..." Bill glanced up at her, then down at his open menu (which he'd spent a few seconds absentmindedly thumbing through right after being seated), a slightly embarrassed smile on his face.

"I think we're still figuring out what we want," said Yvonne, also smiling but sans embarrassment.

In a flash the server was gone again.

Bill was scanning the menu, frowning. "Why did we pick this place again? Somebody was raving about it, right?"

Keesha's Quiches (named very accurately, Bill was now discovering, seeing page after page of no other type of food) was just the sort of trendy restaurant in a trendy location that neither Smede, generally speaking, would ever have considered patronizing.

"Yeah," said Yvonne. "Actually, seems like more than one person mentioned it to us. Hmm... I don't remember who it was. Anyway, what were we talking about?"

"Uh... Francisco."

"Oh, yeah! It was him. He recommended this place. Very strongly."

"Ah. Sounds about right. And what was that other one we were considering, just around the corner from here?"

"Oh—we were never really considering that one." She went back to her phone and began tapping. "Anyway I know who recommended that one—it was Amy, at that happy hour a couple of weeks ago... Ah, here it is. Listen to this. It's called 'Gut Slut: a Probiotic Café.'"

Bill laughed. "Yeah, no wonder we nixed it. So, this happy hour... two weeks ago, you said?"

"Yeah, it was at The Rippled Parasol."

Bill looked blank.

"You know, that mushroom restaurant on La Cienega."

"Oh, yeah. But, hmm... I don't remember going there any time recently..."

"Come on, squeeze your rememberer really hard. It was on a Sunday. Laura and Mike were there, and Jake... Oh, wait! No, you're right—for once. You weren't there."

"I knew it!" Bill grinned.

"That was the day you went to Hearst Castle with Matt."

"Ah, yes. Right. What fun *that* was... Oh! Matt! He was the other one who recommended this place. Said it had a great vibe."

Yvonne chuckled. "Guess maybe we should've considered our sources a bit more!"

"Yes. I thought he also said he'd had the lasagna, but... hmm..." Bill had reached the last page of the menu.

"So he still hasn't tried to dig up that treasure chest?" asked Yvonne.

"Uh..." Bill was perusing the rather small beverage section at the end of the menu. "No. Not that I'm aware of. Actually he seems to have forgotten all about it. Temporarily, no doubt."

"Yes."

"Have you ever heard of 'twice-boiled tea'?"

"No."

Bill's phone began ringing. He looked at it, grimaced, and silenced it.

"Your mother?" Yvonne asked with a smirk.

"No. It's a number I don't recognize. They keep calling and they won't leave a message."

"Well, it *could* be her. Maybe she's using a different phone, to trick you into answering."

"Heh, yeah."

"Next time they call, you should just answer it. Or else just block the number."

"Yeah, I thought about blocking it, but... I mean, it's possible it's actually something valid..."

"Well, just answer it next time."

"Actually, I already know when the next time will be. They always call twice, with exactly two minutes between the two attempts. Bizarre."

"Hey, any chance it could be Steve Ledbetter?"

"Nah, he's in my contacts. Oh, unless he's trying to trick me, like Mom."

"Right."

"Ah, Steve... Hey, you know, it's funny—when I was working in that office all those years ago, where I met Steve, there was this other guy who worked there, who was also named Steve. Steve Fox. Seemed like a great guy, and a funny guy. I didn't really know him, but, I'd overhear him chatting with other people and I always thought, 'He seems like a really cool guy. I think I'd really like to get to know him'..."

"But you never did."

"Nope. Never found an opportunity that met my shy-polite-unassuming standards."

"Well..."

"But Steve Ledbetter, the one I had zero interest in getting to know, *he* approached *me*. And he wanted to be friends. So, of course, we are."

Yvonne chuckled.

Bill's phone started ringing again.

"Just answer it," said Yvonne as she began standing up from her chair. "I need to use the restroom anyway."

Bill stared at the phone screen, with its unrecognized number and its little green and red icons, for several seconds as Yvonne walked away from the table. Finally he decided to go for it.

"Hello?"

"Yes, hello. I'm trying to reach William Smede." It was an adult male voice with a generic American accent.

"Speaking," said Bill tentatively.

"William, this is Brad Harbinger."

"Uh... Do we know each other?"

A quick chuckle. "Yes. Orange County High School."

"Oh. Wow. Uh... Hi... Brad... How are you?"

Bill was wracking his brain, trying to picture this guy or recall something about him. The name did sound vaguely familiar.

"I'm doing well. Very well, in fact. And yourself?"

"Yeah, I'm, uh... I'm fine. Thanks."

"That's good to hear."

"So... uh... to what do I owe the pleasure?"

"Well, I need to ask a favor of you."

"You do?"

"Yes. You see, I've accumulated quite a large amount of monetary wealth over the years, and I need to make sure my assets are secure."

"Okay..."

"But I don't trust so-called professionals. Bankers, money managers, stockbrokers, accountants, and so forth. I distrust them in two ways: they're incompetent and they're corrupt."

"All of them?"

"Sadly, I believe, yes—most of them. And how can one truly be sure?"

"Hmm."

"So, I want to entrust you, William, with a small piece of my fortune. I'm dividing it up among a number of trustworthy... uh, trustees. But nobody is one hundred percent trustworthy—not even you. No offense."

"No, of course not..."

"So, what do you say, William? Will you help me?"

"Uh... I don't know, Brad. I mean... why me?"

"Because you knew me before I was rich."

"But, I don't know you now."

"That's why you're perfect."

"But, we were never that close."

"Like I said, perfect. Come on, William. I need you."

"Uh... I don't know... How much money are we talking about here, anyway?"

"Well the details would need to be ironed out. But probably in the neighborhood of 75 million dollars."

"Jesus Christ."

Brad chuckled. "I understand, William—it's not the sort of figure a person like you comes across every day. But don't worry. A person like me does."

"Uh... I don't know, Brad. I mean... what exactly would I have to... *do?*"

"We'll iron out the details when we meet in person. Come on, William. Just meet with me. You don't have to commit to anything."

"Uh... I don't know..."

"Come on!"

Bill let out a long sigh. He felt a small amount of dread and a large amount of resignation. "Okay. I'll meet with you."

Gary Williams felt euphoric and lighter than air as he burst out of his pen, in the marathon starting area adjacent to FTX Arena, and began rocketing effortlessly through the crisp, fragrant, wonderful Miami morning. It was almost like a dream.

Shortly after passing the 6-mile marker, he noticed a runner, moving at about the same pace as him six feet to his left, who was the spitting image of a former CuppaJoe co-worker named Stu Lowdlee who'd had a hang-up about never combining two enjoyable experiences (so that each could be fully savored). He found many of life's experiences enjoyable, and was never seen consuming both food and drink in the same sitting, nor having a conversation while doing either of these. As Gary recalled, Stu's time at the company had been rather short.

Coming across the Venetian Causeway, Gary saw a fellow runner, stopped next to the guardrail (perhaps to catch her breath and/or take in the beautiful scenery), who bore a striking resemblance to another of his co-workers, Gretchen Casperback. Gary had always respected

Gretchen's work, and had lamented her departure for Starbucks after seven years at CuppaJoe. He had always suspected, however, that she thought a bit too highly of her own intellect and generally fancied herself the smartest person in any room. And he'd been tickled, and slightly baffled, by her mentioning, on several occasions, that she had a deep, lifelong, fundamental, critical need to be the more intelligent one in a relationship. Gary'd had the opportunity to meet Gretchen's husband a few times at corporate social events and to confirm that she'd succeeded brilliantly in her aim.

As he was passing by all the government buildings, on Miami Avenue between 5th Street and 3rd Street, he was reminded of yet another co-worker by a runner who overtook him on the right (quite quickly and seemingly with great ease, causing Gary to wonder what the man's strategy might be and where he'd been from the start of the race until now). This runner's face and hair looked astonishingly similar (at least from the left side and the back) to those of Shane Calloway, who'd been working in Gary's office for the past three years and could frequently be found in the break room engaged in brief spells of non-work-related chitchat.

Shane was an avid reader of science journalism, particularly psychology, and often shared his latest discoveries with whomever would listen. Gary smiled and shook his head remembering a time recently when he'd been treated to a synopsis of a new therapy for extreme fear of needles, being developed by two researchers at Stanford, consisting mainly of threatening the subject—and, in some instances, gently stabbing them—with knives. Thus far the approach had proved phenomenally successful, though it was not, Shane had hastened to point out, entirely free from adverse side effects.

While running along 6th Street beside the 500 Brickell towers, just shy of the 14-mile marker, Gary glanced to his right and witnessed a small drone dropping an Amazon package into a parked car's trunk (which opened and closed with no apparent human involvement). He marveled at the state of modern technology, then wondered if CuppaJoe might be able to ramp up a drone-based coffee delivery system, then panicked about missing an important meeting to discuss the new packaging proposal, then remembered that it was tomorrow and he'd be back in plenty of time for it.

As he was executing a U-turn on the Rickenbacker Causeway, Gary was delighted to spot his good friend Andrea standing on the sidelines, cheering him on, then puzzled and frightened as he slowly realized she had beckoned him over, produced her little dog Winston and a leash from an unknown stowage location, handed both to Gary, and then instantly vanished, seemingly in a puff of smoke.

Gary quickly stopped fretting about his new predicament and settled on the plan that he and Winston would run the remainder of the course together, side by side, as partners, with a six-feet-long strip of leather connecting one's neck to the other's hand for safety.

Unfortunately, Winston proved to lack either the ability or the inclination (or maybe both) to run as fast as Gary, or anywhere remotely near that fast. This huge discrepancy in their rate of travel, along with Gary's perpetual pumping arm motions, meant that Winston was alternately dragged along the pavement and yanked off of it, over and over again. He also periodically received unintentional kicks from other runners who hadn't noticed him down there.

Gary's next tack was to run with Winston tucked under his arm, which would've worked well if only Gary hadn't felt hopelessly compelled to pump his arms continuously. Consequently, during this stage of the dog-care-plus-marathon combo effort, Winston took delivery of vast quantities of vigorous squeezing and rubbing, and tumbled to the ground dozens of times.

Eventually Gary decided that, though he couldn't entrust just some random spectator with temporarily caring for Winston, it would probably be fine to leave the pooch with a race official, or perhaps even one of the volunteers manning the numerous refreshment stations. However, he gave up on this idea after receiving a very hard, very fast "No" from all fifty people he approached about it.

Next, Gary tried several variations of strapping Winston to his body with the leash—right leg, left leg, arms, back, chest, abdomen, head. He found them all equally uncomfortable (and, by the look of it, so did Winston) and each included a gradual self-loosening of the leash that culminated in Winston once again falling onto the road.

Finally, Gary determined that he could, just barely, grip Winston's torso in one hand and keep hold of the dog while charging forward and pumping his arms. He then proceeded to do just that, continuously, for the final seven and a half miles of the course. But just as he was about to cross the finish line in Bayfront Park, he noticed that he was no longer holding Winston, and no longer wearing any clothes; then he slipped on a banana peel and fell face-first onto the pavement, and everything went black, and his ears were assaulted by an unbelievably loud electronic beeping sound. What on earth *is* that?

Gary sat bolt upright in bed, dazed and covered in sweat. The beeping sound was his 4:15 A.M. alarm. He managed to reach over and silence it as reality came flooding back to him, along with an intense wave of relief. He was in his hotel room. The race had not yet begun.

"Woo," he said out loud, but this time he really meant "Phew." Then he shook his head and muttered, "My goodness. It felt so real."

The actual Miami Marathon unfolded much more happily for Gary. He enjoyed excellent weather and persistent high energy throughout the entire race, with no injuries and virtually no aches and pains, and finished with a fairly respectable time of five hours and thirteen minutes. And he was not handed a dog to look after (although he did encounter Andrea, cheering him on from the sidelines, and succumbed to the temptation to briefly pause his running endeavors so she could quickly show him her favorite ice cream parlor, which was located just two blocks off the course).

His journey back to California, however, was a different story altogether. The plane encountered severe turbulence five minutes after taking off, which sent Gary into white knuckles mode; and to his immense horror (but only mild surprise), this continued, with what felt like hurricane-grade intensity, all the way across the country.

"So, yeah," Gary said five days later, safely out of the sky and back in his home, seated at his dining table in front of a half-eaten plate of beef stroganoff and a glass of water, "I've been giving it a lot of thought lately... Such an interesting question. Do we have free will? Dang. It's deep, you know?" He laughed. "I don't think there's any way to be sure of the answer."

There was a brief silence during which all three of his dinner companions slowly nodded their heads.

Then he went on: "But, I think we do. I mean, I *feel* it. When I'm faced with a decision, I just… somehow I just *know*, deep down, this decision can truly go either way. It's up to me!"

After another laugh and another short pause, he looked at Yvonne Smede, seated across from him, and said, "So what do you guys think? Do we have free will?"

"Honestly," she said, gently and with a smile, "I don't know and I don't care."

"I'm with you!" announced Scott Portcullis, sitting to Gary's left.

"Well," said Bill Smede, reluctant but pushed forward by Gary's eager, expectant gaze, "I agree it's an interesting question, and, I have actually thought about it, some. And, I think what I believe is: to the extent that we even exist, yes, we do have free will.

"What I mean is, our existence as sentient, aware beings—our consciousness… it's on another, sort of, level, I guess, from the physical world. The mind exists in a virtual world. I mean, it certainly depends on material things like a brain… and, you know, below that, cells and molecules and atoms. And, probably, I think, it arises *from* those material things. But, it's a separate thing… On its own plane…"

Met with bemused faces all around, Bill hesitated, but decided he'd come this far, he might as well finish his thought.

"So, at the lowest levels of the material world, I think it all comes down to a fixed set of cause-and-effect rules, maybe combined with some element of total randomness—you know, that can't be predicted or controlled at all. But the human mind doesn't exist down there. We exist up here." He held his hand up, horizontally, a foot above the tabletop. "And up here, we do make the choices. Like Gary said."

The group was silent for a moment. Then Bill added, "Just because it might've been predetermined, by physics, that you would make a given choice, doesn't mean you didn't choose. You did."

After another moment of silence, Gary said, "So what you're actually saying is, no, we don't have free will!"

He started laughing and the others all followed his lead.

When the laughter had subsided, Bill asked, "So, Scott, how are things at work now? Last time we got together you were saying…?"

"Right," said Scott. "We were wrapping up a major project then, and I was under the gun. So no, that's all finished now, which is good…"

"But?"

"But, now, this guy Laird Rasmussen, who got a lot of the credit for the success of that project—*undeservedly*, I might add—has more clout than ever before, and a bigger ego, I think, and he's… He's just a…"

"A total asshole?" Bill ventured, smiling.

"Yes. Thank you. I didn't want to say it…"

"No problem."

"Yeah, he really is. I know people have different perspectives and different motivations for their behavior, and… I know sometimes they might be coming from a place of pain or fear or misunderstanding. So, I try to sympathize, if I can."

"Me too, babe," said Gary. "So important. Try to walk in their shoes. Everybody is human, right? Everybody deserves sympathy."

"Yeah, I guess," Scott replied. "But, it's pretty tough with Laird. He just seems… sadistic. I think he actually enjoys being cruel to people. Just, cruelty for its own sake."

"Ouch!" Gary exclaimed. "Well, yeah, that is pretty tough."

"I think sympathy for sadists is possible," said Yvonne. "In theory. Not saying *I* feel it. But, you know, maybe they can't help it if they enjoy other people's suffering. They're only doing what they love and deriving pleasure from it, like all of us do."

"Hah!" Gary exclaimed in amusement.

"Good point," said Bill.

"Anyway," said Scott, "assholes come and go. I'm sure this one will go at some point. But, however much you blame or don't blame the guy for who he is, lately he's been making life at the office worse for me. Thankfully I've got Wendy around to vent to, or talk about baseball or whatever."

"Oh," said Yvonne, "how's it going with that baseball thing you do? What is it again?"

Scott frowned. "Cooperstown Universe. The season ended. I never made MasterBlaster."

"Oh, sorry to hear."

"It's okay. Not a big deal."

"What was the issue?"

"Well, it was… hmm… I guess there really was no issue. It was just, harder than I'd thought."

Yvonne gave a sympathetic smile.

"I wasn't good enough, I wasn't smart enough..."

"And goshdarnit," said Bill, "nobody liked you."

Glancing around and quickly realizing that nobody else at the table understood his joke, he added, "Never mind. I know how you feel, Scott. I'm generally not good enough or smart enough for most things... which is why I attempt so few."

To Bill's relief, Scott seemed not the least bit offended and perhaps even (very) mildly amused.

"It's okay, babe," offered Gary, then grinned widely and added, "I know next year you're gonna kick some serious behind! Master-blasting them all!"

"Mmm, I don't know," Scott replied. "I think I might give up on C.U. It kind of seems like a waste of time."

"Maybe you can get into the stamps with me," Gary excitedly suggested. (As he'd informed the Smedes shortly after their arrival, Gary had recently begun to develop a passion for stamp collecting.)

"Maybe," said Scott.

For the next two minutes they all ate their stroganoff and nobody spoke. Then Gary started up again.

"Let's hear a funny story," he said. "Anybody got a funny story?"

"Bill has one," said Yvonne.

"I do?"

"From this afternoon. The cans."

"Ah, yes. So for years we just recycled our aluminum cans with all the other recycling. But I always kind of thought, in the back of my mind, 'Maybe we should be taking these to one of those redemption centers instead.' You know, might as well get a little cash back."

"We never buy cans of anything," said Gary. "How does it work?"

"You feed them into a machine and it gives you back the CRV. Five cents per can. But the thing is, these machines only exist at special recycling centers, and the nearest one is five miles away, in West Hollywood."

"Gotcha."

"I mean, I can recycle *shit* right around the corner from my condo, but I gotta drive five miles in order to recycle aluminum. Go figure."

Gary laughed loudly. The other two smiled.

"So I load up our cans, in these big plastic trash bags—the huge ones, you know, for like, outdoor use—and I put them in the trunk of the car and make my way over to West Hollywood, very slowly, of course—there's no special lane for can returns. So, I finally get there, park the car, get out, open the trunk, and the cans start falling out, all over the parking lot. I grab hold of the bags, but in a stupid way that only makes it worse by, like, squeezing more cans out the top.

"So I spend five minutes scurrying around, finding all of them, picking them up, and putting them back in the bags. Then I take the bags out of the trunk and place them in this shopping cart that was just sitting around nearby, 'cause they're bulky and it seems like an easy way to transport them across the parking lot.

"But as I'm merrily pushing my cart along, the top of one of the bags comes open again and the cans start falling everywhere. So I have to stop, and move the cart off to the side, and then run around all over the damn place again, dodging cars and waving at the drivers in that friendly, embarrassed, 'Hey, I'm a complete idiot' kind of way, and some of them are running over the cans and crushing them..."

"Good story," said Scott.

It was clear Yvonne agreed, both from her face and from the fact she'd volunteered to listen to it for the second time today.

Gary had been laughing continuously, with varying intensity, throughout.

Bill continued: "So I finally gather them all up again, and make sure the bags are tightly cinched up, and I make it to the entrance to the place, and it turns out they're already closed for the day. So I wheel my cart back to the car, and load the bags back into the trunk, and go on my phone to try to figure out where's the *second* closest recycling center, and are they still open. And it was in Inglewood, and they *were* still open, allegedly, and I tried to go there but got stuck in this horrendous traffic jam..."

Now Scott and Yvonne were laughing too.

"And after like an hour, I gave up and just turned around and went home. So we still have all the cans and I'm thinking, probably, fuck that—I'll just throw them in the curbside bin like I've always done."

"Love it!" exclaimed Gary.

"Wow," said Scott.

"Oh!" Yvonne suddenly said. "Gary, your marathon stuff—you haven't even mentioned it. What's the latest?"

Gary's smile shrunk slightly but remained on his face. "Aw, it's over. I'm not going to the big one."

"You're not?"

"Nah. I didn't make it. Didn't qualify for it."

"Oh no, I'm so sorry."

"Aw, it's okay…" Gary said with a chuckle and a dismissive wave of his hand.

"So, Miami didn't go well?"

"Well, I thought it did… until the following day, got a call from the referee folks and they'd been analyzing data from the race and they said they had to disqualify me because apparently I missed one of their electronic checkpoints…"

"Wow, seriously?"

Scott, who'd been frowning and shaking his head, explained, "He left the course for a few minutes. Thought he rejoined it at the same point, but, must've gotten confused somehow…"

"I thought I rejoined it at the same point," Gary echoed with a shrug and a sheepish face.

"But wasn't there something," asked Bill, "like, you didn't actually need that particular race in order to qualify?"

"Yeah," said Gary, "it would've been good enough just to have the other colors I got, but, trouble is, my 'green,' turns out it didn't actually count for the G.R.C.C., because it wasn't in my home country and I didn't get special authorization for that…"

Scott, still frowning and shaking his head, said "Such *damn* complicated rules!"

"Wow," said Yvonne again.

"Bummer," said Bill.

Gary chuckled. "Aw, it's okay, guys. It just wasn't meant to be. Actually I don't know if running is really my thing, anyway. My heart's just not really in it, you know? Now when I sit down with my stamps— now that's a different story. My heart is soaring!"

A barely audible "Hmm" escaped from Scott's throat.

Chapter 22

This is exactly how I always pictured England looking, thought Amy Lee on a Saturday in mid-February as she gazed out the window of a traditional London black cab at the quaint rooftops, green hillsides, misty rain, and cloudy, dark gray sky rushing past. (In fact she'd never pictured how England looked until this very moment.) Then she leaned forward to address the driver, a dour white man in his sixties with big, unkempt tufts of silver hair protruding out from under a newsboy cap.

"I just can't get over it! Your steering wheel is on the wrong freakin' side of the car!"

He gave her a quick glance in the rearview mirror and said nothing, the same response he'd provided when she'd shouted "Hey, look—a real castle!" as they were passing about a mile from Windsor Castle, and also when she'd told him about the bizarre sign she'd seen above a pedestrian tunnel at Heathrow Airport that read, "Subway to Underground – No Trolleys."

The man had spoken—sort of—several times during the journey, in quiet, nearly indecipherable (but oh so charming!) utterances apparently related to their route and directed, it seemed, at himself or perhaps at nobody. But he clearly hadn't the slightest interest in conducting any verbal exchange whatsoever with his passenger.

This attitude didn't at all dissuade Amy from trying, but as it happened, she thought of nothing else to say, post-steering-wheel-remark, until she was thanking and paying her rather strange driver after they'd transitioned from the M4 to the curiously named A329(M), which quickly became simply the A329 (with muttering from the front seat that sounded like "Jewel, carriage, whey"), then onto the smaller surface roads of the town of Bracknell, and had finished making their way to Amy's destination in the residential district known as Great Hollands (front seat muttering: "Ow, zinger, state").

She found the fare of £100 (not including the £25 tip she cheerfully added (at which the driver seemed pleased but somewhat taken aback)) surprisingly steep, but reminded herself that this was a foreign currency and, though she couldn't recall the exchange rate she'd been given when purchasing her stack of British cash, most likely a hundred pounds was much less than a hundred dollars.

As the taxi pulled away, Amy knocked on the front door of 62 Holbeck—a boxy, ugly, narrow townhouse made of brick and possibly some concrete—feeling the same mild anxiety she'd felt four and a half months ago standing on strangers' doorsteps in Coleman, Michigan.

Immediately from within came the sounds of a barking dog (in Amy's mind, a very large, very vicious one) and of a screaming human (producing the words "I got it! I got it! Nobody else get it!" in an accent reminiscent of the one beloved American actor Dick Van Dyke had so poorly attempted to adopt in the 1964 film "Mary Poppins").

A moment later, the door was flung open to visually reveal the sources of these sounds, which turned out to be a very small, not the least bit scary-looking dog and a short, scrawny white girl of about 10 years, respectively, both of whom were now simply staring at Amy in silence.

"Why hello there!" she said to the girl, smiling widely.

The girl, still staring, began giggling.

"Is your mom home?" Amy enquired.

The giggling intensified. "My ma'am! I haven't got a ma'am, have I!"

"Oh, um… Well, how 'bout your—"

"Mummy!" the girl called out toward the inside of the house as she turned and headed that way. "There's a Yank at the door!"

"I love it," Amy said with a chuckle.

The dog, who'd continued staring at Amy until the girl had turned away, was now moving its head slowly, repeatedly back and forth to look alternately at Amy's face and at some point inside the house, seemingly trying to decide whether to stay or go.

A steady stream of various hard-to-identify but generally chaotic, clanging-banging type noises was flowing into Amy's ears from parts unknown within the building.

These mysterious sounds persisted as a new one joined them and gradually drew nearer—an adult female voice saying, "Deary me, I haven't done the washing up. What am I like! Bloody hell—this lounge is a tip!"

The voice's owner—a white woman about the same age, height and build as Amy, with blue eyes and frizzy, shoulder-length brown hair—suddenly appeared in the doorway.

"Yes, can I help?" she asked with an open-mouthed smile revealing that all of her remaining teeth (about 75% of a full set) were crooked and dark yellow. (Unbeknownst to Amy, this placed the woman's dental state only slightly below average among Brits.)

"Hi!" said Amy. "Sorry to bother you. I'm looking for Essie Lee. Does she live here?"

"Nah, 'fraid not, love," the woman replied. "She used to live here. Had a job driving a lorry for them folks up there on the trading estate, didn't she. And she rented a room from us, here... But, um... she, um... She had to move out."

"Do you happen to know where she went? Any info you can give me would be very much appreciated!"

"You family of hers? She never mentioned having any family in America..."

Amy laughed. "Well, it's funny you should ask that. The honest answer is: I don't know! That's why I'm trying to find her, actually."

"Yeah?"

"Yeah... Um, this is going to sound kinda crazy, but... I think it's possible she might be my mother!"

"Cor blimey!" the woman exclaimed.

Amy laughed again. "I know, right?"

"Well, she said she was headed up north, to Rugby. Said she had family there. Seems she has family all over!"

"Hah, right!" Amy said with a big grin. "So, you don't have, like, an address for her or anything?"

"Nope, sorry, love—got nothing, I'm afraid. She wasn't what I'd call... a close friend, if you know what I mean..."

"Sure, no problem. Well, I won't take up any more of your time. Thank you so much for everything, you've been incredibly helpful!"

Precisely six hours later, having spent about half of the intervening time riding on a train (an experience Amy ultimately felt was worth every penny of its stunningly high price, as the extremely low speed and frequent stops (at towns and villages that included Squiffington, Nardbury, Shallow Wickets, Brookford-on-Brook, Bellend-over-Pate, Stoneham-upon-Wexley-under-Tunbridge, and Wart) allowed a traveler to really take in and savor the whole atmosphere), she raised a pint glass to her lips, smiling broadly, and took her first-ever sip of Fuller's London Pride. Ordinarily she mainly drank cocktails and wine, and when she occasionally had a beer always chose a light American lager. But her new friends, currently surrounding her on three sides, had strongly urged her to try a "bitter." Might as well experience some local color while here, they'd reasoned, and Amy wholeheartedly agreed.

"Ooh," she said, scrunching up her face. "Not sure if I like that."

"You have to give it a chance," said Simon, a grossly overweight white man in his mid-forties seated to Amy's left, who was also having a pint of London Pride. "Nobody likes how it tastes at first."

"Hmm... Okay, if you say so," she replied with a smile, then tentatively took another sip.

"Sometimes it helps to play a drinking game," suggested the bartender, Colin, a moderately overweight white man in his mid-forties who was enjoying a half-pint of Strongbow he'd helped himself to after depositing money Amy had intended as a tip into the cash register. (Amy found very odd the notion that tipping at the bar wasn't customary but buying the bartender a drink (and then they drink on the job!) *was*, but had been assured by her new friends that this was indeed the case.)

"Well I can't help you there," said Nigel, a slender, toned white man in his mid-forties seated to Amy's right, who was clutching a pint of tap water (and who'd managed, within two minutes of meeting Amy, to mention that he went to the gym seven days a week and that he was a non-drinker but definitely not because of alcoholism).

"Oh!" said Simon, his face lighting up. "There was this one me and my mates used to play at college... Oh, what was it called? When it was your turn—yeah?—you could choose what sort of challenge you had to complete. So, you could choose something more physical, like trying to slap somebody's hand before they could pull it away... or you could choose something more mental, like... I think it had to do with saying a lie or the truth..."

"That totally reminds me of this game *I* used to play," said Amy, "with my girlfriends. It wasn't a drinking game. Well, we drank while we were playing it, but... Anyways, so, it was a card game, but... like you said, we had to choose... except, you chose at the beginning and then that was your role for the rest of the game.

"So yeah, you'd choose between something more physical, which always involved slapping down a card. Then you were called a 'slapper.' Or, you could choose a verbal thing where you would like, tell a story with the cards. It was kinda complicated, but... you somehow had to 'clean' the story... Wait, no, it was you 'scrub' the story, gradually changing it and removing certain unwanted cards. Yeah, that was it. Then you were called a 'scrubber.' So, yeah, so... every girl there was either a slapper or a scrubber..."

Amy noticed that all three of her companions were doubled over in fits of laughter, then began laughing herself. "Yeah, it was pretty silly!" she said.

"Are you taking the piss?" asked Nigel between laughs.

"What?" Amy looked quizzically around at all of them. "Um, I don't need to go to the bathroom right now, if that's what you mean..."

As the other two began laughing even harder, Colin smiled warmly and said, "Never mind, dear. We're two nations divided by a common language."

"Hah! Love it," said Amy. "So, anyways, are you sure you don't know Essie Lee?"

"Nope, don't think so," said Colin. "You know his full name? Like, what's the 'S' stand for?"

"She. Essie's a woman. Her full name is Estuary."

"Hmm, nope, sorry—don't ring a bell. Either of you...?"

Colin and Amy looked back and forth between Simon and Nigel, both of whom had finally stopped laughing and were now shaking their heads, shrugging and displaying puzzled faces.

"Knew a girl called Bessie once," Colin added, then shook his head and grinned, thinking back. "Only bird I ever met who enjoyed doing that 'pull my finger' thing. You know—the thing where you fart?"

"Oh my god, don't get me started!" Amy exclaimed. "My husband, Jake, and his friend, Lester, they just think farting is the most hilarious thing in the world."

"Well, it *is* quite funny," remarked Simon.

"Okay, yeah—it can be pretty funny, the sound of it or whatever. But those two, they go too far with it. They've had this thing, like, ever since college, where, they like, try to sneak up and fart in each other's face. So gross."

The three men all chuckled in amusement.

"Oh," Amy continued, "there was this one time, a few years ago... So funny. Jake came out in the morning and saw somebody was sleeping on the couch, and he thought it was Lester, because, the night before... Well, doesn't matter. Anyways, he thought it was Lester, but it wasn't. It was my mom. And he farted in her face!"

All four of them burst into hearty laughter.

Momentarily catching her breath, Amy said, "She was so pissed!"

"Probably didn't even notice, then," offered Simon, amidst guffaws.

Amy had no idea what he meant but responded with "Right!"

After several seconds, the energy level had declined back down to normal and Colin asked, "So, is your husband here with you, in England?"

"Nah," Amy replied. "He stayed home with the kids. Tickets were just so expensive, and he had this sci-fi convention thing... Not a big deal." She smiled and shrugged. "Traveling with kids can be pretty freakin' hard anyways!"

"Too right," said Simon.

Nigel leaned in closer and said, "Amy, what do you reckon is your best quality? Is it your natural beauty? Or is it your electric personality?"

"Always on the pull, Nigel is," Simon mumbled in Colin's direction.

Amy chuckled and said, "Neither one, actually. I think I'd say my best quality is what I call having good 'social judgment'...

"So, what I mean is, I have a finely tuned sense of communications between myself and others. Verbal and non-verbal. I can read where somebody else is coming from and... I'm very good at, um, providing clear communication to people. Giving them what they want, accommodating their feelings. *And,* I'm also very good at receiving and understanding and... absorbing... whatever communication they're giving to me."

Amy's friends were all smiling pleasantly at her, their eyes turning ever so slightly glassy.

She went on, "I wasn't always so controlled—so, you know, 'tuned in.' When I was young—oh, lordy!—I would just blurt out anything that came into my head, to anyone who'd listen. No filter! Didn't matter if what I was saying was relevant, or interesting... or even appropriate!

"And, on the flip side, when it came to other people telling me stuff, I always wanted to know everything! Even when it was none of my business. And I would just, you know, pester them, relentlessly…"

The men's smiles had almost completely faded away.

"Anyways, *I* believe that, the way I used to be… you know, with really bad social judgment… Having to learn to recognize that weakness, and, become aware, and, endure so many bad situations it caused, I think, is what allowed me to cultivate such great social judgment like I have today. I kinda turned my greatest weakness into my greatest strength!"

After a moment of nobody speaking, the smiles came back and Nigel said, "Fascinating, Amy."

"Another round?" asked Colin.

"Yes!" cried Simon.

"Ooh, I don't know," said Amy, glancing down at her phone. "I really gotta find Essie and, honestly, I'm starting to think I'm not gonna find her in here."

"What was it, made you think you might?" Colin enquired.

"Oh, just, this chick out on the street out there…"

From the train station, Amy had followed signs into the center of Rugby until finding herself on a dense, bustling stretch of road (which, despite apparently being named Albert Street and not being particularly elevated, had been referred to as "the high street" by multiple passersby) and then had simply begun asking anybody whose attention she could capture about Essie.

Receiving puzzled looks from her companions, Amy continued, "Yeah, this chick said she kinda knew Essie, just casually. Didn't know where she lives, but, said Essie is, like, always, *always* hanging out in The Frog and Peach."

"This is The Duke's Head," said Colin.

"Yep!" Simon chimed in.

Nigel just frowned and knitted his brow.

"Oh my god," said Amy. "Are you serious?"

"Yep, 'fraid so," said Simon.

"The Frog and Peach is next door," said Colin. "Their sign is really near to our entrance. That's prob'ly why you got confused."

"I can't believe I actually found you!"

Amy couldn't believe she'd actually found Essie. But it was true. There they stood, face to face, a mere 18 inches separating them, in a bare corner of the main room of The Frog and Peach. Five minutes had passed since Amy had attempted (unsuccessfully, thanks to her gentlemen friends) to pay her tab at The Duke's Head.

"Who the fuck are you?" asked Essie gruffly, for the second time in the past 30 seconds. Her accent sounded like a bizarre hybrid—mainly American, probably, but with little British twists. Not pleasant on the ears. Her voice also had a raspy quality, like it belonged to someone who'd smoked approximately ten million cigarettes.

"Like I said, my name's Amy Lee. I think…"—a quick giggle, an equal mix of thrill, amusement, and nerves—"I think I might be your daughter."

"The fuck you are," Essie replied calmly, reaching out with one hand to deposit a collection of little darts on—and retrieve a very tall can of beer from—a shelf bolted to a nearby wall.

"Excuse me?" said Amy.

Essie took a long swig, then said, "I've got no fucking American daughter."

"Well, um…"

"Anyway you're a bit old to be a daughter of mine, ain't ya. Bit ugly, too."

Amy had been studying Essie's appearance the whole time, searching for similarities between them. Same height, and maybe, just maybe, she could see it in the face, but, so hard to tell. Essie was rail thin, to put it mildly—emaciated might be more accurate—with astonishingly wrinkled skin riddled with discolorations and pockmarks. She looked about 85 years old.

"Um, I was told," Amy said, "by a friend of your mother's, that… when you were young, you gave up a baby for adoption."

Essie said nothing and took another gulp of beer.

"And I was hoping that, um, maybe, you might have some records… or that you might remember something about—"

"Fucking hell. Look, I been pregnant loads of times. Some were adopted. Some were aborted—by doctors and by me own body. Some of 'em, I raised. Ungrateful little shits."

"Um, well…"—this time the giggle was all nerves—"This would've been… your first-ever pregnancy, I think…"

"Stayed nice and tight through it all, though," said Essie. "Bet you got a bucket fanny, bitch."

"Um, so, when you were—"

"Oh, take a fucking hint. I got no fucking records, and no fucking memories neither. And I got no fucking time for *you*."

"I'm really sorry for troubling you," said Amy. "But, please, if there's any—"

She was interrupted by a blob of spit striking her on the nose.

"Piss off back to America, bitch," said Essie. "And go fuck yourself. You fucking worthless heap of shit."

For the first time in decades, Amy Lee found herself utterly speechless.

———————————

At that very moment, inside the main building of the Shady Oaks Luxury Assisted Maturity Estate in Culver City, California, 58-year-old Roy "Fats" Cleary (who was actually quite a thin man) was energetically strolling down the corridor, grinning and whistling a happy tune. His euphoric mood resulted from the new knowledge that he was now cured of the horrific mental illness from which he'd suffered for the past 30 years. He'd learned this ten minutes ago in the office of Dr. Homer Pendleton, who'd recently deduced, from Roy's latest test results (which were identical to all the previous ones) and the revised definition of partial non-polarized dissociative evocative disorder published last month by the National Association of Psychiatrists, that Roy didn't have it.

As Roy passed by the door of Apartment 1751 on his way back to his own apartment, he still hadn't realized the full implication of his other new knowledge (involving his insurance policy no longer covering any portion of the rather hefty bill for his accommodation at Shady Oaks), received five minutes ago from Dr. Pendleton's administrative assistant: that he would soon be moving back in with his son and daughter-in-law and their three young children and their two poorly trained dogs.

Inside #1751, seated on his sofa, Albert Forrester (a.k.a. Gramps) was saying, "So, in reality, they'd put all the foods in completely the wrong order."

His daughter, Yvonne Smede, sat next to him, (somewhat) patiently listening to what may or may not have been the conclusion of a fairly lengthy, detailed analysis of a recent unfortunate incident in the Shady Oaks cafeteria.

Now Gramps paused, narrowing his eyes and staring at some faraway point, momentarily deeper in thought.

"Of course," he then said, "what is 'reality,' after all? I might say, or you might say, what's going on around us here is reality, but, that's not entirely true."

"Yeah, interesting," Yvonne responded, smiling. "Actual, objective reality is impossible to pin down. We're constantly filtering everything we take in through our personal beliefs and desires, warping it. Plus probably missing a bunch of stuff—just ignoring it because it's not interesting or important... or because we can only handle so much input, or even because it doesn't fit with our, you know, paradigm, of how things are..."

"What? No, that's a load of horseshit," said Gramps. "No, I'm talking about: there isn't just one reality. The multiverse."

"Oh. Well, that's an interesting idea, too."

"Not just an idea, darling. They've proven it. The scientists who study... uh, time and space, and reality. I was reading a thing about it the other day. There are a million universes out there. There's a million of you, and a million of me."

Yvonne made a "Mmm" sound to indicate listening with interest.

"Wish I could've been the me who has more money and more hair. And maybe a bit taller..."

Yvonne chuckled.

"I'm serious. He's out there somewhere. Bastard. And he's picking up that sweet little piece of ass, Miriam. Mmm-mmm. Tasty."

Yvonne rolled her eyes.

"Stuck-up old hag won't give this version of me the time of day. Did I tell you about her?"

"Uh, I think you might've—"

"Oh! Did I tell you I bumped into Loretta? Well, nearly bumped into her. She managed to sneak into the line right behind me when I was signing up for the bridge tournament."

"I don't think it's actually a tournament—"

"And she grabbed my ass! Can you believe it? The nerve of her. I didn't even dignify that with an acknowledgment of any kind. Didn't even turn around."

"So, how do you know for sure it was Loretta?"

"Reminds me of that time, a couple years ago, remember? When I took you to see the Marshall Tucker Band at the county fair?"

"Yeah." Another eyeroll.

"And that young gal behind us grabbed my ass."

"Uh-huh." Yvonne had heard this story at least half a dozen times before, had found it rather boring the first time, and had always doubted it was even true.

"Criminy! She was a frisky one. Heh. Tried to dance with her but she wandered off..."

Yvonne's phone began ringing inside her purse.

She pulled it out and looked at it, said, "Excuse me, Dad," then swiped green, put it to her ear, and said, "Hey, what's up?"

"Tell Billy he can talk to you when you get back," Gramps snapped. "This is *my* time."

"Tell him I love him too," said Bill.

"Will do," Yvonne replied, smiling and glancing over at her father to gauge whether he needed any handling (like a verbal shushing, a stern face, or a finger wag). No—he'd already turned his attention to an issue of Guns & Ammo magazine.

"Uh," said Bill, "reason I called is: Alice wanted to fix that loose bracket on the den door slider thing, you know?"

Alice, standing next to Bill, said, "I don't want to. I said I was willing to."

"Right. Anyway, we found the screw, and... It's a... It's a Phillips-head... Sort of, uh, I guess medium sized..."

"Okay," said Yvonne, still unsure why this conversation was happening.

"Do you know if we have a screwdriver like that?"

"Well, the first place I'd look is in the tools box under the bathroom sink."

"Ah, right. Let's see here..."

Bill arrived at the bathroom sink and, throughout the process of hunching over, retrieving the box and rummaging through it, emitted a series of his characteristic grunts and groans, which elicited a somewhat-irritated-but-mostly-resigned sigh from Yvonne. Many people, her included, suspected Bill of deliberately (maybe semi-consciously) making these noises for dramatic effect, to ensure his audience knew he was struggling or suffering. In fact, he produced far more of them when he was all alone.

"Nope," he finally said. "I don't see one in there."

"Well my only other thought would be: Patrick keeps some tools in his room."

"Okay. I'll try there… "

"I'd better get going. Good luck."

"Oh, okay. Thanks."

"By the way, Dad's coming back with me, staying over tonight."

"Great."

"Bye!"

"Bye."

Bill reached Patrick's bedroom door as the call ended, and knocked on it. A moment later it opened and Patrick appeared, sporting his usual bedhead.

"Hey, Dad."

"Hey. Uh, I'm looking for a sort of medium-sized Phillips screwdriver. Thought maybe you've got one in there."

"Nope. I don't."

"Are you sure?"

"Yeah."

"Well, mind if I come in and take a look anyway?"

Patrick's face clearly showed that he did mind very much indeed, but, seeing that his father's face clearly showed this was going to happen one way or another, he stepped aside and opened the door wider.

"The tools are over there," he said, vaguely gesturing with his arm toward one corner of the room, as Bill began to trudge through the sea of miscellaneous small objects coating the floor.

"Ah, that should do the trick," he announced almost immediately upon spotting the cardboard box full of tools perched on top of a pile of laundry. He snapped up the relevant screwdriver, held it out for his son to see, and smiled.

"Cool," said Patrick.

"Thanks. See you later," said Bill, then quickly made his way out of the bedroom and down the corridor, and handed the screwdriver to

Alice.

"Here you go. Please make the repair A.S.A.P."

"Okay," said Alice.

Bill continued through into the front half of the condo and hustled around briefly, collecting up his phone, wallet, keys, hat, sunglasses, iPod, earphones, and a small box containing a computer smart card reader. Then he left.

Alice stepped into her den and laid the screwdriver down on her desk. Her preference was to postpone the bracket work until after her friends Anita and Tabitha—currently sitting on the den floor staring at their phone screens—had departed.

"Oh, have you seen the new Ansel Elgort movie?" asked Tabitha without looking up. "He is so hot!"

"He totally is!" agreed Anita, also not looking up.

"It's so stupid," Tabitha went on, "how people always say, in The Fault in Our Stars when he's hooking up with Shailene Woodley, it's like incest, *just* because they played brother and sister in Divergent."

"Yeah!" agreed Anita. "People be dumb!"

"Super dumb," said Tabitha. "He was barely even *in* Divergent!"

Now Anita finally did look up, at Alice.

"Hey Alice," she said, "my friend Jill knows a guy who could probably get us some weed."

Alice stared back at her, silent and expressionless.

"Well, are you interested?"

"No."

"Ooh!" said Tabitha, also looking up now. "My sister has some pills. Like, two or three different kinds. I could probably steal some."

After a moment of mutual staring between the three of them, Anita said, "Aw, Alice never wants to try any of that stuff…"

"I'm going to get a glass of water," Alice said, turning toward the corridor.

"Hey, look!" called out Tabitha.

Alice turned around again.

Tabitha was holding up a Butterfinger candy bar, giggling, her index finger covering the first instance of "er" printed on the wrapper.

Bill was standing on the corner of Santa Monica and Roper 25 minutes later (having just completed his transaction at Mail and Ship in a relatively painless fashion), enormous waves of vehicular traffic slowly oozing past. Gazing up at a billboard featuring a photo of a very determined-looking young man in athletic-style clothing and the words "Forge Your Own Path" (it was not clear what, exactly, was being advertised), he mused over the apparent message, and the tendency of modern American society—in its public expression, at least— to promote and laud things like independence, self-determination, "taking charge," standing your ground, pushing back against authority. We don't hear much about the other attitude, he thought. My attitude. Of following, cooperating. Liking to be told what to do. *Wanting* to be told what to do. Bet it's actually the more prevalent one, by far.

He smiled. Overall he was feeling pretty happy right now (by his standards). It wasn't a workday. He'd had a very pleasant chat with Rufus Fletcher on the way over here, which included being introduced to a new squirrel who, Rufus explained, didn't have a name and refused to take one until all crows had been captured, killed, or driven away. Now Bill was eagerly anticipating a stroll down Landon Avenue, followed by an appointment with a prospective tenant for his apartment—one whom, he felt certain, Joseph Tanur would be unable to find fault with. He'd also temporarily forgotten that his father-in-law was coming for a visit.

Glancing down at his wrist for the second time in the past 18 seconds (the previous one to check on his step count (which had been quite pleasing)), he saw that if he proceeded straight to the apartment he would arrive there about 10 minutes early. Then he had an idea.

It had occurred to Bill periodically in recent years that one block north of Santa Monica lay an east-west street called Pennsylvania Avenue, and that maybe, just maybe, in somewhat the same spirit as Landon Avenue, the property at 1600 might feature some decoration/theming of a presidential nature; but he'd never gotten around to checking it out. Now's the perfect time, he thought, then abruptly turned and began swiftly, purposefully striding northward.

Two minutes later, standing next to a palm tree in front of the very ordinary-looking, completely non-themed apartment building at the corner of Roper and Pennsylvania, whose address was 1600 Roper Boulevard, Bill realized that his thinking had been muddled up all this time—that the east-west addresses around here were in the ten thousands and that 1600 Pennsylvania Avenue, if it existed at all (which it most likely didn't because the state-named streets did not continue nearly far enough east), was located over ten miles away, near downtown.

"Fuck," he said.

The following Friday evening, ten minutes after all six members of The Evils had assembled around the kitchen table in the Lee residence (during which time glasses had been clinked, drinks had been sipped, a discussion had sprung up (then quickly fizzled out) about which human body part is the most valuable (Mike: hands; Laura: brain (pronounced not valid by multiple others in the group, for multiple reasons); Jake: mouth and anus, tied; Amy: eyes; Bill: no opinion; Yvonne: no opinion), and Mike had begun describing his new online business—selling miscellaneous secondhand consumer goods—which he'd cleverly registered in Laos (though had initially believed he was registering in Louisiana) under the domain name ".la" (thereby making it seem L.A.-based to his would-be customers)), they were startled by an extremely loud crash coming from the other side of the front wall of the house.

"What on earth!" exclaimed Jake with a grin, his eyes darting excitedly around the table at the faces of the other five, all of which looked puzzled.

A cat appeared from behind a curtain and made its way to the back of the house at lightning speed, nearly colliding with 5-year-old Brandon Lee, who was making his way in the opposite direction at a similar pace, shouting "I'm gonna check it out!"

He went straight to the front door and began turning the knob, prompting Jake to leap out of his chair (which fell over sideways, striking Bill on the left knee) and lunge in that direction himself.

"Whoa, hang on there, buddy!" he called out to his son.

Brandon flung the door open and started to step out, but then realized somebody was standing there, about to knock.

"Hi there!" said that somebody, a thin, middle-aged black man with shaggy, longish hair, ignoring Brandon and looking at Jake, who was now sidling up behind the little lad.

"Howdy!" said Jake.

"I'm Carl Eisenstein." He extended his hand. "I live next door with my daughter, Tiffany."

Jake shook Carl's hand enthusiastically. "Yeah! Right! I think we've met before..."

"Um, I don't think so. We just moved in a couple weeks ago."

Jake wiggled his eyebrows up and down, continuing to smile, then said, "Cool!"

"Anyway," said Carl, "bad news, I'm afraid. There was a hit-and-run just now, right out here in front of your place."

"Really?" Jake asked excitedly.

"Yeah. The guy drove off so fast, I couldn't get his plate. I think he was drunk. But, um, he really smashed up your car pretty bad."

"Wow!" Jake exclaimed, still grinning.

"The, um..."—Carl briefly glanced back out toward the street—"The green Audi?"

Brandon, who'd been standing in the doorway, staring up at Carl, smiling, continued to do so. Jake turned to look across at his happy hour companions seated around the table, eyebrows raised questioningly.

"We came in the ambulance," said Mike with a shrug.

"We Ubered," said Yvonne.

Amy was chuckling. "Oh, Jake, honey... None of us drive a green Audi. You know that!"

"Right!" Jake exclaimed, turning back to Carl.

"Hmm, okay," said Carl. "Well, that's good news! Um, for you, anyway."

He turned and started swiftly walking away, like he was late for something. "Sorry to bother you!" he called out over his shoulder. "Nice to meet you!"

"Nice meeting you!" Jake replied, then closed the door, turned back toward his friends and said, "What a great guy!"

Brandon sprang back into motion, racing toward the back of the house, gripping his rear end with both hands, a slightly worried expression on his face.

"Oh, bless his little heart," said Amy. "Just realized he needs to poop!"

Jake chortled as he wedged himself back into his seat (which Bill had placed back onto its legs). "Yeah. Sure am glad he's finally potty trained!"

"Oh, it took him forever to go that last little stretch," Amy said. "He was still wearing Pull-Ups when he was four!"

"I know!"

Three of the others were starting to look a bit bored. (Laura was staring at her phone screen.)

"Jennifer was so much quicker," said Amy. "I think she was completely done by, like, two and a half."

"Yes, yes," Jake agreed, eyes gleaming, head bobbing up and down. "Aw, just... Brandon... You know what he used to do?"

This was obviously addressed to everyone, and all of them (even Laura) met Jake's darting gaze and smiled faintly.

"He'd come up to me, you know, when... when he knew he needed to go poop... He'd come up to me and he'd say, 'Daddy, give me a Pull-Up.'"

"God, that's right!" Amy interjected, chuckling.

"And, just... So, I'd give it to him, right? And he'd just... run off to the bedroom, and he'd put on the Pull-Up, and he'd poop into it, and then he'd come running back to me and ask me to change him!"

Jake let out a huge stream of laughter, which was echoed (with far less intensity) by Amy, Mike, and Bill. Yvonne smiled. Laura was back in Phone World.

"Oh, hey," Amy suddenly said, looking at Jake and grinning, "you've got a poop story yourself, mister! And it's *way* more embarrassing than poor little Brandon's!"

"I do?" asked Jake, smiling widely, intrigued.

"Yeah, from last weekend, when you were at Shazam..."

"Oh, yeah!" Jake exclaimed, his eyes lighting up. But then they immediately un-lit, and his face fell, and he added, "But, uh... That story is just... It's pretty embarrassing, honey..."

"Oh, come on," Amy chided. "They don't care! Right, guys?"

She and Jake looked around the table, their eyes met by three fairly interested smiling faces and the top of Laura's head.

"Yeah, tell us," said Mike. "Lord knows I've told *you* some embarrassing shit before." He winked.

Jake's smile was back. "Well, okay," he said. "So, Amy was in England, and..."

"Oh, that's right!" said Laura. "You gotta tell us all about that."

"Of course," she replied. "Yeah, I totally will. Although, honestly, there isn't very much to tell. But, anyways, listen to Jake's story, it's hilarious!"

Jake, who'd been distracted by the talk of England, spent a few seconds bringing his mind back to the topic at hand. Then he continued.

"Right, so, yeah, Amy was over there, and, the kids were staying with my parents, in Cypress, and... I had dinner with this friend of mine, Phil Acktich, who's just... I met him at work, when I worked at the meat packing place. Oh! I gotta tell you about my new job I just started. It's just... just, crazy...

"So anyway... so, yeah, Phil. He's just... kind of a wild man, you know? He likes to party, and, just... He likes to go to trendy places. Just... clubs and restaurants and... nightclubs. Dance clubs. So, we ate at this new, trendy place in West Hollywood. Shazam."

"We'd never eat there," remarked Bill.

"Speak for yourself," Yvonne said with a smirk.

"Oh, have you heard of it?" Jake asked.

"No."

"Well, yeah, so it's like, super trendy, and... They've just got these crazy restrooms. So, the way they do their restrooms is, there's no men's or women's. There's just all these doors, like a whole wall of these doors, and you go inside and lock it and, you know... do your business. And the sinks are outside, along another wall. Anyway, and so, just... Everybody lines up, you know, in front of this wall full of doors, and, if you're at the front of the line, you just... go into the next one that's free."

All present were now listening intently, Laura included.

"But here's the thing! Some of these little... rooms, or whatever... Some of them only have a urinal. They don't have a regular toilet! And I ended up in one of those kind. I just... I don't know what the women do..."

"Check first, is my guess," said Yvonne.

"Yep, yep, I should've checked. It was just... It was crazy, you know? And I just... I couldn't hold it. Just... So, yeah—I pooped in the urinal."

Bill and Mike both burst out laughing at this point, even though they'd already surmised what was coming.

"I couldn't help it!" Jake added, grinning.

"So how did you..." said Mike between laughs. "Aw, never mind..."

"When you came out, what did you say to the next person in line?" Yvonne asked.

"I didn't say anything. I just..."

"Aw, honey, denial!" exclaimed Amy, chuckling. "You gotta deny! You gotta disavow all knowledge and involvement!"

"Oh, god," said Bill to Yvonne. "This reminded me of the 'Bridesmaids' thing, with Jerry..."

Yvonne rolled her eyes.

Amy said, "You mean that movie with... What's her name? Oh my god, she is so funny..."

"Yes, that's what he means," Yvonne replied.

"Melissa McCarthy," said Laura.

"No," said Amy, "not her. She *is* funny, though! But I'm talking about the other one, the main star..."

"So what've you got, Bill?" asked Mike. "I'm warning you, you're gonna be hard pressed to make me laugh as hard as Jake did."

"Humor!" exclaimed Jake with a big smile.

"I think Jake's got it in the bag," said Yvonne.

"Okay," said Bill, "so, you know there's that scene where they all have diarrhea while they're trying on dresses?"

Mike: "Mmm-hmm." Amy: "Yes, hilarious!" Jake: "Yes!" Yvonne: silence. Laura: silence, with attention on her phone.

"Well, years back, Yvonne and I used to sometimes have dinner with one of the teachers at Alice's school who we really liked, an older woman named Rhonda. And Rhonda had this old friend, Jerry, who would tag along sometimes. Cool guy, but sort of odd. I think he wasn't very bright, honestly. And, he was into boxing, and astrology, and playing the lottery. And Rhonda was, well, to say she wasn't into any of that would be a gross understatement. So, kind of surprising they were friends.

"Anyway, Jerry loved Bridesmaids, especially that scene. And he brought it up on *several* occasions during these dinners." Bill began to laugh again. "And, whenever he tried to describe it, he would keep cracking up, and eventually, he'd just collapse into uncontrollable fits, and he'd have to give up on describing it. He could never actually get to the end of the scene because he was laughing so hard! And..."

Bill had to stop speaking because he was laughing so hard.

Looking up from her phone, Laura said, "Kristen Wiig."

"And," Bill continued, "it was extra funny because Rhonda didn't find it funny at all. She'd just look at him like she was thinking, 'Shut up, you idiot.' And this just happened over and over, practically every time we saw them..." He broke down laughing again.

Yvonne, who'd been looking at Bill and shaking her head, now turned to the others and explained, "Bill has told the Jerry story at more dinners than Jerry ever told the Bridesmaids story at."

"True," said Bill between laughs.

The other four were all laughing now, too.

"In our family," Yvonne continued, "Bill is now the butt of the joke. Not Jerry."

"Jake," said Laura after a moment, going back to her phone, "that restaurant where you shit yourself, what was it called again?"

"Shazam," said Amy.

"I didn't..." said Jake. "It was, I... Just, technically..."

"I was thinking maybe we could order some food from them," said Laura, scrolling through the Shazam menu.

"We definitely need to order some from somewhere!" Amy replied.

"Amen to that!" chimed in Mike.

"The food was good!" said Jake. "I had... What did I have again?"

"Patrick ordered recently from this, like, vegan place," said Yvonne. "You know, they do those 'impossible' burgers. He said it was really good, amazingly good. You remember what the place was called?"

"No," said Bill. "I don't remember anything about this. A vegan place?"

"Oh," said Mike, "I think I might know the one. I think they're called like Ocean Moon or something..."

"Oh, I remember now," said Yvonne. "It's Sheer Lunar Sea."

"Right, yes," said Mike, chuckling.

"Hilarious," said Amy.

"Hilarious!" cried Jake.

"Can you bring them up on your phone, babe?" Mike asked Laura.

"Already got 'em," she replied, now scrolling through the menu. "Oh, they're not all vegan. They have one with cheese on it called 'The Improbable Burger'... Oh, and... they have a bunch of salads, too... Hmm. 'The Impossible Salad.' Made entirely from pig parts..."

"Mommy!" screamed 8-year-old Jennifer Lee as she came into view, moving at roughly the same speed recently exhibited by her brother and the fleeing cat.

"What is it, sweetie?" Amy called back.

"Mommy!" Jennifer screamed again as she arrived tableside, causing everyone who hadn't had a part in creating her to shudder slightly.

"Calm down, there, pumpkin," said Jake, chuckling.

"What is it, sweetie?" Amy asked again.

"Brandon took my homework," whined Jennifer.

"Aw, he'll give it back eventually. He just needs to cool off. Don't let him get under your skin."

Jake, who'd risen from his chair (without knocking it over this time) and come around behind his daughter, reached down and scooped her up, saying, "Come on, pumpkin spice. Let's go take care of this."

He draped her over his shoulder and began marching toward the back of the house. She let out a loud, long stream of squealing laughter. A (different) cat appeared from behind a pile of clothes in one corner of the living room, shot across to the opposite corner like a rocket, and vanished again behind a stack of cardboard boxes.

"Thanks, honey," said Amy; then, to the others, "I swear. That girl is so obsessed with school lately. Just, out of the blue!"

"Kids," said Mike with a smile.

"Never experienced such a thing with ours," said Yvonne.

"No," agreed Bill.

"Maybe it's a good thing for her," Amy went on. "It is just, *so* competitive around here with schools. Although, I don't think it has anything to do with a child's performance—it's more like, just, like a random lottery kind of thing."

"Hmm," said Bill. "I don't remember anything like that."

"Yeah, ridiculous—she's in third grade and we already have to start looking at *applying* to different middle schools. These are *public* schools! Isn't every kid entitled to a local public education?"

"Wow," said Mike.

"Gotta love L.A.U.S.D.," said Yvonne.

"Oh my god," said Amy, "did I tell you guys about my friend Linnette? Her daughter's a few years older than Jenny. So, anyways, she made a point of moving into the correct, um, you know, district or neighborhood or whatever, for this one middle school, and she *bought a house* in that neighborhood, that she couldn't really even afford..."

"Wow," said Mike.

"Yeah. And then, bam! They tell her, 'No, sorry, all the spots are filled. Your daughter can't go here.' Un-freakin-believable!"

"That sucks," said Bill.

"So, now she's talking about maybe sending Cindy to Princeton Eastlake..."

"Oh, is that that private school near UCLA?" asked Yvonne.

"Yep, that's the one! Pretentious as hell. Expensive as hell! Lordy. So, I don't know... Actually, I was talking to this woman when I was in England, about their schools—"

"Oh, yeah!" exclaimed Laura. "Tell us about your trip. What did you find out?"

"Basically nothing," said Amy.

"Really? Aw. I thought you were finally going to get all the answers."

"Yeah, so did I! But nah, it was a complete bust. That Essie, holy cow, she's a total nightmare. I mean, you know me—I get along with everyone. But I could *not* get along with her."

"So you still don't know if she's your biological mother?"

"Nope. And now I guess I never will."

"Well, what about the adoption agency?"

Amy laughed. "Yeah. Another dead end. It was kind of insane."

"I thought they said if you showed up in person, they'd give you all the info..."

"Yep. That's what they said. But when I did show up in person, totally different story."

"Wow," said Mike.

"Yep. Wouldn't tell me anything. Wouldn't show me anything. Basically told me to get lost!" She laughed again.

"That's terrible," said Laura.

"Aw, it's okay," said Amy. "My mom was disappointed, of course, but, she actually handled it pretty well. And anyways, I had an awesome time over there! Went around the country, soaking up the culture. Met interesting characters in pubs. Saw where Shakespeare lived. Saw Stonehenge. And Buckingham Palace. I did all that tourist crap." Another laugh. "It was really fun!"

"Cool," said Bill.

"Cool!" echoed Jake, who'd just emerged from the back part of the house and was making his way toward the table, grinning widely. "You had such a great time over there, honey!"

"*Yeah* I did!"

"How were the flights?" asked Yvonne. "It's a long way."

"Yep, they were super long. But, I didn't really mind. Watched some movies. Caught up on some reading."

"Oh!" said Laura. "I discovered this really cool book recently. A novel, called 'Wax Works.' It's a mystery story. Really fascinating. But, here's the unique thing about it: you don't know how long the book is. You never know how much of it you have left."

"Ooh," said Jake, now back in his seat. "Yes! I've got one of those, too..."

"How do they do that?" asked Bill.

"Well, the book is really thick," said Laura. "It's like, at least a thousand pages. But the story is all out of order, so they're constantly telling you to, you know, turn to page so-and-so..."

"Like a 'Choose Your Own Adventure.'"

"Right, except without any choices. And a lot of the pages aren't even part of the story. They just have, like, random stuff printed on them."

"Interesting," said Yvonne.

"It's just plain daffy," said Mike. "If you ask me."

"Mine's different," said Jake. "With mine the book is divided into lots of smaller ones, and it comes with this big box thing, with lots of little compartments, with locks on them with key codes, and... It's just, *so* cool. Just, *so* cool. So, and, like, just... When you get to the end of one of the little books, it tells you how to get the next little book out of one of these compartments."

Mike chuckled. "Might as well go all out, I guess."

"Yeah," Jake continued, "and, just... The box is all decorated with cool designs and stuff... So, and, yeah... It's just... Oh, Bill! I got it from that place in Thousand Oaks, you know, that day I saw you!"

"Ah, right. Cool. Oh, how's it going with your hunt for that super-rare comic? What was it? The field marshal, or...?"

"Yes, yes! Good memory, my friend! But I wasn't looking for it there… But, anyway, yeah, so… No, no, just… I just, uh… I just had to give up on that one. They're all gone. That auction, I just… I couldn't get my foot in the door…"

Jake looked around the table at the others, grinning. Everybody was silent for a moment.

"Too bad," Bill finally said.

"Yeah, just… Too bad… Just…"

"You mentioning your flight," said Mike to Amy, "reminded me of this incident, when we were coming back from Groot Bot." He turned to Laura. "You remember that, babe?"

"Of course. How could I forget?"

"So there was a medical emergency during the flight," Mike explained to the group. "This guy had turned gray. He wasn't moving. He wasn't breathing. His wife was freaking out. And, you know, they made the overhead announcement, asking if there were any doctors on board.

"Well, there were no doctors. The only people who volunteered to help out were me and this other guy who was a veterinarian."

"It was so scary," said Laura.

"Sure was. So me and this vet, we're poking and prodding the guy, slapping him in the face—gently, of course—and, he's totally unresponsive, and we decide, we better get him out of his seat and lay him down on the floor, and… then, you know, maybe try C.P.R."

"Oh my god," said Amy.

"So, we each grab one arm, and we're trying to pull this guy out of his seat, and, he won't budge! We keep pulling harder and harder, until, with each attempt, his whole upper body is like, jerking back and forth, almost like, like a convulsion, you know, except one that's created from, uh… externally. Heh.

"And then, on one of these big, convulsion-like things that the two of us are inflicting on this guy, he wakes up! Suddenly he wakes up, opens his eyes, the color starts coming back into his face…"

"So he was okay?" asked Yvonne.

"Yeah. He was fine. Coughed a couple times, and, he seemed kinda… disoriented. But yeah, basically he was fine. Like nothing had ever happened."

"Cool!" said Jake.

"And the funny part was," added Mike, "ultimately we discovered that, the reason we couldn't get him out of his seat was… he was still wearing his seatbelt!"

All six laughed and Amy said "Oh my god" again.

"That's why I'd rather be in e-commerce than be a paramedic," said Mike as he continued to laugh.

"Oh, yeah," said Amy. "You were telling us about your new business. So you said you're selling 'gently used' items online?"

"Right. Well what they actually are is slightly defective or damaged items, that I bought online myself. Most of which, heh, I managed to get a refund on without returning them."

"So, won't your customers just do the same?" asked Bill.

"Nope. I won't let 'em. If they really want a refund—which, of course, I make as difficult as possible to get—then they absolutely must send the product back to me."

"Okay…"

Laura and Yvonne were both smiling and shaking their heads (one of them while aiming it at a phone screen). Amy and Jake both wore somewhat incredulous (but excitedly smiling) faces.

"When I get it back," Mike continued, "I sell it again to the next sucker. And eventually, somebody is too lazy or too careless, or just too stupid, you know, to go through the process of getting the refund."

"Yeah, I can believe it," said Bill.

"And some of 'em'll even send the thing back to me *and* not take their refund. Double sales. Heh."

"Cool!" said Jake.

"Interesting," said Yvonne.

"All the big retailers do the same thing," said Mike. "Figured I might as well get my slice of the pie, you know?"

"Speaking of pie," said Amy, "I'm starving! Let's take the express rocket to the lunar sea, guys!"

Laura promptly pulled up the menu on her phone again.

Chapter 23

Lying on a sofa in the office of Dr. Linda Swarinsky, on the seventh floor of the "Spartan Tower" wing of the Purple Horseshoe Hotel Casino Conference Center and Professional Building on Las Vegas Boulevard just south of Sahara Avenue, Jarva Coker let out a long, labored sigh.

"I feel like..." she said. "I feel like I am not an equal partner in my relationship. I feel like he's in charge and, and... everything I say and do must meet with his approval, or else I will be punished... not physically, but, in some way."

Dr. Swarinsky, sitting across from Jarva in an easy chair, cocked one eyebrow but otherwise remained expressionless.

Squinting her eyes now, nearly closing them, with a look of analytical concentration on her face, Jarva continued: "And, I do not know... Well, there are four things I don't know. First, to what extent this feeling I have is actually true. Second, if it is true, to what extent it might actually be, in fact, a good thing rather than a bad thing, for our relationship in particular, but even, maybe—who knows?—for people's relationships generally...

"Anyway, third: again, assuming it is true, to what extent it's caused by my personality versus his. Or maybe, neither of those in isolation, but rather, the way they combine with each other.

"And, fourth: again, assuming it is true,"—now her eyes were squeezed tightly shut and she was moving her hands slowly in an intricate but meaningless pattern a few inches from her face—"whether any way exists that it could somehow be changed. Or whether it's just... inevitable..."

Dr. Swarinsky, whose right hand clutched a pen, its tip pressed against a blank page in a little spiral notebook resting on the arm of her chair, was now scrolling through her phone with her left thumb.

Jarva slowly moved her hands down to her sides. Then she opened her eyes, stared up at the ceiling and said, "So?"

"So?" repeated Dr. Swarinsky.

"So, what do you think of what I've just said?"

"What do I think of what you've just said?"

"Yeah. I mean... I'd like you to help me delve into these four questions. To... explore them. And perhaps discover other relevant questions."

"I'm afraid that's all the time we have for today," said Dr. Swarinsky.

"What?" Confused and alarmed, Jarva wriggled around and grabbed her phone off a side table.

"No, we still have three minutes," she said.

"Best not to start on something new with so little time left."

"But, it's not new. It's continuing on the same—"

"Thanks for coming in today, Ms. Cooper."

"It's Coker," said Jarva, now sitting up straight and regarding her therapist with skepticism and a bit of annoyance. "And also, I just remembered, we really have eight minutes left, because you got here five minutes late."

"That doesn't seem likely."

"Yeah, remember? You said—"

"I'm giving you some homework, for our next session. I want you to delve into those four questions I posed. I want you to really explore them. Can you do that for me?"

Ten feet directly beneath where grimacing Jarva's stocking feet pressed against the carpet, Irene Hoffman's head was sporting a big grin. She felt uncharacteristically giddy, despite not having consumed any alcohol. Ah, the intoxication of running a successful business!

"So, yeah," she said, "there I was, in the middle of the hallway, gyrating around like... like a fucking spastic..." She broke down laughing.

Stan Wojcik, seated at a conference table near where Irene was standing, smiled and made an almost instantaneous mental calculation to ignore her extremely non-P.C. choice of words.

"I guess Alex was pretty embarrassed, huh?" he asked.

"Mmm..." Irene responded, considering this momentarily. "Nah, I think she mostly just pitied her poor old lunatic mom... Now, if any of her friends had been there at the time, she would have been..."— she slowed down a lot, for dramatic effect—"Fucking. Mortified." She broke down laughing again.

"What were you listening to?" asked Irene's sister Norma, seated in another conference chair.

"It was 'Drift Away'... I swear, that fucking tune always gets me... It started out as a Life Stroll. I was trying to evaluate the latest algorithms. But then, oh, shit, you know?"

"You were always like that," Norma said with a laugh. "Always dancing around with your Walkman, totally oblivious..."

"Yep, I was always a rock-n-roller..."

"Remember that time I walked in on you, in your bedroom? When you were like, sixteen?"

"Of course! Like it was yesterday."

"That was crazy."

"Yeah there's something about the feeling of warm piss soaking into your jeans that's very memorable!"

"She literally peed herself," Norma said to Stan.

He began gently chuckling as both women howled with laughter.

"That was the same song!" Irene suddenly, delightedly exclaimed.

"What are you guys talking about?" asked Donald Piper, strolling cheerfully into the room, a stack of manila folders tucked under one arm.

"Donald!" snapped Irene, no hint of mirth remaining. "You're not supposed to be here!"

"I know, I know," he replied. "You've already told me like a hundred times."

Irene had strongly encouraged her team, as well as her sister (though not her brother, Daniel, whom she didn't really like (but whose absence had been explained to Norma, who liked him very much, with a bald-faced lie involving the hotel's "large groups policy")), to come to Vegas for the weekend for the purposes of "blowing off some steam and recharging our batteries," as well as to meet with a group of high-powered potential investors (who'd left this room ten minutes ago), but hadn't offered to reimburse anyone for their transportation or lodging (and had paid for her own with company funds). Donald had failed to understand that she'd intended him to stay behind in Orange County and devote his full attention to her tax and bookkeeping clients, whom she'd been making intense efforts to bring back recently with a surprisingly high rate of success.

"You're not supposed to be *here*, in this room," she clarified to

Donald, now standing right in front of her, holding out the manila folders and looking helpless. "I told you to stay in your suite."

"It's not really a suite."

"Whatever! Get your ass back there and keep working on those accounts."

"Um, well, I..." Donald stammered, looking down at the folders, half-believing that Irene might take them from him at any moment. "I had some... um, questions..."

She sighed. "Do you have any capacity whatsoever for thinking?"

Donald pondered this for a second.

"Get gone, little man! Get back to your suite and keep working. We'll talk later."

"Okay," he said as he scurried away with his folders.

"Christ," Irene said, pulling out a cigarette and lighter, "that dude sure is a buzzkill."

"Irene, there's no smoking in here," Stan remarked gently.

"Seriously?! In Vegas?"

Stan smiled and shrugged.

"Fuck it," said Irene, placing the cigarette between her lips. "They'll never know."

"They will know," Stan said, gesturing toward the alarm boxes and sprinklers lacing the walls and ceiling of the conference room.

"Goddammit, fucking piece of shit."

She frustratedly plunked down the cigarette and lighter on the table, then herself into one of the chairs.

"Hey, Stacy," she called out after a couple of seconds, her face pointing in the direction of a phone lying in the center of the table. "What's your situation now?"

"Still can't find the place," said the voice of Stacy Parabola.

"Seriously? Jesus. Do you think you're the worst navigator in the history of automobiles?"

"No."

"I mean, it's right there in the middle of the fucking strip. With its name in thirty-foot-tall letters, and like a gazillion flashing lights all around..."

Silence.

"So, anyway, what did you think of that meeting? You were able to hear us, right?"

"Yeah, I could hear. It didn't sound too promising to me..."

"What did you think, Stormin' Norma?" Irene asked, turning to her sister.

"Oh," Norma replied, taken aback and instantly flustered. "I don't... I really don't understand all this business stuff..."

"Don't sell yourself short," said Irene. "You've got it all, sis— beauty *and* brains. Runs in our family." She grinned and winked. "All you're missing is the self-confidence."

Norma smiled appreciatively but said nothing.

Now Irene turned to Stan. "How 'bout you, Stan the Man?"

"I agree with Stacy. Doesn't seem like they're going to go for it."

"Well," said Irene, "all of you are correct. They are definitely *not* a good fit for us. But that's okay. Actually, this reminds me of something I was reading a few days ago, in my CEO newsletter. Fucking brilliant piece. About maxing out your financial efficiency. The concept is based on a fundamental fact of markets, that we often overlook: they function on averages. On the *typical* producers and consumers. Right?"

Stan and Norma were both smiling.

"So the key is, don't be typical. There are two prongs. First, offer people products, services or whatever that are quite valuable to *them*, but that are not very taxing on *you* to produce. You know, stuff you have a talent for, or special skills, or access to scarce resources, or whatever.

"The second prong is, you consume stuff that's perfectly adequate or enjoyable or whatever, *for you personally*, because of your unique tastes or perspectives or needs or abilities... but *not* generally considered very valuable, or desirable, by the population at large."

Irene's companions were still smiling, though their faces were now a bit strained and Norma's eyes were developing a slight sheen.

"See? Financial efficiency! Gives you a massive edge over everyone else."

"Irene, is this related to our project?" asked Stan.

"Yes! Of course it is!"

Stan waited a moment for more. When none came, he said, "Don't we need these investors, in order to stay afloat?"

"No, Stanley," said Irene, smiling and shaking her head. "We don't need anybody. Not anymore. Our revenue is about to kick into high gear. I just gotta adjust the price of the product up a little."

"I thought you were decreasing the price, in order to move more units."

"It's a delicate dance, my fine computer genius friend. Don't you worry your pretty little head over it. I just need to find the sweet spot, and then, bam!"

Stan wore a rather skeptical face that only conveyed a tiny percentage of the skepticism he felt.

"Did you pay off Chuck Jones yet?" asked the voice of Stacy.

"No," Irene replied. "Why would I?"

"Well, he gives me the creeps. I'd be much more comfortable if we were done dealing with him."

"I paid off everything else," said Irene. "Which is awesome. We are, basically, totally out of debt now. And there's no point in paying Chuck Jones early, 'cause he charges the full-term interest regardless. God, it's a good thing you folks have me around to handle the money stuff."

"And when are you going to pay *us*?"

"Christ. You know, I'm starting to feel like I'm under attack here, people."

"I didn't say anything," Norma pointed out.

"Everybody's going to get paid, okay? Everything's gonna be fine. Just, chill."

Nobody spoke for several seconds.

Then Irene added, "Not to point any fingers, Stan, but you *were* the one who said we should hire the way-more-expensive A.I. company."

Stan smiled and ever so gently responded, "I only mentioned some potential advantages they had. My final recommendation was to go with the cheaper one."

Irene stared at him for a moment, then abruptly stood and began gathering her belongings.

"There's a lot of negative energy in here," she said. "I'm going out for a smoke."

Precisely 48 hours later, Francisco Danilo Rosario, sitting at a small corner table in Los Angeles Bistro International et Affreux (an upscale

French restaurant on Dayton Way in Beverly Hills) wearing a navy blue Armani suit and sporting perfect hair and nails, continued speaking.

"It happens nearly constantly, I daresay with nearly every inhabitant of this planet, despite striking one as a rather unlikely or unusual phenomenon. A person states that he feels a certain way or has a certain attitude, or perhaps even a belief... or asserts that he would, in some given situation, behave in a certain way. These claims, however, are not true, or not entirely true, or... in some cases, the claimant does not even know whether they are true.

"One finds my theory difficult to believe because it illuminates mental processes that occur largely unconsciously. Yet I have become convinced, from observing myself and others, that I am correct. The person in this situation is, without truly realizing it, pretending. He is pretending to be the person he wishes he were, or thinks he rightly should be, or thinks someone else wants him to be."

Sitting across from Francisco, wearing her standard office outfit (dark slacks, not-too-dressy-but-not-too-casual blouse, and sensible shoes), Yvonne Smede, who'd tuned out a few sentences ago, was now (yet again) fretfully checking her PaceTek Ultra, which, though also showing quite a nice step count, was informing her of an alarmingly advanced hour.

"Yvonne," said Francisco, "you seem... tense."

She looked at him and smiled. "There you go with your powers of observation again."

She'd been reluctant to meet for lunch on a workday, but Francisco had pressed her, enthusing about exciting news that wouldn't wait and wasn't appropriate for a phone conversation (which had turned out to be simply that he was presenting something at (or was it just attending?) some symposium in Cleveland this coming weekend—unexciting, would've waited, could've easily been related over the phone). To make matters worse, he'd selected today of all days, after she'd said she had "limited time on Mondays," having misheard her and thought she'd said "unlimited."

Still, she'd anticipated having ample time to get back to the office for her 1:00 meeting (even if that meant accepting a lift from Francisco). But now, 40 minutes after ordering her food (which she'd finally had the opportunity to do 40 minutes after sitting down), it hadn't yet arrived.

"Yvonne, please—tell me what I might do to ease your distress."

"Can you bribe the chef to move my order to the front of the line?"

Francisco chuckled. "Oh, Yvonne. Your eternal wit enchants me. Anyway, I am dreadfully sorry about the excessive wait we have experienced today. Matt led me to believe that the service here was quite expeditious."

"Matt Spratt?"

"Yes. I believe he said a friend of his had been employed here for a period of time."

"So, you two are still hanging out, huh? The odd couple."

"Alas, no. I came to realize that my interactions with Matt, though immensely enjoyable, were detrimental to my overall psychic well-being."

"Really? I'd've thought enjoyment was a positive thing."

"Indeed, one would naturally think so. However, in this case, the enjoyment carried with it too much diversionary power."

"Diversionary?"

"Yes. It hijacked my attention, if you will, diverting it away from important, substantive matters, to... frivolity and... pointless endeavors."

"Hmm..."

"Okay, croque monsieur," said Pierre, the server, arriving tableside with a plate in each hand.

"Actually, I ordered croque madame," said Francisco, "but that is all right."

"Okay, sorry, sir," Pierre replied, placing one of his plates in front of Francisco. "And..."—he looked at his other plate and began moving it toward Yvonne—"croque madame."

Francisco said "Oh" as Pierre laid the plate down.

"I ordered coq au vin," said Yvonne.

"Sorry, ma'am," said Pierre.

"It's okay. But, could you bring a couple of boxes, and the check, please? We're really pressed for time."

"Sure, definitely, right away," Pierre said before hurrying off.

"Sorry, Francisco," said Yvonne, glancing at her wrist again. "I have to get back for a meeting."

"Do not worry about it, Yvonne," he replied. "I understand. We must arrange to get together again soon—perhaps all four of us, next time. Perhaps dinner."

"Four?"

"You, Bill, Felaecia, and I."

"Oh, are you two back together again?"

"Yes, had I not mentioned it? Yes, we underwent a... reconciliation of sorts, I suppose. I came to realize that, despite her numerous shortcomings, Felaecia had always been a stabilizing force in my life—one that I, as it turns out, greatly value."

"Hmm, okay..."

Neither of the friends could think of anything else to say on this subject and, after several seconds of silence, Francisco's mind wandered onto a different one.

"Oh," he said with a slightly giddy smile, "I do not believe I have yet told you about a recent linguistic invention of mine. No doubt you are familiar with the construct of 'and'-slash-'or,' placed between two possibilities, to indicate that either of them might be the case in isolation or that both might be the case."

"Uh, yeah..."

"Well, I have reformulated it as 'or'-slash-'and,' to convey a subtly different meaning, namely that the first possibility is definitely *not* the case in isolation, but the second might be, and, of course, they might both be. Do you understand? Sometimes 'or' does not go both ways, as it were."

"Yeah, I understand. But couldn't you just reverse the order of the two possibilities and connect them with 'and possibly'?"

Pierre reappeared saying "Here you are," then unloaded from his arms onto the table two carry-out containers and a small leather folder.

"Please, allow me to pay, Yvonne," Francisco entreated, snatching up the bill.

"If you insist," she replied with a smirk as she reached across for the croque monsieur. "Just this once." (He always paid, and she'd long ago stopped trying to protest.)

"It has been a great pleasure dining with you, as it has been every time," he remarked as he took his wallet out of his coat.

Yvonne, now in the midst of filling up her takeout box, asked, "Where did you park?"

"Oh, I walked here."

"What? You *always* drive."

Francisco shrugged, then glanced up at a high window on the side wall of the restaurant, which was displaying the top of a palm tree against a bright blue sky. "Such a beautiful late winter day," he said with a smile. "Perfect for a leisurely outdoor stroll."

One hour later, having very hurriedly retraced her steps through a portion of the Beverly Labyrinth (a ritzy, slightly surreal-seeming patch of territory featuring a preponderance of buildings, parks and roads with variations on "Beverly" in their names (today she'd trod on Beverly Drive and Beverly Grove Lane, but not on Beverly Boulevard, Beverly Glen Boulevard, or Beverwil Drive)), dropping her croque monsieur unrecoverably in the middle of the street in the process, and having arrived late for the Lab Team group interview of prospective new employee Norbert "Bert" Hollander, a disheveled, visibly sweaty Yvonne said "Thank you" after listening intently to his highly thoughtful, knowledgeable and articulate answer to what she suspected (correctly) would be the only question she'd have an opportunity to ask him.

"Thank *you*," he replied pleasantly.

"Thanks, Yvonne. Thanks, Bert," said Laura Johnson, team manager and de facto emcee for today's farcical event.

Yvonne had tiptoed into the conference room, laptop tucked under her arm (everyone brought laptops to interviews, and all meetings for that matter, in order to "take notes"), roughly halfway through a monologue from Mona Knox intended to inform Bert of some interesting and useful facts about the Lab Team and to put to him some questions that he'd at least be able to understand and maybe even respond to. She'd failed abysmally on both counts and eventually Laura (who was not wholly lacking in basic human compassion) had rescued a stammering Bert by saying "Let's take this offline."

Now Laura was trying to prompt Fred Nguyen, who was typing feverishly on his laptop, to take his turn. "Okay, Fred... Fred?"

"Oh!" he exclaimed, looking up, startled. "Um... Yes... Yes... Um, Bert, hello. It's a pleasure to meet you. Thanks for coming in today."

"Great to meet you, too," said Bert. "Happy to be here."

"Um... I have a question for you: do you have experience with on-call?"

"With—I'm sorry—'uncle'? I don't believe so. Is that an acronym?"

"Um, no..."

"Fred's asking about your experience with being on call," Yvonne clarified.

"Ah, right," said Bert with a slightly embarrassed face.

"Yes," said Fred. "Thank you, Yvonne."

"No," Bert continued, "I don't actually have much experience with that. Seems like it could be pretty... challenging."

"Oh, it *is*," Fred replied, chuckling. "Let me tell you. Most of the time around here, you're having three kinds of weeks: scared about on-call, on-call, and recovering from on-call." His chuckling intensified into giant waves of laughter, facially animated but very quiet.

"Oh, wow," said Bert, and let out a chuckle of his own (the nervous kind).

Yvonne, who, while keeping an ear out for any noteworthy utterances, had also been scanning her email, where she'd discovered one from nurse Lawrence "Steve" Jorgenson in which he'd requested help with a failing glucometer, clicked Send on a reply she'd quickly composed suggesting docking the device.

"Fred, any other questions?" asked Laura through gritted teeth.

"Yes, yes," he said.

A new email appeared in Yvonne's inbox, from Fred, stating that he would re-send the relevant patient registration message as soon as he had a chance and apologizing profusely for not getting to it faster.

"Um... Now, Bert... I'm wondering... Actually, I'm so sorry. I can't remember what I wanted to ask you."

"That's okay," Bert said with a friendly smile.

A new email appeared in Yvonne's inbox, from Mona, indicating she'd be happy to perform the required message re-send if someone could just remind her of how it's done.

Laura now turned to Rob Harkin, the only team member present who hadn't yet had the chance to interrogate Bert. (Amy Lee was away for a few hours, attending an event at her daughter's school, and Jack Sutton had refused to participate in the interview.)

"Rob?" said Laura, then moved her attention to her laptop.

"Yes," Rob said, looking up from his laptop, where he'd been busily tapping away. "Welcome, Bert. I'm sort of the grandfather of the team." He glanced around the table, grinning, but nobody reacted or even made eye contact.

"You know, I sort of watch over everyone," he continued. "Make sure everyone has what they need."

Bert nodded and smiled.

"I spent a lot of years over on the clinical side. You know, on the real lab team. The *lab* lab team. Heh. Yep. And I've also spent a lot of years over here on this side…"

A new email appeared in Yvonne's inbox, from Rob—a reply to Steve's original message. It simply read, "solution is to re-send the reg msg."

Fred, who'd been looking at his laptop screen, abruptly said, "Bert. Bert. I should probably make more clear what I meant earlier when I spoke about on-call. It's not too bad. It's not bad at all. Not difficult, not stressful. You barely get any calls, and… when you do get calls, there is always a lot of good documentation, and good support from the whole team."

Everyone looked around the table at each other, Yvonne frowning and the other five smiling awkwardly.

____

"This is a waking nightmare," Irene Hoffman said quietly and sincerely, immediately after (and immediately before) taking an aggressive drag on the cigarette tightly pinched between her left thumb and index finger.

It was 9:00 Thursday morning and she was standing on the sidewalk in front of Senter Center (a nearly brand-new five-story office building occupying the eastern half of what had been the site of the old Eddie West Field (the demolition of which (to make way not only for Senter Center but for the extremely spiffy (though half the size of its predecessor) new Eddie West Field) had, by sheer coincidence, begun on the 55th anniversary of the famous soccer match played there between Orange County Soccer Club and Bayern Munich (which had ended in a tie)) on Flower Street in downtown Santa Ana, across from the gigantic Central Justice Center complex), scared out of her wits.

Through a combination of S.O.L. sales unexpectedly taking a sharp nosedive Monday and some small temporal/financial miscalculations on the part of Donald Piper (or, just possibly, Irene herself), she'd reached yesterday—the day her loan from Chuck Jones came due—not only unable to pay him the full amount but unable to pay him anything. During a somewhat heated phone conversation in which she'd related this fact, he'd instructed her to come here this morning to meet with a "colleague" of his to discuss "payment options," adding in a rather ominous tone that should she fail to show up, he would find her and then "produce regrets."

She couldn't recall if she'd ever been this nervous before in her entire life. Certainly not in the past 25 years. Looking down at her cigarette hand, she noticed it was trembling. She stared at the main entrance of Senter Center. It was a door she most decidedly did *not* want to walk through. But, what choice did she have? She took a final drag, dropped the butt and crushed it under her shoe.

"Fuckin' A," she said.

Stepping into Suite 357 five minutes later, Irene was triply surprised. First, the "suite" consisted of a single room—and not a very large one— with only a few pieces of furniture, arranged in a seemingly arbitrary fashion. Second, Dino Bravo, whom Chuck Jones had told her to meet here (granted, she could only *assume* the man seated behind a desk in the middle of the room, atop which sat a nameplate reading "Dino Bravo," was in fact him), looked nothing like she'd imagined: he was young, thin, black, wearing a perfectly tailored navy blue suit, and sporting no visible piercings or tattoos. Third, another person was also here—a young, chubby Asian man wearing a red track suit, curled up in an easy chair a few feet in front of Dino's desk. The men, who apparently had been intently engaged in conversation with each other, both seemed startled by Irene's arrival.

"Good morning," said Dino. "May I help you?"

"Uh..." Irene struggled for words. "Yeah, I guess. I mean, I hope so. I mean, Christ, I don't know..."

Dino waited patiently, smiling, but offered no verbal assistance.

"My name's Irene Hoffman," Irene finally said. "And, uh, Chuck Jones told me to meet you here at 9 A.M. this morning."

"Oh, I see," said Dino. "Well..." He chuckled and performed a mild shake of his head. "Apologies, Ms. Hoffman, but I'm afraid I must ask you to take a seat and wait briefly—just until I'm finished with my friend Roscoe here."

Roscoe, who'd been regarding Irene the entire time with a blank expression, gave her a small nod.

"Uh… okay…" she said, looking around and spotting a small wooden chair in the corner. "Guess I'll just… sit over here while… you guys, uh…"

"So anyway," said Dino, turning back to Roscoe, "as I was saying, your poetry is phenomenal. It's inspired."

"Do you really think so?" Roscoe asked, looking a bit pleased but mostly skeptical.

"Oh, yes."

"Kurt's stuff is pretty good."

"Well, sure, but… yours is better. Much better, in fact. I mean, I would never tell *him* that, of course…"

"Would you tell him the opposite of that?"

"Excuse me?"

"Would you tell Kurt," Roscoe said in a slightly accusatory tone, "that his stuff is way better than mine?"

"Um, well," Dino stammered, "yeah, I suppose, maybe… you know, to spare his feelings… you know, *if* he asked…"

"I asked."

"Yeah, but… that's different…"

"After you told Kurt his stuff is better than mine—you know, to spare his feelings—would you then tell him that of course you'd never tell *me* that?"

"Hang on a second here…"

"And then would you reluctantly admit to him that, in order to spare my feelings, you probably *would* lie to me and say that the opposite of what you really thought was true was true?"

For a couple of seconds, Dino, looking simultaneously confused, embarrassed and offended, seemed poised to speak, but no words came out.

"Screw you, man," said Roscoe, rising from his chair. "You're full of shit."

He stormed out as Dino continued not saying anything.

Irene was standing now, and tentatively inching her way back over toward Dino's desk.

"Uh, Mr. Bravo, sir…?"

He turned to her and smiled. "Ah, yes. Ms. uh… Johnson, was it?"

"Hoffman. Irene Hoffman."

"Hoffman. Right. Sorry. How are you this morning, Ms. Hoffman?"

"Fine. I mean, I don't know. Look, Chuck Jones told me—"

"Ah, yes," said Dino, starting to laugh. "That's right. Well, I don't work for Chuck Jones anymore."

"You don't?"

"Nope. Now I work for her."

Irene, bewildered, whirled around in the direction Dino was pointing to discover that the opposite wall of the room contained a small door she hadn't previously noticed (bearing a sign reading "Unisex Restroom") and that Judy Goldstein had just emerged from it.

The two women, displaying equal and enormous levels of surprise on their faces, shouted out each other's names.

"I didn't know you were actually going to *be* here today!" exclaimed Judy, breaking into a huge smile.

"What the fuck is going on here?" snapped Irene, telegraphing frustration and disgust but feeling far happier than she had a few minutes ago.

Dino laughed again. "Tell me about it! I've had more unexpected visitors today than I could shake a stick at!"

Realizing after a short pause that, for Irene's benefit, he should probably say more, he did. "So, first, Chuck Jones comes in. Wasn't expecting to see *him* here, I can tell you. And he starts rummaging around, pulling things out of drawers and whatnot, and he's telling me he's got an important assignment for me, and yammering on about 'trust' and 'confidence.' I couldn't really make sense of it.

"Then, suddenly, a bunch of cops burst in, waving their guns around! And they handcuff Chuck Jones, and they take him away! And *then*, they've barely been out of the room five seconds, and *this* gal comes waltzing in, all smiling and giggling…"

Judy, already smiling, began giggling and said, "You're welcome!"

"That's what she said to me!" Dino added. "She said, 'You're welcome.' Heh."

"Judy," said Irene, "did you know I was mixed up with Chuck Jones?"

"Oh, yes, of course. I've kept in close contact with everyone on the team since my departure. Well, everyone except you. How come you never return my calls?"

"Because I'm fucking busy, that's why. Anyway... I mean, I don't know... Isn't it kind of weird? I mean, I fired you."

"Well, we're still friends, aren't we?"

"Uh, yeah. I mean—"

"Anyway, what I *didn't* know, until thirteen days ago, was that the D.A. had been building a case against Chuck Jones—a very strong one. Strong enough to pick him up and, almost undoubtedly, hold him without bail until his trial. And then convict the bastard."

"Jesus," said Irene. "How'd you find out all that?"

"Well," Judy replied with a sly grin and an almost-wink of her eye, "my husband is an attorney, too. And, it turns out, he's on a team that's defending this fellow Brock Hightower, a close associate of Chuck Jones. Now, he's not allowed to talk to me about any of this. You know—attorney-client privilege.

"But... "—another almost-wink—"I needed to use his car because mine was in the shop. And he was working from his home office, and he was on a really long conference call with the other lawyers, and, turns out, he wasn't really paying attention. At all. So when I cranked up the engine, his bluetooth connected and the conference call started coming through the speakers. And I just couldn't believe everything I was hearing!"

"Holy shit," said Irene.

"And he just kept having these long conference calls, and, turns out, he *never* pays any attention, and, the others, they never ask him anything. Honestly, my husband isn't that great of an attorney."

Dino laughed.

"So anyway, I just kept finding excuses to go out to the car. Well, actually, I didn't need any excuses because he was in his office with the door shut and he couldn't care less anyway. So, yeah, eventually I knew everything there was to know about Brock Hightower, and a heck of a lot about Chuck Jones to boot—including that the police were ready to arrest him, if only they could find him!"

"Holy shit," Irene said again.

"So, I called them and tipped them off. Anonymously, of course. But then I couldn't resist coming here myself to witness the big take-down!" She let out another giggle.

"Christ," said Irene. "I gotta admit, Judy—you did great work. This is a big relief for me. But, uh... you really don't think there's any chance this douche will be back on the street tomorrow? Or next month? Or next year? I mean. . ."

"No, no, you have nothing to worry about. The case against him is too strong. He's heading to prison for a long time. Over ten thousand days, bare minimum. Without parole."

"Really?" Irene allowed herself to smile just a little.

"Yes, really," Judy squealed. "You can relax!"

Irene turned to Dino. "And what about you?" she asked. "You're not upset about this?"

"Upset?" he repeated incredulously. "No. Not at all. Working for Chuck Jones wasn't a very good fit for me. The role he had me doing, it was called 'Collection, Protection, Inspection.' And it was kind of a drag. I was a lot happier in my younger days, working as a paralegal. Which, now, I get to do again!" He grinned.

"I'm trying to rehabilitate my practice," Judy explained. "And Dino here seems like just the kind of bright, enterprising young soul I need on board!"

Irene was shaking her head and smiling, reeling from the mental bombardment of the last few minutes (and the lifting of an immense emotional weight), struggling to process it all.

"You know," said Dino, still grinning, "to tell you the truth. . . Chuck Jones was kind of an asshole sometimes."

———————————

Two mornings later, Bill Smede was rather surprised, as he pulled up outside Irene's, parked, got out, and ambled up the driveway, that she wasn't already visible, smoking and/or fussing with something, nor did the garage door start going up, nor did she suddenly emerge from the front door as he approached, shooting him a mock sneering face or a real sneering face. He was further surprised (and somewhat horrified) to discover, after ringing the bell and waiting several seconds, that the person answering the door was not Irene but her husband, Keith.

"Hi," he said with a friendly smile. "Come on in."

"Thanks," said Bill.

After closing the door behind Bill, leading him through to the family room and gesturing toward a small sofa (which Bill took as his cue to sit down on it), Keith said, "Irene'll be along shortly. She's in the bathroom."

"Thanks," said Bill.

As he slid into an easy chair directly across from Bill, Keith added, with perhaps a tiny hint of a joyous glint in his eye, "Seems she ate something that didn't agree with her."

"Ah," Bill replied.

A moment later, feeling awkward about the silence between them, he said the only thing he could think of to say. "Pretty quiet in here. Are your kids, uh…"

"Alex is in her room. The boys are at karate camp."

"Karate camp?"

"It's not really a *camp* camp. It's more like a… I don't know what you call it. But it's all day long, and the parents don't have to stay."

"Cool."

Keith's smile widened a bit as he said, "I know it was you."

"Sorry?"

"Who slept with my wife."

Bill said nothing, and (involuntarily) expressed nothing facially. But he felt a very strong desire to be elsewhere.

"It's okay," Keith said after a long pause. "I don't blame you for taking advantage of her. You couldn't help yourself."

"Uh, well…"

"And I'm not mad at her, either. Not anymore. Because I realized, she would never ordinarily sleep with some loser just to hurt me. She was just… in a weird place then. Temporarily weak. Easily manipulated."

"Mmm," Bill said with a slight nod of the head, as he would've done if listening to someone casually relating a not-very-interesting anecdote.

"Nope, all is forgiven," Keith continued. "But, we agreed, in order to make it fair, I get to sleep with someone else, too. Whoever I want."

"Mmm," Bill said again.

"Yep." Keith grinned excitedly. "I chose Aisha, from the school."

"Mmm."

"She's hot. She teaches math. Anyway, it hasn't happened yet because… well, 'cause I haven't really, uh, broke the news to Aisha about it. But, when it does happen, it's gonna be sweet!"

As Keith had said this, the sound of Irene singing quietly and mindlessly to herself "And you don't need to wonder, you're doing fine, lighten up, the pleasure's mine..." had been floating in from the hallway. Now, entering the room, she said, "Christ! My guts are doing a major number on me this morning."

"Sorry to hear," said Bill.

"Yeah, normally I'm like clockwork—once a day, always at 6 A.M. But, holy shit! No pun intended. You know what it was? That god-awful dinner Keith made last night. No doubt in my mind. Remember, honey? Even while I was eating it, I was saying—"

"Yeah, yeah," Keith grumbled. "I remember."

"So what's new with you, dumbass?" Irene asked of Bill.

He shrugged and stammered, "Uh... I guess... nothing, really."

"Oh!" She snapped her fingers and pointed at him. "I have a little gift for you. Stay there."

She dashed back down the hallway and disappeared around a corner.

"Do you like science fiction?" asked Keith.

"Uh, no, not really," said Bill.

"I've been reading this series of short stories... or maybe they're considered novellas? I don't know. Anyway, it's such a cool concept. It takes place in, like, the near future, and... There's this woman who, when she was younger, she had her eggs 'indexed.' So, they've got this technology where they can scan the ovaries and create a genetic profile of each individual egg. So she's got this, like, catalog of her own eggs, and she's become totally fixated on one particular egg."

"Mmm," said Bill.

"Meanwhile, there's this other new technology that's, like, cutting edge, and most people don't even know about it yet, but this woman and her husband, they do know about it and they have access to it. Anyway, it does the same thing on sperm. Well, it doesn't scan the testicles, but, it can scan like a semen sample. And that's what they do—they scan this, uh, you know, this, uh, sample, that the husband... uh, produced. They scan it before it gets frozen. And so they've got the genetic details of *all* those sperm cells."

From an unknown location on the other side of the house came the faint sound of Irene's voice: "What the fuck? Maybe in the garage?"

"So, this woman," Keith went on, "the wife, *again* she's obsessed with the info, and she chooses *one* sperm. You know, out of like, hundreds of millions. She has some fancy software helping her with it, but, she also knows her stuff. She's like a total hardcore scientist or whatever."

"Mmm," said Bill.

"So the stories are about how, as time goes on and technology keeps advancing, she's able to learn more and more about this hypothetical child—Adam, she names him Adam. This hypothetical child that she and her husband maybe could've had, or maybe still *could* have at some point in the future. They don't know. That's part of the intrigue. 'Cause, that indexing thing, and, the sperm technology... Everything's always in motion, you know?"

Some faint crashing and slamming sounds were coming from the direction of the hallway.

"So anyway, this woman forms a deep emotional connection with Adam. She knows what he looks like at different ages. She knows stuff about his personality. She even knows what his voice sounds like. She comes to think of him as real. But he's not there, so, that makes her sad. It's like she's mourning the loss of her son, except he never even existed."

"Nobody wants to hear about your stupid stories," Irene, who was back in the room now, said to Keith; then, to Bill, "Voilà!"

In her hands was an S.O.L. headset. Bill forced a smile.

"The third prototype," Irene announced, beaming. "You can grab the software off the internal site—it's still there."

"Thanks," said Bill, taking the headset from her.

"Oh, and, uh... Shit. That little booster thingie. Never got it back from that fucking punk kid. Did I ever tell you about that?"

"Once or twice."

Keith had risen from his chair and was quietly scuttling off toward the kitchen.

"Yeah," said Irene, "so, anyway..." She sighed wistfully. "End of an era."

"What do you mean?" Bill asked, confused.

"Oh, I didn't tell you? Yeah, had to close down the business. Sales just kept slumping and slumping. There was no fix. I even reached out to those Ass-Backward folks, I was so desperate—hah! But, it was too late."

"Oh, god. I'm really sorry, Irene." Bill felt genuinely bad for her.

"Don't be," she said with a dismissive wave of her hand. "The world wasn't ready for my awesome invention. That's their problem, not mine."

Bill smiled.

"I guess my only regret might be that, in the end I wasn't able to pay my team what I owed them. But, whatever. They're cool with it."

"Oh," said Bill. "Uh, would you like me to—"

"Did I ever tell you? I was just sitting in my dorm room freshman year of college, and, just, out of nowhere, it just hit me—I'm the best. It was a fucking epiphany."

"The best?" Bill asked, puzzled. "The best what?"

"Just, the best, dude. Period. I can do… anything I set my mind to. And if somebody else is doing it, I can do it better."

Bill couldn't help snickering.

"Laugh all you want, William. It's true. Too bad you didn't go to college *with* me. Then maybe you would've been the best, too, instead of being a pussy."

He laughed harder for a moment, then began to reminisce about his own college days, then asked, "You ever feel sad when you think back to earlier times?"

"Nope," said Irene. "Why would I? My life just keeps getting better and better."

"It's not that the past was better," Bill clarified. "It was just… different. Each period of my life was a whole other world. A world that's close to my heart. And which can never be recaptured. I think that's what causes the sadness."

Irene stared at him for a couple of seconds, then said, "You stupid piece of shit. Come on, let's go get some breakfast."

"Okay," he replied with a smile.

"And while we're there I'm going to tell you a fabulous new business idea that is going to blow your mind!"

Chapter 24

Inside L.A. Nail Bar (a nail salon that happened to be located in a strip mall at the corner of Pico and Robertson but which was nearly indistinguishable in name, size, decor, services, and pricing from seventeen other salons within a half-mile radius), Pam Stotz, seated in the pedicure chair farthest from the entrance, was talking up a storm to the woman working on her feet, who went by Lisa but whose real name was Hyun-sook.

"It was unbelievable," said Pam. "My dad strolls into my home office and he says, 'Your mother and I were wondering if you'd like to have lunch at Tres Hermanos.' And I'm like thinking, 'Oh, how nice—they want to take me out for lunch,' right? No! Turns out, I'm driving them there, in *my* car, even though they have a freakin' rental car. What a waste of money, right? Then, when we get there, I order tacos and water. Both of my parents—steak and margaritas. And when the bill comes, they just sit around and wait for *me* to pay it!"

Lisa smiled and grunted, not looking up.

"I mean, they're adults. You'd think they could handle some stuff, right? I mean, they travel all over the freakin' world without me. Oh! They told me about this trip they took to Jamaica recently, and, they were on this sketchy, like, bus thing that was driving them from the airport to the resort. And about halfway through the drive, like in the freakin' middle of nowhere, some old man comes walking out of the trees and walks right into the road, right in front of the bus, and the bus hits him! And the driver just, jumps out, runs over to where the guy is laying in the dirt, *seriously* injured, and, he grabs the guy's ankles and just *drags* him over to the side of the road, then runs back inside the bus and drives away!

"People call it paradise but, I don't know, with stuff like that going on, how much of a paradise could it be, right? My parents are kinda nuts. Me, I stay away from exotic destinations like that. No, thanks! I do dream of maybe one day relocating to some place glamorous, though. Like, maybe Tulsa."

To Pam's right sat Hannah Conklin, emitting a continuous, quiet munching sound and slowly moving her left hand back and forth between her lips and the inside of a large Burger King takeout bag while receiving a pedicure from a woman who went by Betty but whose real name was Soo-jin. Hannah wasn't speaking currently and, in fact, had not spoken a single word since leaving her desk (located on the 17th floor (one of three floors leased by her employer, Collect'm-E) of the Miracle Towers office complex on Wilshire) to head for the salon—not even just after arriving here, as she was a regular and the ladies of L.A. Nail Bar already knew exactly what she wanted.

On the other side of Hannah sat Penny Jones, receiving a pedicure from Mary (real name Eun-jung). Like most human beings, Penny fell somewhere in between Hannah and Pam on the talkativeness scale. She'd been silent the past couple of minutes but now it occurred to her that her nephew's birthday was coming up soon.

"My nephew's birthday is coming up soon," she said to Mary, who smiled and grunted without looking up.

"I know some of the stores where he likes to shop," Penny continued, "so I'm thinking, maybe a gift card? But, I don't know—gift cards seem kind of silly to me. They don't require any thought, any imagination, or creativity, or effort. They're just like giving somebody cash, except they're even worse because you can only use them at that one place."

"Hah! Nope, wrong," said Juice Hughes-Newton from the next chair, in response to Penny's remarks but facing away from her, toward Yvonne Smede, who was seated to Juice's right.

"Gift cards are better than money because they force the person to treat themselves instead of just spending it on practical, boring crap. *And* they're so easy to get. They are the best gift ever. Don't know how I survived back before they became so... uh, plentiful."

Yvonne managed a smile, her first since arriving here. The miniature jacuzzi into which her feet had just been placed by Anna (real name Kyung-hee) felt very pleasant; that, combined with the ever-increasing amount of time since the trauma endured while journeying here from the office, was bringing on relaxation and a sense of peace.

Juice had insisted on picking Yvonne up from the small, paved "emergency parking only" area adjacent to her building, even though Yvonne regularly walked to and from L.A. Nail Bar (and quite enjoyed doing so). While attempting to execute the rather tricky exit from this patch of asphalt back out onto Wilshire, Juice had suddenly realized that a big, bold line of vehicles was rocketing toward the point at which the nose of her BMW X5 protruded out into the roadway, and had then, panic-stricken, thrown it into Reverse and stomped on the gas, not realizing that another car was three feet behind her, nor that those particular three feet were transected by a sidewalk along which was rapidly approaching an innocent young male skateboarder. For a split second, both women had believed that Juice was about to perpetrate a grisly murder, but the lad had then deftly saved his own life by executing a phenomenal aerial stunt that had left him continuing, unscathed, on his merry way, while the back of the X5 crunched dramatically into the front of a 1979 Ford Pinto, greatly upsetting its 88-year-old driver.

Yvonne had been afforded the non-interacting recovery/forgiveness period she'd needed by an unwitting Juice, who'd made a stop on the way to the salon to dash into her favorite bakery for a box of croissants and had then spent the first ten minutes in the pedicure chair alternating her attention between the small screen of the smartphone she clutched in her hand and the slightly larger screen belonging to a T.V. set that was mounted, hospital style, on the wall opposite them. But now she was ready for conversation.

"So anyway, what's going on with you lately, girl?" she asked.

"Hmm," said Yvonne. "Well, our money situation just got better—Bill finally found somebody to take over the lease on that apartment."

"Was that with the asshole landlord?"

"Right. Yeah, Bill brought him like a dozen good candidates and he rejected all of them."

"I hope you had a chance to sow your wild oats while you two were separated."

"Anyway, the landlord had a stroke a few weeks ago and now, apparently, he's incapacitated and his son took over running the property and, lo and behold, the first person Bill brought to the son just sailed right through."

"Oh, it's great when shitty people are finally out of your way. Same thing happened to me recently—Donna Marquez is finished at South

Valley."

"Oh, really?"

"Yep. Supposedly she 'moved on' happily, to, you know, 'pursue another opportunity.' But *I* think what really happened was she was shown the door. Heh." Juice grinned gleefully.

Yvonne made a "Mmm" sound of acknowledgment.

"So, yeah. Karma. So anyway, my job is cushy as hell once again. Just how I like it. And no more of that stupid disciplinary crap, either. That all died with the wicked witch."

"Cool."

"Shame you and I won't be working together, though."

"Yes."

"Oh, speaking of work, a patient asked me yesterday if I'd ever taken the 'hypocritical oath.' I just about died laughing!"

"You are known for your bedside manner."

"Mmm-mmm," said Juice, making a smiling-with-momentarily-tightly-closed-eyes face of contentment and wriggling around a bit in her seat. "This feels *so* nice. You use the massage?"

"Of course," Yvonne replied.

"Me too. Mmm. The whole body experience. Yep, I love being in this chair."

"It sure beats the dentist's chair. In which I spent a thrilling hour last week."

"Oh, did you have to get some work done?"

"No, it was just a cleaning, but... so tedious. It's the same every time. They're always running late, to start with. Then I get in the chair and they try to make some small talk—they pretend they remember stuff about my personal life but they always get it wrong. I wish they wouldn't even bother."

Juice laughed. "I hear you! Totally. Do we have the same dentist?"

"Then they say things like, 'You have some build-up on your teeth.' Yeah, I figured, that's why I'm here. And, 'You should try to floss more often.' Probably true, but I'm not going to, and they should realize that by now."

Juice was chuckling and nodding her head.

"The worst is when they tell me my gums are bleeding after they've stabbed me in the gums with a sharp metal hook. Yeah, no shit."

"Love it," said Juice, not consciously aware that her level of amusement was made just a tiny bit higher by Yvonne's (extraordinarily rare) use of the word "shit."

"And then, right at the end, their parting shot: they give you this free toothbrush to take home, but they've already opened the package and used it in your mouth. You know, to demonstrate proper technique."

"Hah! I love this girl," said Juice, who was now looking at the T.V. screen.

Courtney Kato, a former national television news anchor who'd been well respected but had abruptly ended her journalism career without explanation, had recently launched a web series—in which she and her husband appeared with a rotating roster of guests—that she characterized as "exploratory art" but which everyone else on earth understood was in fact hardcore pornography. Currently one of Ms. Kato's ex-colleagues was presenting a short piece about her new endeavor, in which a portion of its exceedingly vulgar title (displayed in the upper right corner, over the host's shoulder) had been digitally redacted.

"Oh," Yvonne said, "so, what's the latest with your little quest for vengeance?"

"Right!" Juice exclaimed, snapping back into the moment. "Okay, so... Did I tell you it was easy to find Nancy all over the Internet using her real name?"

"Yes."

"But, couldn't find any current contact info, or, really, any current info of any kind, you know? Nothing that I could *use*..."

"Yeah, you told me that, too."

"But you know me—I'm not a quitter!"

"Well..."

"So I talked to a bunch of different people who used to work with her, at various odd jobs she used to have, and... Well, most of them were useless as hell, you know? And so *stupid*. But one of them, at this restaurant, said Nancy had actually come in recently, to have dinner."

"With Ned."

"Oh, I told you already? Yeah, this waitress, who fucking hates Nancy—probably spit in her food!—she pulled the credit card slip and gave me Ned's full name. Ned Vargas."

"Right," said Yvonne. "And, you couldn't find out where he lives but you found his garage."

"Exactly," said Juice. "So, I've been staking the place out, occasionally, you know, when I have time.”

“Great use of it, by the way.”

“And on Tuesday night, it paid off! She was there. And when she left, I followed her. And guess where she went!”

“Uh. . .”

“She went to a pawn shop on Rosecrans. To sell *my* necklace!”

“Seriously?”

“Yes! Of course!”

“You actually saw the necklace?”

“Well, no, but. . . I’m positive that’s what she was doing.”

“Well then you could’ve just gone into the shop right after she left and bought it, right?”

“Yeah, but then I wouldn’t’ve been able to keep following Nasty Nancy. I wanted more intel!”

“Ah, right. So, where did she go next?”

“I don’t know—I lost her. Goddammit! Lost her at the, you know there, by the train tracks and there’s like one intersection like this, and another one—”

“I don’t know that area.”

“Well anyway, not a big deal. I’ll find that bitch again. And meanwhile, I’m going back to that pawn shop tomorrow night.”

“Tomorrow *night*?” Yvonne queried. “Wouldn’t it be safer to go during the day?”

Juice grunted with annoyance. “Mmmf, Paul’s out of town on a retreat and both the kids have shit going on tomorrow. *Both* of them. Can you believe it?”

“Wow.”

Neither woman spoke for several seconds, after which Juice turned her attention back to the T.V. and Yvonne began thinking about tasks awaiting her this afternoon at the office.

Two minutes later, Juice turned back to her friend.

“These days there’s so much of this ‘pick a side’ mentality. You know, ‘us versus them.’ It’s so stupid.”

“Yeah,” agreed Yvonne.

“I can’t believe people buy into that crap, but they do. Stupid people. You know, society is hanging by a thread because of them. And people like us, smart people, have to hold it together. We have to defend. . . well, everything that matters. . . against stupid people.”

Sue Lu Lee, in the midst of routine Saturday lawn care and gardening in the front yard of the Cerritos, California house where she'd been living for the past 40 years, paused and looked eastward to where yet another car was arriving outside her next-door neighbor's place, this time a Cadillac ATS (joining an old Chevy Malibu and an older Isuzu Trooper recently parked curbside, and an even older Corvette convertible in the driveway which, oddly, had arrived twice during the past hour and a half).

She didn't know the names of any of the four people who lived there, but she recognized them all, including the young lady who'd just burst through the front door (whose name was Anika Smede-Hogg) and was giddily sprinting across the driveway to meet the new arrivals.

"They sure are friendly, festive folks over there," she commented with a thick Chinese accent to her husband, John Lee, who was kneeling a few feet away, weeding one of their planters. (The two still abided by an agreement they'd struck long ago as fresh immigrants—one far more important and valuable then than now—to speak only English to each other.)

"Yes, they are," he replied in his usual happy, agreeable fashion.

Sue continued watching as the vehicle's occupants disembarked—first, from the passenger side, a young man and young lady (though not nearly as young as their one-member welcoming party) with facial expressions of mild affection/amusement and utter blankness, respectively, and then, slowly, from the driver's side, a middle-aged man with a rather apprehensive look on his face who seemed to be concentrating intensely on some unknown (and, apparently, entirely internal to his mind) object.

That man, Bill Smede, was urging himself to stay positive as he rounded the rear end of the ATS and stepped onto the curb, entering the final, short stretch of time and space in which to mentally prepare for today's event—a "Welcome to Spring!" party organized by his mother and his sister, ostensibly to celebrate the vernal equinox (which had occurred at some point in the past week or so and which Bill considered barely even noteworthy). At least, he thought, they hadn't ruined his birthday—he'd marked that occasion in exactly the way he'd wanted, enjoying a peaceful, romantic dinner with Yvonne at their favorite restaurant, Sprazzo (which offered the bonus of being walkable from the condo, eliminating the need for driving or Ubering). And at least, he further thought, they'd decided to hold this thing at Debbie's place, which was somewhat larger and considerably closer than their mother's.

He smiled as he watched Anika skipping ahead excitedly while pulling a perhaps slightly reluctant Alice along by the wrist. All three girls (Anika's sister Raylene included) had always gotten along well, despite fairly large differences in personality and age. How old *are* they now, anyway? Bill asked himself. He could never remember. (Raylene was twelve years old and Anika was ten.) At least, he thought, he knew their names and could tell them apart from each other. So that was something—he wasn't the worst uncle in the world.

Now Bill was about halfway between the sidewalk and the house, and Patrick was about halfway between Bill and the house. The girls had just slipped through the doorway, and suddenly it was filled with a deeply horrifying sight: the slouching frame and leering visage of Roger Raderman, ex-partner of Bill's cousin Pippa and all-around insufferable, obnoxious lout. His dark brown hair was, as usual, medium-length and slicked back but somewhat mussed; his varying-length mustache was currently completely shaved off. In one hand he clutched a can of Pabst Blue Ribbon. Yvonne had nearly agreed to join today's outing, but had backed out when Bill had foolishly reminded her of some of Roger's less-than-endearing personality traits.

"Paaaat," he growled playfully at Patrick.

"Hi, Mister Roger," Patrick replied pleasantly as he stepped up onto the tiny front porch. Bill grimaced.

"Ooh, Pat," said Roger, "did you hear what happened at the leper hockey game?"

"Huh?" Patrick replied, totally confused.

"Don't worry about it, Patrick," said Bill, now stepping onto the porch himself.

"Bill Gates!" Roger exclaimed. "How goes it, my man?"

"Uh..." Bill stammered, unable to think of anything to say and trying hard to smile but failing.

Patrick had vanished inside the house. Bill now entered, too, and closed the door behind him (with a heavy sense of sealing his own fate) as Roger resumed the verbal onslaught.

"So listen, here's something that got me thinkin'... Do you believe you're past the midpoint of your life?"

"Yeah, that's—"

"In other words, do you think all the time you've lived so far is *longer* than how much time you've got left?"

"Yeah, well—"

"It's kinda morbid, you know? But also kinda like... philosophical..."

"Yeah I actually ponder that pretty often," Bill finally managed to say. "But I think what fascinates me even more is, periodically I'll calculate what's the midpoint between—"

"Hey, that reminds me," said Roger, "you still managing all that rich dude's money?"

"No. And it wasn't anywhere near all of his money, and 'managing' is a strong term for what I did. 'Pseudo-monitoring' would be more accurate..."

"Well I need to lay my hands on a chunk of it. Got this fantastic investment opportunity. I mean primo. You're gonna love it!"

"Like I said, I'm not working with that guy anymore. But even if—"

"Aw, shit—seriously? What happened, man?"

"He fired me, actually."

"Oh, yeah? What for?"

Bill sighed and shook his head. "He accused me of embezzlement—which, honestly, I don't think was even technically possible for someone in my position, even *if* I'd had the inclination and the wherewithal, neither of which I had..."

Roger guffawed and said, "Hand in the cookie jar, eh? Shame, shame!"

"No, it was all a mistake... *linked to* an issue with this thing he tried to set up so that I would receive a small monetary compensation package for helping him out..." (Bill was now deeply immersed in Fret World and oblivious to the fact that Roger wasn't even pretending to listen, his eyes darting around, looking for new prey.) "...which I kept trying to talk him out of doing but he kept insisting... Mmmf... The whole thing was just such a clusterf—"

The instinctive activation of Bill's personal policy of avoiding swearing in front of children brought him back into the moment, and he realized that his sister was about to come through the entryway, en route from another part of the house to yet another.

"Little Debbie," Roger remarked as she approached. "The host with the most!"

"Hey, little bro!" Debbie said with a delighted smile. "You finally got here!"

She zipped right up next to Bill and gave him a quick peck on the cheek, a maneuver dating back to their childhood which she didn't perform every time they met, but more frequently than he wished.

"Thought maybe you were gonna ditch us," she added, still smiling.

"Yeah," he replied, "sorry I was late... I uh..." He'd done it deliberately and had neglected to choose an official excuse. "I was, uh... I was running late. Sorry."

"Well you're here now, that's what matters."

"Yes!" Roger cried, holding his beer can (from which he'd just taken a swig) aloft.

"Oh!" said Debbie. "You know who else is here? Cranston and Gertrude."

"Oh, really?"

Cranston and Gertrude were Pippa's parents. Bill had known them for as long as he could remember, and had never, as far as he could recall, found either of them the least bit offensive or interesting.

"Yeah," Debbie continued, "aren't they the sweetest? I just love 'em to pieces."

"Speaking of who's here," said Roger, "where's that sexy little minx of a wife of yours?"

"Um..." said Debbie.

"Ooh, and speaking *of*," Roger continued as a short, slightly chubby, thirtysomething Asian woman in a bright red dress sidled up to the group and wrapped an arm around his torso. "This is Sandy. She drove separately because, you know, child safety. Anyway she's kinda my main squeeze now, I guess you might say."

"Nice to meet you!" Sandy exclaimed, too loudly, then grabbed Roger's face with her free hand and engaged him in a long, deep kiss, then turned back to the others and shouted, "Roger being super squeeze man! We maining lots of big squeeze every times!"

Roger chuckled with amusement and possibly a hint of pride (but definitely zero embarrassment). "Hell *yeah* we do," he confirmed. "Gotta be careful about Dora. I think she's gettin' jealous!"

He chuckled some more as Sandy let out a brief, high-pitched giggle and the other two just stood there, stone-faced.

Then he said, "I better watch out the two of them don't get into a catfight!"

More laughter from half the group.

As Bill passed through the kitchen 20 minutes later (having managed to escape his earlier entanglement by excusing himself to go use the bathroom and then remaining there, reading Wikipedia on his phone (today's subject: film director Irvin Kershner), long enough for the other three to disperse), he witnessed 5-year-old Jessica Raderman, on her way from the backyard to the refrigerator, grab a hand towel that was hanging from the oven door handle, wipe it aggressively all over her sweaty face and neck, and carefully place it back in its previous position. He headed toward the dining room, hearing the sound of his sister's voice coming from there (and not hearing the sound of Roger's).

Stepping through the doorway, he saw that two other people (Cranston and Gertrude) were here, as well as one canine, who happened to be the current topic of conversation.

"Yeah, he's just the best," Debbie was saying. "Did you know he's a rescue dog?"

"You mean like Lassie?" asked Gertrude.

"No, *he* doesn't rescue people. *I* rescued *him*."

"You mean like from a burning building or something?"

"No, from the Humane Society."

"Oh my goodness," said Cranston. "What were they doing to him?"

"What? Nothing. Just, he needed a home so I, um... I adopted him."

"Oh, yeah," said Bill, suddenly remembering. "How'd it go with that big-deal competition you entered him in?"

"Ugh, don't remind me," said Debbie. "It didn't go at all. We didn't even qualify for it."

"Oh, really?"

"Yeah. Turns out poor Fritz has quite the anxiety problem."

"Now what's this, dear?" asked Gertrude with a face of concern.

"Well, hello there, Will," said Cranston, awkwardly extending his hand across the two women. Bill gave it a quick grasp and tiny pump.

"Oh, this thing in New York," Debbie explained to her aunt. "The Cup. Anna-Maria Schiaduffa... I guess I was... sort of delusional, you know. She was sort of like, my hero, and I thought that maybe, just maybe, Fritz could..."

"I'm so sorry, dear," offered Gertrude.

"Thanks. Yeah, the show was just last weekend, in New York. Grace went out there anyway, you know, for a gig. We had it all planned out like, way in advance. Shame."

Debbie shrugged and smiled, and Bill, thinking this was probably the end of this subject, muttered "Mmm, shame."

"I watched it live on my laptop," Debbie said. "And it was... just, so gorgeous. Just fantastic. But I couldn't believe who they gave the grand prize to. It was this weird-looking little fluffball, from Florida. Just this weird little, like, blobby ball of fur... Think its name was Wynton..."

There were smiles and a bit of eyebrow motion, but no words, from her three audience members.

"But anyway, they have, like, prizes for different categories, too, and... So, they have this 'large dog' category, which is the one Fritz would've belonged to, and, the winner of that category was this, like... It was the funniest-looking dog I think I've ever seen. You mentioned Lassie, before..."—she made special eye contact with Gertrude— "Well, this dog looked kind of like that, except the middle part of her body, it was like, plumped out, and oval-shaped, I guess—like the shape of a watermelon. And it turns out the breed is called a Melon Collie! Isn't that crazy?"

Bill laughed and said, "Wow."

Gertrude laid her hand on Debbie's shoulder and said "I'm so sorry, dear."

"Will," said Cranston, "I need to go to the john. Do you know where it is?"

An hour later, the four of them were back in this room again, seated at the massive rectangular dining table, about to tuck into heaping servings of sausage potato cream pie alongside Roger Raderman, Sandy Huang, Grace Hogg, and the mastermind of this whole affair, Catherine "Mamsy" Smede. (Patrick had nearly been given a seat here, too, courtesy of his father, but had made it clear that in fact he preferred to keep the spot Debbie and Mamsy had allocated for him at the circular table in the other room and to have his meal there in the company of Alice, Raylene, Anika, Jessica, and Jessica's younger brother, Rodger.)

"Oh, I just love it when the whole family can get together like this!" exclaimed Mamsy giddily.

"Me, too!" declared Gertrude with nearly the same level of enthusiasm.

"So Mamsy," said Roger with a sly grin, "tell us what's been happening in your love life."

"Oh—well, uh," she replied, taken aback by the question but also pleased it had been asked, "recently I've been on a few dates with this gentleman named Douglas. At least, I *think* that's his real name. He also goes by Oliver sometimes..."

"Hah," Roger snorted. "I knew it. You're a silvery old crazy fox, Mamsy." He took a swig of beer.

"Yes," she went on, "we met through this computer thing, 'Maturity Matchmaker' or some such. You remember my friend Dottie? Well she got me set up on it. So anyway, it's a little peculiar: we were in the middle of having coffee last weekend, and, suddenly, he mentioned— just, very casually, like it was nothing at all—that he was a pathological liar..."

Alarmed faces were instantly beamed at Mamsy from all her tablemates except Roger and Sandy, who were now rubbing their noses together and pawing at each other.

"And he suggested maybe, because of this, it'd be better if we didn't go on any more dates."

"Wow," said Bill.

"But then, last night, I asked him about it, at dinner, and he said he wasn't a pathological liar. That's a paradox, isn't it? Very odd. But anyway, it was a lovely dinner. He took me to that place... Oh, what's it called? The restaurant in that giant hotel, next to the Crystal Cathedral..."

"Oh!" Debbie exclaimed. "We were there, at that same hotel! Just, like, a week ago! I don't remember the name, either, but anyway, funniest story... We were there for one of these benefit things, with all of Grace's fashion set. Sorry, babe,"—she turned to her wife—"I'm going to embarrass you with this..."

"Not a problem," Grace replied sincerely, with a happy smile.

"So we're there a few hours, it's getting late, and, we're standing with a group of people near this, like, dance floor area, you know, just sort of watching the folks who're dancing. And, I notice Grace, just, out of the corner of my eye, I notice that she's *swaying*, backwards and forwards… Only a little, but, she just keeps swaying back and forth, and, her eyes are almost shut. And I realize, 'Holy crap, she's drunk as a skunk,' and I start thinking we've got to get her home…"

There was a loud, high-pitched giggle from Sandy and light chuckles from everyone else, including Grace, who commented, "I always have too much when I'm with that crowd. Just something about them."

Debbie continued, "So, we get in the Uber, and, we're heading home, and, Grace says she's gonna throw up. And I'm like, 'Pull over! Stop the car!' But the guy can't hear me or something, I don't know. So then Grace starts puking, and it's just, like, all down her dress and, on the seat, and, on the floor…"

Bill glanced down at his food and frowned. The three members of the older generation were all gazing at Debbie, rapt. Grace was a bit red in the face but still smiling. Roger and Sandy were kissing each other.

"And, the window was already down—'cause she was too hot but I was too cold, which always happens to us… So then she sticks her head out—you know, to try and… throw up outside the car or whatever. But we're going, like, 50 miles an hour and it just goes all over the door and the back part of the car.

"So we finally get home, and Grace goes inside, and then I have to deal with the Uber driver. And I'm figuring he'll probably just charge me a bunch extra for the mess, right? But no, he wants me to help him clean up his car!

"So, I get him the hose, so he can at least wash off the puke from the side of the car, and then I go in the house for a minute, to check on Grace and try to find some rags and stuff. And when I come back out, he's been spraying water all over the back seat and the floor! And then he gets all upset because the inside of his car is all wet…"

Debbie now joined Mamsy, Cranston, Gertrude, Grace and Bill in (various intensities of) laughter.

"I know what you mean about that thing with having different body thermostats," said Roger, who'd just separated his face from Sandy's. "It's the same with me and my cute little baby doll, here. Especially when we're in bed. Whoa, I tell ya—I'm always overheating and she's always freezing her ass off. Sleepin' is pretty easy to figure out but, sometimes, when we're doing the nasty, we gotta get pretty creative..."

All laughter had subsided.

Sandy shouted, "Roger being super creative man! He creating every nasties!" Then she produced an ear-piercing giggle.

"So, yeah," Debbie said after a moment, "I was dealing with that idiot Uber driver for like, probably an hour..."

"Hey Mamsy," said Roger, "do you believe you're past the midpoint of your life?"

Bill was looking down at his dinner again, marveling at the lunacy surrounding him. He reminded himself that staying positive was key, and immediately it occurred to him that he felt some affection toward most of the people currently gathered in this house, and had derived amusement from all of them. A small smile broke out on his face, and the old saying "You can choose your friends but you can't choose your family" ran through his mind. Mulling over the veracity of this statement, he quickly realized that he'd never been able to choose his friends, either.

———————————

At 8:00 that night, Juice Hughes-Newton, having just left her BMW X5 underneath the only functional lamppost in a small, sketchy-looking parking lot, rounded the corner onto Rosecrans Avenue, very near its intersection with Western (and not far from two of Larry Flynt's casinos). She strode purposefully, but her mind was wandering, revisiting the many hours of torture she'd endured today. She didn't notice the gigantic billboard, whose base she was now walking past, informing its audience that one half of the duo who'd hosted a morning talk/comedy/variety radio show here in L.A. called "Nevin & Dean" (which had been a favorite of Juice's back in high school, and which had continued its extraordinarily long run on terrestrial F.M. radio until just a few years ago) could still be enjoyed daily on his solo podcast, recorded in England (where he now resided).

Prior to getting her children, Henry (age 15) and Lateesha (age 10), fed and squared away for the evening with plenty of obligations to prevent their hands from becoming idle, Juice had spent a large chunk of her morning attending Henry's special, extended-length, located-far-from-the-school weekend basketball practice (the ludicrous brainchild of Coach Brubaker, who'd somehow gotten it into his thick head that this was the year his boys were going all the way to State) and a large chunk of her afternoon at Lateesha's located-on-the-opposite-side-of-the-Valley gymnastics meet. At both events, she'd found herself unwillingly engaged in chitchat with some of the other parents, who invariably came across as bumbling, boring dolts.

There was the youngish fellow in a baggy pea-green hoodie who, while incessantly bragging about his son, had continuously kept an index finger jammed up one nostril, perpetually probing around (and, when called out on this by Juice, had claimed he wasn't picking his nose but simply "scratching the inside"). There was the fat gal who'd talked only about food and whose shockingly ugly polka-dot blouse was far too tight, as well as inside-out and backwards. There was the elderly guy sporting what appeared to be a three-day beard who'd claimed that it was actually just three hours' worth of whiskers and that he lived in a nightmarish world of constant shaving, each instance of which caused the growth to speed up further still. There was the woman who'd described in excruciating detail an alleged new technology for monitoring and managing physiological indicators of stress and anxiety, built into a nifty portable device called a "Barostatic Monitor," and had opined that "I ought to have a B.M. whenever I'm driving."

Just after shaking her head and muttering "Fucking idiots," Juice noticed that she'd come upon the entrance to Halstrom's Gold Pawn and Payday Loan.

A large collection of bells, held together by several long strips of twine, produced a very loud jingling noise as she came through the door, and a portly, grizzled, black man seated behind a nearby counter, looking almost as if he'd been expecting her, asked "Can I help you?"

"Yes, sir," she replied, smiling widely and stepping up to the counter. "I believe you can." Juice recognized this man—now staring at her, expressionless—from her reconnaissance mission of four nights ago. He was definitely the one who'd dealt with Nancy.

She continued, "A middle-aged white woman with a stupid face came in here a few days ago and sold you a necklace—a silver chain with a diamond pendant."

The man continued to stare, not speaking or evincing any emotion of any kind.

"Do you remember it?" Juice asked with a hint of impatience.

"Yes," the man replied flatly. "I bought the diamond. Wasn't interested in the chain."

"Well, that diamond was not hers to sell. It belongs to me."

Silence.

"Would you consider giving it to me?"

"No."

"I can get you back your money from that slimy, conniving... witch..."

"I don't have the diamond anymore. I sold it."

"What?! To who?"

Now the man smiled ever so slightly. "I didn't get a name."

"Well... Take a look at your credit card slips. And your surveillance tape."

"There's no way I would do any such thing. But if it makes you feel better, this is a cash business and the surveillance footage gets wiped every 24 hours."

"You know," Juice said, smirking and reaching into her bag, "I can make it worth your while."

"Lady, you are a piece of work," said the man, his smile widening. "I can't help you. I think you better leave."

"Look, if I walk out that door..."—Juice turned her head and eyes in the direction of the exit—"Holy shit!"

Nancy Parsons had just walked past—she was certain of it. She bolted toward the door, flung it open, and stepped out onto the sidewalk.

"Hey, bitch!" she called out to the figure strolling rapidly away from her.

Nancy stopped and turned around. Their eyes locked.

"I want my goddamn necklace!" Juice shouted.

"Jesus Christ!" Nancy exclaimed. "Leave me the fuck alone, you psycho bitch!"

"Never," Juice responded, now on the move.

Nancy turned and began attempting to run, though it was difficult in her six-inch heels. Juice, also wearing high heels, followed suit, accelerating up to the best pseudo-run she could manage.

After several seconds of low-speed chase, Nancy abruptly reached out with her left hand, opened a door, and disappeared behind it.

A moment later, Juice discovered that it led into a lobby of sorts for a building that contained businesses on the lower levels and public parking above. Why didn't I notice this one? she asked herself mentally for a split second. Then, scanning the immediate area, she saw a bank of elevators on the far wall, and to her left, an entrance to a stairwell—with a door that was just swinging shut.

"Aha!" she announced triumphantly.

For the next few minutes, the two women were ascending the stairs, trading insults with each other, Juice consistently a floor and a half below Nancy.

Then Nancy reached the top and went out onto the roof, where Juice found her 30 seconds later, standing ten feet away, by a guardrail at the edge, one arm extended over it.

"Hah!" taunted Juice. "Nowhere left to go!"

"So you want *this*, do you?" Nancy asked, and Juice suddenly realized that the necklace—*her* necklace (minus its diamond)—was dangling from Nancy's fingers, gently swaying in the breeze, suspended 60 feet above the street.

She's bluffing, thought Juice. She wouldn't just give up the necklace—even if she knew I couldn't have it, either. The necklace is too important.

"Well, go fetch!" Nancy commanded in an extra-nasty tone as she flicked her wrist, flinging the necklace into the air. Then she began casually walking off in a different direction, toward where the concrete began sloping gently downward, leading to the other parking levels.

Juice was momentarily stunned. Then she thought, it's a trick. Nancy's going to try to retrieve it. Well not if I get there first!

She sprang into action, sprinting back to the stairwell door, then rocketing down two flights to the highest non-roof level of the building, where she made a snap decision to gamble on switching to the elevator, which paid off—it was already there, waiting, and whisked her back down to the ground floor in short order.

It'd be on the front side of the building, right out here, Juice thought as she burst back out onto the sidewalk and began frantically scanning for both her necklace and her nemesis. Come on—where, where?

Then she spotted it—lying in the road, just a few feet from the curb. Suddenly, a car came roaring down Rosecrans and ran over the necklace, smashing it into several pieces. Then, as Juice stood gazing at those pieces, trying to recover from being startled by the passing car and to absorb the new state of affairs, a street-sweeping truck came trundling along, and she had the opportunity to witness its spinning brushes and spray of water working in concert to quickly (but seemingly in slow motion) usher all the remains of the necklace into a storm drain.

As Juice's mind worked to re-orient itself, she heard the metallic clanging sounds, accompanied by engine and tire noise, of a vehicle exiting the parking garage into an alley. A moment later, a large, black, rather ominous-looking sedan emerged from the alley, turned right onto Rosecrans, proceeded slowly past her and then stopped.

The back window came down to reveal Nancy's face. "Did you get your fucking precious necklace?" she asked with a sneer.

"Let me tell you something, bitch," Juice said with an angry scowl as she began to move toward the car.

The window started sliding up again as, simultaneously, the other three doors opened and three men stepped out, all of them large and rather thuggish in appearance, two of them brandishing baseball bats.

The batless one spoke, and Juice listened.

"Hello there. My name's Ned. I know who you are. I know where you live. I know you got two cute little kids. And I have a friendly warning for you, and it's the only warning you're gonna get. Stay away from me and Nancy. Stay far away. Forever. Or you will wish you did."

Juice continued not to move or speak as the three men got back in the car and it sprang to life with a horrendous squealing of tires, then sped away and disappeared into the night.

Though she hated it with every fiber of her being, she knew this was the end of the line. She raised her face to the heavens and screamed at the top of her lungs, "Fuuuck!!"

Then she got out her phone and started navigating the screens. It was time for a nice, long vent session with her good friend Yvonne.

Chapter 25

Matt Spratt took a long, leisurely gulp from his beer bottle and let out a sigh of pleasure as he surveyed, with great satisfaction, the early April Tuesday afternoon Santa Monica landscape surrounding him: bright blue sky, gentle breeze, sand, surf, palm trees dotted all around, human and canine revelers of every size, shape, age, and color, all having a splendid time; and, in more immediate proximity, the angelic, smiling face of Lindsay LaRoux, a 58-year-old painter and yoga instructor whom Matt had met an hour ago while waiting in line at Hot Dog on a Stick.

"Gorgeous day!" he enthused.

"Sure is," agreed Lindsay.

"Hey, thanks again for the beer," Matt said. "Really hits the spot!"

As he drained the rest of the bottle's contents into his throat, Lindsay remarked, "I don't think you're actually supposed to have it out here…"

Tossing the empty bottle toward a nearby trash can, Matt chuckled and said, inaccurately, "Aw, nobody cares about that."

"Well, anyway," said Lindsay, "are you *finally* going to explain what that shovel is all about?" (Matt had been using his non-beer-and-corndog hand to keep a shovel perched on his shoulder the entire time they'd known each other.)

He grinned gleefully. "Yes, Linnie, my dear. The time has come! You are a very lucky lady."

"Oh, *am* I?" she replied in a sarcastic tone but feeling virtually no skepticism and plenty of amusement and curiosity.

"That's right," said Matt, still smiling but now scanning the horizon in the opposite direction from the ocean for specific markers. "You are part of history in the making. With this shovel I hold in my hand… I am going to dig up... a long-lost, buried treasure chest!"

"Whoa, seriously?"

Having spotted the large rock and twisty-trunked tree he was seeking, both protruding from the cliff face just on the other side of P.C.H., Matt was now carefully stepping backwards and slightly to the left, and holding his free hand straight out in front of his face to aid in alignment.

"Dead serious," he said. "Buried right here on this beach, by a beautiful movie star from the days of old!"

He did an about-face and made several more steps—slow, cautious, deliberate ones, heel-to-toe—which brought him to the small concrete curb forming the boundary between asphalt and sand. Then he turned around again, stretched his arm out, closed one eye, then opened it and closed the other eye, then shuffled a couple of inches to the left.

Sidling up next to him and smiling as widely as he was, Lindsay said, "Wow, this is so cool!"

"Super cool," Matt affirmed. "X marks the spot!" He tapped his index finger against his forehead. "I got the whole treasure map up here."

"Awesome," said Lindsay.

"And now, little lady..."—he held out his hand for her to take— "...we count!"

She excitedly interlocked her fingers with his and, mimicking him, stood rigidly upright and faced straight ahead, eyes on the waves hitting the shore.

"Wait!" Matt said in an abrupt, somewhat officious, somewhat cartoonish voice.

Lindsay looked over at him, puzzled.

"I'm just teasin'," he said with a laugh. "You know, it's like those talking crosswalks up there on Ocean Avenue."

"Hah—right!"

"Okay," said Matt, and they stepped forward together onto the sand.

"One... Two... Three... Four," he counted out loud, concentrating on the movement of his legs, no longer heel-to-toe but just as meticulous, and nearly as slow, as before. "Stay with me. Follow my lead. I've perfected my stride so it exactly matches Marion's... Or, I guess it's Rick's, really..."

Lindsay didn't quite know what he meant, but that was fine. This was fun. Goofy and wacky and fun. She giggled delightedly.

Hand in hand the pair walked 42 paces toward the water with an awkward, robot-style gait, then executed a painstakingly precise 90-degree turn to the right, then 101 paces directly toward the Annenberg Beach House complex, then a left turn, and finally another 27 paces seaward.

"... Twenty-seven." Matt halted his legs and mouth for a second, then cried "This is it!" as he leapt into the air, almost literally clicking his heels together, still clutching Lindsay's hand and his shovel.

Then he let go of Lindsay's hand (first giving it an almost (but not quite) imperceptible little squeeze) and, gripping the shovel shaft with both hands, used the tip of its blade to swiftly scratch two crisscrossing indentations in the sand, each about two feet long and intersecting at their middles, right in between his feet and hers.

"X marks the spot!" he happily proclaimed for the second time in the last five minutes.

Then he dropped the shovel, reached into his shorts pockets and brought out a lighter and a joint.

An hour later, as Matt stood knee-deep in the hole he'd created, lighting a different joint, and Lindsay sat next to the hole, her knees pulled up near her chin and arms wrapped around her legs, they both noticed a figure approaching from the north—surprisingly, the first person who'd passed near them since they'd arrived here.

"Ahoy, mates," he called out as he shuffled hurriedly toward them.

A moment later he stood before them, grinning, looking almost as if he were proud of himself and expected some appreciation to be shown. He was slightly more than five feet tall and completely bald, with skin the same color and texture as well-worn leather saddlebags. Like Matt, he hadn't an ounce of fat on his body, but, unlike Matt, many ounces of muscle. He wore only a Speedo, a gold chain, a gold wristwatch, and a pair of water socks.

"I'm Tainton Legrarduroy," he said. "What are you two getting up to?"

With Matt mid-drag, Lindsay said, "We're on a—"

"I bet that shovel's pretty heavy," Tainton interjected.

Matt glanced down at it, shrugged, exhaled, and said "It can—"

"How far you think you could throw it?" asked Tainton. "Not very far. But *I* could. I could throw it to flippin' kingdom come."

He continued talking as he bent over and snatched up the shovel. "I work out every single day. Nine hours a day. Six in the morning, six at night."

"That's cool, Taint," said Matt. "I'm Matt, by the way."

He extended his hand, but Tainton ignored this and hurled the shovel into the air with a dramatic flailing of all his limbs.

"Holy shit!" exclaimed Lindsay.

The shovel careened through space, spinning and bobbing slightly, the eyes of Lindsay, Tainton and Matt all following its trajectory with facial expressions of horrified bewilderment, smug self-satisfaction and mild bemusement, respectively.

Finally it crashed back to earth, sending up a large cloud of sand, just a few inches from where a young heterosexual couple were sitting on a towel vigorously making out with each other, a millisecond after nearly striking them both in the head. They immediately sprang to their feet, clearly startled and distraught.

The young man, turning in the direction from which the shovel had arrived, shouted angrily, "Hey! What the hell!"

Matt, who'd just taken another drag, held his hand straight up in the air, palm open and fingers apart (except for the two pinching the joint), as a gesture of good will.

He exhaled and then called out, "Sorry, dude!"

For a moment it seemed as if the young man was going to charge at them, but instead he hastily gathered up the blanket and a few other items and took off walking in a different direction with his companion.

"Now it's your turn," said Tainton to Matt.

"Huh?"

"It's your turn for the hammer throw! To prove how weak you are!" His eyes were gleaming.

"God," muttered Lindsay, shaking her head (but grinning ever so minutely).

"Oh," said Matt with a chuckle. "Nah, I... I'm not really into throwing stuff..."

"Now don't be weasel-dieseling about it. Take your lumps."

"Oh, hey,"—Matt extended the stub of his joint toward Tainton—"you want the rest of this?"

Tainton scrunched up his face in disgust. "Don't be loco!" he bellowed. "My body is a temple!"

"Okay, suit yourself, Taint." Matt brought the joint back to his lips for a final drag.

"Oh my god—Matt!" came a female voice from roughly the same direction the shovel had gone.

The three all turned their heads to see a thirtysomething white woman in roller skates rapidly approaching. The tracks in the sand suggested she'd been trudging southward through it, paralleling the shore, and then had made a sharp left turn just now.

"Rorie, is that you?" Matt enquired excitedly, a puff of smoke shooting out of his mouth with the words.

"Hey everyone," she said in a sort of stylized, almost singing, voice as she arrived next to the group. "I'm Aurora."

"Rorie, meet Linnie and Taint," said Matt, gesturing with his arm.

Upon realizing that Aurora was accompanied by a rottweiler, who'd been momentarily occupied with something near her original course but was now right here among them, frantically sniffing everyone's feet and ankles, Tainton suddenly shrieked with alarm.

"Dogs must be leashed on this beach," he announced loudly and sternly. "It's the law!"

"Aw, nobody cares about that," said Matt, reaching out to pat the dog on the head.

"No, it's okay, he's right," said Aurora, who'd already produced a bright red leather leash from her fanny pack. "She's a free spirit, this one! Give her an inch, she'll take a mile!"

"So how do you two know each other?" asked Lindsay.

"Oh, just, from the boardwalk," Aurora replied, snapping the hooked end of the leash onto her dog's collar. "Or, no... from the Stop-n-Shop? It's been a while!" She turned to Matt. "How long has it been?"

"No kidding," he replied with a grin. "Too long, too long. So what are you up to?"

"Oh, just, enjoying this wondrous day... Getting in a little cardio with Nellie, here..."

"Well you came along at a great time. We're about to dig up a buried treasure chest!"

"Seriously?"

"It does seem kinda far-fetched," remarked Lindsay.

"It's for real," Matt said, grinning widely. "Buried right here in this very spot, by silver screen goddess Marion Davies, nearly a hundred years ago!"

Tainton, who'd kept his attention on Nellie this whole time (with an abrupt shift from fear to affection the instant the leash had been attached), now turned to Matt.

"You're not going to find anything that old buried here," he said.

"Oh yeah?"

"They excavated this whole area 20 years ago."

"They dug it up?"

"Sure did. Made a real mess. Ruined the whole vibe of the whole beach. They were building a new something or other."

"Wow," said Matt. "You sure about that?"

"Of course I'm sure. I was right there, watching the whole thing happen. I used to play games, just there." He gestured vaguely to the south.

"Oh, like volleyball?"

Tainton made a sneering utterance, sonically akin to "Pfft," followed by "I would never waste my time with rubbish like that. Real games. Like Russian roulette."

"How did you even know where to dig?" Aurora asked.

"From the treasure map, of course," Matt replied with a smile.

"Ooh! Can I see it?"

"It's all in his head," said Lindsay.

"Yep, every detail," said Matt with a bit of pride and a bit of amusement, again tapping his forehead with his finger.

"Aw," said Aurora, "I was hoping it was a real map."

"Oh, it is!" Matt clarified for her gleefully. "But I gave it to my friend Bill as a souvenir. Me and him, we kinda did this whole thing together, you know? And I knew it'd mean a lot to him, if he could keep the map."

"Why isn't he here for the big moment?" asked Lindsay.

"It's terrible these days," said Tainton, "how you can never crack jokes about any group of people, because they might get offended. I used to have the best jokes about cartographers. But not anymore—you never know when one of them might be listening."

"Maybe we should take a break," suggested Matt. "I'm starving."

"Sure, sounds good to me," said Lindsay.

"Do you know Sidewalk Cafe?"

"Of course!"

"It's a long walk from here, but totally worth it. I'm gonna have their steak and eggs!"

As Lindsay got to her feet and Matt stepped out of the hole he'd dug, he asked, "Anyone else wanna join us?"

"I will!" chirped Aurora, eliciting an almost microscopic wince from Lindsay.

"I can't make it," said Tainton, glancing at his watch. "I need to apply my hair cream."

"Cool," said Matt. "Well, okay then, ladies..." He swept his head and arm gently around to indicate the inclusion of the women and Nellie, then let out a quick laugh. "Let's go!"

"Fuck you!" snarled Bill Smede, seated at his makeshift desk in the main living area of the quite modestly-sized, dilapidated condo he shared with three others.

"What did *I* do?" his wife Yvonne responded from her spot at a real (though extremely small) desk on the other side of the room.

Yvonne knew Bill wasn't addressing her, or anybody nearby, or on the other end of a phone line, or any human on earth for that matter. She knew he reserved such levels of aggression for inanimate objects (typically computers). But this didn't make his outbursts any less irritating.

"It's just this stupid..." he said by way of explanation. "This stupid, fucking..." He trailed off, too absorbed in grappling with his cyber-pain to speak a full sentence.

Upon returning, five minutes ago, from walking a neighborhood loop with Yvonne, Bill had discovered that in his absence all the remote systems he'd been using had conspired to play a cruel joke on him—some logging him out and refusing to let him back in, some freezing up, some just giving him back utter garbage whenever he typed anything. He'd also discovered that Ted Bonar had stealthily slid a tedious and time-consuming task onto his plate, and that he'd been asked by one of the project managers to spend virtually zero hours coming up with a reasonably accurate estimate of how many hundreds of hours, over the next many months, it would take him to complete a highly complex, multi-faceted effort that hadn't yet even been fully defined.

The loop had been a largely miserable experience too, featuring numerous encounters (including one with Mrs. Harris and Max), though it had boosted his step count, of course, and also had involved a rather pleasant (as always) exchange with Rufus Fletcher, after which Bill had tried in vain to count how many squirrels and crows he saw on the rest of the walk (but had managed to successfully tally up the exact quantities of children, dogs, and electric scooters endured).

Patrick Smede strolled in from the back part of the condo and approached his father, his face bearing the slightly anxious expression that inhabited it during 35% of Patrick's waking hours (the rest of which was carved up as follows: 45% intensely focused on screen content, 17% totally blank, 2.8% happy/enthused, 0.2% other).

"Um, hey, Dad?" he said.

Bill sighed and turned to face his son. "Yeah?"

"Um... Could I borrow the car?"

"You don't have a license."

"It's not right now. It's tonight. For, um... this thing me and Len got invited to..."

"Ah, well that changes everything."

"Um... So could I borrow the car?"

"No." Bill turned back to his laptop.

"Okay," said Patrick, then looked thoughtful for a few milliseconds (part of the 0.2%), then strode casually the rest of the way across to the front door and left the condo.

For the next three minutes, the only sounds were clicking and typing. Yvonne and Bill both vaguely intended, any moment now, to issue snarky appraisals of Patrick's behavior, but were too engrossed in their work to actually do it.

Then Alice Smede entered from the same hallway as her brother, earbuds in and backpack on, making a beeline for the same front door through which he'd just disappeared.

Sensing she was being spoken to when "What are *you* doing here?" flew out of Bill's mouth, Alice paused her music, stopped moving her body forward and rotated it marginally in the direction of her parents.

"What," she said.

"Why aren't you at school?" asked Bill.

"There's no school today."

"Really?"

"Only the teachers go. So they can prepare. I told you."

"Well why do you have your backpack?"

"For carrying stuff."

Bill chewed on this for several seconds while using his face to beam a ray of hard skepticism at his daughter. Yvonne had not looked away from her monitor, though she'd been tuned in with her ears to the whole interaction.

Finally Alice, concluding she'd waited the required length of time for any further parental remarks, un-paused her music, proceeded on to the front door and departed.

Bill shrugged and turned back to his screen.

A minute later he shouted, "Goddammit! Fucking piece of shit!"

"Could you try to tone down the vocalization of your sentiments for a few minutes?" asked Yvonne. "Looks like Laura is about to call me."

"Goddammit, fucking piece of shit," Bill stated in a calm, quiet voice.

Yvonne's laptop abruptly began emitting a repetitive, obnoxious noise somewhat reminiscent of a "red alert" aboard a spaceship in a decades-old low-budget science fiction production. She grabbed her headset off the desk, snapped it on, and clicked the mouse button to answer the call.

"Hi, Laura. How are you?"

"Oh, pretty good, I guess," Laura replied from her office chair in the Beth Universal Mount Zion I.T. building. "Except for this morning I forgot to put my mug under the Keurig machine spout, so my coffee poured all over the place, and everybody in the kitchen saw it and that was pretty embarrassing. How 'bout you?"

"Can't complain," said Yvonne. "By which I mean, definitely *can* complain, most likely *will* complain, but have had far more to complain about on numerous days in the past."

Laura chuckled. "Understood. Got any plans for the weekend?"

"Well, my dad is coming for a visit. Can you top that?"

Another chuckle. "Guess I don't really have anything yet... except for keeping Mike out of trouble."

"Up to his old tricks again, huh?"

"God. He signed up with Uber, to be a driver."

"With his ambulance?"

"Yes. He got a few 'luxury upgrades' to the interior when he was having the body work done."

"Hmm, okay..."

"You know, when it got all smashed up, like six weeks ago."

"Not really, but—"

"Outside Amy's place—that little green car got pushed into the back of the ambulance by some hit-and-run maniac."

"Oh, right..."

"Anyway, this Uber thing. So Mike actually *combines* his two jobs—picks up rides while he's on his way to the scene of an accident. And on his way back to the hospital."

Yvonne was cracking up now.

"Says he only does it when he knows it won't affect patient safety. Oh—and speaking of driving, here's his latest thing: he wants to create software that'll hack into a car's back-up camera, and then he can override the system with fake images whenever he wants. So like it'll appear on the screen like there's nothing behind the car, when there really is. 'Cause he says people never use their mirrors anymore, much less actually turn their heads around—they just rely totally on the camera. Which I guess is true."

"So they'll back into something that he puts in their path and then he can sue or collect insurance money or whatever..."

"Right. Exactly. Or back into *him*! That was one idea he had..."

"So how's he planning to 'create software' for this?"

"Oh, he wouldn't do it himself. Actually he said *Bill* put him in touch with someone, down in Orange County, who knows some programming whiz or something. I don't know..."

"Ah, yes," said Yvonne. "Good luck with that."

"He is a very silly man sometimes," Laura said in summary. "I think he needs a vacation. Or I do, anyway."

"Oh—you've got that final island. The very best one."

Laura sighed. "No, we don't."

"You're not going next month?"

"Nope. Can't. It's closed forever. The tide got too high. It's basically underwater now."

"Sorry to hear."

"Yeah, it's a real bummer. I wish we could've known somehow, that this was going to happen. We would've gone there sooner."

Neither woman spoke for nearly a minute as Laura wallowed in regret and Yvonne pondered whether to say anything further on the present topic, ultimately deciding not to.

"So what were you calling about?" she eventually asked.

"Oh, right," said Laura. "Yeah. It's about this thing with the Inpatient Team..."

"Oh, that," Yvonne said with a sigh.

"Did you see the latest from that Kevin guy?"

"Unfortunately."

"I didn't quite understand what he meant..."

"It doesn't matter because he wasn't answering the question I'd asked. In fact, he wasn't talking about anything remotely relevant to this conversation."

"Oh..."

"It's frustrating because I spent a lot of time carefully crafting that email I sent him—to make sure it was absolutely crystal clear: here's the situation, here's the info I need from you, and..."

"Right, right..."

"It's like he didn't even read it. His reply was so short and... thoughtless and... just, worthless."

"Hmm, okay, well... yeah, that's a shame."

"When's Bert coming aboard? So I can pass some of this crap off to him..."

"Oh, I didn't tell you? Yeah, Bert declined our offer. He decided to stay where he was."

"I thought he hated his current job."

"Yeah, I don't know what to tell you. But anyway, Kevin can be pretty cool to work with sometimes. I mean, I really like his passion..."

"Well," said Yvonne, "at the risk of offending you—not to mention sounding like a conceited, self-righteous moralizer—I'm going to put myself out there by saying that passion is highly overrated."

Laura chuckled. "Oh, yeah? Tell me more. Oh—Amy's tapping on my glass, making faces at me. Probably wants to talk about this inpatient stuff. I pinged her about it earlier. Oh, she's leaving now. Guess she saw my headset..."

Yvonne continued, "Anyway, I think passion *can* be a positive quality in a person. But so often it's passion for wrongheaded things, or it blows hot and cold too frequently to yield any good result... or it's just pretend passion—it's really just all about *seeming* passionate. You know, just, showing off, in essence."

Laura chuckled again.

"And in Kevin's case," added Yvonne, "it's all of the above."

"Wow, that's quite a dissertation," said Laura. "Okay, well... Hmm, let's see... Oh, Amy's calling me now, from her desk. Maybe I can conference her in. Hang on a sec..."

The line went completely silent momentarily. Then Laura's voice returned.

"Amy?"

"Yes, ma'am! Read you loud and clear!"

"Yvonne?"

"Yep."

"Okay, great. I never know if it's going to work or not. Okay, so... Amy, you want to weigh in on this stuff?"

"Not sure what stuff you're talking about," said Amy, "but I definitely want to weigh in on... happy hour tonight!"

"Ooh," Laura said, intrigued.

Yvonne rolled her eyes. Thankfully most of her work calls (including this one) did not involve going on camera.

"That's right, bitches," Amy continued. "Taco Loco has moved its three-dollar margaritas night to *Thurs-days*!" (The word "Thursdays" came out slowly and in a sing-songy voice.)

"Yum, sounds great," said Laura.

"I don't know..." said Yvonne, frantically trying to formulate her excuse.

"You're going!" Amy pronounced in an aggressive but playful tone.

A small smile involuntarily broke out on Yvonne's face. Yep, she thought. I probably am.

Bill stepped out onto the landing just in front of the condo entrance and, wearing neither hat nor sunglasses (as he typically didn't don these prior to getting in the car), was immediately stabbed in the eyes by sharp rays of light shooting in from the southeastern sky.

He scrunched up his face and nearly blurted out an obscenity, but caught himself just short of it upon registering the fact that, in that infinitesimal sliver of time between emerging and getting blinded, he'd glimpsed a figure standing on the sidewalk below.

Reaching the bottom of the stairs and taking another look (this time through his sunglasses), Bill discovered that the person he'd seen was his friend Gary Williams from up the street, who was indeed standing, completely still (very unusual for Gary), on the sidewalk, staring at, apparently, nothing.

"Hi, Gary," Bill called out, approaching.

Gary turned around and his face lit up. "Oh, hey, guys!" he exclaimed.

"How's it going?" asked Bill.

"Going good," Gary replied with a big smile, turning back to face the way he had been. "I was just looking at that tree there…"

Disappointed to hear this, Bill, now standing right next to his friend, made a halfhearted attempt to figure out which tree Gary meant, but failed.

"Do you think that's a scarf, or… like a bandana? Or maybe a piece of a… I don't know…"

"What?"

"That red and blue thing there, hanging from that branch there…"

"Oh, *that* tree," said Bill, finally realizing that Gary was referring to one way up the block and on the opposite side of the street, at the corner of Wexler and Utah. "Hmm. No idea."

He paused and glanced at Gary, hoping his mind had moved on to a different, less boring (or even equally boring!) topic. But clearly it hadn't, so he grudgingly added, "To me it kind of looks like two separate… uh, things. One red, one blue."

"Which type of tree is that?" Gary asked. "Is it a sycamore?"

"Hello there!" boomed a cheerful voice from directly across the street. It belonged to 47-year-old Marty McLanahey, dressed in nightclub attire, who was now stepping off the curb just behind—while remotely unlocking, causing a flurry of flashing lights and electronic beeping sounds—his bright green Lamborghini Huracán Evo Spyder.

"Hi, Marty," Bill responded, also giving a quick salutatory wave of his arm and hand.

Gary's attention was no longer on the tree.   "Nice car!"   he remarked.

"Yeah," said Bill.

"So, you know him?"

"Only because of his nice car. Made the mistake of complimenting him on it once, then had to listen to his whole life story."

Marty was now in the driver's seat with the door shut and the window down. He gave the men on the sidewalk a final nod and smile. Then he began slowly reclining and disappeared from view.

"What is he *doing*?" asked Gary.

"He's going to bed," said Bill. "He lives in his car."

"No way!"

"Yep. Says housing costs a fortune and you end up living in a dump anyway, so he thought, why not spend a fortune on something awesome instead..."

Gary laughed, then said, "That's pretty crazy. I haven't ever met anyone before who lived in their vehicle *by choice*. I love it, though. Woo... So, wait—why's he going to bed in the morning?"

"Well he says he stays out all night, you know, partying... and then sleeps all day."

"Heh—if I was going out partying, I'd take that sweet ride with me!"

"Maybe he parties here in this neighborhood... So anyway, what brings *you* out on foot this morning?"

"Oh..."—Gary looked down at a brown paper bag he was holding, then lifted it up a few inches to symbolize showing it to Bill— "Shopping! Down there on Olympic. There's a little hole-in-the-wall place down there with some great specimens."

"Specimens?"

"Stamps. Oh, man, they've got some real rarities down there." Gary now wore a big, giddy grin. "And the stories behind them, ooh, so fascinating..."

"I'm really sorry," said Bill, glancing at his wrist, "but, uh, Yvonne and I need to get going..."

"No worries," replied Gary. "I gotta get home anyway and get these puppies filed and catalogued!"

"Okay, cool. See you later."

"Bye! You guys have a great morning!"

As Gary took off up the sidewalk and Bill turned back toward his building, wondering what had become of Yvonne (whom he'd thought was right behind him coming out of the condo), he was startled to find a different woman standing in the "driveway" (a very short, very steep concrete slope linking the carport to the sidewalk), staring at him, hands on her hips.

Kimberlea Periodontis, age 39, a lifelong Angeleno who in recent times had been working as a patent attorney for a string of tech startups in Santa Monica, lived alone in Number Three, directly beneath the Smedes, and had been there since before they'd moved in. Bill did not recognize her at all.

"I know who you are," she quite sternly said now (after a creepily long stretch of silent glaring).

Bill quickly and hopefully looked behind him, but nobody was there.

"I'm afraid I can't say the same about you," he conceded as he approached Kimberlea, smiling nervously and extending his hand. "I'm Bill. I live—"

"Yeah, I know all about you. You're a disgusting pervert. A real deviant, you are. A filthy..."

"Excuse me?"

"I saw you. Outside my bedroom window."

"What? I think maybe—"

"Don't play innocent with me. I saw you! Last year. It was a Tuesday morning. I remember. Normally my curtains are closed but that day they were open. And there you were..."

"Look, I can assure you—"

"Leering. Prancing around. Playing with your... your... fetish toys. And hollering—all that filthy dirty talk. Very undignified."

"Well I operate under a 'dignity optional' life framework," Bill said with a smile, but neither his face nor his words had any observable impact on Kimberlea.

"Anyway," he continued after a brief pause, "if it was me you saw then I'm sorry for upsetting you."

"What do you mean, 'if'? There is no 'if'! I hope you realize that having you people above me is no picnic."

For an instant Bill pondered how dumb this expression was (because he hated picnics), then brought himself back to the here and now. "Honestly," he said, "if it's the time I think you must mean, I was just locked out and trying to figure out how to get back in."

"Whatever you were doing," she replied, "you exercised terrible judgment. You made wrong choices."

"Yes, absolutely, I..."

"Bill makes the wrong choice about everything," said Yvonne, who'd just come down the stairs from the condo and was now standing right behind Bill. "Except women."

"Oh, there you are," he said, turning around.

"Yeah, sorry—I remembered they handed us a coupon for Diet Coke at the checkout last week so I went back to grab it. But then it took me forever to find it."

"Ah."

"But I finally did." She held it up.

"Cool. Okay, I guess let's get this show on the road. It was nice to meet you, uh..."

As he partially turned around again in the direction Kimberlea had been, he realized she'd walked away and was about to disappear around a corner behind which lay her front door.

"Hmm," he said.

"Such a nice person," commented Yvonne.

Half an hour later, with Bill pushing a shopping cart (an activity that somehow prevented all PaceTek devices from giving their wearers proper credit for steps taken (which was the reason Yvonne never did it)) that he'd just obtained from a collection of them located next to the main entrance of Hank's, the pair trudged through it.

This particular Hank's (one of a dozen on the Westside, hundreds in greater Los Angeles, and nearly a thousand across Southern California) was especially difficult to access. It occupied one sixth of a gigantic three-story building with businesses in the western half and parking in the eastern half. On the lowest level, where cars entered the parking garage (which charged typically exorbitant rates but could be used for up to two hours for free with validation), one of the principal shop floor tenants was a private daycare facility catering to an age range of infant through six years; consequently, the parking area was always riddled with obnoxious parents and their bratty offspring, ambling around as if they owned the place and inspiring the Smedes to keep on moving and take the ATS higher.

Hank's sat on the middle level—a wonderful level on which to park except that everyone else had thought exactly the same thing and already done it; no empty spaces were ever to be found (though perhaps would've been, had a smaller percentage of Mercedes and BMW drivers felt compelled to precisely center their car over the line of white paint intended to separate one from another).

And so it was the top (and farthest from the exit) level, adjacent to less-popular-but-still-very-popular Target, where Bill invariably ended up parking the ATS, after which he and Yvonne usually waited ages for, then rode down on, the world's slowest elevator (which was also a contender for world's tiniest and reliably rendered its occupants packed in like sardines).

But the inside of this Hank's had a unique grandness that seemed to make the ordeal of getting there worthwhile. It boasted a larger square footage than any other grocery store most people who set foot in here had ever set foot in (owing to its expansion, ten years ago, into what had until then been a neighboring retail space (occupied by an ill-fated Best Buy)) and featured an absurdly high ceiling, in the rafters of which birds could often be seen frolicking. Its checkout stands were astonishingly numerous, as were its aisles, which were also astonishingly long and tall. There was a salad bar. There was a sushi bar. There was even an *actual* bar, serving beer and wine starting at 11 A.M. each day. Yes, this Hank's transformed one of life's most ordinary experiences into something truly extraordinary.

Or so Yvonne and Bill had thought back in the early days. It hadn't taken them long to conclude that in fact this Hank's provided them no practical advantages whatsoever. It was every bit as crowded as any other, despite all that additional space. Its wider selection applied only to the types of products they never bought: the hyper-processed, super-junky snack foods of the ignorant, unsophisticated lower classes and the overpriced, ultra-trendy, style-over-substance concoctions favored by snobby, pretentious urban elitists. And they never made use of any of the bars. Still, they'd stuck with this one because it was the closest to home, and no torture was worse than spending time on L.A. roads.

By the time they'd reached their first stop, the CuppaJoe counter (located in the opposite corner of the store from the main entrance, next to a street entrance that served on-the-go Angelenos who just popped in for a coffee or to pick up a few items they could easily carry in their arms), Bill had noticed that his cart was what he called "wonky," meaning that some component of its infinitely mysterious wheels mechanism had some kind of issue that caused phenomena—resistance and/or erratic tracking and/or noises—of a most irritating nature. He'd never yet come across a Hank's cart that wasn't wonky, but kept trying to maintain faith that one day he would.

The line at CuppaJoe this morning was long, but not quite long enough to prompt the Smedes to temporarily abandon their cart and dash out onto the street, around the corner and up a flight of stairs to a pedestrian entrance to Target, just inside of which, oddly enough, was another CuppaJoe counter, which, on the occasions they'd been to it, had seemed to offer a shorter wait time than this one.

As Yvonne stood in line, it occurred to her that she hadn't taken a picture of the fridge-mounted whiteboard containing their shopping list. After confirming with Bill that neither had he (a fact of which she was already 99% certain), she remedied the situation by texting Alice to request the taking and sending of such a picture. Alice responded in her standard fashion—quick, complete, highly word-efficient (in this case, no words at all) compliance—and Yvonne was in possession of the list before receiving her coffee.

After completing their transaction at CuppaJoe, Bill and Yvonne took their hot beverages and their wonky cart and began the slow procession up and down the many long, tall aisles of Hank's, gradually progressing from north to south across the vast floor of the store. In nearly every aisle, they found their path momentarily (or, sometimes, permanently) blocked by a fellow customer meticulously attentive to their own shopping requirements but shockingly oblivious to everything around them, or by a "team member" stocking shelves, wearing earbuds and, apparently, suffering from a deficiency in their peripheral vision. Or, in many cases, by both.

In the cereal aisle, they learned that Special K Protein belonged to the "Buy Five" deal, which allowed savvy shoppers to select five or more of the participating products from around the store in a mix-and-match style and receive $1 off each of them. They decided to hedge their bets, placing three boxes of Special K Protein into the cart. They could always come back for more if necessary, they reasoned.

In the canned vegetables aisle, they discovered there was a digital coupon for the beans they routinely bought, so Yvonne opened up the Hank's app (which Bill had never managed even to install) and began the highly frustrating task of attempting to "clip" the coupon.

This effort went on for the next ten minutes (before ending in failure), during which she and Bill also traded speculative comments about what sort of calculus had led the folks at Hank's corporate H.Q. to determine that their most sound business strategy involved dangling money in front of people, making them dance for it, and then keeping it.

In the midst of a U-turn at the back of the store, Bill noticed a sign on a door reading "Employees Only Please" and elicited a laugh from Yvonne by pointing out the clear fallaciousness of this statement—it was patently obvious to anyone that employees disappoint, and do so regularly.

They shared another laugh in one of the beverage aisles, perusing the ridiculous creations on offer, such as coffee mixed with cola and something calling itself "the perfect blend of chocolate and wine" (which Bill and Yvonne agreed would simply be wine).

In the real wine aisle, they chose three bottles that genuinely appealed to them, then three other bottles from the bottom shelf in order to get the 10% discount for buying six, all the while suspecting correctly, but not actually computing, that the cost of the shitty bottles was more than they were saving on the nice bottles.

At the dairy cooler (at the back of the store again), they found that the Hank's Organic Rejuvenation brand half-gallons of nonfat milk were part of the "Buy Five" deal. They grabbed just one carton, concerned that a second one would spoil before they finished it. They couldn't recall their current count, nor what else they'd seen that was on the deal.

In the produce section, they struggled (as always) to find decent specimens of the very ordinary fruits and vegetables they wanted, while being entertained by little chalkboards bragging about the latest obscure temporary offerings that they'd never dream of buying, such as chilies from Hatch, New Mexico and quinces grown on the shore of the Khan Sea.

At the checkout stand, they were subjected to a relentless barrage of inane chatter from the bagger, which happened every week. They both pondered with curiosity the contrasting, almost totally mute behavior of every non-bagger who worked at Hank's.

After everything had been scanned and Bill had inserted his credit card into the little payment machine and then carefully (and somewhat anxiously) followed the instructions on its screen for removing the card at the correct moment, the cashier thrust a long paper receipt into his hand that looked exactly like every grocery receipt he'd seen since early childhood. Before shoving it into his jeans pocket, he scanned the information at the bottom about his fuel points, which he'd never been able to understand, and once again didn't understand it.

After riding back up on the world's slowest elevator to the top level with their haul, loading it all into the trunk, ditching the cart in a nearby receptacle loaded with Target carts, climbing into the ATS, and winding their way back down to the bottom level, Bill and Yvonne were met at the exit gate with an unexpected demand for payment of $25, and realized upon examining the timestamp on their ticket that they'd arrived here two hours and two minutes ago.

Sitting in the normal stop-and-go traffic on the way home, Yvonne remembered the Diet Coke coupon she'd made a point of going back into the condo to find, which she'd handed to Bill on the drive to Hank's for him to put in his wallet, which he'd done. She then checked with Bill that they'd paid full price for their Diet Coke and that the coupon was still tucked safely inside his wallet; he confirmed this was indeed the case.

A few minutes later, she mentioned to him that neither of them had consulted their list the entire time they were inside of Hank's, then got out her phone, brought the list up on the screen, and began identifying the items they'd neglected to get, of which she eventually determined there were four.

Bill said he was officially going on the record with his firm belief that by the end of the day they'd become aware of four other things they should've bought that had never even made it onto the list.

Ultimately he was proven correct, but by then they'd both forgotten his prediction.

———————————

The next morning at 10:06, Bill was sitting in front of his laptop looking at a many-decades-old trade journal article about a prominent (at the time) L.A. building contractor called Linklater and Sons Construction, for which a man named Archie Wailoverenson had served as site manager on multiple projects in Santa Monica.

"Interesting," Bill muttered as he slowly scrolled.

Though well aware of his own tendency to get sucked into virtually any reading material, he'd mildly surprised himself by taking such a strong interest in something he'd read recently—a piece of personal correspondence that had unexpectedly accompanied the treasure map he'd reluctantly received from his friend Matt—that he'd felt compelled to conduct further research. He'd also begun to feel grateful, for the very first time, for his "Deep Dive" level subscription to the UCLA libraries' digitized archives (without which the article he was currently examining would've been inaccessible), which he'd been pressured by the alumni association into buying five years ago.

Bill's phone, lying on the table next to his laptop, suddenly came to life with light, sound, and vibration. Glancing at it, he saw that a call was coming in from an unrecognized 310 number. He hesitated.

"Hello?" he said into it a moment later, having decided to roll the dice.

"Bill! What's going on?"

"Hey, Matt. Funny, I was just thinking about you."

"Hah! Yeah—I was just thinking about you too, dude. So how's it hanging?"

"Pretty well, I guess," Bill said with a sigh. "Just found out I'm probably going to be seeing my mom and sister next weekend."

"That's cool," said Matt. "They're nice. And your little nieces are sweethearts, too."

"Yeah. Anyway, to what do I owe the pleasure?"

"Oh—right! Yeah I just realized, you and me never go for donuts together…"

"Donuts?"

"Yes! I bet it's been so long since you ate one, you've forgotten how awesome they are."

"Apparently."

"It'd be a great outing for a Sunday morning. It's too late today, but, like, I don't know, maybe next Sunday or whatever…"

"Okay…"

"Yeah I know the perfect place: Blinkie's, up on Topanga Canyon. Most people have never been there, but it rocks."

"Is that the one with the giant donut out front?"

"No, no. That's Randy's. Everybody's been there."

"I haven't."

"Yeah I'm telling you, man—Blinkie's. Great drive, great scenery, *really* great donuts. It'll be awesome."

"Uh… Yeah, sure. Maybe. I mean, it might depend on this thing with my mom…"

"Yeah that's cool, dude," said Matt. "We'll figure it out. Mmm—can't wait!"

"So what's the latest with your big dig?" asked Bill. "Have you done it yet?"

"Yes! I finally did. Just a few days ago, actually."

"Oh, wow. So, tell me all about it."

"Well, honestly, it was kinda… anti-climactic? I didn't get the treasure chest. Oh, did I tell you? I think you were right all along—you know, about the key. I think it really *did* say 'old,' not 'gold.' 'Cause, you know, I mean… that key I got, what the heck kind of padlock would that open, right?"

They both laughed.

"But then I thought, do I really even *need* the key? I mean, I could just, like, use some tools and stuff to just break the lock right off. I mean it's not like I'm gonna want to use the lock again, right?" Another laugh, this time from Matt only.

"So," said Bill, "you didn't get the treasure?"

"Nah. Turns out I was like 20 years too late. It's long gone."

"Someone else dug it up?"

"Sort of. Not really. So, yeah—I met a new friend that day, when I was out there digging. Taint. Holy Toledo, that guy is a trip. But so he knew about this stuff that happened back in, like, whatever year that was, where they did like a major excavation around that whole area there—you know, by where Marion used to live."

"Oh, really?"

"Yeah. They were trying to renovate it or whatever, to attract more beachgoers I guess. But yeah, they had one of those big-ass scooper machines out there, just, pulling up massive chunks of earth, you know? And, the treasure chest was inside one of those chunks and it… just went off to some landfill somewhere. Nobody ever knew!"

"Wow."

"Yeah. At first I thought maybe Taint was confused. I took a lunch break and then I went back to the spot and kept digging for a few more hours but, you know, nothing. So I went home and went online and did some research. Really dug into it—hah!"

Bill gave a small, appreciative chuckle.

"And, yeah, I learned all about what went down there, with the excavation and everything. Pretty cool stuff, actually."

"Well I'm sorry it didn't work out," Bill said, sincerely.

"Aw, it's no biggie. That crafty vixen, Marion... She didn't want anybody to ever find it. But, you know, *maybe*, someday... somebody will! They'll dig it up from that old landfill a hundred years from now. That'd be pretty sweet, wouldn't it?"

"Yes it would."

Bill heard some rustling noises on the line, and a muffled female voice.

Then Matt said, "Sorry, Bill—Cassie here wants to check her Instagram."

"Oh, sure, no problem..."

"I'm gonna hang up the call. But this'll only take a minute, you know, if you want to talk more or whatever..."

"Yeah," said Bill. "No worries. We can, uh... Okay, bye."

He tapped the red icon, lay the phone back down, and pondered Matt's story for several seconds. Then he spent a few minutes studying the two ancient sheets of paper Matt had gifted him (both of which had been here on the table, ready for reference as needed). Then he began mulling over everything he'd learned, these past many months, about the life and times of Marion Davies.

"Interesting," he eventually muttered, having concluded that she almost certainly had never buried a treasure chest—or anything else, for that matter—under the sand near her seaside home.

As he was looking at his phone lying on the table, wondering whether he ought to call Matt back, Yvonne came into the room from the back half of the condo.

"Hey," she said.

"Hey," said Bill.

"Feel like doing a loop?"

He smiled. "Yeah. Let's."

They gathered up their bits and pieces and headed for the front door. Yvonne went out first; Bill lingered briefly, adjusting the fit of his hat and sunglasses.

Yvonne descended the stairs, proceeded out to the sidewalk, and slowly headed south along Wexler, fiddling with her PaceTek Ultra. It was unusually warm out, and she could hear her husband noticing this and swearing about it as he approached from behind.

"How are your steps?" he asked as he joined her at the corner of Wyoming.

"Lousy," she replied.

"Yeah, mine too. Want to make this one a double?"

"Sounds good."

The author wishes to acknowledge that in writing this book he received invaluable encouragement and advice from some very smart, kind, insightful people who generously shared their time and who know he is hugely grateful to them.

The author also wishes to acknowledge that everything about this book that is stupid, boring, offensive, incomprehensible or pointless is entirely his own doing.